Praise for Stieg Larsson's

THE GIRL WHO KICKED THE HORNET'S NEST

"Fully lives up to the excellence of the previous two and . . . brings the saga to a satisfactory conclusion. . . . A **modern masterpiece.**"
—*The Washington Post Book World*

"Satisfying. . . . [Lisbeth Salander] **bursts off the page**, a vibrant, forcefully 'real' character." —*The Plain Dealer*

"[This] heroine with a spine of steel, is, I promise, someone you will never forget. . . . Take advantage of this trilogy. . . . I lingered over pages, languished in them, **not wanting the story to end.**"
—Alan Cheuse, *Chicago Tribune*

"**Enough twists to keep even the most astute reader guessing.**"
—*The Denver Post*

"**Complex, satisfying, clever, moral.** . . . This is a grown-up novel for grown-up readers, who want something **more than a quick fix and a car chase.**"
—*The Guardian* (London)

STIEG LARSSON

THE GIRL WHO KICKED THE HORNET'S NEST

Stieg Larsson, who lived in Sweden, was the editor in chief of the magazine *Expo*, and a leading expert on anti-democratic, right-wing extremist, and Nazi organizations. He died in 2004, shortly after delivering the manuscripts for *The Girl with the Dragon Tattoo*, *The Girl Who Played with Fire*, and *The Girl Who Kicked the Hornet's Nest*.

www.stieglarsson.net

ALSO BY STIEG LARSSON

The Girl with the Dragon Tattoo
The Girl Who Played with Fire

THE GIRL
WHO KICKED THE
HORNET'S NEST

STIEG LARSSON

TRANSLATED FROM THE SWEDISH
BY REG KEELAND

VINTAGE CRIME/BLACK LIZARD

Vintage Books

A Division of Random House, Inc.

New York

FIRST VINTAGE CRIME/BLACK LIZARD MASS-MARKET EDITION,
FEBRUARY 2012

The Library of Congress has cataloged the Knopf edition as follows:
Larsson, Stieg, 1954–2004.
[Luftslottet som sprängdes. English]
The girl who kicked the hornet's nest / by Stieg Larsson ; translated
from the Swedish by Reg Keeland. —1st U.S. ed.
p.   cm.
Originally published in Sweden as *Luftslottet som sprängdes*
by Norstedts, Stockholm, in 2007.
Sequel to: The girl who played with fire.
1. Political corruption—Sweden—Fiction.   2. Revenge—Fiction.
I. Keeland, Reg, 1943–   II. Title.
PT9876.22.A6933L8413   2010
839.738—dc22
2010006361

Vintage Mass-Market ISBN: 978-0-307-74253-7

Book design by Rebecca Aidlin

www.weeklylizard.com

Printed in the United States of America
10   9   8   7   6   5   4   3   2   1

LAKE SILJAN

NORWAY

SWEDEN

Uppsala
STOCKHOLM

Eskilstuna   Strängnäs
              Mariefred
              Järna
          Katrineholm

VÄNERN

Norrköping

Uddevalla

Linköping
ÖSTERGÖTLAND   GOTLAND

Nossebro
Sollebrunn
Lake Anten
Alingsås
GÖTEBORG
  Borås
  Seglora

VÄTTERN

Jönköping

KATTEGAT

Kalmar

Laholm   OLAND

        Karlskrona
Ronneby   BALTIC

Helsingborg
Landskrona

COPEN-
HAGEN   Malmö Ystad
        Trelleborg   BORNHOLM

DENMARK

PART 1

Intermezzo in a Corridor

APRIL 8–12

An estimated 600 women served during the American Civil War. They had signed up disguised as men. Hollywood has missed a significant chapter of cultural history here—or is this history ideologically too difficult to deal with? Historians have often struggled to deal with women who do not respect gender distinctions, and nowhere is that distinction more sharply drawn than in the question of armed combat. (Even today, it can cause controversy having a woman on a typical Swedish moose hunt.)

But from antiquity to modern times, there are many stories of female warriors, of Amazons. The best known find their way into the history books as warrior queens, rulers as well as leaders. They have been forced to act as any Churchill, Stalin, or Roosevelt: Semiramis from Nineveh, who shaped the

Assyrian Empire, and Boudicca, who led one of the bloodiest English revolts against the Roman forces of occupation, to cite just two. Boudicca is honoured with a statue on the Thames at Westminster Bridge, opposite Big Ben. Be sure to say hello to her if you happen to pass by.

On the other hand, history is reticent about women who were common soldiers, who bore arms, belonged to regiments, and took part in battles on the same terms as men, though hardly a war has been waged without women soldiers in the ranks.

CHAPTER 1

Friday, April 8

Dr. Jonasson was woken by a nurse five minutes before the helicopter was expected to land. It was just before 1:30 in the morning.

"What?" he said, confused.

"Rescue Service helicopter coming in. Two patients. An injured man and a younger woman. The woman has gunshot wounds."

"All right," Jonasson said wearily.

Although he had slept for only half an hour, he felt groggy. He was on the night shift in the ER at Sahlgrenska hospital in Göteborg. It had been a strenuous evening.

By 12:30 the steady flow of emergency cases had eased off. He had made a round to check on the state of his patients and then gone back to the staff bedroom to try to rest for a while. He was on duty until 6:00, and seldom got the chance to sleep even if no emergency patients came in. But this time he had fallen asleep almost as soon as he turned out the light.

Jonasson saw lightning out over the sea. He knew that the helicopter was coming in the nick of time. All of a sudden a heavy downpour lashed at the window. The storm had moved in over Göteborg.

He heard the sound of the chopper and watched as it banked through the storm squalls down towards the helipad. For a second he held his breath when the pilot seemed to have difficulty controlling the aircraft. Then it vanished from his field of vision and he heard the engine slowing to land. He took a hasty swallow of his tea and set down the cup.

Jonasson met the emergency team in the admissions area. The other doctor on duty took on the first patient who was wheeled in—an elderly man with his head bandaged, apparently with a serious wound to the face. Jonasson was left with the second patient, the woman who had been shot. He did a quick visual examination: it looked like she was a teenager, very dirty and bloody, and severely wounded. He lifted the blanket that the Rescue Service had wrapped around her body and saw that the wounds to her hip and shoulder were bandaged with duct tape, which he considered a pretty clever idea. The tape kept bacteria out and blood in. One bullet had entered her hip and gone straight through the muscle tissue. He gently raised her shoulder and located the entry wound in her back. There was no exit wound: the round was still inside her shoulder. He hoped it had not penetrated her lung, and since he did not see any blood in the woman's mouth he concluded that probably it had not.

"Radiology," he told the nurse in attendance. That was all he needed to say.

Then he cut away the bandage that the emergency team had wrapped around her skull. He froze when he saw another entry wound. The woman had been shot in the head, and there was no exit wound there either.

Jonasson paused for a second, looking down at the girl. He felt dejected. He often described his job as being like that of a goalkeeper. Every day people came to his place of work in varying conditions but with one objective: to get help.

Jonasson was the goalkeeper who stood between the patient and Fonus Funeral Service. His job was to decide what to do. If he made the wrong decision, the patient might die or perhaps wake up disabled for life. Most often he made the right decision, because the vast majority of injured people had an obvious and specific problem. A stab wound to the lung or a crushing injury after a car crash were both particular and recognizable problems that could be dealt with. The survival of the patient depended on the extent of the damage and on Jonasson's skill.

There were two kinds of injury that he hated. One was a serious burn case, because no matter what measures he took the burns would almost inevitably result in a lifetime of suffering. The second was an injury to the brain.

The girl on the gurney could live with a piece of lead in her hip and a piece of lead in her shoulder. But a piece of lead inside her brain was a trauma of a wholly different magnitude. He was suddenly aware of the nurse saying something.

"Sorry. I wasn't listening."

"It's her."

"What do you mean?"

"It's Lisbeth Salander. The girl they've been hunting for the past few weeks, for the triple murder in Stockholm."

Jonasson looked again at the unconscious patient's face.

He realized at once that the nurse was right. He and the whole of Sweden had seen Salander's passport photograph on billboards outside every newspaper kiosk for weeks. And now the murderer herself had been shot, which was surely poetic justice of a sort.

But that was not his concern. His job was to save his patient's life, irrespective of whether she was a triple murderer or a Nobel Prize winner. Or both.

Then the efficient chaos, the same in every ER the world over, erupted. The staff on Jonasson's shift set about their appointed tasks. Salander's clothes were cut away. A nurse reported on her blood pressure—100/70—while the doctor put his stethoscope to her chest and listened to her heartbeat. It was surprisingly regular, but her breathing was not quite normal.

Jonasson did not hesitate to classify Salander's condition as critical. The wounds in her shoulder and hip could wait until later, with a compress on each, or even with the duct tape that some inspired soul had applied. What mattered was her head. Jonasson ordered tomography with the new and improved CT scanner that the hospital had lately acquired.

Jonasson had a view of medicine that was at times unorthodox. He thought doctors often drew conclusions that they could not substantiate. This meant that they gave up far too easily; alternatively, they spent too much time at the acute stage trying to work out exactly what was wrong with the patient so as to decide on the right treatment. This was correct procedure, of course. The problem was that the patient was in danger of dying while the doctor was still doing his thinking.

But Jonasson had never before had a patient with a bullet in her skull. Most likely he would need a brain surgeon. He had all the theoretical knowledge required to make an incursion into the brain, but he did not by any means consider himself a brain surgeon. He felt inadequate, but all of a sudden he realized that he might be luckier than he deserved. Before he scrubbed up and put on his operating clothes he sent for the nurse.

"There's an American professor from Boston working at the Karolinska hospital in Stockholm. He happens to be in Göteborg tonight, staying at the Elite Park Avenue on Avenyn. He just gave a lecture on brain research. He's a good friend of mine. Could you get the number?"

While Jonasson was still waiting for the X-rays, the nurse came back with the number of the Elite Park Avenue. Jonasson picked up the phone. The night porter at the Elite Park Avenue was very reluctant to wake a guest at that time of night and Jonasson had to come up with a few choice phrases about the critical nature of the situation before his call was put through.

"Good morning, Frank," Jonasson said when the call was finally answered. "It's Anders. Do you feel like coming over to Sahlgrenska to help out in a brain op?"

"Are you bullshitting me?" Dr. Frank Ellis had lived in Sweden for many years and was fluent in Swedish—albeit with an American accent—but when Jonasson spoke to him in Swedish, Ellis always replied in his mother tongue.

"The patient is in her mid-twenties. Entry wound, no exit."

"And she's alive?"

"Weak but regular pulse, less regular breathing, blood

pressure one hundred over seventy. She also has a bullet wound in her shoulder and another in her hip. But I know how to handle those two."

"Sounds promising," Ellis said.

"Promising?"

"If somebody has a bullet in their head and they're still alive, that points to hopeful."

"I understand. . . . Frank, can you help me out?"

"I spent the evening in the company of good friends, Anders. I got to bed at 1:00 and no doubt I have an impressive blood alcohol content."

"I'll make the decisions and do the surgery. But I need somebody to tell me if I'm doing anything stupid. Even a falling-down drunk Professor Ellis is several classes better than I could ever be when it comes to assessing brain damage."

"OK, I'll come. But you're going to owe me one."

"I'll have a taxi waiting outside by the time you get down to the lobby. The driver will know where to drop you, and a nurse will be there to meet you and get you scrubbed in."

"I had a patient a number of years ago, in Boston—I wrote about the case in the *New England Journal of Medicine*. It was a girl the same age as your patient here. She was walking to the university when someone shot her with a crossbow. The arrow entered at the outside edge of her left eyebrow and went straight through her head, exiting from almost the middle of the back of her neck."

"And she survived?"

"She looked like nothing on earth when she came in. We

cut off the arrow shaft and put her head in a CT scanner. The arrow went straight through her brain. By all known reckoning she should have been dead, or at least suffered such massive trauma that she would have been in a coma."

"And what was her condition?"

"She was conscious the whole time. Not only that; she was terribly frightened, of course, but she was completely rational. Her only problem was that she had an arrow through her skull."

"What did you do?"

"Well, I got the forceps and pulled out the arrow and bandaged the wounds. More or less."

"And she lived to tell the tale?"

"Obviously her condition was critical, but the fact is we could have sent her home the same day. I've seldom had a healthier patient."

Jonasson wondered whether Ellis was pulling his leg.

"On the other hand," Ellis went on, "I had a forty-two-year-old patient in Stockholm some years ago who banged his head on a windowsill. He began to feel sick immediately and was taken by ambulance to the ER. When I got to him he was unconscious. He had a small bump and a very slight bruise. But he never regained consciousness and died after nine days in intensive care. To this day I have no idea why he died. In the autopsy report, we wrote brain haemorrhage resulting from an accident, but not one of us was satisfied with that assessment. The bleeding was so minor, and located in an area that shouldn't have affected anything else at all. And yet his liver, kidneys, heart, and lungs shut down one after the other. The older I get, the more I think it's like a game of roulette. I don't believe we'll ever figure out precisely how the brain works." He tapped on the X-ray with a pen. "What do you intend to do?"

"I was hoping you would tell me."

"Let's hear your diagnosis."

"Well, first of all, it seems to be a small-calibre bullet. It entered at the temple, and then stopped about four centimetres into the brain. It's resting against the lateral ventricle. There's bleeding there."

"How will you proceed?"

"To use your terminology, get some forceps and extract the bullet by the same route it went in."

"Excellent idea. I would use the thinnest forceps you have."

"It's that simple?"

"What else can we do in this case? We could leave the bullet where it is, and she might live to be a hundred, but it's also a risk. She might develop epilepsy, migraines, all sorts of complaints. And one thing you really don't want to do is drill into her skull and then operate a year from now when the wound itself has healed. The bullet is located away from the major blood vessels. So I would recommend that you extract it, but . . ."

"But what?"

"The bullet doesn't worry me so much. She's survived this far and that's a good omen for her getting through having the bullet removed too. The real problem is here." He pointed at the X-ray. "Around the entry wound you have all sorts of bone fragments. I can see at least a dozen that are a couple of millimetres long. Some are embedded in the brain tissue. That's what could kill her if you're not careful."

"Isn't that part of the brain associated with numbers and mathematical capacity?" Jonasson said.

Ellis shrugged. "Mumbo jumbo. I have no idea what these particular grey cells are for. You can only do your best. You operate. I'll look over your shoulder."

Mikael Blomkvist looked up at the clock and saw that it was just after 3:00 in the morning. He was handcuffed and increasingly uncomfortable. He closed his eyes for a moment. He was dead tired but running on adrenaline. He opened them again and gave the policeman an angry glare. Inspector Thomas Paulsson had a shocked expression on his face. They were sitting at a kitchen table in a white farmhouse called Gosseberga, somewhere near Nossebro. Blomkvist had heard of the place for the first time less than twelve hours earlier.

There was no denying the disaster that had occurred.

"Imbecile," Blomkvist said.

"Now, you listen here—"

"Imbecile," Blomkvist said again. "I warned you he was dangerous, for Christ's sake. I told you that you would have to handle him like a live grenade. He's murdered at least three people with his bare hands and he's built like a tank. And you send a couple of village policemen to arrest him as if he were some Saturday night drunk."

Blomkvist shut his eyes again, wondering what else could go wrong that night.

He had found Lisbeth Salander just after midnight. She was very badly wounded. He had sent for the police and the Rescue Service.

The only thing that had gone right was that he had persuaded them to send a helicopter to take the girl to Sahlgrenska hospital. He had given them a clear description of her injuries and the bullet wound in her head, and some bright spark at the Rescue Service got the message.

Even so, it had taken over half an hour for the Puma from the helicopter unit in Säve to arrive at the farmhouse. Blomkvist had gotten two cars out of the barn. He switched on their headlights to illuminate a landing area in the field in front of the house.

The helicopter crew and two paramedics had proceeded in a routine and professional manner. One of the medics tended to Salander while the other took care of Alexander Zalachenko, known locally as Karl Axel Bodin. Zalachenko was Salander's father and her worst enemy. He had tried to kill her, but he had failed. Blomkvist had found him in the woodshed at the farm with a nasty-looking gash—probably from an axe—in his face and some shattering damage to one of his legs which Blomkvist did not bother to investigate.

While he waited for the helicopter, he did what he could for Salander. He took a clean sheet from a linen cupboard and cut it up to make bandages. The blood had coagulated at the entry wound in her head, and he did not know whether he dared to put a bandage on it or not. In the end he fixed the fabric very loosely around her head, mostly so that the wound would not be exposed to bacteria or dirt. But he had stopped the bleeding from the wounds in her hip and shoulder in the simplest possible way. He had found a roll of duct tape and had used it to close the wounds. The medics remarked that this, in their experience, was a brand-new form of bandage. He had also bathed Salander's face with a wet towel and done his best to wipe off the dirt.

He had not gone back to the woodshed to tend to Zalachenko. He honestly did not give a damn about the man. But he did call Erika Berger, editor in chief of *Millennium* magazine, on his mobile and told her the situation.

"Are *you* all right?" Berger asked him.

"I'm OK," Blomkvist said. "Lisbeth is the one who's in real danger."

"That poor girl," Berger said. "I read Björck's Säpo report this evening. How should I deal with it?"

"I don't have the energy to think that through right now," Blomkvist said. Security Police matters were going to have to wait until the next day, even if the report could help vindicate Lisbeth.

As he talked to Berger, he sat on the floor next to the bench and kept a watchful eye on Salander. He had taken off her shoes and her pants so that he could bandage the wound to her hip, and now his hand rested on the pants, which he had dropped on the floor next to the bench. There was something in one of the pockets. He pulled out a Palm Tungsten T3.

He frowned and looked long and hard at the hand-held computer. When he heard the approaching helicopter he stuffed it into the inside pocket of his jacket and then went through all her other pockets. He found another set of keys to the apartment in Mosebacke and a passport in the name of Irene Nesser. He put these swiftly into a side pocket of his laptop case.

. . .

The first patrol car from the station in Trollhättan arrived a few minutes after the helicopter landed. Next to arrive was Inspector Paulsson, who took charge immediately. Blomkvist began to explain what had happened. He very soon realized that Paulsson was a pompous, rigid drill-sergeant type. He did not seem to take in anything that Blomkvist said. It was when Paulsson arrived that things really started to go awry.

The only thing he seemed capable of grasping was that the badly damaged girl being cared for by the medics on the floor next to the kitchen bench was the triple murderer Lisbeth Salander. And above all, it was important that he make the arrest. Three times Paulsson had asked the urgently occupied medical orderly whether the girl could be arrested on the spot. In the end the orderly stood up and shouted at Paulsson to keep the hell out of his way.

Paulsson had then turned his attention to the wounded man in the woodshed, and Blomkvist heard the inspector report over his radio that Salander had evidently attempted to kill yet another person.

By now Blomkvist was so infuriated with Paulsson, who had obviously not paid attention to a word he had said, that he yelled at him to call Inspector Bublanski in Stockholm without delay. Blomkvist had even taken out his mobile and offered to dial the number for him, but Paulsson was not interested.

Blomkvist then made two mistakes.

First, he patiently but firmly explained that the man who had committed the murders in Stockholm was Ronald Niedermann, who was built like a heavily armoured robot and suffered from a disease called congenital analgesia, and who at that moment was sitting in a ditch on the road to Nossebro tied to a traffic sign. Blomkvist told Paulsson exactly where Niedermann was to be found, and urged him to send a platoon armed with automatic weapons to pick him up. Paulsson finally asked how Niedermann had come to be in that ditch, and Blomkvist freely admitted that he himself had put him there, and had managed only by holding a gun on him the whole time.

"Assault with a deadly weapon," was Paulsson's immediate response.

At this point Blomkvist should have realized that Paulsson was dangerously stupid. He should have called Bublanski himself and asked him to intervene, to bring some clarity to the fog in which Paulsson was apparently enveloped. Instead he made his second mistake: he offered to hand over the weapon he had in his jacket pocket—the Colt 1911 Government model that he had found earlier that day at Salander's apartment in Stockholm. It was the weapon he had used to disarm and disable Niedermann—not a straightforward matter with that giant of a man.

After which Paulsson swiftly arrested Blomkvist for possession of an illegal weapon. He then ordered his two officers to drive over to the Nossebro road. They were to find out if there was any truth to Blomkvist's story that a man was sitting in a ditch there, tied to a MOOSE CROSSING sign. If this was the case, the officers were to handcuff the person in question and bring him to the farm in Gosseberga.

Blomkvist had objected at once, pointing out that Niedermann was not a man who could be arrested and handcuffed just like that: he was a maniacal killer, for God's sake. When Blomkvist's objections were ignored by Paulsson, the exhaustion of the day made him reckless. He told Paulsson he was an incompetent fool and yelled at him that the officers should fucking forget about untying Niedermann until they had called for backup. As a result of this outburst, he was handcuffed and pushed into the back seat of Paulsson's car. Cursing, he watched as the policemen drove off in their patrol car. The only glimmer of light in the darkness was that Salander had been carried to the helicopter, which was even now disappearing over the treetops in the direction of Göteborg. Blomkvist felt utterly helpless: he could only hope that she would be given the very best care. She was going to need it, or she would die.

Jonasson made two deep incisions all the way down to the cranium and peeled back the skin around the entry wound. He used clamps to secure the opening. An OR nurse inserted a suction tube to remove any blood. Then came the awkward part, when he had to use a drill to enlarge the hole in the skull. The procedure was excruciatingly slow.

Finally he had a hole big enough to gain access to Salander's brain. With infinite care he inserted a probe into the brain and enlarged the wound channel by a few millimetres. Then he inserted a thinner probe and located the bullet. From the X-ray he could see that the bullet had turned and was lying at an angle of forty-five degrees to the entry channel. He used the probe cautiously to prise at the edge of the bullet, and after a few unsuccessful attempts he managed to lift it very slightly so that he could turn it in the right direction.

Finally he inserted narrow forceps with serrated jaws. He gripped the base of the bullet, got a good hold on it, then pulled the forceps straight out. The bullet emerged with almost no resistance. He held it up to the light for a few seconds and saw that it appeared intact; then he dropped it into a bowl.

"Swab," he said, and his request was instantly met.

He glanced at the ECG, which showed that his patient still had regular heart activity.

"Forceps."

He pulled down the powerful magnifying glass hanging overhead and focused on the exposed area.

"Careful," Ellis said.

Over the next forty-five minutes Jonasson picked out no fewer than thirty-two tiny bone chips from around the entry wound. The smallest of these chips could scarcely be seen with the naked eye.

As Blomkvist tried in frustration to manoeuvre his mobile out of the breast pocket of his jacket—it proved to be an impossible task with his hands cuffed behind his back, nor was it clear to him how he was going to be able to use it— several more vehicles containing both uniformed officers and technical personnel arrived at the Gosseberga farm. They were detailed by Paulsson to secure forensic evidence in the woodshed and to do a thorough examination of the farmhouse, from which several weapons had already been confiscated. By now resigned to his futility, Blomkvist had observed their comings and goings from his vantage point in Paulsson's vehicle.

An hour passed before it dawned on Paulsson that his officers had not yet returned from their mission to retrieve

Niedermann. He had Blomkvist brought into the kitchen, where he was required once more to provide precise directions to the spot.

Blomkvist closed his eyes.

He was still in the kitchen with Paulsson when the armed response team sent to relieve the first two officers reported back. One had been found dead with a broken neck. The other was still alive, but he had been savagely beaten. The men had been discovered near a MOOSE CROSSING sign by the side of the road. Their service weapons and the marked police car were gone.

Inspector Paulsson had started out with a relatively manageable situation: now he had a murdered policeman and an armed killer on the run.

"Imbecile," Blomkvist said again.

"It won't help to insult the police."

"That certainly seems to be true in your case. But I'm going to report you for dereliction of duty and you won't even know what hit you. Before I'm through with you, you're going to be celebrated as the dumbest policeman in Sweden on every newspaper billboard in the country."

The notion of being the object of public ridicule appeared at last to have an effect on Inspector Paulsson. His face was lined with anxiety.

"What do you propose?"

"I don't propose, I *demand* that you call Inspector Bublanski in Stockholm. This minute. His number's in my mobile in my breast pocket."

Inspector Modig woke with a start when her mobile rang at the other end of the bedroom. She saw to her dismay that it was just after 4:00 in the morning. Then she looked at her husband, who was snoring peacefully. He would probably sleep through an artillery barrage. She staggered out of bed, unplugged her mobile from the charger, and fumbled for the Talk button.

Jan Bublanski, she thought. *Who else?*

"Everything has gone to hell down in Trollhättan," her senior officer said without bothering to greet her or apologize. "The X2000 to Göteborg leaves at 5:10. Take a taxi."

"What's happened?"

"Blomkvist found Salander, Niedermann, *and* Zalachenko. Got himself arrested for insulting a police officer, resisting arrest, and possession of an illegal weapon. Salander was taken to Sahlgrenska with a bullet in her head. Zalachenko is there too, with an axe wound to his skull. Niedermann got away. And he killed a policeman tonight."

Modig blinked twice, registering how exhausted she felt. Most of all she wanted to crawl back into bed and take a month's vacation.

"The X2000 at 5:10. OK. What do you want me to do?"

"Meet Jerker Holmberg at Central Station. You're to contact an Inspector Thomas Paulsson at the Trollhättan police. He seems to be responsible for much of the mess tonight. Blomkvist described him as an Olympic-class idiot."

"You've talked to Blomkvist?"

"Apparently he's been arrested and cuffed. I managed to persuade Paulsson to let me talk to him for a moment. I'm on my way to Kungsholmen right now, and I'll try to work out what's going on. We'll keep in touch by mobile."

Modig looked at the time again. Then she called a taxi and jumped into the shower for a minute. She brushed her teeth, pulled a comb through her hair, and dressed in long black pants, a black T-shirt, and a grey jacket. She put her police revolver in her shoulder bag and picked out a dark-red leather coat. Then she shook enough life into her husband to explain where she was off to, and that he had to deal with the kids in the morning. She walked out the front door just as the taxi pulled up.

She did not have to search for her colleague, Criminal Inspector Holmberg. She assumed he would be in the restaurant car, and that is where she found him. He had already bought coffee and sandwiches for her. They sat in silence for five minutes as they ate their breakfast. Finally Holmberg pushed his coffee cup aside.

"Maybe I should get some training in some other field," he said.

Some time after 4:00 in the morning, Criminal Inspector Marcus Erlander from the violent crimes division of the Göteborg police arrived in Gosseberga and took over the investigation from the overburdened Paulsson. Erlander was a short, round man in his fifties with grey hair. One of the first things he did was to have Blomkvist released from his hand-cuffs, and then he produced rolls and coffee from a thermos. They sat in the living room for a private conversation.

"I've spoken with Bublanski," Erlander said. "Bubble and I have known each other for many years. We are both sorry that you were subjected to Paulsson's rather primitive way of operating."

"He succeeded in getting a policeman killed tonight," Blomkvist said.

Erlander said: "I knew the man personally. He served in

Göteborg before he moved to Trollhättan. He has a three-year-old daughter."

"I'm sorry. I tried to warn Paulsson."

"So I heard. You were quite emphatic, it seems, and that's why you were cuffed. You were the one who exposed that billionaire financier Wennerström last year. Bublanski says you're a shameless journalist bastard and an insane investigative reporter, but that you just might know what you're talking about. Can you bring me up to speed?"

"What happened here tonight is the culmination of the murders of two friends of mine in Enskede, Dag Svensson and Mia Johansson. And the murder of a person who was no friend of mine . . . a lawyer named Bjurman, also Lisbeth Salander's guardian."

Erlander made notes between taking sips of his coffee.

"As you no doubt know, the police have been looking for Salander since Easter. She was a suspect in all three murders. First of all, you have to realize that Salander is not only not guilty of these murders, she has been a victim in the whole affair."

"I haven't had the least connection to the Enskede business, but after everything that was in the media about her it seems a bit hard to swallow that Salander could be completely innocent."

"Nonetheless, that's how it is. She's innocent. Period. The killer is Ronald Niedermann, the man who murdered your officer tonight. He works for Karl Axel Bodin."

"The Bodin who's in Sahlgrenska with an axe in his skull?"

"The axe isn't still in his head. I assume it was Salander who nailed him. His real name is Alexander Zalachenko and he's Lisbeth's father. He was a hit man for Russian military intelligence. He defected in the seventies, and was then on the books of Säpo until the collapse of the Soviet Union. He's been running his own criminal network ever since."

Erlander scrutinized the man across from him. Blomkvist's face was shiny with sweat, but he looked both frozen and deathly tired. Until now he had sounded perfectly rational, but Paulsson—whose opinion had little influence on Erlander—had warned him that Blomkvist had been babbling on about Russian agents and German hit men, hardly routine elements in Swedish police work. Blomkvist had apparently reached the point in his story at which Paulsson had decided to ignore everything else he might say. But there was one policeman dead and another severely wounded on the road to Nossebro, so Erlander was willing to listen. But he could not keep a trace of incredulity out of his voice.

"OK. A Russian agent."

Blomkvist smiled weakly, only too aware of how odd his story sounded.

"A *former* Russian agent. I can document every one of my claims."

"Go on."

"Zalachenko was a top spy in the sixties and seventies. He defected and was granted asylum by Säpo. In his old age he became a gangster. As far as I understand it, it's not a unique situation in the wake of the Soviet Union's collapse."

"OK."

"As I said, I don't know exactly what happened here tonight, but Lisbeth tracked down her father, whom she hadn't seen for fifteen years. Zalachenko abused her mother so viciously that she spent most of her life in a nursing home. He tried to murder Lisbeth, and through Niedermann he was the architect of the murders of Svensson and Johansson. Plus, he was behind the kidnapping of Salander's friend Miriam Wu—you probably heard of boxer Paolo Roberto's title bout in Nykvarn, as a result of which Wu was rescued from certain death."

"If Salander hit her father in the head with an axe she isn't exactly innocent."

"She has been shot three times. I think we could assume her actions were on some level self-defence. I wonder . . ."

"Yes?"

"She was so covered with dirt, with mud, that her hair was one big lump of dried clay. Her clothes were full of sand, inside and out. It looked as though she might have been buried during the night. Niedermann is known to have a habit of burying people alive. The police in Södertälje have found two graves in the place that's owned by Svavelsjö Motorcycle Club, outside Nykvarn."

"Three, as a matter of fact. They found one more late last night. But if Salander was shot and buried, how was she able to climb out and start wandering around with an axe?"

"Whatever went on here tonight, you have to understand that Salander is exceptionally resourceful. I tried to persuade Paulsson to bring in a dog unit—"

"It's on its way now."

"Good."

"Paulsson arrested you for insulting a police officer. . . ."

"I will dispute that. I called him an imbecile and an incompetent fool. Under the circumstances, neither of these epithets could be considered wide of the mark."

"Hmm. It's not a wholly inaccurate description. But you were also arrested for possession of an illegal weapon."

"I made the mistake of trying to hand over a weapon to him. I don't want to say anything more about that until I talk to my lawyer."

"All right. We'll leave it at that. We have more serious issues to discuss. What do you know about this Niedermann?"

"He's a murderer. And there's something wrong with him. He's well over six feet tall and built like a tank. Ask Paolo Roberto, who boxed with him. He suffers from a disease called congenital analgesia, which means the transmitter substance in his nerve synapses doesn't function. He feels no pain. He's German, was born in Hamburg, and in his teens he was a skinhead. Right now he's on the run and he'll be seriously dangerous to anyone he runs into."

"Do you have an idea where he might be heading?"

"No. I only know that I had him neatly trussed, all ready to be arrested, when that idiot from Trollhättan took charge of the situation."

Annika Giannini woke with a start. She saw that it was 5:58 a.m. She had her first client meeting at 8:00. She turned to look at her husband, Enrico, who was sleeping peacefully and probably would not be awake before 8:00. She blinked hard a few times and got up to turn on the coffeemaker before she took her shower. She dressed in black pants, a white polo shirt, and a muted brick-red jacket. She made two slices of toast with cheese, orange marmalade, and a sliced avocado, and carried her breakfast into the living room in time for the 6:30 television news. She took a sip of coffee and had just opened her mouth to take a bite of toast when she heard the headlines.

One policeman killed and another seriously wounded. Drama last night as triple murderer Lisbeth Salander is finally captured.

At first she could not make any sense of it. Was it Salander who had killed a policeman? The news item was sketchy, but bit by bit she gathered that a man was being sought for the killing. A nationwide alert had gone out for a man in his mid-thirties, as yet unnamed. Salander herself was critically injured and at Sahlgrenska hospital in Göteborg.

Annika switched to the other channel, but she learned nothing more about what had happened. She reached for her mobile and called her brother, Mikael Blomkvist. She only got his voicemail. She felt a small twinge of fear. He had called on his way to Göteborg. He had been tracking Salander. And a murderer who called himself Ronald Niedermann.

As it was growing light, an observant police officer found traces of blood on the ground behind the woodshed. A police dog followed the trail to a narrow trench in a clearing in a wood about a quarter of a mile northeast of the farmhouse.

Blomkvist went with Inspector Erlander. Grimly they studied the site. Much more blood had obviously been shed in and around the trench.

They found a damaged cigarette case that seemed to have been used as a scoop. Erlander put it in an evidence bag and labelled the find. He also gathered samples of blood-soaked clumps of dirt. A uniformed officer drew his attention to a cigarette butt—a filterless Pall Mall—some distance from the hole. This too was saved in an evidence bag and labelled. Blomkvist remembered having seen a pack of Pall Malls on the kitchen counter in Zalachenko's house.

Erlander glanced up at the lowering rain clouds. The storm that had ravaged Göteborg earlier in the night had obviously passed to the south of the Nossebro area, but it was only a matter of time before the rain came. He instructed one of his men to get a tarpaulin to cover the trench and its immediate surroundings.

"I think you're right," Erlander said to Blomkvist as they walked back to the farmhouse. "An analysis of the blood will probably establish that Salander was shot and buried here, and I'm beginning to expect that we'll find her fingerprints on the cigarette case. Somehow she managed to survive and dig herself out and—"

"And somehow get back to the farm and swing an axe into Zalachenko's skull," Blomkvist finished for him. "She can be a moody bitch."

"But how on earth did she handle Niedermann?"

Blomkvist shrugged. He was as bewildered as Erlander on that score.

CHAPTER 2

Friday, April 8

Modig and Holmberg arrived at Göteborg Central Station just after 8:00 a.m. Bublanski had called to give them new instructions. They could forget about finding a car to take them to Gosseberga. They were to take a taxi to police headquarters on Ernst Fontells Plats, the seat of the County Criminal Police in western Götaland. They waited for almost an hour before Inspector Erlander arrived from Gosseberga with Blomkvist. Blomkvist said hello to Modig, having met her before, and shook hands with Holmberg, whom he did not know. One of Erlander's colleagues joined them with an update on the hunt for Niedermann. It was a brief report.

"We have a team working under the auspices of the County Criminal Police. An APB has gone out, of course. The missing patrol car was found in Alingsås early this morning. The trail ends there for the moment. We have to suppose that he switched vehicles, but we've had no report of a car being stolen thereabouts."

"Media?" Modig asked, with an apologetic glance at Blomkvist.

"It's a police killing and the press is out in force. We'll be holding a press conference at 10:00."

"Does anyone have any information on Lisbeth Salander's condition?" Blomkvist said. He felt strangely uninterested in everything to do with the hunt for Niedermann.

"She was operated on during the night. They removed a bullet from her head. She hasn't regained consciousness yet."

"Is there any prognosis?"

"As I understand it, we won't know anything until she wakes up. But the surgeon says he has high hopes that she'll survive, barring unforeseen complications."

"And Zalachenko?"

"Who?" Erlander's colleague said. He had not yet been brought up to date with all the details.

"Karl Axel Bodin."

"I see . . . yes, he was operated on last night too. He had a very deep gash across his face, and another just below one kneecap. He's in bad shape, but the injuries aren't life-threatening."

Blomkvist absorbed this news.

"You look tired," Modig said.

"You got that right. I'm into my third day with hardly any sleep."

"Believe it or not, he actually slept in the car coming down from Nossebro," Erlander said.

"Could you manage to tell us the whole story from the beginning?" Holmberg said. "It feels to us as though the score between the private investigators and the police investigators is about three to nothing."

Blomkvist gave him a wan smile. "That's a line I'd like to hear from Officer Bubble."

They made their way to the police cafeteria to have breakfast. Blomkvist spent half an hour explaining step by step how he had pieced together the story of Zalachenko. When he had finished, the detectives sat in silence.

"There are a few holes in your account," Holmberg said at last.

"That's possible," Blomkvist said.

"You didn't say, for example, how you came to be in possession of the top secret Säpo report on Zalachenko."

"I found it yesterday at Lisbeth Salander's apartment when I finally worked out where she was. She probably found it in Bjurman's summer cabin."

"So you've discovered Salander's hideout?" Modig said.

Blomkvist nodded.

"And?"

"You'll have to find out for yourselves where it is. Salander put a lot of effort into establishing a secret address for herself, and I have no intention of revealing its whereabouts."

Modig and Holmberg exchanged an anxious look.

"Mikael . . . this is a murder investigation," Modig said.

"You still don't get it, do you? Lisbeth Salander is in fact innocent and the police have destroyed her reputation in unprecedented ways. 'Lesbian Satanist gang' . . . Where the hell do you get this stuff? Not to mention her being sought in connection with three murders she had nothing to do with. If she wants to tell you where she lives, then I'm sure she will."

"But there's another gap I don't really understand," Holmberg said. "How does Bjurman come into the story in the first place? You say he was the one who started the whole thing by contacting Zalachenko and asking him to kill Salander. Why would he do that?"

"My guess is that he hired Zalachenko to get rid of Salander. The plan was for her to end up in that warehouse in Nykvarn."

"He was her guardian. What motive would he have had to get rid of her?"

"It's complicated."

"I can do complicated."

"He had a hell of a good motive. He had done something that Salander knew about. She was a threat to his entire future and well-being."

"What had he done?"

"I think it would be best if you gave Salander a chance to explain the story herself." He looked Holmberg steadily in the eye.

"Let me guess," Modig said. "Bjurman subjected his ward to some sort of sexual assault."

Blomkvist shrugged and said nothing.

"You don't know about the tattoo Bjurman had on his abdomen?"

"What tattoo?" Blomkvist was taken aback.

"An amateurish tattoo across his belly with a message that said: 'I am a sadistic pig, a pervert, and a rapist.' We've been wondering what that was about."

Blomkvist burst out laughing.

"What's so funny?"

"I've always wondered what she did to get her revenge. But listen, I don't want to discuss this for the same reason I've already given. She's the real victim here. She's the one who has to decide what she is willing to tell you. Sorry."

He looked almost apologetic.

"Rapes should always be reported to the police," Modig said.

"I'm with you on that. But this rape took place two years ago, and Lisbeth still hasn't talked to the police about it. Which means that she doesn't intend to. It doesn't matter how much I disagree with her about the matter; it's her decision. Anyway . . ."

"Yes?"

"She had no good reason to trust the police. The last time she tried explaining what a pig Zalachenko was, she was locked up in a mental hospital."

Richard Ekström, the leader of the preliminary investigation, had butterflies in his stomach as he asked his team leader, Inspector Bublanski, to take a seat across from him. Ekström straightened his glasses and stroked his well-groomed goatee. He felt that the situation was chaotic and ominous. For several weeks they had been hunting Lisbeth Salander. He himself had proclaimed her far and wide to be mentally imbalanced, a dangerous psychopath. He had leaked information that would have backed him up in an upcoming trial. Everything had looked so good.

There had been no doubt in his mind that Salander was guilty of three murders. The trial should have been a straightforward matter, a pure media circus with himself at centre stage. Then everything had gone haywire, and he found himself with a completely different murderer and a chaos that seemed to have no end in sight. *That bitch Salander.*

"Well, this is a fine mess we've landed in," he said. "What have you come up with this morning?"

"A nationwide APB has been sent out on this Ronald Niedermann, but there's no sign of him. At present he's being sought only for the murder of a police officer, but I anticipate we'll have grounds for charging him with the three murders here in Stockholm. Maybe you should call a press conference."

Bublanski added the suggestion of a press conference out of sheer spite. Ekström hated press conferences.

"I think we'll hold off on the press conference for the time being," he snapped.

Bublanski had to stop himself from smiling.

"In the first place, this is a matter for the Göteborg police," Ekström said.

"Well, we do have Modig and Holmberg on the scene in Göteborg, and we've begun to cooperate—"

"We'll hold off on the press conference until we know more," Ekström repeated in a brittle tone. "What I want to know is: how certain are you that Niedermann really is involved in the murders in Stockholm?"

"My gut feeling? I'm 100 percent convinced. On the other hand, the case isn't exactly rock solid. We have no witnesses to the murders, and there is no satisfactory forensic evidence. Magge Lundin and Sonny Nieminen of the Svavelsjö MC are refusing to say anything—they're claiming they've never heard of Niedermann. But he's going to go to prison for the murder of a policeman."

"Precisely," said Ekström. "The killing of the officer is the main thing right now. But tell me this: is there anything at all to even suggest that Salander might be involved in some way in the murders? Could she and Niedermann have committed the murders together?"

"I very much doubt it, and if I were you I wouldn't voice that theory in public."

"So how is she involved?"

"This is an intricate story, as Mikael Blomkvist claimed from the very beginning. It revolves around this Zala . . . Alexander Zalachenko."

Ekström flinched at the mention of the name Blomkvist.

"Go on," he said.

"Zala is a Russian hit man—apparently without a grain of conscience—who defected in the seventies, and Lisbeth Salander was unlucky enough to have him as her father. He was sponsored or supported by a faction within Säpo that tidied up after any crimes he committed. A police officer attached to Säpo also saw to it that Salander was locked up in a children's psychiatric clinic. She was twelve and had threatened to blow Zalachenko's identity, his alias, his whole cover."

"This is a bit difficult to digest. It's hardly a story we can make public. If I understand the matter correctly, all this stuff about Zalachenko is highly classified."

"Nevertheless, it's the truth. I have documentation."

"May I see it?"

Bublanski pushed across the desk a folder containing a police report dated 1991. Ekström surreptitiously scanned the stamp, which indicated that the document was top secret, and the registration number, which he at once identified as belonging to the Security Police. He leafed rapidly through the hundred or so pages, reading paragraphs here and there. Eventually he put the folder aside.

"We have to try to tone this down, so that the situation doesn't get completely out of our control. So Salander was locked up in an asylum because she tried to kill her father, this Zalachenko. And now she has attacked him with an axe. By any interpretation that would be attempted murder. And she has to be charged with shooting Magge Lundin in Stallarholmen."

"You can arrest whomever you want, but I would tread carefully if I were you."

"There's going to be an enormous scandal if Säpo's involvement gets leaked."

Bublanski shrugged. His job was to investigate crimes, not to clean up after scandals.

"This bastard from Säpo, this Gunnar Björck. What do you know about his role?"

"He's one of the major players. He's on sick leave for a slipped disk and lives in Smådalarö at present."

"OK . . . we'll keep the lid on Säpo's involvement for the time being. The focus right now is to be on the murder of a police officer."

"It's going to be hard to keep this under wraps."

"What do you mean?"

"I sent Andersson to bring in Björck for a formal interrogation. That should be happening"—Bublanski looked at his watch—"yes, about now."

"You *what*?"

"I was rather hoping to have the pleasure of driving out to Smådalarö myself, but the events surrounding last night's killing took precedence."

"I didn't give anyone permission to arrest Björck."

"That's true. But it's not an arrest. I'm just bringing him in for questioning."

"Whichever, I don't like it."

Bublanski leaned forward, almost as if to confide in the other man.

"Richard, this is how it is. Salander has been subjected to a number of infringements of her rights, starting when she was a child. I do not mean for this to continue on my watch. You have the option to remove me as leader of the investigation . . . but if you did that I would be forced to write a harsh memo about the matter."

Ekström looked as if he had just swallowed something very sour.

Gunnar Björck, on sick leave from his job as assistant chief of the immigration division of the Security Police, opened the door of his summer house in Smådalarö and looked up at a powerfully built blond man with a crew cut who wore a black leather jacket.

"I'm looking for Gunnar Björck."

"That's me."

"Curt Andersson, County Criminal Police." The man held up his ID.

"Yes?"

"You are requested to accompany me to Kungsholmen to assist the police in their investigations into the case involving Lisbeth Salander."

"Uh . . . there must be some sort of misunderstanding."

"There's no misunderstanding," Andersson said.

"You don't understand. I'm a police officer myself. Save yourself making a big mistake: check it out with your superior officers."

"My superior is the one who wants to talk to you."

"I have to make a call and—"

"You can make your call from Kungsholmen."

Björck felt suddenly resigned. *It's happened. I'm going to be arrested. That goddamn fucking Blomkvist. And fucking Salander.*

"Am I being arrested?" he said.

"Not at the moment. But we can arrange for that if you like."

"No . . . no, of course I'll come with you. Naturally I'd want to assist my colleagues in the police force."

"All right, then," Andersson said, walking into the hallway to keep a close eye on Björck as he turned off the coffee machine and picked up his coat.

In the late morning it dawned on Blomkvist that his rental car was still at the Gosseberga farm, but he was so exhausted that he did not have the strength or the means to get out there to fetch it, much less drive safely for any distance. Erlander kindly arranged for a crime scene tech to take the car back on his way home.

"Think of it as compensation for the way you were treated last night."

Blomkvist thanked him and took a taxi to City Hotel on Lorensbergsgatan. He booked in for the night for 800 kronor and went straight to his room and undressed. He sat naked on the bed and took Salander's Palm Tungsten T3 from the inside pocket of his jacket, weighing it in his hand. He was still amazed that it had not been confiscated when Paulsson frisked him, but Paulsson presumably thought it was Blomkvist's own, and he had never been formally taken into custody and searched. He thought for a moment and then slipped it into a compartment of his laptop case, where he had also put Salander's DVD marked "Bjurman," which Paulsson had also missed. He knew that technically he was withholding evidence, but these were the things that Salander would no doubt prefer not to have fall into the wrong hands.

He turned on his mobile and saw that the battery was low, so he plugged in the charger. He made a call to his sister, Advokat Giannini.

"Hi, Annika."

"What did you have to do with the policeman's murder last night?" she asked him at once.

He told her succinctly what had happened.

"So Salander is in intensive care."

"Correct, and we won't know the extent or severity of her injuries until she regains consciousness, but now she's really going to need a lawyer."

Giannini thought for a moment. "Do you think she'd want me for her lawyer?"

"Probably she wouldn't want any lawyer at all. She isn't the type to ask anyone for help."

"Mikael . . . I've said this before: it sounds like she might need a criminal lawyer. Let me look at the documentation you have."

"Talk to Erika and ask her for a copy."

As soon as Blomkvist hung up, he called Berger himself. She did not answer her mobile, so he tried her number at the *Millennium* offices. Henry Cortez answered.

"Erika's out somewhere," he said.

Blomkvist briefly explained what had happened and asked Cortez to pass the information to Erika.

"I will. What do you want us to do?" Cortez said.

"Nothing today," Blomkvist said. "I have to get some sleep. I'll be back in Stockholm tomorrow if nothing else comes up. *Millennium* will have an opportunity to present its version of the story in the next issue, but that's almost a month away."

He flipped his mobile shut and crawled into bed. He was asleep within thirty seconds.

Assistant County Police Chief Carina Spångberg tapped her pen against her glass of water and asked for quiet. Nine people were seated around the conference table in her office at police headquarters. Three women and six men: the head of the violent crimes division and his assistant head; three criminal inspectors, including Erlander; the Göteborg police public information officer; preliminary investigation leader Agneta Jervas from the prosecutor's office; and Inspectors Modig and Holmberg from the Stockholm police. They were included as a sign of goodwill and to demonstrate that Göteborg wished to cooperate with their colleagues from the capital. Possibly also to show them how a real police investigation should be run.

Spångberg, who was frequently the lone woman in a male landscape, had a reputation for not wasting time on formalities or mere courtesies. She explained that the county police chief was at the Europol conference in Madrid, that he had cut short his trip as soon as he learned that one of his police officers had been murdered, but that he was not expected back before late that night. Then she turned directly to the head of the violent crimes division, Anders Pehrzon, and asked him to brief the assembled company.

"It's been about ten hours since our colleague was murdered on Nossebrovägen. We know the name of the killer,

Ronald Niedermann, but we still don't have a picture of him."

"In Stockholm we have a photograph of him that's about twenty years old. Paolo Roberto got it through a boxing club in Germany, but it's almost unusable," Holmberg said.

"All right. The patrol car that Niedermann is thought to have driven away was found in Alingsås this morning, as you all know. It was parked on a side street a quarter of a mile from the railway station. We haven't had a report yet of any car thefts in the area this morning."

"What's the status of the search?"

"We're keeping an eye on all trains arriving in Stockholm and Malmö. There is a nationwide APB out and we've alerted the police in Norway and Denmark. Right now we have about thirty officers working directly on the investigation, and of course the whole force is keeping their eyes peeled."

"No leads?"

"No, nothing yet. But someone with Niedermann's distinctive appearance is not going to go unnoticed for long."

"Does anyone know about the wounded officer's condition?" asked one of the inspectors from Violent Crimes.

"He's at Sahlgrenska. His injuries seem to be similar to those of a car crash victim—it's hardly credible that anyone could do such damage with his bare hands: leg broken, ribs crushed, cervical vertebrae injured, plus there's a risk that he may be paralysed."

They all took stock of their colleague's plight for a few moments until Spångberg turned to Erlander.

"Marcus, tell us what really happened at Gosseberga."

"Thomas Paulsson happened at Gosseberga."

A ripple of groans greeted this response.

"Can't someone give that man early retirement? He's a walking catastrophe."

"I know all about Paulsson," Spångberg interjected. "But I haven't heard any complaints about him in the last . . . well, not for the past two years. In what way has he become harder to handle?"

"The police chief up there is an old friend of Paulsson's, and he's probably been trying to protect him. With all good intentions, of course, and I don't mean to criticize him. But last night Paulsson's behaviour was so bizarre that several of his people mentioned it to me."

"In what way bizarre?"

Erlander glanced at Modig and Holmberg. He was embarrassed to be discussing flaws in their organization in front of the visitors from Stockholm.

"As far as I'm concerned, the strangest thing was that he detailed one of the techs to make an inventory of everything in the woodshed—where we found the Zalachenko guy."

"An inventory of *what* in the woodshed?" Spångberg wanted to know.

"He said he needed to know exactly how many pieces of wood were in there. So that the report would be accurate."

There was a charged silence around the conference table before Erlander went on.

"And this morning it came out that Paulsson has been taking at least two different antidepressants. He should have been on sick leave, but no-one knew about his condition."

"What condition?" Spångberg said sharply.

"Well, obviously I don't know what's wrong with him—patient confidentiality and all that—but he's taking both strong tranquilizers and stimulants. He was high as a kite all night."

"Good God," said Spångberg emphatically. She looked like the thundercloud that had swept over Göteborg that morning. "I want Paulsson in here for a chat. Right now."

"He collapsed this morning and was admitted to the hospital, suffering from exhaustion. It was just our bad luck that he happened to be on rotation."

"Did he arrest Mikael Blomkvist last night?"

"He wrote a report citing disorderly conduct, resisting arrest, and illegal possession of a weapon. That's what he put in the report."

"What does Blomkvist say?"

"He concedes that he was insulting, but he claims it was in self-defence. He says that the resistance consisted of a forceful verbal attempt to prevent two officers from going to pick up Niedermann alone, without backup."

"Witnesses?"

"Well, there is the surviving officer. I don't believe Paulsson's claim of resisting arrest. It's a typical pre-emptive retaliation to undermine potential complaints from Blomkvist."

"But Blomkvist managed to overpower Niedermann all by himself, did he not?" Prosecutor Jervas said.

"By holding a gun on him."

"So Blomkvist had a gun. Then there was some basis for his arrest after all. Where did he get the weapon?"

"Blomkvist won't discuss it without his lawyer being there. And Paulsson arrested Blomkvist when he was trying to hand in the weapon to the police."

"Could I make a small, informal suggestion?" Modig said cautiously.

Everyone turned to her.

"I have met Mikael Blomkvist on several occasions in the course of this investigation. I have found him quite likeable, even though he is a journalist. I suppose you're the one who has to make the decision about charging him . . ." She looked at Jervas, who nodded. "All this stuff about insults and resisting arrest is just nonsense. I assume you will ignore it."

"Probably. Illegal weapons are more serious."

"I would urge you to wait and see. Blomkvist has put the pieces of this puzzle together all by himself; he's way ahead of us on the police force. It will be to our advantage to stay on good terms with him and ensure his cooperation, rather than unleash him to condemn the entire police force in his magazine and elsewhere in the media."

After a few seconds, Erlander cleared his throat. If Modig dared to stick her neck out, he could do the same.

"I agree with Sonja. I too think Blomkvist is a man we could work with. I've apologized to him for the way he was treated last night. He seems ready to let bygones be bygones. Besides, he has integrity. He somehow tracked down where Salander was living, but he won't give us the address. He's not afraid to get into a public scrap with the police . . . and he's most certainly in a position where his voice will carry just as much weight in the media as any report from Paulsson."

"But he refuses to give the police any information about Salander."

"He says that we'll have to ask her ourselves, if that time ever comes. He says he absolutely won't discuss a person who is not only innocent but who also has had her rights so severely violated."

"What kind of weapon is it?" Jervas said.

"It's a Colt 1911 Government. Serial number unknown. Forensics has it, and we don't know yet whether it is connected to any known crime in Sweden. If it is, that will put the matter in a rather different light."

Spångberg raised her pen.

"Agneta, it's up to you to decide whether you want to initiate a preliminary investigation against Blomkvist. But I advise that you wait for the report from forensics. So let's move on. This character Zalachenko . . . what can our colleagues from Stockholm tell us about him?"

"The truth is," Modig said, "that until yesterday afternoon we had never heard of either Zalachenko or Niedermann."

"I thought you were busy looking for a lesbian Satanist gang in Stockholm. Was I wrong?" one of the Göteborg detectives said. His colleagues all frowned. Holmberg was studying his fingernails. Modig had to take the question.

"Within these four walls, I can tell you that we have our equivalent of Inspector Paulsson, and all that stuff about a lesbian Satanist gang is probably a smokescreen originating mainly from him."

Modig and Holmberg then described in detail the investigation as it had developed. When they had finished there was a long silence around the table.

"If all this about Gunnar Björck is true and it comes out, Säpo's ears are going to be burning," the assistant head of the violent crimes division concluded.

Jervas raised her hand. "It sounds to me as though your suspicions are for the most part based on assumptions and circumstantial evidence. As a prosecutor I would be uneasy about the lack of unassailable evidence."

"We're aware of that," Holmberg said. "We think we know

what happened in general, but there are questions that still have to be answered."

"I gather you're still busy with excavations in Nykvarn," Spångberg said. "How many killings do you reckon this case involves?"

Holmberg rubbed his eyes wearily. "We started with two, then three murders in Stockholm. Those are the ones that prompted the hunt for Salander: the deaths of Advokat Bjurman, the journalist Dag Svensson, and Mia Johansson, an academic. In the area around the warehouse in Nykvarn we have so far found three graves—well, three bodies. We've identified a known dealer and petty thief who was found dismembered in one trench. We found a woman's body in a second trench—she's still unidentified. And we haven't dug up the third yet. It appears to be older than the others. Furthermore, Blomkvist has made a connection to the murder several months ago of a prostitute in Södertälje."

"So, with the policeman dead in Gosseberga, we're talking about at least eight murders. That's a horrendous statistic. Do we suspect this Niedermann of all of them? If so, he has to be treated as a madman, a mass murderer."

Modig and Holmberg exchanged glances. It was now a matter of how far they wanted to align themselves with such assertions. Finally Modig spoke up.

"Even though crucial evidence is lacking, my superior, Inspector Bublanski, and I are tending towards the belief that Blomkvist is correct in claiming that the first three murders were committed by Niedermann. That would require us to believe that Salander is innocent. With respect to the graves in Nykvarn, Niedermann is linked to the site through the kidnapping of Salander's friend Miriam Wu. There is a strong likelihood that she too would have been his victim. But the warehouse is owned by a relative of the president of Svavelsjö Motorcycle Club, and until we're able to identify the remains, we won't be able to draw any conclusions."

"That petty thief you identified . . ."

"Forty-four, a dealer, and delinquent in his youth. Off-hand I would guess the murder has to do with an internal shake-up of some sort. Svavelsjö MC is mixed up in several kinds of criminal activity, including the distribution of methamphetamine. Nykvarn may be a cemetery in the woods for people who crossed them, but . . ."

"Yes?"

"This young prostitute who was murdered in Söder-tälje . . . the autopsy revealed that she died as a result of a staggeringly vicious assault. She looked as if she had been beaten to death. But the actual cause of her injuries could not be established. Blomkvist made a pretty acute observation. She had injuries that could very well have been inflicted by a man's bare hands."

"Niedermann?"

"It's a reasonable assumption. But there's no proof yet."

"So how do we proceed?" Spångberg wondered.

"I have to confer with Bublanski," Modig said. "But a logical step would be to interrogate Zalachenko. We're interested in hearing what he has to say about the murders in Stockholm, and for you it's a matter of finding out what was Niedermann's role in Zalachenko's business. He might even be able to point you in the direction of Niedermann."

One of the detectives from Göteborg said: "What have we found at the farm in Gosseberga?"

"We found four revolvers. A Sig Sauer that had been dismantled and was being oiled on the kitchen table. A Polish P-83 Wanad on the floor next to the bench in the kitchen. A Colt 1911 Government—that's the pistol that Blomkvist tried to hand in to Paulsson. And finally a .22-calibre Browning, which is pretty much a toy gun alongside the others. We rather think that it was the weapon used to shoot Salander, given that she's still alive with a slug in her brain."

"Anything else?"

"We found and confiscated a bag containing about 200,000 kronor. It was in an upstairs room used by Niedermann."

"How do you know it was his room?"

"Well, he does wear a size XXL. Zalachenko is at most a medium."

"Do you have anything on Zalachenko or Bodin in your records?" Holmberg said.

Erlander shook his head.

"Of course, it depends on how we interpret the confiscated weapons. Apart from the more sophisticated weaponry and an unusually high-tech video surveillance system at the farm, we found nothing to distinguish it from any other farmhouse. The house itself is spartan, no frills."

Just before noon there was a knock on the door and a uniformed officer delivered a document to Spångberg.

"We've received a call," she said, "about a missing person in Alingsås. A dental hygienist by the name of Anita Kaspersson left her home by car at 7:30 this morning. She took her child to day care and should have arrived at her place of work by 8:00. But she never did. The dental office is about a hundred fifty yards from the spot where the patrol car was found."

Erlander and Modig both looked at their wristwatches.

"Then he has a four-hour head start. What kind of car is it?"

"A dark blue 1991 Renault. Here's the registration number."

"Send out an APB on the vehicle at once. He could be in Oslo by now, or Malmö, or maybe even Stockholm."

They brought the conference to a close by deciding that Modig and Erlander would together interrogate Zalachenko.

Cortez frowned and followed Berger with his gaze as she cut across the hall from her office to the kitchenette. She emerged moments later with a cup of coffee, went back into her office, and closed the door.

Cortez could not put his finger on what was wrong. *Millennium* was the kind of small office where co-workers were close. He had worked part-time at the magazine for four years, and during that time the team had weathered some phenomenal storms, especially during the period when Blomkvist was serving a three-month sentence for libel and the magazine almost went under. Then their colleague Dag Svensson was murdered, and his girlfriend too.

Through all these storms, Berger had been the rock that nothing seemed capable of shifting. He was not surprised that she had called to wake him early that morning and put him and Lotta Karim to work. The Salander affair had cracked wide open, and Blomkvist had somehow gotten himself involved in the killing of a policeman in Göteborg. So far, everything was under control. Karim had parked herself at police headquarters and was doing her best to get some solid information out of someone. Cortez had spent the morning making calls, piecing together what had happened overnight. Blomkvist was not answering his phone, but from a number of sources Cortez had a fairly clear picture of the events of the night before.

Berger, on the other hand, had been distracted all morning. It was rare for her to close the door to her office. That usually happened only when she had a visitor or was working intently on some problem. This morning she had not had a single visitor, and she was not—so far as he could judge—working. On several occasions when he had knocked on the door to relay some news, he had found her sitting in the chair by the window. She seemed lost in thought, as she listlessly watched the stream of people walking down below on Götgatan. She had paid scant attention to his reports.

Something was wrong.

The doorbell interrupted his ruminations. He went to open it and found the lawyer Annika Giannini. Cortez had met Blomkvist's sister a few times, but he did not know her well.

"Hello, Annika," he said. "Mikael isn't here today."

"I know. I want to talk to Erika."

Berger barely looked up from her position by the window, but she quickly pulled herself together when she saw who it was.

"Hello," she said. "Mikael isn't here today."

Giannini smiled. "I know. I'm here for Björck's Säpo report. Micke asked me to take a look at it in case it turns out that I represent Salander."

Berger nodded. She got up, took a folder from her desk, and handed it to Giannini.

Giannini hesitated a moment, wondering whether to leave the office. Then she made up her mind and, uninvited, sat down across from Berger.

"OK, what's going on with you?"

"I'm about to resign from *Millennium*, and I haven't been able to tell Mikael. He's been so tied up in this Salander mess that there hasn't been the right opportunity, and I can't tell the others before I tell him. Right now I just feel like shit."

Giannini bit her lower lip. "So you're telling me instead. Why are you leaving?"

"I'm going to be editor in chief of *Svenska Morgon-Posten*."

"Jesus. Well, in that case, congratulations seem to be in order rather than any weeping or gnashing of teeth."

"Annika . . . this isn't the way I had planned to end my time at *Millennium*. In the middle of chaos. But the offer came like a bolt from the blue, and I can't say no. I mean, it's the chance of a lifetime. I got the offer just before Dag and Mia were shot, and there's been such turmoil here that I buried it. And now I have the world's worst guilty conscience."

"I understand. But now you're afraid of telling Micke."

"It's an utter disaster. I haven't told anybody. I thought I wouldn't be starting at *SMP* until after the summer, and that there would still be time to tell everyone. But now they want me to start ASAP."

She fell silent and stared at Annika. She looked on the verge of tears.

"This is, in point of fact, my last week at *Millennium*. Next week I'll be on a trip, and then . . . I need about two weeks off to recharge my batteries. I start at *SMP* on the first of May."

"Well, what would have happened if you'd been run over by a bus? Then they would have been without an editor in chief with only a moment's notice."

Erika looked up. "But I haven't been run over by a bus. I've been deliberately keeping quiet about my decision."

"I can see this is a difficult situation, but I have a feeling that Micke and Christer Malm and the others will be able to work things out. I think you ought to tell them right away."

"All right, but your damned brother is in Göteborg today. He's asleep and has turned off his mobile."

"I know. There aren't many people who are as stubborn as Mikael about not being available when you need him. But Erika, this isn't about you and Micke. I know that you've worked together for twenty years or so and you've had your ups and downs, but you have to think about Christer and the others on the staff too."

"I've been keeping it under wraps all this time. Mikael's going to—"

"Micke's going to go through the roof, of course he is. But if he can't handle the fact that you screwed up one time in twenty years, then he isn't worth the time you've put in for him."

Berger sighed.

"Pull yourself together," Giannini told her. "Call Christer in, and the rest of the staff. Right now."

Malm sat motionless for a few seconds. Berger had gathered her colleagues into *Millennium*'s small conference room with only a few minutes' notice, just as he was about to leave early. He glanced at Cortez and Karim. They were as astonished as he was. Malin Eriksson, the managing editor, had not known anything either, nor had Monika Nilsson, the reporter, or the advertising manager, Magnusson. Blomkvist was the only one absent from the meeting. He was in Göteborg being his usual Blomkvist self.

Good God. Mikael doesn't know anything about it either, thought Malm. *How on earth is he going to react?*

Then he realized that Berger had stopped talking, and it was as silent as the grave in the conference room. He shook his head, stood up, and spontaneously gave Berger a hug and a kiss on the cheek.

"Congrats, Ricky," he said. "Editor in chief of *SMP*. That's not a bad step up from this sorry little rag."

Cortez came to life and began to clap. Berger held up her hands.

"Stop," she said. "I don't deserve any applause today." She looked around at her colleagues in the cramped editorial office. "Listen, I'm terribly sorry that it had to be this way. I wanted to tell you sooner, but the news sort of got drowned out by all the turmoil surrounding Dag and Mia. Mikael and Malin have been working like demons, and it just didn't ever seem like the right time or place. And that's how we've arrived at this point today."

Eriksson realized with terrible clarity how understaffed the paper was, and how empty it was going to seem without Berger. No matter what happened, or whatever problem arose, Berger had been a boss she could always rely on. No wonder the biggest daily had recruited her. But what was going to happen now? Erika had always been a crucial part of *Millennium*.

"There are a few things we have to get straight. I'm perfectly aware that this is going to create difficulties in the office. I didn't want it to, but that's the way things are. First of all: I won't abandon *Millennium*. I'm going to stay on as a partner and will attend board meetings. I won't, of course, have any influence in editorial matters."

Malm nodded thoughtfully.

"Second, I officially leave on the last day of April. But today is my last day of work. Next week I'll be travelling, as you know. It's been planned for a long time. And I've decided not to come back here to put in any days during the transition period." She paused for a moment. "The next issue of the magazine is ready in the computer. There are a few minor things that need fixing. It will be my final issue. I'm clearing my desk tonight."

There was absolute silence in the room.

"The selection of a new editor in chief will have to be discussed and made by the board. It's something that you all on the staff will have to talk through."

"Mikael," Malm said.

"No. Never Mikael. He's surely the worst possible editor in chief you could pick. He's perfect as publisher and damned good at editing articles and tying up loose ends in material that is going to be published. He's the fixer. The editor in chief has to be the one who takes the initiative. Mikael also has a tendency to bury himself in his own stories and be totally off the radar for weeks at a time. He's at his best when things heat up, but he's incredibly bad at routine work. You all know that."

Malm muttered his assent and then said: "*Millennium* functioned because you and Mikael were a good balance for each other."

"That's not the only reason. You remember when Mikael

was up in Hedestad sulking for almost a whole year? *Millennium* functioned without him precisely the way the magazine is going to have to function without me now."

"What's your plan?"

"My choice would be for you, Christer, to take over as editor in chief."

"Not on your life." Malm threw up his hands.

"But since I knew that's what you would say, I have another solution. Malin. You can start as acting editor in chief from today."

"Me?" Eriksson said. She sounded shocked.

"Yes, you. You've been damned good as managing editor."

"But I—"

"Give it a try. I'll be out of my office tonight. You can move in on Monday morning. The May issue is done—we've already worked hard on it. June is a double issue, and then you have a month off. If it doesn't work, the board will have to find somebody else for August. Henry, you'll take Malin's place as managing editor. Then we'll need to hire a new employee. But that will be up to all of you, and to the board."

She studied the group thoughtfully.

"One more thing. For all practical purposes, *SMP* and *Millennium* are not competitors, but nevertheless I don't want to know any more than I already do about the content of the next two issues. All such matters should be discussed with Malin, effective immediately."

"What should we do about this Salander story?" Cortez said.

"Discuss it with Mikael. I know something about Salander, but I'm putting what I know in mothballs. I won't take it to *SMP*." Berger suddenly felt an enormous wave of relief. "That's about it," she said, and she ended the meeting by getting up and going back to her office without another word.

Millennium's staff sat in silence.

It was not until an hour later that Eriksson knocked on Berger's door.

"Hello there."

"Yes?" said Berger.

"The staff would like to have a word."

"What is it?"

"Out here."

Berger got up and went to the door. They had set a table with cake and Friday afternoon coffee.

"We think we should have a party and give you a real send-off in due course," Malm said. "But for now, coffee and cake will have to do."

Berger smiled, for the first time in a long time.

CHAPTER 3

Friday, April 8–
Saturday, April 9

Zalachenko had been awake for eight hours when Inspectors Modig and Erlander came to his room at 7:00 in the evening. He had undergone an extensive operation in which a significant section of his jaw was realigned and fixed with titanium screws. His head was wrapped in so many bandages that you could see only his left eye and a narrow slit of mouth. A doctor had explained that the axe blow had crushed his cheekbone and damaged his forehead, peeling off a large part of the flesh on the right side of his face and tugging at his eye socket. His injuries were causing him immense pain. He had been given large doses of painkillers, yet was relatively lucid and able to talk. But the officers were warned not to tire him.

"Good evening, Herr Zalachenko," Modig said. She introduced herself and her colleague.

"My name is Karl Axel Bodin," Zalachenko said laboriously through clenched teeth. His voice was steady.

"I know exactly who you are. I've read your file from Säpo."

This, of course, was not true.

"That was a long time ago," Zalachenko said. "I'm Karl Axel Bodin now."

"How are you doing? Are you able to have a conversation?"

"I want to report a serious crime. I have been the victim of attempted murder by my daughter."

"We know. That matter will be dealt with at the appropriate time," Erlander said. "But we have more urgent issues to talk about."

"What could be more urgent than attempted murder?"

"Right now we need information from you about three murders in Stockholm, at least three murders in Nykvarn, and a kidnapping."

"I don't know anything about that. Who was murdered?"

"Herr Bodin, we have good reason to believe that your associate, thirty-five-year-old Ronald Niedermann, is guilty of these crimes," Erlander said. "Last night he also murdered a police officer from Trollhättan."

Modig was surprised that Erlander had acquiesced to Zalachenko's wish to be called Bodin. Zalachenko turned his head a little so that he could see Erlander. His voice softened slightly.

"That is . . . unfortunate to hear. I know nothing about Niedermann's affairs. I have not killed any policeman. I was the victim of attempted murder myself last night."

"There's a manhunt under way for Ronald Niedermann even as we speak. Do you have any idea where he might hide?"

"I am not aware of the circles he moves in. I . . ." Zalachenko hesitated a few seconds. His voice took on a confidential tone. "I must admit, just between us, that sometimes I worry about Niedermann."

Erlander bent towards him.

"What do you mean?"

"I have discovered that he can be a violent person. . . . I am actually afraid of him."

"You mean you felt threatened by Niedermann?" Erlander said.

"Precisely. I'm old and handicapped. I cannot defend myself."

"Could you explain your relationship to Niedermann?"

"I'm disabled." Zalachenko gestured towards his feet. "This is the second time my daughter has tried to kill me. I hired Niedermann as an assistant a number of years ago. I thought he could protect me, but he has actually taken over my life. He comes and goes as he pleases. . . . I have nothing more to say about it."

"What does he help you with?" Modig broke in. "Doing things that you can't do yourself?"

Zalachenko gave Modig a long look with his only visible eye.

"I understand that your daughter threw a Molotov cocktail into your car in the early nineties," Modig said. "Can you explain what prompted her to do that?"

"You would have to ask my daughter. She is mentally ill." His tone was again hostile.

"You mean that you can't think of any reason why Lisbeth Salander attacked you in 1991?"

"My daughter is mentally ill. There is substantial documentation."

Modig cocked her head. Zalachenko's answers were much more aggressive and hostile when she asked the questions. She saw that Erlander had noticed the same thing. *OK. Good cop, bad cop.* Modig raised her voice.

"You don't think that her actions could have anything to do with the fact that you had beaten her mother so badly that she suffered permanent brain damage?"

Zalachenko turned his head towards Modig.

"That is all bullshit. Her mother was a whore. It was probably one of her johns who beat her up. I just happened to be passing by."

Modig raised her eyebrows. "So you're completely innocent?"

"Of course I am."

"Zalachenko . . . let me repeat that to see if I've understood you correctly. You say that you never beat your girlfriend, Agneta Sofia Salander, Lisbeth's mother, despite the fact that the whole business is the subject of a long report, stamped TOP SECRET, written at the time by your handler at Säpo, Gunnar Björck."

"I was never convicted of anything. I have never been charged. I cannot help it if some idiot in the Security Police fantasizes in his reports. If I had been a suspect, they would have at the very least questioned me."

Modig made no answer. Zalachenko seemed to be grinning beneath his bandages.

"So I wish to press charges against my daughter. For trying to kill me."

Modig sighed. "I'm beginning to understand why she felt an uncontrollable urge to slam an axe into your head."

Erlander cleared his throat. "Excuse me, Herr Bodin. We

should get back to any information you might have about Ronald Niedermann's activities."

Modig made a call to Inspector Bublanski from the corridor outside Zalachenko's hospital room.

"Nothing," she said.

"*Nothing?*" Bublanski said.

"He's lodging a complaint with the police against Salander—for aggravated assault and attempted murder. He says that he had nothing to do with the murders in Stockholm."

"And how does he explain the fact that Salander was buried in a trench on his property in Gosseberga?"

"He says he had a cold and was asleep most of the day. If Salander was shot in Gosseberga, it must have been something that Niedermann decided to do."

"So what do we have?"

"She was shot with a Browning, .22 calibre. Which is why she's still alive. We found the weapon. Zalachenko admits that it's his."

"I see. In other words, he knows we're going to find his prints on the gun."

"Exactly. But he says that the last time he saw the gun, it was in his desk drawer."

"Which means that the excellent Herr Niedermann took the weapon while Zalachenko was asleep and shot Salander. This is one cold bastard. Do we have any evidence to the contrary?"

Modig thought for a few seconds before she replied. "Zalachenko is well versed in Swedish law and police procedure. He doesn't admit to a thing, and he has Niedermann as a scapegoat. I don't have any idea what we can prove. I asked Erlander to send his clothes to forensics and have them examined for traces of gunpowder, but he's bound to say that he was doing target practice two days ago."

Salander was aware of the smell of almonds and ethanol. It felt as if she had alcohol in her mouth and she tried to swallow, but her tongue felt numb and paralysed. She tried to open her eyes, but she could not. In the distance she heard a voice that seemed to be talking to her, but she could not understand the words. Then she heard the voice quite clearly.

"I think she's coming around."

She felt someone touch her forehead and tried to brush away the intrusive hand. At the same moment she felt intense pain in her left shoulder. She forced herself to relax.

"Can you hear me, Lisbeth?"

Go away.

"Can you open your eyes?"

Who was this fucking idiot harping on at her?

Finally she did open her eyes. At first she just saw strange lights, until a figure appeared in the centre of her field of vision. She tried to focus her gaze, but the figure kept slipping away. She felt as if she had a stupendous hangover, and the bed seemed to keep tilting backwards.

"Pnkllrs," she said.

"Say that again?"

"'diot," she said.

"That sounds good. Can you open your eyes again?"

She opened her eyes to narrow slits. She saw the face of a complete stranger and memorized every detail. A blond man with intense blue eyes and a tilted, angular face about a foot from hers.

"Hello. My name is Anders Jonasson. I'm a doctor. You're in a hospital. You were injured and you're waking up after an operation. Can you tell me your name?"

"Pshalandr," Salander said.

"Good. Would you do me a favour and count to ten?"

"One, two, four . . . no . . . three, four, five, six . . ."

Then she passed out.

Dr. Jonasson was pleased with the response he had gotten. She had said her name and started to count. That meant that she still had her cognitive abilities somewhat intact and was not going to end up a vegetable. He wrote down her wake-up time as 9:06 p.m., about sixteen hours after he had finished the operation. He had slept most of the day and then drove back to the hospital at around 7:00 in the evening. He was actually off that day, but he had some paperwork to catch up on.

And he could not resist going to intensive care to look in on the patient whose brain he had rooted around in early that morning.

"Let her sleep awhile, but check her EEG regularly. I'm worried there might be swelling or bleeding in the brain. She seemed to have sharp pain in her left shoulder when she tried to move her arm. If she wakes up again you can give her two milligrams of morphine per hour."

He felt oddly exhilarated as he left by the main entrance of Sahlgrenska.

Anita Kaspersson, a dental hygienist who lived in Alingsås, was shaking all over as she stumbled through the woods. She had severe hypothermia. She wore only a pair of wet pants and a thin sweater. Her bare feet were bleeding. She had managed to free herself from the barn where the man had tied her up, but she could not untie the rope that bound her hands behind her back. Her fingers had no feeling in them at all.

She felt as if she were the last person on earth, abandoned by everyone.

She had no idea where she was. It was dark, and she had no sense of how long she had been aimlessly walking. She was amazed to still be alive.

Then she saw a light through the trees and stopped.

For several minutes she did not dare to approach the light. She pushed through some bushes and stood in the yard of a one-storey house of grey brick. She looked around her in astonishment.

She staggered to the door and turned to kick it with her heel.

Salander opened her eyes and saw a light in the ceiling. After a minute she turned her head and became aware that she had on a neck brace. She had a heavy, dull headache and acute pain in her left shoulder. She closed her eyes.

Hospital, she thought. *What am I doing here?*

She felt exhausted, could hardly get her thoughts in order. Then the memories came rushing back to her. For several seconds she was seized by panic as the fragmented images of how she had dug herself out of a grave came flooding over her. Then she clenched her teeth and concentrated on breathing.

She was alive, but she was not sure whether that was a good thing.

She could not piece together all that had happened, but

she summoned up a foggy mosaic of images from the wood-shed and how she had swung an axe in fury and struck her father in the face. Zalachenko. Was he alive or dead?

She could not clearly remember what had happened with Niedermann. She had a memory of being surprised that he had run away, and she did not know why.

Suddenly she remembered having seen Kalle Fucking Blomkvist. Perhaps she had dreamed the whole thing, but she remembered a kitchen—it must have been the kitchen in the Gosseberga farmhouse—and she thought she remembered seeing him coming towards her. *I must have been hallucinating.*

The events in Gosseberga already seemed like the distant past, or possibly a ridiculous dream. She concentrated on the present and opened her eyes again.

She was in a bad way. She did not need anyone to tell her that. She raised her right hand and felt her head. There were bandages. Then she remembered it all. *Niedermann. Zalachenko. The old bastard had a pistol too. A .22-calibre Browning.* Which, compared to all other handguns, had to be considered a toy. That was why she was still alive.

I was shot in the head. I could stick my finger in the entry wound and touch my brain.

She was surprised to be alive. Yet she felt indifferent. If death was the black emptiness from which she had just woken up, then death was nothing to worry about. She would hardly notice the difference. With this esoteric thought she closed her eyes and fell asleep again.

She had been dozing only a few minutes when she became aware of movement and opened her eyelids to a narrow slit.

She saw a nurse in a white uniform bending over her. She closed her eyes and pretended to be asleep.

"I think you're awake," the nurse said.

"Mmm," Salander said.

"Hello. My name is Marianne. Do you understand what I'm saying?"

Salander tried to nod, but her head was immobilized by the brace.

"No, don't try to move. You don't have to be afraid. You've been hurt and had surgery."

"Could I have some water?" Salander whispered.

The nurse gave her a beaker with a straw to drink water through. As she swallowed the water she saw another person appear on her left side.

"Hello, Lisbeth. Can you hear me?"

"Mmm."

"I'm Dr. Helena Endrin. Do you know where you are?"

"Hospital."

"You're at Sahlgrenska hospital in Göteborg. You've had an operation and you're in the intensive care unit."

"Umm-hmm."

"There is no need to be afraid."

"I was shot in the head."

Endrin hesitated for a moment, then said, "That's right. So you remember what happened."

"The old bastard had a pistol."

"Ah . . . yes, well, someone did."

"A .22."

"I see. I didn't know that."

"How badly hurt am I?"

"Your prognosis is positive. You were in pretty bad shape,

but we think you have a good chance of making a full recovery."

Salander weighed this information. Then she tried to fix her eyes on the doctor. Her vision was blurred.

"What happened to Zalachenko?"

"Who?"

"The old bastard. Is he alive?"

"You must mean Karl Axel Bodin."

"No, I don't. I mean Alexander Zalachenko. That's his real name."

"I don't know anything about that. But the elderly man who came in at the same time as you is critical but out of danger."

Salander's heart sank. She considered the doctor's words.

"Where is he?"

"He's down the hall. But don't worry about him for the time being. You have to concentrate on getting well."

Salander closed her eyes. She wondered whether she could manage to get out of bed, find something to use as a weapon, and finish the job. But she could scarcely keep her eyes open. She thought, *He's going to get away again.* She had missed her chance to kill Zalachenko.

"I'd like to examine you for a moment. Then you can go back to sleep," Dr. Endrin said.

Blomkvist was suddenly awake, and he did not know why. He did not know where he was, and then he remembered that he had booked himself a room in City Hotel. It was as dark as coal. He fumbled to turn on the bedside lamp and looked at the clock: 2:00 a.m. He had slept fifteen hours straight.

He got up and went to the bathroom. He would not be

able to get back to sleep. He took a long shower. Then he put on his jeans and sweatshirt. He called the front desk to ask if he could get coffee and a sandwich at this early hour. The night porter said that was possible.

He put on his sports jacket and went downstairs. He ordered a coffee and a cheese and liver pâté sandwich. He bought the *Göteborgs-Posten*. The arrest of Lisbeth Salander was front-page news. He took his breakfast back to his room and read the paper. The reports were somewhat confused, but they were on the right track. Ronald Niedermann, thirty-five, was being sought for the killing of a policeman. The police wanted to question him also in connection with several murders in Stockholm. The police had released nothing about Salander's condition, and the name Zalachenko was not mentioned. He was referred to only as a sixty-five-year-old landowner from Gosseberga, and apparently the media had taken him for an innocent victim.

When Blomkvist finished reading, he flipped open his mobile and saw that he had twenty new messages. Three were messages to call Berger. Two were from his sister, Annika. Fourteen were from reporters at various newspapers who wanted to talk to him. One was from Malm, who had sent him the brisk advice: *It would be best if you took the first train home.*

Blomkvist frowned. That was unusual, coming from Malm. The text had been sent at 7:06 the night before. He stifled the impulse to call and wake someone up at 3:00 in the morning. Instead he booted up his iBook and plugged the cable into the broadband jack. He found that the first train to Stockholm left at 5:20, and there was nothing new in *Aftonbladet* online.

He opened a new Word document, lit a cigarette, and sat for three minutes staring at the blank screen. Then he began to type.

```
Her name is Lisbeth Salander. Sweden has gotten
to know her through police reports and press
releases and the headlines in the evening papers.
She is twenty-six years old and not even five
feet tall. She has been called a psychopath, a
murderer, and a lesbian Satanist. There has been
almost no limit to the fantasies that have been
circulated about her. In this issue, Millennium
will tell the story of how government officials
conspired against Salander in order to protect a
pathological murderer. . . .
```

He wrote steadily for fifty minutes, primarily a recapitulation of the night on which he had found Dag Svensson and Mia Johansson and why the police had focused on Salander as the suspected killer. He quoted the newspaper headlines about lesbian Satanists and the media's apparent hope that the murders might have involved S & M sex.

He checked the clock and quickly closed his iBook. He packed his bag and went down to the front desk. He paid with a credit card and took a taxi to Göteborg Central Station.

Blomkvist went straight to the dining car and ordered more coffee and sandwiches. He opened his iBook again and read through his text. He was so absorbed that he did not notice Inspector Modig until she cleared her throat and asked if she could join him. He looked up, smiled sheepishly, and closed his computer.

"On your way home?"

"You too, I see."

She nodded. "My colleague is staying another day."

"Do you know anything about how Salander is? I've been sound asleep since I last saw you."

"She had an operation soon after she was brought in and was awake in the early evening. The doctors think she'll make a full recovery. She was incredibly lucky."

Blomkvist nodded. It dawned on him that he had not been worried about her. He had assumed that she would survive. Any other outcome was unthinkable.

"Has anything else of interest happened?" he said.

Modig wondered how much she should say to a reporter, even to one who knew more of the story than she did. On the other hand, she had sat down at his table, and by now maybe a hundred other reporters had been briefed at police headquarters.

"I don't want to be quoted," she said.

"I'm simply asking out of personal interest."

She told him that a nationwide manhunt was under way for Ronald Niedermann, particularly in the Malmö area.

"And Zalachenko? Have you questioned him?"

"Yes, we questioned him."

"And?"

"I can't tell you anything about that."

"Come on, Sonja. I'll know exactly what you talked about less than an hour after I get to my office in Stockholm. And I won't write a word of what you tell me."

She hesitated for a while before she met his gaze.

"He made a formal complaint against Salander, that she

tried to kill him. She risks being charged with aggravated assault and attempted murder."

"And in all likelihood she'll claim self-defence."

"I hope she will," Modig said.

"That doesn't sound like an official line."

"Bodin—Zalachenko—is as slippery as an eel, and he has answers to all our questions. I'm convinced that things are more or less as you told us yesterday, and that means that Salander has been subjected to a lifetime of injustice—since she was twelve."

"That's the story I'm going to publish," Blomkvist said.

"It won't be popular with some people."

Modig hesitated again. Blomkvist waited.

"I talked with Bublanski half an hour ago. He didn't go into any detail, but the preliminary investigation against Salander for the murder of your friends seems to have been shelved. The focus has shifted to Niedermann."

"Which means that . . ." He let the question hang in the air between them.

Modig shrugged.

"Who's going to take over the investigation of Salander?"

"I don't know. What happened in Gosseberga is primarily Göteborg's problem. I would guess that somebody in Stockholm will be assigned to compile all the material for a prosecution."

"I see. What do you think the odds are that the investigation will be transferred to Säpo?"

Modig shook her head.

Just before they reached Alingsås, Blomkvist leaned towards her. "Sonja, I think you understand how things stand. If the Zalachenko story gets out, there'll be a massive scandal. Säpo conspired with a psychiatrist to lock Salander up in an asylum. The only thing they can do now is to stonewall and go on claiming that Salander is mentally ill, and that committing her in 1991 was justified."

Modig nodded.

"I'm going to do everything I can to counter any such claims. I believe that Salander is as sane as you or I. Odd, certainly, but her intellectual gifts are undeniable." He paused to let what he had said sink in. "I'm going to need somebody on the inside I can trust."

She met his gaze. "I'm not competent to judge whether or not Salander is mentally ill."

"But you are competent to say whether or not she was the victim of a miscarriage of justice."

"What are you suggesting?"

"I'm only asking you to let me know if you discover that Salander is being subjected to another miscarriage of justice."

Modig said nothing.

"I don't want details of the investigation or anything like that. I just need to know what's happening with the charges against her."

"It sounds like a good way for me to get kicked off the force."

"You would be a source. I would never, ever mention your name."

He wrote an email address on a page torn from his notebook.

"This is an untraceable Hotmail address. You can use it if

you have anything to tell me. Don't use your official address, obviously; just set up your own temporary Hotmail account."

She put the address in the inside pocket of her jacket. She did not make him any promises.

Inspector Erlander woke at 7:00 on Saturday morning to the ringing of his phone. He heard voices from the TV and smelled coffee from the kitchen, where his wife was already doing her morning chores. He had returned to his apartment in Mölndal at 1:00 in the morning, having been on duty for twenty-two hours, so he was far from wide awake when he reached to answer it.

"Rikardsson, night shift. Are you awake?"

"No," Erlander said. "What's happened?"

"News. Anita Kaspersson has been found."

"Where?"

"Outside Seglora, south of Borås."

Erlander visualized the map in his head.

"South," he said. "He's taking the back roads. He must have driven up the 180 through Borås and swung south. Have we alerted Malmö?"

"Yes, and Helsingborg, Landskrona, and Trelleborg. And Karlskrona. I'm thinking of the ferry to the east."

Erlander rubbed the back of his neck.

"He has almost a twenty-four-hour head start now. He could be clean out of the country. How was Kaspersson found?"

"She turned up at a house on the outskirts of Seglora."

"She what?"

"She knocked—"

"You mean she's alive?"

"I'm sorry; I'm not expressing myself clearly. The Kaspersson woman kicked on the door of a house at 3:10 this morning, scaring the hell out of a couple and their kids, who were all asleep. She was barefoot and suffering from severe hypothermia. Her hands were tied behind her back. She's at the hospital in Borås, reunited with her husband."

"Amazing. I think we all assumed she was dead."

"Sometimes you can be surprised. But here's the bad news: Assistant County Police Chief Spångberg has been here since 5:00 this morning. She's made it plain that she wants you to rush over to Borås to interview the woman."

It was Saturday morning and Blomkvist assumed that the *Millennium* offices would be empty. He called Malm as the train was coming into Stockholm and asked him what had prompted the tone of his text message.

"Have you had breakfast?" Malm said.

"On the train."

"OK. Come over to my place and I'll make you something more substantial."

"What's this about?"

"I'll tell you when you get here."

Blomkvist took the tunnelbana to Medborgarplatsen and walked to Allhelgonagatan. Malm's boyfriend, Arnold Magnusson, opened the door to him. No matter how hard Blomkvist tried, he could never rid himself of the feeling that he was looking at an advertisement for something. Magnusson was often onstage at the Dramaten, and was one of Sweden's most popular actors. It was always a shock to meet him in person. Blomkvist was not ordinarily impressed by celebrity, but Magnusson had such a distinctive appearance and was so familiar from his roles, in particular for playing the irascible but honest Inspector Frisk in a wildly popular TV series. Blomkvist always expected him to behave just like Gunnar Frisk.

"Hello, Micke," Magnusson said.

"Hello," Blomkvist said.

"In the kitchen."

Malm was serving up freshly made waffles with cloudberry jam and coffee. Blomkvist's appetite was revived even before he sat down. Malm wanted to know what had happened in Gosseberga. Blomkvist gave him a succinct account. He was into his third waffle before he remembered to ask what was going on.

"We had a little problem at *Millennium* while you were away Blomkvisting in Göteborg."

Blomkvist looked at Malm intently.

"What was that?"

"Oh, nothing serious. Erika has taken the job of editor in chief at *Svenska Morgon-Posten*. She finished at *Millennium* yesterday."

It was several seconds before Blomkvist could absorb the whole impact of the news. He sat there stunned, but did not doubt the truth of it.

"Why didn't she tell anyone before?" he said at last.

"Because she wanted to tell you first, and you've been running around being unreachable, and because she probably thought you had your hands full with the Salander story. Then she found herself with an unbearably guilty conscience and was feeling terrible. And not one of us had noticed a thing."

Blomkvist shut his eyes. "Goddamnit," he said.

"I know. Now it turns out that you're the last one in the office to find out. I wanted to have the chance to tell you myself so that you'd understand what happened and not think anyone was doing anything behind your back."

"No, I don't think that. But, Jesus. It's wonderful that she got the job, if she wants to work at *SMP*, but what the hell are we going to do?"

"Malin's going to be acting editor in chief starting with the next issue."

"Eriksson?"

"Unless you want to be editor in chief . . ."

"Good God, no."

"That's what I thought."

"Have you appointed a managing editor?"

"Henry. He's been with us four years. Hardly an apprentice any longer."

"Do I have a say in this?"

"No," Malm said.

Blomkvist gave a dry laugh. "Right. We'll let it stand the way you've decided. Malin is tough, but she's unsure of herself. Henry shoots from the hip a little too often. We'll have to keep an eye on both of them."

"Yes, we will."

Blomkvist sat in silence, cradling his coffee. It would be damned empty without Berger, and he wasn't sure how things would turn out at the magazine.

"I have to call Erika and—"

"No, better not."

"What do you mean?"

"She's sleeping at the office. Go and wake her up or something."

Blomkvist found Berger sound asleep on the sofa bed in her office. She had been up until all hours emptying her desk and bookshelves of all personal belongings and sorting papers that she wanted to keep. She had filled five large boxes. He looked at her for a while from the doorway before he went in and sat down on the edge of the sofa and woke her.

"Why in heaven's name don't you go over to my place and sleep if you have to sleep on the job," he said.

"Hi, Mikael," she said.

"Christer told me."

She started to say something, but he bent down and kissed her on the cheek.

"Are you livid?"

"Insanely," he said.

"I'm sorry. I couldn't turn it down. But it feels wrong, to leave all of you in the lurch in such a bad situation."

"I'm hardly the person to criticize you for abandoning ship. I left you in the lurch in a situation much worse than this."

"The two have nothing to do with each other. You took a break. I'm leaving for good and I didn't tell anybody. I'm so sorry."

Blomkvist gave her a wan smile.

"When it's time, it's time." Then he added in English, "A woman's gotta do what a woman's gotta do, and all that crap."

Berger smiled. Those were the words she had said to him

when he moved to Hedeby. He reached out his hand and mussed her hair affectionately.

"I can understand why you'd want to quit this madhouse—but to be the head of Sweden's most turgid old-boy newspaper? That's going to take some time to sink in."

"There are quite a few women working there nowadays."

"Bullshit. Check the masthead. It's status quo all the way. You must be a raving masochist. Shall we go and have some coffee?"

Berger sat up. "I have to know what happened in Göteborg."

"I'm writing the story now," Blomkvist said. "And there's going to be war when we publish it. We'll put it out at the same time as the trial. I hope you're not thinking of taking the story with you to *SMP*. The fact is I need you to write something on the Zalachenko story before you leave here."

"Micke . . . I . . ."

"Your very last editorial. Write it whenever you like. It almost certainly won't be published before the trial, whenever that might be."

"I'm not sure that's such a good idea. What do you think it should be about?"

"Morality," Blomkvist said. "And the story of why one of our colleagues was murdered because the government didn't do its job fifteen years ago."

Berger knew exactly what kind of editorial he wanted. She had been at the helm when Svensson was murdered, after all. She suddenly felt in a much better mood.

"OK," she said. "My last editorial."

CHAPTER 4

Saturday, April 9–
Sunday, April 10

By 1:00 on Saturday afternoon, Prosecutor Fransson in Södertälje had finished her deliberations. The burial ground in the woods in Nykvarn was a miserable mess, and the violent crimes division had racked up a huge amount of overtime since Wednesday, when Paolo Roberto had fought his boxing match with Niedermann in the warehouse there. They were dealing with at least three homicides, the bodies found buried on the property, along with the kidnapping and assault of Salander's friend Miriam Wu, and arson to top it all off.

The incident in Stallarholmen was connected with the discoveries at Nykvarn, and was actually the purview of the Strängnäs police district in Södermanland county. Carl-Magnus Lundin of the Svavelsjö Motorcycle Club was a key player in the whole thing, but he was in the hospital in Södertälje with one foot in a cast and his jaw wired shut. Accordingly, all of these crimes came under county police jurisdiction, which meant that Stockholm would have the last word.

On Friday the court hearing was held. Lundin was formally charged in connection with Nykvarn. It had eventually been established that the warehouse was owned by the Medimport Company, which in turn was owned by a fifty-two-year-old cousin of Lundin who lived in Puerto Banús, Spain. She had no criminal record.

Fransson closed the folder that held all the preliminary investigation papers. There would need to be another hundred pages of detailed work before they were ready to go to trial. But right now she had to make decisions on several matters. She looked up at her police colleagues.

"We have enough evidence to charge Lundin with participating in the kidnapping of Miriam Wu. Paolo Roberto has identified him as the man who drove the van. I'm also going to charge him with probable involvement in arson. We'll wait to charge him with the murders of the three individuals we dug up on the property, at least until each of them has been identified."

The officers nodded. That was what they had been expecting.

"What'll we do about Sonny Nieminen?"

Fransson leafed through to the section on Nieminen in the papers on her desk.

"This is a man with an impressive criminal history. Robbery, possession of illegal weapons, assault, manslaughter, and drug crime. He was arrested with Lundin at Stallarholmen. I'm convinced that he's involved, but we don't have the evidence to persuade a court."

"He says he's never been to the Nykvarn warehouse and

that he just happened to be out with Lundin on a motorcycle ride," said the detective responsible for Stallarholmen on behalf of the Södertälje police. "He claims he had no idea what Lundin was up to in Stallarholmen."

Fransson wondered whether she could somehow arrange to hand the entire business over to Prosecutor Ekström in Stockholm.

"Nieminen refuses to say anything about what happened," the detective went on, "but he vehemently denies being involved in any crime."

"You'd think he and Lundin were the victims themselves," Fransson said, drumming her fingertips in annoyance. "Lisbeth Salander," she added, her voice scored with scepticism. "We're talking about a girl who looks as if she's barely entered puberty and who's less than five feet tall. She doesn't look strong enough to take on either Nieminen or Lundin, let alone both of them."

"Unless she was armed. A pistol would compensate for her physique."

"But that doesn't quite fit with our reconstruction of what happened."

"No. She used Mace and kicked Lundin in the balls and face with such aggression that she crushed one of his testicles and then broke his jaw. The shot in Lundin's foot must have happened after she kicked him. But I can't swallow the scenario that says she was the one who was armed."

"The lab has identified the weapon used on Lundin. It's a Polish P-83 Wanad using Makarov ammo. It was found in Gosseberga outside Göteborg, and it has Salander's prints on it. We can pretty much assume that she took the pistol with her to Gosseberga."

"Sure. But the serial number shows that the pistol was stolen four years ago in the robbery of a gun shop in Örebro. The thieves were eventually caught, but they had ditched the gun. It was a local thug with a drug problem who hung out around Svavelsjö MC. I'd much rather place the pistol with either Lundin or Nieminen."

"It could be as simple as Lundin carrying the pistol and Salander disarming him. Then a shot was fired accidentally that hit him in the foot. I mean, it can't have been her intention to kill him, since he's still alive."

"Or else she shot him in the foot out of sheer sadism. Who knows? But how did she deal with Nieminen? He has no visible injuries."

"He does have one, or rather two: small burn marks on his chest."

"What sort of burns?"

"I'm guessing a Taser."

"So Salander was supposedly armed with a Taser, a Mace canister, and a pistol. How much would all that stuff weigh? No, I'm quite sure that either Lundin or Nieminen was carrying the gun, and she took it from him. We're not going to be sure how Lundin got himself shot until one of the parties involved starts talking."

"All right."

"As things now stand, Lundin has been charged for the reasons I mentioned earlier. But we don't have a damned thing on Nieminen. I'm thinking of turning him loose this afternoon."

Nieminen was in a vile mood when he left the cells at Södertälje police station. His mouth was dry, so his first stop was a corner shop, where he bought a Pepsi. He guzzled it down on the spot. He bought a pack of Lucky Strikes and a tin of Göteborgs Rapé snuff. He flipped open his mobile and checked the battery, then dialled the number of Hans-Åke Waltari, thirty-three years old and number three in Svavelsjö MC's hierarchy. It rang four times before Waltari picked up.

"Nieminen. I'm out."

"Congrats."

"Where are you?"

"Nyköping."

"What the fuck are you doing in Nyköping?"

"We decided to lay low when you and Magge were busted—until we knew the lay of the land."

"So now you know the lay of the land. Where is everybody?"

Waltari told him where the other five members of Svavelsjö MC were located. The news neither pleased Nieminen nor made him any calmer.

"So who the fuck is minding the store while all of you hide away like a bunch of pussies?"

"That's not fair. You and Magge take off on some fucking job we don't know shit about, and all of a sudden you're mixed up in a shoot-out with that fucking slut the cops are after, Magge gets shot, and you're busted. Then they start digging up bodies at our warehouse in Nykvarn."

"So?"

"So? So we were starting to wonder if maybe you and Magge were hiding something from the rest of us."

"And what the fuck would that be? We're the ones who took the job for the sake of the club."

"Well, no-one ever told me that the warehouse was doubling as a woodland cemetery. Who were those stiffs?"

Nieminen had a vicious retort on the tip of his tongue, but he stopped himself. Waltari might be an idiot, but this was no time to start an argument. The important thing right now was to consolidate their forces. After stonewalling his way through five police interrogations, it was not a good idea to start boasting that he actually knew something on a mobile less than 200 yards from a police station.

"Forget the bodies," he said. "I don't know anything about that. But Magge is in deep shit. He's going to be in the slammer for a while, and while he's gone, I'm running the club."

"OK. What happens now?" Waltari said.

"Who's keeping an eye on the property?"

"Benny stayed at the clubhouse to hold the fort. They searched the place the day you were arrested. They didn't find anything."

"Benny Karlsson?" Nieminen yelled. "Benny K.'s hardly dry behind the ears."

"Take it easy. He's with that blond fucker you and Magge always hang out with."

Sonny froze. He glanced around and walked away from the door of the corner shop.

"What did you say?" he asked in a low voice.

"That blond monster you and Magge hang out with. He showed up and needed a place to hide."

"Goddamnit, Waltari! They're looking for him all over the fucking country!"

"Yeah . . . that's why he needed somewhere to hide. What were we supposed to do? He's your and Magge's pal."

Nieminen shut his eyes for ten full seconds. Niedermann

had brought Svavelsjö MC a lot of jobs and good money for several years. But he was absolutely not a friend. He was a dangerous bastard and a psychopath—a psychopath that the police were looking for with a vengeance. Nieminen did not trust Niedermann for one second. The best thing would be if he turned up with a bullet in his head. Then the manhunt would at least ease up a bit.

"So what did you do with him?"

"Benny's taking care of him. He took him out to Viktor's."

Viktor Göransson was the club's treasurer and financial expert, who lived just outside Järna. He was trained in accounting and had begun his career as financial adviser to a Yugoslav who owned a string of bars, until the whole gang ended up in the slammer for fraud. He had met Lundin at Kumla prison in the early nineties. He was the only member of Svavelsjö MC who normally wore a jacket and tie.

"Waltari, get in your car and meet me in Södertälje. I'll be outside the train station in forty-five minutes."

"All right. But what's the rush?"

"I have to get a handle on the situation. Do you want me to take the bus?"

Waltari sneaked a look at Nieminen, sitting quiet as a mouse as they drove out to Svavelsjö. Unlike Lundin, Nieminen was never very easy to deal with. He had the face of a model and looked weak, but he had a short fuse and was a dangerous fucker, especially when he had been drinking. Just then he was sober, but Waltari felt uneasy about having Nieminen as their leader in the future. Lundin had somehow always managed to keep Nieminen in line. He wondered how things would unfold now with Lundin out of the way.

At the clubhouse, Benny was nowhere to be seen. Nieminen called him twice on his mobile but got no answer.

They drove to Nieminen's place, about half a mile farther down the road. The police had carried out a search, but they had evidently found nothing of value to the Nykvarn investigation. Which was why Nieminen had been released.

He took a shower and changed his clothes while Waltari waited patiently in the kitchen. Then they walked about 150 yards into the woods behind Nieminen's property and scraped away the thin layer of soil that concealed a chest containing six handguns, including an AK5, a stack of ammunition, and around four pounds of explosives. This was Nieminen's arms cache. Two of the guns were Polish P-83 Wanads. They came from the same batch as the weapon that Salander had taken from him at Stallarholmen.

Nieminen drove away all thoughts of Salander. It was an unpleasant subject. In the cell at Södertälje police station he had played the scene over and over in his head: how he and Lundin had arrived at Advokat Bjurman's summer house and found Salander apparently just leaving.

Events had been rapid and unpredictable. He had ridden over there with Lundin to burn the damned summer cabin down. On the instructions of that goddamned blond fucker. And then they had stumbled upon that bitch Salander—all alone, five feet tall, thin as a stick. Nieminen wondered how much she actually weighed. And then everything had gone to hell, exploded in a brief orgy of violence neither of them was prepared for.

Objectively, he could describe the chain of events. Salander had a canister of Mace, which she sprayed in Lundin's face. Lundin should have been ready, but he wasn't. She kicked him twice, and you don't need a lot of muscle to fracture a jaw. She took him by surprise. That could be explained.

But then she took him too, Sonny Nieminen, a man who could make well-trained men cower. She moved so fast. He hadn't been able to pull his gun. She had taken him out easily, as if brushing off a mosquito. It was humiliating. She had a Taser. She had . . .

He could not remember a thing when he came to. Lundin had been shot in the foot and then the police showed up. After some palaver over jurisdiction between Strängnäs and Södertälje, he wound up in the cells in Södertälje. Plus she had stolen Magge's Harley.

She had cut the badge out of his leather jacket—the very symbol that made people step aside in the line at the bar, that gave him a status that was beyond most people's wildest dreams. She had humiliated him.

Nieminen was boiling over. He had kept his mouth shut through the entire series of police interrogations. He would never be able to tell anyone what had happened in Stallarholmen. Until that moment, Salander had meant nothing to him. She was a little side project that Lundin was messing around with . . . again commissioned by that fucking Niedermann. Now he hated her with a fury that astonished him. Usually he was cool and analytical, but he knew that at some time in the future he would have to pay her back and erase the shame. But first he had to get a grip on the chaos that Svavelsjö MC had landed in because of Salander and Niedermann.

Nieminen took the two remaining Polish guns, loaded them, and handed one to Waltari.

"Do we have a plan?"

"We're going to drive over and have a talk with Nieder-mann. He isn't one of us, and he doesn't have a criminal record. I don't know how he's going to react if they catch him, but if he talks he could send us all to the slammer. We'd be sent down so fast it'd make your head spin."

"You mean we should . . ."

Nieminen had already decided that Niedermann had to be gotten rid of, but he knew that it would be a bad idea to frighten off Waltari before they were in place.

"I don't know. We'll see what he has in mind. If he's plan-ning to get out of the country as fast as hell then we could help him on his way. But as long as he risks being busted, he's a threat to us."

The lights were off at Göransson's place when Nieminen and Waltari drove up in the twilight. That was not a good sign. They sat in the car and waited.

"Maybe they're out," Waltari said.

"Right. They went to the bar with Niedermann," Niemi-nen said, opening the car door.

The front door was unlocked. Nieminen switched on an overhead light. They went from room to room. The house was well kept and neat, which was probably because of her, whatever-her-name-was, the woman Göransson lived with.

They found Göransson and his girlfriend in the base-ment, stuffed in a laundry room.

Nieminen bent down and looked at the bodies. He reached out a finger to touch the woman whose name he could not remember. She was ice-cold and stiff. That meant they had been dead maybe twenty-four hours.

Nieminen did not need the help of a pathologist to work out how they had died. Her neck had been broken when her head was turned 180 degrees. She was dressed in a T-shirt and jeans and had no other injuries that Nieminen could see.

Göransson, on the other hand, wore only his underpants. He had been beaten, had blood and bruises all over his body. His arms were bent in impossible directions, like twisted tree limbs. The battering he had been subjected to could only be defined as torture. He had been killed, as far as Nieminen could judge, by a single blow to the neck. His larynx was rammed deep into his throat.

Nieminen went up the stairs and out the front door. Waltari followed him. Nieminen walked the fifty yards to the barn. He flipped the latch and opened the door.

He found a dark blue 1991 Renault.

"What kind of car does Göransson have?" Nieminen said.

"He drove a Saab."

Nieminen nodded. He fished some keys out of his jacket pocket and opened a door at the far end of the barn. One quick look around told him that they were too late. The heavy weapons cabinet stood wide open.

Nieminen grimaced. "About 800,000 kronor," he said.

"What?"

"Svavelsjö MC had about 800,000 kronor stashed in this cabinet. It was our treasury."

Only three people knew where Svavelsjö MC kept the cash that was waiting to be invested and laundered: Göransson, Lundin, and Nieminen. Niedermann was on the run. He needed cash. He knew that Göransson was the one who handled the money.

Nieminen shut the door and walked slowly away from the

barn. His mind was spinning as he tried to digest the catastrophe. Part of Svavelsjö MC's assets were in the form of bonds that he could access, and some of their investments could be reconstructed with Lundin's help. But a large number of them had been listed only in Göransson's head, unless he had given clear instructions to Lundin. Which Nieminen doubted—Lundin had never been good with finances. Nieminen estimated that Svavelsjö MC had lost upwards of 60 percent of its assets with Göransson's death. It was a devastating blow. Above all, they needed the cash to take care of day-to-day expenses.

"What do we do now?" Waltari said.

"We'll go and tip off the police about what happened here."

"Tip off the *police*?"

"Yes, damn it. My prints are all over the house. I want Göransson and his bitch to be found as soon as possible, so that forensics can work out that they died while I was still locked up."

"I get it."

"Good. Go and find Benny. I want to talk to him. If he's still alive, that is. And then we'll track down Niedermann. We'll need every contact we have in the clubs all over Scandinavia to keep their eyes peeled. I want that bastard's head on a platter. He's probably riding around in Göransson's Saab. Find out the registration number."

When Salander woke up it was 2:00 on Saturday afternoon and a doctor was poking at her.

"Good morning," he said. "My name is Benny Svantesson. I'm a doctor. Are you in pain?"

"Yes," Salander said.

"I'll make sure you get some painkillers in a minute. But first I'd like to examine you."

He squeezed and poked her lacerated body. Salander was extremely aggravated by the time he had finished, but she held back; she was exhausted and decided it would be better to keep quiet than to tarnish her stay at Sahlgrenska with a fight.

"How am I doing?" she said.

"You'll pull through," the doctor said and made some notes before he stood up. This was not very informative.

After he left, a nurse came in and helped Salander with a bedpan. Then she was allowed to go back to sleep.

Zalachenko, alias Karl Axel Bodin, was given a liquid lunch. Even small movements of his facial muscles caused sharp pains in his jaw and cheekbone, and chewing was out of the question.

But the pain was manageable. Zalachenko was used to pain. Nothing could compare with the pain he had undergone for several weeks, months even, fifteen years before, when he had burned like a torch in his car. The follow-up care had been a marathon of agony.

The doctors had decided that his life was no longer at risk, but still he was severely injured. In view of his age, he would stay in the intensive care unit for a few more days.

On Saturday he had five visitors.

At 10:00 a.m. Inspector Erlander returned. This time he had left that damned Modig woman behind and instead was accompanied by Inspector Holmberg, who was much more agreeable. They asked pretty much the same questions about

Niedermann as they had the night before. He had his story straight and did not slip up. When they started plying him with questions about his possible involvement in trafficking and other criminal activities, he again denied all knowledge of any such thing. He was living on a disability pension, and he had no idea what they were talking about. He blamed Niedermann for everything and offered to help them in any way he could to find the fugitive.

Unfortunately, there was not much he could help with, practically speaking. He had no knowledge of the circles Niedermann moved in, or whom he might go to for protection.

At around 11:00 he had a brief visit from a representative of the prosecutor's office, who formally advised him that he was a suspect in the aggravated assault and attempted murder of Lisbeth Salander. Zalachenko patiently explained that on the contrary, *he* was the victim of a crime, that in point of fact it was Salander who had attempted to murder *him*. The prosecutor's office offered him legal assistance in the form of a public defence lawyer. Zalachenko said that he would mull over the matter.

Which he had no intention of doing. He already had a lawyer, and the first thing he had to do that morning was call him and tell him to get down there right away. Martin Thomasson was therefore the fourth guest of the day at Zalachenko's sickbed. He wandered in with a carefree expression, ran a hand through his thick blond hair, adjusted his glasses, and shook hands with his client. He was a chubby and very charming man. True, he was suspected of running errands for the Yugoslav mafia, a matter which was still under investigation, but he was also known for winning his cases.

Zalachenko had been referred to Thomasson through a

business associate five years earlier, when he needed to restructure certain funds connected to a small financial firm that he owned in Liechtenstein. They were not dramatic sums, but Thomasson's skill had been exceptional, and Zalachenko had avoided paying taxes on them. He then engaged Thomasson on a couple of other matters. Thomasson knew that the money came from criminal activity, but it didn't seem to faze him. Ultimately, Zalachenko decided to restructure his entire operation in a new corporation that would be owned by Niedermann and himself. He approached Thomasson and proposed that the lawyer come in as a third, silent partner to handle the financial side of the business. Thomasson accepted at once.

"So, Herr Bodin, none of this looks like much fun."

"I have been the victim of aggravated assault and attempted murder," Zalachenko said.

"I can see as much. A certain Lisbeth Salander, if I understood correctly."

Zalachenko lowered his voice: "Our partner Niedermann, as you know, has really screwed things up."

"Indeed."

"The police suspect that I am involved."

"Which of course you are not. You're a victim, and it's important that we see to it at once that this is the image presented to the press. Ms. Salander has already received a good deal of negative publicity. . . . Let me deal with the situation."

"Thank you."

"But I have to remind you right from the start that I'm not a criminal lawyer. You're going to need a specialist. I'll arrange to hire one that you can trust."

. . .

The fifth visitor of the day arrived at 11:00 on Saturday night and managed to get past the nurses by showing an ID card and stating that he had urgent business. He was shown to Zalachenko's room. The patient was still awake, and grumbling.

"My name is Jonas Sandberg," he introduced himself, holding out a hand that Zalachenko ignored.

He was in his thirties. He had blond hair and was casually dressed in jeans, a checked shirt, and a leather jacket. Zalachenko scrutinized him for fifteen seconds.

"I was wondering when one of you was going to show up."

"I work for SIS, Swedish Internal Security," Sandberg said, and showed Zalachenko his ID.

"I doubt that," said Zalachenko.

"I beg your pardon?"

"You may be employed by SIS, but I doubt that's who you're working for."

Sandberg looked around the room, then he pulled up the guest chair.

"I came here late so as not to attract attention. We've discussed how we can help you, and now we have to reach some sort of agreement about what's going to happen. I'm just here to get your version of the story and find out what your intentions are, so that we can work out a common strategy."

"What sort of strategy do you have in mind?"

"Herr Zalachenko . . . I'm afraid that a process has been set in motion in which the deleterious effects are hard to foresee," Sandberg said. "We've talked it through. It's going to be difficult to explain away the grave in Gosseberga, and the fact that the girl was shot three times. But let's not lose hope altogether. The conflict between you and your daughter can explain your fear of her and why you took such drastic measures . . . but I'm afraid we're talking about your doing some time in prison."

Zalachenko suddenly felt elated and would have burst out laughing had he not been so trussed up. He managed a slight curl of his lips. Anything more would be just too painful.

"So that's our strategy?"

"Herr Zalachenko, you are aware of the concept of damage control. We have to arrive at a common strategy. We'll do everything in our power to assist you with a lawyer and so on, but we need your cooperation, as well as certain guarantees."

"You'll get only one guarantee from me. First, you will see to it that all this disappears." He waved his hand. "Niedermann is the scapegoat, and I guarantee that no-one will ever find him."

"There's forensic evidence that—"

"Fuck the forensic evidence. It's a matter of how the investigation is carried out and how the facts are presented. My guarantee is this: if you don't wave your magic wand and make all this disappear, I'm inviting the media to a press conference. I know names, dates, events. I don't think I need to remind you who I am."

"You don't understand—"

"I understand perfectly. You're an errand boy. So go to your superior and tell him what I've said. He'll understand. Tell him that I have copies of . . . everything. I can take you all down."

"We have to come to an agreement."

"This conversation is over. Get out of here. And tell them that next time they should send a grown man for me to discuss things with."

Zalachenko turned his head away from his visitor. Sandberg looked at Zalachenko for a moment. Then he shrugged and got up. He was almost at the door when he heard Zalachenko's voice again.

"One more thing."

Sandberg turned.

"Salander."

"What about her?"

"She has to disappear."

"How do you mean?"

Sandberg looked so nervous that Zalachenko had to smile, though the pain drilled into his jaw.

"I see that you milksops are too sensitive to kill her, and that you don't even have the resources to have it done. Who would do it . . . you? But she has to disappear. Her testimony has to be declared invalid. She has to be committed to a mental institution for life."

Salander heard footsteps in the corridor. She had never heard those footsteps before.

Her door had been open all evening and the nurses had been in to check on her every ten minutes. She had heard a man explain to a nurse right outside her door that he had to see Herr Karl Axel Bodin on an urgent matter. She had heard him offering his ID, but no words were exchanged that gave her any clue as to who he was or what sort of ID he had.

The nurse had asked him to wait while she went to see

whether Herr Bodin was awake. Salander concluded that his ID, whatever it said, must have been persuasive.

She heard the nurse go down the corridor to the left. It took her seventeen steps to reach the room, and the male visitor took fourteen steps to cover the same distance. That gave an average of fifteen and a half steps. She estimated the length of a step at twenty-four inches, which multiplied by fifteen and a half told her that Zalachenko was in a room about thirty feet down the corridor to the left. She estimated that the width of her room was about fifteen feet, which should mean that Zalachenko's room was two doors down from hers.

According to the green numerals on the digital clock on her bedside cabinet, the visit lasted precisely nine minutes.

Zalachenko lay awake for a long time after the man who called himself Jonas Sandberg had left. He assumed that it was not his real name; in his experience, Swedish amateur spies had a real obsession with using false names even when it was not in the least bit necessary. In which case Sandberg, or whatever the hell his name was, was the first indication that Zalachenko's predicament had come to the attention of the Section. Considering the media attention, this would have been hard to avoid. But the visit did confirm that his predicament was a matter of anxiety to them. As well it might be.

He weighed the pros and cons, lined up the possibilities, and rejected various options. He was fully aware that everything had gone about as badly as it could have. In a well-ordered world he would be at home in Gosseberga now, Niedermann would be safely out of the country, and Salander would be buried in a hole in the ground. Despite the fact that he had a reasonable grasp of what had happened, for the life of him he could not comprehend how she had managed to dig herself out of Niedermann's trench, make her way to his farm, and damn near destroy him with two blows of an axe. She was extraordinarily resourceful.

On the other hand, he understood quite well what had happened to Niedermann, and why he had run for his life instead of staying to finish Salander off. He knew that something was not quite right in Niedermann's head, that he saw visions—ghosts, even. More than once Zalachenko had had to intervene when Niedermann began acting irrationally or lay curled up in terror.

This worried Zalachenko. He was convinced that since Niedermann had not yet been captured, he must have been acting rationally during the twenty-four hours since his flight from Gosseberga. Probably he would go to Tallinn, where he would seek protection among contacts in Zalachenko's criminal empire. What worried him in the short term was that he could never predict when Niedermann might be struck by his mental paralysis. If it happened while he was trying to escape, he would make mistakes, and if he made mistakes he would end up in prison. He would never surrender voluntarily, which meant that policemen would die and Niedermann probably would as well.

This thought upset Zalachenko. He did not want Niedermann to die. Niedermann was his son, and physically an almost perfect specimen. But regrettable as it was, Niedermann must not be captured alive. He had never been arrested, and Zalachenko could not predict how he would react under interrogation. He doubted that Niedermann would be able to keep quiet, as he should. So it would be a good thing if he were killed by the police. Zalachenko would grieve for his son, but the alternative was worse. If Niedermann talked, Zalachenko himself would have to spend the rest of his life in prison.

But it was now forty-eight hours since Niedermann had fled, and he had not yet been caught. That was good. It was an indication that Niedermann was functioning, and a functioning Niedermann was invincible.

In the long term there was another worry. He wondered how Niedermann would get along on his own, without his father there to guide him. Over the years he had noticed that if he stopped giving instructions or gave Niedermann too much latitude to make his own decisions, he would slip into an indolent state of indecision.

Zalachenko acknowledged for the umpteenth time that it was a shame his son did not possess certain qualities. Ronald Niedermann was without doubt a very talented person who had physical attributes to make him a formidable and feared individual. He was also an excellent and cold-blooded organizer. His problem was that he utterly lacked the instinct to lead. He always needed somebody to tell him what he was supposed to be organizing.

But for the time being all this lay outside Zalachenko's control. Right now he had to focus on himself. His situation was precarious, perhaps more precarious than ever before.

He did not think that Advokat Thomasson's visit earlier in the day had been particularly reassuring. Thomasson was and remained a corporate lawyer, and no matter how effective he was in that respect, he would not be a great support in this other business.

And then there had been the visit of Jonas Sandberg, or whatever his name was. Sandberg offered a considerably stronger lifeline. But that lifeline could also be a trap. Zalachenko had to play his cards right, and he would have to take control of the situation. Control was everything.

In the end he had his own resources to fall back on. For the moment he needed medical attention, but in a couple of days, maybe a week, he would have regained his strength. If things came to a head, he might have only himself to rely on. That meant he would have to disappear, from right under the noses of the policemen circling around him. He would need a hideout, a passport, and some cash. Thomasson could provide all that. But first he would have to get strong enough to make his escape.

At 1:00 a.m. the night nurse looked in. He pretended to be asleep. When she closed the door he arduously sat up and swung his legs over the edge of the bed. He sat still for a while, testing his sense of balance. Then he cautiously put his left foot down on the floor. Luckily the axe blow had struck his already crippled right leg. He reached for his prosthesis, stored in the cabinet next to his bed, and attached it to his stump. Then he stood up, keeping his weight on his uninjured leg. As he shifted his weight, a sharp pain shot through his right leg.

He gritted his teeth and took a step. He would need crutches, and he was sure that the hospital would offer him some soon. He braced himself against the wall and limped over to the door. It took him several minutes, and he had to stop after each step to deal with the pain.

He rested on one leg as he pushed open the door a crack and peered out into the corridor. He did not see anyone, so he stuck his head out a little farther. He heard faint voices to the left and turned to look. The night nurses were at their station about twenty yards down on the other side of the corridor.

He turned his head to the right and saw the exit at the other end.

Earlier in the day he had enquired about Lisbeth Salander's condition. He was, after all, her father. The nurses obviously had been instructed not to discuss other patients. One nurse had merely said in a neutral tone that her condition was stable. But she had unconsciously glanced to her left.

In one of the rooms between his own and the exit was Lisbeth Salander.

He carefully closed the door, limped back to the bed, and detached his prosthesis. He was drenched in sweat when he finally slipped under the covers.

Inspector Holmberg returned to Stockholm at lunchtime on Sunday. He was hungry and exhausted. He took the tunnelbana to City Hall, walked to police headquarters on Bergsgatan, and went up to Inspector Bublanski's office. Modig and Andersson had already arrived. Bublanski had called the meeting on Sunday because he knew that preliminary investigation leader Richard Ekström was busy elsewhere.

"Thanks for coming in," said Bublanski. "I think it's time we had a discussion in peace and quiet to try to make sense of this mess. Jerker, do you have anything new?"

"Nothing I haven't already told you on the phone. Zalachenko isn't budging an inch. He's innocent of everything and won't talk. Just that—"

"Yes?"

"Sonja, you were right. He's one of the nastiest people I've ever met. It might sound stupid to say that. Policemen aren't supposed to think in those terms, but there's something really scary beneath his calculating façade."

"OK." Bublanski cleared his throat. "What have we got? Sonja?"

She smiled weakly.

"The investigative reporter won this round. I can't find Zalachenko in any public registry, but a Karl Axel Bodin seems to have been born in 1942 in Uddevalla. His parents were Marianne and Georg Bodin. They died in an accident in 1946. Karl Axel Bodin was brought up by an uncle living in Norway. So there is no record of him until the seventies, when he moved back to Sweden. Mikael Blomkvist's story that he's a GRU agent who defected from the Soviet Union seems impossible to verify, but I'm inclined to think he's right."

"And what does that mean?"

"The obvious explanation is that he was given a false identity. It must have been done with the consent of the authorities."

"You mean the Security Police, Säpo?"

"That's what Blomkvist claims. But exactly how it was done I don't know. It presupposes that his birth certificate and a number of other documents were falsified and then slipped into our public records. I don't dare to comment on the legal ramifications of such an action. It probably depends on who made the decision. But for it to be legal, the decision would have to have been made at senior government level."

Silence descended in Bublanski's office as the four criminal inspectors considered these implications.

"OK," said Bublanski. "The four of us are just dumb police officers. If people in government are mixed up in this, I don't intend to interrogate them."

"Hmm," said Andersson. "This could lead to a constitutional crisis. In the United States you can cross-examine members of the government in a normal court of law. In Sweden you have to do it through a constitutional committee."

"But we could ask the boss," said Holmberg.

"Ask the boss?" said Bublanski.

"Thorbjörn Fälldin. He was prime minister at the time."

"So we'll just cruise up to wherever he lives and ask the former prime minister if he faked identity documents for a defecting Russian spy. I don't think so."

"Fälldin lives in Ås, in Härnösand. I grew up a few miles from there. My father's a member of the Centre Party and knows Fälldin well. I've met him several times, both as a kid and as an adult. He's a very approachable person."

Three inspectors gave Holmberg an astonished look.

"You know Fälldin?" Bublanski said dubiously.

Holmberg nodded. Bublanski pursed his lips.

"To tell the truth," said Holmberg, "it would solve a number of issues if we could get the former prime minister to give us a statement—at least we'd know where we stand in all this. I could go up there and talk to him. If he won't say anything, so be it. But if he does, we might save ourselves a lot of time."

Bublanski weighed the suggestion. Then he shook his head. Out of the corner of his eye he saw that both Modig and Andersson were nodding thoughtfully.

"Holmberg, it's nice of you to offer, but I think we'll put that idea on the back burner for now. So, back to the case. Sonja."

"According to Blomkvist, Zalachenko came here in 1976. As far as I can work out, there's only one person he could have gotten that information from."

"Gunnar Björck," said Andersson.

"What has Björck told us?" Holmberg asked.

"Not much. He says it's all classified and that he can't discuss anything without permission from his superiors."

"And who are his superiors?"

"He won't say."

"So what's going to happen to him?"

"I arrested him for violation of the prostitution laws. We have excellent documentation in Dag Svensson's notes. Ekström was upset, but since I had already filed a report, he could get himself into trouble if he closes the preliminary investigation," Andersson said.

"I see. Violation of the prostitution laws. That might result in a fine of ten times his daily income."

"Probably. But we have him in the system and can call him in again for questioning."

"But now we're getting a little too involved in Säpo's business. That might cause a bit of turbulence."

"The problem is that none of this could have happened if Säpo weren't involved somehow. It's possible that Zalachenko really was a Russian spy who defected and was granted political asylum. It's also possible that he worked for Säpo as an expert or source or whatever title you want to give him, and that there was good reason to offer him a false identity and anonymity. But there are three problems. First, the investigation carried out in 1991 that led to Lisbeth Salander's being locked away was illegal. Second, Zalachenko's activities since then have nothing whatsoever to do with national security. Zalachenko is an ordinary gangster who's probably mixed up in several murders and other criminal activities. And third, there is no doubt that Lisbeth Salander was shot and buried alive on his property in Gosseberga."

"Speaking of which, I'd really like to read the infamous report," said Holmberg.

Bublanski's face clouded over.

"Jerker, this is how it is: Ekström laid claim to it on Friday, and when I asked for it back he said he'd make me a copy, which he never did. Instead he called me and said that he had spoken with the prosecutor general and there was a problem. According to the PG, the 'top secret' classification means that the report may not be disseminated or copied. The PG has called in all copies until the matter is investigated. Which meant that Sonja had to relinquish the copy she had too."

"So we no longer have the report?"

"No."

"Damn," said Holmberg. "The whole thing stinks."

"I know," said Bublanski. "Worst of all, it means that someone is acting against us, and acting very quickly and efficiently. The report was what finally put us on the right track."

"So we have to work out who's acting against us," said Holmberg.

"Just a moment," said Modig. "We also have Peter Teleborian. He contributed to our investigation by profiling Lisbeth Salander."

"Exactly," said Bublanski in a darker tone of voice. "And what did he say?"

"He was very concerned about her safety and wished her well. But when the discussion was over, he said she was lethally dangerous and might well resist arrest. We based a lot of our thinking on what he told us."

"And he got Hans Faste all worked up," said Holmberg. "Have we heard anything from Faste, by the way?"

"He took some time off," Bublanski replied curtly. "The question now is how *we* should proceed."

They spent the next two hours discussing their options. The only practical decision they made was that Modig should return to Göteborg the next day to see whether Salander had anything to say. When they finally broke up, Modig and Andersson walked together down to the garage.

"I was just thinking . . ." Andersson stopped.

"Yes?"

"It's just that when we talked to Teleborian, you were the only one in the group who offered any opposition when he answered our questions."

"Yes?"

"Well . . . er . . . good instincts," he said.

Andersson was not known for handing out praise, and it was definitely the first time he had ever said anything positive or encouraging to Modig. He left her standing by her car in astonishment.

CHAPTER 5

Sunday, April 10

Blomkvist had spent Saturday night with Berger. They lay in bed and talked through the details of the Zalachenko story. Blomkvist trusted Berger implicitly and was never for a second inhibited by the fact that she was going to be working for a rival paper. Nor had Berger any thought of taking the story with her. It was *Millennium*'s scoop, even though she may have felt a certain frustration that she was not going to be the editor of that particular issue. It would have been a fine ending to her years at *Millennium*.

They also discussed the future structure of the magazine. Berger was determined to retain her shares in *Millennium* and to remain on the board, even if she had no say over the magazine's contents.

"Give me a few years at the daily and then, who knows? Maybe I'll come back to *Millennium* before I retire," she said.

And as for their own complicated relationship, why should it be any different? Except that of course they would not be meeting so often. It would be as it was in the eighties, before *Millennium* was founded and when they worked in separate offices.

"I imagine we'll have to book appointments with each other," Berger said with a faint smile.

On Sunday morning they said a hasty goodbye before Berger drove home to her husband, Greger Beckman.

After she was gone Blomkvist called the hospital in Sahlgrenska and tried to get some information about Salander's condition. Nobody would tell him anything, so finally he called Inspector Erlander, who took pity on him and vouchsafed that, given the circumstances, Salander's condition was fair and the doctors were cautiously optimistic. He asked if he would be able to visit her. Erlander told him that Salander was officially under arrest and that the prosecutor would not allow any visitors, but in any case she was in no condition to be questioned. Erlander said he would call if her condition took a turn for the worse.

When Blomkvist checked his mobile, he saw that he had forty-two messages and texts, almost all of them from journalists. There had been wild speculation in the media after it was revealed that Blomkvist was the one who had found Salander, and had probably saved her life. He was obviously closely connected with the development of events.

He deleted all the messages from reporters and called his sister, Annika, to invite himself for Sunday lunch. Then he called Dragan Armansky, CEO of Milton Security, who was at his home in Lidingö.

"You certainly have a way with headlines," Armansky said.

"I tried to reach you earlier this week. I got a message that you were looking for me, but I just didn't have time—"

"We've been doing our own investigation at Milton. And I understood from Holger Palmgren that you had some information. But it seems you were far ahead of us."

Blomkvist hesitated before he said: "Can I trust you?"

"How do you mean exactly?"

"Are you on Salander's side or not? Can I believe that you want the best for her?"

"I'm her friend. Although, as you know, that's not necessarily the same thing as saying that she's my friend."

"I understand that. But what I'm asking is whether or not you're willing to put yourself in her corner and get into a pitched battle with her enemies."

"I'm on her side," he said.

"Can I share information with you and discuss things with you without the risk of your leaking it to the police or to anyone else?"

"I can't get involved in criminal activity," Armansky said.

"That's not what I asked."

"You can absolutely rely on me as long as you don't reveal that you're engaged in any sort of criminal activity."

"Good enough. We need to meet."

"I'm coming into the city this evening. Dinner?"

"I don't have time today, but I'd be grateful if we could meet tomorrow night. You and I and perhaps a few other people might need to sit down for a chat."

"You're welcome at Milton. Shall we say 6:00?"

"One more thing . . . I'm seeing my sister, the lawyer Annika Giannini, later this morning. She's considering taking on Salander as a client, but she can't work for nothing. I can pay part of her fee out of my own pocket. Would Milton Security be willing to contribute?"

"That girl is going to need a damned good criminal lawyer. Your sister might not be the best choice, if you'll forgive me for saying so. I've already talked to Milton's chief lawyer and he's looking into it. I was thinking of Peter Althin or someone like that."

"That would be a mistake. Salander needs a totally different kind of legal support. You'll see what I mean when we talk. But would you be willing, in principle, to help?"

"I'd already decided that Milton ought to hire a lawyer for her—"

"Is that a yes or a no? I know what happened to her. I know roughly what's behind it all. And I have a strategy."

Armansky laughed.

"OK. I'll listen to what you have to say. If I like it, I'm in."

Blomkvist kissed his sister on the cheek and immediately asked: "Are you going to be representing Lisbeth Salander?"

"I'm going to have to say no. You know I'm not a criminal lawyer. Even if she's acquitted of murder, there's going to be a long list of other charges. She's going to need someone with a completely different sort of clout and experience than I have."

"You're wrong. You're a lawyer and you're a recognized authority in women's rights. In my considered view you're precisely the lawyer she needs."

"Mikael . . . I don't think you really appreciate what this involves. It's a complex criminal case, not a straightforward case of sexual harassment or violence against a woman. If I take on her defence, it could turn out to be a disaster."

Blomkvist smiled. "You're missing the point. If she had been charged with the murders of Dag and Mia, for example,

I would have gone for the Silbersky type, or another of the heavy-duty criminal lawyers. But this trial is going to be about entirely different things."

"I think you'd better explain."

They talked for almost two hours over sandwiches and coffee. By the time Mikael had finished his account, Annika had been persuaded. Mikael picked up his mobile and made another call to Inspector Erlander in Göteborg.

"Hello; it's Blomkvist again."

"I don't have any news on Salander," Erlander said, plainly irritated.

"Which I assume is good news. But *I* actually have some news."

"What's that?"

"Well, she now has a lawyer named Annika Giannini. She's with me right now, so I'll put her on."

Blomkvist handed the phone across the table.

"My name is Annika Giannini and I've signed on to represent Lisbeth Salander. I need to get in touch with my client so that she can approve me as her defence lawyer. And I need the phone number of the prosecutor."

"As far as I know," Erlander said, "a public defence lawyer has already been appointed."

"That's nice to hear. Did anyone ask Lisbeth Salander her opinion?"

"Quite frankly, we haven't had the opportunity to speak with her yet. We hope to be able to do so tomorrow, if she's well enough."

"Fine. Then I'll tell you here and now that until Fröken Salander says otherwise, you may regard me as her legal representative. You may not question her unless I am present.

You can say hello to her and ask her whether she accepts me as her lawyer or not. But that is all. Is that understood?"

"Yes," Erlander said with an audible sigh. He was not entirely sure what the letter of the law was on this point. "Our number one objective is to discover if she has any information as to where Ronald Niedermann might be. Is it OK to ask her about that . . . even if you're not present?"

"That's fine; you may ask her questions relating to the police hunt for Niedermann. But you may not ask her any questions relating to any possible charges against her. Agreed?"

"I think so, yes."

Inspector Erlander got up from his desk and went upstairs to tell the preliminary investigation leader, Agneta Jervas, about his conversation with Giannini.

"She was obviously hired by Blomkvist. I can't believe Salander knows anything about it."

"Giannini works in women's rights. I heard her lecture once. She's sharp, but completely unsuitable for this case."

"It's up to Salander to decide."

"I might have to contest the decision in court. For the girl's own sake she has to have a proper defence, and not some celebrity chasing headlines. Hmm. Salander has also been declared legally incompetent. I don't know whether that affects things."

"What should we do?"

Jervas thought for a moment. "This is a complete mess. I don't know who's going to be in charge of this case, or if it'll be transferred to Ekström in Stockholm. In any event, she has to have a lawyer. OK . . . ask her if she wants Giannini."

. . .

When Blomkvist got home at 5:00 in the afternoon he turned on his iBook and took up the thread of the text he had begun writing at the hotel in Göteborg. When he had worked for seven straight hours, he had identified the most glaring holes in the story. There was still much research to be done. One question he could not answer—based on the existing documentation—was who in Säpo, apart from Gunnar Björck, had conspired to lock Salander away in the asylum. Nor had he gotten to the heart of the relationship between Björck and the psychiatrist Peter Teleborian.

Finally he shut down the computer and went to bed. He felt as soon as he lay down that for the first time in weeks he could relax and sleep peacefully. The story was under control. No matter how many questions remained unanswered, he already had enough material to set off a landslide of headlines.

Late as it was, he picked up the phone to call Berger and update her. And then he remembered that she had left *Millennium*. Suddenly he found it difficult to sleep.

A man carrying a brown briefcase stepped carefully down from the 7:30 p.m. train at Stockholm Central Station. He stood for a moment in the sea of travellers, getting his bearings. He had started out from Laholm just after 8:00 in the morning. He stopped in Göteborg to have lunch with an old friend before resuming his journey to Stockholm. He had not been to Stockholm for two years. In fact, he had not planned to visit the capital ever again. Even though he had lived there for large parts of his working life, he always felt a little out of place in Stockholm, a feeling that had grown stronger with every visit he made since his retirement.

He walked slowly through the station, bought the evening papers and two bananas at Pressbyrån, and paused to watch two Muslim women in veils hurry past him. He had nothing against women in veils. But he was bothered by the fact that they had to dress like that in the middle of Stockholm. In his opinion, Somalia was a much better place for that sort of attire.

He walked the 300 yards to Freys Hotel, next to the old post office on Vasagatan. That was where he had stayed on previous visits. The hotel was centrally located and clean. And it was inexpensive, which was a factor since he was paying for the journey himself. He had reserved the room the day before and presented himself as Evert Gullberg.

When he got up to the room he went straight to the bathroom. He had reached the age when he had to use the toilet rather often. It had been several years since he had slept through a whole night.

When he had finished he took off his hat, a narrow-brimmed, dark-green English felt hat, and loosened his tie. He was six feet tall and weighed 150 pounds, which meant he was thin and wiry. He wore a houndstooth jacket and dark grey trousers. He opened the brown briefcase and unpacked two shirts, a second tie, and underwear, which he arranged in the chest of drawers. Then he hung his overcoat and jacket in the wardrobe behind the door.

It was too early to go to bed. It was too late to bother going for an evening walk, something he might not enjoy in any case. He sat down in the obligatory chair in the hotel room and looked around. He switched on the TV and muted the volume. He thought about calling reception and ordering coffee, but decided it was too late. Instead he opened the minibar, poured a miniature bottle of Johnnie Walker into a glass, and added very little water. He opened the evening papers and read everything that had been written that day about the search for Ronald Niedermann and the case of Lisbeth Salander. After a while he took out a leather-bound notebook and made some notes.

Gullberg, formerly senior administrative officer at the Security Police, was now seventy-eight years old and had been retired for thirteen years. But intelligence officers never really retire, they just slip into the shadows.

After the war, when Gullberg was nineteen years old, he had joined the navy. He did his military service first as an officer cadet and was then accepted for officer training. But instead of the usual assignment at sea that he had anticipated, he was sent to Karlskrona as a signal tracker in the navy's intelligence service. He had no difficulty with the work, which was mostly figuring out what was going on on the other side of the Baltic. But he found it dull and uninteresting. Through the service's language school, however, he did learn Russian and Polish. These linguistic skills were one of the reasons he was recruited by the Security Police in 1950, during the time when the impeccably mannered Georg Thulin was head of the third division of Säpo. When Gullberg started, the total budget of the secret police was 2.7 million kronor for a staff of ninety-six people. When he formally retired in 1992, the budget of the Security Police was in excess of 350 million kronor, and he had no idea how many employees the Firm had.

Gullberg had spent his life on His Majesty's Secret Service, or perhaps more accurately in the secret service of the social-democratic welfare state. Which was an irony, since he had faithfully voted for the moderates in one election after another, except in 1991, when he deliberately voted against the moderates because he believed that Carl Bildt was a realpolitik catastrophe. He had voted instead for Ingvar Carlsson. The years of "Sweden's best government" had also confirmed his worst fears. The moderate government had come to power when the Soviet Union was collapsing, and in his opinion no government had been less prepared to meet the new political opportunities emerging in the East, or to make use of the art of espionage. On the contrary, the Bildt government had cut back the Soviet desk for financial reasons and had at the same time gotten themselves involved in the international mess in Bosnia and Serbia—as if Serbia could ever threaten Sweden. The result was that a fabulous opportunity to plant long-term informants in Moscow had been lost. Someday, when relations would once again worsen—which according to Gullberg was inevitable—absurd demands would be made on the Security Police and the military intelligence service, as if they could wave a magic wand and produce agents on demand.

Gullberg had begun at the Russia desk of the third division of the state police, and after two years in the job had undertaken his first tentative field work in 1952 and 1953 as an air force attaché with the rank of captain at the embassy in Moscow. Strangely enough, he was following in the footsteps of another well-known spy. Some years earlier that post had been occupied by the notorious Colonel Stig Wennerström.

Back in Sweden, Gullberg had worked in Counter-Espionage, and ten years later he was one of the younger Security Police officers who, working under Otto Daniels-son, exposed Wennerström and eventually got him a life sentence for treason at Långholmen prison.

When the Security Police was reorganized under Per Gunnar Vinge in 1964 and became the Security Division of the National Police Board, or Swedish Internal Security—SIS—the major increase in personnel began. By then Gullberg had worked at the Security Police for fourteen years, and had become one of its trusted veterans.

Gullberg had never used the designation "Säpo" for Säkerhetspolisen, the Security Police. He used the term "SIS" in official contexts, and among colleagues he would also refer to "the Company" or "the Firm," or merely "the Division"—but never "Säpo." The reason was simple. The Firm's most important task for many years was so-called personnel control; that is, the investigation and registration of Swedish citizens who might be suspected of harbouring communist or subversive views. Within the Firm the terms "communist" and "traitor" were synonymous. The later conventional use of the term "Säpo" was actually something that the potentially subversive communist publication *Clarté* had coined as a pejorative name for the communist-hunters within the police force. For the life of him Gullberg could never imagine why his former boss P. G. Vinge had titled his memoirs *Säpo Chief 1962–1970*.

It was the reorganization of 1964 that had shaped Gullberg's future career.

The designation SIS indicated that the secret state police had been transformed into what was described in the memos from the justice department as a modern police organization. This involved recruiting new personnel, and continual problems breaking them in. In this expanding organization the "Enemy" was presented with dramatically improved opportunities to place agents within the division. This meant in turn that internal security had to be intensified—the Security Police could no longer be a club of former officers, where everyone knew everyone else, and where the most common qualification for a new recruit was that his father was or had been an officer.

In 1963 Gullberg was transferred from Counter-Espionage to Personnel Control, a role that took on added significance in the wake of Wennerström's exposure as a double agent. During that period the foundation was laid for the "registry of political opinions," a list which towards the end of the sixties amounted to around 300,000 Swedish citizens who were believed to harbour undesirable political sympathies. Checking the backgrounds of Swedish citizens was one thing, but the crucial question was how security control within SIS itself would be implemented.

The Wennerström debacle had given rise to an avalanche of dilemmas within the Security Police. If a colonel on the defence staff—he was also the government's adviser on matters involving nuclear weapons and security policy—could work for the Russians, it followed that the Russians might have an equally senior agent within the Security Police. Who would guarantee that the top ranks and middle management at the Firm were not working for the Russians? Who, in short, was going to spy on the spies?

In August 1964 Gullberg was summoned to an afternoon meeting with the assistant chief of the Security Police, Hans

Wilhelm Francke. The other participants at the meeting were two individuals from the top echelon of the Firm, the assistant head of Secretariat and the head of Budget. Before the day was over, Gullberg had been appointed head of a newly created division with the working title of "the Special Section." The first thing he did was to rename it "Special Analysis." That held for a few minutes, until the head of Budget pointed out that SA was not much better than SS. The organization's final name became "the Section for Special Analysis," the SSA, and in daily parlance, "the Section," to differentiate it from "the Division" or "the Firm," which referred to the Security Police as a whole.

"The Section" was Francke's idea. He called it "the last line of defence." An ultra-secret unit that was given strategic positions within the Firm, but which was invisible, it was never referred to in writing, even in budget memoranda, and therefore could not be infiltrated. Its task was to watch over national security. Francke had the authority to make it happen. He needed the Budget chief and the Secretariat chief to create the hidden substructure, but they were old colleagues, friends from dozens of skirmishes with the Enemy.

During the first year, the Section consisted of Gullberg and three hand-picked colleagues. Over the next ten years it grew to include no more than eleven people, of whom two were administrative secretaries of the old school and the remainder were professional spy-hunters. It was a structure with only two ranks. Gullberg was the chief. He would ordinarily meet each member of his team every day. Efficiency was valued more highly than background.

Formally, Gullberg was subordinate to a line of people in the hierarchy under the head of Secretariat of the Security

Police, to whom he had to deliver monthly reports, but in practice he had been given a unique position with exceptional powers. He, and he alone, could decide to put Säpo's top bosses under the microscope. If he wanted to, he could even turn Per Gunnar Vinge's life inside out. (Which he also did.) He could initiate his own investigations or carry out telephone tapping without having to justify his objective or even report it to a higher level. His model was the legendary James Jesus Angleton, who had a similar position in the CIA, and whom he came to know personally.

The Section became a micro-organization within the Division—outside, above, and parallel to the rest of the Security Police. This also had geographical consequences. The Section had its offices at Kungsholmen, but for security reasons almost the whole team was moved out of police headquarters to an eleven-room apartment in Östermalm that had been discreetly remodelled into a fortified office. It was staffed twenty-four hours a day, since the faithful old retainer and secretary Eleanor Badenbrink was installed in permanent lodgings in two of its rooms closest to the entrance. Badenbrink was an implacable colleague in whom Gullberg had implicit trust.

In the organization, Gullberg and his employees disappeared from public view—they were financed through a special fund, but they did not exist anywhere in the formal structure of the Security Police, which reported to the police commission or the justice department. Not even the head of SIS knew about the most secret of the secret, whose task it was to handle the most sensitive of the sensitive.

At the age of forty, Gullberg consequently found himself in a situation where he did not have to explain his actions to any living soul and could initiate investigations of anyone he chose.

It was clear to Gullberg that the Section for Special Analysis could become a politically sensitive unit, and the job description was expressly vague. The written record was meagre in the extreme. In September 1964, Prime Minister Erlander signed a directive that guaranteed the setting aside of funds for the Section for Special Analysis, which was understood to be essential to the nation's security. This was one of twelve similar matters which the assistant chief of SIS, Hans Wilhelm Francke, brought up during an afternoon meeting. The document was stamped TOP SECRET and filed in the special protocol of SIS.

The signature of the prime minister meant that the Section was now a legally approved institution. The first year's budget amounted to 52,000 kronor. That the budget was so low was a stroke of genius, Gullberg thought. It meant that the creation of the Section appeared to be just another routine matter.

In a broader sense, the signature of the prime minister meant that he had sanctioned the need for a unit that would be responsible for "internal personnel control." At the same time, it could be interpreted as the prime minister giving his approval to the establishment of a body that would also monitor particularly sensitive individuals outside SIS, such as the prime minister himself. It was this last which created potentially acute political problems.

Evert Gullberg saw that his whisky glass was empty. He was not fond of alcohol, but it had been a long day and a long journey. At this stage of life he did not think it mattered whether he decided to have one glass of whisky or two. He poured himself the miniature Glenfiddich.

The most sensitive of all issues, of course, was Olof Palme.*

Gullberg remembered every detail of Election Day 1976. For the first time in modern history, Sweden had voted for a conservative government. Most regrettably it was Thorbjörn Fälldin who became prime minister, not Gösta Bohman, a man infinitely better qualified. But above all, Palme was defeated, and for that Gullberg could breathe a sigh of relief.

Palme's suitability as prime minister had been the object of more than one lunch conversation in the halls of SIS. In 1969, Vinge had been dismissed from the service after he gave voice to the view, shared by many inside the Division, that Palme might be an agent of influence for the KGB. Vinge's view was not even controversial in the climate prevailing inside the Firm. Unfortunately, he had openly discussed the matter with County Governor Lassinanti on a visit to Norrbotten. Lassinanti had been astonished and had informed the government chancellor, with the result that Vinge was summoned to explain himself at a one-on-one meeting.

To Gullberg's frustration, the question of Palme's possible Russian contacts was never resolved. Despite persistent attempts to establish the truth and uncover the crucial evidence—the smoking gun—the Section had never found any proof. In Gullberg's eyes this did not mean that Palme was innocent, but rather that he was an especially cunning and intelligent spy who was not tempted to make the same mistakes that other Soviet spies had made. Palme continued

---

* Asterisks throughout the book refer to explanatory notes on p. 821–22.

to baffle them, year after year. In 1982 the Palme question arose again when he became prime minister for the second time. Then the assassin's shots rang out on Sveavägen and the matter became irrelevant.

Nineteen seventy-six had been a problematic year for the Section. Within SIS—among the few people who actually knew about the existence of the Section—a certain amount of criticism had surfaced. During the past ten years, sixty-five employees from within the Security Police had been dismissed from the organization on the grounds of presumed political unreliability. Most of the cases, however, could never be proven, and some senior officers began to wonder whether the Section was run by paranoid conspiracy theorists.

Gullberg still raged to recall the case of an officer hired by SIS in 1968 whom he had personally evaluated as unsuitable. He was Inspector Bergling, a lieutenant in the Swedish army who later turned out to be a colonel in the Soviet military intelligence service, the GRU. On four separate occasions, Gullberg tried to have Bergling removed, but each time his efforts were stymied. Things did not change until 1977, when Bergling became the object of suspicion outside the Section as well. His became the worst scandal in the history of the Swedish Security Police.

Criticism of the Section had increased during the first half of the seventies, and by mid-decade Gullberg had heard several proposals that the budget be reduced, and even suggestions that the operation was altogether unnecessary.

The criticism meant that the Section's future was questioned. That year the threat of terrorism was made a priority in SIS. In terms of espionage it was a sad chapter in their history, dealing as they were mainly with confused youths flirting with Arab or pro-Palestinian elements. The big question within the Security Police was to what extent Personnel Control would be given special authority to investigate foreign citizens residing in Sweden, or whether this would continue to be the exclusive domain of the immigration division.

Out of this somewhat esoteric bureaucratic debate, a need had arisen for the Section to assign a trusted colleague to the operation who could reinforce its control: espionage, in fact, against members of the immigration division.

The job fell to a young man who had worked at SIS since 1970, and whose background and political loyalty made him eminently qualified to work alongside the officers in the Section. In his free time he was a member of an organization called the Democratic Alliance, which was described by the social-democratic media as extremely right-wing. Within the Section this was no obstacle. Three others were members of the Democratic Alliance too, and the Section had in fact been instrumental in the formation of the group. It had also contributed a small part of its funding. It was through this organization that the young man was brought to the attention of the Section and recruited.

His name was Gunnar Björck.

It was an improbable stroke of luck that when Alexander Zalachenko walked into Norrmalm police station on Election Day 1976 and requested asylum, it was a junior officer named Gunnar Björck who received him in his capacity as administrator of the immigration division. An agent already connected to the most secret of the secret.

Björck recognized Zalachenko's importance at once and

broke off the interview to install the defector in a room at the Hotel Continental. It was Gullberg whom Björck notified when he sounded the alarm, and not his formal boss in the immigration division. The call came just as the voting booths had closed, and all signs pointed to the fact that Palme was going to lose. Gullberg had just come home and was watching the election coverage on TV. At first he was sceptical about the information that the excited young officer was telling him. Then he drove down to the Continental, not 250 yards from the hotel room where he found himself today, to assume control of the Zalachenko affair.

That night Gullberg's life underwent a radical change. The notion of secrecy took on a whole new dimension. He saw immediately the need to create a new structure around the defector.

He decided to include Björck in the Zalachenko unit. It was a reasonable decision, since Björck already knew of Zalachenko's existence. Better to have him on the inside than a security risk on the outside. Björck was moved from his post within the immigration division to a desk in the apartment in Östermalm.

In the drama that followed, Gullberg chose from the beginning to inform only one person in SIS, namely the head of Secretariat, who already had an overview of the activities of the Section. The head of Secretariat sat on the news for several days before he explained to Gullberg that the defection was so big that the chief of SIS would have to be informed, as well as the government.

By that time the new chief of SIS knew about the Section for Special Analysis, but he had only a vague idea of what the

Section actually did. He had come on board recently to clean up the shambles of what was known as the Internal Bureau affair, and was already on his way to a higher position within the police hierarchy. The chief of SIS had been told in a private conversation with the head of Secretariat that the Section was a secret unit appointed by the government. Its mandate put it outside regular operations, and no questions should be asked. Since this particular chief was a man who never asked questions that might yield unpleasant answers, he acquiesced. He accepted that there was something known only as SSA and that he should have nothing more to do with the matter.

Gullberg was willing to accept this situation. He issued instructions that required even the chief of SIS not to discuss the topic in his office without taking special precautions. It was agreed that Zalachenko would be handled by the Section for Special Analysis.

The outgoing prime minister was certainly not to be informed. Because of the merry-go-round associated with a change of government, the incoming prime minister was fully occupied appointing ministers and negotiating with other conservative parties. It was not until a month after the government was formed that the chief of SIS, along with Gullberg, drove to Rosenbad to inform the incoming prime minister. Gullberg had objected to telling the government at all, but the chief of SIS had stood his ground—it was constitutionally indefensible not to inform the prime minister. Gullberg used all his eloquence to convince the prime minister not to allow information about Zalachenko to pass beyond his own office; there was, he insisted, no need for the foreign minister, the minister of defence, or any other member of the government to be informed.

It had upset Fälldin that an important Soviet agent had sought asylum in Sweden. The prime minister had begun to talk about how, for the sake of fairness, he would be obliged to take up the matter at least with the leaders of the other two parties in the coalition government. Gullberg was expecting this objection and played the strongest card he had available. He explained in a low voice that if that happened, he would be forced to tender his resignation immediately. This was a threat that made an impression on Fälldin. It was intended to convey that the prime minister would bear the responsibility if the story ever got out and the Russians sent a death squad to liquidate Zalachenko. And if the person responsible for Zalachenko's safety had seen fit to resign, such a revelation would be a political disaster for the prime minister.

Fälldin, still relatively unsure in his role, had acquiesced. He approved a directive that was immediately entered into the secret protocol, making the Section responsible for Zalachenko's safety and debriefing. It also laid down that information about Zalachenko would not leave the prime minister's office. By signing this directive, Fälldin had in practice demonstrated that he had been informed, but it also prevented him from ever discussing the matter. In short, he could forget about Zalachenko. But Fälldin had required that one person in his office, a hand-picked state secretary, also be informed. He would function as a contact person in matters relating to the defector. Gullberg allowed himself to agree to this. He did not anticipate having any problem handling a state secretary.

The chief of SIS was pleased. The Zalachenko matter was now constitutionally secured, which in this case meant that the chief had covered his back. Gullberg was pleased as well. He had managed to create a quarantine, which meant that he would be able to control the flow of information. He alone controlled Zalachenko.

When he got back to Östermalm he sat at his desk and wrote down a list of the people who knew about Zalachenko: himself; Björck; the operations chief of the Section, Hans von Rottinger; Assistant Chief Fredrik Clinton; the Section's secretary, Eleanor Badenbrink; and two officers whose job it was to compile and analyse any intelligence information that Zalachenko might contribute. Seven individuals who over the coming years would constitute a special Section within the Section. He thought of them as the Inner Circle.

Outside the Section, the information was known by the chief of SIS, the assistant chief, and the head of Secretariat. Besides them, the prime minister and a state secretary. A total of twelve. Never before had a secret of this magnitude been known to such a very small group.

Then Gullberg's expression darkened. The secret was known also to a thirteenth person. Björck had been accompanied at Zalachenko's original reception by a lawyer, Nils Erik Bjurman. To include Bjurman in the special Section would be out of the question. Bjurman was not a real security policeman—he was really no more than a trainee at SIS—and he did not have the requisite experience or skills. Gullberg considered various alternatives and then chose to steer Bjurman carefully out of the picture. He used the threat of imprisonment for life, for treason, if Bjurman were to breathe so much as one syllable about Zalachenko, and at the same time he offered inducements, promises of future assignments, and finally he used flattery to bolster Bjurman's feeling of importance. He arranged for Bjurman to be hired by a well-regarded law firm, which then provided him with a steady stream of assignments to keep him busy. The only problem was that Bjurman was such a mediocre lawyer that he was hardly capable of exploiting his opportunities. He left the firm after ten years and opened his own practice, which eventually became a law office at Odenplan.

Over the following years Gullberg kept Bjurman under discreet but regular surveillance. That was Björck's job. It was not until the end of the eighties that he stopped monitoring Bjurman, at which time the Soviet Union was heading for collapse and Zalachenko had ceased to be a priority.

For the Section, Zalachenko had at first been thought of as a potential breakthrough in the Palme mystery. Palme had accordingly been one of the first subjects that Gullberg discussed with him during the long debriefing.

The hopes for a breakthrough, however, were soon dashed, since Zalachenko had never operated in Sweden and had little knowledge of the country. On the other hand, Zalachenko had heard the rumour of a "Red Jumper," a highly placed Swede—or possibly other Scandinavian politician—who worked for the KGB.

Gullberg drew up a list of names that were connected to Palme: Carl Lidbom, Pierre Schori, Sten Andersson, Marita Ulvskog, and a number of others. For the rest of his life, Gullberg would come back again and again to that list, but he never found an answer.

Gullberg was suddenly a big player: he was welcomed with respect in the exclusive club of selected warriors, all known to one another, where the contacts were made through personal friendship and trust, not through official channels and bureaucratic regulations. He met James Jesus Angleton, and he got to drink whisky at a discreet club in London with the chief of MI6. He was one of the elite.

He was never going to be able to tell anyone about his triumphs, not even in posthumous memoirs. And there was the ever-present anxiety that the Enemy would notice his overseas journeys, that he might attract attention, that he might involuntarily lead the Russians to Zalachenko. In that respect, Zalachenko was his worst enemy.

During the first year, the defector had lived in an anonymous apartment owned by the Section. He did not exist in any registry or in any public document. Those within the Zalachenko unit thought they had plenty of time before they had to plan his future. Not until the spring of 1978 was he given a passport in the name of Karl Axel Bodin, along with a laboriously crafted personal history—a fictitious but verifiable background in Swedish records.

By that time it was already too late. Zalachenko had gone and fucked that stupid whore Agneta Sofia Salander, née Sjölander, and he had heedlessly told her his real name—Zalachenko. Gullberg began to believe that Zalachenko was not quite right in the head. He suspected that the Russian defector *wanted* to be exposed. It was as if he needed a platform. How else to explain the fact that he had been so fucking stupid?

There were whores, there were periods of excessive drinking, and there were incidents of violence with bouncers and others. On three occasions Zalachenko was arrested by the Swedish police for drunkenness, and twice more in connection with fights in bars. Every time, the Section had to intervene discreetly and bail him out, seeing to it that documents disappeared and records were altered. Gullberg assigned Björck to babysit the defector almost around the clock. It was not an easy job, but there was no alternative.

Everything could have gone fine. By the early eighties Zalachenko had calmed down and begun to adapt. But he never gave up the whore Salander—and worse, he had become the father of Camilla and Lisbeth Salander.

Lisbeth Salander.

Gullberg pronounced the name with displeasure.

Ever since the girls were nine or ten, he had had a bad feeling about Lisbeth. He did not need a psychiatrist to tell him that she was not normal. Björck had reported that she was vicious and aggressive towards her father and that she seemed to be not in the least afraid of him. She did not say much, but she expressed her dissatisfaction in a thousand other ways. She was a problem in the making, but how gigantic this problem would become was something Gullberg could never have imagined in his wildest dreams. What he most feared was that the situation in the Salander family would give rise to a social welfare report that named Zalachenko. Time and again he urged the man to cut his ties and disappear from their lives. Zalachenko would give his word, and then would always break it. He had other whores. He had plenty of whores. But after a few months he was always back with the Salander woman.

That bastard Zalachenko. An intelligence agent who let his cock rule any part of his life was obviously not a good intelligence agent. It was as though the man thought himself above all normal rules. If he could have screwed the whore without beating her up every time, that would have been one thing, but Zalachenko was guilty of repeated assault against his girlfriend. He seemed to find it amusing to beat her just to provoke his babysitters in the Zalachenko group.

Gullberg had no doubt that Zalachenko was a sick fuck, but he was in no position to pick and choose among defecting GRU agents. He had only one, a man very aware of his value to Gullberg.

The Zalachenko unit had taken on the role of clean-up patrol. It was undeniable. Zalachenko knew that he could take liberties and that the unit would resolve whatever problems there might be. When it came to Agneta Sofia Salander, he exploited his hold over them to the maximum.

Not that there weren't warnings. When Salander was twelve, she stabbed Zalachenko. His wounds had not been life-threatening, but he was taken to St. Göran's hospital and the group had more of a mop-up job to do than ever. Gullberg then made it crystal clear to Zalachenko that he must never have any more dealings with the Salander family, and Zalachenko had promised. A promise he kept for more than six months, before he turned up at Agneta Sofia Salander's place and beat her so savagely that she ended up in a nursing home for the rest of her life.

But Gullberg had not foreseen that the Salander girl would go so far as to make a Molotov cocktail. That day had been utter chaos. All manner of investigations loomed, and the future of the Zalachenko unit—of the whole Section, even—had hung by a thread. If Salander talked, Zalachenko's cover was at risk, and if that were to happen a number of operations put in place across Europe over the past fifteen years might have to be dismantled. Furthermore, there was a possibility that the Section would be subjected to official scrutiny, and that had to be prevented at all costs.

Gullberg had been consumed with worry. If the Section's archives were opened, a number of practices would be revealed that were not always consistent with the dictates of the constitution, not to mention their years of investigations of Palme and other prominent Social Democrats. Just a few years after Palme's assassination that was still a sensitive issue. Prosecution of Gullberg and several other employees of the Section would inevitably follow. Even worse, some ambitious journalist would float the theory that the Section was behind the assassination of Palme, and that in turn would lead to even more damaging speculation and investigation. The most worrying aspect of all this was that the command of the Security Police had changed so much that not even the overall chief of SIS now knew about the existence of the Section. All contacts with SIS stopped at the desk of the new assistant chief of Secretariat, and he had been on the staff of the Section for ten years.

A mood of acute panic, even fear, overtook the unit. It was in fact Björck who proposed the solution. Peter Teleborian, a psychiatrist, had become associated with SIS's department of Counter-Espionage in a different case. He had been key as a consultant in connection with Counter-Espionage's surveillance of a suspected industrial spy. At a critical stage of the investigation, they needed to know how the person in question might react if subjected to a great deal of stress. Teleborian had offered concrete advice, and SIS had succeeded in averting a suicide, managing to turn the spy in question into a double agent.

After Salander's attack on Zalachenko, Björck had surreptitiously engaged Teleborian as an outside consultant to the Section.

The solution to the problem had been very simple. Karl Axel Bodin would disappear into rehabilitative custody. Agneta Sofia Salander would necessarily disappear into an institution for long-term care. All the police reports on the case were collected at SIS and transferred by way of the assistant head of Secretariat to the Section.

Teleborian was assistant head physician at St. Stefan's psychiatric clinic for children in Uppsala. All that was needed was a legal psychiatric report, which Björck and Teleborian drafted together, and then a brief and, as it turned out, uncontested decision in a district court. It was a question only of how the case was presented. The constitution had nothing to do with it. It was, after all, a matter of national security.

Besides, Salander was obviously insane. A few years in an institution would do her nothing but good. Gullberg had approved the operation.

This solution to their multiple problems presented itself at a time when the Zalachenko unit was on its way to being dissolved. The Soviet Union had ceased to exist, and Zalachenko's usefulness was definitively a thing of the past.

The unit procured a generous severance package from Security Police funds. They arranged for him to have the best rehabilitative care, and after six months they put him on a flight to Spain. From that moment on, they made it clear to Zalachenko that he and the Section were going their separate ways. It had been one of Gullberg's last responsibilities. One week later he reached retirement age and handed the reins to his chosen successor, Fredrik Clinton. Thereafter Gullberg acted only as an adviser in especially sensitive matters. He stayed in Stockholm for another three years and worked almost daily at the Section, but the number of his assignments decreased, and gradually he disengaged himself. He then returned to his hometown of Laholm and did some work from there. At first he had travelled frequently to Stockholm, but he made these journeys less and less often, and eventually not at all.

He had not even thought about Zalachenko for months, until the morning he discovered the daughter in every newspaper headline.

Gullberg followed the story in a state of bewilderment. It was no accident, of course, that Bjurman had been Salander's guardian; on the other hand, he couldn't see why the old Zalachenko story should surface. Salander was obviously deranged, so it was no surprise that she had killed these people, but that Zalachenko might have any connection to the affair had not dawned on him. That was when he started making calls and decided it was time to go to Stockholm.

The Section was faced with its worst crisis since the day he had created it.

Zalachenko dragged himself to the toilet. Now that he had crutches, he could move around his room. On Sunday he forced himself through short, sharp training sessions. The pain in his jaw was still excruciating, and he could manage only liquid food, but he could get out of his bed and begin to cover small distances. Having lived so long with a prosthesis, he was used to crutches. He practiced moving noiselessly on them, manoeuvring back and forth around his bed. Every time his right foot touched the floor, a terrible pain shot up his leg.

He gritted his teeth. He thought about the fact that his daughter was very close by. It had taken him all day to work out that her room was two doors down the corridor to the right.

The night nurse had been gone ten minutes; everything was quiet; it was 2:00 in the morning. Zalachenko laboriously got up and fumbled for his crutches. He listened at the door but heard nothing. He pulled open the door and went into the corridor. He heard faint music from the nurses' station. He made his way to the end of the corridor, pushed open the door, and looked into the empty landing where the elevators were. Going back down the corridor, he stopped at the door to his daughter's room and rested there on his crutches for half a minute, listening.

Salander opened her eyes when she heard a scraping sound. It was as though someone was dragging something along the corridor. For a moment there was only silence, and she wondered if she was imagining things. Then she heard the same sound again, moving away. Her uneasiness grew.

Zalachenko was out there somewhere.

She felt fettered to her bed. Her skin itched under the neck brace. She felt an intense desire to move, to get up. Gradually she succeeded in sitting up. That was all she could manage. She sank back onto the pillow.

She ran her hand over her neck brace and located the fastenings that held it in place. She opened them and dropped the brace to the floor. Immediately it was easier to breathe.

What she wanted more than anything was a weapon, and to have the strength to get up and finish the job once and for all.

With difficulty she propped herself up, switched on the night light, and looked around the room. She could see nothing that would serve her purpose. Then her eyes fell on a nurses' table on the wall across from her bed. Someone had left a pencil there.

She waited until the night nurse had come and gone, which tonight she seemed to be doing about every half hour. Presumably the reduced frequency of the nurse's visits meant that the doctors had decided her condition had improved; over the weekend the nurses had checked on her at least once every ten minutes. She could hardly notice any difference herself.

When she was alone she gathered her strength, sat up, and swung her legs over the side of the bed. She had electrodes taped to her body to record her pulse and breathing, but the wires stretched in the direction of the pencil. She put her weight on her feet and stood up. Suddenly she swayed, off balance. For a second she felt as though she would faint, but she steadied herself against the bed and concentrated her gaze on the table in front of her. She took small, wobbly steps, reached out and grabbed the pencil.

Then she retreated slowly to the bed. She was exhausted.

After a while she managed to pull the sheet and blanket up to her chin. She studied the pencil. It was a plain wooden pencil, newly sharpened. It would make a passable weapon—for stabbing a face or an eye.

She laid it next to her hip and fell asleep.

CHAPTER 6

Monday, April 11

Blomkvist got up just after 9:00 and called Eriksson at *Millennium*.

"Good morning, editor in chief," he said.

"I'm still in shock that Erika is gone and you want me to take her place. Her office is empty."

"Then it would probably be a good idea to spend the day moving in there."

"I feel extremely self-conscious."

"Don't be. Everyone agrees that you're the best choice. And if need be, you can always come to me or Christer."

"Thank you for your trust in me."

"You've earned it," Blomkvist said. "Just keep working the way you always do. We'll deal with any problems as and when they crop up."

He told her he was going to be at home all day writing. Eriksson realized that he was reporting in to her the way he had with Berger.

"OK. Is there anything you want us to do?"

"No. On the contrary . . . if you have any instructions for

me, just call. I'm still on the Salander story, trying to find out what's happening there, but for everything else to do with the magazine, the ball's in your court. You make the decisions. You'll have my support if you need it."

"And what if I make a wrong decision?"

"If I see or hear anything out of the ordinary, we'll talk it through. But it would have to be something very unusual. Generally there aren't any decisions that are 100 percent right or wrong. You'll make your decisions, and they might not be the same ones Erika would have made or even that I would have made. But your decisions are the ones that count."

"All right."

"If you're a good boss, then you'll discuss any concerns with the others. First with Henry and Christer, then with me, and we'll raise any problems at the editorial meetings."

"I'll do my best."

"Good luck."

He sat down on the sofa in the living room with his iBook on his lap and worked without any breaks all day. When he was finished, he had a rough draft of two articles totalling twenty-one pages focused on the deaths of Svensson and Johansson—what they were working on, why they were killed, and who the killer was. He estimated that he would have to produce twice as much text again for the summer issue. He also had to resolve how to profile Salander in the article without violating her trust. He knew things about her that she would never want published.

Gullberg had a single slice of bread and a cup of black coffee in Freys café. Then he took a taxi to Artillerigatan in Öster-malm. At 9:15 he introduced himself on the entry phone and was buzzed inside. He took the elevator to the seventh floor, where he was received by Birger Wadensjöö, the new chief of the Section.

Wadensjöö had been one of the latest recruits to the Section around the time Gullberg retired. He wished that the decisive Fredrik was still there. Clinton had succeeded Gullberg and was the chief of the Section until 2002, when diabetes and coronary artery disease had forced him into retirement. Gullberg did not have a clear sense of what Wadensjöö was made of.

"Welcome, Evert," Wadensjöö said, shaking hands with his former chief. "It's good of you to take the time to come in."

"Time is more or less all I have," Gullberg said.

"You know how it goes. I wish we had the leisure to stay in touch with faithful old colleagues."

Gullberg ignored the insinuation. He turned left into his old office and sat at the round conference table by the window. He assumed it was Wadensjöö who was responsible for the Chagall and Mondrian reproductions. In his day, plans of the warships *Kronan* and *Wasa* had hung on the walls. He had always dreamed about the sea, and he was in fact a naval officer, although he had spent only a few brief months at sea during his military service. There were computers now, but otherwise the room looked almost exactly as when he had left. Wadensjöö poured coffee.

"The others are on their way," he said. "I thought we could have a few words first."

"How many in the Section are still here from my day?"

"Apart from me, only Otto Hallberg and Georg Nyström. Hallberg is retiring this year, and Nyström is turning sixty.

Otherwise it's new recruits. You've probably met some of them before."

"How many are working for the Section today?"

"We've reorganized a bit."

"And?"

"There are seven full-timers. So we've cut back. But there's a total of thirty-one employees of the Section within SIS. Most of them never come here. They take care of their normal jobs and do some discreet moonlighting for us should the need or opportunity arise."

"Thirty-one employees."

"Plus the seven here. You were the one who created the system, after all. We've just fine-tuned it. Today we have what's called an internal and external organization. When we recruit somebody, they're given a leave of absence for a time to go to our school. Hallberg is in charge of training, which is six weeks for the basics. We do it out at the Naval School. Then they go back to their regular jobs in SIS, but now they work for us."

"I see."

"It's an excellent system. Most of our employees have no idea of the others' existence. And here in the Section we function principally as report recipients. The same rules apply as in your day. We have to be a single-level organization."

"Do you have an operations unit?"

Wadensjöö frowned. In Gullberg's day the Section had a small operations unit consisting of four people under the command of the shrewd Hans von Rottinger.

"Well, not exactly. Von Rottinger died five years ago. We have a younger talent who does some field work, but usually we use someone from the external organization if necessary. Of course, things have become more complicated technically, for example when we need to arrange a telephone tap or enter an apartment. Nowadays there are alarms and other devices everywhere."

Gullberg nodded. "Budget?"

"About eleven million a year total. A third goes to salaries, a third to overheads, and a third to operations."

"The budget has shrunk."

"A little. But we have fewer people, which means that the operations budget has actually increased."

"Tell me about our relationship to SIS."

Wadensjöö shook his head. "The chief of Secretariat and the chief of Budget belong to us. Formally, the chief of Secretariat is the only one who has insight into our activities. We're so secret that we don't exist. But in practice, two assistant chiefs know of our existence. They do their best to ignore anything they hear about us."

"Which means that if problems arise, the present SIS leadership will have an unpleasant surprise. What about the defence leadership and the government?"

"We cut off the defence leadership some ten years ago. And governments come and go."

"So if the shit hits the fan, we're on our own?"

Wadensjöö nodded. "That's the drawback with this arrangement. The advantages are obvious. But our assignments have also changed. There's a new realpolitik in Europe since the Soviet Union collapsed. Our work is less and less about identifying spies. It's about terrorism, and about evaluating the political suitability of individuals in sensitive positions."

"That's what it was always about."

There was a knock at the door. Gullberg looked up to see a smartly dressed man of about sixty and a younger man in jeans and a tweed jacket.

"Come in. . . . Evert Gullberg, this is Jonas Sandberg. He's been working here for four years and is in charge of operations. He's the one I told you about. And Georg Nyström you know."

"Hello, Georg," Gullberg said.

They all shook hands. Then Gullberg turned to Sandberg. "So where do you come from?"

"Most recently from Göteborg," Sandberg said lightly. "I went to see him."

"Zalachenko?"

Sandberg nodded.

"Have a seat, gentlemen," Wadensjöö said.

"Björck," Gullberg said, frowning when Wadensjöö lit a cigarillo. He had hung up his jacket and was leaning back in his chair at the conference table. Wadensjöö glanced at Gullberg and was struck by how thin the old man had become.

"He was arrested for violation of the prostitution laws last Friday," Nyström said. "The matter has gone to court, but in effect he confessed and slunk home with his tail between his legs. He lives out in Smådalarö, but he's on disability leave. The press hasn't picked up on it yet."

"He was once one of the very best we had here in the Section," Gullberg said. "He played a key role in the Zalachenko affair. What's happened to him since I retired?"

"Björck is probably one of the very few internal colleagues who left the Section and went back to external operations. He was out flitting around even in your day."

"Well, I do recall he needed a little rest and wanted to expand his horizons. He was on leave of absence from the Section for two years in the eighties when he worked as intelligence attaché. He had worked like a fiend with Zalachenko, practically around the clock from 1976 on, and I thought he needed a break. He was gone from 1985 to 1987, when he came back here."

"You could say that he quit the Section in 1994 when he went over to the external organization. In 1996 he became assistant chief of the immigration division and ended up in a stressful position. His official duties took up a great deal of his time. Naturally he's stayed in contact with the Section throughout, and we had conversations with him about once a month until recently."

"He's ill?"

"It's nothing serious, but very painful. He has a slipped disk. He's had recurring trouble with it over the past few years. Two years ago he was on sick leave for four months. Then he was taken ill again in August last year. He was supposed to start work again in January, but his sick leave was extended, and now it's a question of waiting for an operation."

"And he spent his sick leave running around with prostitutes?" Gullberg said.

"Yes. He's not married, and his dealings with whores appear to have been going on for many years, if I've understood correctly," said Sandberg, who had been silent for almost half an hour. "I've read Dag Svensson's manuscript."

"I see. But can anyone explain to me what actually happened?"

"As far as we can tell, it was Björck who initiated this

whole mess. How else can we explain the report from 1991 ending up in the hands of Advokat Bjurman?"

"Another man who spends his time with prostitutes?" Gullberg said.

"Not as far as we know, and he wasn't mentioned in Svensson's material. He was, however, Lisbeth Salander's guardian."

Wadensjöö sighed. "You could say it was my fault. You and Björck arrested Salander in 1991, when she was sent to the psychiatric hospital. We expected her to be away for much longer, but she became acquainted with a lawyer, Holger Palmgren, who managed to spring her loose. She was then placed with a foster family. By that time you had retired."

"And then what happened?"

"We kept an eye on her. In the meantime her twin sister, Camilla, was placed in a foster home in Uppsala. When they were seventeen, Lisbeth started digging into her past. She was looking for Zalachenko, and she went through every public registry she could find. Somehow—we're not sure how it happened—she came to the conclusion that her sister knew where Zalachenko was."

"Was it true?"

Wadensjöö shrugged. "I have no idea. The sisters had not seen each other for several years when Lisbeth Salander confronted Camilla and tried to persuade her to tell her what she knew. It ended in a violent argument and a spectacular fight between the sisters."

"Then what?"

"We kept close track of Lisbeth during those months. We had also informed Camilla that her sister was violent and mentally ill. She was the one who got in touch with us after

Lisbeth's unexpected visit, and thereafter we increased our surveillance of her."

"The sister was your informant?"

"Camilla was mortally afraid of her sister. Lisbeth had aroused attention in other quarters as well. She had several run-ins with people from the social welfare agency, and in our estimation she still represented a threat to Zalachenko's anonymity. Then there was the incident in the tunnelbana."

"She attacked a paedophile—"

"Precisely. She was obviously prone to violence, and mentally disturbed. We thought that it would be best for all concerned if she disappeared into some institution again and availed herself of the opportunities there, so to speak. Clinton and von Rottinger were the ones who took the lead. They engaged the psychiatrist Teleborian again and through a representative filed a request in the district court to get her institutionalized for a second time. Palmgren stood up for Salander, and against all odds the court decided to follow his recommendation—so long as she was placed under guardianship."

"But how did Bjurman get involved?"

"Palmgren had a stroke in the fall of 2002. We still flag Salander for monitoring whenever she turns up in any database, and I saw to it that Bjurman became her new guardian. Bear in mind that he had no clue she was Zalachenko's daughter. The brief was simply for Bjurman to sound the alarm if she started blabbing about Zalachenko."

"Bjurman was an idiot. He should never have been allowed to have anything to do with Zalachenko, even less with his daughter." Gullberg looked at Wadensjöö. "That was a serious mistake."

"I know," Wadensjöö said. "But he seemed the right choice at the time. I never would have dreamed that—"

"Where's the sister today? Camilla Salander."

"We don't know. When she was nineteen she packed her bag and ran away from her foster family. We haven't heard a peep out of her since."

"Go on."

"I have a man in the regular police who has spoken with Prosecutor Ekström," Sandberg said. "The officer running the investigation, Inspector Bublanski, thinks that Bjurman raped Salander."

Gullberg looked at Sandberg with astonishment.

"Raped her?" he said.

"Bjurman had a tattoo across his belly which read 'I am a sadistic pig, a pervert, and a rapist.'"

Sandberg put a colour photograph from the autopsy on the table. Gullberg stared at it with distaste.

"Zalachenko's daughter is supposed to have given him that?"

"It's hard to find another explanation. And she's not known for being a shrinking violet. She kicked the shit out of two thugs from Svavelsjö MC."

"Zalachenko's daughter," Gullberg repeated. He turned to Wadensjöö. "You know what? I think you ought to recruit her for the Section."

Wadensjöö looked so startled that Gullberg had to explain that he was joking.

"OK. Let's take it as a working hypothesis that Bjurman raped her and she somehow took her revenge. What else?"

"The only one who could tell us exactly what happened, of course, is Bjurman, and he's dead. But the thing is, he shouldn't have had a clue that she was Zalachenko's daughter; it's not in any public records. But somehow, somewhere along the way, Bjurman discovered the connection."

"But, Goddamnit, Wadensjöö! *She* knew who her father was and could have told Bjurman at any time."

"I know. We . . . that is, *I* simply wasn't thinking straight."

"That is unforgivably incompetent," Gullberg said.

"I've kicked myself a hundred times about it. But Bjurman was one of the very few people who knew of Zalachenko's existence, and my thought was that it would be better if he rather than some other unknown guardian discovered she was Zalachenko's daughter. She could have told anyone."

Gullberg pulled on his earlobe. "All right. Continue."

"It's all hypothetical," Nyström said. "But our supposition is that Bjurman assaulted Salander and that she struck back and did that." He pointed at the tattoo in the autopsy photograph.

"Her father's daughter," Gullberg said. There was more than a trace of admiration in his voice.

"With the result that Bjurman made contact with Zalachenko, hoping to get rid of the daughter. As we know, Zalachenko had good reason to hate the girl. And he gave the contract to Svavelsjö MC and this Niedermann that he hangs out with."

"But how did Bjurman get in touch—" Gullberg fell silent. The answer was obvious.

"Björck," Wadensjöö said. "Björck gave him the contact."

"Damn," Gullberg said.

In the morning two nurses came to change her bed linen. They found the pencil.

"Oops. How did this get here?" one of them said, putting the pencil in her pocket. Salander looked at her with murder in her eyes.

She was once more without a weapon, but she was too weak to protest.

Her headache was unbearable, and she was given strong painkillers. Her left shoulder stabbed like a knife if she moved carelessly or tried to shift her weight. She lay on her back with the brace around her neck. It was supposed to be left on for a few more days, until the wound in her head began to heal. This morning she had a temperature of 102. Dr. Endrin could tell that there was an infection. Salander didn't need a thermometer to work that out.

She realized that once again she was confined to an institutional bed, even though this time there was no strap holding her down. That would have been unnecessary. She couldn't sit up, let alone leave the room.

At lunchtime on Monday she had a visit from Dr. Jonasson.

"Hello. Do you remember me?"

She shook her head.

"I was the one who woke you after surgery. I operated on you. I just wanted to hear how you're doing and if everything is going well."

Salander looked at him, her eyes wide. It should have been obvious that everything was not going well.

"I heard you took off your neck brace last night."

She acknowledged as much with her eyes.

"We put the neck brace on for a reason—you have to keep your head still for the healing process to get started." He looked at the silent girl. "OK," he said at last. "I just wanted to check on you."

He was at the door when he heard her voice.

"It's Jonasson, right?"

He turned and smiled at her in surprise. "That's right. If you remember my name, then you must have been more alert than I thought."

"And you were the one who operated to remove the bullet?"

"That's right."

"Please tell me how I'm doing. I can't get a sensible answer from anyone."

He went back to her bedside and looked her in the eye.

"You were lucky. You were shot in the head, but the bullet did not, I believe, injure any vital areas. The risk is that you could have bleeding in your brain. That's why we want you to stay still. You also have an infection. The wound in your shoulder seems to be the cause. It's possible that you'll need another operation—on your shoulder—if we can't arrest the infection with antibiotics. You're going to have some painful times ahead while your body heals. But as things look now, I'm optimistic that you'll make a full recovery."

"Can this cause brain damage?"

He hesitated before nodding. "Yes, there is that possibility. But all signs indicate that you made it through fine. There's also a possibility that you'll develop scar tissue in your brain, which might cause trouble . . . for instance, you might develop epilepsy or some other problem. But to be honest, it's all speculation. Right now, things look good. You're healing. And if problems crop up along the way, we'll deal with them. Is that a clear enough answer?"

She shut her eyes to say yes. "How long do I have to lie here like this?"

"You mean in the hospital? It will be at least a couple of weeks before we can let you go."

"No, I mean how long before I can get up and start walking and moving around?"

"That depends on how the healing progresses. But count on two weeks before we can start you on some sort of physical therapy."

She gave him a long look. "You wouldn't happen to have a cigarette, would you?" she said.

Dr. Jonasson burst out laughing and shook his head. "Sorry. There's no smoking allowed in the hospital. But I can see to it that you get a nicotine patch or some gum."

She thought for a moment before she looked at him again. "How's the old bastard doing?"

"Who? You mean—"

"The one who came in the same time as I did."

"No friend of yours, I presume. Well, he's going to survive, and he's been up walking around on crutches. He's actually in worse shape than you are, and he has a very painful facial wound. As I understand it, you slammed an axe into his head."

"He tried to kill me," Salander said in a low voice.

"That doesn't sound good. I have to go. Do you want me to come back and look in on you again?"

Salander thought for a moment, then she signalled yes. When he was gone she stared at the ceiling. *Zalachenko has been given crutches. That was the sound I heard last night.*

Sandberg, the youngest person at the meeting, was sent out to get some food. He came back with sushi and light beer and passed both around the conference table. Gullberg felt a thrill of nostalgia. This was just the way it was in his day, when some operation went into a critical phase and they had to work around the clock.

The difference, he observed, was that in his day nobody would have come up with the wild idea of ordering raw fish. He wished Sandberg had ordered Swedish meatballs with mashed potatoes and lingonberries. On the other hand, he wasn't really hungry, so he pushed the sushi aside. He ate a piece of bread and drank some mineral water.

They continued the discussion over their meal. They had to decide what to do. The situation was urgent.

"I never knew Zalachenko," Wadensjöö said. "What was he like?"

"Much as he is today, I assume," Gullberg said. "Phenomenally intelligent, with a damn near photographic memory. But in my opinion he's a pig. And not quite right in the head."

"Jonas, you talked to him yesterday. What's your take?" Wadensjöö said.

Sandberg put down his chopsticks.

"He's got us over a barrel. I've already told you about his ultimatum. Either we make the whole thing disappear, or he cracks the Section wide open."

"How the hell do we make something disappear that's been plastered all over the media?" Nyström said.

"It's not a question of what we can or can't do. It's a question of his need to control us," Gullberg said.

"Would he, in your opinion, talk to the press?" Wadensjöö said.

Gullberg hesitated. "It's almost impossible to answer that

question. Zalachenko doesn't make empty threats, and he's going to do what's best for him. In that respect he's predictable. If it benefits him to talk to the media . . . if he thought he could get an amnesty or a reduced sentence, then he'd do it. Or if he felt betrayed and wanted to get even."

"Regardless of the consequences?"

"Especially regardless of the consequences. For him the point is to be seen as tougher than all of us."

"If Zalachenko were to talk, it's not certain that anyone would believe him. And to prove anything they'd have to get ahold of our archives."

"Do you want to take the chance? Let's say Zalachenko talks. Who's going to talk next? What do we do if Björck signs an affidavit confirming his story? And Clinton, sitting at his dialysis machine . . . what would happen if he turned religious and felt bitter about everything and everyone? What if he wanted to make a confession? Believe me, if anyone starts talking, it's the end of the Section."

"So . . . what should we do?"

Silence settled over the table. It was Gullberg who spoke first.

"There are several parts to this problem. First of all, we can agree on what the consequences would be if Zalachenko talked. The entire legal system would come crashing down on our heads. We would be demolished. My guess is that several employees of the Section would go to prison."

"Our activity is completely legal . . . we're actually working under the auspices of the government."

"Spare me the bullshit," Gullberg said. "You know as well as I do that a loosely formulated document that was written in the mid-sixties isn't worth a damn today. I don't think any one of us could even imagine what would happen if Zalachenko talked."

Silence descended once again.

"So our starting point has to be to persuade Zalachenko to keep his mouth shut," Nyström said at last.

"And to persuade him to keep his mouth shut, we have to be able to offer him something substantial. The problem is that he's unpredictable. He would burn us out of sheer malice. We have to think about how we can keep him in check."

"And what about his demand," Sandberg said, "that we make the whole thing disappear and put Salander back in an asylum?"

"Salander we can handle. It's Zalachenko who's the problem. But that leads us to the second part: damage control. Teleborian's report from 1991 has been leaked, and it's potentially as serious a threat as Zalachenko."

Nyström cleared his throat. "As soon as we realized that the report was out and in the hands of the police, I took certain measures. I went through Forelius, our lawyer in SIS, and he got ahold of the prosecutor general. The PG ordered the report confiscated from the police—it's not to be disseminated or copied."

"How much does the PG know?" Gullberg said.

"Not a thing. He's acting on an official request from SIS. It's classified material, and the PG has no alternative."

"Who in the police has read the report?"

"There were two copies, which were read by Bublanski, his colleague Inspector Modig, and finally the preliminary investigation leader, Richard Ekström. We can assume that another two police officers"—Nyström leafed through his notes—"that Curt Andersson and Jerker Holmberg, at least, are aware of the contents."

"So, four police officers and one prosecutor. What do we know about them?"

"Prosecutor Ekström, forty-two, regarded as a rising star. He's been an investigator at Justice and has handled a number of cases that got a fair bit of attention. Zealous. PR-savvy. Careerist."

"Social Democrat?" Gullberg said.

"Probably. But not active."

"Bublanski is leading the investigation. I saw him in a press conference on TV. He didn't seem comfortable in front of the cameras."

"He's older and has an exceptional record, but he also has a reputation for being crusty and obstinate. He's quite conservative."

"And the woman . . . who's she?"

"Sonja Modig. Married, thirty-nine, two kids. Has advanced rather quickly in her career. I talked to Teleborian, who described her as emotional. She asks questions non-stop."

"Next."

"Andersson is a tough customer. He's thirty-eight and comes from the gangs unit in Söder. He landed in the spotlight when he shot dead some hooligan a couple of years ago. Acquitted of all charges, according to the report. He was the one Bublanski sent to arrest Björck."

"I see. Keep in mind that he shot someone dead. If there's any reason to cast doubt on Bublanski's group, we can always single him out as a rogue policeman. I assume we still have relevant media contacts. And the last guy?"

"Holmberg, fifty-five. Comes from Norrland and is in fact a specialist in crime scene investigation. He was offered supervisory training a few years ago but turned it down. He seems to like his job."

"Are any of them politically active?"

"No. Holmberg's father was a city councillor for the Centre Party in the seventies."

"It seems to be a modest group. We can assume they're fairly tight-knit. Could we isolate them somehow?"

"There's a fifth officer involved," Nyström said. "Hans Faste, forty-seven. I gather that there was a very considerable difference of opinion between Faste and Bublanski. So much so that Faste took sick leave."

"What do we know about him?"

"I get mixed reactions when I ask. He has an exemplary record with no real criticisms. A pro. But he's tricky to deal with. The disagreement with Bublanski seems to have been about Salander."

"In what way?"

"Faste appears to have become obsessed by one newspaper story about a lesbian Satanist gang. He really doesn't like Salander and seems to regard her existence as a personal insult. He may himself be behind half of the rumours. I was told by a former colleague that he has difficulty working with women."

"Interesting," Gullberg said slowly. "Since the newspapers have already written about a lesbian gang, it would make sense to continue promoting that story. It won't exactly bolster Salander's credibility."

"But the officers who've read Björck's report are a big

problem," Sandberg said. "Is there any way we can isolate them?"

Wadensjöö lit another cigarillo. "Well, Ekström is the head of the preliminary investigation. . . ."

"But Bublanski's leading it," Nyström said.

"Yes, but he can't go against an administrative decision." Wadensjöö turned to Gullberg. "You have more experience than I do, but this whole story has so many different threads and connections. . . . It seems to me that it would be wise to get Bublanski and Modig away from Salander."

"That's good, Wadensjöö," Gullberg said. "And that's exactly what we're going to do. Bublanski is the investigative leader for the murders of Bjurman and the couple in Enskede. Salander is no longer a suspect. Now it's all about this German, Ronald Niedermann. Bublanski and his team have to focus on Niedermann. Salander is not their assignment anymore. Then there's the investigation at Nykvarn; three cold-case killings. And there's a connection to Niedermann there too. That investigation is presently allocated to Södertälje, but it ought to be brought into a single investigation. That way Bublanski would have his hands full for a while. And who knows? Maybe he'll catch Niedermann. Meanwhile, Hans Faste . . . do you think he might come back on duty? He sounds like the right man to investigate the allegations against Salander."

"I see what you're thinking," Wadensjöö said. "It's all about getting Ekström to split the two cases. But that's only if we can control Ekström."

"That shouldn't be such a big problem," Gullberg said. He glanced at Nyström, who nodded.

"I can take care of Ekström," he said. "I'm guessing that he's wishing he'd never heard of Zalachenko. He turned over Björck's report as soon as SIS asked him for it, and he's agreed to comply with every request that may have a bearing on national security."

"What do you have in mind?" Wadensjöö said.

"Allow me to manufacture a scenario," Nyström said. "I assume that we're going to tell him in a subtle way what he has to do to avoid an abrupt end to his career."

"The most serious problem is going to be the third part," Gullberg said. "The police didn't get ahold of Björck's report by themselves . . . they got it from a journalist. And the press, as you are all aware, is a real problem here. *Millennium.*"

Nyström turned a page in his notebook. "Mikael Blomkvist."

Everyone around the table had heard of the Wennerström affair and knew the name.

"Svensson, the journalist who was murdered, was freelancing at *Millennium*. He was working on a story about sex trafficking. That was how he lit upon Zalachenko. It was Blomkvist who found Svensson's and his girlfriend's bodies. In addition, Blomkvist knows Salander and has always believed in her innocence."

"How the hell can he know Zalachenko's daughter? That sounds like too big a coincidence."

"We don't think it is a coincidence," Wadensjöö said. "We believe that Salander is in some way the link between all of them, but we don't yet know how."

Gullberg drew a series of concentric circles on his notepad. At last he looked up.

"I have to think about this for a while. I'm going for a walk. We'll meet again in an hour."

Gullberg's excursion lasted nearly three hours. He had walked for only about ten minutes before he found a café that served many unfamiliar types of coffee. He ordered a cup of regular black coffee and sat at a corner table near the entrance. He spent a long time thinking things over, trying to dissect the various aspects of their dilemma. Occasionally he would jot down notes in a pocket diary.

After an hour and a half a plan had begun to take shape.

It was not a perfect plan, but after weighing all the options, he concluded that the problem called for a drastic solution.

As luck would have it, the human resources were available. It was doable.

He got up to find a phone booth and called Wadensjöö.

"We'll have to postpone the meeting a bit longer," he said. "There's something I have to do. Can we meet again at 2:00 p.m.?"

Gullberg went down to Stureplan and hailed a taxi. He gave the driver an address in the suburb of Bromma. When he was dropped off, he walked south one block and rang the doorbell of a small, semi-detached house. A woman in her forties opened the door.

"Good afternoon. I'm looking for Fredrik Clinton."

"Who should I say is here?"

"An old colleague."

The woman nodded and showed him into the living room, where Clinton rose slowly from the sofa. He was only sixty-eight, but he looked much older. His ill health had taken a heavy toll.

"Gullberg," Clinton said in surprise.

For a long moment they stood looking at each other. Then the two old agents embraced.

"I thought I'd never see you again," Clinton said. He pointed to the front page of the morning paper, which had a photograph of Niedermann and the headline POLICE KILLER HUNTED IN DENMARK. "I assume that's what's brought you out here."

"How are you?"

"I'm sick," Clinton said.

"I can see that."

"If I don't get a new kidney I'm not long for this world. And the likelihood of my getting one in this people's republic is pretty slim."

The woman came to the living-room doorway and asked if Gullberg would like anything.

"A cup of coffee, thank you," he said. When she was gone he turned to Clinton. "Who's that?"

"My daughter."

It was fascinating that despite the collegial atmosphere they had shared for so many years at the Section, hardly any of them socialized with each other in their free time. Gullberg knew the most minute character traits, the strengths and weaknesses, of all his colleagues, but he had only a vague notion of their family lives. Clinton had probably been Gullberg's closest colleague for twenty years. Gullberg knew that he had been married and had children, but he did not know the daughter's name, his late wife's name, or even where

Clinton usually spent his vacations. It was as if everything outside the Section was sacred, not to be discussed.

"What can I do for you?" asked Clinton.

"Can I ask you what you think of Wadensjöö?"

Clinton shook his head. "I don't want to get into it."

"That's not what I asked. You know him. He worked with you for ten years."

Clinton shook his head again. "He's the one running the Section today. What I think is no longer of any interest."

"Can he handle it?"

"He's no idiot."

"But?"

"He's an analyst. Extremely good at puzzles. Instinctual. A brilliant administrator who balanced the budget, and did it in a way we didn't think was possible."

Gullberg nodded. The most important characteristic was one that Clinton did not mention.

"Are you ready to come back to work?"

Clinton looked up. He hesitated for a long time.

"Evert . . . I spend nine hours every other day on a dialysis machine at the hospital. I can't go up stairs without gasping for breath. I simply have no energy. No energy at all."

"I need you. One last operation."

"I can't."

"Yes, you can. And you can still spend nine hours every other day on dialysis. You can take the elevator instead of going up the stairs. I'll even arrange for somebody to carry you back and forth on a stretcher if necessary. It's your mind I need."

Clinton sighed. "Tell me."

"Right now we're confronted with an exceptionally complicated situation that requires operational expertise. Wadensjöö has a young kid, still wet behind the ears, named Jonas Sandberg; he's the entire operations department. And I don't think Wadensjöö has the drive to do what needs to be done. He might be a genius at finessing the budget, but he's afraid to make operational decisions, and he's afraid to get the Section involved in the necessary field work."

Clinton gave him a feeble smile.

"The operation has to be carried out on two separate fronts. One part concerns Zalachenko. I have to get him to listen to reason, and I think I know how I'm going to do it. The second part has to be handled from here, in Stockholm. The problem is that there isn't anyone in the Section who can actually run it. I need you to take command. One last job. Sandberg and Nyström will do the legwork; you control the operation."

"You don't understand what you're asking."

"Yes, I do. But you're going to have to make up your mind whether to take on the assignment or not. Either we ancients step in and do our bit, or the Section will cease to exist a few weeks from now."

Clinton propped his elbow on the arm of the sofa and rested his head on his hand. He thought about it for two minutes.

"Tell me your plan," he said at last.

Gullberg and Clinton talked for a long time.

Wadensjöö stared in disbelief when Gullberg returned at 2:57 with Clinton in tow. Clinton looked like a skeleton. He seemed to have difficulty breathing; he kept one hand on Gullberg's shoulder.

"What in the world . . . ?" Wadensjöö said.

"Let's get the meeting moving again," Gullberg said briskly.

They settled themselves again around the table in Wadensjöö's office. Clinton sank silently onto the chair that was offered.

"You all know Fredrik Clinton," Gullberg said.

"Indeed," Wadensjöö said. "The question is, what's he doing here?"

"Clinton has decided to return to active duty. He'll be leading the Section's operations department until the present crisis is over." Gullberg raised a hand to forestall Wadensjöö's objections. "Clinton is tired. He's going to need assistance. He has to go regularly to the hospital for dialysis. Wadensjöö, assign two personal assistants to help him with all the practical matters. But let me make this quite clear: with regard to this affair, it's Clinton who will be making the operational decisions."

He paused for a moment. No-one voiced any objections.

"I have a plan. I think we can handle this matter successfully, but we're going to have to act fast so that we don't squander the opportunity," he said. "It depends on how decisive you can be in the Section these days."

"Let's hear it," Wadensjöö said.

"First of all, we've already discussed the police. This is what we're going to do. We'll try to isolate them in a lengthy investigation, sidetracking them into the search for Niedermann. That will be Nyström's task. Whatever happens, Niedermann is of no importance. We'll arrange for Faste to be assigned to investigate Salander."

"That may not be such a bright idea," Nyström said. "Why

don't I just go and have a discreet talk with Prosecutor Ekström?"

"And if he gets difficult?"

"I don't think he will. He's ambitious and on the lookout for anything that will benefit his career. I might be able to use some leverage if I need to. He would hate to be dragged into any sort of scandal."

"Good. Stage two is *Millennium* and Mikael Blomkvist. That's why Clinton has returned to duty. This will require extraordinary measures."

"I don't think I'm going to like this," Wadensjöö said.

"Probably not. But *Millennium* can't be manipulated in the same straightforward way. On the other hand, the magazine is a threat because of one thing only: Björck's 1991 police report. I presume that the report now exists in two places, possibly three. Salander found the report, but Blomkvist somehow got ahold of it. Which means that there was some degree of contact between the two of them while Salander was on the run."

Clinton held up a finger and uttered his first words since he had arrived.

"It also tells us something about the character of our adversary. Blomkvist is not afraid to take risks. Remember the Wennerström affair."

Gullberg nodded. "Blomkvist gave the report to his editor in chief, Erika Berger, who in turn messengered it to Bublanski. So Berger has read it too. We have to assume that they made a copy for safekeeping. I'm guessing that Blomkvist has a copy and that there's one at the editorial offices."

"That sounds reasonable," Wadensjöö said.

"*Millennium* is a monthly, so they won't be publishing it

tomorrow. We've got a little time—find out exactly how long before the next issue is published—but we have to confiscate both those copies of the police report. And we can't go through the prosecutor general."

"I understand."

"So we're talking about an operation, getting into Blomkvist's apartment and *Millennium*'s offices. Can you handle that, Jonas?"

Sandberg glanced at Wadensjöö.

"Evert, you have to understand that we don't do things like that anymore," Wadensjöö said. "It's a new era. We deal more with computer hacking and electronic surveillance. We don't have the resources for what you'd think of as an operations unit."

Gullberg leaned forward. "Wadensjöö, you're going to have to arrange some resources pretty damn fast. Hire some people. Hire a bunch of skinheads from the Yugo mafia who can whack Blomkvist over the head if necessary. But those two copies have to be recovered. If they don't have the copies, they don't have the evidence. If you can't manage a simple job like that, then you might as well sit here with your thumb up your ass until the constitutional committee comes knocking on your door."

Gullberg and Wadensjöö glared at each other for a long moment.

"I can handle it," Sandberg said suddenly.

"Are you sure?"

Sandberg nodded.

"Good. Starting now, Clinton is your boss. He's the one you take your orders from."

Sandberg nodded his agreement.

"It's going to involve a lot of surveillance," Nyström said. "I can suggest a few names. We have a man in the external organization, Mårtensson—he works as a bodyguard in SIS. He's fearless and shows promise. I've been considering bringing him in here. I've even thought that he could take my place one day."

"That sounds good," Gullberg said. "Clinton can decide."

"I'm afraid there might be a third copy," Nyström said.

"Where?"

"This afternoon I found out that Salander has hired a lawyer. Her name is Annika Giannini. She's Blomkvist's sister."

Gullberg pondered this news. "You're right. Blomkvist will have given his sister a copy. He must have. In other words, we have to keep tabs on all three of them—Berger, Blomkvist, and Giannini—until further notice."

"I don't think we have to worry about Berger. There was a report today that she's going to be the new editor in chief at *Svenska Morgon-Posten*. She's finished with *Millennium*."

"Check her out anyway. As far as *Millennium* is concerned, we're going to need telephone taps and bugs in everyone's homes, and at the offices. We have to check their email. We have to know whom they meet and whom they talk to. And we would very much like to know what strategy they're planning. Above all, we have to get those copies of the report. A whole lot of stuff, in other words."

Wadensjöö sounded doubtful. "Evert, you're asking us to run an operation against an influential magazine and the editor in chief of *SMP*. That's just about the riskiest thing we could do."

"Understand this: you have no choice. Either you roll up your sleeves or it's time for somebody else to take over here."

The challenge hung like a cloud over the table.

"I think I can handle *Millennium*," Sandberg said at last. "But none of this solves the basic problem. What do we do with Zalachenko? If he talks, anything else we pull off is useless."

"I know. That's my part of the operation," Gullberg said. "I think I have an argument that will persuade Zalachenko to keep his mouth shut. But it's going to take some preparation. I'm leaving for Göteborg later this afternoon."

He paused and looked around the room. Then he fixed his eyes on Wadensjöö.

"Clinton will make the operational decisions while I'm gone," he said.

Not until Monday evening did Dr. Endrin decide, in consultation with her colleague Dr. Jonasson, that Salander's condition was stable enough for her to have visitors. First, two police inspectors were given fifteen minutes to ask her questions. She looked at the officers in sullen silence as they came into her room and pulled up chairs.

"Hello. My name is Marcus Erlander, criminal inspector. I work in the violent crimes division here in Göteborg. This is my colleague Inspector Modig from the Stockholm police."

Salander said nothing. Her expression did not change. She recognized Modig as one of the officers on Bublanski's team. Erlander gave her a cool smile.

"I've been told that you don't generally communicate much with the authorities. Let me put it on record that you do not have to say anything at all. But I would be grateful if you would listen to what we have to say. We have a number of things to discuss with you, but we don't have time to go into them all today. There'll be opportunities later."

Salander still said nothing.

"First of all, I'd like to let you know that your friend Mikael Blomkvist has told us that a lawyer by the name of Annika Giannini is willing to represent you, and that she knows about the case. He says that he already mentioned her name to you in connection with something else. I need you to confirm that this would be your intention. I'd also like to know if you want Giannini to come here to Göteborg, the better to represent you."

Annika Giannini. Blomkvist's sister. He had mentioned her in an email. Salander had not thought about the fact that she would need a lawyer.

"I'm sorry, but I have to insist that you answer the question. A yes or no will be fine. If you say yes, the prosecutor here in Göteborg will contact Advokat Giannini. If you say no, the court will appoint a defence lawyer on your behalf. Which do you prefer?"

Salander considered the choice. She assumed that she really would need a lawyer, but having Kalle Fucking Blomkvist's sister working for her was hard to stomach. On the other hand, some unknown lawyer appointed by the court would probably be worse. She rasped out a single word:

"Giannini."

"Good. Thank you. Now I have a question for you. You don't have to say anything before your lawyer gets here, but this question does not, as far as I can see, affect you or your welfare. The police are looking for a German citizen by the name of Ronald Niedermann, wanted for the murder of a policeman."

Salander frowned. She had no clue as to what had happened to Niederman after he ran from the woodshed.

"The Göteborg police are anxious to arrest him as soon as possible. My colleague here would like to question him also in connection with the three recent murders in Stockholm. You should know that you are no longer a suspect in those cases. So we are asking for your help. Do you have any idea . . . can you give us any help at all in finding this man?"

Salander flicked her eyes suspiciously from Erlander to Modig and back.

They don't know that he's my brother.

Then she considered whether she wanted Niedermann caught or not. Most of all she wanted to take him to a hole in the ground in Gosseberga and bury him. Finally she shrugged. Which she should not have done, because pain flew through her left shoulder.

"What day is it today?" she said.

"Monday."

She thought about that. "The first time I heard the name Ronald Niedermann was last Thursday. I tracked him to Gosseberga. I have no idea where he is or where he might go, but he'll try to get out of the country as soon as he can."

"Why would he flee abroad?"

Salander thought about it. "Because while Niedermann was out digging a grave for me, Zalachenko told me that things were getting too hot and that it had already been decided that Niedermann should leave the country for a while."

Salander had not exchanged this many words with a police officer since she was twelve.

"Zalachenko . . . so that's your father?"

Well, at least they've worked that one out. Probably thanks to Kalle Fucking Blomkvist.

"I have to tell you that your father has made a formal accusation to the police stating that you tried to murder him. The case is now at the prosecutor's office, and he has to decide whether to bring charges. But you have already been placed under arrest on a charge of aggravated assault, for having struck Zalachenko on the head with an axe."

There was a long silence. Then Modig leaned forward and said in a low voice, "I just want to say that we on the police force don't put much faith in Zalachenko's story. Have a serious discussion with your lawyer so we can come back later and have another talk."

The detectives stood up.

"Thanks for the help with Niedermann," Erlander said.

Salander was surprised that the officers had treated her in such a professional, almost friendly manner. She thought about what the Modig woman had said. There had to be some ulterior motive, she decided.

CHAPTER 7

Monday, April 11–
Tuesday, April 12

At 5:45 p.m. on Monday, Blomkvist closed the lid on his iBook and got up from the kitchen table in his apartment on Bellmansgatan. He put on a jacket and walked to Milton Security's offices in Slussen. He took the elevator up to the reception on the fourth floor and was immediately shown into a conference room. It was 6:00 p.m. on the dot, but he was the last to arrive.

"Hello, Dragan," he said and shook hands. "Thank you for being willing to host this informal meeting."

Blomkvist looked around the room. There were four others there: his sister, Salander's former guardian Holger Palmgren, Malin Eriksson, and former criminal inspector Sonny Bohman, who now worked for Milton Security. At Armansky's instruction Bohman had been following the Salander investigation from the start.

Palmgren was on his first outing in more than two years. Dr. Sivarnandan of the Ersta rehabilitation home had been less than enchanted at the idea of letting him out, but Palmgren himself had insisted. He had come by special transport for the disabled, accompanied by his personal assistant and trainer, Johanna Karolina Oskarsson, whose salary was paid from a fund that had been mysteriously established to provide Palmgren with the best possible care. Oskarsson was sitting in an office next to the conference room. She had brought a book with her. Blomkvist closed the door behind him.

"For those of you who haven't met her before, this is Malin Eriksson, *Millennium*'s editor in chief. I asked her to be here because what we're going to discuss will also affect her job."

"OK," Armansky said. "Everyone's here. I'm all ears."

Blomkvist stood at Armansky's whiteboard and picked up a marker. He looked around.

"This is probably the craziest thing I've ever been involved with," he said. "When this is all over I'm going to found an association called 'The Knights of the Idiotic Table,' and its purpose will be to arrange an annual dinner where we tell stories about Lisbeth Salander. You're all members."

He paused.

"So, this is how things really are," he said, and he began to make a list of headings on Armansky's whiteboard. He talked for a good thirty minutes. Afterwards, the discussion went on for almost three hours.

Gullberg sat down next to Clinton when their meeting was over. They spoke in low voices for a few minutes before Gullberg stood up. The old comrades shook hands.

Gullberg took a taxi to Freys, packed his briefcase, and checked out. He took the late-afternoon train to Göteborg.

He chose first class and had the compartment to himself. When he passed Årstabron he took out a ballpoint pen and a notepad. He thought for a long while and then began to write. He filled half a page before he stopped and tore the sheet off the pad.

Forged documents had never been his department or his expertise, but here the task was simplified by the fact that the letters he was writing would be signed by him. What complicated the issue was that not a word of what he was writing was true.

By the time the train went through Nyköping he had already discarded a number of drafts, but he was starting to get a sense for how the letters should be phrased. When they arrived in Göteborg he had twelve letters he was satisfied with. He made sure he had left clear fingerprints on each sheet.

At Göteborg Central Station he tracked down a photocopier and made copies of the letters. Then he bought envelopes and stamps and posted the letters in a box with a 9:00 p.m. collection.

Gullberg took a taxi to City Hotel on Lorensbergsgatan, where Clinton had already booked a room for him. It was the same hotel Blomkvist had spent the night in several days before. He went straight to his room and sat on the bed. He was completely exhausted and realized that he had eaten only two slices of bread all day. Yet he was not hungry. He undressed, stretched out in bed, and fell asleep almost at once.

Salander woke with a start when she heard the door open. She knew right away that it was not one of the night nurses. She opened her eyes to two narrow slits and saw a silhouette with crutches in the doorway. Zalachenko was watching her in the light that came from the corridor.

Without moving her head she glanced at the digital clock: 3:10 a.m.

She then glanced at the bedside table and saw the water glass. She calculated the distance. She could just reach it without having to move her body.

It would take a few seconds to stretch out her arm and break off the rim of the glass with a firm rap against the hard edge of the table. It would take half a second to shove the broken edge into Zalachenko's throat if he leaned over her. She looked for other options, but the glass was her only reachable weapon.

She relaxed and waited.

Zalachenko stood in the doorway for two minutes without moving. Then gingerly he closed the door.

She heard the faint scraping of the crutches as he quietly retreated down the corridor.

Five minutes later she propped herself up on her right elbow, reached for the glass, and took a long drink of water. She swung her legs over the edge of the bed. With effort she stood up, pulled the electrodes off her arms and chest, and swayed unsteadily. It took her a few seconds to gain control over her body. She hobbled to the door and leaned against the wall to catch her breath. She was in a cold sweat. Then she turned icy with rage.

Fuck you, Zalachenko. Let's end this right here and now.

She needed a weapon.

The next moment she heard quick heels clacking in the corridor.

Shit. The electrodes.

"What in God's name are you doing up?" the night nurse said.

"I had to . . . go . . . to the toilet," Salander said breathlessly.

"Get back into bed at once."

She took Salander's hand and helped her into the bed. Then she got a bedpan.

"When you have to go to the toilet, just ring for us. That's what this button is for."

Blomkvist woke up at 10:30 on Tuesday, showered, put on coffee, and then sat down with his iBook. After the meeting at Milton Security the previous evening, he had come home and worked until 5:00 a.m. The story was finally beginning to take shape. Zalachenko's biography was still vague—all he had was what he had blackmailed Björck to reveal, as well as the handful of details Palmgren had been able to provide. Salander's story was pretty much done. He explained step by step how she had been targeted by a gang of Cold War mongers at SIS and locked away in a psychiatric hospital to stop her from blowing the whistle on Zalachenko.

He was pleased with what he had written. There were still some holes that he would have to fill, but he knew that he had one hell of a story. It would be a news sensation, and there would be volcanic eruptions high up in the government bureaucracy.

He smoked a cigarette while he thought.

He could see two particular gaps that needed attention. One was manageable. He had to deal with Teleborian, and he was looking forward to that assignment. When he was finished with him, the renowned children's psychiatrist would be one of the most detested men in Sweden. That was one thing.

The second thing was more complicated.

The men who conspired against Salander—he thought of them as the Zalachenko club—were inside the Security Police. He knew one, Gunnar Björck, but Björck could not possibly be the only man responsible. There had to be a group . . . a division or unit of some sort. There must be chiefs, operations managers. There had to be a budget. But he had no idea how to go about identifying these people, where even to start. He had only the vaguest notion of how Säpo was organized.

On Monday he had begun his research by sending Cortez to the second-hand bookshops on Södermalm, to buy every book which in any way dealt with the Security Police. Cortez had come to his apartment in the afternoon with six books: *Espionage in Sweden* by Mikael Rosquist (Tempus, 1988); *Säpo Chief 1962–1970* by P. G. Vinge (Wahlström & Widstrand, 1988); *Secret Forces* by Jan Ottosson and Lars Magnusson (Tiden, 1991); *Power Struggle for Säpo* by Erik Magnusson (Corona, 1989); *An Assignment* by Carl Lidbom (Wahlström & Widstrand, 1990); and—somewhat surprisingly—*An Agent in Place* by Thomas Whiteside (Viking, 1966), which dealt with the Wennerström affair. The Wennerström affair of the sixties, not Blomkvist's own much more recent Wennerström affair.

He had spent much of Monday night and the early hours of Tuesday morning reading or at least skimming the books. When he had finished he made some observations. First, most of the books published about the Security Police were from the late eighties. An Internet search showed that there was hardly any current literature on the subject.

Second, there did not seem to be any intelligible basic overview of the activities of the Swedish secret police over the years. This may have been because many documents were stamped TOP SECRET and were therefore off limits, but there did not seem to be any single institution, researcher, or media that had carried out a critical examination of Säpo.

He also noticed another odd thing: there was no bibliography in any of the books Cortez had found. On the other hand, the footnotes often referred to articles in the evening newspapers, or to interviews with some old, retired Säpo hand.

The book *Secret Forces* was fascinating but largely dealt with the time before and during the Second World War. Blomkvist regarded P. G. Vinge's memoir as propaganda, written in self-defence by a severely criticized Säpo chief who was eventually fired. *An Agent in Place* contained so much inaccurate information about Sweden in the first chapter that he threw the book into the wastepaper basket. The only two books with any real ambition to portray the work of the Security Police were *Power Struggle for Säpo* and *Espionage in Sweden*. They contained data, names, and organizational charts. He found Magnusson's book to be especially worthwhile reading. Even though it did not offer any answers to his immediate questions, it provided a good account of Säpo as a structure, as well as of its primary concerns over several decades.

The biggest surprise was Lidbom's *An Assignment*, which described the problems encountered by the former Swedish ambassador to France when he was commissioned to examine Säpo in the wake of the Palme assassination and the Ebbe Carlsson affair. Blomkvist had never before read anything by Lidbom, and he was taken aback by the sarcastic tone combined with razor-sharp observations. But even Lidbom's book brought Blomkvist no closer to an answer to his questions, even if he was beginning to get an idea of what he was up against.

He opened his mobile and called Cortez.

"Hi, Henry. Thanks for the legwork yesterday."

"What do you need now?"

"A little more legwork."

"Micke, I hate to say this, but I have a job to do. I'm managing editor now."

"An excellent career advancement."

"What is it that you want?"

"Over the years there have been a number of public reports on Säpo. Carl Lidbom did one. There must be several others like it."

"I see."

"Order everything you can find from Parliament: budgets, public reports, interpellations, and the like. And get Säpo's annual reports as far back as you can find them."

"Yes, master."

"Good man. And, Henry . . ."

"Yes?"

"I don't need them until tomorrow."

Salander spent the whole day brooding about Zalachenko. She knew that he was only two doors away, that he wandered in the corridors at night, and that he had come to her room at 3:10 that morning.

She had tracked him to Gosseberga fully intending to kill him. She had failed, with the result that Zalachenko was alive and tucked into bed just thirty feet from where she was. And she was in hot water. She could not tell how bad the situation was, but she supposed that she would have to escape and discreetly disappear abroad herself if she did not want to risk being locked up in some nuthouse again with Teleborian as her keeper.

The problem was that she could scarcely sit upright in bed. She did notice improvements. The headache was still there, but it came in waves instead of being constant. The pain in her left shoulder had subsided a bit, but it resurfaced whenever she tried to move.

She heard footsteps outside the door and saw a nurse open it to admit a woman wearing black pants, a white blouse, and a dark jacket. She was pretty, slender, with dark hair in a boyish hairstyle. She radiated a cheerful confidence. She was carrying a black briefcase. Salander saw at once that she had the same eyes as Blomkvist.

"Hello, Lisbeth. I'm Annika Giannini," she said. "May I come in?"

Salander studied her without expression. All of a sudden she did not have the slightest desire to meet Blomkvist's sister and regretted that she had accepted this woman as her lawyer.

Giannini came in, shut the door behind her, and pulled up a chair. She sat there for some time, looking at her client.

The girl looked terrible. Her head was wrapped in bandages. She had purple bruises around her bloodshot eyes.

"Before we begin to discuss anything, I have to know whether you really do want me to be your lawyer. Normally

I'm involved in civil cases, in which I represent victims of rape or domestic violence. I'm not a criminal defence lawyer. I have, however, studied the details of your case, and I would very much like to represent you, if I may. I should also tell you that Mikael Blomkvist is my brother—I think you already know that—and that he and Dragan Armansky are paying my fee."

She paused, but when she got no response she continued.

"If you want me to be your lawyer, it's you I will be working for. Not for my brother or for Armansky. I have to tell you too that I will receive advice and support during any trial from your former guardian, Holger Palmgren. He's tough, and he dragged himself out of his sickbed to help you."

"Palmgren?"

"Yes."

"Have you seen him?"

"Yes."

"How's he doing?"

"He's absolutely furious, but strangely he doesn't seem to be at all worried about you."

Salander smiled lopsidedly. It was the first time she had smiled at Sahlgrenska hospital.

"How are you feeling?"

"Like a sack of shit."

"Well then. Do you want me to be your lawyer?"

"Yes. But I'll pay your fee myself. I don't want a single öre from Armansky or Kalle Blomkvist. But I can't pay before I have access to the Internet."

"I understand. We'll deal with that problem when it arises. In any case, the state will be paying most of my salary. I'll get started by giving you a message from Mikael. It sounds a little cryptic, but he says you'll know what he means."

"Oh?"

"He wants you to know that he's told me most of the story, except for a few details, of which the first concerns the skills he discovered in Hedestad."

He knows that I have a photographic memory . . . and that I'm a hacker. He's kept quiet about that.

"OK."

"The other is the DVD. I don't know what he's referring to, but he was adamant that it's up to you to decide whether you tell me about it or not. Do you know what he's referring to?"

The film of Bjurman raping me.

"Yes."

"That's good, then." Giannini was suddenly hesitant. "I'm a little miffed at my brother. Even though he hired me, he'll only tell me what he feels like telling me. Do you intend to hide things from me too?"

"I don't know. Could we leave that question for later?" Salander said.

"Certainly. We're going to be talking to each other quite a lot. I don't have time for a long conversation now—I have to meet Prosecutor Jervas in forty-five minutes. I just wanted to confirm that you really do want me to be your lawyer. But there's something else I need to tell you."

"Yes?"

"It's this: if I'm not present, you're not to say a single word to the police, no matter what they ask you. Even if they provoke you or accuse you. Can you promise me?"

"No problem."

. . .

Gullberg was completely exhausted after all his efforts on Monday. He did not wake until 9:00 on Tuesday morning, four hours later than usual. He went to the bathroom to shower and brush his teeth. He stood for a long time looking at his face in the mirror before he turned off the light and went to get dressed. He chose the only clean shirt he had left in the brown briefcase and put on a brown-patterned tie.

He went down to the hotel's breakfast room and had a cup of black coffee and a slice of wheat toast with cheese and a little marmalade on it. He drank a glass of mineral water.

Then he went to the hotel lobby and called Clinton's mobile from the public telephone.

"It's me. Status report?"

"A lot of BS."

"Fredrik, can you handle this?"

"Yes; it's like the old days. But it's a shame von Rottinger isn't still with us. He was better at planning operations than I."

"You were equally good. You could have switched places at any time. Which you quite often did."

"It's a matter of intuition. He was always a little sharper."

"Tell me, how are you all doing?"

"Sandberg is brighter than we thought. We brought in some external help in the form of Mårtensson. He's a gofer, but he's usable. We have taps on Blomkvist's landline and mobile. We'll take care of Giannini's and the *Millennium* office phones today. We're looking at the blueprints for all the relevant offices and apartments. We'll be going in as soon as it can be done."

"First thing is to locate all the copies—"

"I've already done that. We've had some unbelievable luck. Giannini called Blomkvist this morning. She actually asked him how many copies there were in circulation, and it turned out that Blomkvist only has one. Berger copied the report, but she sent the copy on to Bublanski."

"Good. No time to waste."

"I know. But it has to be done in one fell swoop. If we don't get all the copies simultaneously, it won't work."

"True."

"It's a bit complicated, since Giannini left for Göteborg this morning. I've sent a team of externals to tail her. They're flying down right now."

"Good." Gullberg could not think of anything more to say. "Thanks, Fredrik," he said at last.

"My pleasure. This is a lot more fun than sitting around waiting for a kidney."

They said goodbye. Gullberg paid his hotel bill and went out to the street. The ball was in motion. Now it was just a matter of mapping out the moves.

He started by walking to the Elite Park Avenue Hotel, where he asked to use the fax machine. He didn't want to do it at the hotel where he had been staying. He faxed copies of the letters he had written the day before. Then he went out onto Avenyn to look for a taxi. He stopped at a trash can and tore up the copies of his letters.

Giannini was with Prosecutor Jervas for fifteen minutes. She wanted to know what charges the prosecutor intended to bring against Salander, but she soon realized that Jervas was not yet sure of her plan.

"Right now I'll settle for charges of aggravated assault and attempted murder. I refer to the fact that Salander hit her father with an axe. I take it that you will plead self-defence?"

"Maybe."

"To be honest with you, Niedermann is my priority at the moment."

"I understand."

"I've been in touch with the prosecutor general. Discussions are ongoing as to whether to combine all the charges against your client under the jurisdiction of a prosecutor in Stockholm and tie them in with what happened here."

"I assumed that the case would be handled in Stockholm," Giannini said.

"Fine. But I need an opportunity to question the girl. When can we do that?"

"I have a report from her doctor, Anders Jonasson. He says that Salander won't be in a condition to participate in an interview for several days yet. Apart from her injuries, she's on powerful painkillers."

"I received a similar report, and as you no doubt realize, this is frustrating. I repeat that my priority is Niedermann. Your client says that she doesn't know where he's hiding."

"She doesn't know Niedermann at all. She happened to identify him and track him down to Gosseberga, to Zalachenko's farm."

"We'll meet again as soon as your client is strong enough to be interviewed," Jervas said.

Gullberg had a bunch of flowers in his hand when he got into the elevator at Sahlgrenska hospital at the same time as a short-haired woman in a dark jacket. He held the elevator door open for her and let her go first to the reception desk on the ward.

"My name is Annika Giannini. I'm a lawyer and I'd like to see my client again. Lisbeth Salander."

Gullberg turned his head very slowly and looked in surprise at the woman. He glanced down at her briefcase as the nurse checked Giannini's ID and consulted a list.

"Room twelve," the nurse said.

"Thank you. I know the way." She walked off down the corridor.

"May I help you?"

"Thank you, yes. I'd like to leave these flowers for Karl Axel Bodin."

"He's not allowed visitors."

"I know. I just want to leave the flowers."

"We'll take care of them."

Gullberg had brought the flowers with him mainly as an excuse. He wanted to get an idea of how the ward was laid out. He thanked the nurse and followed the sign to the staircase. On the way, he passed Zalachenko's door, room fourteen according to Jonas Sandberg.

He waited in the stairwell. Through a glass pane in the door he saw the nurse take the bouquet into Zalachenko's room. When she returned to her station, Gullberg pushed open the door to room fourteen and stepped quickly inside.

"Good morning, Alexander," he said.

Zalachenko looked up in surprise at his unannounced visitor. "I thought you'd be dead by now," he said.

"Not quite yet."

"What do you want?"

"What do you think?"

Gullberg pulled up a chair and sat down.

"Probably to see me dead."

"Well, that's gratitude for you. How could you be so fucking stupid? We give you a whole new life and you wind up here."

If Zalachenko could have laughed he would have. In his opinion, the Swedish Security Police were amateurs. That applied to Gullberg, and equally to Björck. Not to mention that complete idiot Bjurman.

"Once again we have to haul you out of the furnace."

The expression did not sit well with Zalachenko, who thought back to his gasoline bomb attack.

"Spare me the lectures. Just get me out of this mess."

"That's what I wanted to discuss with you."

Gullberg put his briefcase on his lap, took out a notebook, and turned to a blank page. Then he gave Zalachenko a long, searching look.

"There's one thing I'm curious about . . . were you really going to betray us after all we've done for you?"

"What do you think?"

"It depends how crazy you are."

"Don't call me crazy. I'm a survivor. I do what I have to do to survive."

Gullberg shook his head. "No, Alexander, you do what you do because you're evil and rotten. You wanted a message from the Section. I'm here to deliver it. We're not going to lift a finger to help you this time."

All of a sudden Zalachenko looked uncertain. He studied Gullberg, trying to figure out if this was some puzzling bluff.

"You don't have a choice," he said.

"There's always a choice," Gullberg said.

"I'm going to—"

"You're not going to do anything at all."

Gullberg took a deep breath, unzipped the outside pocket of his case, and pulled out a 9mm Smith & Wesson with a gold-plated butt. The revolver was a present he had received from British Intelligence twenty-five years earlier as a reward for an invaluable piece of information: the name of a clerical officer at MI5 who in good Philby style was working for the Russians.

Zalachenko looked astonished. Then he burst out laughing.

"And what are you going to do with that? Shoot me? You'll spend the rest of your miserable life in prison."

"I don't think so."

Zalachenko was suddenly very unsure whether Gullberg was bluffing.

"There will be a scandal of enormous proportions."

"Again, I don't think so. There'll be a few headlines, but in a week nobody will even remember the name Zalachenko."

Zalachenko's eyes narrowed.

"You motherfucker," Gullberg said then with such coldness in his voice that Zalachenko froze.

Gullberg squeezed the trigger and put the bullet right in the centre of Zalachenko's forehead just as the patient was starting to swing his prosthesis over the edge of the bed. Zalachenko was thrown back onto the pillow. His good leg kicked four, five times before he was still. Gullberg saw a red flower-shaped splatter on the wall behind the bed. He became aware that his ears were ringing after the shot and he rubbed his left one with his free hand.

Then he stood up, put the muzzle to Zalachenko's temple, and squeezed the trigger twice. He wanted to be sure this time that the bastard really was dead.

Salander sat up with a start the instant she heard the first shot. Pain stabbed through her shoulder. When the next two shots came she tried to get her legs over the edge of the bed.

Giannini had been there for only a few minutes. She sat paralysed and tried to work out which direction the sharp reports had come from. She could tell from Salander's reaction that something deadly was brewing.

"Lie still," she shouted. She put her hand on Salander's chest and shoved her client down onto the bed.

Then Giannini crossed the room and pulled open the door. She saw two nurses running towards another room two doors away. The first nurse stopped short on the threshold. "No, don't!" she screamed and then took a step back, colliding with the second nurse.

"He's got a gun. Run!"

Giannini watched as the two nurses took cover in the room next to Salander's.

The next moment she saw a thin, grey-haired man in a houndstooth jacket walk into the corridor. He had a gun in his hand. Annika recognized him as the man who had come up in the elevator with her.

Then their eyes met. He appeared confused. He aimed the revolver at her and took a step forward. She pulled her head back in and slammed the door shut, looking around in desperation. A nurses' table stood right next to her. She rolled it quickly over to the door and wedged the tabletop under the door handle.

She heard a movement and turned to see Salander just starting to clamber out of bed again. In a few quick steps she crossed the floor, wrapped her arms around her client, and lifted her up. She tore electrodes and IV tubes loose as she carried her to the bathroom and set her on the toilet seat. Then she turned and locked the bathroom door. She dug her mobile out of her jacket pocket and dialled 112.

Gullberg went to Salander's room and tried the door handle. It was blocked. He couldn't move it even an inch.

For a moment he stood indecisively outside the door. He knew that the lawyer, Giannini, was in the room, and he wondered if a copy of Björck's report might be in her briefcase. But he couldn't get into the room, and he did not have the strength to force the door.

That hadn't been part of the plan anyway. Clinton would take care of Giannini. Gullberg's only job was Zalachenko.

He looked around the corridor and saw that he was being watched by nurses, patients, and visitors. He raised the pistol and fired at a picture hanging on the wall. His spectators vanished as if by magic.

He glanced one last time at the door to Salander's room. Then he walked decisively back to Zalachenko's room and closed the door. He sat in the guest chair and looked at the Russian defector who had been such an intimate part of his own life for so many years.

He sat still for almost ten minutes before he heard movement in the corridor and was aware that the police had arrived. By now he wasn't thinking of anything in particular.

Then he raised the revolver one last time, held it to his temple, and squeezed the trigger.

. .

As the situation developed, the futility of attempting suicide in the middle of a hospital became apparent. Gullberg was transported at top speed to the hospital's trauma unit, where Dr. Jonasson received him and immediately initiated a battery of measures to maintain his vital functions.

For the second time in less than a week Jonasson performed emergency surgery, extracting a full-metal-jacketed bullet from human brain tissue. After a five-hour operation, Gullberg's condition was critical. But he was still alive.

Yet Gullberg's injuries were considerably more serious than those Salander had sustained. He hovered between life and death for several days.

Blomkvist was at the Kaffebar on Hornsgatan when he heard on the radio that a sixty-five-year-old unnamed man, suspected of attempting to murder the fugitive Lisbeth Salander, had been shot and killed at Sahlgrenska hospital in Göteborg. He left his coffee untouched, picked up his laptop case, and hurried off towards the editorial offices on Götgatan. He had crossed Mariatorget and was just turning up St. Paulsgatan when his mobile beeped. He answered on the run.

"Blomkvist."

"Hi, it's Malin."

"I heard the news. Do we know who the killer was?"

"Not yet. Henry is chasing it down."

"I'm on the way in. Be there in five minutes."

Blomkvist ran into Cortez at the entrance to the *Millennium* offices.

"Ekström's holding a press conference at 3:00," Cortez said. "I'm going to Kungsholmen now."

"What do we know?" Blomkvist shouted after him.

"Ask Malin," Cortez said, and was gone.

Blomkvist headed into Berger's—wrong; Eriksson's—office. She was on the phone and writing furiously on a yellow Post-it. She waved him away. Blomkvist went into the kitchenette and poured coffee with milk into two mugs marked with the logos of the KDU and SSU political parties. When he returned she had just finished her call. He gave her the SSU mug.

"OK," she said. "Zalachenko was shot dead at 1:15." She looked at Blomkvist. "I just spoke to a nurse at Sahlgrenska. She says that the murderer was an elderly man who arrived with flowers for Zalachenko minutes before the murder. He shot Zalachenko in the head several times and then shot himself. Zalachenko is dead. The murderer is still alive and in surgery."

Blomkvist breathed more easily. Ever since he had heard the news at the Kaffebar he had had his heart in his throat and a panicky feeling that Salander might have been the killer. That really would have thrown a monkey wrench into his plan.

"Do we have the name of the shooter?"

Eriksson shook her head as the phone rang again. She took the call, and from the conversation Blomkvist gathered that it was a stringer in Göteborg whom Eriksson had sent to Sahlgrenska. He went to his own office and sat down.

It felt as if it was the first time in weeks that he had even been to his office. There was a pile of unopened mail, which he shoved firmly to one side. He called his sister.

"Giannini."

"It's Mikael. Did you hear what happened at Sahlgrenska?"

"You could say so."

"Where are you?"

"At the hospital. That bastard aimed at me too."

Blomkvist sat speechless for several seconds before he fully took in what his sister had said.

"What the hell . . . you were there?"

"Yes. It was the most horrendous thing I've ever experienced."

"Are you hurt?"

"No. But he tried to get into Lisbeth's room. I blockaded the door and locked us in the bathroom."

Blomkvist's whole world suddenly felt off balance. His sister had almost . . .

"How is she?" he said.

"She's not hurt. Or, I mean, she wasn't hurt in today's drama at least."

He let that sink in.

"Annika, do you know anything at all about the murderer?"

"Not a thing. He was an older man, neatly dressed. I thought he looked rather bewildered. I've never seen him before, but I came up in the elevator with him a few minutes before it all happened."

"And Zalachenko is dead, no question?"

"Yes. I heard three shots, and according to what I've overheard he was shot in the head all three times. But it's been utter chaos here, with a thousand policemen, and they're evacuating a ward for acutely ill and injured patients who really ought not to be moved. When the police arrived one of them tried to question Lisbeth before they even bothered to ask what shape she's in. I had to read them the riot act."

. . .

Inspector Erlander saw Giannini through the doorway to Salander's room. The lawyer had her mobile pressed to her ear, so he waited for her to finish her call.

Two hours after the murder there was still chaos in the corridor. Zalachenko's room was sealed off. Doctors had tried resuscitation immediately after the shooting, but they soon gave up. He was beyond all help. His body was sent to the pathologist, and the crime scene investigation proceeded as best it could under the circumstances.

Erlander's mobile chimed. It was Fredrik Malmberg from the investigative team.

"We've got a positive ID on the murderer," Malmberg said. "His name is Evert Gullberg, and he's seventy-eight years old."

Seventy-eight. Quite elderly for a murderer.

"And who the hell is Evert Gullberg?"

"Retired. Lives in Laholm. Apparently he was a tax lawyer. I got a call from someone at SIS, who told me that they had recently initiated a preliminary investigation against him."

"When and why?"

"I don't know when. But apparently he had a habit of sending crazy and threatening letters to people in government."

"Such as who?"

"The minister of justice, for one."

Erlander sighed. *So, a madman. A fanatic.*

"This morning Säpo got calls from several newspapers that had received letters from Gullberg. The Ministry of Justice also called, because Gullberg had made specific death threats against Karl Axel Bodin."

"I want copies of the letters."

"From Säpo?"

"Yes, damn it. Drive up to Stockholm and pick them up in person if necessary. I want them on my desk when I get back to HQ. Which will be in about an hour."

He thought for a second and then asked one more question.

"Was it Säpo that called you?"

"That's what I told you."

"I mean, they called you, not vice versa?"

"Exactly."

Erlander closed his mobile.

He wondered what had gotten into Säpo to make them, out of the blue, feel the need to get in touch with the police— of their own accord. Ordinarily you couldn't get a word out of them.

Wadensjöö flung open the door to the room at the Section where Clinton was resting. Clinton sat up cautiously.

"Just what the hell is going on?" Wadensjöö shrieked. "Gullberg has murdered Zalachenko and then shot himself in the head."

"I know," Clinton said.

"You *know*?" Wadensjöö yelled. He was bright red in the face and looked as if he was about to have a stroke. "He shot himself, for Christ's sake. He tried to commit suicide. Is he out of his mind?"

"You mean he's alive?"

"For the time being, yes, but he has massive brain damage."

Clinton sighed. "Such a shame," he said with real sorrow in his voice.

"*Shame?*" Wadensjöö burst out. "Gullberg is out of his mind. Don't you understand what—"

Clinton cut him off.

"Gullberg has cancer of the stomach, colon, and bladder. He's been dying for several months, and in the best case he had only a few months left."

"Cancer?"

"He's been carrying that gun around for the past six months, determined to use it as soon as the pain became unbearable and before the disease turned him into a vegetable. But he was able to do one last favour for the Section. He went out in grand style."

Wadensjöö was almost beside himself. "You knew? You knew that he was thinking of killing Zalachenko?"

"Naturally. His assignment was to make sure that Zalachenko never got a chance to talk. And as you know, you couldn't threaten or reason with that man."

"But don't you understand what a scandal this could turn into? Are you just as nuts as Gullberg?"

Clinton got to his feet laboriously. He looked Wadensjöö in the eye and handed him a stack of faxes.

"It was an operational decision. I mourn for my friend, but I'll probably be following him pretty soon. As far as a scandal goes . . . A retired tax lawyer wrote paranoid letters to newspapers, the police, and the Ministry of Justice. Here's a sample of them. Gullberg blames Zalachenko for everything from the Palme assassination to trying to poison the Swedish people with chlorine. The letters are plainly the work of a lunatic and were illegible in places, with capital letters, underlining, and exclamation marks. I especially like the way he wrote in the margin."

Wadensjöö read the letters with rising astonishment. He put a hand to his brow.

Clinton said: "Whatever happens, Zalachenko's death will have nothing to do with the Section. It was just some demented retiree who fired the shots." He paused. "The important thing is that starting from now, you have to get with the programme. And don't rock the boat." He fixed his gaze on Wadensjöö. There was steel in the sick man's eyes. "What you have to understand is that the Section functions as the spearhead for the total defence of the nation. We're Sweden's last line of defence. Our job is to watch over the security of our country. Everything else is unimportant."

Wadensjöö regarded Clinton with doubt in his eyes.

"We're the ones who don't exist," Clinton went on. "We're the ones nobody will ever thank. We're the ones who have to make the decisions that nobody else wants to make. Least of all the politicians." His voice quivered with contempt as he spoke those last words. "Do as I say and the Section might survive. For that to happen, we have to be decisive and resort to tough measures."

Wadensjöö felt panic rise in his chest.

Cortez wrote feverishly, trying to get down every word that was said from the podium at the police press office at Kungsholmen. Prosecutor Ekström had begun. He explained that it had been decided that the investigation into the police killing in Gosseberga—for which Ronald Niedermann was being sought—would be placed under the jurisdiction of a prosecutor in Göteborg. The rest of the investigation concerning Niedermann would be handled by Ekström himself. Niedermann was a suspect in the murders of Dag Svensson and Mia Johansson. No mention was made of Advokat Bjurman. Ekström also had to investigate and bring charges against Lisbeth Salander, who was under suspicion for a long list of crimes.

He explained that he had decided to go public with the information in light of the events that had occurred in Göteborg that day, including the fact that Salander's father, Karl Axel Bodin, had been shot dead. The immediate reason for calling the press conference was that he wanted to deny the rumours already being circulated in the media. He had himself received a number of calls concerning these rumours.

"Based on current information, I am able to tell you that Karl Axel Bodin's daughter, who is being held for the aggravated assault and attempted murder of her father, had nothing to do with this morning's events."

"Then who was the murderer?" a reporter from *Dagens Eko* shouted.

"The man who at 1:15 today fired the fatal shots at Karl Axel Bodin before attempting to commit suicide has now been identified. He is a seventy-eight-year-old man who has been undergoing treatment for a terminal illness and the psychiatric problems associated with it."

"Does he have any connection to Lisbeth Salander?"

"No. The man is a tragic figure who evidently acted alone, in accordance with his own paranoid delusions. The Security Police recently initiated an investigation of this man because he had written a number of confused letters to well-known politicians and the media. As recently as this morning, newspaper and government offices received letters in which he threatened to kill Karl Axel Bodin."

"Why didn't the police give Bodin protection?"

"The letters naming Bodin were sent only last night, and thus arrived at the same time as the murder was being committed. There was no time to act."

"What's the killer's name?"

"We will not give out that information until his next of kin have been notified."

"What sort of background does he have?"

"As far as I understand, he previously worked as an accountant and tax lawyer. He has been retired for fifteen years. The investigation is still under way, but as you can appreciate from the letters he sent, it is a tragedy that could have been prevented if there had been more support within society."

"Did he threaten anyone else?"

"I have been advised that he did, yes, but I do not have any details to pass on to you."

"What will this mean for the case against Salander?"

"For the moment, nothing. We have Karl Axel Bodin's own testimony from the officers who interviewed him, and we have extensive forensic evidence against her."

"What about the reports that Bodin tried to murder his daughter?"

"That is under investigation, but there are strong indications that he did indeed attempt to kill her. As far as we can determine at the moment, it was a case of deep antagonism in a tragically dysfunctional family."

Cortez scratched his ear. He noticed that the other reporters were taking notes as feverishly as he was.

• • •

Gunnar Björck felt an almost unquenchable panic when he heard the news about the shooting at Sahlgrenska hospital. He had terrible pain in his back.

It took him an hour to make up his mind. Then he picked up the phone and tried to call his old protector in Laholm. There was no answer.

He listened to the news and heard a summary of what had been said at the press conference. Zalachenko had been shot by a seventy-eight-year-old tax specialist.

Good Lord. Seventy-eight years old.

He tried again to call Gullberg, but again in vain.

Finally his uneasiness took the upper hand. He could not stay in the borrowed summer cabin in Smådalarö. He felt vulnerable and exposed. He needed time and space to think. He packed clothes, painkillers, and toiletries. He did not want to use his own phone, so he limped to the phone booth at the grocer's to call Landsort and book himself a room in the old lighthouse. Landsort was the end of the world, and few people would look for him there. He booked the room for two weeks.

He glanced at his watch. He would have to hurry to make the last ferry. He went back to the cabin as fast as his aching back would permit. He made straight for the kitchen and checked that the coffee machine was turned off. Then he went to the hall to get his bag. He happened to look into the living room and stopped short in surprise.

At first he could not grasp what he was seeing.

In some mysterious way the ceiling lamp had been taken down and placed on the coffee table. In its place hung a rope from a hook, right above a stool that was usually in the kitchen.

Björck looked at the noose, failing to understand.

Then he heard movement behind him and felt his knees buckle.

Slowly he turned to look.

Two men stood there. They were eastern European, by the look of them. He had no will to react when calmly they took him in a firm grip under both arms, lifted him off the ground, and carried him to the stool. When he tried to resist, pain shot like a knife through his back. He was almost paralysed as he felt himself being lifted onto the stool.

Sandberg was accompanied by a man who went by the nickname of Falun and who in his youth had been a professional burglar. He had, in time, retrained as a locksmith. Hans von Rottinger had first hired Falun for the Section in 1986 for an operation that involved forcing entry into the home of the leader of an anarchist group. After that, Falun had been hired from time to time until the mid-nineties, when there was less demand for this type of operation. Early that morning Clinton had revived the contact and given Falun an assignment. Falun would make 10,000 kronor tax-free for a job that would take about ten minutes. In return he had pledged not to steal anything from the apartment that was the target of the operation. The Section was not a criminal enterprise, after all.

Falun did not know exactly what interests Clinton represented, but he assumed it had something to do with the military. He had read Jan Guillou's books, and he did not ask any questions. But it felt good to be back in the saddle again after so many years of silence from his former employer.

His job was to open the door. He was expert at breaking

and entering. Even so, it still took five minutes to force the lock to Blomkvist's apartment. Then Falun waited on the landing as Sandberg went in.

"I'm in," Sandberg said into a hands-free mobile.

"Good," Clinton said into his earpiece. "Take your time. Tell me what you see."

"I'm in the hall with a wardrobe and a hat-rack on my right. Bathroom on the left. Otherwise there's one very large room, about five hundred square feet. There's a small kitchen alcove at the far end on the right."

"Is there a desk?"

"He seems to work at the kitchen table or sitting on the living-room sofa. . . . Wait."

Clinton waited.

"Yes. Here we are, a folder on the kitchen table. And Björck's report is in it. It looks like the original."

"Very good. Anything else of interest on the table?"

"Books. P. G. Vinge's memoirs. *Power Struggle for Säpo* by Erik Magnusson. Four or five more of the same."

"Is there a computer?"

"No."

"A safe?"

"No . . . not that I can see."

"Take your time. Go through the apartment inch by inch. Mårtensson reports that Blomkvist is still at the office. You're wearing gloves, right?"

"Of course."

Erlander had a chat with Giannini in a brief interlude between one or the other or both of them talking on their mobiles. He went into Salander's room and held out his hand to introduce himself. Then he said hello to Salander and asked her how she was feeling. Salander looked at him, expressionless. He turned to Giannini.

"I need to ask some questions."

"All right."

"Can you tell me what happened this morning?"

Giannini related what she had seen and heard and how she had reacted up until the moment she had barricaded herself with Salander in the bathroom. Erlander glanced at Salander and then back to her lawyer.

"So you're sure that he came to the door of this room?"

"I heard him trying to push down the door handle."

"And you're perfectly sure about that? It's not difficult to imagine things when you're scared or excited."

"I definitely heard him at the door. He had seen me and pointed his pistol at me; he knew that this was the room I was in."

"Do you have any reason to believe that he had planned, beforehand that is, to shoot you too?"

"I have no way of knowing. When he took aim at me I pulled my head back in and blockaded the door."

"Which was the sensible thing to do. And it was even more sensible of you to carry your client to the bathroom. These doors are so thin that the bullets would have gone clean through them if he had fired. What I'm trying to figure out is whether he wanted to attack you personally or whether he was just reacting to the fact that you were looking at him. You were the person nearest to him in the corridor."

"Apart from the two nurses."

"Did you get the sense that he knew you, or perhaps recognized you?"

"No, not really."

"Could he have recognized you from the papers? You've had a lot of publicity over several widely reported cases."

"It's possible. I can't say."

"And you'd never seen him before?"

"I'd seen him in the elevator; that's the first time I set eyes on him."

"I didn't know that. Did you talk?"

"No. I got in at the same time he did. I was vaguely aware of him for just a few seconds. He had flowers in one hand and a briefcase in the other."

"Did you make eye contact?"

"No. He was looking straight ahead."

"Who got in first?"

"We got in more or less at the same time."

"Did he look confused or—"

"I couldn't say one way or the other. He got into the elevator and stood perfectly still, holding the flowers."

"What happened then?"

"We got out of the elevator on the same floor, and I went to visit my client."

"Did you come straight here?"

"Yes . . . no. That is, I went to the reception desk and showed my ID. The prosecutor has forbidden my client to have visitors."

"Where was this man then?"

Giannini hesitated. "I'm not quite sure. He was behind me, I think. No, wait. He got out of the elevator first, but stopped and held the door for me. I couldn't swear to it, but I think he went to the reception desk too. I was just quicker on my feet than he was. But the nurses would know."

Elderly, polite, and a murderer, Erlander thought.

"Yes, he did go to the reception desk," he confirmed. "He did talk to the nurse, and he left the flowers at the desk, on her instructions. But you didn't see that?"

"No. I have no recollection of any of that."

Erlander had no more questions. Frustration was gnawing at him. He had had the feeling before and had trained himself to interpret it as an alarm triggered by instinct. Something was eluding him, something that was not right.

The murderer had been identified as Evert Gullberg, a former accountant and sometime business consultant and tax lawyer. A man in advanced old age. A man against whom Säpo had lately initiated a preliminary investigation because he was a nutcase who wrote threatening letters to public figures.

Erlander knew from long experience that there were plenty of nutcases out there, some pathologically obsessed ones who stalked celebrities and looked for love by hiding in woods near their villas. When their love was not reciprocated, it could quickly turn to violent hatred. There were stalkers who travelled from Germany or Italy to follow a twenty-one-year-old lead singer in a pop band from gig to gig, and who then got upset because she would not drop everything to start a relationship with them. There were violent individuals who harped on and on about real or imaginary injustices and who sometimes turned to threatening behaviour. There were psychopaths and conspiracy theorists, nutcases who had the gift to read messages hidden from the normal world.

There were plenty of examples of these fools taking the

leap from fantasy to action. Was not the assassination of Anna Lindh* the result of precisely such a crazy impulse?

But Inspector Erlander did not like the idea that a mentally ill accountant, or whatever he was, could wander into a hospital with a bunch of flowers in one hand and a pistol in the other. Or that he could, for God's sake, execute someone who was the object of a police investigation—*his* investigation. A man whose name in the public registry was Karl Axel Bodin but whose real name, according to Blomkvist, was Zalachenko. A fucking defected Soviet Russian agent and professional gangster.

At the very least, Zalachenko was a witness, but in the worst case he was involved up to his neck in a series of murders. Erlander had been allowed to conduct two brief interviews with Zalachenko, and at no time during either had he been swayed by the man's protestations of innocence.

His murderer had shown interest also in Salander, or at least in her lawyer. He had tried to get into her room.

And then he had attempted suicide. According to the doctors, he had probably succeeded, even if his body had not yet absorbed the message that it was time to shut down. It was highly unlikely that Evert Gullberg would ever be brought before a court.

Erlander did not like the situation, not for a moment. But he had no proof that Gullberg's shots had been anything other than what they seemed. So he had decided to play it safe. He looked at Giannini.

"I've decided that Salander should be moved to a different room. There's a room in the connecting corridor to the right of the reception area that would be better from a security point of view. It's in direct line-of-sight of the reception desk and the nurses' station. No visitors will be permitted other than you. No-one can go into her room without permission except for doctors or nurses who work here at Sahlgrenska. And I'll see to it that a guard is stationed outside her door around the clock."

"Do you think she's in danger?"

"I know of nothing to indicate that she is. But I want to play it safe."

Salander listened attentively to the conversation between her lawyer and her adversary, a member of the police. She was impressed that Giannini had replied so precisely and lucidly, and in such detail. She was even more impressed by her lawyer's grace under pressure.

Otherwise she had had a monstrous headache ever since Giannini had dragged her out of bed and carried her into the bathroom. Instinctively she wanted as little as possible to do with the hospital staff. She did not like asking for help or showing any sign of weakness. But the headaches were so overpowering that she could not think straight. She reached out and rang for a nurse.

Giannini had planned her visit to Göteborg as a brisk, necessary prologue to long-term work. She wanted to get to know Salander, question her about her actual condition, and present a draft outline of the strategy that she and Blomkvist had cobbled together to deal with the legal proceedings. She had originally intended to return to Stockholm that evening, but because of the dramatic events at Sahlgrenska, she still had not had a real conversation with Salander. Her client was in much worse shape than she had been led to believe. She was suffering from acute headaches and a high fever, which prompted a doctor by the name of Endrin to prescribe a strong painkiller, an antibiotic, and rest. Consequently, as soon as her client had been moved to a new room and a security guard had been posted outside, Giannini was asked, quite firmly, to leave.

It was already 4:30 p.m. She hesitated. She could go back to Stockholm knowing that she might have to take the train to Göteborg again as soon as the following day. Or she could stay overnight. But her client might be too ill to deal with a visit tomorrow as well. She had not booked a hotel room. As a lawyer who mainly represented abused women without any great financial resources, she tried to avoid padding her bill with expensive hotel charges. She called home first and then rang Lillian Josefsson, a lawyer colleague who was a member of the Women's Network and an old friend from law school.

"I'm in Göteborg," she said. "I was thinking of going home tonight, but certain things happened today that require me to stay overnight. Is it OK if I sleep at your place?"

"Oh, please do; that would be fun. We haven't seen each other in ages."

"I'm not interrupting anything?"

"No, of course not. But I've moved. I'm now on a side street off Linnégatan. But I do have a guest room. And we can go out to a bar later if we feel like it."

"If I have the energy," Giannini said. "What time is good?"

They agreed that Giannini should turn up at around 6:00.

Giannini took the bus to Linnégatan and spent the next hour in a Greek restaurant. She was famished, and ordered a shish kebab with salad. She sat for a long time thinking about the day's events. She was a little shaky now that the adrenaline had worn off, but she was pleased with herself. In a time of great danger she had been cool, calm, and collected. She had instinctively made the right decisions. It was a pleasant feeling to know that her reactions were up to an emergency.

After a while she took her Filofax from her briefcase and opened it to the notes section. She read through it carefully. She was filled with doubt about the plan that her brother had outlined to her. It had sounded logical at the time, but it didn't look so good now. Even so, she did not intend to back out.

At 6:00 she paid her bill and walked to Lillian's place on Olivedalsgatan. She punched in the door code her friend had given her. She stepped into the stairwell and was looking for a light switch when the attack came out of the blue. She was slammed up against a tiled wall next to the door. She banged her head hard, felt a rush of pain, and fell to the ground.

The next moment she heard footsteps moving swiftly away and then the front door opening and closing. She struggled to her feet and put her hand to her forehead. There was blood on her palm. What the hell? She went out onto the street and just caught a glimpse of someone turning the corner towards Sveaplan. In shock, she stood still for about a minute. Then she walked back to the door and punched in the code again.

Suddenly she realized that her briefcase was gone. She had been robbed. It took a few seconds before the horror of it sank in. *Oh no. The Zalachenko folder.* She felt the alarm spreading up from her diaphragm.

Slowly she sat down on the staircase.

Then she jumped up and dug into her jacket pocket. *The Filofax. Thank God.* Leaving the restaurant, she had stuffed it into her pocket instead of putting it back in her briefcase. It contained the draft of her strategy in the Salander case, point by detailed point.

Then she stumbled up the stairs to the fifth floor and pounded on her friend's door.

Half an hour had passed before she had recovered enough to call her brother. She had a black eye and a gash above her eyebrow that was still bleeding. Lillian had cleaned it with alcohol and put a bandage on it. No, she did not want to go to the hospital. Yes, she would like a cup of tea. Only then did she begin to think rationally again. The first thing she did was call Blomkvist.

He was still at *Millennium,* where he was searching for information about Zalachenko's murderer with Cortez and Eriksson. He listened with increasing dismay to Giannini's account of what had happened.

"No bones broken?" he said.

"Black eye. I'll be OK after I've had a chance to calm down."

"Did you disturb a robbery, was that it?"

"Mikael, my briefcase was stolen, with the Zalachenko report you gave me."

"Not a problem. I can make another copy—"

He broke off as he felt the hair rise on the back of his neck. *First Zalachenko. Now Annika.*

He closed his iBook, stuffed it into his shoulder bag, and left the office without a word, moving fast. He jogged home to Bellmansgatan and up the stairs.

The door was locked.

As soon as he entered the apartment he saw that the folder

he had left on the kitchen table was gone. He did not even bother to look for it. He knew exactly where it had been. He sank onto a chair at the kitchen table as thoughts whirled through his head.

Someone had been in his apartment. Someone who was trying to cover Zalachenko's tracks.

His own copy and his sister's copy were gone.

Bublanski still had the report.

Or did he?

Blomkvist got up and went to the phone, but stopped with his hand on the receiver. Someone had been in his apartment. He looked at his phone with the utmost suspicion and took out his mobile.

But how easy is it to eavesdrop on a mobile conversation?

He slowly put the mobile down next to his landline and looked around.

I'm dealing with pros here, obviously. People who could bug an apartment as easily as get into one without breaking a lock.

He sat down again.

He looked at his laptop case.

How hard is it to hack into my email? Salander can do it in five minutes.

He thought for a long time before he went back to the landline and called his sister. He chose his words with care.

"How are you doing?"

"I'm fine, Micke."

"Tell me what happened from the moment you arrived at Sahlgrenska until you were attacked."

It took ten minutes for Giannini to give him her account. Blomkvist did not say anything about the implications of what she told him, but asked questions until he was satisfied. He sounded like an anxious brother, but his mind was working on a completely different level as he reconstructed the key points.

She had decided to stay in Göteborg at 4:30 that afternoon. She called her friend on her mobile, gotten the address and door code. The robber was waiting for her inside the stairwell at 6:00 on the dot.

Her mobile was being monitored. It was the only possible explanation.

Which meant that his was being monitored too.

Foolish to think otherwise.

"And the Zalachenko report is gone," Giannini repeated.

Blomkvist hesitated. Whoever had stolen the report already knew that his copy too had been stolen. It would only be natural to mention that.

"Mine too," he said.

"What?"

He explained that he had come home to find that the blue folder on his kitchen table was gone.

"It's a disaster," he said in a gloomy voice. "That was the crucial part of the evidence."

"Micke, I'm so sorry."

"Me too," Blomkvist said. "Damn it! But it's not your fault. I should have published the report the day I got it."

"What do we do now?"

"I have no idea. This is the worst thing that could have happened. It will turn our whole plan upside down. We don't have a shred of evidence left against Björck or Teleborian."

They talked for another two minutes before Blomkvist ended the conversation.

"I want you to come back to Stockholm tomorrow," he said.

"I have to see Salander."

"Go and see her in the morning. We have to sit down and think about where we go from here."

When Blomkvist hung up he sat on the sofa staring into space. Whoever was listening to their conversation knew now that *Millennium* had lost Björck's report, along with the correspondence between Björck and Dr. Teleborian. They could be satisfied that Blomkvist and Giannini were distraught.

If nothing else, Blomkvist had learned from the preceding night's study of the history of the Security Police that disinformation was the basis of all espionage activity. And he had just planted disinformation that in the long run might prove invaluable.

He opened his laptop case and took out the copy of the Zalachenko report he'd made for Armansky, which he had not yet managed to deliver. It was the only remaining copy, and he did not intend to waste it. On the contrary, he would make five more copies and put them in safe places.

Then he called Eriksson. She was about to lock up for the day.

"Where did you disappear to in such a hurry?" she said.

"Could you stay there a few minutes, please? There's something I have to discuss with you before you leave."

He had not had time to do his laundry for several weeks. All his shirts were in the hamper. He packed a razor and *Power Struggle for Säpo* along with the last remaining copy of Björck's report. He went to Dressman and bought four shirts, two pairs of trousers, and some underwear and took the clothes with him to the office. Eriksson waited while he took a quick shower, wondering what was going on.

"Someone broke into my apartment and stole the Zalachenko report. Someone mugged Annika in Göteborg and stole her copy. I have proof that her phone is tapped, which may well mean that mine is too. Maybe yours at home and all the *Millennium* phones have been bugged. And if someone took the trouble to break into my apartment, they'd be pretty dumb if they didn't bug it as well."

"I see," said Eriksson in a flat voice. She glanced at the mobile on the desk in front of her.

"Keep working as usual. Use the mobile, but don't give away any information. Tomorrow, tell Henry."

"He went home an hour ago. He left a stack of public reports on your desk. But what are you doing here?"

"I plan to sleep here tonight. If they shot Zalachenko, stole the reports, and bugged my apartment today, there's a good chance they've just gotten started and haven't done the office yet. People have been here all day. I don't want the office to be empty tonight."

"You think that the murder of Zalachenko . . . ? But the murderer was a geriatric psycho."

"Malin, I don't believe in coincidence. Somebody is covering Zalachenko's tracks. I don't care who people think that old lunatic was or how many crazy letters he wrote to government ministers. He was a hired killer of some sort. He went there to kill Zalachenko . . . and maybe Lisbeth too."

"But he committed suicide, or tried to. What hired killer would do that?"

Blomkvist thought for a moment. He met the editor in chief's gaze.

"Maybe someone who's seventy-eight and doesn't have much to lose. He's mixed up in all this, and when we finish digging we'll prove it."

Eriksson studied Blomkvist's face. She had never before seen him so composed and unflinching. She shuddered. Blomkvist noticed her reaction.

"One more thing. We're no longer in a battle with a gang of criminals; this time it's with a government department. It's going to be tough."

Eriksson nodded.

"I didn't imagine things would go this far. Malin, what happened today makes very plain how dangerous this could get. If you want out, just say the word."

She wondered what Berger would have said. Then stubbornly she shook her head.

PART 2

Hacker Republic

MAY 1–22

An Irish law from the year 697 forbids women to be soldiers—which means that women *had* been soldiers previously. Peoples who over the centuries have recruited female soldiers include Arabs, Berbers, Kurds, Rajputs, Chinese, Filipinos, Maoris, Papuans, Micronesians, and American Indians.

There is a wealth of legend about fearsome female warriors from ancient Greece. These tales speak of women who were trained in the art of war from childhood—in the use of weapons, and how to cope with physical privation. They lived apart from the men and went to war in their own regiments. The tales tell us that they conquered men on the field of battle. Amazons occur in Greek literature in the *Iliad* of Homer, for example, in 600 BC.

It was the Greeks who coined the term "Amazon."

The word literally means "without breast." It is said that in order to facilitate the drawing of a bow, the female's right breast was removed, either in early childhood or with a red-hot iron after she became an adult. Even though the Greek physicians Hippocrates and Galen are said to have agreed that this operation would enhance the ability to use weapons, it is doubtful whether such operations were actually performed. Herein lies a linguistic riddle—whether the prefix "a-" in their language does indeed mean "without." It has been suggested that it means the opposite—that an Amazon was a woman with especially large breasts. Nor is there a single example in any museum of a drawing, amulet, or statue of a woman without her right breast, which should have been a common motif had the legend about breast amputation been based on fact.

CHAPTER 8

Sunday, May 1– Monday, May 2

Berger took a deep breath as the elevator door opened and she walked into the editorial offices of *Svenska Morgon-Posten*. It was 10:15 in the morning. She was dressed for work in black pants, a red sweater, and a dark jacket. It was glorious May 1 weather, and on her way through the city she had noticed that the workers' groups had begun to gather. It dawned on her that she had not been part of such a parade in more than twenty years.

For a moment she stood, alone and invisible, next to the elevator doors. *First day on the job.* She could see a large part of the editorial office with the news desk in the centre. She saw the glass doors of the editor in chief's office, which was now hers.

She was not at all sure right now that she was the person to lead the sprawling organization that comprised *SMP*. It was a gigantic step up from *Millennium,* with a minimal staff, to a daily newspaper with eighty reporters and another ninety people in administration, with IT personnel, layout artists, photographers, and advertising reps. Add to that a publishing house, a production company, and a management company. More than 230 people.

As she stood there she asked herself whether the whole thing hadn't been an enormous mistake.

Then the older of the two receptionists noticed who had just come into the office. She got up, came out from behind the counter, and extended her hand.

"Fru Berger, welcome to *SMP*."

"Call me Erika. Hello."

"Beatrice. Welcome. Shall I show you where to find Editor in Chief Morander? I should say 'outgoing editor in chief.' "

"Thank you; I see him sitting in the glass cage over there," said Berger with a smile. "I can find my way, but thanks for the offer."

She walked briskly through the newsroom and was aware of the drop in noise level. She felt everyone's eyes upon her. She stopped at the half-empty news desk and gave a friendly nod.

"We'll introduce ourselves properly in a while," she said, and then walked over to knock on the door of the glass cubicle.

The departing editor in chief, Håkan Morander, had spent twelve years in the glass cage. Just like Berger, he had been headhunted from outside the company—so he had once taken that very same first walk to his office. He looked up at her, puzzled, and then stood up.

"Hello, Erika," he said. "I thought you were starting tomorrow."

"I couldn't stand sitting at home one more day. So here I am."

Morander held out his hand. "Welcome. I can't tell you how glad I am that you're taking over."

"How are you feeling?" Berger said.

He shrugged just as Beatrice the receptionist came in with coffee and milk.

"It feels as though I'm already operating at half speed. Actually, I don't want to talk about it. You walk around feeling like a teenager and immortal your whole life, and suddenly there isn't much time left. But one thing's for sure—I don't intend to spend the rest of it in this glass cage."

He rubbed his chest. He had heart and artery problems, which was the reason for his going and why Berger was to start several months earlier than originally announced.

Berger turned and looked out over the landscape of the newsroom. She saw a reporter and a photographer heading for the elevator, perhaps on their way to cover the May Day parade.

"Håkan, if I'm being a nuisance or if you're busy today, I'll come back tomorrow or the day after."

"Today's task is to write an editorial on the demonstrations. I could do it in my sleep. If the pinkos want to start a war with Denmark, then I have to explain why they're wrong. If the pinkos want to avoid a war with Denmark, I have to explain why they're wrong."

"Denmark?"

"Correct. The message on May Day has to touch on the immigrant integration question. The pinkos, of course, no matter what they say, are wrong."

He burst out laughing.

"Always so cynical?"

"Welcome to *SMP*."

Erika had never had an opinion about Morander. He was an anonymous power figure among the elite of editors in chief. In his editorials he came across as boring and conservative. Expert in complaining about taxes, and a typical libertarian when it came to freedom of the press. But she had never met him in person.

"Do you have time to tell me about the job?"

"I'm gone at the end of June. We'll work side by side for two months. You'll discover positive things and negative things. I'm a cynic, so mostly I see the negative things."

He got up and stood next to her to look through the glass at the newsroom.

"You'll discover that you're going to have a number of adversaries out there—daily editors and veterans among the editors who have created their own little empires. They have their own club that you can't join. They'll try to stretch the boundaries, to push through their own headlines and angles. You'll have to fight hard to hold your own."

Berger nodded.

"Your night editors are Billinger and Karlsson . . . they're a whole chapter unto themselves. They hate each other and, important, they don't work the same shift, but they both act as if they're publishers and editors in chief. Then there's Anders Holm, the news editor—you'll be working with him a lot. You'll have your share of clashes with him. In point of fact, he's the one who gets *SMP* out every day. Some of the reporters are prize prima donnas, and some of them should really be put out to pasture."

"Have you got any good colleagues?"

Morander laughed again.

"Oh yes, but you're going to have to decide for yourself

which ones you can get along with. Some of the reporters out there are seriously good."

"How about management?"

"Magnus Borgsjö is the CEO. He was the one who recruited you. He's charming. A bit old school and yet at the same time a bit of a reformer, but he's above all the one who makes the decisions. Some of the board members, including several from the family which owns the paper, mostly seem to sit and kill time, while others flutter around, professional board-member types."

"You don't seem to be exactly enamoured of your board."

"There's a division of labour. We put out the paper. They take care of the finances. They're not supposed to interfere with the content, but situations do crop up. To be honest, Erika, between the two of us, this is going to be tough."

"Why's that?"

"Circulation has dropped by nearly 150,000 copies since the glory days of the sixties, and there may soon come a time when *SMP* is no longer profitable. We've reorganized, cut more than 180 jobs since 1980. We went over to tabloid format—which we should have done twenty years sooner. *SMP* is still one of the big papers, but it wouldn't take much for us to be regarded as a second-class paper. If it hasn't already happened."

"Why did they pick me, then?" Berger said.

"Because the median age of our readers is fifty-plus, and the growth in readers in their twenties is almost zero. The paper has to be rejuvenated. And the reasoning among the board was to bring in the most improbable editor in chief they could think of."

"A woman?"

"Not just any woman. *The* woman who crushed Wenner-ström's empire, who is considered the queen of investigative journalism, and who has a reputation for being the toughest. Picture it. It's irresistible. If *you* can't rejuvenate this paper, nobody can. *SMP* isn't just hiring Erika Berger, we're hiring the whole mystique that goes with your name."

When Blomkvist left Café Copacabana, next to the Kvarter cinema in Hornstull, it was just past 2:00 p.m. He put on his dark glasses and turned up Bergsundsstrand on his way to the tunnelbana. He noticed the grey Volvo parked at the corner right away. He passed it without slowing down. Same registration, and the car was empty.

It was the seventh time he had seen the car in four days. He had no idea how long it had been in his neighbourhood. It was pure chance that he had noticed it at all. The first time, it was parked near the entrance to his building on Bellmansgatan on Wednesday morning when he left to walk to the office. He happened to read the registration number, which began with KAB, and he paid attention because those were the initials of Zalachenko's holding company, Karl Axel Bodin Inc. He would not have thought any more about it except that he spotted the car again a few hours later when he was having lunch with Cortez and Eriksson at Medborgarplatsen. That time the Volvo was parked on a side street near the *Millennium* offices.

He wondered whether he was becoming paranoid, but when he visited Palmgren the same afternoon at the rehabilitation home in Ersta, the car was in the visitors' parking lot. That could not have been chance. Blomkvist began to keep an eye on everything around him. And when he saw the car again the next morning he was not surprised.

Not once had he seen its driver.

A call to the national vehicle registry revealed that the car belonged to a Göran Mårtensson of Vittangigatan in Vällingby. An hour's research turned up the information that Mårtensson held the title of business consultant and owned a private company whose address was a P.O. box on Fleminggatan in Kungsholmen. Mårtensson's CV was an interesting one. In 1983, at eighteen, he had done his military service with the coast guard, and then enrolled in the army. By 1989 he had advanced to lieutenant, and then he switched to study at the police academy in Solna. Between 1991 and 1996 he worked for the Stockholm police. In 1997 he was no longer on the official roster of the external service, and in 1999 he had registered his own company.

So—Säpo.

An industrious investigative journalist could get paranoid on less than this. Blomkvist concluded that he was under surveillance, but it was being carried out so clumsily that he could hardly have helped but notice.

Or was it clumsy? The only reason he first noticed the car was the registration number, which just happened to mean something to him. But for the KAB, he would not have given the car a second glance.

On Friday KAB was conspicuous by its absence. Blomkvist could not be absolutely sure, but he thought he had been tailed by a red Audi that day. He had not managed to catch the registration number. On Friday the Volvo was back.

. . .

Exactly twenty seconds after Blomkvist left Café Copacabana, Malm raised his Nikon in the shadows of Café Rosso's awning across the street and took a series of twelve photographs of the two men who followed Blomkvist out of the café and past the Kvarter cinema.

One of the men looked to be in his late thirties or early forties and had blond hair. The other seemed a bit older, with thinning reddish-blond hair and sunglasses. Both were dressed in jeans and leather jackets.

They parted company at the grey Volvo. The older man got in, and the younger one followed Blomkvist towards the Hornstull tunnelbana station.

Malm lowered the camera. Blomkvist had given him no good reason for insisting that he patrol the neighbourhood near the Copacabana on Sunday afternoon looking for a grey Volvo with a registration beginning KAB. Blomkvist told him to position himself where he could photograph whoever got into the car, probably just after 3:00. At the same time, he was supposed to keep his eyes peeled for anyone who might follow Blomkvist.

It sounded like the prelude to a typical Blomkvist adventure. Malm was never quite sure whether Blomkvist was paranoid by nature or if he had paranormal gifts. Since the events in Gosseberga his colleague had certainly become withdrawn and hard to communicate with. Nothing unusual about this. But when Blomkvist was working on a complicated story—Malm had observed the same obsessive and secretive behaviour in the weeks before the Wennerström story broke—it became more pronounced.

On the other hand, Malm could see for himself that Blomkvist was indeed being tailed. He wondered vaguely what new nightmare was in the works. Whatever it was, it would soak up all of *Millennium*'s time, energy, and resources. Malm didn't think it was a great idea for Blomkvist to set off on some wild scheme just when the magazine's editor in chief had deserted to the Big Daily, and now *Millennium*'s laboriously reconstructed stability was suddenly hanging in the balance once again.

But Malm had not participated in any parade—apart from Gay Pride—in at least ten years. He had nothing better to do on this May Day Sunday than humour his wayward publisher. He sauntered after the man tailing Blomkvist even though he had not been instructed to do so, but he lost sight of him on Långholmsgatan.

One of the first things Blomkvist did when he realized that his mobile was bugged was to send Cortez out to buy some used handsets. Cortez bought a job lot of Ericsson T10s for a song. Blomkvist then opened some anonymous cash-card accounts on Comviq and distributed the mobiles to Eriksson, Cortez, Giannini, Malm, and Armansky, keeping one for himself. They were to be used only for conversations that absolutely must not be overheard. Day-to-day stuff they could and should do on their own mobiles. Which meant that they all had to carry two mobiles with them.

Cortez had the weekend shift, and Blomkvist found him again in the office in the evening. Since the murder of Zalachenko, Blomkvist had devised a 24/7 roster, so that *Millennium*'s office was always staffed and someone slept there every night. The roster included himself, Cortez, Eriksson, and Malm. Lotta Karim was notoriously afraid of the dark and would never for the life of her have agreed to be by herself overnight at the office. Nilsson was not afraid of the dark, but she worked so furiously on her projects that she was encouraged to go home when the day was done. Magnusson was getting on in years and as advertising manager had nothing to do with the editorial side. He was also about to go on vacation.

"Anything new?"

"Nothing special," Cortez said. "Today is all about May 1, naturally enough."

"I'm going to be here for a couple of hours," Blomkvist told him. "Take a break and come back around 9:00."

After Cortez left, Blomkvist got out his anonymous mobile and called Daniel Olsson, a freelance journalist in Göteborg. Over the years, *Millennium* had published several of his articles, and Blomkvist had great faith in his ability to gather background material.

"Hi, Daniel. Mikael Blomkvist here. Can you talk?"

"Sure."

"I need someone for a research job. You can bill us for five days, and you don't have to produce an article at the end of it. Well, you can write an article on the subject if you want and we'll publish it, but it's the research we're after."

"Fine. Tell me."

"It's sensitive. You can't discuss this with anyone except me, and you can communicate with me only via Hotmail. You must not even mention that you're doing research for *Millennium*."

"This sounds like fun. What are you looking for?"

"I want you to do a workplace report on Sahlgrenska hospital. We're calling the report 'ER,' and it's to look at the differences between reality and the TV series. I want you to go to the hospital and observe the work in the emergency ward and the intensive care unit for a couple of days. Talk with doctors, nurses, and cleaners—everybody who works there, in fact. What are their working conditions like? What do they actually *do*? That sort of stuff. Photographs too, of course."

"Intensive care?" Olsson said.

"Exactly. I want you to focus on the follow-up care given to severely injured patients in corridor 11C. I want to know the whole layout of the corridor, who works there, what they look like, and what sort of background they have."

"Unless I'm mistaken, a certain Lisbeth Salander is a patient on 11C."

Olsson was not born yesterday.

"How interesting," Blomkvist said. "Find out which room she's in, who's in the neighbouring rooms, and what the routines are in that section."

"I have a feeling that this story is going to be about something altogether different," Olsson said.

"As I said, all I want is the research you come up with."

They exchanged Hotmail addresses.

Salander was lying on her back on the floor when Nurse Marianne came in.

"Hmm," she said, thereby indicating her doubts about the wisdom of this style of conduct in the intensive care unit. But it was, she accepted, her patient's only exercise space.

Salander was sweating. She had spent thirty minutes trying to do arm lifts, stretches, and sit-ups on the recommendation of her physical therapist. She had a long list of the movements she was to perform each day to strengthen the muscles in her shoulder and hip in the wake of her operation three weeks earlier. She was breathing hard and felt wretchedly out of shape. She tired easily, and her left shoulder was tight and hurt at the very least effort. But she was on the path to recovery. The headaches that had tormented her after surgery had subsided and came back only sporadically.

She realized that she was sufficiently recovered now that she could have walked out of the hospital, or at any rate hobbled out, if that had been possible, but it was not. First of all, the doctors had not yet declared her fit, and second, the door to her room was always locked and guarded by a fucking hit man from Securitas, who sat on his chair in the corridor.

She was healthy enough to be moved to a normal rehabilitation ward, but after going back and forth about this, the police and hospital administration had agreed that Salander should remain in room 18 for the time being. The room was easier to guard, there was round-the-clock staff close by, and the room was at the end of an L-shaped corridor. And in corridor 11C the staff were security-conscious after the killing of Zalachenko; they were familiar with her situation. Better not to move her to a new ward with new routines.

Her stay at Sahlgrenska was in any case going to come to an end in a few more weeks. As soon as the doctors discharged her, she would be transferred to Kronoberg prison in Stockholm to await trial. And the person who would decide when it was time for that was Dr. Jonasson.

It was ten days after the shooting in Gosseberga before Dr. Jonasson gave permission for the police to conduct their first real interview, which Giannini viewed as being to Salander's advantage. Unfortunately, Dr. Jonasson had made it difficult even for Giannini to have access to her client, and that was annoying.

After the tumult of Zalachenko's murder and Gullberg's attempted suicide, Jonasson had done an evaluation of Salander's condition. He took into account that Salander must be under a great deal of stress as the suspect for three murders plus the near fatal assault on her late father. Jonasson had no idea whether she was guilty or innocent, and as a doctor he was not the least bit interested in the answer to that question. He simply concluded that Salander was suffering from stress, that she had been shot three times, and that one bullet had entered her brain and almost killed her. She had a fever that would not abate, and she had severe headaches.

He had played it safe. Murder suspect or not, she was his patient, and his job was to make sure she got well. So he filled out a "no visitors" form that had no connection whatsoever to the one that was set in place by the prosecutor. He prescribed various medications and complete bedrest.

But Jonasson also realized that isolation was an inhumane way of punishing people; in fact, it bordered on torture. No-one felt good when they were separated from all their friends, so he decided that Salander's lawyer should serve as a proxy friend. He had a serious talk with Giannini and explained that she could have access to Salander for one hour a day. During this hour she could talk with her or just sit quietly and keep her company, but their conversations should not deal with Salander's problems or impending legal battles.

"Lisbeth Salander was shot in the head and was very seriously injured," he explained. "I think she's out of danger, but there is always a risk of bleeding or some other complication. She needs to rest, and she has to have time to heal. Only when that has happened can she begin to confront her legal problems."

Giannini understood Dr. Jonasson's reasoning. She had some general conversations with Salander and hinted at the outline of the strategy that she and Blomkvist had planned, but Salander was simply so drugged and exhausted that she would fall asleep while Giannini was speaking.

Armansky studied Malm's photographs of the men who had followed Blomkvist from the Copacabana. They were in sharp focus.

"No," he said. "Never seen them before."

Blomkvist nodded. They were in Armansky's office on Monday morning. Blomkvist had come into the building via the garage.

"The older one is Göran Mårtensson, who owns the Volvo. He followed me like a guilty conscience for at least a week, but it could have been longer."

"And you reckon that he's Säpo."

Blomkvist referred to Mårtensson's CV. Armansky hesitated.

You could take it for granted that the Security Police invariably made fools of themselves. That was the natural order of things, not for Säpo alone but probably for intelligence services all over the world. The French secret police had sent frogmen to New Zealand to blow up the Greenpeace ship *Rainbow Warrior,* for God's sake. That had to be the most idiotic intelligence operation in the history of the world, with the possible exception of President Nixon's lunatic break-in at Watergate. With such cretinous leadership it was no wonder that scandals occurred. Their successes were never reported. But the media jumped all over the Security Police whenever anything improper or foolish came to light, and with all the wisdom of hindsight.

On the one hand, the media regarded Säpo as an excellent news source, and almost any political blunder gave rise to headlines: "Säpo suspects that . . ." A Säpo statement carried a lot of weight in a headline.

On the other hand, politicians of various affiliations, along with the media, were particularly diligent in condemning exposed Säpo agents if they had spied on Swedish citizens. Armansky found this entirely contradictory. He did not have anything against the existence of Säpo. Someone had to take responsibility for preventing national-Bolshevist crackpots—who had read too much Bakunin or whoever the hell these neo-Nazis read—from patching together a bomb made of fertilizer and oil and parking it in a van outside Rosenbad. Säpo was necessary, and Armansky did not think a little discreet surveillance was such a bad thing, so long as its objective was to safeguard the security of the nation.

The problem, of course, was that an organization assigned to spy on citizens must remain under strict public scrutiny. There had to be a high level of constitutional oversight. But it was almost impossible for members of Parliament to have oversight of Säpo, even when the prime minister appointed a special investigator who, on paper at least, was supposed to have access to everything. Armansky had Blomkvist's copy of Lidbom's book *An Assignment,* and he was reading it with gathering astonishment. If this were the United States, a dozen or so senior Säpo hands would have been arrested for obstruction of justice and forced to appear before a public committee in Congress. In Sweden, apparently, they were untouchable.

The Salander case demonstrated that something was out of joint inside the organization. But when Blomkvist came over to give him a secure mobile, Armansky's first thought was that the man was paranoid. It was only when he heard the details and studied Malm's photographs that he reluctantly admitted that Blomkvist had good reason to be suspicious. It did not bode well, but rather indicated that the conspiracy that had tried to eliminate Salander fifteen years earlier was not a thing of the past.

There were simply too many incidents for this to be coincidence. Never mind that Zalachenko had supposedly been murdered by a maniac. It had happened at the same time that both Blomkvist and Giannini were robbed of the document that was the cornerstone in the burden of proof. That was a shattering misfortune. And then the key witness, Gunnar Björck, had gone and hanged himself.

"Are we agreed that I pass this on to my contact?" Armansky said, gathering up Blomkvist's documentation.

"And this is a person that you say you can trust?"

"An individual of the highest moral standing."

"Inside *Säpo*?" Blomkvist said with undisguised scepticism.

"We have to be of one mind. Both Holger and I have accepted your plan and are cooperating with you. But we can't clear this matter up all by ourselves. We have to find allies within the bureaucracy if this is not going to end in calamity."

"OK." Blomkvist nodded reluctantly. "I've never had to give out information on a story before it's published."

"But in this case you already have. You've told me, your sister, and Holger."

"True enough."

"And you did it because even you recognize that this is far more than just a scoop in your magazine. For once you're not an objective reporter, but a participant in unfolding events. And as such, you need help. You're not going to win on your own."

Blomkvist gave in. He had not, in any case, told the *whole* truth, either to Armansky or to his sister. He still had one or two secrets that he shared only with Salander.

He shook hands with Armansky.

CHAPTER 9

Wednesday, May 4

Three days after Berger started as acting editor in chief of *SMP*, current Editor in Chief Håkan Morander died at lunchtime. He had been in the glass cage all morning, while Berger and assistant editor Peter Fredriksson met the sports editors so that she could get to know her colleagues and find out how they worked. Fredriksson was forty-five years old and also relatively new to the paper. He was taciturn but pleasant, with broad experience. Berger had already decided that she would be able to depend on Fredriksson's insights when she took command of the ship. She was spending a good part of her time evaluating the people she might be able to count on and could then make part of her new regime. Fredriksson was definitely a candidate.

When they got back to the news desk they saw Morander get up and come over to the door of the glass cage. He looked startled.

Then he leaned forward, grabbed the back of a chair, and held on to it for a few seconds before he collapsed to the floor.

He was dead before the ambulance arrived.

There was a confused atmosphere in the newsroom throughout the afternoon. CEO Borgsjö arrived at 2:00 and gathered the employees for a brief memorial to Morander. He spoke of how Morander had dedicated more than a decade of his life to the newspaper, and the price that the work of a newspaperman can sometimes exact. Finally he called for a minute's silence.

Berger realized that several of her new colleagues were looking at her. *The unknown quantity.*

She cleared her throat, and without being invited to, without knowing what she would say, took half a step forward and spoke in a firm voice: "I knew Håkan Morander for all of three days. That's too short a time, but from even the little I managed to know of him, I can honestly say that I would have wanted very much to know him better."

She paused when she saw out of the corner of her eye that Borgsjö was staring at her. He seemed surprised that she was saying anything at all. She took another pace forward.

"Your editor in chief's untimely departure will create problems in the newsroom. I was supposed to take over from him in two months, and I was counting on having the time to learn from his experience."

She saw that Borgsjö had opened his mouth as if to say something himself.

"That won't happen now, and we're going to go through a period of adjustment. But Morander was editor in chief of a daily newspaper, and this paper will come out tomorrow too. There are now nine hours left before we go to press and four before the front page has to be resolved. May I ask . . . who among you was Morander's closest confidant?"

A brief silence followed as the staff looked at one another. Finally Berger heard a voice from the left side of the room.

"That would probably be me."

It was Gunnar Magnusson, assistant editor of the front page, who had worked on the paper for thirty-five years.

"Somebody has to write an obit. I can't do it . . . that would be presumptuous of me. Could you possibly write it?"

Magnusson hesitated a moment but then said, "I'll do it."

"We'll use the whole front page and move everything else back."

Magnusson nodded.

"We need images." She glanced to her right and met the eye of the photo editor, Lennart Torkelsson. He nodded.

"We have to get busy on this. Things might be a bit rocky at first. When I need help making a decision, I'll ask your advice and I'll depend on your skill and experience. You know how the paper is made, and I still have a lot to learn."

She turned to Fredriksson.

"Peter, Morander put a great deal of trust in you. You will have to be something of a mentor to me for the time being, and carry a heavier load than usual. I'm asking you to be my adviser."

He nodded. What else could he do?

She returned to the subject of the front page.

"One more thing. Morander was writing his editorial this morning. Gunnar, could you get into his computer and see whether he finished it? Even if it's not quite rounded out, we'll publish it. It was his last editorial, and it would be a crying shame not to print it. The paper we're making today is still Håkan Morander's paper."

Silence.

"If any of you need a little personal time, or want to take a break to think for a while, do it, please. You all know our deadlines."

Silence. She noticed that some people were nodding their approval.

"Go to work, boys and girls," she said in English in a low voice.

Holmberg threw up his hands in a helpless gesture. Bublanski and Modig looked dubious. Andersson's expression was neutral. They were scrutinizing the results of the preliminary investigation that Holmberg had completed that morning.

"Nothing?" Modig said. She sounded surprised.

"Nothing," Holmberg said, shaking his head. "The pathologist's final report arrived this morning. Nothing to indicate anything but suicide by hanging."

They looked once more at the photographs taken in the living room of the summer cabin in Smådalarö. Everything pointed to the conclusion that Gunnar Björck, assistant chief of the immigration division of the Security Police, had climbed onto a stool, tied a rope to the lamp hook, placed it around his neck, and then with great resolve kicked the stool across the room. The pathologist was unable to supply the exact time of death, but he had established that it occurred on the afternoon of April 12. The body had been discovered on April 19 by none other than Inspector Andersson. This happened because Bublanski had repeatedly tried to get ahold of Björck. Annoyed, he finally sent Andersson to bring him in.

Sometime during that week, the lamp hook in the ceiling came away and Björck's body fell to the floor. Andersson had seen the body through a window and called in the alarm.

Bublanski and the others who arrived at the summer house had treated it as a crime scene from the word go, taking it for granted that Björck had been garrotted by someone. Later that day the forensic team found the lamp hook. Holmberg had been assigned to work out how Björck had died.

"There's nothing whatsoever to suggest a crime, or that Björck was not alone at the time," Holmberg said.

"The lamp?"

"The ceiling lamp has fingerprints from the owner of the cabin—who put it up two years ago—and Björck himself. Which indicates that he took the lamp down."

"Where did the rope come from?"

"From the flagpole in the garden. Someone cut off about six feet of rope. There was a Mora sheath knife on the windowsill outside the back door. According to the owner of the house, it's his knife. He normally keeps it in a tool drawer under the kitchen counter. Björck's prints were on the handle and the blade, as well as on the tool drawer."

"Hmm," Modig said.

"What sort of knots?" Andersson said.

"Granny knots. Even the noose was just a loop. It's probably the only thing that's a bit odd. Björck was a sailor; he would have known how to tie proper knots. But who knows how much attention a person contemplating suicide would pay to the knots on his own noose?"

"What about drugs?"

"According to the toxicology report, Björck had traces of a strong painkiller in his blood. That medication had been prescribed for him. He also had traces of alcohol, but the percentage was negligible. In other words, he was more or less sober."

"The pathologist wrote that there were graze wounds."

"A graze over an inch long on the outside of his left knee. A scratch, really. I've thought about it, but it could have come about in a dozen different ways . . . for instance, if he walked into the corner of a table or a bench."

Modig held up a photograph of Björck's distorted face. The noose had cut so deeply into his flesh that the rope itself was hidden in the skin of his neck. The face was grotesquely swollen.

"He hung there for something like twenty-four hours before the hook gave way. All the blood was either in his head—the noose having prevented it from running into his body—or in the lower extremities. When the hook came out and his body fell, his chest hit the coffee table, causing deep bruising there. But this injury happened long after the time of death."

"Hell of a way to die," said Andersson.

"I don't know. The noose was so thin that it pinched deep and stopped the blood flow. He was probably unconscious within a few seconds, and dead in one or two minutes."

Bublanski closed the preliminary report with distaste. He did not like this. He absolutely did not like the fact that Zalachenko and Björck had, so far as they could tell, both died on the same day. But no amount of speculating could change the fact that the crime scene investigation offered no grain of support to the theory that a third party had helped Björck on his way.

"He was under a lot of pressure," Bublanski said. "He knew that the whole Zalachenko affair was in danger of being exposed and that he risked a prison sentence for sex-trade crimes, plus being hung out to dry in the media. I wonder which scared him more. He was sick, had been suffering chronic pain for a long time. . . . I don't know. I wish he had left a letter."

"Many suicides don't."

"I know. OK. We'll put Björck to one side for now. We have no choice."

Berger could not bring herself to sit at Morander's desk right away, or to move his belongings aside. She arranged for Magnusson to talk to Morander's family so that the widow could come herself when it was convenient, or send someone to sort out his things.

Instead she had an area cleared off the central desk in the heart of the newsroom, and there she set up her laptop and took command. It was chaotic. But three hours after she had taken the helm of *SMP* in such appalling circumstances, the front page went to press. Magnusson had put together a four-column article about Morander's life and career. The page was designed around a black-bordered portrait, almost all of it above the fold, with his unfinished editorial to the left and a frieze of photographs along the bottom edge. The layout was not perfect, but it had a strong emotional impact.

Just before 6:00, as Berger was going through the headlines on page two and discussing the text with the head of copyediting, Borgsjö approached and touched her shoulder. She looked up.

"Could I have a word?"

They went together to the coffee machine in the cafeteria.

"I just wanted to say that I'm really very pleased with the way you took control today. I think you surprised us all."

"I didn't have much choice. But I may stumble a bit before I really get going."

"We understand that."

"We?"

"I mean the staff and the board. The board especially. But after what happened today, I'm more than ever persuaded that you were the ideal choice. You came here in the nick of time, and you took charge in a very difficult situation."

Berger almost blushed. But she had not done that since she was fourteen.

"Could I give you a piece of advice?"

"Of course."

"I heard that you had a disagreement about a headline with Anders Holm."

"We didn't agree on the angle in the article about the government's tax proposal. He inserted an opinion into the headline in the news section, which is supposed to be neutral. Opinions should be reserved for the editorial page. And while I'm on this topic . . . I'll be writing editorials from time to time, but as I told you, I'm not active in any political party, so we have to solve the problem of who's going to be in charge of the editorial section."

"Magnusson can take over for the time being," said Borgsjö.

Erika shrugged. "It makes no difference to me whom you appoint. But it should be somebody who clearly stands for the newspaper's views. That's where they should be aired, not in the news section."

"Quite right. What I wanted to say was that you'll probably have to give Holm some concessions. He's worked at *SMP* a long time, and he's been news chief for fifteen years. He knows what he's doing. He can be surly sometimes, but he's irreplaceable."

"I know. Morander told me. But when it comes to policy he's going to have to toe the line. I'm the one you hired to run the paper."

Borgsjö thought for a moment and said: "We're going to have to solve these problems as they come up."

Giannini was both tired and irritated on Wednesday evening as she boarded the X2000 at Göteborg Central Station. She felt as if she had been living on the X2000 for a month. She bought a coffee in the restaurant car, went to her seat, and opened the folder of notes from her last conversation with Salander. Who was also the reason why she was feeling tired and irritated.

She's hiding something. That little fool is not telling me the truth. And Micke is hiding something too. God knows what they're playing at.

She also decided that since her brother and her client had not so far communicated with each other, the conspiracy—if it was one—had to be a tacit agreement that had developed naturally. She did not understand what it was about, but it had to be something that her brother considered important enough to conceal.

She was afraid that it was a moral issue, because that was one of his weaknesses. He was Salander's friend. She knew her brother. She knew that he was loyal to the point of foolhardiness once he had made someone a friend, even if the friend was impossible and obviously flawed. She also knew that he could accept any number of idiocies from his friends, but that there was a boundary and it could not be overstepped. Where exactly this boundary was seemed to vary from one person to another, but she knew he had broken completely with people who had previously been close friends because they had done something that he regarded as beyond the pale. And he was inflexible. The break was forever.

Giannini understood what went on in her brother's head. But she had no idea what Salander was up to. Sometimes she thought that there was nothing going on in there at all.

She had gathered that Salander could be moody and withdrawn. Until she met her in person, Giannini had supposed it must be some phase, and that it was a question of gaining her trust. But after a month of conversations—ignoring the fact that the first two weeks had been wasted time because Salander was hardly able to speak—their communication was still distinctly one-sided.

Salander seemed at times to be in a deep depression and had not the slightest interest in dealing with her situation or her future. She simply did not grasp or did not care that the only way Giannini could provide her with an effective defence would be if she had access to all the facts. There was no way she was going to be able to work in the dark.

Salander was sulky, and often just silent. When she did say something, she took a long time to think, and she chose her words carefully. Often she did not reply at all, and sometimes she would answer a question that Giannini had asked several days earlier. During the police interviews, Salander had sat in utter silence, staring straight ahead. With rare exceptions, she had refused to say a single word to the police. The exceptions were on those occasions when Inspector Erlander had asked her what she knew about Niedermann. Then she looked up at him and answered every question in a perfectly matter-of-fact way. As soon as he changed the subject, she lost interest.

On principle, she knew, Salander never talked to the authorities. In this case, that was an advantage. Despite the fact that she kept urging her client to answer questions from the police, deep inside she was pleased with Salander's silence. The reason was simple. It was a consistent silence. It contained no lies that could entangle her, no contradictory reasoning that would look bad in court.

But she was astonished at how imperturbable Salander was. When they were alone she had asked her why she so provocatively refused to talk to the police.

"They'll twist what I say and use it against me."

"But if you don't explain yourself, you risk being convicted anyway."

"Then that's how it'll have to be. I didn't make all this mess. And if they want to convict me, it's not my problem."

Salander had in the end described to her lawyer almost everything that had happened at Stallarholmen. All except for one thing. She would not explain how Magge Lundin had ended up with a bullet in his foot. No matter how much she asked and nagged, Salander would just stare at her and smile her crooked smile.

She had also told Giannini what had happened in Gosseberga. But she had not said anything about why she had confronted her father. Had she gone there expressly to murder him—as the prosecutor claimed—or was it to make him listen to reason?

When Giannini raised the subject of her former guardian, Nils Bjurman, Salander said only that she was not the one who shot him. That particular murder was no longer one of the charges against her. And when Giannini reached the very crux of the whole chain of events, the role of Dr. Teleborian in the psychiatric clinic in 1991, Salander lapsed into such inexhaustible silence that it seemed she might never utter a word again.

This is getting us nowhere, Giannini decided. *If she won't trust me, we're going to lose the case.*

Salander sat on the edge of her bed, looking out the window. She could see the building on the other side of the parking lot. She had sat undisturbed and motionless for an hour, ever since Giannini had stormed out and slammed the door behind her. She had a headache again, but it was mild and distant. Yet she felt uncomfortable.

She was irritated with Giannini. From a practical point of view she could see why her lawyer kept going on and on about details from her past. Rationally, she understood it. Giannini needed to have all the facts. But Salander did not have the remotest wish to talk about her feelings or her actions. Her life was her own business. It was not her fault that her father had been a pathological sadist and murderer. It was not her fault that her brother was a murderer. And thank God nobody yet knew that he was her brother, which would otherwise no doubt also be held against her in the psychiatric evaluation that sooner or later would inevitably be conducted. She was not the one who had killed Svensson and Johansson. She was not responsible for appointing a guardian who turned out to be a pig and a rapist.

And yet it was *her* life that was going to be turned inside out. She would be forced to explain herself and to beg for forgiveness because she had defended herself.

She just wanted to be left in peace. When it came down to it, she was the one who would have to live with herself. She did not expect anyone to be her friend. Annika Fucking Giannini was most likely on her side, but it was the professional friendship of a professional person who was her lawyer. Kalle Fucking Blomkvist was out there somewhere— Giannini was for some reason reluctant to talk about her brother, and Salander never asked. She did not expect that he would be quite so interested now that the Svensson murder was solved and he had his story.

She wondered what Armansky thought of her after all that had happened.

She wondered how Holger Palmgren viewed the situation.

According to Giannini, both of them said they would be in her corner, but those were words. They could not do anything to solve her private problems.

She wondered how Miriam Wu felt about her.

She wondered what she thought of herself, and came to the realization that she felt mostly indifference towards her entire life.

She was interrupted when the Securitas guard put the key in the door to let in Dr. Jonasson.

"Good evening, Fröken Salander. And how are you feeling today?"

"OK," she said.

He checked her chart and saw that she was free of her fever. She had gotten used to his visits, which came a couple of times a week. Of all the people who touched her and poked at her, he was the only one in whom she had a measure of trust. She never felt that he was giving her strange looks. He visited her room, chatted for a while, and examined her to check on her progress. He did not ask any questions about Niedermann or Zalachenko, or whether she was off her rocker or why the police kept her locked up. He seemed to be interested only in how her muscles were working, how the healing in her brain was progressing, and how she felt in general.

Besides, he had—literally—rooted around in her brain. Someone who rummaged around in your brain had to be treated with respect. To her surprise she found Dr. Jonasson's visits pleasant, despite the fact that he poked at her and fussed over her fever chart.

"Do you mind if I check?"

He made his usual examination, looking at her pupils, listening to her breathing, taking her pulse and her blood pressure, and checking how she swallowed.

"How am I doing?"

"You're on the road to recovery. But you have to work harder on the exercises. And you're picking at the scab on your head. You need to stop that." He paused. "May I ask a personal question?"

She looked at him. He waited until she nodded.

"That dragon tattoo . . . Why did you get it?"

"You didn't see it before?"

He smiled all of a sudden.

"I mean, I've *glanced* at it, but when you were uncovered I was pretty busy stopping the bleeding and extracting bullets and so on."

"Why do you ask?"

"Out of curiosity, nothing more."

Salander thought for a while. Then she looked at him.

"I got it for reasons that I don't want to discuss."

"Forget I asked."

"Do you want to see it?"

He looked surprised. "Sure. Why not?"

She turned her back and pulled the hospital gown off her shoulder. She sat so that the light from the window fell on her back. He looked at her dragon. It was beautiful and professionally done, a work of art.

After a while she turned her head.

"Satisfied?"

"It's beautiful. But it must have hurt like hell."

"Yes," she said. "It hurt."

Jonasson left Salander's room somewhat confused. He was satisfied with the progress of her physical rehabilitation. But he could not work out this strange girl. He did not need a master's degree in psychology to know that she was not doing very well emotionally. The tone she used with him was polite, but filled with suspicion. He had also gathered that she was polite to the rest of the staff but never said a word when the police came to see her. She was locked up inside her shell and kept her distance from those around her.

The police had locked her in her hospital room, and a prosecutor intended to charge her with attempted murder and aggravated assault. He was amazed that such a small, thin girl had the physical strength for this sort of violent criminality, especially when the violence was directed at full-grown men.

He had asked about her dragon tattoo in the hope of finding a personal topic he could discuss with her. He was not particularly interested in why she had decorated herself in such a way, but he supposed that since she had chosen such a striking tattoo, it must have a special meaning for her. He thought simply that it might be a way to start a conversation.

His visits to her were outside his schedule, since Dr. Endrin was assigned to her case. But Jonasson was head of the trauma unit, and he was proud of what had been achieved that night when Salander was brought into the ER. He had made the right decision, electing to remove the bullet. As far as he could see, she had no complications in the form of memory lapses, diminished bodily function, or other handicaps from the injury. If she continued to heal at the same pace, she would leave the hospital with a scar on her scalp, but with no other visible damage. Scars on her soul were another matter.

Returning to his office, he discovered a man in a dark suit leaning against the wall outside his door. He had a thick head of hair and a well-groomed goatee.

"Dr. Jonasson?"

"Yes?"

"My name is Peter Teleborian. I'm the head physician at St. Stefan's psychiatric clinic in Uppsala."

"Yes, I recognize you."

"Good. I'd like to have a word in private with you if you have a moment."

Jonasson unlocked the door and ushered the visitor in. "How can I help you?"

"It's about one of your patients, Lisbeth Salander. I need to visit her."

"You'll have to get permission from the prosecutor. She's under arrest, and all visitors are prohibited. Any applications for visits must also be referred in advance to Salander's lawyer."

"Yes, yes, I know. I thought we might be able to cut through all the red tape in this case. I'm a physician, so you could let me have the opportunity to visit her on medical grounds."

"Yes, there might be a case for that, but I can't see what your objective is."

"For several years I was Lisbeth Salander's psychiatrist, when she was institutionalized at St. Stefan's. I followed up with her until she turned eighteen, when the district court released her back into society, albeit under guardianship. I should perhaps mention that I opposed that action. Since then she has been allowed to drift aimlessly, and the consequences are there for all to see today."

"Indeed?"

"I feel a great responsibility towards her still, and would value the chance to gauge how much deterioration has occurred over the past decade."

"Deterioration?"

"Compared to when she was receiving qualified care as a teenager. I thought we might be able to come to an understanding here, as one doctor to another."

"While I have it fresh in my mind, perhaps you could help me with a matter I don't quite understand . . . as one doctor to another, that is. When Lisbeth Salander was admitted to Sahlgrenska hospital I performed a comprehensive medical examination on her. A colleague sent for the forensic report on the patient. It was signed by a Dr. Jesper H. Löderman."

"That's correct. I was Dr. Löderman's assistant when he was in practice."

"I see. But I noticed that the report was vague in the extreme."

"Really?"

"It contains no diagnosis. It almost seems to be an academic study of a patient who refuses to speak."

Teleborian laughed. "Yes, she certainly isn't easy to deal with. As it says in the report, she consistently refused to participate in conversations with Dr. Löderman. With the result that he was bound to express himself rather imprecisely. Which was entirely correct on his part."

"And yet the recommendation was that she should be institutionalized?"

"That was based on her prior history. We had experience with her pathology compiled over many years."

"That's exactly what I don't understand. When she was admitted here, we sent for a copy of her file from St. Stefan's. But we still haven't received it."

"I'm sorry about that. But it's been classified top secret by order of the district court."

"And how are we supposed to give her the proper care here if we can't have access to her records? The medical responsibility for her right now is ours, no-one else's."

"I've taken care of her since she was twelve, and I don't think there is any other doctor in Sweden with the same insight into her clinical condition."

"Which is what?"

"Lisbeth Salander suffers from a serious mental disorder. Psychiatry, as you know, is not an exact science. I would hesitate to confine myself to an exact diagnosis, but she has obvious delusions with distinct paranoid schizophrenic characteristics. Her clinical status also includes periods of manic depression, and she lacks empathy."

Jonasson looked intently at Dr. Teleborian for ten seconds

before he said: "I won't argue a diagnosis with you, Dr. Teleborian, but have you ever considered a significantly simpler
diagnosis?"

"Such as?"

"For example, Asperger's syndrome. Of course, I haven't
done a psychiatric evaluation of her, but if I had to hazard a
guess, I would consider some form of autism. That would
explain her inability to relate to social conventions."

"I'm sorry, but Asperger's patients do not generally set fire
to their parents. Believe me, I've never met such a clearly
defined sociopath."

"I consider her to be withdrawn, but not a paranoid
sociopath."

"She is extremely manipulative," Teleborian said. "She acts
the way she thinks you would expect her to act."

Jonasson frowned. Teleborian was contradicting his own
reading of Salander. If there was one thing Jonasson felt sure
of about her, it was that she was not manipulative. On the
contrary, she was a person who stubbornly kept her distance
from those around her and showed no emotion at all. He
tried to reconcile the picture that Teleborian was painting
with his own image of Salander.

"And you've seen her only for a short period, when she has
been forced to be passive because of her injuries. I have witnessed her violent outbursts and unreasoning hatred. I have
spent years trying to help Lisbeth Salander. That's why I'm
here. I propose a cooperation between Sahlgrenska hospital
and St. Stefan's."

"What sort of cooperation are you talking about?"

"You're responsible for her medical condition, and I'm
convinced that it's the best care she could receive. But I'm

extremely worried about her mental state, and I would like to be included at an early stage. I'm ready to offer all the help I can."

"I see."

"So I do need access to her to do a first-hand evaluation of her condition."

"Unfortunately, I cannot help you."

"I beg your pardon?"

"As I said, she's under arrest. If you want to initiate any psychiatric treatment of her, you'll have to apply to Prosecutor Jervas here in Göteborg. She's the one who makes the decisions on these things. And it would have to be done, I repeat, in cooperation with Salander's lawyer, Annika Giannini. If it's a matter of a forensic psychiatric report, then the district court would have to issue you a warrant."

"It was just that sort of bureaucratic procedure I wanted to avoid."

"Understood, but I'm responsible for Salander, and if she's going to be taken to court in the near future, we need to have clear documentation of all the measures we have taken. So we're bound to observe the bureaucratic procedures."

"All right. Then I might as well tell you that I've already received a formal commission from Prosecutor Ekström in Stockholm to do a forensic psychiatric report. It will be needed in connection with the trial."

"Then you can also obtain formal access to visit her through the appropriate channels without sidestepping regulations."

"But while we're discussing bureaucracy, there is a risk that her condition may continue to deteriorate. I'm only interested in her well-being."

"So am I," Jonasson said. "And between us, I can tell you

that I see no sign of mental illness. She has been badly treated and is under a lot of pressure. But I see no evidence whatsoever that she is schizophrenic or suffering from paranoid delusions."

When at long last he realized that it was fruitless trying to persuade Jonasson to change his mind, Teleborian got up abruptly and took his leave.

Jonasson sat for a while, staring at the chair Teleborian had been sitting in. It was not unusual for other doctors to contact him with advice or opinions on treatment. But that usually happened only with patients whose doctors were already managing their treatment. He had never before seen a psychiatrist land like a flying saucer, ignore all the protocols, and more or less demand to be given access to a patient—a patient whom he obviously had not been treating for several years. After a while Jonasson glanced at his watch and saw that it was almost 7:00. He picked up the phone and called Martina Karlgren, the psychologist at Sahlgrenska who had been made available to trauma patients.

"Hello. I'm assuming you've already left for the day. Am I disturbing you?"

"No problem. I'm at home, but just puttering."

"I'm curious about something. You've spoken to our notorious patient, Lisbeth Salander. Could you give me your impression of her?"

"Well, I've visited her three times and offered to talk with her. Every time she declined in a friendly but firm way."

"What's your impression of her?"

"What do you mean?"

"Martina, I know that you're not a psychiatrist, but you're

an intelligent and sensible person. What general impression did you get of her nature, her state of mind?"

After a while Karlgren said: "I'm not sure how I should answer that question. I saw her twice soon after she was admitted, but she was in such wretched shape that I didn't make any real contact with her. Then I visited her about a week ago, at the request of Helena Endrin."

"Why did Helena ask you to visit her?"

"Salander is starting to recover. She mainly just lies there staring at the ceiling. Dr. Endrin wanted me to look in on her."

"And what happened?"

"I introduced myself. We chatted for a couple of minutes. I asked how she was feeling and whether she felt the need to have someone to talk to. She said that she didn't. I asked if I could help her with anything. She asked me to smuggle in a pack of cigarettes."

"Was she angry, or hostile?"

"No, I wouldn't say that. She was calm, but she kept her distance. I considered her request for cigarettes more of a joke than a serious need. I asked if she wanted something to read, whether I could bring her books of any sort. At first she said no, but later she asked if I had any scientific journals that dealt with genetics and brain research."

"With *what*?"

"Genetics."

"*Genetics?*"

"Yes. I told her that there were some popular science books on the subject in our library. She wasn't interested in those. She said she'd read books on the subject before, and she named some standard works that I'd never heard of. She was more interested in pure research in the field."

"Good grief."

"I said that we probably didn't have any more advanced books in the patient library—we have more Philip Marlowe than scientific literature—but that I'd see what I could dig up."

"And did you?"

"I went upstairs and borrowed some copies of *Nature* magazine and the *New England Journal of Medicine.* She was pleased and thanked me for taking the trouble."

"But those journals contain mostly scholarly papers and pure research."

"She reads them with obvious interest."

Jonasson sat speechless for a moment.

"And how would you rate her mental state?"

"Withdrawn. She hasn't discussed anything of a personal nature with me."

"Do you have the sense that she's mentally ill? Manic-depressive or paranoid?"

"No, no, not at all. If I thought that, I'd have sounded the alarm. She's strange, no doubt about it, and she has big problems and is under stress. But she's calm and matter-of-fact and seems to be able to cope with her situation. Why do you ask? Has something happened?"

"No, nothing's happened. I'm just trying to take stock of her."

CHAPTER 10

Saturday, May 7–
Thursday, May 12

Blomkvist put his laptop case on the desk. It contained the findings of Olsson, the stringer in Göteborg. He watched the flow of people on Götgatan. That was one of the things he liked best about his office. Götgatan was full of life at all hours of the day and night, and when he sat by the window he never felt isolated, never alone.

He was under great pressure. He had kept working on the articles that were to go into the summer issue, but he had finally realized there was so much material that not even an issue devoted entirely to the topic would be sufficient. He had ended up in the same situation as during the Wennerström affair, and he had again decided to publish all the articles as a book. He had enough text already for 150 pages, and he estimated that the final book would run to 320 or 336 pages.

The easy part was done. He had written about the murders of Svensson and Johansson and described how he happened to be the one who came upon the scene. He had dealt with why Salander had become a suspect. He spent a chapter debunking first what the press had written about Salander, then what Prosecutor Ekström had claimed, and thereby indirectly the entire police investigation. After long deliberation he had toned down his criticism of Bublanski and his team. He did this after studying a video from Ekström's press conference, in which it was clear that Bublanski was uncomfortable in the extreme and obviously annoyed at Ekström's rapid conclusions.

After the introductory drama, he had gone back in time and described Zalachenko's arrival in Sweden, Salander's childhood, and the events that led to her being locked away in St. Stefan's in Uppsala. He was careful to annihilate both Teleborian and the now dead Björck. He presented the psychiatric report of 1991 and explained why Salander had become a threat to certain unknown civil servants who had taken it upon themselves to protect the Russian defector. He quoted from the correspondence between Teleborian and Björck.

He then described Zalachenko's new identity and his criminal operations. He described his assistant Niedermann, the kidnapping of Miriam Wu, and Paolo Roberto's intervention. Finally, he summed up the dénouement in Gosseberga which led to Salander's being shot and buried alive, and explained how a policeman's death was a needless catastrophe because Niedermann had already been captured.

Then the story became more sluggish. Blomkvist's problem was that the account still had gaping holes in it. Björck had not acted alone. Behind this chain of events there had to be a larger group with resources and political influence. Nothing else made sense. But he had eventually come to the conclusion that the unlawful treatment of Salander would not have been sanctioned by the government or the bosses of the Security Police. Behind this conclusion lay no exaggerated trust in government, but rather his faith in human nature. An operation of that type could never have been kept secret if it were politically motivated. Someone would have called in a favour and gotten someone to talk, and the press would have uncovered the Salander affair several years earlier.

He thought of the Zalachenko club as small and anonymous. He could not identify any one of them, except possibly Mårtensson, a policeman with a secret appointment who devoted himself to shadowing the publisher of *Millennium*.

It was now clear that Salander would definitely go to trial.

Ekström had brought a charge of aggravated assault in the case of Magge Lundin, and aggravated assault and attempted murder in the case of Karl Axel Bodin.

No trial date had yet been set, but Blomkvist's colleagues had learned that Ekström was planning for July, depending on the state of Salander's health. Blomkvist understood the reasoning. A trial during the peak vacation season would attract less attention than one at any other time of the year.

Blomkvist's plan was to have the book printed and ready to distribute on the first day of the trial. He and Malm had thought of a paperback edition, shrink-wrapped and sent out with the special summer issue. Various assignments had been given to Cortez and Eriksson, who were to produce articles on the history of the Security Police, the IB affair,* and the like.

He frowned as he stared out the window.

It's not over. The conspiracy is continuing. It's the only way to explain the tapped phones, the attack on Annika, and the double theft of the Salander report. Perhaps the murder of Zalachenko is a part of it too.

But he had no evidence.

Together with Eriksson and Malm, he had decided that *Millennium* would publish Svensson's book about sex trafficking, also to coincide with the trial. It was better to present the package all at once, and besides, there was no reason to delay publication. On the contrary—the book would never be able to attract the same attention at any other time. Eriksson and Cortez were Blomkvist's principal assistants for the Salander book. Karim and Malm (against his will) had thus become temporary assistant editors at *Millennium,* with Nilsson as the only available reporter. One result of this increased workload was that Eriksson had had to contract several freelancers to produce articles for future issues. It was expensive, but they had no choice.

Blomkvist wrote a note on a yellow Post-it, reminding himself to discuss the rights to the book with Svensson's family. Svensson's parents lived in Örebro and were his sole heirs. Blomkvist did not really need permission to publish the book in Svensson's name, but he wanted to go and see them to get their approval. He had postponed the visit because he had had too much to do, but now it was time to take care of the matter.

Then there were a hundred other details. Some of them concerned how he should present Salander in the articles. To make the ultimate decision he needed to have a personal conversation to get her approval to tell the truth, or at least parts of it. And he could not have that conversation because she was under arrest and no visitors were allowed.

In that respect, his sister was no help either. She followed the regulations slavishly and had no intention of acting as Blomkvist's go-between. Nor did Giannini tell him anything about what she and her client discussed, other than the parts that concerned the conspiracy against her—Giannini needed help with those. It was frustrating, but all very correct. Consequently Blomkvist had no clue whether Salander had revealed that her previous guardian had raped her, or that she had taken revenge by tattooing a shocking message on his stomach. As long as Giannini did not mention the matter, neither could he.

But Salander's being isolated presented one other acute problem. She was a computer expert and a hacker, which Blomkvist knew but Giannini did not. Blomkvist had promised Salander that he would never reveal her secret, and he had kept his promise. But now he had a great need for her skills in that field.

Somehow he had to establish contact with her.

He sighed as he opened Olsson's folder again. There was a photocopy of a passport application form for one Idris Ghidi, born 1950. A man with a moustache, olive skin, and black hair going grey at the temples.

He was Kurdish, a refugee from Iraq. Olsson had dug up much more on Ghidi than on any other hospital worker. Ghidi had apparently aroused media attention for a time, and had appeared in several articles.

Born in the city of Mosul in northern Iraq, he graduated as an engineer and had been part of the "great economic leap forward" in the seventies. In 1984 he was a teacher at the College of Construction Technology in Mosul. He had not been known as a political activist, but he was a Kurd, and so a potential criminal in Saddam Hussein's Iraq. In 1987 Ghidi's father was arrested on suspicion of being a Kurdish militant. No elaboration was forthcoming. He was executed in January 1988. Three months later Idris Ghidi was seized by the Iraqi secret police, taken to a prison outside Mosul, and tortured there for eleven months to make him confess. What he was expected to confess, Ghidi never discovered, so the torture continued.

In March 1989, one of Ghidi's uncles paid the equivalent of 50,000 Swedish kronor to the local leader of the Ba'ath Party, as compensation for the injury Ghidi had caused the Iraqi state. Two days later he was released into his uncle's custody. He weighed eighty-six pounds and was unable to walk. Before his release, his left hip was smashed with a sledgehammer to discourage any mischief in the future.

He hovered between life and death for several weeks. When, slowly, he began to recover, his uncle took him to a farm well away from Mosul and there, over the summer, his strength returned and he was eventually able to walk again with crutches. He would never regain full health. The question was: what was he going to do in the future? In August he learned that his two brothers had been arrested. He would never see them again. When his uncle heard that Saddam Hussein's police were looking once more for Ghidi, he arranged, for a fee equivalent to 30,000 kronor, to get him across the border into Turkey and from there with a false passport to Europe.

Idris Ghidi landed at Arlanda Airport in Sweden on October 19, 1989. He did not know a word of Swedish, but he had been told to go to the passport police and immediately to ask for political asylum, which he did in broken English. He was sent to a refugee camp in Upplands Väsby. There he would spend almost two years, until the immigration authorities decided that Ghidi did not have sufficient grounds for a residency permit.

By this time Ghidi had learned Swedish and obtained treatment for his shattered hip. He had two operations and could now walk without crutches. During that period the Sjöbo debate* had been conducted in Sweden, refugee camps had been attacked, and Bert Karlsson had formed the New Democracy Party.

The reason why Ghidi had appeared so frequently in the press archives was that at the eleventh hour he got a new lawyer who went directly to the press, and they published reports on his case. Other Kurds in Sweden got involved, including members of the prominent Baksi family. Protest meetings were held and petitions were sent to Minister of Immigration Birgit Friggebo, with the result that Ghidi was granted both a residency permit and a work visa in the kingdom of Sweden. In January 1992 he left Upplands Väsby a free man.

Ghidi soon discovered that being a well-educated and experienced construction engineer counted for nothing. He worked as a newspaper boy, a dishwasher, a doorman, and a taxi driver. He liked being a taxi driver, except for two things: he had no local knowledge of the streets in Stockholm county, and he could not sit still for more than an hour before the pain in his hip became unbearable.

In May 1998 he moved to Göteborg after a distant relative who owned an office-cleaning firm took pity on him. He was given a job on a cleaning crew at Sahlgrenska hospital, with which the company had a contract. The work was routine.

He swabbed floors six days a week, including, as Olsson's ferreting had revealed, corridor 11C.

Blomkvist studied the photograph of Idris Ghidi from the passport application. Then he logged on to the media archive and picked out several of the articles on which Olsson's report was based. He read attentively. He lit a cigarette. The smoking ban at *Millennium* had been relaxed soon after Berger left. Cortez now kept an ashtray on his desk.

Finally Blomkvist read what Olsson had produced about Dr. Anders Jonasson.

Blomkvist did not see the grey Volvo on Monday, nor did he have the feeling that he was being watched or followed, but he walked briskly from the Academic bookshop to the side entrance of NK department store, and then straight through and out the main entrance. Anybody who could keep up surveillance inside the bustling NK would have to be superhuman. He turned off both his mobiles and walked through the Galleria to Gustav Adolfs Torg, past the Parliament building, and into Gamla Stan. Just in case anyone was still following him, he took a zigzag route through the narrow streets of the old city until he reached the right address and knocked at the door of Black/White Publishing.

It was 2:30 in the afternoon. He didn't have an appointment, but the editor, Kurdo Baksi, was in and delighted to see him.

"Hello there," he said heartily. "Why don't you ever come and visit me anymore?"

"I'm here to see you right now," Blomkvist said.

"Sure, but it's been three years since the last time."

They shook hands.

Blomkvist had known Baksi since the eighties. In fact, Blomkvist had been one of the people who gave Baksi practical help when he started the magazine *Black/White* with an issue that he produced secretly at night at the Trade Union Confederation offices. Baksi had been caught in the act by Per-Erik Åström—the same man who went on to be the paedophile hunter at Save the Children—who in the eighties was the research secretary at the Trade Union Confederation. He had discovered stacks of pages from *Black/White*'s first issue, along with an oddly subdued Baksi in one of the copy rooms. Åström had looked at the front page and said: "God Almighty, that's not how a magazine is supposed to look." After that, Åström had designed the logo that was on *Black/White*'s masthead for fifteen years before *Black/White* magazine went to its grave and became the book publishing house Black/White. At the same time, Blomkvist had been suffering through an appalling period as IT consultant at the Trade Union Confederation—his only venture into the IT field. Åström had enlisted him to proofread and give *Black/White* some editorial support. Baksi and Blomkvist had been friends ever since.

Blomkvist sat on a sofa while Baksi got coffee from a machine in the hallway. They chatted for a while, the way you do when you haven't seen someone for some time, but they were constantly interrupted by Baksi's mobile. He would have urgent-sounding conversations in Kurdish or possibly Turkish or Arabic or some other language that Blomkvist did not understand. It had always been this way on his other visits to Black/White Publishing. People called from all over the world to talk to Baksi.

"My dear Mikael, you look worried. What's on your mind?" he said at last.

"Could you turn off your phone for a few minutes?"

Baksi turned off his phone.

"I need a favour. A really important favour, and it has to be done immediately and cannot be mentioned outside this room."

"Tell me."

"In 1989 a refugee by the name of Idris Ghidi came to Sweden from Iraq. When he was faced with the prospect of deportation, he received help from your family until he was granted a residency permit. I don't know if it was your father or somebody else in the family who helped him."

"It was my uncle Mahmut. I know Ghidi. What's going on?"

"He's working in Göteborg. I need his help to do a simple job. I'm willing to pay him."

"What kind of job?"

"Do you trust me, Kurdo?"

"Of course. We've always been friends."

"The job is very odd. I don't want to say what it entails right now, but I assure you it's in no way illegal, nor will it cause any problems for you or for Ghidi."

Baksi gave Blomkvist a searching look. "You don't want to tell me what it's about?"

"The fewer people who know, the better. But I need your help for an introduction—so that Idris will listen to me."

Baksi went to his desk and opened an address book. He looked through it for a minute before he found the number. Then he picked up the phone. The conversation was in Kurdish. Blomkvist could see from Baksi's expression that he started out with words of greeting and small talk before he got serious and explained why he was calling. After a while he said to Blomkvist: "When do you want to meet him?"

"Friday afternoon, if that would work. Ask if I can visit him at home."

Baksi spoke for a short while before he hung up.

"Idris lives in Angered," he said. "Do you have the address?"

Blomkvist nodded.

"He'll be home by 5:00 on Friday afternoon. You're welcome to visit him there."

"Thanks, Kurdo."

"He works at Sahlgrenska hospital as a cleaner," Baksi said.

"I know."

"I couldn't help reading in the papers that you're mixed up in this Salander story."

"That's right."

"She was shot."

"Yes."

"I heard she's at Sahlgrenska."

"That's also true."

Baksi knew that Blomkvist was busy planning some sort of mischief, which he was famous for doing. They might not have been best friends, but they never argued either, and Blomkvist had never hesitated if Baksi asked him a favour.

"Am I going to get mixed up in something I ought to know about?"

"You're not going to get involved. Your role was only to do me the kindness of introducing me to one of your acquaintances. And, I repeat, I won't ask him to do anything illegal."

This assurance was enough for Baksi. Blomkvist stood up. "I owe you one."

"We always owe each other one."

Cortez put down the phone and drummed so loudly with his fingertips on the edge of his desk that Nilsson glared at him. But she could see that he was lost in thought, and since she was feeling irritated in general she decided not to take it out on him.

She knew that Blomkvist was doing a lot of whispering with Cortez and Eriksson and Malm about the Salander story, while she and Karim were expected to do all the grunt work for the next issue of a magazine that hadn't had any real leadership since Berger left. Eriksson was fine, but she lacked the experience and gravitas of Berger. And Cortez was just a young whippersnapper.

Nilsson was not unhappy that she had been passed over, nor did she want their jobs—that was the last thing she wanted. Her own job was to keep tabs on the government departments and Parliament on behalf of *Millennium*. She enjoyed the work, and she knew it inside out. Besides, she was overloaded with part-time jobs, like writing a column in a trade journal every week, and various volunteer tasks for Amnesty International and the like. She wasn't interested in being editor in chief of *Millennium* and working a minimum of twelve hours a day as well as sacrificing her weekends.

She did, however, feel that something had changed at *Millennium*. The magazine suddenly felt foreign. She could not put her finger on what was wrong.

As always, Blomkvist was irresponsible and kept vanishing on another of his mysterious trips, coming and going as he pleased. He was a part owner of *Millennium*, fair enough; he could decide for himself what he wanted to do, but Jesus, a little sense of responsibility wouldn't hurt.

Malm was also part owner, and he was about as much help as he was when he was on vacation. He was talented, no question, and he could step in and take over the reins when Berger was away or busy, but usually he just followed through with what other people had already decided. He was brilliant at anything involving graphic design or presentations, but he was out of his depth when it came to planning a magazine.

Nilsson frowned.

No, she was being unfair. What bothered her was that something had happened at the office. Blomkvist was working with Eriksson and Cortez, and the rest of them were somehow excluded. Those three had formed an inner circle and were always shutting themselves in Berger's office . . . well, Eriksson's office, and then they'd all come trooping out in silence. Under Berger's leadership the magazine had always been a collective.

Blomkvist was working on the Salander story and wouldn't share any part of it. This was nothing new. He hadn't said a word about the Wennerström story either— not even Berger had known—but this time he had two confidants.

In a word, Nilsson was pissed off. She needed a vacation. She needed to get away for a while. Then she saw Cortez putting on his corduroy jacket.

"I'm going out for a while," he said. "Could you tell Malin that I'll be back in two hours?"

"What's going on?"

"I think I've got a lead on a story. A really good story.

About toilets. I want to check a few things, but if this pans out we'll have a fantastic article for the June issue."

"Toilets," Nilsson muttered.

Berger clenched her teeth and put down the article about the forthcoming Salander trial. It was short, two columns, intended for page five, under national news. She looked at the text for a minute and pursed her lips. It was 3:30 on Thursday. She had been working at *SMP* for exactly twelve days. She picked up the phone and called Holm, the news editor.

"Hello, it's Berger. Could you find Johannes Frisk and bring him to my office ASAP?"

She waited patiently until Holm sauntered into the glass cage with the reporter Frisk in tow. Berger looked at her watch.

"Twenty-two," she said.

"Twenty-two what?" said Holm.

"Twenty-two minutes. That's how long it's taken you to get up from the editorial desk, walk the fifty feet to Frisk's desk, and drag yourself over here with him."

"You said there was no rush. I was pretty busy."

"I did not say there was no rush. I asked you to get Frisk and come to my office. I said ASAP, and I meant ASAP, not tonight or next week or whenever you feel like getting your butt out of your chair."

"But I don't think—"

"Shut the door."

She waited until Holm had closed the door behind him and studied him in silence. He was without doubt an extremely competent news editor. His role was to make sure that the pages of *SMP* were filled every day with the correct text, logically organized, and appearing in the order and position they had decided on in the morning meeting. This meant that Holm juggled a colossal number of tasks every day. And he did it without ever dropping a ball.

The problem with him was that he consistently ignored the decisions Berger made. She had done her best to find a formula for working with him. She had tried friendly reasoning and direct orders, she had encouraged him to think for himself, and generally she had done everything she could think of to make him understand how she wanted the newspaper to be shaped.

Nothing made any difference.

An article she had rejected in the afternoon would appear in the newspaper sometime after she had gone home. *We had a hole we needed to fill, so I had to put in something.*

The headline that Berger had decided to use was suddenly replaced by something entirely different. It was not always a bad choice, but it would be done without her consultation. As an act of defiance.

It was always a matter of details. An editorial meeting at 2:00 was suddenly moved to 1:30 without her being told, and most of the decisions were already made by the time she arrived. *I'm sorry . . . in the rush I forgot to let you know.*

For the life of her, Berger couldn't see why Holm had adopted this attitude towards her, but she knew that calm discussions and friendly reprimands didn't work. Until now she hadn't confronted him in front of other colleagues in the newsroom. Now it was time to express herself more clearly, and this time in front of Frisk, which would ensure that the exchange became common knowledge.

"The first thing I did when I started here was to tell you

that I had a special interest in everything to do with Lisbeth Salander. I explained that I wanted information in advance on all proposed articles, and that I wanted to look at and approve everything to be published. I've reminded you about this at least half a dozen times, most recently at the editorial meeting on Friday. Which part of these instructions do you not understand?"

"All the articles that are planned or in production are on the daily memo on our intranet. They're sent to your computer. You're always kept informed," Holm said.

"Bullshit," Berger said. "When the city edition of the paper landed in my mailbox this morning we had a three-column story about Salander and the developments in the Stallarholmen incident in our best news spot."

"That was Margareta Orring's article. She's a freelancer; she didn't turn it in until 7:00 last night."

"Margareta called me with the proposal at 11:00 yesterday morning. You approved it and gave her the assignment at 11:30. You didn't say a word about it at the 2:00 meeting."

"It's in the daily memo."

"Oh, right . . . here's what it says in the daily memo: quote, Margareta Orring, interview with Prosecutor Martina Fransson re: narcotics bust in Södertälje, unquote."

"The basic story was an interview with Martina Fransson about the confiscation of anabolic steroids. A would-be Svavelsjö biker was busted for that," Holm said.

"Exactly. And not a word in the daily memo about Svavelsjö MC, or that the interview would be focused on Magge Lundin and Stallarholmen, and therefore the investigation of Salander."

"I assume it came up during the interview—"

"Anders, I don't know why, but you're standing here lying to my face. I spoke to Margareta and she said that she clearly explained to you what her interview was going to focus on."

"I must not have realized that it would centre on Salander. Then I got an article late in the evening. What was I supposed to do, kill the whole story? Orring turned in a good piece."

"There I agree with you. It's an excellent story. But that's now your third lie in about the same number of minutes. Orring turned it in at 3:20 in the afternoon, long before I went home at 6:00."

"Berger, I don't like your tone of voice."

"Great. Then I can tell you that I like neither your tone nor your evasions nor your lies."

"It sounds as if you think I'm organizing some sort of conspiracy against you."

"You still haven't answered the question. And item two: today this piece by Johannes shows up on my desk. I can't recall having any discussion about it at the 2:00 meeting. Why has one of our reporters spent the day working on Salander without anybody telling me?"

Frisk squirmed. He was bright enough to keep his mouth shut.

Holm said, "We're putting out a newspaper, and there must be hundreds of articles you don't know about. We have routines here at *SMP*, and we all have to adapt to them. I don't have time to give special treatment to specific articles."

"I didn't ask you to give special treatment to specific articles. I asked you for two things: first, that I be informed of everything that has a bearing on the Salander case. Second, I want to approve everything we publish on that topic. So, one more time . . . what part of my instructions did you not understand?"

Holm sighed and adopted an exasperated expression.

"OK," Berger said. "I'll make myself crystal clear. I am not going to argue with you about this. Let's see if you understand this message. If it happens again I'm going to relieve you of your job as news editor. You'll hear bang-boom, and then you'll find yourself editing the family page or the comics or something like that. I cannot have a news editor whom I can't trust or work with and who devotes his precious time to undermining my decisions. Understood?"

Holm threw up his hands in a gesture that indicated he considered Berger's accusations to be absurd.

"Do you understand me? Yes or no?"

"I heard what you said."

"I asked if you understood. Yes or no?"

"Do you really think you can get away with this? This paper comes out because I and the other cogs in the machinery work our butts off. The board is going to—"

"The board is going to do as I say. I'm here to revamp this paper. I have a carefully worded agreement that gives me the right to make far-reaching editorial changes at section editors' level. I can get rid of the dead meat and recruit new blood from outside if I choose. And Holm . . . you're starting to look like dead meat to me."

She fell silent. Holm met her gaze. He was furious.

"That's all," Berger said. "I suggest you consider very carefully what we've talked about today."

"I don't think—"

"It's up to you. That's all. Now go."

He turned on his heel and left the glass cage. She watched him disappear into the editorial sea in the direction of the cafeteria. Frisk stood up and made to follow.

"Not you, Johannes. You stay here and sit down."

She picked up his article and read it one more time.

"You're here on a temporary basis, I gather."

"Yes. I've been here five months—this is my last week."

"How old are you?"

"Twenty-seven."

"I apologize for putting you in the middle of a duel between me and Holm. Tell me about this story."

"I got a tip this morning and took it to Holm. He told me to follow up on it."

"I see. It's about the police investigating the possibility that Lisbeth Salander was mixed up in the sale of anabolic steroids. Does this story have any connection to yesterday's article about Södertälje, in which steroids also appeared?"

"Not that I know of, but it's possible. This thing about steroids has to do with her connection to boxers. Paolo Roberto and his pals."

"Paolo Roberto uses steroids?"

"What? No, of course not. It's more about the boxing world in general. Salander used to train at a gym in Söder. But that's the angle the police are taking. Not me. And somewhere the idea seems to have popped up that she might have been involved in selling steroids."

"So there's no actual substance to this story at all, just a rumour?"

"It's no rumour that the police are looking into the possibility. Whether they're right or wrong, I have no idea yet."

"OK, Johannes. I want you to know that what I'm discussing with you now has nothing to do with my dealings with Holm. I think you're an excellent reporter. You write well and you have an eye for detail. In short, this is a good story. My problem is that I don't believe it."

"I can assure you that it's quite true."

"And I have to explain to you why there's a fundamental flaw in the story. Where did the tip come from?"

"From a source within the police."

"Who?"

Frisk hesitated. It was an automatic response. Like every other journalist the world over, he was unwilling to name his source. On the other hand, Berger was editor in chief, and therefore one of the few people who could demand that information from him.

"An officer named Faste in the violent crimes division."

"Did he call you or did you call him?"

"He called me."

"Why do you think he called you?"

"I interviewed him a couple of times during the hunt for Salander. He knows who I am."

"And he knows you're twenty-seven and a temp and that you're useful when he wants to plant information that the prosecutor wants put out."

"Sure, I understand all that. But I get a tip from the police investigation and go over and have a coffee with Faste and he tells me this. He is correctly quoted. What am I supposed to do?"

"I'm convinced that you quoted him accurately. What should have happened is that you should have taken the information to Holm, who should have knocked on the door of my office and explained the situation, and together we would have decided what to do."

"I get it. But I—"

"You left the material with Holm, who's the news editor. You acted correctly. But let's analyse your article. First of all, why would Faste want to leak this information?"

Frisk shrugged.

"Does that mean that you don't know, or that you don't care?"

"I don't know."

"If I were to tell you that this story is untrue, and that Salander doesn't have a thing to do with anabolic steroids, what would you say then?"

"I can't prove otherwise."

"No indeed. But you think we should publish a story that might be a lie just because we have no proof that it's a lie."

"No, we have a journalistic responsibility. But it's a balancing act. We can't refuse to publish when we have a source who makes a specific claim."

"We can ask why the source might want this information to get out. Let me explain why I gave orders that everything to do with Salander has to cross my desk. I have special knowledge of the subject that no-one else at *SMP* has. The legal department has been informed that I possess this knowledge but cannot discuss it with them. *Millennium* is going to publish a story that I am contractually bound not to reveal to *SMP*, despite the fact that I work here. I obtained the information in my capacity as editor in chief of *Millennium*, and right now I'm caught between two loyalties. Do you see what I mean?"

"Yes."

"What I learned at *Millennium* tells me that I can say without a doubt that this story is a lie, and its purpose is to damage Salander before the trial."

"It would be hard to do her any more damage, considering all the revelations that have already come out about her."

"Revelations that are largely lies and distortions. Hans Faste is one of the key sources for the claims that Salander is a paranoid and violence-prone lesbian devoted to Satanism and S & M. And the media as a whole bought Faste's propaganda simply because he appears to be a serious source and it's always cool to write about S & M. Now he's trying a new angle, which will put her at a disadvantage in the public consciousness, and which he wants *SMP* to help disseminate. Sorry, but not on my watch."

"I understand."

"Do you? Good. Then I can sum up everything I said in one sentence. Your job description as a journalist is to question and scrutinize critically— never to repeat claims uncritically, no matter how highly placed the sources in the bureaucracy. Don't ever forget that. You're a damn good writer, but that talent is completely worthless if you forget your job description."

"Right."

"I intend to kill this story."

"I understand."

"This doesn't mean that I distrust you."

"Thank you."

"So that's why I'm sending you back to your desk with a proposal for a new story."

"All right."

"The whole thing has to do with my contract with *Millen-*

nium. I'm not allowed to reveal what I know about the Salander story. At the same time, I'm editor in chief of a newspaper that's in danger of skidding because the newsroom doesn't have the information that I have. And we can't allow that to happen. This is a unique situation and applies only to Salander. That's why I've decided to choose a reporter and steer him in the right direction so that we won't end up with our pants down when *Millennium* comes out."

"And you think that *Millennium* will be publishing something noteworthy about Salander?"

"I don't think so, I know so. *Millennium* is sitting on a scoop that will turn the Salander story on its head, and it's driving me crazy that I can't go public with it."

"You say you're rejecting my article because you know that it isn't true. That means there's something in the story that all the other reporters have missed."

"Exactly."

"I'm sorry, but it's difficult to believe that the entire Swedish media has been duped in the same way. . . ."

"Salander has been the object of a media frenzy. That's when normal rules no longer apply, and any drivel can be printed."

"So you're saying that Salander isn't exactly what she seems to be."

"Try out the idea that she's innocent of these accusations, that the picture painted of her in the media is nonsense, and that there are forces at work you haven't even dreamed of."

"Is that the truth?"

Berger nodded.

"So what I just handed in is part of a continuing campaign against her."

"Precisely."

Frisk scratched his head. Berger waited until he had finished thinking.

"What do you want me to do?"

"Go back to your desk and start working on another story. You don't have to stress out about it, but just before the trial begins we might be able to publish a whole feature that examines the accuracy of all the statements that have been made about Salander. Start by reading through the clippings, list everything that's been said about her, and check off the allegations one by one."

"All right."

"Think like a reporter. Investigate who's spreading the story, why it's being spread, and ask yourself whose interests it might serve."

"But I probably won't be at *SMP* when the trial starts. This is my last week."

Berger took a plastic folder from a desk drawer and laid a sheet of paper in front of him.

"I've extended your assignment by three months. You'll finish off this week with your ordinary duties and report in here on Monday."

"Thank you."

"If you want to keep working at *SMP*, that is."

"Of course I do."

"You're contracted to do investigative work outside the normal editorial job. You'll report directly to me. You're going to be a special correspondent assigned to the Salander trial."

"The news editor is going to have something to say—"

"Don't worry about Holm. I've talked with the head of the

legal department and fixed it so there won't be any hassle there. But you're going to be digging into the background, not news reporting. Does that sound good?"

"It sounds fantastic."

"All right, then. That's all. I'll see you on Monday."

As she waved him out of the glass cage she saw Holm watching her from the other side of the news desk. He lowered his gaze and pretended that he had not been looking at her.

CHAPTER 11

Friday, May 13– Saturday, May 14

Blomkvist made sure that he was not being watched when he walked from the *Millennium* offices early on Friday morning to Salander's old apartment block on Lundagatan. He had to meet Idris Ghidi in Göteborg. The question was how to travel there without being observed or leaving a trail. He decided against the train, since he didn't want to use a credit card. Normally he would borrow Berger's car, but that was no longer possible. He had thought about asking Cortez or someone else to rent a car for him, but that too would leave a trace.

Finally he came up with the obvious solution. He had the keys to Salander's burgundy Honda. It had been parked outside her building since March. He adjusted the seat and saw that the gas tank was half full. Then he backed out and headed across Liljeholmsbron towards the E4.

At 2:50 he parked on a side street off Avenyn in Göteborg. He had a late lunch at the first café he saw. At 4:10 he took the tram to Angered and got off in the centre of town. It took twenty minutes to find Idris Ghidi's address. He was about ten minutes late for their meeting.

Ghidi opened the door, shook hands with Blomkvist, and invited him into a living room with spartan furnishings. He had a limp. He asked Blomkvist to take a seat at the table next to a dresser on which were a dozen framed photographs, which Blomkvist studied.

"My family," Ghidi said.

He spoke with a thick accent. Blomkvist suspected that he would not pass the language test recommended by the People's Party of Sweden.

"Are those your brothers?"

"My two brothers on the left were murdered by Saddam in the eighties. That's my father in the middle. My two uncles were murdered by Saddam in the nineties. My mother died in 2000. My three sisters are still alive. Two are in Syria and my little sister is in Madrid."

Ghidi poured Turkish coffee.

"Kurdo Baksi sends his greetings."

"Kurdo said you wanted to hire me for a job, but not what it was. I have to tell you, right away, that I won't take the job if it's illegal. I can't afford to get mixed up in anything like that."

"There is nothing illegal in what I'm going to ask you to do. But it is unusual. The job itself will last for a couple of weeks. It must be done each day, but it will take only a minute of your time. For this I'm willing to pay you a thousand kronor a week, which I won't report to the tax authorities."

"I understand. What is it I have to do?"

"One of your jobs at Sahlgrenska hospital—six days a week, if I understand correctly—is to clean corridor 11C, the intensive care unit."

Ghidi nodded.

Blomkvist leaned forward and explained his plan.

Prosecutor Ekström took stock of his visitor. It was the third time he had met Superintendent Nyström. He saw a lined face framed by short grey hair. Nyström had first come to see him in the days following the murder of Karl Axel Bodin. He had offered credentials to indicate that he worked for SIS. They had had a long, subdued conversation.

"It's important that you understand this: in no way am I trying to influence how you might act or how you do your job. I would also emphasize that under no circumstances can you make public the information I give you," Nyström said.

"I understand."

Truth be told, Ekström did not entirely understand, but he didn't want to look like an idiot by asking questions. He understood that the death of Bodin/Zalachenko was a case that had to be handled with the utmost discretion. He also understood that Nyström's visit was off the record, although endorsed by the highest authorities within the Security Police.

"This is a matter of life or death," Nyström had said at their first meeting. "As far as the Security Police are concerned, everything related to the Zalachenko case is top secret. I can tell you that he is a defector, a former agent of Soviet military intelligence, and a key player in the Russians' offensive against Western Europe in the seventies."

"That's what Blomkvist at *Millennium* is evidently alleging."

"And in this instance Blomkvist is quite correct. He's a journalist who happened to stumble upon one of the most secret operations ever conducted by Swedish defence."

"He's going to publish the information."

"Of course. He represents the media, with all the advantages and drawbacks. We live in a democracy and naturally we cannot influence what is written in the press. The problem in this case is that Blomkvist knows only a fraction of the truth about Zalachenko, and much of what he thinks he knows is wrong."

"I see."

"What Blomkvist doesn't grasp is that if the truth about Zalachenko comes out, the Russians will swiftly identify our informants and sources in Russia. People who have risked their lives for democracy will be in danger of being killed."

"But isn't Russia a democracy now too? I mean, if this had been during the communist days—"

"That's an illusion. This is about people who spied formerly within the Soviet Union—no regime in the world would stand for that, even if it happened many years ago. And a number of these sources are still active."

No such agents existed, but Ekström couldn't know that. He was bound to take Nyström at his word. And he couldn't help feeling flattered that he was being given information—off the record, of course—that was among the most secret to be found in Sweden. He was slightly surprised that the Swedish Security Police had been able to penetrate the Russian military to the degree Nyström was describing, but he perfectly understood that this was information that absolutely could not be disseminated.

"When I was assigned to make contact with you, we did an extensive investigation of your background," Nyström said.

The seduction always involved discovering someone's weaknesses. Prosecutor Ekström's weakness was his belief in his own importance. Like everyone else, he appreciated flattery. The trick was to make him feel that he had been specially chosen.

"We have confirmed that you are a man who enjoys enormous respect within the police force . . . and of course in government circles."

Ekström looked pleased. That unnamed individuals in government circles had great confidence in him implied that he could count on their gratitude if he played his cards right.

"Simply stated, my assignment is to provide you with background as necessary, and as discreetly as possible. You must understand how improbably complicated this story has become. For one thing, a preliminary investigation is under way, for which you bear the primary responsibility. No-one—not in the government or the Security Police or anywhere else—can interfere in how you run this investigation. Your job is to ascertain the truth and bring the guilty parties to court. One of the most crucial functions in a democratic state."

Ekström nodded.

"It would be a national catastrophe if the whole truth about Zalachenko were to leak out."

"So what exactly is the purpose of your visit?"

"First, to make you aware of the sensitive nature of the situation. I don't think Sweden has been in such an exposed position since the end of the Second World War. One might say that, to a certain extent, the fate of Sweden rests in your hands."

"Who is your superior?"

"I'm sorry, but I cannot reveal the name of anyone working on this case. Let me just say that my instructions come from the very highest levels."

Good Lord. He's acting on orders from the government. But he can't say without unleashing a political firestorm.

Nyström saw that Ekström had swallowed the bait.

"What I am able to do, however, is provide you with information. I have been given the authority to use my own judgement in giving you material that is among the most highly classified in this country."

"I see."

"This means that if you have questions about something, whatever it may be, you should turn to me. You must not talk to anyone else in the Security Police, only to me. My assignment is to be your guide in this labyrinth, and if clashes between various interests threaten to arise, then we will assist each other in finding solutions."

"I understand. In that case I should say how grateful I am that you and your colleagues are willing to facilitate matters for me."

"We want the legal process to take its course even though this is a difficult situation."

"Good. I assure you that I will exercise the utmost discretion. This isn't the first time I've handled top secret information, after all."

"No, we are quite aware of that."

Ekström had a dozen questions that Nyström meticulously noted, and then answered as best he could. On this third visit Ekström would be given answers to several of the questions he had asked earlier. Among them, and most crucially: what was the truth surrounding Björck's report from 1991?

"That is a serious matter." Nyström adopted a concerned expression. "Since this report surfaced, we have had an analysis group working almost around the clock to discover exactly what happened. We are now close to the point where we can draw conclusions. And they are most unpleasant."

"I can well imagine. That report alleges that the Security Police and the psychiatrist Peter Teleborian cooperated to place Lisbeth Salander in psychiatric care."

"If only that were the case," Nyström said with a slight smile.

"I don't understand."

"If that was all there was to it, the matter would be simple. Then a crime would have been committed and an indictment could be brought. The difficulty is that this report doesn't correspond with other reports that we have in our archives." Nyström took out a blue folder and opened it. "What I have here is the report that Gunnar Björck actually wrote in 1991. Here too are the original documents from the correspondence between him and Teleborian. The two versions do not agree."

"Please explain."

"The appalling thing is that Björck has hanged himself. Presumably because of the threat of revelations about his sexual deviations. Blomkvist's magazine was going to expose him. That drove him to such depths of despair that he took his own life."

"Well . . ."

"The original report is an account of Lisbeth Salander's attempt to murder her father, Alexander Zalachenko, with a gasoline bomb. The first thirty pages of the report that Blomkvist discovered agree with the original. These pages, frankly, contain nothing remarkable. It's not until page thirty-three, where Björck draws conclusions and makes recommendations, that the discrepancy arises."

"What discrepancy?"

"In the original version Björck presents five well-argued recommendations. We don't need to hide the fact that they concern playing down the Zalachenko affair in the media and so forth. Björck proposes that Zalachenko's rehabilitation—he suffered very severe burns—be carried out abroad. And similar things. He also recommends that Salander be offered the best conceivable psychiatric care."

"I see. . . ."

"The problem is that a number of sentences were altered in a very subtle way. On page thirty-four there is a paragraph in which Björck appears to suggest that Salander be branded psychotic, so that she will not be believed if anyone should start asking questions about Zalachenko."

"And this suggestion is not in the original report."

"Precisely. Gunnar Björck's own report never suggested anything of the kind. Aside from anything else, that would have been against the law. He recommended that she be given the care she quite clearly needed. In Blomkvist's copy, this was made out to be a conspiracy."

"Could I read the original?"

"Be my guest. But I have to take the report with me when I go. And before you read it, let me direct your attention to the appendix containing the subsequent correspondence between Björck and Teleborian. It is almost entirely fabricated. Here it's not a matter of subtle alterations, but of gross falsifications."

"Falsifications?"

"I think that's the only appropriate description. The original shows that Peter Teleborian was assigned by the district court to do a forensic psychiatric examination of Lisbeth

Salander. Nothing out of the ordinary there. Salander was twelve years old and had tried to kill her father—it would have been very strange if that shocking event had not resulted in a psychiatric report."

"That's true."

"If you had been the prosecutor, I assume that you would have insisted on both social and psychiatric investigations."

"Of course."

"Even then Teleborian was a well-respected child psychiatrist who had also worked in forensic medicine. He was given the assignment, conducted a normal investigation, and came to the conclusion that the girl was mentally ill. I don't have to use their technical terms."

"No, no . . ."

"Teleborian wrote this in a report that he sent to Björck. The report was then given to the district court, which decided that Salander should be cared for at St. Stefan's. Blomkvist's version is missing the entire investigation conducted by Teleborian. In its place is an exchange between Björck and Teleborian, which has Björck instructing Teleborian to falsify a mental examination."

"And you're saying that it's an invention, a forgery?"

"No question about it."

"But who would be interested in creating such a thing?"

Nyström put down the report and frowned. "Now you're getting to the heart of the problem."

"And the answer is . . . ?"

"We don't know. That's the question our analytical group is working very hard to answer."

"Could it be that Blomkvist made some of it up?"

Nyström laughed. "That was one of our first thoughts too. But we don't think so. We incline to the view that the falsification was done a long time ago, presumably more or less simultaneously with the writing of the original report. And that leads to one or two disagreeable conclusions. Whoever did the falsification was extremely well informed. In addition, whoever did it had access to the very typewriter that Björck used."

"You mean . . ."

"We don't know *where* Björck wrote the report. It could have been at his home or at his office or somewhere else altogether. We can imagine two alternatives. Either the person who did the falsification was someone in the psychiatric or forensic medicine department, who for some reason wanted to involve Teleborian in a scandal, or the falsification was done for a completely different purpose by someone inside the Security Police."

"For what possible reason?"

"This happened in 1991. There could have been a Russian agent inside SIS who had picked up Zalachenko's trail. Right now we're examining a large number of old personnel files."

"But if the GRU had found out it should have leaked years ago."

"You're right. But don't forget that this was during the period when the Soviet Union was collapsing and the GRU was dissolved. We have no idea what went wrong. Maybe it was a planned operation that was shelved. The GRU were masters of forgery and disinformation."

"But why would Soviet military intelligence want to plant such a forgery?"

"We don't know that either. But the most obvious purpose would have been to involve the Swedish government in a scandal."

Ekström pinched his lip. "So what you're saying is that the medical assessment of Salander is correct?"

"Oh yes. Salander is, to put it in colloquial terms, stark raving mad. No doubt about that. The decision to commit her to an institution was absolutely correct."

"*Toilets?*" Eriksson sounded as if she thought Cortez was pulling her leg.

"Toilets," Cortez repeated.

"You want to run a story on toilets? In *Millennium*?"

Eriksson could not help laughing. She had observed his ill-concealed enthusiasm when he sauntered into the Friday meeting, and she recognized all the signs of a reporter who had a story in the works.

"Explain."

"It's really quite simple," Cortez said. "The biggest industry in Sweden by far is construction. It's an industry that in practice cannot be outsourced overseas, even if Skanska opens an office in London and stuff like that. No matter what, the houses have to be built in Sweden."

"But that's nothing new."

"No, but what *is* new is that the construction industry is a couple of light-years ahead of all other Swedish industries when it comes to competition and efficiency. If Volvo built cars the same way, the latest model would cost about one million kronor, maybe even two million. For most of industry, cutting prices is the constant challenge. For the construction industry it's the opposite. The price per square foot keeps going up. The state subsidizes the cost with taxpayers' money just so that the prices aren't prohibitive."

"Is there a story in that?"

"Wait. It's complicated. Let's say the price curve for hamburgers had been the same since the seventies—so a Big Mac would cost about 150 kronor or more. I don't want to guess what it would cost with fries and a Coke, but my salary at *Millennium* might not cover it. How many people around this table would go to McDonald's and buy a burger for 150 kronor?"

Nobody said a word.

"Understandable. But when NCC bangs together some sheet-metal cubes for exclusive rental at Gåshaga on Lidingö, they ask 10 to 12,000 kronor a month for a three-cube apartment. How many of you are paying that much?"

"I couldn't afford it," Nilsson said.

"No, of course not. But you already live in a one-bedroom apartment by Danvikstull which your father bought for you twenty years ago, and if you were to sell it you'd probably get a million and a half for it. But what does a twenty-year-old who wants to move out of the family home do? He can't afford to. So he sublets or sub-sublets or lives at home with his mother until he retires."

"So where do the toilets come into the picture?" Malm said.

"I'm getting to that. The question is, why are apartments so fucking expensive? Because the people commissioning the buildings don't know how to set the price. To put it simply, a developer calls up Skanska, says they want a hundred apartments, and asks what it will cost. Skanska calculates it, comes back and says it'll cost around 500 million kronor. Which means that the price per square foot will be X kronor and it would cost 10,000 a month if you wanted to move in. But unlike the McDonald's example, you don't really have a choice—you have to live somewhere. So you have to pay the going rate."

"Henry, dear, please get to the point."

"But that *is* the point. Why should it cost 10,000 a month to live in those crappy dumps in Hammarbyhamnen? Because the construction companies don't give a damn about keeping prices down. The customer's going to have to pay, come what may. One of the big costs is building materials. The trade in building materials goes through wholesalers who set their own prices. Since there isn't any real competition there, a bathtub retails for 5,000 kronor in Sweden. The same bathtub from the same manufacturer retails for the equivalent of 2,000 kronor in Germany. There is no added cost that can satisfactorily explain the price difference."

There was impatient muttering around the table.

"You can read about a lot of this in a report from the government's Construction Cost Delegation, which was active in the late nineties. Since then not much has happened. No one is talking to the construction companies about the unreasonable prices. The buyers cheerfully pay what they are told it costs, and in the end the price burden falls on the renters or the taxpayers."

"Henry, the toilets?"

"The little that has changed since the Construction Cost Delegation's report has happened at the local level, and primarily outside Stockholm. There are buyers who got fed up with the high construction prices. One example is Karlskrona Homes, which builds houses less expensively than anyone else by buying the materials themselves. And Svensk Handel has also gotten into the game. They think that the price of construction materials is absurd, so they've been trying to make it easier for companies to buy less expensive products that are equally good. And that led to a little clash at the Construction Fair in Älvsjö last year. Svensk Handel had brought in a man from Thailand who was selling toilets for 500 kronor apiece."

"And what happened?"

"His nearest competitor was a Swedish wholesale outfit called Vitavara Inc., which sells genuine Swedish toilets for 1,700 kronor apiece. And shrewd municipal buyers started to scratch their heads and wonder why they were shelling out 1,700 kronor when they could get a similar toilet from Thailand for 500."

"Better quality, maybe," Karim said.

"No. The exact same."

"Thailand," Malm said. "That sounds like child labour and stuff like that. Which could explain the low price."

"Not so," Cortez said. "Child labour exists mostly in the textile and souvenir industries in Thailand. And the paedophile industry, of course. The United Nations keeps an eye on child labour, and I've checked out this company. They're a reputable manufacturer. It's a big, modern, respectable operation producing appliances and plumbing goods."

"All right . . . but we're talking about low-wage countries, and that means you risk writing an article proposing that Swedish industry should be outbid by Thai industry. Fire the Swedish workers and close the factories here, and import everything from Thailand. You won't win any points with the Trade Union Confederation."

A smile spread over Cortez's face. He leaned back and looked ridiculously pleased with himself.

"No again," he said. "Guess where Vitavara Inc. makes its toilets to sell at 1,700 kronor apiece?"

Silence fell over the room.

"Vietnam," Cortez said.

"You've got to be kidding," Eriksson said.

"They've been making toilets there for at least ten years. Swedish workers were already out of that race in the nineties."

"Oh, shit."

"But here comes my point. If you imported directly from the factory in Vietnam, the price would be in the order of 390 kronor. Guess how you can explain the price difference between Thailand and Vietnam?"

"Don't tell me that—"

"Oh yes. Vitavara Inc. subcontracts the work to an outfit called Fong Soo Industries. They're on the UN list of companies that use child labour—at least they were in an investigation from 2001. But the majority of the workers are convicts."

Eriksson burst out laughing. "This is great. This is really great. I'm sure you're going to be a journalist when you grow up. How fast can you have the story ready?"

"Two weeks. I have a lot of international trade stuff to check out. And then we need a bad guy for the story, so I'm going to see who owns Vitavara Inc."

"Then we could run it in the June issue?"

"No problem."

Inspector Bublanski listened to Prosecutor Ekström without expression. The meeting had lasted forty minutes, and Bublanski was feeling an intense desire to reach out and grab the copy of *The Law of the Swedish Kingdom* that lay on the edge of Ekström's desk and ram it down the prosecutor's throat. He wondered what would happen if he acted on his impulse. There would certainly be headlines in the evening papers, and it would probably result in an assault charge. He pushed the thought away. The whole point of the socialized human being was to not give in to that sort of impulse, regardless of how belligerently an opponent might behave. Of course it was usually after somebody had given in to such impulses that Inspector Bublanski was called in.

"I take it we're in agreement," Ekström said.

"No, we are not in agreement," Bublanski said, getting to his feet. "But you're the leader of the preliminary investigation."

He muttered to himself as he turned down the hall to his office, summoning Andersson and Modig as he went. They were the only colleagues available to him that afternoon, as Holmberg had regrettably opted to take a two-week vacation.

"My office," Bublanski said. "Bring some coffee."

After they settled in, Bublanski looked at the notes from his meeting with Ekström.

"As the situation stands, our preliminary investigation leader has dropped all charges against Lisbeth Salander relating to the murders for which she was being sought. She is no longer part of the preliminary investigation as far as we're concerned."

"That can be considered a step forward, at any rate," Modig said.

Andersson, as usual, said nothing.

"I'm not so sure about that," Bublanski said. "Salander is still suspected in connection with the events at Stallarholmen and Gosseberga. But we're no longer involved with those investigations. We have to concentrate on finding Niedermann and working on the graves in the woods at

Nykvarn. On the other hand, it's now clear that Ekström is going to bring charges against Salander. The case has been transferred to Stockholm, and an entirely new investigation has been set up for the purpose."

"Oh, really?" Modig said.

"And who do you think is going to investigate Salander?" Bublanski said.

"I'm fearing the worst."

"Hans Faste is back on duty, and he's going to assist Ekström."

"That's insane. Faste is grossly unsuited to investigate anything at all to do with Salander."

"I know that. But Ekström has a good argument. Faste has been out on sick leave, and this would be the perfect, simple case for him to focus on."

Silence.

"The long and the short of it is that we're to hand over all our material on Salander to him this afternoon."

"And this story about Gunnar Björck and Säpo and the 1991 report . . ."

" . . . is going to be handled by Faste and Ekström."

"I don't like this," Modig said.

"Nor do I. But Ekström's the boss, and he has backing from higher up in the bureaucracy. In other words, our job is still to find the killer. Curt, what's the situation?"

Andersson shook his head. "Niedermann seems to have been swallowed up by the earth. I have to admit that in all my years on the force I've never seen anything like it. We haven't had any tip-offs, and we don't have a single informer who knows him or has any idea where he might be."

"That sounds fishy," Modig said. "But he's being sought for the police murder in Gosseberga, for aggravated assault on another officer, for the attempted murder of Salander, and for the aggravated kidnapping and assault of the dental hygienist Anita Kaspersson, as well as for the murders of Svensson and Johansson. In every instance there's good forensic evidence."

"That helps a bit, at least. How's it going with the case of Svavelsjö MC's treasurer?"

"Viktor Göransson—and his girlfriend, Lena Nygren. We have forensic evidence that ties Niedermann to the scene. Fingerprints and DNA from Göransson's body. Niedermann must have bloodied his knuckles pretty badly during the beating."

"Anything new on Svavelsjö MC?"

"Nieminen has taken over as club president while Lundin remains in custody, awaiting trial for the kidnapping of Miriam Wu. There's a whisper that Nieminen has offered a big reward to anyone who can provide information on Niedermann's whereabouts."

"If the entire underworld is looking for him, it's even stranger that he hasn't been found. What about Göransson's car?"

"Since we found Kaspersson's car at Göransson's place, we're sure that Niedermann switched vehicles. But we have no trace of the car he took."

"So we have to ask ourselves, one, is Niedermann still hiding out somewhere in Sweden? Two, if so, with whom? Three, is he out of the country? What do we think?"

"We have nothing to indicate that he's left the country, but really that seems his most logical course."

"Where did he ditch the car?"

Modig and Andersson shook their heads. Nine times out of ten, police work was uncomplicated when it came to looking for one specific individual. It was about initiating a logical sequence of inquiries. Who were his friends? Who had he been in prison with? Where did his girlfriend live? Who did he drink with? In what area was his mobile last used? Where was his vehicle? At the end of that sequence the fugitive would generally be found.

The problem with Niedermann was that he had no friends, no girlfriend, and no listed mobile, and he had never been in prison.

The inquiries had concentrated on finding Göransson's car, which Niedermann was presumed to be using. They had expected the car to turn up in a matter of days, probably in some parking lot in Stockholm. But there was still no sign of it.

"If he's out of the country, where would he be?"

"He's a German citizen, so the obvious thing would be for him to head for Germany."

"He seems not to have had any contact with his old friends in Hamburg."

Andersson waved his hand. "If his plan was to go to Germany, why would he drive to Stockholm? Shouldn't he have made for Malmö and the bridge to Copenhagen, or for one of the ferries?"

"I know. And Inspector Erlander in Göteborg has been focusing his search in that direction from day one. The Danish police have been informed about Göransson's car, and we know for sure that he didn't take any of the ferries."

"But he did drive to Stockholm and to Svavelsjö, and there he murdered the club's treasurer and—we can assume—made off with an unspecified sum of money. What would his next step be?"

"He has to get out of Sweden," Bublanski said. "The most direct option would be to take one of the ferries across the Baltic. Göransson and his girlfriend were murdered late on the night of April 9. Niedermann could have taken the ferry the next morning. We got the alarm roughly sixteen hours after they died, and we've had an APB out on the car ever since."

"If he took the morning ferry, then Göransson's car would be parked at one of the ports," Modig said.

"Perhaps we haven't found the car because Niedermann drove out of the country to the north via Haparanda? It's a big detour around the Gulf of Bothnia, but in sixteen hours he could have been in Finland."

"Sure, but soon after he would have had to abandon the car in Finland, and it should have been found by now."

They sat in silence. Finally Bublanski got up and stood at the window.

"Could he have found a hiding place where he's just lying low, a summer cabin or—"

"I don't think it would be a summer cabin. This time of year every cabin owner is out checking their property."

"And he wouldn't try anywhere connected to Svavelsjö MC. They're the last people he'd want to run into."

"The entire underworld can be ruled out as well. . . . Any girlfriend we don't know about?"

They could speculate, but they had no facts.

. . .

When Andersson left for the day, Modig went back to Bublanski's office and knocked on the door jamb. He waved her in.

"Do you have a couple of minutes?" she said.

"What's up?"

"Salander. I don't like this business with Ekström and Faste and a new trial. You've read Björck's report. I've read Björck's report. Salander was unlawfully committed in 1991 and Ekström knows it. What the hell is going on?"

Bublanski took off his reading glasses and tucked them into his breast pocket. "I don't know."

"No idea at all?"

"Ekström claims that Björck's report and the correspondence with Teleborian were falsified."

"Bullshit. If it were fake, then Björck would have said so when we brought him in."

"Ekström says Björck refused to discuss it, on the grounds that it was top secret. I was given a dressing down because I jumped the gun and brought him in."

"I'm beginning to have strong reservations about Ekström."

"He's getting squeezed from all sides."

"That's no excuse."

"We don't have a monopoly on the truth, Sonja. Ekström says he's received evidence that the report is a fake—that there is no real report with that protocol number. He also says that the forgery is a good one and that the content is a clever blend of truth and fantasy."

"Which part is truth and which part is fantasy, that's what I need to know," Modig said.

"The frame story is pretty much correct. Zalachenko is

Salander's father, and he was a bastard who beat her mother. The problem is the usual one—the mother never wanted to make a complaint, so it went on for several years. Björck was given the job of finding out what happened when Salander tried to kill her father. He corresponded with Teleborian, but the correspondence we've seen is apparently a forgery. Teleborian did a routine psychiatric examination of Salander and concluded that she was mentally unbalanced. A prosecutor decided not to take the case any further. She needed care, and she got it at St. Stefan's."

"If it is a forgery, who did it and why?"

Bublanski shrugged. "As I understand it, Ekström is going to commission one more thorough evaluation of Salander."

"I can't accept that."

"It's not our case anymore."

"And Faste has replaced us. Jan, I'm going to the media if these bastards piss all over Salander one more time."

"No, Sonja. You won't. First of all, we no longer have access to the report, so you have no way of backing up your claims. You're going to look paranoid, and then your career will be over."

"I still have the report," Modig said in a low voice. "I made a copy for Curt, but I never had a chance to give it to him before the prosecutor general collected the others."

"If you leak that report, you'll not only be fired but you'll be guilty of gross misconduct."

Modig sat in silence for a moment and looked at her superior.

"Sonja, don't do it. Promise me."

"No, Jan. I can't promise that. There's something very sick about this whole story."

"You're right, it is sick. But since we don't know who the enemy is at the moment, you're not going to do anything."

Modig tilted her head to one side. "Are you going to do anything?"

"I'm not going to discuss that with you. Trust me. It's Friday night. Take a break; go home. This discussion never took place."

Niklas Adamsson, the Securitas guard, was studying for a test in three weeks' time. It was 1:30 on Saturday afternoon when he heard the sound of rotating brushes from the low-humming floor polisher and saw that it was the dark-skinned immigrant who walked with a limp. The man would always nod politely but never laughed if Adamsson said anything humorous. Adamsson watched as he took a bottle of cleaning fluid and sprayed the reception counter-top twice before wiping it with a rag. Then he took his mop and swabbed the corners in the reception area where the brushes of the floor polisher couldn't reach. The guard put his nose back into his book about the national economy and kept reading.

It took ten minutes for the cleaner to work his way over to Adamsson's spot at the end of the corridor. They nodded to each other. Adamsson stood to let the man clean the floor around his chair outside Salander's room, as he did almost every day since he had been posted outside the room. Adamsson couldn't remember the cleaner's name—something foreign—but he didn't feel the need to check his ID. For one thing, the man was not allowed to clean inside the prisoner's room—that was done by two cleaning women in the morning—and besides, he didn't seem to be any sort of threat.

When the cleaner had finished in the corridor, he opened the door to the room next to Salander's. Adamsson glanced his way, but this was no deviation from the daily routine. This was where the cleaning supplies were kept. In the course of the next five minutes the man emptied his bucket, cleaned the brushes, and replenished the cart with plastic bags for the wastepaper baskets. Finally he manoeuvred the cart into the cubbyhole.

Ghidi was aware of the guard in the corridor. It was a young blond man who was usually there two or three days a week, reading books. Part-time guard, part-time student. He was about as aware of his surroundings as a brick.

Ghidi wondered what Adamsson would do if someone actually tried to get into the Salander woman's room.

He also wondered what Blomkvist was really after. He had read about the eccentric journalist in the newspapers, and had made the connection to the woman in 11C, expecting that he would be asked to smuggle something in for her. But he didn't have access to her room and had never even seen her. Whatever he had expected, it wasn't this.

He couldn't see anything illegal about his task. He looked through the crack in the doorway at Adamsson, who was once more reading his book. He checked that nobody else was in the corridor. He reached into the pocket of his smock and took out a Sony Ericsson Z600 mobile. Ghidi had seen in an advertisement that it cost around 3,500 kronor and had all the latest features.

He took a screwdriver from his pocket, stood on tiptoe, and unscrewed the three screws in the round white cover of a vent in the wall of Salander's room. He pushed the phone as far into the vent as he could, just as Blomkvist had asked him to. Then he screwed the cover back on.

It took him forty-five seconds. The next day it would take less. He was supposed to get down the mobile, change the batteries, and put it back in the vent. He would then take the used batteries home and recharge them overnight.

That was all Ghidi had to do.

But this wasn't going to be any help to Salander. On her side of the wall there was presumably a similar screwed-on cover. She would never be able to get at the phone, unless she had a screwdriver and a ladder.

"I know that," Blomkvist had said. "But she doesn't have to reach the phone."

Ghidi was to do this every day until Blomkvist told him it was no longer necessary.

And for this job Ghidi would be paid 1,000 kronor a week, straight into his pocket. And he could keep the phone when the job was over.

He knew, of course, that Blomkvist was up to some sort of funny business, but he couldn't work out what it was. Putting a mobile into an air vent inside a locked cleaning supplies room, turned on but not uplinked, was so crazy that Ghidi couldn't imagine what use it could be. If Blomkvist wanted a way of communicating with the patient, he would be better off bribing one of the nurses to smuggle the phone in to her.

On the other hand, he had no objection to doing Blomkvist this favour. He was better off not asking any questions.

. . .

Jonasson slowed his pace when he saw a man with a briefcase leaning on the wrought-iron gates outside his apartment building on Hagagatan. He looked somehow familiar.

"Dr. Jonasson?" he said.

"Yes?"

"Apologies for bothering you on the street outside your home. It's just that I didn't want to track you down at work, and I do need to talk to you."

"What's this about, and who are you?"

"My name is Blomkvist, Mikael Blomkvist. I'm a journalist, and I work at *Millennium* magazine. It's about Lisbeth Salander."

"Oh, now I recognize you. You were the one who called the paramedics. Was it you who put duct tape on her wounds?"

"Yes."

"That was a smart thing to do. But I don't discuss my patients with journalists. You'll have to speak to the PR department at Sahlgrenska, like everyone else."

"You misunderstand me. I don't want information, and I'm here in a completely private capacity. You don't have to say a word or give me any information. Quite the opposite: I want to give you some."

Jonasson frowned.

"Please hear me out," Blomkvist said. "I don't go around accosting surgeons on the street, but what I have to tell you is very important. Can I buy you a cup of coffee?"

"Tell me what it's about."

"It's about Lisbeth Salander's future and well-being. I'm a friend."

Jonasson thought that if it had been anyone other than Blomkvist he would have refused. But Blomkvist was a man in the public eye, and Jonasson couldn't imagine that this would be some sort of monkey business.

"I won't under any circumstances be interviewed, and I won't discuss my patient."

"Perfectly understood," Blomkvist said.

Jonasson accompanied Blomkvist to a nearby café.

"So what's this all about?" he said when they had gotten their coffee.

"First of all, I'm not going to quote you, or even mention you in anything I write. And as far as I'm concerned this conversation never took place. That said, I am here to ask you a favour. But I have to explain why, so that you can decide whether you can or you can't do it."

"I don't like the sound of this."

"All I ask is that you hear me out. It's your job to take care of Lisbeth's physical and mental health. As her friend, it's my job to do the same. I can't poke around in her skull and extract bullets, but I have another skill that is as crucial to her welfare."

"Which is?"

"I'm an investigative journalist, and I've found out the truth about what happened to her."

"OK."

"I can tell you in general terms what it's about and you can come to your own conclusions."

"All right."

"I should also say that Annika Giannini, Lisbeth's lawyer—you've met her, I think—is my sister, and I'm the one paying her to defend Salander."

"I see."

"I can't, obviously, ask Annika to do this favour. She has to keep her conversations with Lisbeth confidential. I assume you've read about Lisbeth in the newspapers."

Jonasson nodded.

"She's been described as psychotic, and as a mentally ill lesbian mass murderer. All that is nonsense. Lisbeth Salander is not psychotic. She is probably as sane as you and I. And her sexual preferences are nobody's business."

"If I've understood the matter correctly, there's been some reassessment of the case. Now it's this German who's being sought in connection with the murders."

"Yes. Niedermann is a murderer utterly without conscience. But Lisbeth has enemies. Big, nasty enemies. Some of them are in the Security Police."

Jonasson looked at Blomkvist in astonishment.

"When Lisbeth was twelve, she was put in a children's psychiatric clinic in Uppsala. Why? Because she had stirred up a secret that Säpo was trying at any price to keep a lid on. Her father, Alexander Zalachenko—otherwise known as Karl Axel Bodin, who was murdered in your hospital—was a Soviet defector, a spy, a relic from the Cold War. He also beat up Lisbeth's mother year after year. When Lisbeth was twelve, she struck back and tried to kill him with a Molotov cocktail. That was why she was locked up."

"I don't understand. If she tried to kill her father, then surely there was good reason to take her in for psychiatric treatment."

"The story I am going to publish is that Säpo knew that Zalachenko was abusive—the beating that provoked Lisbeth's attack put her mother in a nursing home for the rest of her life—but they chose to protect him because he was a source of valuable information. So they faked a diagnosis to make sure that Lisbeth was committed."

Jonasson looked so sceptical that Blomkvist had to laugh.

"I can document every detail. And I'm going to write a full account in time for Lisbeth's trial. Believe me, it's going to cause an uproar."

"Go on."

"I'm going to expose two doctors who were errand boys for Säpo, and who helped bury Lisbeth in the asylum. I'm going to hang them out to dry. One of them is a well-known and respected person."

"If a doctor was mixed up in something like this, it's a blot on the entire profession."

"I don't believe in collective guilt. It concerns only those directly involved. The same is true of Säpo. I don't doubt that there are excellent people working in Säpo. This is about a small group of conspirators. When Lisbeth was eighteen they tried to institutionalize her again. This time they failed, and she was instead put under guardianship. In the trial, whenever it is, they're once again going to try to throw as much shit at her as they can. I—or rather, my sister, Annika—will fight to see that she is acquitted, and that her declaration of incompetence is revoked."

"I see."

"But she needs ammunition. So that's the background for this tactic. I should probably also mention that there are some individuals in the police force who are actually on Lisbeth's side in all this. But not the prosecutor who brought the charges against her. In short, Lisbeth needs help before the trial."

"I'm not a lawyer."

"No. But you're Lisbeth's doctor, and you have access to her."

Jonasson's eyes narrowed.

"What I'm thinking of asking you is unethical and might also be illegal."

"Indeed?"

"But morally it's the right thing to do. Her constitutional rights are being violated by the very people who ought to be protecting her. Let me give you an example. Lisbeth is not allowed to have visitors, and she can't read newspapers or communicate with the outside world. The prosecutor has also pushed through a prohibition of disclosure for her lawyer. Annika has obeyed the rules. However, the prosecutor himself is the primary source of leaks to the reporters who keep writing all the shit about Lisbeth."

"Really?"

"This story, for example." Blomkvist held up a week-old evening newspaper. "A source within the investigation claims that Lisbeth is non compos mentis, which prompted the newspaper to speculate about her mental state."

"I read the article. It's nonsense."

"So you don't think she's crazy."

"I won't comment on that. But I do know that no psychiatric evaluations have been done. Accordingly, the article is nonsense."

"I can prove that the person who leaked this information is a police officer named Hans Faste. He works for Prosecutor Ekström."

"Hmm."

"Ekström is going to insist that the trial take place behind closed doors, so that no outsider can examine or evaluate the evidence against Lisbeth. But what's worse, because the prosecutor has isolated Lisbeth, she won't be able to do the research she needs to prepare her defence."

"Isn't that supposed to be done by her lawyer?"

"As you must have gathered by now, Lisbeth is an extraordinary person. She has secrets I happen to know about but can't reveal to my sister. But Lisbeth should be able to choose whether she wants to make use of them in her trial."

"I see."

"And in order to do that, she needs this."

Blomkvist laid Salander's Palm Tungsten T3 handheld computer and a battery charger on the table between them.

"This is the most important weapon Lisbeth has in her arsenal—she has to have it."

Jonasson looked suspiciously at the Palm.

"Why not give it to her lawyer?"

"Because Lisbeth is the only one who knows how to get at the evidence."

Jonasson sat for a while, still not touching the computer.

"Let me tell you one or two things about Dr. Peter Teleborian," Blomkvist said, taking a folder from his briefcase.

It was just after 8:00 on Saturday evening when Armansky left his office and walked to the synagogue of the Söder congregation on St. Paulsgatan. He knocked on the door, introduced himself, and was admitted by the rabbi himself.

"I have an appointment to meet someone I know here," Armansky said.

"One flight up. I'll show you the way."

The rabbi offered him a yarmulke for his head, which

Armansky hesitantly put on. He had been brought up in a Muslim family and he felt foolish wearing it.

Bublanski was also wearing a yarmulke.

"Hello, Dragan. Thanks for coming. I've borrowed a room from the rabbi so we can speak undisturbed."

Armansky sat down across from Bublanski.

"I presume you have good reason for such secrecy."

"I'm not going to drag this out: I know that you're a friend of Salander's."

Armansky nodded.

"I need to know what you and Blomkvist have cooked up to help her."

"Why would we be cooking something up?"

"Because Prosecutor Ekström has asked me a dozen times how much you at Milton Security actually knew about the Salander investigation. It's not a casual question—he's concerned that you're going to spring something that could result in repercussions . . . in the media."

"I see."

"And if Ekström is worried, it's because he knows or suspects that you've got something brewing. Or at least he's talked to someone who has suspicions."

"Someone?"

"Dragan, let's not play games. You know Salander was the victim of an injustice in the early nineties, and I'm afraid she's going to get the same medicine when the trial begins."

"You're a police officer in a democracy. If you have information to that effect you should take action."

Bublanski nodded. "I'm thinking of doing just that. The question is, how?"

"Tell me what you want to know."

"I want to know what you and Blomkvist are up to. I assume you're not just sitting there twiddling your thumbs."

"It's complicated. How do I know I can trust you?"

"There's a report from 1991 that Blomkvist discovered . . ."

"I know about it."

"I no longer have access to the report."

"Nor do I. The copies that Blomkvist and his sister—now Salander's lawyer—had in their possession have both disappeared."

"Disappeared?"

"Blomkvist's copy was taken during a break-in at his apartment, and Giannini's was stolen when she was mugged in Göteborg. All this happened on the day Zalachenko was murdered."

Bublanski said nothing for a long while.

"Why haven't we heard anything about this?"

"Blomkvist put it like this: there's only one right time to publish a story, and an endless number of wrong times."

"But you two . . . he'll publish it?"

Armansky gave a curt nod.

"A nasty attack in Göteborg and a break-in here in Stockholm. On the same day," Bublanski said. "That means our adversary is well organized."

"I should probably also mention that we know Giannini's phone is tapped."

"Someone is committing a whole bunch of crimes."

"The question is, who?"

"That's what I'm wondering. Most likely it's Säpo—they would have an interest in suppressing Björck's report. But Dragan, we're talking about the Swedish Security Police, a government agency. I can't believe this would be sanctioned by Säpo. I don't even believe Säpo has the expertise to do anything like this."

"I'm having trouble digesting it myself. Not to mention that someone saunters into Sahlgrenska and blows Zalachenko's head off. And at the same time, Gunnar Björck, author of the report, hangs himself."

"So you think there's a single hand behind all this? I know Inspector Erlander, who did the investigation in Göteborg. He said there was nothing to indicate that the murder was other than the impulsive act of a sick man. And we did a thorough investigation of Björck's place. Everything points towards a suicide."

"Gullberg, seventy-eight years old, suffering from cancer, recently treated for depression. Our operations chief, Johan Fräklund, has been looking into his background."

"And?"

"He did his military service in Karlskrona in the forties, studied law, and eventually became a tax adviser. Had an office here in Stockholm for thirty years: low profile, private clients . . . whoever they might have been. Retired in 1991. Moved back to his hometown of Laholm in 1994. Unremarkable, except—"

"Except what?"

"Except for one or two surprising details. Fräklund cannot find a single reference to Gullberg anywhere. He's never referred to in any newspaper or trade journal, and there's no-one who can tell us who his clients were. It's as if he never actually existed in the professional world."

"What are you saying?"

"Säpo is the obvious link. Zalachenko was a Soviet defector. Who else but Säpo would have taken charge of him?

Then there's the question of a coordinated strategy to get Salander locked away in an institution. Now we have burglaries, muggings, and telephone tapping. But I don't think Säpo is behind this. Blomkvist calls them 'the Zalachenko club,' a small group of dormant Cold War mongers who hide out in some dark hallway at Säpo."

"So what can we do?" Bublanski said.

CHAPTER 12

Sunday, May 15–
Monday, May 16

Superintendent Torsten Edklinth, director of Constitutional Protection at the Security Police, slowly swirled his glass of red wine and listened attentively to the CEO of Milton Security, who had called out of the blue and insisted Edklinth come to Sunday dinner at his place on Lidingö. Armansky's wife, Ritva, had made a delicious casserole. They had eaten well and talked politely about nothing in particular. Edklinth was wondering what was on Armansky's mind. After dinner Ritva repaired to the sofa to watch TV and left them at the table. Armansky began to tell him the story of Lisbeth Salander.

Edklinth and Armansky had known each other for twelve years, ever since a female member of Parliament had received death threats. She'd reported the matter to the head of her party, and Parliament's security detail was informed. In due course the matter came to the attention of the Security Police. At that time, Personal Protection had the smallest budget of any unit. The member of Parliament was given surveillance during the course of her official appearances but was left to her own devices at the end of the working day, the time when she was obviously more vulnerable. She began to have doubts about the ability of the Security Police to protect her.

She arrived home late one evening to discover that someone had broken in, daubed sexually explicit epithets on her living-room walls, and masturbated in her bed. She immediately hired Milton Security to take over her personal protection. She did not advise Säpo of this decision. The next morning, when she was due to appear at a school in Täby, there was a confrontation between the government security forces and her Milton bodyguards.

At that time, Edklinth was acting deputy chief of Personal Protection. He instinctively disliked a situation in which private muscle was doing what a government department was supposed to do. But he recognized that the member of Parliament had reason enough for complaint. Instead of exacerbating the issue, he invited Milton Security's CEO to lunch. They agreed that the situation might be more serious than Säpo had at first assumed, and Edklinth realized that Armansky's people not only had the skills for the job, but also that they were as well trained and probably better equipped. They solved the immediate problem by giving Armansky's people responsibility for bodyguard services, while the Security Police took care of the criminal investigation and paid the bill.

The two men discovered that they liked each other a good deal, and they enjoyed working together on a number of assignments in subsequent years. Edklinth had great respect for Armansky, so when he was invited to dinner and to have a private conversation, he was willing to listen.

But he had not anticipated Armansky's lobbing a bomb with a sizzling fuse into his lap.

"You're telling me that the Security Police is involved in flagrant criminal activity."

"No," Armansky said. "You misunderstand me. I'm saying that some people within the Security Police are involved in such activity. I don't believe that this activity is sanctioned by the leadership of SIS, or that it has government approval."

Edklinth studied Malm's photographs of a man getting into a car with a registration number that began with the letters KAB.

"Dragan . . . this isn't a practical joke?"

"I wish it were."

The next morning Edklinth was in his office at police headquarters, meticulously cleaning his glasses. He was a grey-haired man with big ears and a powerful face, but for the moment his expression was more puzzled than powerful. He had spent most of the night worrying about how to deal with the information Armansky had given him.

They were not pleasant thoughts. The Security Police was an institution in Sweden that all parties (well, almost all) agreed had an indispensable value. This led them to distrust the group and at the same time concoct imaginative conspiracy theories about it. The scandals had undoubtedly been many, especially in the leftist-radical seventies when a number of constitutional blunders had certainly occurred. But after five governmental—and roundly criticized—Säpo investigations, a new generation of civil servants had come through. They represented a younger school of activists recruited from the financial, weapons, and fraud units of the state police.

They were officers used to investigating real crimes, not chasing political mirages. The Security Police had been modernized, and the Constitutional Protection Unit in particular had taken on a new, conspicuous role. Its task, as set out in the government's instructions, was to uncover and prevent threats to the internal security of the nation, that is, "unlawful activity that uses violence, threat, or coercion for the purpose of altering our form of government, inducing decision-making political entities or authorities to take decisions in a certain direction, or preventing individual citizens from exercising their constitutionally protected rights and liberties."

In short, to defend Swedish democracy against real or presumed anti-democratic threats. They were chiefly concerned with the anarchists and the neo-Nazis: the anarchists because they persisted in practicing civil disobedience, the neo-Nazis because they were by definition the enemies of democracy.

After completing his law degree, Edklinth had worked as a prosecutor, and then twenty-one years ago joined the Security Police. He had at first worked in the field in the Personal Protection Unit, then within the Constitutional Protection Unit as an analyst and administrator. Eventually he became director of the agency, the head of the police forces responsible for the defence of Swedish democracy. He considered himself a democrat. The constitution had been established by Parliament, and it was his job to see that it stayed intact.

Swedish democracy is based on a single premise: the Right to Free Speech (RFS). This guarantees the inalienable right to say, think, and believe anything whatsoever. It embraces all Swedish citizens, from the crazy neo-Nazi living in the woods to the rock-throwing anarchist—and everyone in between.

Every other basic right, such as the Formation of Government and the Right to Freedom of Organization, are simply practical extensions of the Right to Free Speech. On this law democracy stands or falls.

All democracy has its limits, and the limits to the RFS are set by the Freedom of the Press regulation (FP). This defines four restrictions on democracy. It is forbidden to publish child pornography and the depiction of certain violent sexual acts, regardless of how artistic the originator believes the depiction to be. It is forbidden to incite or exhort someone to commit a crime. It is forbidden to defame or slander another person. It is forbidden to engage in the persecution of an ethnic group.

Press freedom has also been enshrined by Parliament and is based on the socially and democratically acceptable restrictions of society, that is, the social contract that makes up the framework of a civilized society. The core of the legislation states that no person has the right to harass or humiliate another person.

Since RFS and FP are laws, some sort of authority is needed to guarantee the observance of these laws. In Sweden this function is divided between two institutions.

The first is the office of the prosecutor general, assigned to prosecute crimes against FP. This did not please Torsten Edklinth. In his view, the prosecutor general was too lenient with cases concerning what were, in his view, direct crimes against the Swedish constitution. The prosecutor general usually replied that the principle of democracy was so important that it was only in an extreme emergency that he should step in and bring a charge. This attitude, however, had come under question more and more in recent years, particularly after Robert Hårdh, the general secretary of the

Swedish Helsinki Committee, submitted a report which examined the prosecutor general's lack of initiative over a number of years. The report claimed that it was almost impossible to charge and convict anyone under the law of persecution against an ethnic group.

The second institution is the Security Police division for Constitutional Protection, and Superintendent Edklinth took on this responsibility with the utmost seriousness. He thought it was the most important post a Swedish policeman could hold, and he wouldn't have exchanged his appointment for any other position in the entire Swedish legal system or police force. He was the only policeman in Sweden whose official job description was to function as a political police officer. It was a delicate task requiring great wisdom and judicial restraint, since far too many countries have shown that a political police department can easily transform itself into the principal threat to democracy.

The media and the public assumed for the most part that the main function of the Constitutional Protection Unit was to keep track of Nazis and militant vegans. These types of groups did attract interest from the Constitutional Protection Unit, but a great many institutions and phenomena also fell under the auspices of the division. If the king, for example, or the commander-in-chief of the armed forces, happened to decide that Parliament should be replaced by a dictatorship, they would very swiftly come under observation by the Constitutional Protection Unit. Or, to give a second example, if a group of police officers decided to stretch the laws so that an individual's constitutionally guaranteed rights were infringed, then it was the Constitutional Protection Unit's duty to react. In such serious instances the investigation also came under the authority of the prosecutor general.

The problem, of course, was that the Constitutional Protection Unit had only an analytical and investigative function, and no operations arm. That was why generally either the regular police or other divisions within the Security Police stepped in when neo-Nazis were to be arrested.

In Edklinth's opinion, this state of affairs was deeply unsatisfactory. Almost every democratic country maintains an independent constitutional court in some form, with a mandate to see to it that authorities do not ride roughshod over the democratic process. In Sweden the task is that of the prosecutor general or the parliamentary ombudsman, who, however, can only pursue recommendations forwarded to them by other departments. If Sweden had a constitutional court, then Salander's lawyer could instantly charge the Swedish government with the violation of her constitutional rights. The court could then order all the documents on the table and summon anyone it pleased, including the prime minister, to testify until the matter was resolved. But in the current situation, the most her lawyer could do was file a report with the parliamentary ombudsman, who didn't have the authority to walk into the Security Police and start demanding documents and other evidence.

Over the years, Edklinth had been an impassioned advocate of the establishment of a constitutional court. He could then more easily act upon the information he had been given by Armansky. But as things stood, Edklinth lacked the legal authority to initiate a preliminary investigation.

He took a pinch of snuff.

If Armansky's information was correct, Security Police

officers in senior positions had looked the other way when a series of savage assaults were committed against a Swedish woman. Then her daughter was locked up in a mental hospital on the basis of a fabricated diagnosis. Finally, they had given carte blanche to a former Soviet intelligence officer to commit crimes involving weapons, narcotics, and sex trafficking. Edklinth grimaced. He did not even want to begin to estimate how many counts of illegal activity must have taken place. Not to mention the burglary at Blomkvist's apartment, the attack on Salander's lawyer—which Edklinth could not bring himself to accept was part of the same pattern—and possible involvement in the murder of Zalachenko.

It was a mess, and Edklinth didn't feel the slightest desire to get mixed up in it. Unfortunately, he had become involved from the moment Armansky invited him to dinner.

How now to handle the situation? Technically, the answer was simple. If Armansky's account was true, Lisbeth Salander had at the very least been deprived of the opportunity to exercise her constitutionally protected rights and liberties. From a constitutional standpoint, this was the first can of worms. Decision-making political bodies had been induced to make certain decisions. This too touched on the core of the responsibility delegated to the Constitutional Protection Unit. Edklinth, a policeman, had knowledge of a crime, and thus he had the obligation to submit a report to a prosecutor. In real life, the answer was not so simple. It was, to put it mildly, complicated.

Inspector Monica Figuerola, in spite of her unusual name, was born in Dalarna to a family that had lived in Sweden at least since the time of Gustavus Vasa in the sixteenth century.

She was a woman whom people usually paid attention to, for several reasons. She was thirty-six, blue eyed, and six feet tall. She had short, light blond, naturally curly hair. She was attractive and dressed in a way that she knew made her more so. And she was in exceptionally good shape.

She had been a top-level gymnast in her teens and almost qualified for the Olympic team when she was seventeen. She had given up classic gymnastics but still worked out obsessively at the gym five nights a week. She exercised so often that the endorphins her body produced functioned as a drug that made it difficult for her to stop training. She ran, lifted weights, played tennis, did karate. She had cut back on bodybuilding, that extreme variant of bodily glorification, some years ago. In those days she was spending two hours a day pumping iron. Even so, she trained so hard and her body was so muscular that malicious colleagues still called her Herr Figuerola. When she wore a sleeveless T-shirt or a summer dress, no-one could fail to notice her biceps and powerful shoulders.

Her intelligence too intimidated many of her male colleagues. She had left school with top grades, studied to become a police officer at twenty, then served for nine years in Uppsala and studied law in her spare time. For fun, she said, she had also studied for a degree in political science.

When she left patrol duty to become a criminal inspector, it was a great loss to Uppsala street safety. She worked first in the violent crimes division and then in the unit that specialized in financial crime. In 2000 she applied to the Security Police in Uppsala, and by 2001 she had moved to Stockholm. She first worked in Counter-Espionage, but she was almost immediately hand-picked by Edklinth for the Constitutional

Protection Unit. He happened to know Figuerola's father and had followed her career over the years.

When at long last Edklinth concluded that he had to act on Armansky's information, he called Figuerola into his office. She had been at Constitutional Protection for less than three years, which meant she was still more of a real police officer than a desk warrior.

She was dressed that day in tight blue jeans, turquoise sandals with a low heel, and a navy blue jacket.

"What are you working on at the moment, Monica?"

"We're following up on the robbery of the grocer's in Sunne."

Figuerola was the head of a department of five officers working on political crimes. They relied heavily on computers connected to the incident-reporting network of the regular police. Nearly every report submitted in any police district in Sweden passed through the computers in Figuerola's department. The software scanned every report and reacted to 310 keywords—*nigger,* for example, or *skinhead, swastika, immigrant, anarchist, Hitler salute, Nazi, National Democrat, traitor, Jew-lover,* or *nigger-lover.* If such a keyword cropped up, the report would be printed out and scrutinized.

The Constitutional Protection Unit publishes an annual report, "Threats to National Security," which supplies the only reliable statistics on political crime. These statistics are based on reports filed with local police authorities. The Security Police did not normally spend time investigating robberies of groceries, but in the case of the robbery of the shop in Sunne, the computer had reacted to three keywords: *immigrant, shoulder patch,* and *nigger.* Two masked men had robbed at gunpoint a shop owned by an immigrant. They had taken 2,780 kronor and a carton of cigarettes. One of the robbers had a mid-length jacket with a Swedish flag shoulder patch. The other had screamed "Fucking nigger" several times at the manager and forced him to lie on the floor.

This was enough for Figuerola's team to initiate the preliminary investigation: to inquire whether the robbers had a connection to the neo-Nazi gang in Värmland, and whether the robbery could be defined as a racist crime. If so, the incident might be included in that year's statistical compilation, which would then itself be incorporated within the European statistics put together by the EU's office in Vienna.

"I have a difficult assignment for you," Edklinth said. "It's a job that could land you in big trouble. Your career might be ruined. But if things go well, it could be a major step forward for you."

"I'm all ears."

"I'm thinking of moving you to the Constitutional Protection operations unit."

"Forgive me for mentioning this, but Constitutional Protection doesn't have an operations unit."

"Yes, it does," Edklinth said. "I established it this morning. At present it consists of you."

"I see," said Figuerola hesitantly.

"The task of Constitutional Protection is to defend the constitution against what we call 'internal threats,' most often those on the extreme left or the extreme right. But what do we do if a threat to the constitution comes from within our own organization?"

For the next half hour he told her what Armansky had told him the night before.

"Who is the source of these claims?" Figuerola said when the story was ended.

"Focus on the information, not the source."

"What I'm wondering is whether you consider the source to be reliable."

"I consider the source to be totally reliable. I've known this person for many years."

"It all sounds a bit . . . I don't know. Improbable?"

"I know. It's the stuff of a spy novel."

"How do you expect me to go about tackling it?"

"Starting now, you're released from all other duties. Your task, your only task, is to investigate the truth of this story. You have to either verify or dismiss the claims one by one. You report directly and only to me."

"I see what you mean when you say I might land in it up to my neck."

"But if the story is true—if even a fraction of it is true—then we have a constitutional crisis on our hands."

"Where do you want me to begin?"

"Start with the simple things. First, read the Björck report. Then identify the people who are allegedly tailing this guy Blomkvist. According to my source, the car belongs to Göran Mårtensson, a police officer living on Vittangigatan in Vällingby. Then identify the other person in the pictures taken by Blomkvist's photographer. The younger blond man here."

Figuerola was making notes.

"Then look into Gullberg's background. I'd never heard his name before, but my source believes there's a connection between him and the Security Police."

"So somebody here at SIS put out a contract on a former spy using a seventy-eight-year-old man. I don't believe it."

"Nevertheless, check it out. Your entire investigation has to be carried out without a single person other than me knowing anything at all about it. Before you take any action I want to be informed. I don't want to see any rings on the water."

"This is one hell of an investigation. How am I going to do all this alone?"

"You won't have to. You have to do only the first check. If you come back and say that you didn't find anything, then everything is fine. If you come back having found *anything* as my source describes it, then we'll decide what to do."

Figuerola spent her lunch hour pumping iron in the police gym. Lunch consisted of black coffee and a meatball sandwich with beet salad, which she took back to her office. She closed her door, cleared her desk, and started reading the Björck report while she ate.

She also read the appendix with the correspondence between Björck and Dr. Teleborian. She made a note of every name and every incident in the report that had to be verified. After two hours she got up, went to the coffee machine, and got a refill. When she left her office she locked the door, part of the routine at SIS.

Back at her desk, the first thing she did was check the report's protocol number. She called the registrar and was informed that no report with that protocol number existed. Her second check was to consult a media archive. That yielded better results. The evening papers and a morning paper had reported a person being badly injured in a car fire on Lundagatan on the date in question in 1991. The victim of the incident was a middle-aged man, but no name was given. One evening paper reported that, according to a witness, the fire had been started deliberately by a young girl.

Gunnar Björck, the author of the report, was a real person. He was a senior official in the immigration unit, lately on sick leave and now, very recently, deceased—a suicide.

The personnel department had no information about what Björck had been working on in 1991. The file was stamped TOP SECRET, even for other employees at SIS. Which was routine.

It was a straightforward matter to establish that Salander had lived with her mother and twin sister on Lundagatan in 1991 and spent the following two years at St. Stefan's children's psychiatric clinic. In these sections at least, the record corresponded with the report's contents.

Peter Teleborian, now a well-known psychiatrist often seen on TV, had worked at St. Stefan's in 1991 and was today its senior physician.

Figuerola then called the assistant head of the personnel department.

"We're working on an analysis here in CP that requires evaluating a person's credibility and general mental health. I need to consult a psychiatrist or some other professional who's approved to handle classified information. Dr. Peter Teleborian was mentioned to me, and I was wondering whether I could hire him."

It took a while before she got an answer.

"Dr. Teleborian has been an external consultant for SIS in

a couple of instances. He has security clearance, and you can discuss classified information with him in general terms. But before you approach him, you have to follow the bureaucratic procedure. Your supervisor must approve the consultation and make a formal request for you to be allowed to approach Dr. Teleborian."

Her heart sank. She had verified something that could be known only to a very restricted group of people. Teleborian had indeed had dealings with SIS.

She put down the report and focused her attention on other aspects of the information that Edklinth had given her. She studied the photographs of the two men who had allegedly followed the journalist Blomkvist from Café Copacabana on May 1.

She consulted the vehicle registry and found that Göran Mårtensson was the owner of a grey Volvo with the registration number legible in the photographs. Then she got confirmation from the SIS personnel department that he was employed there. Her heart sank again.

Mårtensson worked in Personal Protection. He was a bodyguard. He was one of the officers responsible on formal occasions for the safety of the prime minister. For the past few weeks he had been loaned to Counter-Espionage. His leave of absence had begun on April 10, a couple of days after Zalachenko and Salander had landed in Sahlgrenska hospital. But that sort of temporary reassignment was not unusual—covering a shortage of personnel here or there in an emergency situation.

Then Figuerola called the assistant chief of Counter-Espionage, a man she knew and had worked for during her short time in that department. Was Göran Mårtensson working on anything important, or could he be borrowed for an investigation in Constitutional Protection?

The assistant chief of Counter-Espionage was puzzled. Inspector Figuerola must have been misinformed. Mårtensson had not been reassigned to Counter-Espionage. Sorry.

Figuerola stared at her receiver for two minutes. In Personal Protection they believed that Mårtensson had been loaned out to Counter-Espionage. Counter-Espionage said that they definitely had *not* borrowed him. Transfers of that kind had to be approved by the chief of Secretariat. She reached for the phone to call him, but stopped short. If Personal Protection had loaned out Mårtensson, then the chief of Secretariat must have approved the decision. But Mårtensson was not at Counter-Espionage, which the chief of Secretariat must be aware of. And if Mårtensson was loaned out to some department that was tailing journalists, then the chief of Secretariat would have to know about that too.

Edklinth had told her he didn't want any rings in the water. To raise the matter with the chief of Secretariat might be to chuck a very large stone into a pond.

Berger sat at her desk in the glass cage. It was 10:30 on Monday morning. She badly needed the cup of coffee she had just gotten from the machine in the cafeteria. The first hours of her workday had been taken up entirely with meetings, starting with one lasting fifteen minutes in which Assistant Editor Fredriksson presented the guidelines for the day's work. She was increasingly dependent on Fredriksson's judgement due to her loss of confidence in Anders Holm.

The second was an hour-long meeting with the CEO, Magnus Borgsjö; *SMP*'s CFO, Christer Sellberg; and Ulf Flodin, the budget chief. The discussion was about the slump in advertising and the downturn in single-copy sales. The budget chief and the CFO were both determined to cut the newspaper's overhead.

"We made it through the first quarter of this year thanks to a marginal rise in advertising sales and the fact that two senior, highly paid employees retired. Those positions have not been filled," Flodin said. "We'll probably close out the present quarter with a small deficit. But the free papers, *Metro* and *Stockholm City,* are cutting into our ad revenue in Stockholm. My prognosis is that the third quarter will produce a significant loss."

"So how do we counter that?" Borgsjö said.

"The only option is cutbacks. We haven't laid anyone off since 2002. But before the end of the year we will have to eliminate ten positions."

"Which positions?" Berger said.

"We need to work on the 'cheese plane' principle—shave a job here and a job there. The sports desk has six and a half jobs at the moment. We should cut that to five full-timers."

"As I understand it, the sports desk is on its knees already. What you're proposing means that we'll have to cut back on sports coverage."

Flodin shrugged. "I'll gladly listen to other suggestions."

"I don't have any better suggestions, but the principle is this: if we cut personnel, then we have to produce a smaller newspaper, and if we make a smaller newspaper, the number of readers will drop, and the number of advertisers too."

"The eternal vicious circle," Sellberg said.

"I was hired to turn this downward trend around," said Berger. "I see my job as taking an aggressive approach to change the newspaper and make it more attractive to readers. I can't do that if I have to cut staff." She turned to Borgsjö. "How long can the paper continue to bleed? How big a deficit can we take before we hit the limit?"

Borgsjö pursed his lips. "Since the early nineties *SMP* has eaten into a great many old consolidated assets. We have a stock portfolio that has dropped in value by about 30 percent compared to ten years ago. A large portion of these funds were used for investments in IT. We've also had enormous expenses."

"I gather that *SMP* has developed its own text editing system, the AXT. What did that cost?"

"About five million kronor to develop."

"Why did *SMP* go to the trouble of developing its own software? There are inexpensive commercial programmes already on the market."

"Well, Erika, that may be true. Our former IT chief talked us into it. He persuaded us that it would be less expensive in the long run, and that *SMP* would also be able to licence the programme to other newspapers."

"Did any of them buy it?"

"Yes, as a matter of fact—a local paper in Norway."

"Meanwhile," Berger said in a dry voice, "we're sitting here with PCs that are five or six years old. . . ."

"It's simply out of the question that we invest in new computers in the coming year," Flodin said.

The discussion had gone back and forth. Berger was aware that her objections were being systematically stonewalled by Flodin and Sellberg. For them, cost cutting was what counted, which was understandable enough from the point of view of a budget chief and a CFO, but it was unacceptable for a newly appointed editor in chief. What irritated her most was that they kept brushing off her arguments with patronizing smiles, making her feel like a teenager being quizzed on her homework. Without actually uttering a single inappropriate word, they displayed an attitude that was so antediluvian it was almost comical. *You shouldn't worry your pretty head over complex matters, little girl.*

Borgsjö wasn't much help. She didn't sense the same condescension from him, but he was biding his time and letting the other participants at the meeting say their piece.

She sighed and plugged in her laptop. She had nineteen new emails. Four were spam. Someone wanted to sell her Viagra, cybersex with "The Sexiest Lolitas on the Net" for only $4.00 per minute, "Animal Sex, the Juiciest Horse Fuck in the Universe," and a subscription to fashion.nu. The tide of this crap never receded, no matter how many times she tried to block it. Another seven messages were those so-called Nigeria letters from the widow of the former head of a bank in Abu Dhabi offering her ludicrous sums of money if she would only assist with a small sum of start-up money, and other such junk.

There was the morning memo, the lunchtime memo, three emails from Fredriksson updating her on developments in the day's lead story, one from her accountant, who wanted a meeting to discuss the implications of her move from *Millennium* to *SMP*, and a message from her dental hygienist suggesting a time for her quarterly visit. She put the appointment in her calendar and realized at once that she would have to change it because she had a major editorial conference planned for that day.

Finally she opened the last one, sent from <centraled@ smpost.se> with the subject line

[Attn: Editor in Chief].

Slowly she put down her coffee cup.

```
YOU WHORE! YOU THINK YOU'RE SOMETHING,
YOU FUCKING CUNT: DON'T THINK YOU CAN
COME HERE AND THROW YOUR WEIGHT
AROUND. YOU'RE GOING TO GET FUCKED IN
THE CUNT WITH A SCREWDRIVER, WHORE! THE
SOONER YOU DISAPPEAR THE BETTER.
```

Berger looked up and searched for the news editor, Holm. He was not at his desk, nor could she see him in the newsroom. She checked the sender and then picked up the phone and called Peter Fleming, the IT manager.

"Good morning, Peter. Who uses the address <centraled @smpost.se>?"

"That isn't a valid address at *SMP*."

"I just got an email from that address."

"It's a fake. Does the message contain a virus?"

"I wouldn't know. At least, the antivirus programme didn't react."

"OK. It's very simple to fake an apparently legitimate address. There are sites on the Net that you can use to send anonymous mail."

"Is it possible to trace an email like that?"

"Almost impossible, even if the person in question is so stupid that he sends it from his home computer. You might be able to trace the IP number to a server, but if he uses an account that he set up at Hotmail, for instance, the trail will fizzle out."

Berger thanked him. She thought for a moment. It was not the first time she had received a threatening email or a message from a crackpot. This one was obviously referring to her new job as editor in chief. She wondered whether it was some lunatic who had read about her in connection with Morander's death, or whether the sender was in the building.

Figuerola thought long and hard about how to investigate Gullberg. One advantage of working at Constitutional Protection was that she had the authority to access almost any police report in Sweden that might have any connection to racially or politically motivated crimes. Zalachenko was technically an immigrant, and her job included tracking violence against persons born abroad to decide whether or not the crime was racially motivated. Accordingly, she had the right to involve herself in the investigation of Zalachenko's murder, to determine whether Gullberg, the known killer, had a connection to any racist organization, or whether he was overheard making racist remarks at the time of the murder. She requisitioned the report. She found the letters that had been sent to the minister of justice and discovered that alongside the diatribe and the insulting personal attacks were also the words *nigger-lover* and *traitor*.

By then it was 5:00 p.m. Figuerola locked all the material in her safe, shut down her computer, washed her coffee mug, and clocked out. She walked briskly to a gym at St. Eriksplan and spent the next hour doing some easy strength training.

When she was finished she went home to her one-bedroom apartment on Pontonjärgatan, showered, and ate a late but nutritious dinner. She considered calling Daniel Mogren, who lived three blocks down the same street. Mogren was a carpenter and bodybuilder and had been her training partner off and on for three years. In recent months they had also had sex as friends.

Sex was almost as satisfying as a rigorous workout at the gym, but at a mature thirty-plus or, rather, forty-minus, Figuerola had begun to think that maybe she ought to start looking for a steady partner and a more permanent living arrangement. Maybe even children. But not with Mogren.

She decided that she didn't feel like seeing anyone that evening. Instead she went to bed with a book on the history of the ancient world.

CHAPTER 13

Tuesday, May 17

Figuerola woke at 6:10 on Tuesday morning, took a long run along Norr Mälarstrand, showered, and clocked in at police headquarters at 8:10. She prepared a memorandum on the conclusions she had reached the day before.

At 9:00 Edklinth arrived. She gave him twenty minutes to deal with his mail, then knocked on his door. She waited while he read her four pages. At last he looked up.

"The chief of Secretariat," he said.

"He must have approved loaning out Mårtensson. So he must know that Mårtensson is not at Counter-Espionage, even though according to Personal Protection that's where he is."

Edklinth took off his glasses and polished them thoroughly with a paper napkin. He had met Chief of Secretariat Albert Shenke at meetings and internal conferences on countless occasions, but he couldn't claim to know the man well. Shenke was rather short, with thin reddish-blond hair and a waistline that had expanded over the years. He was about fifty-five and had worked at SIS for at least twenty-five years, possibly longer. He had been chief of Secretariat for a decade, and was assistant chief before that. Edklinth thought of him as a taciturn man who could act ruthlessly when necessary. He had no idea what he did in his free time, but he had a memory of having once seen him in the garage of the police building in casual clothes, with a golf bag slung over his shoulder. He had also run into him once at the opera.

"There was one thing that struck me," Figuerola said.

"What's that?"

"Evert Gullberg. He did his military service in the forties and became a tax attorney, and then in the fifties he vanished into thin air."

"And?"

"When we were discussing this yesterday, we talked about him as if he were some sort of hired killer."

"It sounds far-fetched, I know, but—"

"It struck me that there is so little background on him it seems almost like a smokescreen. Both IB and SIS established cover companies outside the building in the fifties and sixties."

"I was wondering when you'd think of that," Edklinth said.

"I'd like permission to go through the personnel files from the fifties," Figuerola said.

"No," Edklinth said, shaking his head. "We can't go into the archives without authorization from the chief of Secretariat, and we don't want to attract attention until we have more to go on."

"So what next?"

"Mårtensson," Edklinth said. "Find out what he's working on."

. . .

Salander was studying the vent window in her room when she heard the key turn in the door. In came Jonasson. It was past 10:00 on Tuesday night. He had interrupted her planning how to break out of Sahlgrenska hospital.

She had measured the window and discovered that her head would fit through it and that she would not have much problem squeezing the rest of her body through. It was three storeys to the ground, but a combination of torn sheets and a ten-foot extension cord from a floor lamp would solve that problem.

She had plotted her escape step by step. The problem was what she would wear. She had underwear, a hospital nightshirt, and a pair of plastic flip-flops that she had managed to borrow. She had 200 kronor in cash from Annika Giannini to pay for sweets from the hospital snack shop. That should be enough for a cheap pair of jeans and a T-shirt at the Salvation Army store, if she could find one in Göteborg. She would have to spend what was left of the money on a call to Plague, a fellow member of Hacker Republic. Then everything would work out. She planned on landing in Gibraltar a few days after she escaped, and from there she would create a new identity somewhere in the world.

Jonasson sat in the guest chair. She sat on the edge of her bed.

"Hello, Lisbeth. I'm sorry I haven't come to see you the past few days, but I've been up to my ears in the ER, and I've also been made a mentor for a couple of interns."

She hadn't expected Jonasson to make special visits to see her.

He picked up her chart and studied her temperature graph

and the record of medications. Her temperature was steady, between 98.6 and 98.9 degrees, and for the past week she had not taken any headache tablets.

"Dr. Endrin is your doctor. Do you get along with her?"

"She's all right," Salander said without enthusiasm.

"Is it OK if I do an examination?"

She nodded. He took a penlight out of his pocket and bent over to shine it into her eyes, to see how her pupils contracted and expanded. He asked her to open her mouth and examined her throat. Then he placed his hands gently around her neck and moved her head back and forth and to the sides a few times.

"You don't have any pain in your neck?" he said.

She shook her head.

"How's the headache?"

"I feel it now and then, but it passes."

"The healing process is ongoing. The headache will eventually disappear altogether."

Her hair was still so short that he hardly needed to push aside the tufts to feel the scar above her ear. It was healing, but there was a small scab.

"You've been scratching the wound. You shouldn't do that."

She nodded. He took her left elbow and raised the arm.

"Can you lift it by yourself?"

She lifted her arm.

"Do you have any pain or discomfort in the shoulder?"

She shook her head.

"Does it feel tight?"

"A little."

"I think you have to do a bit more physical therapy on your shoulder muscles."

"It's hard when you're locked up like this."

He smiled at her. "That won't last. Are you doing the exercises the therapist recommended?"

She nodded.

He pressed his stethoscope against his wrist for a moment to warm it. Then he sat on the edge of the bed and untied the strings of her nightshirt, listened to her heart, and took her pulse. He asked her to lean forward and placed the stethoscope on her back to listen to her lungs.

"Cough."

She coughed.

"OK, you can do up your nightshirt and get into bed. From a medical standpoint, you're just about recovered."

She expected him to get up and say he would come back in a few days, but he stayed, sitting on the bed. He seemed to be thinking about something. Salander waited patiently.

"Do you know why I became a doctor?" he said.

She shook her head.

"I come from a working-class family. I always thought I wanted to be a doctor. I'd actually thought about becoming a psychiatrist when I was a teenager. I was terribly intellectual."

Salander looked at him with sudden alertness as soon as he mentioned the word *psychiatrist*.

"But I wasn't sure I could handle the studies. So when I finished school I studied to be a welder and I even worked as one for several years. I thought it was a good idea to have something to fall back on if the medical studies didn't work out. And being a welder wasn't so different from being a doctor. It's all about patching things up. Now I'm working here at Sahlgrenska and patching up people like you."

She wondered if he was pulling her leg.

"Lisbeth, I'm wondering . . ."

He then said nothing for such a long time that Salander almost asked what he wanted. But she waited for him to speak.

"Would you be angry if I asked you a personal question? I want to ask you as a private individual, not as a doctor. I won't make any record of your answer, and I won't discuss it with anyone else. And you don't have to answer if you don't want to."

"What is it?"

"Since you were shut up at St. Stefan's when you were twelve, you've refused to respond when any psychiatrist has tried to talk to you. Why is that?"

Salander's eyes darkened, but they were utterly expressionless as she looked at Jonasson. She sat in silence for two minutes.

"Why do you want to know?" she said at last.

"To be honest, I'm not really sure. I think I'm trying to understand something."

Her lips curled a little. "I don't talk to crazy-doctors because they never listen to what I have to say."

Jonasson laughed. "OK. Tell me . . . what do you think of Peter Teleborian?"

Jonasson threw out the name so unexpectedly that Salander almost jumped. Her eyes narrowed.

"What the hell is this, Twenty Questions? What are you after?" Her voice sounded like sandpaper.

Jonasson leaned forward, almost too close.

"Because a—what did you call it—a crazy-doctor by the name of Peter Teleborian, who's somewhat renowned in my profession, has been to see me twice in the past few days, trying to convince me to let him examine you."

Salander felt an icy chill run down her spine.

"The district court is going to appoint him to do a forensic psychiatric assessment of you."

"And?"

"I don't like the man. I've told him he can't see you. Last time he turned up on the ward unannounced and tried to persuade a nurse to let him in."

Salander pressed her lips tight.

"His behaviour was a bit odd and a little too eager. So I want to know what you think of him."

This time it was Jonasson's turn to wait patiently for Salander's reply.

"Teleborian is a beast," she said at last.

"Is it something personal between the two of you?"

"You could say that."

"I've also had a conversation with an official who wants me to let Teleborian see you."

"And?"

"I asked what sort of medical expertise he thought he had to assess your condition and then I told him to go to hell. More diplomatically than that, of course. And one last question. Why are you talking to me?"

"You asked me a question, didn't you?"

"Yes, but I'm a doctor and I've studied psychiatry. So why are you talking to me? Should I take it to mean that you have a certain amount of trust in me?"

She did not reply.

"Then I'll choose to interpret it that way. I want you to

know this: you are my patient. That means that I work for you and not for anyone else."

She gave him a suspicious look. He looked back at her for a moment. Then he spoke in a lighter tone of voice.

"From a medical standpoint, as I said, you're more or less healthy. But unfortunately you're a bit too healthy."

"Why 'unfortunately'?"

He gave her a cheerful smile. "You're getting better too fast."

"What do you mean?"

"It means that I have no legitimate reason to keep you isolated here. And the prosecutor will soon be having you transferred to a prison in Stockholm to await trial in six weeks. I'm guessing that such a request will arrive next week. And that means that Teleborian will be given the chance to observe you."

She sat utterly still. Jonasson seemed distracted, and he bent over to arrange her pillow. He spoke as if thinking out loud.

"You don't have much of a headache or any fever, so Dr. Endrin is probably going to discharge you." He stood up suddenly. "Thanks for talking to me. I'll come back and see you before you're transferred."

He was already at the door when she spoke.

"Dr. Jonasson?"

He turned towards her.

"Thank you."

He nodded curtly once before he went out and locked the door.

Salander stared for a long time at the locked door. And then she lay back and stared up at the ceiling.

That was when she felt that there was something hard beneath her head. She lifted the pillow and saw to her surprise a small cloth bag that had definitely not been there before. She opened it and stared in amazement at a Palm Tungsten T3 hand-held computer and battery charger. Then she looked more closely at the computer and saw the little scratch on the top left corner. Her heart skipped a beat. *It's my Palm. But how . . . ?* In amazement she glanced over at the locked door. Jonasson was a catalogue of surprises. In great excitement, she turned on the computer and discovered that it was password-protected.

She stared in frustration at the blinking screen. It seemed to be challenging her. *How the hell did they think I would . . . ?* Then she looked in the cloth bag and found at the bottom a scrap of folded paper. She unfolded it and read a line written in an elegant script:

You're the hacker; work it out! Kalle B.

Salander laughed aloud for the first time in weeks. *Touché.* She thought for a few seconds. Then she picked up the stylus and wrote the number combination 9277, which corresponded to the letters W-A-S-P on the keyboard. It was a code that Kalle Fucking Blomkvist had been forced to work out when he got into her apartment on Fiskargatan uninvited and tripped the burglar alarm.

It did not work.

She tried 52553, which corresponded to the letters K-A-L-L-E.

That did not work either. Since Blomkvist presumably intended that she should use the computer, he must have chosen a simple password. He had used the signature Kalle, which normally he hated. She free-associated. She thought for a moment. It must be some insult. Then she typed in 74774, which corresponded to the word *P-I-P-P-I*—Pippi Fucking Longstocking.

The computer started up.

There was a smiley face on the screen with a cartoon speech balloon:

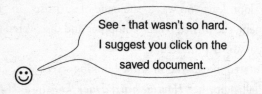

She found the document [Hi, Sally] at the top of the list. She clicked on it and read:

First of all, this is only between you and me.
Your lawyer, my sister, Annika, has no idea that
you have access to this computer. It has to stay
that way.

I don't know how much you understand of what is
happening outside your locked room, but strangely
enough (despite your personality), you have a
number of loyal idiots working on your behalf. I
have already established an elite body called The
Knights of the Idiotic Table. We will be holding
an annual dinner at which we'll have fun talking
crap about you. (No, you're not invited.)

So, to the point. Annika is doing her best to
prepare for your trial. One problem, of course,

is that she's working for you and is bound and
fettered by one of those damned confidentiality
oaths. So she can't tell me what the two of you
discuss, which in this case is a bit of a handi-
cap. Luckily she does accept information.

We have to talk, you and I.

Don't use my email.

I may be paranoid, but I have reason to suspect
that I'm not the only one reading it. If you want
to deliver something, go to Yahoo group [Idiotic_
Table]. ID Pippi and password p9i2p7p7i. Mikael

_____

Salander read his letter twice, staring in bewilderment at
the Palm. After a period of computer celibacy, she was suffering from massive cyber-abstinence. And she wondered which
big toe Blomkvist had been thinking with when he smuggled
her a computer but forgot that she needed a mobile to connect to the Net.

She was still thinking when she heard footsteps in the corridor. She turned the computer off at once and shoved it
under her pillow. As she heard the key in the door she realized that the cloth bag and charger were still in view on the
bedside table. She reached out and slid the bag under the
covers and pressed the coil of cord into her crotch. She lay
passively looking up at the ceiling when the night nurse came
in, said a polite hello, and asked how she was doing and
whether she needed anything.

Salander told her that she was doing fine and that she
wanted a pack of cigarettes. This request was turned down in

a firm but friendly tone. She was given a pack of nicotine gum. As the nurse was closing the door, Salander glimpsed the guard on his chair out in the corridor. She waited until she heard the nurse's steps receding before she once again picked up her Palm.

She turned it on and searched for connectivity.

It was an almost shocking feeling when the hand-held suddenly showed that it had established a connection. *Contact with the Net. Unbelievable.*

She jumped out of bed so fast that she felt a pain in her injured hip. *How?* She walked all the way around the room, examining every nook and cranny. No, there was no mobile. And yet she had connectivity. Then a crooked grin spread across her face. The connection was radio-controlled and locked into a mobile via Bluetooth, which had a range of ten to twelve yards. Her eyes lit upon an air vent just below the ceiling.

Kalle Fucking Blomkvist had somehow planted a mobile just outside her room. That could be the only explanation.

But why not smuggle in the mobile too? Ah, of course. The batteries.

Her Palm had to be recharged only once every three days. A mobile that was connected, if she surfed it hard, would burn out its batteries in much less time. Blomkvist—or more likely somebody he had hired and who was *out there*—would have to change the batteries at regular intervals.

But he had sent in the charger for her Palm. *He isn't so stupid after all.*

Salander began by deciding where to keep the hand-held. She had to find a hiding place. There were outlets by the door and in the panel behind the bed, which provided electricity for her bedside lamp and digital clock. There was a recess where a radio had been removed. She smiled. Both the battery charger and the Palm could fit in there. She could use the outlet inside the bedside table to charge the Palm during the day.

Salander was happy. Her heart was pounding hard when she started up the hand-held for the first time in two months and ventured onto the Internet.

Surfing on a Palm hand-held with a tiny screen and a stylus was not the same thing as surfing on a PowerBook with a seventeen-inch screen. But she was connected. From her bed at Sahlgrenska she could now reach the entire world.

She started by going to a website that advertised rather uninteresting pictures by an unknown and not especially skilled amateur photographer named Gil Bates in Jobsville, Pennsylvania. Salander had once checked it out and confirmed that the town of Jobsville did not exist. Nevertheless, Bates had taken more than 200 photographs of the community and created a gallery of small thumbnails. She scrolled down to image 167 and clicked to enlarge it. It showed the church in Jobsville. She put her cursor on the spire of the church tower and clicked. She instantly got a pop-up dialog box that asked for her ID and password. She took out her stylus and wrote the word *Remarkable* on the screen as her ID and A(89)Cx#magnolia as the password.

She got a dialog box with the text [Error—you have the wrong password] and a button that said [OK—try again]. Lisbeth knew that if she clicked on [OK—try again] and tried a different password, she would get the same dialog box again—for years and years, for as long as she kept trying. Instead she clicked on the *o* in *Error*.

The screen went blank. Then an animated door opened and a Lara Croft–like figure stepped out. A speech bubble materialized with the text [WHO GOES THERE?]. She clicked on the bubble and wrote Wasp. She got the instant reply [PROVE IT—OR ELSE . . .] as the animated Lara Croft unlocked the safety catch on her gun. Salander knew it was no empty threat. If she entered the wrong password three times in a row the site would shut down and the name Wasp would be struck from the membership list. Carefully she entered the password MonkeyBusiness.

The screen changed again and now had a blue background with the text:

[Welcome to Hacker Republic, citizen Wasp. It has been 56 days since your last visit. There are 11 citizens online. Do you want to (a) Browse the Forum, (b) Send a Message, (c) Search the Archive, (d) Talk, (e) Get Laid?]

She clicked on (d) Talk and then went to the menu selection [Who's online?] and got a list with the names Andy, Bambi, Dakota, Jabba, BuckRogers, Mandrake, Pred, Slip, SisterJen, SixOfOne, and Trinity.

<Hi gang.> Wasp wrote.

<Wasp. That really U?> SixOfOne wrote. <Look who's back.>

<Where you been keeping yourself?> Trinity wrote.

<Plague said you were in some trouble.> Dakota wrote.

Salander was not sure, but she suspected that Dakota was

a woman. The other citizens online, including the one who called himself SisterJen, were guys. Hacker Republic had a total (the last time she was connected) of sixty-two citizens, of whom four were female.

<Hi, Trinity.> Wasp wrote. <Hi, everybody.>

<Why are you saying hi to Trin? Is there something on G and is there something wrong with the rest of us?> Dakota wrote.

<We've been dating.> Trinity wrote. <Wasp only hangs out with intelligent people.>

He got abuse from five directions at once.

Of the sixty-two citizens, Wasp had met two face-to-face. Plague, who for some strange reason was not online, was one. Trinity was the other. He was English and lived in London. Two years earlier she had met him for a few hours when he helped her and Blomkvist in the hunt for Harriet Vanger by doing an illegal tapping of a landline in St. Albans. Salander fumbled with the clumsy stylus and wished she had a keyboard.

<Still there?> Mandrake wrote.

She punched letters. <Sorry. Only have a Palm. Slow going.>

<What happened to your computer?> Pred wrote.

<My computer is OK. It's me that's the problem.>

<Tell big brother.> Slip wrote.

<I'm under arrest by the government.>

<What? Why?> Three chatters at once.

Salander summed up her situation in five lines, which were greeted by a worried muttering.

<How are you doing?> Trinity wrote.

<I have a hole in my head.>

<I can't tell the difference.> Bambi wrote.

<Wasp has always had air in her head.> SisterJen wrote, and that was followed by a spate of disparaging remarks about Wasp's mental abilities. Salander smiled. The conversation resumed with a contribution from Dakota.

<Wait. This is an attack against a citizen of Hacker Republic. How are we going to respond?>

<Nuclear attack on Stockholm?> SixOfOne wrote.

<No, that would be overdoing it a bit.> Wasp wrote.

<A little tiny bomb?>

<Go jump in the lake, Six00.>

<We could shut down Stockholm.> Mandrake wrote.

<A virus to shut down the government?>

The citizens of Hacker Republic did not generally spread computer viruses. On the contrary—they were hackers and consequently implacable adversaries of those idiots who created viruses whose sole purpose was to sabotage the Net and crash computers. The citizens were information junkies and wanted a functioning Internet that they could hack.

But their proposal to shut down the Swedish government was not an idle threat. Hacker Republic comprised a very exclusive club of the best of the best, an elite force that any defence organization in the world would have paid enormous sums to use for cyber-military purposes, if the citizens could be persuaded to feel any kind of loyalty to any state. Which was not very likely.

But they were every one of them computer wizards, and they were well versed in the art of contriving viruses. Nor did they need much convincing to carry out particular campaigns if the situation warranted. Some years earlier a citizen of Hacker Republic, who in his private life was a software developer in California, had been cheated out of a patent by a hot dot-com company that had the nerve to take the citizen to court. This caused the activists in Hacker Republic to devote a startling amount of energy for six months to hacking and destroying every computer owned by that company. All the company's secrets and emails—along with some fake documents that might lead people to think that its CEO was involved in tax fraud—were gleefully posted on the Net, along with information about the CEO's now not-so-secret mistress and pictures from a party in Hollywood in which he could be seen snorting cocaine. The company went under in six months, and several years later some members of the "people's militia" in Hacker Republic, who did not easily forget an enemy, were still haunting the former CEO.

If fifty of the world's foremost hackers decided to launch a coordinated attack against an entire country, the country might survive, but not without serious problems. The costs would certainly run into the billions if Salander gave it the thumbs-up. She thought for a moment.

<Not right now. But if things don't go the way I need them to I might ask for help.>

<Just say the word.> Dakota wrote.

<It's been a long time since we messed with a government.> Mandrake wrote.

<I have a suggestion for reversing the tax-

```
payment system. A programme that could be
custom-tailored for a small country like Nor-
way.> Bambi wrote.
<Great, but Stockholm is in Sweden.> Trinity
wrote.
<Same difference. Here's what you could
do . . . >
```

Salander leaned back against the pillow and followed the conversation with a smile. She wondered why she, who had such difficulty talking about herself with people of flesh and blood, could blithely reveal her most intimate secrets to a bunch of completely unknown freaks on the Internet. The fact was that if Salander could claim to have any sort of family or group affiliation, then it was with these lunatics. None of them actually had a hope of helping her with the problems she had with the Swedish state. But she knew that if the need arose, they would devote both time and cunning to performing effective demonstrations of their powers. Through this network she could also find herself hideouts abroad. It had been Plague's contacts on the Net who had provided her with a Norwegian passport in the name of Irene Nesser.

Salander had no idea who the citizens of Hacker Republic were, and she had only a vague notion of what they did when they were not on the Net—the citizens were uniformly vague about their identities. SixOfOne had once claimed that he was a black, male American of Catholic origin living in Toronto. He could just as easily be white, female, and Lutheran, and living in Skövde.

The one she knew best was Plague—he had introduced

her to the family, and nobody became a member of this exclusive club without very strong recommendations. And for anyone to become a member they had also to be known personally to one other citizen.

On the Net, Plague was an intelligent and socially gifted citizen. In real life he was a severely overweight and socially challenged thirty-year-old living on disability benefits in Sundbyberg. He bathed too seldom and his apartment smelled like a monkey house. Salander visited him only once in a blue moon. She was content to confine her dealings with him to the Net.

As the chat continued, Wasp downloaded mail that had been sent to her private mailbox at Hacker Republic. One was from another member, Poison, and contained an improved version of her programme Asphyxia 1.3, which was available in the Republic's archive for its citizens. Asphyxia was a programme that could control other people's computers via the Internet. Poison said that he had used it successfully, and that his updated version included the latest versions of Unix, Apple, and Windows. She emailed him a brief reply and thanked him for the upgrade.

During the next hour, as evening approached in the United States, another half-dozen citizens had come online and welcomed back Wasp before joining the debate. When Salander logged off, the others were discussing to what extent the Swedish prime minister's computer could be made to send civil but crazy emails to other heads of state. A working group had been formed to explore the matter. Salander logged off by writing a brief message:

```
<Keep talking but don't do anything unless I OK
it. I'll come back when I can uplink again.>
```

Everyone sent her hugs and kisses and admonished her to keep the hole in her head warm.

Only when Salander had logged out of Hacker Republic did she go into Yahoo and log on to the private newsgroup [Idiotic_Table]. She discovered that the group had two members—herself and Blomkvist. The mailbox had one message, sent on May 15. It was titled [Read this first].

Hi, Sally. The situation is as follows:

The police haven't found your apartment and don't have access to the DVD of Bjurman's rape. The disk is very strong evidence. I don't want to turn it over to Annika without your approval. I have the keys to your apartment and a passport in name of Nesser.

But the police do have the backpack you had in Gosseberga. I don't know if it contains anything compromising.

Salander thought for a moment. *Don't think so. A half-empty thermos of coffee, some apples, a change of clothes. No problem.*

You're going to be charged with aggravated assault against and the attempted murder of Zalachenko, and aggravated assault against Carl-Magnus Lundin at Stallarholmen—i.e., because you shot him in the foot and broke his jaw when you kicked him. But a source in the police whom I

trust tells me that the evidence in each case is
vague. The following is important:

(1) Before Zalachenko was shot he denied everything and claimed that it could only have been
Niedermann who shot and buried you. He laid a
charge against you for attempting to murder him.
The prosecutor is going to go on about this
being the second time you have tried to kill
him.

(2) Neither Lundin nor Sonny Nieminen has said a
word about what happened at Stallarholmen. Lundin
has been arrested for kidnapping Miriam. Nieminen
has been released.

Salander had already discussed all of this with Giannini.
She *had* told Giannini everything that had happened in
Gosseberga, but she had refrained from telling her anything
about Bjurman.

What I think you haven't understood are the rules
of the game.

It's like this. Säpo got saddled with Zalachenko
in the middle of the Cold War. For fifteen years
he was protected, no matter what he did. Careers
were built on Zalachenko. On any number of occasions they cleaned up after his rampages. This is
all criminal activity: Swedish authorities helping to cover up crimes against individual
citizens.

If this gets out, there'll be a scandal that will affect both the conservative and social democratic parties. Above all, people in high places within Säpo will be exposed as accomplices in criminal and immoral activities. Even though by now the statute of limitations has run out on the specific instances of crime, there'll still be a scandal. It involves big shots who are either retired now or close to retirement.

They will do everything they can to reduce the damage to themselves and their group, and that means you'll once again be a pawn in their game. But this time it's not a matter of them sacrificing a pawn—it'll be a matter of them actively needing to limit the damage to themselves personally. So you'll have to be locked up again.

This is how it will work. They know that they can't keep the lid on the Zalachenko secret for long. I have got the story, and they know that sooner or later I'm going to publish it. It doesn't matter so much, of course, now that he's dead. What matters to them is their own survival. The following points are therefore high on their agenda:

(1) They have to convince the district court (the public, in effect) that the decision to lock you up in St. Stefan's in 1991 was a legitimate one, that you really were mentally ill.

(2) They have to separate the "Salander affair" from the "Zalachenko affair." They'll try to create a situation where they can say, "Certainly Zalachenko was a fiend, but that had nothing to do with the decision to lock up his daughter. She was locked up because she was deranged—any claims to the contrary are the sick fantasies of bitter journalists. No, we did not assist Zalachenko in any crime—that's the delusion of a mentally ill teenage girl."

(3) The problem is that if you're acquitted, it would mean that the district court finds that you're not a nutcase. And that would have to mean that locking you up in 1991 was illegal. So they have to condemn you, at all costs, to the locked psychiatric ward. If the court determines that you are mentally ill, the media's interest in continuing to dig around in the "Salander affair" will die away. That is how the media work.

Are you with me?

_____

All of this she had already worked out for herself. The problem was that she didn't know what she should do.

Lisbeth—seriously—this battle is going to be decided in the mass media, and not in the courtroom. Unfortunately, the trial is going to be held behind closed doors "to protect your privacy."

The day that Zalachenko was shot there was a robbery at my apartment. There were no signs on my door of a break-in, and nothing was touched or moved—except for one thing. The folder from Bjurman's summer cabin with Björck's report was taken. At the same time, my sister was mugged and her copy of the report was also stolen. That folder is your most important evidence.

I have let it be known that our Zalachenko documents are gone, disappeared. In fact I had a third copy that I was going to give to Armansky. I made several copies of that one and have tucked them away in safe places.

Our opponents—who include several high-powered figures and certain psychiatrists—are of course also preparing for the trial, together with Prosecutor Ekström. I have a source who provides me with some info on what's going on, but I suspect that you might have a better chance of finding out the relevant information. This is urgent.

The prosecutor is going to try to get you locked up in the psychiatric ward. Assisting him is your old friend Peter Teleborian.

Annika won't be able to go out and do a media campaign in the same way that the prosecution can (and does), leaking information as they see fit. Her hands are tied.

But I'm not encumbered by that sort of restric-
tion. I can write whatever I want—and I also have
an entire magazine at my disposal.

Two important details are still needed:

(1) First of all, I want to have something that
shows that Prosecutor Ekström is working with
Teleborian in some inappropriate manner, and that
the objective once more is to confine you to a
nuthouse. I want to be able to go on any talk
show on TV and present documentation that annihi-
lates the prosecution's game.

(2) To wage a media war I must be able to appear
in public to discuss things that you may consider
your private business. Privacy in this situation
is wildly overrated in view of all that has been
written about you since Easter. I have to be able
to construct a completely new media image of you,
even if that, in your opinion, means invading
your privacy—preferably with your approval. Do
you understand what I mean?

She opened the archive in [Idiotic_Table]. It contained
twenty-six documents.

CHAPTER 14

Wednesday, May 18

Figuerola got up at 5:00 on Wednesday morning and went for an unusually short run before she showered and dressed in black jeans, a white top, and a lightweight grey linen jacket. She made coffee, poured it into a thermos, and then made sandwiches. She also strapped on a shoulder holster and took her Sig Sauer from the gun cabinet. Just after 6:00 she drove her white Saab 9–5 to Vittangigatan in Vällingby.

Mårtensson's apartment was on the top floor of a three-storey building in the suburbs. The day before, she had assembled everything that could be found out about him in the public archives. He was unmarried, but that did not mean that he wasn't living with someone. He had no black marks in police records, and no great fortune, and he did not seem to lead a fast life. He very seldom called in sick.

The one conspicuous thing about him was that he had licences for no fewer than sixteen weapons. Three of them were hunting rifles; the others were handguns of various types. As long as he had a licence, of course, there was no crime, but Figuerola harboured a deep scepticism about anyone who collected weapons on such a scale.

The Volvo with the registration beginning KAB was in the parking lot about thirty yards from where Figuerola herself parked. She poured black coffee into a paper cup and ate a lettuce and cheese baguette. Then she peeled an orange and sucked each segment to extinction.

At morning rounds, Salander was out of sorts and had a bad headache. She asked for a Tylenol, which she was immediately given.

After an hour the headache had grown worse. She rang for the nurse and asked for another Tylenol. That didn't help either. By lunchtime she had such a headache that the nurse called Dr. Endrin, who examined her patient briskly and prescribed a powerful painkiller.

Salander held the tablets under her tongue and spat them out as soon as she was alone.

At 2:00 in the afternoon she threw up. This recurred at around 3:00.

At 4:00 Jonasson came up to the ward just as Dr. Endrin was about to go home. They conferred briefly.

"She feels sick and she has a strong headache. I gave her Dexofen. I don't understand what's going on with her. She's been doing so well lately. It might be some sort of flu . . ."

"Does she have a fever?" asked Jonasson.

"No. She had 98.6 an hour ago."

"I'm going to keep an eye on her overnight."

"I'll be going on vacation for three weeks," Endrin said. "Either you or Svantesson will have to take over her case. But Svantesson hasn't had much to do with her. . . ."

"I'll arrange to be her primary care doctor while you're on vacation."

"Good. If there's a crisis and you need help, do call."

They paid a short visit to Salander's sickbed. She was lying with the sheet pulled up to the tip of her nose, and she looked miserable. Jonasson put his hand on her forehead and felt that it was damp.

"I think we'll have to do a quick examination."

He thanked Dr. Endrin, and she left.

At 5:00 Jonasson discovered that Salander had developed a temperature of 100, which was noted on her chart. He visited her three times that evening and noted that her temperature had remained at 100—too high, certainly, but not so high as to present a real problem. At 8:00 he ordered a cranial X-ray.

When the X-rays came through he studied them intently. He could not see anything remarkable, but he did observe that there was a barely visible darker area immediately adjacent to the bullet hole. He wrote a carefully worded and noncommittal comment on her chart: *Radiological examination gives a basis for definitive conclusions, but the condition of the patient has deteriorated steadily during the day. It cannot be ruled out that there is a minor bleed that is not visible on the images. The patient should be confined to bedrest and kept under strict observation until further notice.*

Berger had received twenty-three emails by the time she arrived at *SMP* at 6:30 on Wednesday morning.

One of them had the address <editorial-sr@swedishradio .com>. The text was short. A single word.

WHORE

She raised her index finger to delete the message. At the last moment she changed her mind. She went back to her inbox and opened the message that had arrived two days before. The sender was <centraled@smpost.se>. So . . . two emails with the word *whore* and a phoney sender from the world of mass media. She created a new folder called [Mediafool] and saved both messages. Then she got busy on the morning memo.

Mårtensson left home at 7:40 that morning. He got into his Volvo and drove towards the city but turned off to go across Stora Essingen and Gröndal into Södermalm. He drove down Hornsgatan and across to Bellmansgatan via Brännkyrkagatan. He turned left onto Tavastgatan at the Bishop's Arms pub and parked at the corner.

Just as Figuerola reached the Bishop's Arms, a van pulled out and left a parking space on Bellmansgatan at the corner with Tavastgatan. From her ideal location at the top of the hill she had an unobstructed view. She could just see the back window of Mårtensson's Volvo. Straight ahead of her, on the steep slope down towards Pryssgränd, was Bellmansgatan 1. She was looking at the building from the side, so she could not see the front door itself, but as soon as anyone came out onto the street, she would see them. She had no doubt that this particular address was the reason for Mårtensson's being there. It was Blomkvist's building.

Figuerola could see that the area surrounding Bellmansgatan 1 would be a nightmare to keep under surveillance. The only spot from which the door to the building could be observed directly was from the promenade and footbridge on upper Bellmansgatan near the Maria lift and the Laurinska building. There was nowhere there to park a car, and the person doing the surveillance would stand exposed on the footbridge like a swallow perched on an old telephone wire in the country. The intersection of Bellmansgatan and Tavastgatan, where Figuerola had parked, was basically the only place where she could sit in her car and have a view of the whole. She had been incredibly lucky. Yet it was not a particularly good place because any alert observer would see her in her car. But she did not want to leave the car and start walking around the area. She was too easily noticeable. In her role as undercover officer her looks worked against her.

Blomkvist emerged at 9:10. Figuerola noted the time. She saw him look up at the footbridge on upper Bellmansgatan. He started up the hill straight towards her.

She opened her handbag and unfolded a map of Stockholm, which she placed on the passenger seat. Then she opened a notebook and took a pen from her jacket pocket. She pulled out her mobile and pretended to be talking, keeping her head bent so that the hand holding her phone hid part of her face.

She saw Blomkvist glance down Tavastgatan. He knew he was being watched and he must have seen Mårtensson's Volvo, but he kept walking without showing any interest in the car. *Acts calm and cool. Somebody should have opened the car door and scared the shit out of him.*

The next moment he passed Figuerola's car. She was obviously trying to find an address on the map while she talked on the phone, but she could sense Blomkvist looking at her as he passed. *Suspicious of everything around him.* She saw him in the side-view mirror on the passenger side as he went on down towards Hornsgatan. She had seen him on TV a couple of times, but this was the first time she had seen him in person. He was wearing blue jeans, a T-shirt, and a grey jacket. He carried a shoulder bag and he walked with a long, loose stride. A nice-looking man.

Mårtensson appeared at the corner by the Bishop's Arms and watched Blomkvist go. He had a large sports bag over his shoulder and was just finishing a call on his mobile. Figuerola expected him to follow his quarry, but to her surprise he crossed the street right in front of her car and turned down the hill towards Blomkvist's building. A second later a man in blue overalls passed her car and caught up with Mårtensson. *Hello, where did you come from?*

They stopped outside the door to Blomkvist's building. Mårtensson punched in the code and they disappeared into the stairwell. *They're checking the apartment. Amateur night. What the hell does he think he's doing?*

Then Figuerola raised her eyes to the rear-view mirror and gave a start when she saw Blomkvist again. He was standing about ten yards behind her, close enough that he could keep an eye on Mårtensson and his buddy by looking over the crest of the steep hill down towards Bellmansgatan 1. She watched his face. He was not looking at her. But he had seen Mårtensson go in through the front door of his building. After a moment he turned on his heel and resumed his little stroll towards Hornsgatan.

Figuerola sat motionless for thirty seconds. *He knows he's being watched. He's keeping track of what goes on around him. But why doesn't he react? A normal person would react, and pretty strongly at that.... He must have something up his sleeve.*

. . .

Blomkvist hung up and rested his gaze on the notebook on his desk. The national vehicle registry had just informed him that the car he had seen at the top of Bellmansgatan with the blond woman inside was owned by Monica Figuerola, born in 1969, and living on Pontonjärgatan in Kungsholmen. Since it was a woman in the car, Blomkvist assumed it was Figuerola herself.

She had been talking on her mobile and looking at a map that was unfolded on the passenger seat. Blomkvist had no reason to believe that she had anything to do with the Zalachenko club, but he made a note of every deviation from the norm in his working day, and especially around his neighbourhood.

He called Karim in.

"Who is this woman, Lotta? Dig up her passport picture, where she works, and anything else you can find."

Sellberg looked rather startled. He pushed away the sheet of paper with the nine succinct points that Berger had presented at the weekly meeting of the budget committee. Flodin looked similarly concerned. Borgsjö appeared neutral, as always.

"This is impossible," Sellberg said with a polite smile.

"How so?" Berger said.

"The board will never go along with this. It defies all rhyme or reason."

"Shall we take it from the top?" Berger said. "I was hired to make *SMP* profitable again. To do that I have to have something to work with, don't you think?"

"Well, yes, but—"

"I can't wave a magic wand and conjure up the contents of

a daily newspaper by sitting in my glass cage and just wishing for things."

"You don't understand the hard economic facts."

"That's possible. But I understand making newspapers. And the reality is that over the past fifteen years, *SMP*'s personnel has been reduced by 118. Half were graphic artists and so on, replaced by new technology . . . but the number of reporters contributing to copy was reduced by 48 during that period."

"Those were necessary cuts. If the staff hadn't been cut, the paper would have folded long ago. At least Morander understood the necessity of the reductions."

"Well, let's wait and see what's necessary and what isn't. In three years, nineteen reporter jobs have disappeared. In addition, we now have a situation in which nine positions at *SMP* are vacant and are being to some extent covered by temps. The sports desk is dangerously understaffed. There should be nine employees there, and for more than a year two positions have remained unfilled."

"It's a question of saving money. It's that simple."

"The culture section has three unfilled positions. The business section has one. The legal desk does not even in practice exist; there we have a chief editor who borrows reporters from the news desk for each of his features. And so on. *SMP* hasn't done any serious coverage of the civil service and government agencies for at least eight years. We depend for that on freelancers and the material from the TT wire service. And as you know, TT shut down its civil service desk some years ago. In other words, there isn't a single news desk in Sweden covering the civil service and the government agencies."

"The newspaper business is in a vulnerable position—"

"The reality is that *SMP* should either be shut down immediately, or the board should find a way to take an aggressive stance. Today we have fewer employees responsible for producing more copy every day. The articles they turn out are terrible, superficial, and they lack credibility. That's why *SMP* is losing its readers."

"You don't understand the situation—"

"I'm tired of hearing that I don't understand the situation. I'm not some temp who's just here for the bus fare."

"But your proposal is crazy."

"Why is that?"

"You're proposing that the newspaper should not be profitable."

"Listen, Sellberg, this year you will be paying out a huge amount of money in dividends to the paper's twenty-three stockholders. Add to this the unforgivably absurd bonuses that will cost *SMP* almost 10 million kronor for nine individuals who sit on *SMP*'s board. You've awarded yourself a bonus of 400,000 kronor for administering cutbacks. Of course, it's a long way from being a bonus as huge as the ones that some of the directors of Skandia grabbed. But in my eyes you're not worth a bonus of so much as one single öre. Bonuses should be paid to people who do something to strengthen *SMP*. The plain truth is that your cutbacks have weakened *SMP* and deepened the crisis we now find ourselves in."

"That is grossly unfair. The board approved every measure I proposed."

"Of course the board approved your measures, because you guaranteed a dividend each year. That's what has to stop, and now."

"So you're suggesting in all seriousness that the board should decide to abolish dividends and bonuses. What makes you think the stockholders would agree to that?"

"I'm proposing a zero-profit operating budget this year. That would mean savings of almost twenty-one million kronor and the chance to beef up *SMP*'s staff and finances. I'm also proposing wage cuts for management. I'm being paid a monthly salary of 88,000 kronor, which is utter insanity for a newspaper that can't add a job to its sports desk."

"So you want to cut your own salary? Is this some sort of wage communism you're advocating?"

"Don't bullshit me. You make 112,000 kronor a month, if you add in your annual bonus. *That's* crazy. If the newspaper were stable and bringing in a tremendous profit, then you could pay out as much as you wanted in bonuses. But this is no time for you to be increasing your own bonus. I propose cutting all management salaries by half."

"What you don't understand is that our stockholders bought stock in the paper because they want to make money. That's called capitalism. If you arrange for them to lose money, then they won't want to be stockholders any longer."

"I'm not suggesting they should lose money, though it might come to that. Ownership implies responsibility. As you yourself pointed out, capitalism is what matters here. *SMP*'s owners want to make a profit. But it's the market that decides whether you make a profit or take a loss. By your reasoning, you want the rules of capitalism to apply solely to the *employees* of *SMP*, while you and the stockholders will be exempt."

Sellberg rolled his eyes and sighed. He cast an entreating glance at Borgsjö, but the CEO was intently studying Berger's nine-point programme.

. . .

Figuerola waited for forty-nine minutes before Mårtensson and his companion in overalls came out of Bellmansgatan 1. As they started up the hill towards her, she very steadily raised her Nikon, with its 300mm telephoto lens, and took two pictures. She put the camera in the space under her seat and was just about to fiddle with her map when she happened to glance towards the Maria lift. Her eyes opened wide. At the end of upper Bellmansgatan, right next to the gate to the Maria lift, stood a dark-haired woman with a digital camera filming Mårtensson and his companion. *What the hell? Is there some sort of spy convention on Bellmansgatan today?*

The two men parted at the top of the hill without exchanging a word. Mårtensson went back to his car on Tavastgatan. He pulled away from the curb and disappeared from view.

Figuerola looked into her rear-view mirror, in which she could still see the back of the man in the blue overalls. She then saw that the woman with the camera had stopped filming and was heading past the Laurinska building in her direction.

Heads or tails? She already knew who Mårtensson was and what he was up to. The man in the blue overalls and the woman with the camera were unknown entities. But if she left her car, she risked being seen by the woman.

She sat still. In her rear-view mirror she saw the man in the blue overalls turn into Brännkyrkagatan. She waited until the woman reached the crossing in front of her, but instead of following the man in the overalls, the woman turned 180 degrees and went down the steep hill towards Bellmansgatan 1. Figuerola guessed that she was in her mid-thirties. She had short dark hair and was dressed in dark jeans and a black jacket. As soon as she was a little way down the hill, Figuerola pushed open her car door and ran towards Brännkyrka-gatan. She could not see the blue overalls. The next second a Toyota van pulled away from the curb. Figuerola saw the man in half-profile and memorized the registration number. But if she got the registration wrong she would be able to trace him anyway. The sides of the van advertised LARS FAULSSON LOCK AND KEY SERVICE—with a phone number.

There was no need to follow the van. She walked calmly back to the top of the hill just in time to see the woman disappear through the door of Blomkvist's building.

She got back into her car and wrote down both the registration and phone numbers for Lars Faulsson. There was a lot of mysterious traffic around Blomkvist's address that morning. She looked up towards the roof of Bellmans-gatan 1. She knew that Blomkvist's apartment was on the top floor, but from the blueprints from the city construction office she knew that it was on the other side of the building, with dormer windows looking out on Gamla Stan and the waters of Riddarfjärden. An exclusive address in a fine old cultural quarter. She wondered whether he was an ostentatious nouveau riche.

Ten minutes later the woman with the camera came out of the building again. Instead of going back up the hill to Tavastgatan, she continued down the hill and turned right at the corner of Pryssgränd. *Hmm.* If she had a car parked down on Pryssgränd, Figuerola was out of luck. But if she was walking, there was only one way out of the dead end— up to Brännkyrkagatan via Pustegränd and towards Slussen.

Figuerola decided to leave her car behind and turned

left in the direction of Slussen on Brännkyrkagatan. She had almost reached Pustegränd when the woman appeared, coming up towards her. *Bingo.* She followed her past the Hilton on Södermalmstorg and past the Stadsmuseum at Slussen. The woman walked quickly and purposefully, without once looking around. Figuerola gave her a lead of about thirty yards. When she went into Slussen tunnelbana Figuerola picked up her pace, but stopped when she saw the woman head for the Pressbyrån kiosk instead of through the turnstiles.

She watched the woman as she stood in line at the kiosk. She was about five foot seven and looked to be in pretty good shape. She was wearing running shoes. Seeing her with both feet planted firmly as she stood by the window of the kiosk, Figuerola suddenly had the feeling that she was a policewoman. She bought a tin of Catch Dry snuff and went back out onto Södermalmstorg and turned right across Katarinavägen.

Figuerola followed her. She was almost certain the woman had not seen her. The woman turned the corner at McDonald's and Figuerola hurried after her, but when she got to the corner, the woman had vanished without a trace. Figuerola stopped short in consternation. *Shit.* She walked slowly past the entrances to the buildings. Then she caught sight of a brass plate that read MILTON SECURITY.

Figuerola walked back to Bellmansgatan.

She drove to Götgatan, where the offices of *Millennium* were, and spent the next half hour walking around the streets in the area. She did not see Mårtensson's car. At lunchtime she returned to police headquarters in Kungsholmen and spent two hours thinking as she pumped iron in the gym.

· · ·

"We have a problem," Cortez said.

Eriksson and Blomkvist looked up from the manuscript of the book about the Zalachenko case. It was 1:30 in the afternoon.

"Take a seat," Eriksson said.

"It's about Vitavara Inc., the company that makes the 1,700 kronor toilets in Vietnam."

"What's the problem?" Blomkvist said.

"Vitavara Inc. is a wholly owned subsidiary of Svea Construction Inc."

"I see. That's a very large firm."

"Yes, it is. The chairman of the board is Magnus Borgsjö, a professional board member. He's also the CEO of *Svenska Morgon-Posten* and owns about 10 percent of it."

Blomkvist gave Cortez a sharp look. "Are you sure?"

"Yep. Berger's boss is a fucking crook, a man who exploits child labour in Vietnam."

Assistant Editor Fredriksson looked to be in a bad mood as he knocked on the door of Berger's glass cage at 2:00 in the afternoon.

"What is it?"

"Well, this is a little embarrassing, but somebody in the newsroom got an email from you."

"From me? So? What does it say?"

He handed her some printouts of emails addressed to Eva Carlsson, a twenty-six-year-old temp on the culture pages. According to the headers the sender was <erika.berger@smpost.se>:

Darling Eva. I want to caress you and kiss
your breasts. I'm hot with excitement and
can't control myself. I beg you to
reciprocate my feelings. Could
we meet? Erika

_____

And then two emails on the following days:

Dearest, darling Eva. I beg you not to
reject me. I'm crazy with desire. I want to
have you naked. I have to have you. I'm
going to make you so happy. You'll never
regret it. I'm going to kiss every inch of
your naked skin, your lovely breasts, and
your delicious grotto. Erika

_____

Eva. Why don't you reply? Don't be afraid of me.
Don't push me away. You're no innocent. You know
what it's all about. I want to have sex with you,
and I'm going to reward you handsomely. If you're
nice to me, then I'll be nice to you. You've
asked for an extension of your temporary job. I
have the power to extend it and even make it a
full-time position. Let's meet tonight at 9:00 by
my car in the garage. Yours, Erika

_____

"All right," Berger said. "And now she's wondering if I
really sent these to her, is that it?"

"Not exactly . . . I mean . . . geez."

"Peter, please speak up."

"She sort of halfway believed the first email, although she was surprised by it. But she realized this isn't exactly your style and then . . ."

"Then?"

"Well, she thinks it's embarrassing and doesn't know what to do. Part of it is probably that she's very impressed by you and likes you a lot . . . as a boss, I mean. So she came to me and asked for my advice."

"And what did you tell her?"

"I said that someone had faked your address and is obviously harassing her. Or possibly both of you. I said I'd talk to you about it."

"Thank you. Could you please ask her to come to my office in ten minutes?"

In the meantime Berger composed her own email.

It has come to my attention that an employee of SMP has received a number of emails that appear to come from me. The emails contain vulgar sexual innuendos. I have also received similar emails from a sender who purports to be "centraled" at SMP. No such address exists.

I have consulted the head of the IT department, who informs me that it is very easy to fake a sender's address. I don't understand how it's done, but there are sites on the Internet where such things can be arranged. I have to draw the conclusion that some sick individual is doing this.

```
I want to know if any other colleagues have
received strange emails. If so, I would like them
to inform Fredriksson of this immediately. If
these unpleasant pranks continue we will have to
consider reporting them to the police.

Erika Berger, Editor in Chief
```

She printed a copy of the email and then pressed Send so that the message went out to all employees in the company. At that moment, Eva Carlsson knocked on the door.

"Hello. Have a seat," Berger said. "Peter told me that you got an email from me."

"Well, I didn't really think it came from you."

"Thirty seconds ago you *did* get an email from me. I wrote it all by myself and sent it to everyone in the company."

She handed Carlsson the printout.

"OK. I get it," the girl said.

"I'm really sorry that somebody decided to target you for this ugly campaign."

"You don't have to apologize for the actions of some asshole."

"I just want to make sure that you don't have any lingering suspicions that I had anything to do with these emails."

"I never believed you sent them."

"Thanks," Berger said with a smile.

Figuerola spent the afternoon gathering information. She started by ordering passport photographs of Faulsson. Then she ran a check in the criminal records and got a hit at once.

Lars Faulsson, forty-seven years old and known by the nickname Falun, had begun his criminal career stealing cars at seventeen. In the seventies and eighties he was arrested twice and charged with breaking and entering, burglary, and receiving stolen goods. The first time, he was given a light prison sentence; the second time, he got three years. At that time he was regarded as "up and coming" in criminal circles and had been questioned as a suspect in three other burglaries, one of which was a relatively complicated and widely reported safe-cracking heist at a department store in Västerås. When he got out of prison in 1984 he kept his nose clean—or at least he did not pull any jobs that got him arrested and convicted again. But he had retrained himself to be a locksmith (of all professions), and in 1987 he started his own company, Lars Faulsson Lock and Key Service, with an address near Norrtull in Stockholm.

Identifying the woman who had filmed Mårtensson and Faulsson proved to be easier than she had anticipated. She simply called Milton Security and explained that she was looking for a female employee she had met a while ago and whose name she had forgotten. She could give a good description of the woman. The switchboard told her that it sounded like Susanne Linder, and put her through. When Linder answered the phone, Figuerola apologized and said she must have dialled the wrong number.

The public registry listed eighteen Susanne Linders in Stockholm county, three of them around thirty-five years old. One lived in Norrtälje, one in Stockholm, and one in Nacka. She requisitioned their passport photographs and identified at once the woman she had followed from Bellmansgatan as the Susanne Linder who lived in Nacka.

She set out her day's work in a memo and went in to see Edklinth.

Blomkvist closed Cortez's research folder and pushed it away with distaste. Malm put down the printout of his article, which he had read four times. Cortez sat on the sofa in Eriksson's office looking guilty.

"Coffee," Eriksson said, getting up. She came back with four mugs and the coffeepot.

"This is a great sleazy story," Blomkvist said. "First-class research. Documentation to the hilt. Perfect dramaturgy with a bad guy who swindles Swedish tenants through the system—which is legal—but who is so greedy and so fucking stupid that he outsources to this company in Vietnam."

"Very well written too," Malm said. "The day after we publish this, Borgsjö is going to be persona non grata. TV is going to pick this up. He's going to be right up there with the directors of Skandia. A genuine scoop for *Millennium*. Well done, Henry."

"But this thing with Erika is a real fly in the ointment," Blomkvist said.

"Why should that be a problem?" Eriksson said. "Erika isn't the villain. We have to be free to examine any chairman of the board or CEO, even if he happens to be her boss."

"It's a hell of a dilemma," Blomkvist said.

"Erika hasn't completely left *Millennium*," Malm said. "She owns 30 percent and sits on our board. In fact, she's chairman of the board until we can elect Harriet Vanger at the next board meeting, and that won't be until August. Plus, Erika is working at *SMP* and you're about to expose her boss."

Glum silence.

"So what the hell are we going to do?" Cortez said. "Do we kill the article?"

Blomkvist looked Cortez straight in the eye. "No, Henry. We're not going to kill the article. That's not the way we do things at *Millennium*. But this is going to take some legwork. We can't just dump it on Erika's desk as a newspaper headline."

Malm waved a finger in the air. "We're really putting Erika on the spot. She'll have to sell her share of *Millennium* and leave our board . . . or in the worst case, she could get fired by *SMP*. Either way she would have a terrible conflict of interest. Honestly, Henry, I agree with Mikael that we should publish the story, but we may have to postpone it for a month."

"Because we're facing a conflict of loyalties too," Blomkvist said.

"Should I call her?"

"No, Christer," Blomkvist said. "I'll call her and arrange to meet. Tonight."

Figuerola gave a summary of the circus that had sprung up around Blomkvist's building on Bellmansgatan. Edklinth felt the floor sway slightly beneath his chair.

"An employee of SIS goes into Blomkvist's building with an ex-safebreaker, now retrained as a locksmith."

"Correct."

"What do you think they did in the stairwell?"

"I don't know. But they were in there for forty-nine minutes. My guess is that Faulsson opened the door and Mårtensson spent the time in Blomkvist's apartment."

"And what did they do there?"

"It couldn't have been to plant bugs, because that takes only a minute or so. Mårtensson must have been looking through Blomkvist's papers or whatever else he keeps at his place."

"But Blomkvist has already been warned . . . they stole Björck's report from there."

"Right. He knows he's being watched, and he's watching the ones who are watching him. He's calculating."

"Calculating what?"

"I mean, he has a plan. He's gathering information and is going to expose Mårtensson. That's the only reasonable explanation."

"And this Linder woman?"

"Susanne Linder, former police officer."

"Police officer?"

"She graduated from the police academy and worked for six years on the Södermalm crime team. She resigned abruptly. There's nothing in her file that says why. She was out of a job for several months before she was hired by Milton Security."

"Armansky," Edklinth said thoughtfully. "How long was she in the building?"

"Nine minutes."

"Doing what?"

"Since she was filming Mårtensson and Faulsson on the street I'm guessing that she's documenting their activities. That means that Milton Security is working with Blomkvist and has placed surveillance cameras in his apartment or in the stairwell. She probably went in to collect the film."

Edklinth sighed. The Zalachenko story was beginning to get tremendously complicated.

"Thank you. You go home. I have to think about this."

Figuerola went to the gym at St. Eriksplan.

Blomkvist used his second mobile when he punched in Berger's number at *SMP*. He interrupted a discussion she was having with her editors about what angle to give an article on international terrorism.

"Oh, hello, it's you . . . wait a second."

Berger put her hand over the mouthpiece.

"I think we're done," she said, and gave them one last instruction. When she was alone she said: "Hello, Mikael. Sorry not to have been in touch. I'm just so swamped here. There are a thousand things I have got to learn. How's the Salander stuff going?"

"Good. But that's not why I called. I have to see you. Tonight."

"I wish I could, but I have to be here until 8:00. And I'm dead tired. I've been at it since dawn. What's it about?"

"I'll tell you when I see you. But it's not good."

"I'll come to your place at 8:30."

"No. Not at mine. It's a long story, but my apartment is unsuitable for the time being. Let's meet at Samir's Cauldron for a beer."

"I'm driving."

"Then we'll have a light beer."

Berger was slightly annoyed when she walked into Samir's Cauldron. She was feeling guilty because she had not contacted Blomkvist even once since the day she had walked into *SMP*.

Blomkvist waved from a corner table. She stopped in the doorway. For a second he seemed a stranger. *Who's that over there? God, I'm so tired.* Then he stood and kissed her on the cheek, and she realized to her dismay that she had not even thought about him for several weeks and that she missed him terribly. It was as though her time at *SMP* had been a dream and she might suddenly wake up on the sofa at *Millennium*. It felt unreal.

"Hello, Mikael."

"Hello, editor in chief. Have you eaten?"

"It's 8:30. I don't have your disgusting eating habits."

Samir came over with the menu and she realised she was hungry. She ordered a beer and a small plate of calamari with Greek potatoes. Blomkvist ordered couscous and a beer.

"How are you?" she said.

"These are interesting times we're living in. I'm swamped too."

"And Salander?"

"She's part of what makes it so interesting."

"Micke, I'm not going to steal your story."

"I'm not trying to evade your question. The truth is that right now everything is a little confused. I'd love to tell you the whole thing, but it would take half the night. How do you like being editor in chief?"

"It's not exactly *Millennium*. I fall asleep like a blown-out candle as soon as I get home, and when I wake up, I see spreadsheets before my eyes. I've missed you. Can't we go back to your place and sleep? I don't have the energy for sex, but I'd love to curl up and sleep next to you."

"I'm sorry, Ricky. The apartment isn't a good place right now."

"Why not? Has something happened?"

"Well, some spooks have bugged the place and they listen, presumably, to every word I say. I've had cameras installed to record what happens when I'm not home. I don't think we should let the state archives have footage of your naked posterior."

"Are you kidding?"

"No. But that wasn't why I had to see you tonight."

"What is it? Tell me."

"Well, I'll be very direct. We've come across a story that will sink your CEO. It's about using child labour and exploiting political prisoners in Vietnam. We're looking at a conflict of interest."

Berger put down her fork and stared at him. She saw at once that he was not being funny.

"This is how things stand," he said. "Borgsjö is chairman and majority stockholder of a company called Svea Construction, which in turn is sole owner of a subsidiary called Vitavara Inc. They make toilets at a factory in Vietnam which has been condemned by the UN for using child labour."

"Run that by me again."

Blomkvist told her the details of the story that Cortez had compiled. He opened his laptop bag and took out a copy of the documentation. Berger read slowly through the article. Finally she looked up and met Blomkvist's eyes. She felt unreasoning panic mixed with disbelief.

"Why the hell is it that the first thing *Millennium* does after I leave is to start running background checks on *SMP*'s board members?"

"That's not what happened, Ricky." He explained how the story had developed.

"And how long have you known about this?"

"Since today; since this afternoon. I feel deeply uncomfortable about how this has unfolded."

"And what are you going to do?"

"I don't know. We have to publish. We can't make an exception just because it deals with your boss. But not one of us wants to hurt you." He threw up his hands. "We're all extremely unhappy about the situation. Henry especially."

"I'm still a member of *Millennium*'s board. I'm a part owner. It's going to be viewed as—"

"I know exactly how it's going to be viewed. You're going to land in a shitload of trouble at *SMP*."

Berger felt weariness settling over her. She clenched her teeth and stifled an impulse to ask Blomkvist to sit on the story.

"Goddamnit," she said. "And there's no doubt in your mind . . . ?"

Blomkvist shook his head. "I spent the whole afternoon going over Henry's documentation. We have Borgsjö ready for the slaughter."

"So what are you planning, and when?"

"What would you have done if we'd uncovered this story two months ago?"

Berger looked intently at her friend, who had also been her lover over the past twenty years. Then she lowered her eyes.

"You know what I would have done."

"This is a disastrous coincidence. None of it is directed at you. I'm terribly, terribly sorry. That's why I insisted on seeing you at once. We have to decide what to do."

"We?"

"Listen, the story was slated to run in the June issue. I've killed that idea. The earliest it could come out is August, and it can be postponed further if you need more time."

"I understand." Her voice took on a bitter tone.

"I suggest we don't decide anything now. Take the documentation and go home and think it over. Don't do anything until we can agree on a common strategy. We have time."

"A common strategy?"

"You either have to resign from *Millennium*'s board before we publish, or resign from *SMP*. You can't wear both hats."

She nodded. "I'm so linked to *Millennium* that no-one will believe I didn't have a hand in this, whether I resign or not."

"There is an alternative. You could take the story to *SMP* and confront Borgsjö and demand his resignation. I'm quite sure Henry would agree to that. But don't do anything until we all agree."

"So I start by getting the person who recruited me fired."

"I'm sorry."

"He isn't a bad person."

"I believe you. But he's greedy."

Berger got up. "I'm going home."

"Ricky, I—"

She interrupted him. "I'm just dead tired. Thanks for warning me. I'll let you know."

She left without kissing him, and he had to pay the bill.

Berger had parked 200 yards from the restaurant and was halfway to her car when she felt such strong heart palpitations that she had to stop and lean against a wall. She felt sick.

She stood for a long time breathing in the mild May air. She had been working fifteen hours a day since May 1. That was almost three weeks. How would she feel after three years? Was that how Morander had felt before he dropped dead in the newsroom?

After ten minutes she went back to Samir's Cauldron and ran into Blomkvist as he was coming out the door. He stopped in surprise.

"Erika . . ."

"Mikael, don't say a word. We've been friends so long—nothing can destroy that. You're my best friend, and this feels exactly like the time you disappeared to Hedestad two years ago, only vice versa. I feel stressed out and unhappy."

He put his arms around her. She felt tears in her eyes.

"Three weeks at *SMP* have already done me in," she said.

"Now, now. It takes more than that to do in Erika Berger."

"Your apartment is compromised. And I'm too tired to drive home. I'd fall asleep at the wheel and die in a crash. I've decided. I'm going to walk to the Scandic Crown and book a room. Come with me."

"It's called the Hilton now."

"Same difference."

They walked the short distance without talking. Blomkvist had his arm around her shoulder. Berger glanced at him and saw that he was just as tired as she was.

They went straight to the front desk, took a double room, and paid with Berger's credit card. When they got to the room, they undressed, showered, and crawled into bed.

Berger's muscles ached as though she had just run the Stockholm marathon. They cuddled for a while and then both fell asleep in seconds.

Neither of them had noticed the man in the lobby who was watching them as they stepped into the elevator.

CHAPTER 15

Thursday, May 19–
Sunday, May 22

Salander spent most of Wednesday night and early Thursday morning reading Blomkvist's articles and the chapters of the *Millennium* book that were more or less finished. Since Prosecutor Ekström had tentatively referred to a trial in July, Blomkvist had set June 20 as his deadline for going to press. That meant that Blomkvist had about a month to finish writing and patching up all the holes in his text.

She could not imagine how he could finish in time, but that was his problem, not hers. Her problem was how to respond to his questions.

She took her Palm and logged on to the Yahoo group [Idiotic_Table] to check whether he had put up anything new in the past twenty-four hours. He had not. She opened the document that he had called [Central Questions]. She knew the text by heart already, but she read through it again anyway.

He outlined the strategy that Giannini had already explained to her. When her lawyer spoke to her she had listened with only half an ear, almost as though it had nothing to do with her. But Blomkvist, knowing things about her that Giannini did not, could present a more forceful strategy. She skipped down to the fourth paragraph.

```
The only person who can decide your future is
you. It doesn't matter how hard Annika works
for you, or how much Armansky and Palmgren and
I, and others, want to support you. I'm not
going to try to convince you one way or the
other. You have to decide for yourself. You
can turn the trial to your advantage or you
can let them convict you. But if you want to
win, you're going to have to fight.
```

She disconnected and looked up at the ceiling. Blomkvist was asking her for permission to tell the truth in his book. He was not going to mention the fact of Bjurman's raping her, and he had already written that section. He had filled in the gaps by saying that Bjurman had made a deal with Zalachenko which collapsed when Bjurman lost control. Therefore Niedermann was obliged to kill him. Blomkvist did not speculate about Bjurman's motives.

Kalle Fucking Blomkvist was complicating life for her.

At 2:00 in the morning she opened the word-processing programme on her Palm. She clicked on New Document, took out the stylus, and began to tap on the letters on the digital keypad.

> My name is Lisbeth Salander. I was born on
> April 30, 1978. My mother was Agneta Sofia
> Salander. She was twenty-two when I was born.
> My father was a psychopath, killer, and bat-
> terer whose name was Alexander Zalachenko. He
> previously worked in western Europe for the
> Soviet military intelligence service GRU.

It was a slow process, writing with the stylus on the key-pad. She thought through each sentence before she tapped it in. She did not make a single change to what she had written. She worked until 4:00, then turned off her computer and put it in the charger in the recess at the back of her bedside table. By that time she had produced a document corresponding to two single-spaced pages.

Twice since midnight the duty nurse had put her head around the door, but Salander could hear her a long way off, and even before she turned the key the computer was hidden and the patient asleep.

Berger woke at 7:00. She felt far from rested, but she had slept uninterrupted for eight hours. She glanced at Blomkvist, who was still sleeping soundly beside her.

She turned on her mobile to check for messages. Greger Beckman, her husband, had called eleven times. *Shit. I forgot to call.* She dialled the number and explained where she was and why she had not come home. He was angry.

"Erika, don't do that again. It has nothing to do with Mikael, but I've been worried sick all night. I was terrified that something had happened. You know you have to call and tell me if you're not coming home. You can't ever forget something like that."

Beckman was completely OK with the fact that Blomkvist was his wife's lover. Their affair was carried on with his assent. But every time she had decided to sleep at Blomkvist's, she had called her husband to tell him.

"I'm sorry," she said. "I just collapsed in exhaustion last night."

He grunted.

"Try not to be furious with me, Greger. I can't handle it right now. You can give me hell tonight."

He grunted some more and promised to scold her when she got home. "OK. How's Mikael doing?"

"He's dead to the world." She burst out laughing. "Believe it or not, we were fast asleep moments after we got here. That's never happened."

"This is serious, Erika. I think you ought to see a doctor."

When she hung up she called the office and left a message for Fredriksson. Something had come up and she would be in a little later than usual. She asked him to cancel a meeting she had arranged with the culture editor.

She found her shoulder bag, ferreted out a toothbrush, and went to the bathroom. Then she got back into bed and woke Blomkvist.

"Hurry up—go and wash your face and brush your teeth."

"What . . . Huh?" He sat up and looked around in bewilderment. She had to remind him that he was at the Slussen Hilton. He nodded.

"So. To the bathroom with you."

"Why the hurry?"

"Because as soon as you come back I need you to make

love to me." She glanced at her watch. "I have a meeting at 11:00 that I can't postpone. I have to look presentable, and it'll take me at least half an hour to put on my face. And I'll have to buy a new shift dress or something on the way to work. That gives us only two hours to make up for a whole lot of lost time."

Blomkvist headed for the bathroom.

Holmberg parked his father's Ford in the drive of former prime minister Thorbjörn Fälldin's house in Ås just outside Ramvik in Härnösand county. He got out of the car and looked around. At the age of seventy-nine, Fälldin could hardly still be an active farmer, and Holmberg wondered who did the sowing and harvesting. He knew he was being watched from the kitchen window. That was the custom in the village. He himself had grown up in Hälledal outside Ramvik, very close to Sandöbron, which was one of the most beautiful places in the world. At least Holmberg thought so.

He knocked on the front door.

The former leader of the Centre Party looked old, but he seemed alert, and vigorous.

"Hello, Thorbjörn. My name is Jerker Holmberg. We've met before but it's been a few years. My father is Gustav Holmberg, a delegate for the Centre in the seventies and eighties."

"Yes, I recognize you, Jerker. Hello. You're a policeman down in Stockholm now, aren't you? It must be ten or fifteen years since I last saw you."

"I think it's probably longer than that. May I come in?"

Holmberg sat at the kitchen table while Fälldin poured them some coffee.

"I hope all's well with your father. But that's not why you came, is it?"

"No. Dad's doing fine. He's out repairing the roof of the cabin."

"How old is he now?"

"He turned seventy-one two months ago."

"Is that so?" Fälldin said, joining Holmberg at the kitchen table. "So what's this visit all about then?"

Holmberg looked out the window and saw a magpie land next to his car and peck at the ground. Then he turned to Fälldin.

"I am sorry for coming to see you without warning, but I have a big problem. It's possible that when this conversation is over, I'll be fired from my job. I'm here on a work issue, but my boss, Criminal Inspector Jan Bublanski of the violent crimes division in Stockholm, doesn't know I'm here."

"That sounds serious."

"Just say that I'd be on very thin ice if my superiors found out about this visit."

"I understand."

"On the other hand, I'm afraid that if I don't do something, there's a risk that a woman's rights will be shockingly violated, and to make matters worse, it'll be the second time it's happened."

"You'd better tell me the whole story."

"It's about a man named Alexander Zalachenko. He was an agent for the Soviets' GRU and defected to Sweden on Election Day in 1976. He was given asylum and began to work for Säpo. I have reason to believe that you know his story."

Fälldin regarded Holmberg attentively.

"It's a long story," Holmberg said, and he began to tell

Fälldin about the preliminary investigation in which he had been involved for the past few months.

Erika Berger finally rolled over onto her stomach and rested her head on her fists. She broke out in a big smile.

"Mikael, have you ever wondered if the two of us aren't completely nuts?"

"What do you mean?"

"It's true for me, at least. I'm smitten by an insatiable desire for you. I feel like a crazy teenager."

"Oh, yes?"

"And then I want to go home and go to bed with my husband."

Blomkvist laughed. "I know a good therapist."

She poked him in the stomach. "Mikael, it's starting to feel like this thing with *SMP* was one big fucking mistake."

"Bullshit. It's a huge opportunity for you. If anyone can inject life into that dying body, it's you."

"Maybe so. But that's just the problem. *SMP* feels like a cadaver. And then you dropped that bombshell about Borgsjö."

"You have to let things settle down."

"I know. But the thing with Borgsjö is going to be a real problem. I don't have the faintest idea how to handle it."

"Nor do I. But we'll think of something."

She was quiet for a moment.

"I miss you."

"I miss you too."

"How much would it take for you to come to *SMP* and be the news editor?"

"I wouldn't do it for anything. Isn't what's-his-name, Holm, the news editor?"

"Yes. But he's an idiot."

"You got that right."

"Do you know him?"

"I certainly do. I worked for him for three months as a temp in the mid-eighties. He's a prick who plays people off against each other. Besides . . ."

"Besides what?"

"It's nothing."

"Tell me."

"Some girl, Ulla something, who was also a temp, claimed that he sexually harassed her. I don't know how much was true, but the union did nothing about it and her contract wasn't extended."

Berger looked at the clock and sighed. She got up from the bed and made for the shower. Blomkvist did not move when she came out, dried herself, and dressed.

"I think I'll doze for a while," he said.

She kissed his cheek and waved as she left.

Figuerola parked seven cars behind Mårtensson's Volvo on Luntmakargatan, close to the corner of Olof Palmes Gata. She watched as Mårtensson walked to the machine to pay his parking fee. He then walked onto Sveavägen.

Figuerola decided not to pay for a ticket. She would lose him if she went to the machine and back, so she followed him. He turned left onto Kungsgatan, and went into Kungstornet. She waited three minutes before she followed him into the café. He was on the ground floor talking to a

blond man who looked to be in very good shape. A police-
man, she thought. She recognized him as the other man
Malm had photographed outside the Copacabana on May
Day.

She bought herself a coffee and sat at the opposite end of
the café and opened her *Dagens Nyheter*. Mårtensson and his
companion were talking in low voices. She took out her
mobile and pretended to make a call, although neither of the
men was paying her any attention. She took a photograph
with the mobile that she knew would be only 72 dpi—low
quality, but it could be used as evidence that the meeting had
taken place.

After about fifteen minutes the blond man stood up and
left the café. Figuerola cursed. Why had she not stayed outside? She would have recognized him when he came out. She
wanted to leap up and follow him. But Mårtensson was still
there, calmly nursing his coffee. She did not want to draw
attention to herself by leaving so soon after his unidentified
companion.

And then Mårtensson went to the toilet. As soon as he
closed the door Figuerola was on her feet and back out on
Kungsgatan. She looked up and down the block, but the
blond man was gone.

She took a chance and hurried to the corner of Sveavägen.
She could not see him anywhere, so she went down to the
tunnelbana concourse, but it was hopeless.

She turned back towards Kungstornet, feeling stressed.
Mårtensson had left too.

Berger swore when she got back to where she had parked her
BMW the night before.

The car was still there, but during the night some bastard had punctured all four tyres. *Goddamn fucking piss rats,* she fumed.

She called the vehicle recovery service, told them that she did not have time to wait, and put the key in the exhaust pipe. Then she went down to Hornsgatan and hailed a taxi.

Lisbeth Salander logged on to Hacker Republic and saw that Plague was online. She pinged him.

<Hi, Wasp. How's Sahlgrenska?>

<Restful. I need your help.>

<Shoot.>

<I never thought I'd have to ask this.>

<It must be serious.>

<Göran Mårtensson, living in Vällingby. I need access to his computer.>

<OK.>

<Everything on it has to be copied to Blomkvist at Millennium.>

<I'll deal with it.>

<Big Brother is bugging Blomkvist's phone and probably his email. You'll have to send the material to a Hotmail address.>

<OK.>

<If I can't be reached for any reason, Blomkvist is going to need your help. He has to be able to contact you.>

<Oh?>

<He's a bit square, but you can trust him.>

<Hmm.>

```
<How much do you want?>
```

Plague went quiet for a few seconds. `<Does this have
something to do with your situation?>`

```
<Yes.>
<Then I'll do it for nothing.>
<Thanks. But I always pay my debts. I'm going
to need your help all the way to the trial.
I'll send you 30,000.>
<Can you afford it?>
<I can.>
<Then OK.>
<I think we're going to need Trinity too. Can
you persuade him to come to Sweden?>
<To do what?>
<What he's best at. I'll pay him a standard
fee + expenses.>
<OK. What is this job?>
```

She explained what she needed to have done.

On Friday morning Jonasson was faced with an obviously
irritated Inspector Faste on the other side of his desk.

"I don't understand this," Faste said. "I thought Salander
had recovered. I came to Göteborg for two reasons: to interview her and to get her ready to be transferred to a cell in
Stockholm, where she belongs."

"I'm sorry for your wasted journey," Jonasson said. "I'd be
glad to discharge her because we certainly don't have any
beds to spare here. But—"

"Could she be faking?"

Jonasson smiled politely. "I really don't think so. You see,
Lisbeth Salander was shot in the head. I removed a bullet

from her brain, and it was fifty-fifty whether she would survive. She did survive, and her prognosis has been exceedingly satisfactory . . . so much so that my colleagues and I were getting ready to discharge her. Then yesterday she had a setback. She complained of severe headaches and developed a fever that has been fluctuating up and down. Last night she had a temperature of 100 and vomited on two occasions. During the night the fever subsided; she was almost back down to normal and I thought the episode had passed. But when I examined her this morning her temperature had gone up to over 102. That is serious."

"So what's wrong with her?"

"I don't know, but the fact that her temperature is fluctuating indicates that it's not flu or any other viral infection. Exactly what's causing it I can't say—it could be something as simple as an allergy to her medication or to something else she's come into contact with."

He clicked on an image on his computer and turned the screen towards Faste.

"I had a cranial X-ray done. There's a darker area here, as you can see, right next to her gunshot wound. I can't determine what it is. It could be scar tissue as a product of the healing process, but it could also be a minor haemorrhage. And until we've found out what's wrong, I can't release her, no matter how urgent it may be from a police point of view."

Faste knew better than to argue with a doctor, since they were the closest things to God's representatives here on earth. Policemen possibly excepted.

"What is going to happen now?"

"I've ordered complete bedrest and put her physical therapy on hold—she needs therapeutic exercise because of the wounds in her shoulder and hip."

"Understood. I'll have to call Prosecutor Ekström in Stockholm. This will come as a bit of a surprise. What can I tell him?"

"Two days ago I was ready to approve a discharge, possibly for the end of this week. As the situation is now, it will take longer. You'll have to prepare him for the fact that probably I won't be in a position to make a decision in the coming week, and that it might be two weeks before you can move her to Stockholm. It depends on her rate of recovery."

"The trial has been set for July."

"Barring the unforeseen, she should be on her feet well before then."

Bublanski cast a sceptical glance at the muscular woman on the other side of the table. They were drinking coffee in the outdoor area of a café on Norr Mälarstrand. It was Friday, May 20, and the warmth of summer was in the air. Inspector Monica Figuerola, her ID said, SIS. She had caught up with him just as he was leaving for home and suggested a conversation over a cup of coffee.

At first he had been surly, but she had very straightforwardly conceded that she had no authority to interview him and that he was perfectly free to tell her nothing at all if he did not want to. He asked her what her business was, and she told him that she had been assigned by her boss to form an unofficial picture of what was true and not true in the so-called Zalachenko case, also known in some quarters as the Salander case.

"What would you like to know?" Bublanski said at last.

"Tell me what you know about Salander, Mikael Blomkvist, Gunnar Björck, and Zalachenko. How do the pieces fit together?"

They talked for more than two hours.

Edklinth thought long and hard about how to proceed. After five days of investigations, Figuerola had given him a number of indisputable indications that something was rotten within SIS. He recognized the need to move very carefully until he had enough information. He found himself, furthermore, with a constitutional dilemma: he did not have the authority to conduct secret investigations, and most assuredly not against his colleagues.

Accordingly, he had to contrive some cause that would legitimize what he was doing. If worst came to worst, he could always fall back on the fact that it was a policeman's duty to investigate a crime—but the breach was now so sensitive from a constitutional standpoint that he would surely be fired if he took a single wrong step. So he spent the whole of Friday brooding alone in his office.

Finally he concluded that Armansky was right, no matter how improbable it might seem. There really was a conspiracy inside SIS, and a number of individuals were acting outside of, or parallel to, regular operations. Because this had been going on for many years—at least since 1976, when Zalachenko arrived in Sweden—it had to be organized and sanctioned from the top. Exactly how high the conspiracy went he had no idea.

He wrote three names on a pad:

Göran Mårtensson, Personal Protection. Criminal Inspector.

*Gunnar Björck, assistant chief of immigration
    division. Deceased (suicide?).*
Albert Shenke, chief of Secretariat, SIS.

Figuerola was of the view that the chief of Secretariat must have been calling the shots when Mårtensson in Personal Protection was supposedly moved to Counter-Espionage, although he was not in fact working there. He was too busy monitoring the movements of journalist Mikael Blomkvist, and that didn't have anything at all to do with the operations of Counter-Espionage.

Some other names from outside SIS had to be added to the list:

Peter Teleborian, psychiatrist
Lars Faulsson, locksmith

Teleborian had been hired by SIS as a psychiatric consultant on specific cases in the late eighties and early nineties— on three occasions, to be exact—and Edklinth had examined the reports in the archive. The first had been extraordinary: Counter-Espionage had identified a Russian informer inside the Swedish telecom industry, and the spy's background indicated that he might be inclined to suicide in the event that his actions were exposed. Teleborian had done a strikingly good analysis, which helped them turn the informer so that he could become a double agent. His other two reports had involved less significant evaluations: one was of an employee inside SIS who had an alcohol problem, and the second was an analysis of the bizarre sexual behaviour of an African diplomat.

Neither Teleborian nor Faulsson—especially not Faulsson—had any position inside SIS. And yet through their assignments they were connected to ... *to what?*

The conspiracy was intimately linked to the late Alexander Zalachenko, the defected GRU agent who had apparently turned up in Sweden on Election Day in 1976. A man no-one had ever heard of before. *How was that possible?*

Edklinth tried to imagine what reasonably would have happened if he had been sitting at the chief's desk at SIS in 1976 when Zalachenko defected. What would he have done? Absolute secrecy would have been essential. The defection could only be known to a small group without risking that the information might leak back to the Russians, and ... How small a group?

An operations department?

An unknown operations department?

If the affair had been appropriately handled, Zalachenko's case should have ended up in Counter-Espionage. Ideally he should have come under the auspices of the military intelligence service, but they had neither the resources nor the expertise to run this sort of operational activity. So, SIS it was.

But Counter-Espionage never had him. Björck was the key; he had been one of the people who handled Zalachenko. And yet Björck never had anything to do with Counter-Espionage. Björck was a mystery. Officially he had held a post in the immigration division since the seventies, but in reality he had scarcely been seen in the department before the nineties, when suddenly he became assistant chief.

And yet Björck was the primary source of Blomkvist's information. How had Blomkvist been able to persuade Björck to reveal such explosive material? And to a journalist at that.

Prostitutes. Björck messed around with teenage prostitutes, and *Millennium* was going to expose him. Blomkvist must have blackmailed Björck.

Then Salander came into the picture.

The deceased lawyer Nils Bjurman worked in the immigration division at the same time as the deceased Björck. They were the ones who had taken care of Zalachenko. But what did they do with him?

Somebody must have made the decision. With a defector of such importance the order must have come from the highest level.

From the government. It must have been backed by the government. Anything else would be unthinkable.

Edklinth felt cold shivers of apprehension. This was all conceivable in practice. It made sense.

But what happened in 1991 did not make sense. Björck had hired Teleborian to lock Salander up in a psychiatric hospital for children under the pretense that she was mentally deranged. That was a crime. That was such a monstrous crime that Edklinth felt yet more apprehensive.

Somebody must have made that decision. It simply could not have been the government. Ingvar Carlsson had been prime minister at the time, and then Carl Bildt.* But no politician would dare to be involved in such a decision, which contradicted all law and justice and which would result in a disastrous scandal if it were ever discovered.

If the government was involved, then Sweden wasn't one iota better than any dictatorship in the entire world.

It was impossible.

And what about the events of April 12? Zalachenko was

conveniently murdered at Sahlgrenska hospital by a mentally ill fanatic at the same time as a burglary was committed at Blomkvist's apartment and Advokat Giannini was mugged. In both latter instances, copies of Björck's strange report dating from 1991 were stolen. Armansky had contributed this information, but it was completely off the record. No police report was ever filed.

And at the same time, Björck—a person with whom Edklinth wished he could have had a serious talk—hangs himself.

Edklinth didn't believe in coincidence on such a grand scale. Inspector Bublanski didn't believe in it either. Neither did Blomkvist. Edklinth took up his felt pen once more:

> *Evert Gullberg, seventy-eight years old.*
> *Tax specialist. ???*

Who the hell was Evert Gullberg?

He considered calling up the chief of SIS but restrained himself for the simple reason that he did not know how far up in the organization the conspiracy reached. He didn't know whom to trust.

For a moment he considered turning to the regular police. Jan Bublanski was the leader of the investigation concerning Ronald Niedermann, and obviously he would be interested in any related information. But from a purely political standpoint, it was out of the question.

He felt a great weight on his shoulders.

There was only one constitutionally correct option left, which might provide some protection if he ended up in hot water. He would have to turn to the chief to secure political support for what he was working on.

It was just before 4:00 on Friday afternoon. He picked up the phone and called the minister of justice, whom he had known for many years and had dealings with at numerous departmental meetings. He got him on the line within five minutes.

"Hello, Torsten. It's been a long time. What's the problem?"

"To tell you the truth, I think I'm calling to check how much credibility I have with you."

"Credibility? That's a peculiar question. As far as I'm concerned you have *absolute* credibility. What makes you ask such a dramatic question?"

"It's prompted by a dramatic and extraordinary request. I need to have a meeting with you and the prime minister, and it's urgent."

"Whoa!"

"If you'll forgive me, I'd rather explain when we can talk in private. Something so remarkable came across my desk that I believe both you and the prime minister need to be informed."

"Does it have anything to do with terrorists and threat assessments?"

"No. It's more serious than that. I'm putting my reputation and career on the line by calling you with this request."

"I see. That's why you asked about your credibility. How soon do you need the meeting with the PM?"

"This evening if possible."

"Now you've got me worried."

"Unfortunately, there's good reason for you to be worried."

"How long will the meeting take?"

"Probably an hour."

"Let me call you back."

The minister of justice called back ten minutes later and said that the prime minister would meet with Edklinth at his residence at 9:30 that evening. Edklinth's palms were sweating when he put down the phone. *By tomorrow morning my career could be over.*

He called Figuerola.

"Hello, Monica. At 9:00 tonight you have to report for duty. You'd better dress nicely."

"I always dress nicely," Figuerola said.

The prime minister gave the director of Constitutional Protection a long, wary look. Edklinth had a sense that cogs were whirring at high speed behind the PM's glasses.

The PM shifted his gaze to Figuerola, who hadn't said a word during the presentation. He saw an unusually tall and muscular woman looking back at him with a polite, expectant expression. Then he turned to the minister of justice, who had paled over the course of the presentation.

Then the PM took a deep breath, removed his glasses, and stared for a moment into the distance.

"I think we need a little more coffee," he said.

"Yes, please," Figuerola said.

Edklinth nodded and the minister of justice poured coffee from a thermos carafe.

"Let me be absolutely certain I understood you correctly," the prime minister said. "You suspect that there's a conspiracy within the Security Police that is acting outside its constitutional mandate, and that over the years this conspiracy has committed what could be categorized as serious criminal acts."

"Yes."

"And you're coming to me because you don't trust the leadership of the Security Police?"

"No, not exactly," Edklinth said. "I decided to turn directly to you because this sort of activity is unconstitutional. But I don't know the objective of the conspiracy, or whether I've misinterpreted something. For all I know, the activity may be legitimate and sanctioned by the government. Then I risk proceeding on faulty information, thereby compromising some secret operation."

The prime minister looked at the minister of justice. Both understood that Edklinth was hedging his bets.

"I've never heard of anything like this. Do you know anything about it?"

"Absolutely not," the minister of justice said. "There's nothing in any report I've seen from the Security Police that could have a bearing on this matter."

"Blomkvist thinks there's a faction within Säpo. He refers to it as the Zalachenko club," Edklinth said.

"I'd never even heard that Sweden had taken in and protected a Russian defector of such importance," the PM said. "He defected during the Fälldin administration, you say?"

"I don't believe Fälldin would have covered up something like this," the minister of justice said. "This kind of defection would have been given the highest priority, and would have been passed over to the next administration."

Edklinth cleared his throat. "Fälldin's conservative government was succeeded by Olof Palme's. It's no secret that some of my predecessors at SIS had a certain opinion of Palme—"

"You're suggesting that somebody forgot to inform the social democratic government?"

Edklinth nodded. "Let's remember that Fälldin was in power for two separate mandates. Each time, the coalition government collapsed. First he handed over to Ola Ullsten, who had a minority government in 1979. The government collapsed again when the moderates jumped ship, and Fälldin governed together with the People's Party. I'm guessing that the government secretariat was in turmoil during those transition periods. It's also possible that knowledge of Zalachenko was confined to so small a circle that Prime Minister Fälldin had no real oversight, so he never had anything to hand over to Palme."

"In that case, who's responsible?" the PM said.

All except Figuerola shook their heads.

"I assume this is bound to leak to the media," the PM said.

"Blomkvist and *Millennium* are going to publish it. In other words, we're caught between the proverbial rock and hard place." Edklinth was careful to use the word *we*.

The PM nodded. He realized the gravity of the situation. "Then I'll have to start by thanking you for coming to me with this matter as soon as you did. I don't usually agree to this sort of unscheduled meeting, but the minister here said that you were a prudent person, and that something serious must have happened if you wanted to see me outside all normal channels."

Edklinth exhaled a little. Whatever happened, the wrath of the prime minister was not going to come down on him.

"Now we just have to decide how we're going to handle it. Do you have any suggestions?"

"Perhaps," Edklinth said tentatively.

He was silent for so long that Figuerola cleared her throat. "May I say something?"

"Please do," the PM said.

"If it's true that the government doesn't know about this operation, then it's illegal. The person responsible in such a case is the criminal civil servant—or civil servants—who overstepped his authority. If we can verify all the claims Blomkvist is making, it means that a group of officers within SIS have been devoting themselves to criminal activity for a long time. The problem would then unfold in two parts."

"How do you mean?"

"First we have to ask the question: How could this have been possible? Who is responsible? How did such a conspiracy develop within the framework of an established police organization? I myself work for SIS, and I'm proud of it. How can this have gone on for so long? How could this activity have been both concealed and financed?"

"Go on," the PM said.

"Whole books will probably be written about this first part. It's clear that there must have been financing, at least several million kronor annually, I'd say. I looked over the budget of the Security Police and found nothing resembling an allocation for the Zalachenko club. But, as you know, there are a number of hidden funds controlled by the chief of Secretariat and chief of Budget that I have no access to."

The prime minister nodded grimly. Why did Säpo always have to be such a nightmare to administer?

"The second part is: who is involved? And very specifically, which individuals should be arrested? From my standpoint, the answers to all these questions depend on the decision you make in the next few minutes," she said to the PM.

Edklinth was holding his breath. If he could have kicked Figuerola in the shin he would have done so. She had cut through all the rhetoric and intimated that the prime minister himself was responsible. He had considered coming to the same conclusion, but not before a long and diplomatic circumlocution.

"What decision do you think I should make?"

"I believe we have common interests. I've worked at Constitutional Protection for three years. I consider this office of central importance to Swedish democracy. The Security Police has worked satisfactorily within the framework of the constitution in recent years. Naturally, I don't want the scandal to affect SIS. For us it's important to bear in mind that this is a case of criminal activity perpetrated by a small number of individuals."

"Activity of this kind is most definitely not sanctioned by the government," the minister of justice said.

Figuerola nodded and thought for a few seconds. "It is, in my view, essential that the scandal should not implicate the government—which is what would happen if the government tried to suppress the story."

"The government does not cover up criminal activity," the minister of justice said.

"No, but let's assume, hypothetically, that the government might want to do so. There would be a scandal of enormous proportions."

"Go on," the PM said.

"The situation is complicated by the fact that we in Constitutional Protection are being forced to conduct an operation which is itself against regulations in order to investigate this matter. So we want everything to be legitimate and in keeping with the constitution."

"As do we all," the PM said.

"In that case I suggest that you—in your capacity as prime minister—instruct Constitutional Protection to investigate this mess with the utmost urgency," Figuerola said. "Give us a written order and the authority we need."

"I'm not sure that what you propose is legal," the minister of justice said.

"It is legal. The government has the power to adopt a wide range of measures in the event that breaches of the constitution are threatened. If a group from the military or police starts pursuing an independent foreign policy, a de facto coup has taken place in Sweden."

"Foreign policy?" the minister of justice said.

The PM nodded all of a sudden.

"Zalachenko was a defector from a foreign power," Figuerola said. "The information he contributed was supplied, according to Blomkvist, to foreign intelligence services. If the government was not informed, a coup has taken place."

"I follow your reasoning," the PM said. "Now let me say my piece."

He got up and walked once around the table before stopping in front of Edklinth.

"You have a very talented colleague. She has hit the nail on the head."

Edklinth swallowed and nodded. The PM turned to the minister of justice.

"Get in touch with the undersecretary of state and the head of the legal department. By tomorrow morning I want a document drawn up granting the Constitutional Protection Unit extraordinary authority to act in this matter. Their assignment is to determine the truth behind the assertions we have discussed, to gather documentation about its extent, and to identify the individuals responsible or in any way involved. The document must not state that you are conducting a preliminary investigation—I may be wrong, but I think only the prosecutor general could appoint a preliminary investigation leader in this situation. But I can give you the authority to conduct a one-man investigation. What you are doing is therefore an official public report. Do you understand?"

"Yes. But I should point out that I myself am a former prosecutor."

"We'll have to ask the head of the legal department to take a look at this and determine exactly what is formally correct. In any case, you alone are responsible for your investigation. You will choose the assistants you require. If you find evidence of criminal activity, you must turn this information over to the PG, who will decide on the charges."

"I'll have to look up exactly what applies, but I think you'll have to inform the speaker of Parliament and the constitutional committee. This is going to leak out fast," the minister of justice said.

"In other words, we have to work faster," the PM said.

Figuerola raised a hand.

"What is it?" the PM said.

"There are two problems remaining. First, will *Millen-*

nium's publication clash with our investigation? And second, Lisbeth Salander's trial will be starting in a couple of weeks."

"Can we find out when *Millennium*'s going to publish?"

"We could ask," Edklinth said. "The last thing we want to do is to interfere with the press."

"With regard to this girl Salander . . . ," the minister of justice began, and then he paused for a moment. "It would be terrible if she really has been subjected to the injustices that *Millennium* claims. Could it be possible?"

"I'm afraid it is," Edklinth said.

"In that case we have to see to it that she is given redress for these wrongs, and above all that she is not subjected to new injustices," the PM said.

"And how would that work?" asked the minister of justice. "The government cannot interfere in an ongoing prosecution case. That would be against the law."

"Could we talk to the prosecutor?"

"No," Edklinth said. "As prime minister, you may not influence the judicial process in any way."

"In other words, Salander will have to take her chances in court," the minister of justice said. "Only if she loses the trial and appeals to the government can the government step in and pardon her or require the PG to investigate whether there are grounds for a new trial. But this applies only if she's sentenced to prison. If she's sentenced to a secure psychiatric facility, the government cannot do a thing. Then it's a medical matter, and the prime minister has no jurisdiction to determine whether or not she is sane."

At 10:00 on Friday night, Salander heard the key turn in the door. She instantly switched off her Palm and slipped it under the mattress. When she looked up she saw Jonasson closing the door.

"Good evening, Fröken Salander," he said. "And how are you doing this evening?"

"I have a splitting headache and I feel feverish."

"That doesn't sound so good."

Salander looked to be not particularly bothered by either the fever or the headache. Jonasson spent ten minutes examining her. He noticed that over the course of the evening her fever had again risen dramatically.

"It's a shame that you should be having this setback when you've been recovering so well over the past few weeks. Unfortunately, I now won't be able to discharge you for at least two more weeks."

"Two weeks should be sufficient."

The distance by land from London to Stockholm is roughly 1,180 miles. In theory that would be about twenty hours' driving. In fact it had taken almost twenty hours to reach the northern border of Germany with Denmark. The sky was filled with leaden thunderclouds, and when the man known as Trinity found himself on Sunday in the middle of the Øresundsbron, there was a downpour. He slowed and turned on his windshield wipers.

Trinity thought it was sheer hell driving in Europe, since everyone on the Continent insisted on driving on the wrong side of the road. He had packed his van on Friday morning and taken the ferry from Dover to Calais, then crossed Belgium by way of Liège. He crossed the German border at Aachen and then took the Autobahn north towards Hamburg and on to Denmark.

His companion, Bob the Dog, was asleep in the back. They had taken turns driving, and apart from a couple of hour-long stops along the way, they had maintained a steady fifty-five miles an hour. The van was eighteen years old and wasn't able to go much faster anyway.

There were easier ways of getting from London to Stockholm, but it wasn't likely that he would be able to take more than sixty pounds of electronic gear on a normal flight. They had crossed six national borders, but they had not been stopped once, either by customs or by passport control. Trinity was an ardent fan of the EU, whose regulations simplified his visits to the Continent.

Trinity had been born in Bradford, but he had lived in north London since childhood. He had had a miserable formal education, and then attended a vocational school and earned a certificate as a trained telecommunications technician. For three years after his nineteenth birthday he had worked as an engineer for British Telecom. Once he understood how the telephone network functioned and realized how hopelessly antiquated it was, he switched to being a private security consultant, installing alarm systems and managing burglary protection. For special clients he would also offer his video surveillance and telephone-tapping services.

Now thirty-two years old, he had a theoretical knowledge of electronics and computer science that allowed him to challenge any professor in the field. He had lived with computers since he was ten, and he hacked his first computer when he was thirteen.

It had whetted his appetite, and when he was sixteen he had advanced to the extent that he could compete with the best in the world. There was a period in which he spent every waking minute in front of his computer screen, writing his own programmes and planting insidious tendrils on the Internet. He infiltrated the BBC, the Ministry of Defence, and Scotland Yard. He even managed—for a short time—to take command of a nuclear submarine on patrol in the North Sea. It was for the best that Trinity belonged to the inquisitive rather than the malicious type of computer marauder. His fascination was extinguished the moment he had cracked a computer, gained access, and appropriated its secrets.

He was one of the founders of Hacker Republic. And Wasp was one of its citizens.

It was 7:30 on Sunday evening as he and Bob the Dog approached Stockholm. When they passed IKEA at Kungens Kurva in Skärholmen, Trinity flipped open his mobile and dialled a number he had memorized.

"Plague," Trinity said.

"Where are you guys?"

"You said to call when we passed IKEA."

Plague gave him directions to the youth hostel on Långholmen where he had booked a room for his colleagues from England. Since Plague hardly ever left his apartment, they agreed to meet at his place at 10:00 the next morning.

Plague decided to make an exceptional effort and washed the dishes, generally cleaned up, and opened the windows in anticipation of his guests' arrival.

PART 3

Disk Crash

MAY 27–JUNE 6

The historian Diodorus from Sicily, second century BC
(who is regarded as an unreliable source by other historians), describes the Amazons of Libya, which at that
time was a name used for all of north Africa west of
Egypt. This Amazon reign was a gynaecocracy; that is,
only women were allowed to hold high office, including in the military. According to legend, the realm was
ruled by a Queen Myrina, who with 30,000 female soldiers and 3,000 female cavalry swept through Egypt
and Syria and all the way to the Aegean, defeating a
number of male armies along the way. After Queen
Myrina finally fell in battle, her army scattered.

But the army did leave its imprint on the region.
The women of Anatolia took to the sword to crush an
invasion from the Caucasus, after the male soldiers
were all slaughtered in a far-reaching genocide. These

women trained in the use of all types of weapons, including bow and arrow, spear, battleaxe, and lance. They copied their bronze breastplates and armour from the Greeks.

They rejected marriage as subjugation. So that they might have children they were granted a leave of absence, during which they copulated with randomly selected males from nearby towns.

Only a woman who had killed a man in battle was allowed to give up her virginity.

CHAPTER 16

Friday, May 27– Tuesday, May 31

Blomkvist left the *Millennium* offices at 10:30 on Friday night. He took the stairs down to the ground floor, but instead of going out onto the street he turned left and went through the basement, across the inner courtyard, and through the building behind theirs onto Hökens Gata. He ran into a group of youths on their way from Mosebacke, but no-one seemed to be paying him any attention. Anyone watching the building would think that he was spending the night at *Millennium,* as he often did. He had established that pattern as early as April. Actually it was Malm who had the night shift.

He spent fifteen minutes walking down the alleys and boulevards around Mosebacke before he headed for Fiskargatan 9. He opened the door using the code and took the stairs to the top-floor apartment, where he used Salander's keys to get in. He turned off the alarm. He always felt a bit bemused when he went into the apartment: twenty-one rooms, of which only three were furnished.

He made coffee and sandwiches before he went into Salander's office and booted up her PowerBook.

From the moment in mid-April when Björck's report was stolen and Blomkvist realized he was under surveillance, he had established his own headquarters at Salander's apartment. He had transferred the most crucial documentation to her desk. He spent several nights a week at the apartment, slept in her bed, and worked on her computer. She had wiped her hard drive clean before she left for Gosseberga and the confrontation with Zalachenko. Blomkvist supposed that she had not planned to come back. He had used her system disks to restore her computer to a functioning state.

Since April he had not even plugged in the broadband cable to his own machine. He logged on to her broadband connection, started up the ICQ chat programme, and pinged up the address she had created for him through the Yahoo group [Idiotic_Table].

<Hi, Sally.>

<Talk to me.>

<I've been working on the two chapters we discussed earlier this week. New version is on Yahoo. How's it going with you?>

<Finished with 17 pages. Uploading now.>

Ping.

<OK. Got 'em. Let me read, then we'll talk later.>

<I've got more.>

<More what?>

<I created another Yahoo group called The_Knights.>

Blomkvist smiled.

<The Knights of the Idiotic Table.>

<Password yacaraca12.>

<Four members. You, me, Plague, and Trinity.>

<Your mysterious night-time buddies.>

<Protection.>

<OK.>

<Plague has copied info from Prosecutor
Ekström's computer. We hacked it in April.
If I lose the Palm he'll keep you informed.>

<Good. Thanks.>

Blomkvist logged in to ICQ and went into the newly created Yahoo group [The_Knights]. All he found was a link from Plague to an anonymous URL which consisted solely of numbers. He copied the address into Explorer, hit the Return key, and came to a website somewhere on the Internet that contained the sixteen gigabytes of Ekström's hard drive.

Plague had obviously made it simple for himself by copying over Ekström's entire hard drive, and Blomkvist spent more than an hour sorting through its contents. He ignored the system files, software, and endless files containing preliminary investigations that seemed to stretch back several years. He downloaded four folders. Three of them were called [PrelimInv/Salander], [Slush/Salander], and [PrelimInv/Niedermann]. The fourth was a copy of Ekström's email folder made at 2:00 p.m. the previous day.

"Thanks, Plague," Blomkvist said to himself.

He spent three hours reading through Ekström's preliminary investigation and strategy for the trial. Not surprisingly, much of it dealt with Salander's mental state. Ekström wanted an extensive psychiatric examination and had sent a lot of messages with the object of getting her transferred to Kronoberg prison as a matter of urgency.

Blomkvist could tell that Ekström was making no headway in his search for Niedermann. Bublanski was the leader of that investigation. He had succeeded in gathering some forensic evidence linking Niedermann to the murders of Svensson and Johansson, as well as to the murder of Bjurman. Blomkvist's own three long interviews in April had set them on the trail of this evidence. If Niedermann were ever apprehended, Blomkvist would have to be a witness for the prosecution. At long last DNA from sweat droplets and two hairs from Bjurman's apartment were matched to items from Niedermann's room in Gosseberga. The same DNA was found in abundant quantities on the remains of Svavelsjö MC's Göransson.

On the other hand, Ekström had remarkably little on the record about Zalachenko.

Blomkvist lit a cigarette and stood by the window looking out towards Djurgården.

Ekström was leading two separate preliminary investigations. Criminal Inspector Faste was the investigative leader in all matters dealing with Salander. Bublanski was working only on Niedermann.

When the name Zalachenko turned up in the preliminary investigation, the logical thing for Ekström to do would have been to contact the general director of the Security Police to determine who Zalachenko actually was. Blomkvist could find no such enquiry in Ekström's email, journal, or notes. But among the notes Blomkvist found several cryptic sentences.

The Salander investigation is fake. Björck's original doesn't match Blomkvist's version. Classify Top Secret.

Then a series of notes claiming that Salander was paranoid and a schizophrenic.

Correct to lock up Salander 1991.

He found what linked the investigations in the Salander slush, that is, the supplementary information that the prosecutor considered irrelevant to the preliminary investigation, and which would therefore not be presented at the trial or make up part of the chain of evidence against her. This included almost everything that had to do with Zalachenko's background.

The investigation was totally inadequate.

Blomkvist wondered to what extent this was a coincidence and to what extent it was contrived. Where was the boundary? And was Ekström aware that there was a boundary?

Could it be that someone was deliberately supplying Ekström with believable but misleading information?

Finally Blomkvist logged into Hotmail and spent ten minutes checking the half-dozen anonymous email accounts he had created. Each day he had checked the address he had given to Criminal Inspector Modig. He had no great hope that she would contact him, so he was mildly surprised when he opened the in-box and found an email from <ressallskap9april@ hotmail.com>. The message consisted of a single line:

Café Madeleine, upper level, 11:00 a.m. Saturday.

Plague pinged Salander at midnight and interrupted her in the middle of a sentence she was writing about her time

with Holger Palmgren as her guardian. She cast an irritated
glance at the display.

<What do you want?>

<Hi, Wasp; nice to hear from you too.>

<Yeah yeah. What is it?>

<Teleborian.>

She sat up in bed and looked eagerly at the screen of
her Palm.

<Tell me.>

<Trinity fixed it in record time.>

<How?>

<The crazy-doctor won't stay in one place.
He travels between Uppsala and Stockholm
all the time and we can't do a hostile
takeover.>

<I know. How?>

<He plays tennis twice a week. About two
hours. Left his computer in the car in a
garage.>

<Aha.>

<Trinity easily disabled the car alarm to
get the computer. Took him 30 minutes to
copy everything via Firewire and install
Asphyxia.>

<Where?>

Plague gave her the URL of the server where he kept Teleborian's hard drive.

<To quote Trinity, this is one nasty shit.>

<?>

<Check his hard drive.>

Salander disconnected from Plague and accessed the server he had directed her to. She spent nearly three hours scrutinizing folder after folder on Teleborian's computer.

She found correspondence between Teleborian and a person with a Hotmail address who sent encrypted email. Since she had access to Teleborian's PGP key, she easily decoded the correspondence. His name was Jonas, no last name. Jonas and Teleborian had an unhealthy interest in seeing that Salander did not thrive.

Yes, we can prove that there is a conspiracy.

But what really interested Salander were the forty-seven folders containing close to 9,000 photographs of explicit child pornography. She clicked on image after image of children aged about fifteen or younger. A number of pictures were of infants. The majority were of girls. Many of them were sadistic.

She found links to at least a dozen people abroad who traded child porn with one another.

Salander bit her lip, but her face was otherwise expressionless.

She remembered the nights when, as a twelve-year-old, she had been strapped down in a stimulus-free room at St. Stefan's. Teleborian had come into the room again and again to look at her in the glow of the night light.

She knew. He had never touched her, but she had always known.

She should have dealt with Teleborian years ago. But she had repressed the memory of him. She had chosen to ignore his existence.

After a while she pinged Blomkvist on ICQ.

. . .

Blomkvist spent the night at Salander's apartment on Fiskargatan. He did not shut down the computer until 6:30 a.m. and fell asleep with photographs of gross child pornography whirling through his mind. He woke at 10:15 and rolled out of Salander's bed, showered, and called a taxi to pick him up outside Södra theatre. He got out at Birger Jarlsgatan at 10:55 and walked to Café Madeleine.

Modig was waiting for him with a cup of black coffee in front of her.

"Hi," Blomkvist said.

"I'm taking a big risk here," she said without greeting.

"Nobody will hear of our meeting from me."

She seemed stressed.

"One of my colleagues recently went to see former prime minister Fälldin. He went there on his own initiative, and his job is on the line now too."

"I understand."

"I need a guarantee of anonymity for both of us."

"I don't even know which colleague you're talking about."

"I'll tell you later. I want you to promise to give him protection as a source."

"You have my word."

She looked at her watch.

"Are you in a hurry?"

"Yes. I have to meet my husband and kids at the Sturegallerian in ten minutes. He thinks I'm still at work."

"And Bublanski knows nothing about this?"

"No."

"Right. You and your colleague are sources and you have complete source protection. Both of you. As long as you live."

"My colleague is Jerker Holmberg. You met him down in Göteborg. His father is a Centre Party member, and Jerker has known Prime Minister Fälldin since he was a child. He seems to be pleasant enough. So Jerker went to see him and asked about Zalachenko."

Blomkvist's heart began to pound.

"Jerker asked Fälldin what he knew about the defection, but Fälldin didn't reply. When Holmberg told him that we suspect Salander was locked up by the people who were protecting Zalachenko, well, that really upset him."

"Did he say how much he knew?"

"Fälldin told him that the chief of Säpo at the time and a colleague came to visit him very soon after he became prime minister. They told a fantastic story about a Russian defector who had come to Sweden, told him that it was the most sensitive military secret Sweden possessed, that there was nothing in Swedish military intelligence that was anywhere near as important. Fälldin said he didn't know how to handle it, that there was no-one with much experience in government, the Social Democrats having been in power for more than forty years. He was advised that he alone had to make the decisions, and that if he discussed it with his government colleagues then Säpo would wash their hands of it. He remembered the whole thing as being very unpleasant."

"What *did* he do?"

"He realized he had no choice but to do what the gentlemen from Säpo proposed. He issued a directive putting Säpo in sole charge of the defector. He pledged never to discuss the matter with anyone. Fälldin was never ever told Zalachenko's name."

"Extraordinary."

"After that he heard almost nothing more during his two terms in office. But he did do something extremely shrewd. He insisted that an undersecretary of state be let in on the secret, in case there was a need for a go-between for the government secretariat and those who were protecting Zalachenko."

"Did he remember who it was?"

"It was Bertil K. Janeryd, now Swedish ambassador in The Hague. When it was explained to Fälldin how serious this preliminary investigation was, he sat down and wrote to Janeryd."

Modig pushed an envelope across the table.

Dear Bertil,

> *The secret we both protected during my administration is now the subject of some very serious questions. The person referred to in the matter is now deceased and can no longer come to harm. But other people can.*

> *It is of the utmost importance that we obtain answers to the necessary questions.*

> *The person who bears this letter is working unofficially and has my trust. I urge you to listen to his story and answer his questions.*

> *Use your famous good judgement.*

> *T.F.*

"This letter is referring to Holmberg?"

"No. Jerker asked Fälldin not to put in a name. He said that he couldn't know who would be going to The Hague."

"You mean . . . ?"

"Jerker and I have discussed it. We're already out on ice so thin that we'll need paddles rather than ice picks. We have no authority to travel to Holland to interview the ambassador. But you could do it."

Blomkvist folded the letter and was putting it into his jacket pocket when Modig grabbed his hand. Her grip was hard.

"Information for information," she said. "We want to hear everything Janeryd tells you."

Blomkvist nodded. Modig stood up.

"Hang on. You said that Fälldin was visited by two people from Säpo. One was the chief of Säpo. Who was the other?"

"Fälldin met him only on that one occasion and couldn't remember his name. No notes were taken at the meeting. He remembered him as thin with a narrow moustache. But he did recall that the man was introduced as the boss of the Section for Special Analysis, or something like that. Fälldin later looked at an organizational chart of Säpo and couldn't find that department."

The Zalachenko club, Blomkvist thought.

Modig seemed to be weighing her words.

"At the risk of ending up dead," she said at last, "there is one record that neither Fälldin nor his visitors thought of."

"What was that?"

"Fälldin's visitors' logbook at Rosenbad. Jerker requisitioned it. It's a public document."

"And?"

Modig hesitated once again. "The book states only that the prime minister met with the chief of Säpo along with a colleague to discuss general questions."

"Was there a name?"

"Yes. E. Gullberg."

Blomkvist could feel the blood rush to his head.

"Evert Gullberg," he said.

Blomkvist called from Café Madeleine on his anonymous mobile to book a flight to Amsterdam. The plane would take off from Arlanda at 2:50. He walked to Dressman on Kungsgatan and bought a shirt and a change of underwear, and then he went to a pharmacy to buy a toothbrush and other toiletries. He checked carefully to see that he was not being followed and hurried to catch the Arlanda Express.

The plane landed at Schiphol airport at 4:50, and by 6:30 he was checking in to a small hotel about fifteen minutes' walk from The Hague's Centraal station.

He spent two hours trying to locate the Swedish ambassador and made contact by telephone at around 9:00. He used all his powers of persuasion and explained that he was there on a matter of great urgency. The ambassador finally relented and agreed to meet him at 10:00 on Sunday morning.

Then Blomkvist went out and had a light dinner at a restaurant near his hotel. He was asleep by 11:00.

Ambassador Janeryd was in no mood for small talk when he offered Blomkvist coffee at his residence on Lange Voorhout.

"Well, what is it that's so urgent?"

"Alexander Zalachenko. The Russian defector who came to Sweden in 1976," Blomkvist said, handing him the letter from Fälldin.

Janeryd looked surprised. He read the letter and laid it on the table beside him.

Blomkvist explained the background and why Fälldin had written to him.

"I . . . I can't discuss this matter," Janeryd said at last.

"I think you can."

"No. I can only speak of it with the constitutional committee."

"There's a great probability that you will have to do just that. But this letter tells you to use your own good judgement."

"Fälldin is an honest man."

"I don't doubt that. And I'm not looking to damage either you or Fälldin. Nor do I ask you to tell me a single military secret that Zalachenko may have revealed."

"I don't know any secrets. I didn't even know that his name was Zalachenko. I only knew him by his cover name, Ruben. But it's absurd that you should think I would discuss it with a journalist."

"Let me give you one very good reason why you should," Blomkvist said and sat up straight in his chair. "This whole story is going to be published very soon. And when that happens, the media will either tear you to pieces or describe you as an honest civil servant who made the best of an impossible situation. You were the one Fälldin assigned to be the go-between with those who were protecting Zalachenko. I already know that."

Janeryd was silent for almost a minute.

"Listen, I never had any information, not the remotest idea of the background you've described. I was young. . . . I didn't know how I should deal with these people. I met them about twice a year during the time I worked for the government. I was told that Ruben—your Zalachenko—was alive and healthy, that he was cooperating, and that the information he provided was invaluable. I was never privy to the details. I had no 'need to know.'"

Blomkvist waited.

"The defector had operated in other countries and knew nothing about Sweden, so he was never a major factor for security policy. I informed the prime minister on a couple of occasions, but there was never very much to report."

"I see."

"They always said that he was being handled in the customary way and that the information he provided was being processed through the appropriate channels. What could I say? If I asked for clarification, they smiled and said that it was outside my security clearance level. I felt like an idiot."

"You never considered the fact that there might be something wrong with the arrangement?"

"No. There was nothing wrong with the arrangement. I took it for granted that Säpo knew what they were doing and had the appropriate routines and experience. But I can't talk about this."

Janeryd had by this time been talking about it for several minutes.

"OK. But all this is beside the point. Only one thing is important right now."

"What?"

"The names of the individuals you had your meetings with."

Janeryd gave Blomkvist a puzzled look.

"The people who were looking after Zalachenko went far beyond their jurisdiction. They've committed serious criminal acts, and they'll be the subject of a preliminary investigation. That's why Fälldin sent me to see you. He doesn't know who they are. You were the one who met them."

Janeryd blinked and pressed his lips together.

"One was Evert Gullberg. . . . He was the top man."

Janeryd nodded.

"How many times did you meet him?"

"He was at every meeting except one. There were about ten meetings during the time Fälldin was prime minister."

"Where did you meet?"

"In the lobby of some hotel. Usually the Sheraton. Once at the Amaranth on Kungsholmen and sometimes at the Continental pub."

"And who else was at the meetings?"

"It was a long time ago; I don't remember."

"Try."

"There was a . . . Clinton. Like the American president."

"First name?"

"Fredrik. I saw him four or five times."

"Others?"

"Hans von Rottinger. I knew him through my mother."

"Your mother?"

"Yes, my mother knew the von Rottinger family. Hans von Rottinger was always a pleasant guy. Before he turned up out of the blue at a meeting with Gullberg, I had no idea that he worked for Säpo."

"He didn't," Blomkvist said.

Janeryd turned pale.

"He worked for something called the Section for Special Analysis," Blomkvist said. "What were you told about that group?"

"Nothing. I mean, just that they were the ones who took care of the defector."

"Right. But isn't it strange that they don't appear anywhere in Säpo's organizational chart?"

"That's ridiculous."

"It is, isn't it? So how did they set up the meetings? Did they call you, or did you call them?"

"Neither. The time and place for each meeting was set at the preceding one."

"What happened if you needed to get in contact with them? For instance, to change the time of a meeting or something like that?"

"I had a number to call."

"What was the number?"

"I couldn't possibly remember."

"Who answered if you called the number?"

"I don't know. I never used it."

"Next question. Who did you hand everything over to?"

"How do you mean?"

"When Fälldin's term came to an end. Who took your place?"

"I don't know."

"Did you write a report?"

"No. Everything was classified. I couldn't even take notes."

"And you never briefed your successor?"

"No."

"So what happened?"

"Well . . . Fälldin left office, and Ola Ullsten came in. I was told that we would have to wait until after the next election. Then Fälldin was re-elected and our meetings were resumed.

Then came the election in 1985. The Social Democrats won, and I assume that Palme appointed somebody to take over from me. I transferred to the foreign ministry and became a diplomat. I was posted to Egypt, and then to India."

Blomkvist went on asking questions for another few minutes, but he was sure that he already had everything Janeryd could tell him. Three names.

Fredrik Clinton.

Hans von Rottinger.

And Evert Gullberg—the man who had shot Zalachenko.

The Zalachenko club.

He thanked Janeryd for the meeting and walked the short distance along Lange Voorhout to Hotel Des Indes, from which he took a taxi to Centraal. It was not until he was in the taxi that he reached into his jacket pocket and stopped the tape recorder.

Berger looked up and scanned the half-empty newsroom beyond the glass cage. Holm was off that day. She saw no-one who showed any interest in her, either openly or covertly. Nor did she have reason to think that anyone on the editorial staff wished her ill.

The email had arrived a minute before. The sender was <editorial@aftonbladet.com>. Why *Aftonbladet*? The address was another fake.

Today's message contained a JPEG, which she opened in Photoshop.

The image was pornographic: a naked woman with exceptionally large breasts, a dog collar around her neck. She was on all fours and being mounted from the rear.

The woman's face had been replaced with Berger's. It was not a skilled collage, but probably that was not the point. The picture was from her old byline at *Millennium* and could be downloaded off the Net.

At the bottom of the picture was one word, written with the spray function in Photoshop.

Whore.

This was the ninth anonymous message she had received containing the word *whore,* sent apparently by someone at a well-known media outlet in Sweden. She had a cyber-stalker on her hands.

The telephone tapping was a more difficult task than the computer monitoring. Trinity had no trouble locating the cable to Prosecutor Ekström's home phone. The problem was that Ekström seldom or never used it for work-related calls. Trinity did not even consider trying to bug Ekström's work phone at police HQ on Kungsholmen. That would have required extensive access to the Swedish cable network, which he did not have.

But Trinity and Bob the Dog devoted the best part of a week to identifying and separating out Ekström's mobile from the background noise of about 200,000 other mobiles within half a mile of police headquarters.

They used a technique called Random Frequency Tracking System. The technique was not uncommon. It had been developed by the U.S. National Security Agency, and was built into an unknown number of satellites that performed pinpoint monitoring of capitals around the world, as well as flashpoints of special interest.

The NSA had enormous resources and used a vast network in order to capture a large number of mobile conversations in a certain region simultaneously. Each individual call was separated and processed digitally by computers programmed to react to certain words, such as *terrorist* or *Kalashnikov*. If such a word occurred, the computer automatically sent an alarm, which meant that some operator would go in manually and listen to the conversation to decide whether it was of interest or not.

It was a more complex problem to identify a specific mobile. Each mobile has its own unique signature—a fingerprint—in the form of the phone number. With exceptionally sensitive equipment the NSA could focus on a specific area to separate out and monitor mobile calls. The technique was simple but not 100 percent effective. Outgoing calls were particularly hard to identify. Incoming calls were simpler because they were preceded by the fingerprint that would enable the phone in question to receive the signal.

The difference between Trinity's and the NSA's attempting to eavesdrop could be measured in economic terms. The NSA had an annual budget of several billion U.S. dollars, close to 12,000 full-time agents, and access to cutting-edge technology in IT and telecommunications. Trinity had a van with sixty pounds of electronic equipment, much of which was home-made stuff that Bob the Dog had set up. Through its global satellite monitoring, the NSA could train highly sensitive antennae on a specific building anywhere in the world. Trinity had an antenna constructed by Bob the Dog which had an effective range of about 500 yards.

The relatively limited technology to which Trinity had access meant that he had to park his van on Bergsgatan or one of the nearby streets and laboriously calibrate the equipment until he had identified the fingerprint that represented Ekström's mobile number. Since he did not know Swedish, he had to relay the conversations via another mobile to Plague, who did the actual eavesdropping.

For five days, Plague, who was looking more and more hollow-eyed, listened in vain to a vast number of calls to and from police headquarters and the surrounding buildings. He heard fragments of ongoing investigations, uncovered planned lovers' trysts, and taped hours and hours of conversations of no interest whatsoever. Late on the evening of the fifth day, Trinity sent a signal which a digital display instantly identified as Ekström's mobile number. Plague locked the parabolic antenna on to the exact frequency.

The technology of RFTS worked primarily on incoming calls to Ekström. Trinity's parabolic antenna captured the search for Ekström's mobile number as it was sent through the ether.

Because Trinity could record the calls from Ekström, he also got voiceprints that Plague could process.

Plague ran Ekström's digitized voice through a programme called VPRS, Voiceprint Recognition System. He specified a dozen commonly occurring words, such as *OK* or *Salander*. When he had five separate examples of a word, he charted it with respect to the time it took to speak the word, what tone of voice and frequency range it had, whether the end of the word went up or down, and a dozen other markers. The result was a graph. In this way Plague could also monitor outgoing calls from Ekström. His parabolic antenna would be permanently listening out for a call containing Ekström's characteristic graph curve for one of a dozen commonly occurring words. The technology was not perfect, but roughly half of all the calls that Ekström made on his mobile from anywhere near police headquarters were monitored and recorded.

The system had an obvious weakness. As soon as Ekström left police headquarters, it was no longer possible to monitor his mobile, unless Trinity knew where he was and could park his van in the immediate vicinity.

With the authorization from the highest level, Edklinth had been able to set up a legitimate operations department. He picked four colleagues, purposely selecting younger talent who had experience on the regular police force and had been only recently recruited to SIS. Two had a background in the fraud division, one had been with the financial police, and one was from the violent crimes division. They were summoned to Edklinth's office and told of their assignment as well as the need for absolute secrecy. He made plain that the investigation was being carried out at the express order of the prime minister. Inspector Figuerola was named as their chief, and she directed the investigation with a force that matched her physical appearance.

But the investigation proceeded slowly. This was largely due to the fact that no-one was quite sure who or what should be investigated. On more than one occasion Edklinth and Figuerola considered bringing Mårtensson in for questioning. But they decided to wait. Arresting him would reveal the existence of the investigation.

Finally, on Tuesday, eleven days after the meeting with the prime minister, Figuerola came to Edklinth's office.

"I think we've got something."

"Sit down."

"Evert Gullberg. One of our investigators had a talk with Marcus Erlander, who's leading the investigation into Zalachenko's murder. According to Erlander, SIS contacted the Göteborg police just two hours after the murder and gave them information about Gullberg's threatening letters."

"That was fast."

"A little too fast. SIS faxed nine letters that Gullberg had supposedly written. There's just one problem."

"What's that?"

"Two of the letters were sent to the justice department— to the minister of justice and to the deputy minister."

"I know that."

"Yes, but the letter to the deputy minister wasn't logged in at the department until the following day. It arrived with a later delivery."

Edklinth stared at Figuerola. He felt very afraid that his suspicions were going to turn out to be justified. Figuerola went implacably on.

"So we have SIS sending a fax of a threatening letter that hadn't yet reached its addressee."

"Good Lord," Edklinth said.

"It was someone in Personal Protection who faxed them through."

"Who?"

"I don't think he's involved in the case. The letters landed on his desk in the morning, and shortly after the murder he was told to get in touch with the Göteborg police."

"Who gave him the instruction?"

"The chief of Secretariat's assistant."

"Good God, Monica. Do you know what this means? It means that SIS was involved in Zalachenko's murder."

"Not necessarily. But it definitely does mean that some individuals within SIS had knowledge of the murder before it was committed. The only question is: who?"

"The chief of Secretariat . . ."

"Yes. But I'm beginning to suspect that this Zalachenko club is out of house."

"How do you mean?"

"Mårtensson. He was moved from Personal Protection and is working on his own. We've had him under surveillance around the clock for the past week. He hasn't had contact with anyone within SIS as far as we can tell. He gets calls on a mobile that we cannot monitor. We don't know what number it is, but it's not his normal number. He did meet with the fair-haired man, but we haven't been able to identify him."

Edklinth frowned. At the same instant Anders Berglund knocked on the door. He was one of the new team, the officer who had worked with the financial police.

"I think I've found Evert Gullberg," Berglund said.

"Come in," Edklinth said.

Berglund put a dog-eared black-and-white photograph on the desk. Edklinth and Figuerola looked at the picture, which showed a man that both of them immediately recognized. He was being led through a doorway by two broad-shouldered-plain-clothes police officers. The legendary double agent Colonel Stig Wennerström.*

"This print comes from Åhlén and Åkerlund Publishers and was used in *Se* magazine in the spring of 1964. The photograph was taken in the course of the trial. Behind Wennerström you can see three people. On the right, Detective Superintendent Otto Danielsson, the policeman who arrested him."

"Yes . . ."

"Look at the man on the left behind Danielsson."

They saw a tall man with a narrow moustache who was wearing a hat. He reminded Edklinth vaguely of the writer Dashiell Hammett.

"Compare his face with this passport photograph of Gullberg, taken when he was sixty-six."

Edklinth frowned. "I wouldn't be able to swear it's the same person—"

"But it is," Berglund said. "Turn the print over."

On the reverse was a stamp saying that the picture belonged to Åhlén & Åkerlund Publishers and that the photographer's name was Julius Estholm. The text was written in pencil: *Stig Wennerström flanked by two police officers on his way into Stockholm district court. In the background O. Danielsson, E. Gullberg, and H. W. Francke.*

"Evert Gullberg," Figuerola said. "He was SIS."

"No," Berglund said. "Technically speaking, he wasn't. At least not when this picture was taken."

"Oh?"

"SIS wasn't established until four months later. In this photograph he was still with the Security Police."

"Who's H. W. Francke?" Figuerola said.

"Hans Wilhelm Francke," Edklinth said. "Died in the early nineties, but was assistant chief of the Security Police in the late fifties and early sixties. He was a bit of a legend, just like Otto Danielsson. I actually met him a couple of times."

"Is that so?" Figuerola said.

"He left SIS in the late sixties. Francke and P. G. Vinge never saw eye to eye, and he was more or less forced to resign at the age of fifty or fifty-five. Then he opened his own shop."

"His own *shop*?"

"He became a consultant in security for industry. He had an office on Stureplan, but he also gave lectures from time to time at SIS training sessions. That's where I met him."

"What did Vinge and Francke quarrel about?"

"They were just very different. Francke was a bit of a cowboy who saw KGB agents everywhere, and Vinge was a bureaucrat of the old school. Vinge was fired shortly thereafter. A bit ironic, that, because he thought Palme was working for the KGB."

Figuerola looked at the photograph of Gullberg and Francke standing side by side.

"I think it's time we had another talk with Justice," Edklinth told her.

"*Millennium* came out today," Figuerola said.

Edklinth shot her a glance.

"Not a word about the Zalachenko affair," she said.

"So we've got a month before the next issue. Good to know. But we have to deal with Blomkvist. In the middle of all this mess he's like a hand grenade with the pin pulled."

CHAPTER 17

Wednesday, June 1

Blomkvist had no warning that someone was in the stairwell
when he reached the landing outside his top-floor apartment
at Bellmansgatan 1. It was 7:00 in the evening. He stopped
short when he saw a woman with short blond curly hair sitting on the top step. He recognized her right away as Monica
Figuerola of SIS from the passport photograph Karim had
located.

"Hello, Blomkvist," she said cheerfully, closing the book
she had been reading. Blomkvist looked at the book and saw
that it was in English, on the idea of God in the ancient
world. He studied his unexpected visitor as she stood up. She
was wearing a short-sleeved summer dress and had laid a
brick-red leather jacket over the top stair.

"We need to talk to you," she said.

She was tall, taller than he was, and that impression was
magnified by the fact that she was standing two steps above
him. He looked at her arms and then at her legs and saw that
she was much more muscular than he was.

"You spend a couple of hours a week at the gym," he said.

She smiled and took out her ID.

"My name is—"

"Monica Figuerola, born in 1969, living on Pontonjär-gatan on Kungsholmen. You came from Borlänge and you've worked with the Uppsala police. For three years you've been working in SIS, Constitutional Protection. You're an exercise fanatic and you were once a top-class athlete, almost made it onto the Swedish Olympic team. What do you want with me?"

She was surprised, but she quickly regained her composure.

"Fair enough," she said in a low voice. "You know who I am—so you don't have to be afraid of me."

"I don't?"

"There are some people who need to have a talk with you in peace and quiet. Since your apartment and mobile seem to be bugged and we have reason to be discreet, I've been sent to invite you."

"And why would I go anywhere with somebody who works for Säpo?"

She thought for a moment. "Well . . . you could just accept a friendly personal invitation, or if you prefer, I could hand-cuff you and take you with me." She smiled sweetly. "Look, Blomkvist. I understand that you don't have many reasons to trust anyone from SIS. But it's like this: not everyone who works there is your enemy, and my superiors really want to talk to you. So, which do you prefer? Handcuffed or voluntarily?"

"I've been handcuffed by the police once already this year. And that was enough. Where are we going?"

She had parked around the corner, down on Pryssgränd.

When they were settled in her new Saab 9–5, she flipped open her mobile and pressed a speed-dial number.

"We'll be there in fifteen minutes."

She told Blomkvist to fasten his seat belt and drove over Slussen to Östermalm and parked on a side street off Artillerigatan. She sat still for a moment and looked at him.

"This is a friendly invitation, Blomkvist. You're not risking anything."

Blomkvist said nothing. He was reserving judgement until he knew what this was all about. She punched in the code on the street door. They took the elevator to the fifth floor, to an apartment with the name Martinsson on the door.

"We've borrowed the place for tonight's meeting," she said, opening the door. "To your right, into the living room."

The first person Blomkvist saw was Torsten Edklinth, which was no surprise since Säpo was deeply involved in what had happened, and Edklinth was Figuerola's boss. The fact that the director of Constitutional Protection had gone to the trouble of bringing him in said that somebody was nervous.

Then he saw a figure by the window. The minister of justice. That was a surprise.

Then he heard a sound to his right and saw the prime minister get up from an armchair. He hadn't for a moment expected that.

"Good evening, Herr Blomkvist," the PM said. "Excuse us for summoning you to this meeting on such short notice, but we've discussed the situation and agreed that we need to talk to you. May I offer you some coffee, or something else to drink?"

Blomkvist looked around. He saw a dining-room table of

dark wood that was cluttered with glasses, coffee cups, and the remnants of sandwiches. They must have been there for a couple of hours already.

"Ramlösa," he said.

Figuerola poured him a mineral water. They sat down on the sofas as she stayed in the background.

"He recognized me and knew my name, where I live, where I work, and the fact that I'm a workout fanatic," Figuerola said to no-one in particular.

The prime minister glanced quickly at Edklinth and then at Blomkvist. Blomkvist realized at once that he was in a position of some strength. The prime minister needed something from him and presumably had no idea how much Blomkvist knew or did not know.

"How did you know who Inspector Figuerola was?" Edklinth said.

Blomkvist looked at the director of Constitutional Protection. He could not be sure why the prime minister had set up a meeting with him in a borrowed apartment in Östermalm, but he suddenly felt inspired. There were not many ways it could have come about. It was Armansky who had set this in motion by giving information to someone he trusted. Which must have been Edklinth, or someone close to him. Blomkvist took a chance.

"A mutual friend spoke with you," he said to Edklinth. "You sent Figuerola to find out what was going on, and she discovered that some Säpo activists are running illegal phone taps and breaking into my apartment and stealing things. This means that you have confirmed the existence of what I call the Zalachenko club. It made you so nervous that you knew you had to take the matter further, but you sat in your office for a while and didn't know in which direction to go. So you went to the justice minister, and he in turn went to the prime minister. And now here we all are. What is it that you want from me?"

Blomkvist spoke with a confidence that suggested he had a source right at the heart of the affair and had followed every step Edklinth had taken. He knew that his guesswork was on the mark when Edklinth's eyes widened.

"The Zalachenko club spies on me, I spy on them," Blomkvist went on. "And you spy on the Zalachenko club. This situation makes the prime minister both angry and uneasy. He knows that at the end of this conversation awaits a scandal that the government might not survive."

Figuerola understood that Blomkvist was bluffing, and she knew how he had been able to surprise her by knowing her name and bio.

He saw me in my car on Bellmansgatan. He took the registration number and looked me up. But the rest is guesswork.

She did not say a word.

The prime minister certainly looked uneasy now.

"Is that what awaits us?" he said. "A scandal to bring down the government?"

"The survival of the government isn't my concern," Blomkvist said. "My role is to expose shit like the Zalachenko club."

The prime minister said: "And my job is to run the country in accordance with the constitution."

"Which means that my problem is definitely the government's problem. But not vice versa."

"Could we stop going around in circles? Why do you think I arranged this meeting?"

"To find out what I know and what I intend to do with it."

"Partly right. But more precisely, we've landed in a constitutional crisis. Let me first say that the government has absolutely no hand in this matter. We have been caught napping, without a doubt. I've never heard mention of this . . . what you call the Zalachenko club. The minister here has never heard a word about this matter either. Torsten Edklinth, an official high up in SIS who has worked in Säpo for many years, has never heard of it."

"It's still not my problem."

"I appreciate that. What I'd like to know is when you mean to publish your article, and exactly what it is you intend to publish. And this has nothing to do with damage control."

"Does it not?"

"Herr Blomkvist, the worst possible thing I could do in this situation would be to try to influence the shape or content of your story. Instead, I am going to propose a cooperation."

"Please explain."

"Since we have now had confirmation that a conspiracy exists within an exceptionally sensitive part of the administration, I have ordered an investigation." The PM turned to the minister of justice. "Please explain what the government has directed."

"It's very simple," said the minister of justice. "Torsten Edklinth has been given the task of finding out whether we can confirm this. He is to gather information that can be turned over to the prosecutor general, who in turn must decide whether charges should be brought. It is a very clear instruction. And this evening Edklinth has been reporting on how the investigation is proceeding. We've had a long discussion about the constitutional implications—of course we want it to be handled properly."

"Naturally," Blomkvist said in a tone that indicated he had scant trust in the prime minister's assurances.

"The investigation has already reached a sensitive stage. We have not yet identified exactly who is involved. That will take time. And that's why we sent Inspector Figuerola to invite you to this meeting."

"It wasn't exactly an invitation."

The prime minister frowned and glanced at Figuerola.

"It's not important," Blomkvist said. "Her behaviour was exemplary. Please come to the point."

"We want to know your publication date. This investigation is being conducted in great secrecy. If you publish before Edklinth has completed it, it could be ruined."

"And when would you like me to publish? After the next election, I suppose?"

"You decide that for yourself. It's not something I can influence. Just tell us, so that we know exactly what our deadline is."

"I see. You spoke about cooperation . . ."

The PM said: "Yes, but first let me say that under normal circumstances I would not have dreamed of asking a journalist to come to such a meeting."

"Presumably in normal circumstances you would be doing everything you could to keep journalists away from a meeting like this."

"Yes. But I understand that you're driven by several factors. You have a reputation for not pulling your punches when there's corruption involved. In this case there are no differences of opinion to divide us."

"Aren't there?"

"No, not in the least. Or rather, the differences that exist might be of a legal nature, but we share an objective. If this Zalachenko club exists, it is not merely a criminal conspiracy—it is a threat to national security. These activities must be stopped, and those responsible must be held accountable. On that point we would be in agreement, correct?"

Blomkvist nodded.

"I understand that you know more about this story than anyone else. We suggest that you share your knowledge. If this were a regular police investigation of an ordinary crime, the leader of the preliminary investigation could decide to summon you for an interview. But, as you can appreciate, this is an extreme state of affairs."

Blomkvist weighed the situation for a moment.

"And what do I get in return—if I do cooperate?"

"Nothing. I'm not going to haggle with you. If you want to publish tomorrow morning, then do so. I won't get involved in any horse-trading that might be constitutionally dubious. I'm asking you to cooperate in the interests of the country."

"In this case 'nothing' could be quite a lot," Blomkvist said. "For one thing, I'm very, very angry. I'm furious at the state and the government and Säpo and all these fucking bastards who for no reason at all locked up a twelve-year-old girl in a mental hospital until she could be declared incompetent."

"Lisbeth Salander has become a government matter," the PM said, and smiled. "Mikael, I am personally very upset over what happened to her. Please believe me when I say that those responsible will be held accountable. But before we can do that, we have to know who they are."

"My priority is that Salander should be acquitted and declared competent."

"I can't help you with that. I'm not above the law, and I can't direct what prosecutors and the courts decide. She has to be acquitted by a court."

"OK," Blomkvist said. "You want my cooperation. Give me some insight into Edklinth's investigation, and I'll tell you when and what I plan to publish."

"I can't give you that insight. That would be placing myself in the same relation to you as the minister of justice's predecessor once stood to the journalist Ebbe Carlsson."*

"I'm not Ebbe Carlsson," Blomkvist said calmly.

"I know that. On the other hand, Edklinth can decide for himself what he can share with you within the framework of his assignment."

"Hmm," Blomkvist said. "I want to know who Evert Gullberg was."

Silence fell over the group.

"Gullberg was presumably for many years the chief of that division within SIS which you call the Zalachenko club," Edklinth said.

The prime minister gave him a sharp look.

"I think he knows that already," Edklinth said by way of apology.

"That's correct," Blomkvist said. "He started at Säpo in the fifties. In the sixties he became chief of some outfit called the Section for Special Analysis. He was the one in charge of the Zalachenko affair."

The PM shook his head. "You know more than you ought to. I would very much like to discover how you came by all this information. But I'm not going to ask."

"There are holes in my story," Blomkvist said. "I need to fill them. Give me information and I won't try to compromise you."

"As prime minister I'm not in a position to deliver any such information. And Edklinth is on very thin ice if he does so."

"Don't bullshit me. I know what you want and you know what I want. If you give me information, then you'll be my sources—with all the enduring anonymity that implies. Don't misunderstand me. . . . I'll tell the truth as I see it in what I publish. If you are involved, I will expose you and do everything I can to ensure that you are never re-elected. But as of yet I have no reason to believe that is the case."

The prime minister glanced at Edklinth. After a moment he nodded. Blomkvist took it as a sign that the prime minister had just broken the law—if only of the more academic type—by giving his consent to sharing classified information with a journalist.

"This can all be solved quite simply," Edklinth said. "I have my own investigative team, and I decide for myself which colleagues to recruit for the investigation. You can't be employed by the investigation because that would mean you would be obliged to sign an oath of confidentiality. But I can hire you as an external consultant."

Berger's life had been filled with meetings and work around the clock from the minute she stepped into Morander's shoes.

It was not until Wednesday night, almost two weeks after

Blomkvist had given her Cortez's research papers on Borgsjö, that she had time to address the issue. As she opened the folder, she realized that her procrastination also had to do with the fact that she didn't really want to deal with the problem. She already knew that calamity was inevitable.

She arrived home in Saltsjöbaden at 7:00, unusually early, and it was only when she had to turn off the alarm in the hall that she remembered her husband was away. She had given him an especially long kiss that morning because he was flying to Paris to give some lectures and wouldn't be back until the weekend. She had no idea where he was giving the lectures, or what they were about.

She went upstairs, ran a bath, and undressed. She took Cortez's folder with her and spent the next half hour reading through the whole story. She couldn't help but smile. The boy was going to be a formidable reporter. He was twenty-six years old and had been at *Millennium* for four years, right out of journalism school. She felt a certain pride. The story had *Millennium*'s stamp on it from beginning to end; every *t* was crossed, every *i* dotted.

But she also felt tremendously depressed. Borgsjö was a good man, and she liked him. He was soft-spoken, sharp-witted, and charming, and he seemed unconcerned with prestige. Besides, he was her employer. *How the hell could he have been so fucking stupid?*

She wondered whether there might be another explanation or some mitigating circumstances, but she already knew it would be impossible to explain this away.

She put the folder on the windowsill and stretched out in the bath to ponder the situation.

Millennium was going to publish the story, no question. If she had still been there, she wouldn't have hesitated. That *Millennium* had leaked the story to her in advance was nothing but a courtesy; they wanted to reduce the damage to her personally. If the situation had been reversed—if *SMP* had made some damaging discovery about *Millennium*'s chairman of the board (which happened to be her)—they wouldn't have hesitated either.

Publication would be a serious blow to Borgsjö. The damaging thing was not that his company, Vitavara Inc., had imported goods from a company on the United Nations blacklist of companies using child labour (and in this case slave labour too in the form of convicts, undoubtedly some of them political prisoners). The really damaging thing was that Borgsjö knew about all this and still went on ordering toilets from Fong Soo Industries. It was a mark of the sort of greed that did not go down well with the Swedish people in the wake of the revelations about other criminal capitalists such as Skandia's former president.

Borgsjö would naturally claim that he did not know about the conditions at Fong Soo, but Cortez had solid evidence. If Borgsjö took that tack he would be exposed as a liar. In June 1997 Borgsjö had gone to Vietnam to sign the first contracts. He had spent ten days there on that occasion and toured the company's factories. If he claimed not to have known that many of the workers there were only twelve or thirteen years old, he would look like an idiot.

Cortez had demonstrated that in 2001, the UN commission on child labour had added Fong Soo Industries to its list of companies that exploit child labour, and that this had then been the subject of magazine articles. Two organizations against child labour, one of them the globally recognized International Joint Effort Against Child Labour in London, had written letters to companies that had placed orders with Fong Soo. Seven letters had been sent to Vitavara Inc., and two of those were addressed to Borgsjö personally. The organization in London had been very willing to supply the evidence. And Vitavara Inc. had not replied to any of the letters.

Worse still, Borgsjö went to Vietnam twice more, in 2001 and 2004, to renew the contracts. This was the coup de grâce. It would be impossible for Borgsjö to claim ignorance.

The inevitable media storm could lead to only one thing. If Borgsjö was smart, he would apologize and resign from his positions on various boards. If he decided to fight, he would be annihilated.

Berger did not care if Borgsjö was or was not chairman of the board of Vitavara Inc. What mattered to her was that he was the CEO of *SMP*. At a time when the newspaper was on the edge and a campaign of rejuvenation was under way, *SMP* could not afford to keep him.

Berger's decision was made.

She would go to Borgsjö, show him the document, and thereby hope to persuade him to resign before the story was published.

If he dug in his heels, she would call an emergency board meeting, explain the situation, and force the board to dismiss Borgsjö. And if they did not, she would have to resign, effective immediately.

She had been thinking for so long that the bathwater was now cold. She showered and towelled herself off and went to the bedroom to put on a bathrobe. Then she picked up her mobile and called Blomkvist. No answer. She went downstairs to put on some coffee, and for the first time since she had started at *SMP*, she looked to see whether there was a film on TV that she could watch to relax.

As she walked into the living room, she felt a sharp pain in her foot. She looked down and saw blood. She took another step and pain shot through her entire foot; she had to hop over to an antique chair to sit down. She lifted her foot and saw to her dismay that a shard of glass had pierced her heel. At first she felt faint. Then she steeled herself and took hold of the shard and pulled it out. The pain was appalling, and blood gushed from the wound.

She pulled open a drawer in the hall where she kept scarves, gloves, and hats. She found a scarf and wrapped it around her foot and tied it tight. That was not going to be enough, so she reinforced it with another improvised bandage. The bleeding had apparently subsided.

She looked at the bloodied piece of glass in amazement. *How did this get here?* Then she discovered more glass on the hall floor. Jesus Christ. She looked into the living room and saw that the picture window was shattered and the floor was covered in glass.

She went back to the front door and put on the outdoor shoes she had kicked off as she came home. That is, she put on one shoe and stuck the toes of her injured foot into the other, and hopped into the living room to take stock of the damage.

Then she found the brick in the middle of the living-room floor.

She limped over to the balcony door and went out to the garden. Someone had sprayed in three-foot-high letters on the back wall:

WHORE

It was just after 9:00 in the evening when Figuerola held the car door open for Blomkvist. She went around the car and got into the driver's seat.

"Should I drive you home, or do you want to be dropped off somewhere?"

Blomkvist stared straight ahead. "I haven't got my bearings yet, to be honest. I've never had a confrontation with a prime minister before."

Figuerola laughed. "You played your cards very well," she said. "I would never have guessed you were such a good poker player."

"I meant every word."

"Of course; but what I meant was that you pretended to know a lot more than you actually do. I realized that when I worked out how you identified me."

Blomkvist turned and looked at her profile.

"You wrote down my car registration when I was parked on the hill outside your building. You made it sound as if you knew what was being discussed at the prime minister's secretariat."

"Why didn't you say anything?" Blomkvist said.

She gave him a quick look and turned onto Grev Turegatan. "The rules of the game. I shouldn't have picked that spot, but there wasn't anywhere else to park. You keep a sharp eye on your surroundings, don't you?"

"You were sitting with a map spread out on the front seat, talking on the phone. I took down your registration and ran a routine check. I check out every car that catches my attention. I usually draw a blank. In your case I discovered that you worked for Säpo."

"I was following Mårtensson."

"Aha. So simple."

"Then I discovered that you were tailing him using Susanne Linder at Milton Security."

"Armansky's detailed her to keep an eye on what goes on around my apartment."

"And since she went into your building I assume that Milton has put in some sort of hidden surveillance of your apartment."

"That's right. We have an excellent film of how they break in and go through my papers. Mårtensson carries a portable photocopier with him. Have you identified Mårtensson's sidekick?"

"He's unimportant. A locksmith with a criminal record who's probably being paid to open your door."

"Name?"

"Protected source?"

"Naturally."

"Lars Faulsson. Forty-seven. Alias Falun. Convicted of safe-cracking in the eighties and some other minor stuff. Has a shop at Norrtull."

"Thanks."

"But let's save the secrets till we meet again tomorrow."

The meeting had ended with an agreement that Blomkvist would come to Constitutional Protection the next day to set in motion an exchange of information. Blomkvist was thinking. They were just passing Sergels Torg in the city centre.

"You know what? I'm incredibly hungry. I had a late lunch and was going to make some pasta when I got home, but I was waylaid by you. Have you eaten?"

"A while ago."

"Take us to a restaurant where we can get some decent food."

"All food is decent."

He looked at her. "I thought you were a health-food fanatic."

"No, I'm a workout fanatic. If you work out, you can eat whatever you want. Within reason."

She braked at the Klaraberg viaduct and considered the options. Instead of turning down towards Södermalm she kept going straight to Kungsholmen.

"I don't know what the restaurants are like in Söder, but I know an excellent Bosnian place at Fridhemsplan. Their *burek* is fantastic."

"Sounds good," Blomkvist said.

Salander tapped her way, letter by letter, through her report. She had worked an average of five hours each day. She was careful to express herself precisely. She left out all the details that could be used against her.

That she was locked up had turned out to be a blessing. She always had plenty of warning to put away her Palm when she heard the rattling of a key ring or a key being put in the lock.

```
I was about to lock up Bjurman's cabin outside
Stallarholmen when Carl-Magnus Lundin and Sonny
Nieminen arrived on motorbikes. Since they had
```

been searching for me in vain for a while on
behalf of Zalachenko and Niedermann, they were
surprised to see me there. Magge Lundin got off
his motorbike and declared, "I think the dyke
needs some cock." Both he and Nieminen acted so
threatening that I had no choice but to resort to
my right of self-defence. I left the scene on
Lundin's motorbike, which I then abandoned at the
shopping centre in Älvsjö.

There was no reason to volunteer the information that
Lundin had called her a whore or that she had bent down
and picked up Nieminen's P-83 Wanad and punished Lundin
by shooting him in the foot. The police could probably work
that out for themselves, but it was up to them to prove it. She
did not intend to make their job any easier by confessing to
something that would lead to a prison sentence.

The text had grown to thirty-three pages, and she was
nearing the end. In some sections she was particularly reticent about details and went to a lot of trouble not to supply
any evidence that could back up in any way the many claims
she was making. She went so far as to obscure some obvious
evidence and instead moved on to the next link in the chain
of events.

She scrolled back and read through a section where she
told how Advokat Bjurman had violently and sadistically
raped her. That was the part she had spent the most time on,
and one of the few she had rewritten several times before she
was satisfied. The section took up nineteen lines in her
account. She reported in a matter-of-fact manner how he
had hit her, thrown her onto her stomach on the bed, taped

her mouth, and handcuffed her. She then related how he had repeatedly committed acts of sexual violence against her, including anal penetration. She went on to report how at one point during the rape he had wound a piece of clothing—her own T-shirt—around her neck and strangled her for such a long time that she temporarily lost consciousness. Then there were several lines where she identified the implements he had used during the rape, which included a short whip, an anal plug, a rough dildo, and clamps, which he attached to her nipples.

She frowned and studied the text. At last she raised the stylus and tapped out a few more lines of text.

```
On one occasion when I still had my mouth taped
shut, Bjurman commented on the fact that I had
several tattoos and piercings, including a ring in
my left nipple. He asked if I liked being pierced
and then left the room. He came back with a
needle, which he pushed through my right nipple.
```

The matter-of-fact tone gave the text such a surreal touch that it sounded like an absurd fantasy.

The story simply did not sound credible.

That was her intention.

At that moment she heard the rattle of the guard's key ring. She turned off the Palm at once and put it in the recess at the back of the bedside table. It was Giannini. She frowned. It was 9:00 in the evening and Giannini did not usually appear this late.

"Hello, Lisbeth."

"Hello."

"How are you feeling?"

"I'm not finished yet."

Giannini sighed. "Lisbeth, they've set the trial date for July 13."

"That's OK."

"No, it's not OK. Time is running out, and you're not telling me anything. I'm beginning to think that I made a colossal mistake taking this job. If we're going to have the slightest chance, you have to trust me. We have to work together."

Salander studied her for a long moment. Finally she leaned her head back and looked up at the ceiling.

"I know what we're supposed to be doing. I understand Mikael's plan. And he's right."

"I'm not so sure about that."

"But I am."

"The police want to interrogate you again. A detective named Hans Faste from Stockholm."

"Let him interrogate me. I won't say a word."

"You have to hand in a statement."

Salander gave Giannini a sharp look. "I repeat: I won't say a word to the police. When we get to that courtroom the prosecutor won't have a single syllable from any interrogation to fall back on. All they'll have is the statement that I'm composing now, large parts of which will seem preposterous. And they're going to get it a few days before the trial."

"So when are you actually going to sit down with a pen and paper and write this statement?"

"You'll have it in a few days. But it can't go to the prosecutor until just before the trial."

Giannini looked sceptical. Salander suddenly gave her a cautious smile. "You talk about trust. Can I trust you?"

"Of course you can."

"OK. Could you smuggle me in a hand-held computer so that I can keep in touch with people online?"

"No, of course not. If it were discovered I'd be charged with a crime and lose my licence to practice."

"But if someone else got one in, would you report it to the police?"

Giannini raised her eyebrows. "If I didn't know about it . . ."

"But if you did know about it, what would you do?"

"I'd shut my eyes. How about that?"

"This hypothetical computer is soon going to send you a hypothetical email. When you've read it I want you to come again."

"Lisbeth—"

"Wait. It's like this. The prosecutor is dealing with a marked deck. I'm at a disadvantage no matter what I do, and the purpose of the trial is to get me committed to a secure psychiatric ward."

"I know."

"If I'm going to survive, I have to fight dirty."

Finally Giannini nodded.

"When you came to see me the first time," Salander said, "you had a message from Blomkvist. He said that he'd told you almost everything, with a few exceptions. One of those exceptions had to do with the skills he discovered I had when we were in Hedestad."

"That's correct."

"He was referring to the fact that I'm extremely good with computers. So good that I can read and copy what's on Ekström's machine."

Giannini went pale.

"You can't be involved in this. And you can't use any of that material at the trial," Salander said.

"You're right about that."

"So you know nothing about it."

"OK."

"But someone else—your brother, let's say—could publish selected excerpts from it. You'll have to think about this possibility when you plan your strategy."

"I understand."

"Annika, this trial is going to turn on who uses the toughest methods."

"I know."

"I'm happy to have you as my lawyer. I trust you and I need your help."

"Hmm."

"But if you get difficult about the fact that I'm going to use unethical methods, then we'll lose the trial."

"Right."

"And if that were the case, I need to know now. I'd have to get myself a new lawyer."

"Lisbeth, I can't break the law."

"You don't have to break any law. But you do have to shut your eyes to the fact that I am. Can you manage that?"

Salander waited patiently for almost a minute before Annika nodded.

"Good. Let me tell you the main points that I'm going to put in my statement."

Figuerola had been right. The *burek* was fantastic. Blomkvist studied her carefully as she came back from the ladies'.

She moved as gracefully as a ballerina, but she had a body like . . . hmm. Blomkvist could not help being fascinated. He repressed an impulse to reach out and feel her leg muscles.

"How long have you been working out?" he said.

"Since I was a teenager."

"And how many hours a week do you do it?"

"Two hours a day. Sometimes three."

"Why? I mean, I understand why people work out, but . . ."

"You think it's excessive."

"I'm not sure exactly what I think."

She smiled and did not seem at all irritated by his questions.

"Maybe you're just bothered by seeing a woman with muscles. Do you think it's a turn-off, or unfeminine?"

"No, not at all. It suits you somehow. You're very sexy."

She laughed.

"I'm cutting back on the training now. Ten years ago I was doing rock-hard bodybuilding. It was cool. But now I have to be careful that the muscles don't turn to fat. I don't want to get flabby. So I lift weights once a week and spend the rest of the time doing some cross-training, or running, playing badminton, or swimming, that sort of thing. It's exercise more than hard training."

"I see."

"The reason I work out is that it feels great. That's a normal phenomenon among people who do extreme training. The body produces a pain-suppressing chemical and you become addicted to it. If you don't run every day, you get withdrawal symptoms after a while. You feel an enormous sense of well-being when you give something your all. It's almost as powerful as good sex."

Blomkvist laughed.

"You should start working out yourself," she said. "You're getting a little thick in the waist."

"I know," he said. "I have a constant guilty conscience. Sometimes I start running regularly and lose a few pounds. Then I get involved in something and don't get time to do it again for a month or two."

"You've been pretty busy these last few months. I've been reading a lot about you. You beat the police by several lengths when you tracked down Zalachenko and identified Niedermann."

"Lisbeth Salander was faster."

"How did you find out Niedermann was in Gosseberga?"

Blomkvist shrugged. "Routine research. I wasn't the one who found him. It was our managing editor—well, now our editor in chief—Malin Eriksson who managed to dig him up through the corporate records. He was on the board of Zalachenko's company, KAB Import."

"That simple . . ."

"And why did you become a Säpo activist?" he said.

"Believe it or not, I'm something as old-fashioned as a democrat. I mean, the police are necessary, and a democracy needs a political safeguard. That's why I'm proud to be working at Constitutional Protection."

"Is it really something to be proud of?" said Blomkvist.

"You don't like the Security Police."

"I don't like institutions that are beyond normal parliamentary scrutiny. It's an invitation to abuse of power, no matter how noble the intentions. Why are you so interested in the religion of antiquity?"

Figuerola looked at Blomkvist.

"You were reading a book about it on my staircase," he said.

"The subject fascinates me."

"I see."

"I'm interested in a lot of things. I've studied law and political science while I've worked for the police. Before that I studied both philosophy and the history of ideas."

"Do you have any weaknesses?"

"I don't read fiction, I never go to the cinema, and I watch only the news on TV. How about you? Why did you become a journalist?"

"Because there are institutions like Säpo that lack parliamentary oversight and which have to be exposed from time to time. I don't really know. I suppose my answer to that is the same one you gave me: I believe in a constitutional democracy and sometimes it has to be protected."

"The way you did with Hans-Erik Wennerström?"

"Something like that."

"You're not married. Are you and Erika Berger together?"

"Erika Berger's married."

"So all the rumours about you two are nonsense. Do you have a girlfriend?"

"No-one steady."

"So the rumours might be true after all."

Blomkvist smiled.

Malin Eriksson worked at her kitchen table at home in Årsta until the small hours. She sat bent over spreadsheets of *Millennium*'s budget and was so engrossed that Anton, her boyfriend, eventually gave up trying to have a conversation with her. He washed the dishes, made a late snack, and put on some coffee. Then he left her in peace and sat down to watch a repeat of *CSI*.

Malin had never before had to cope with anything more complex than a household budget, but she had worked alongside Berger balancing the monthly books, and she understood the principles. Now she was suddenly editor in chief, and with that role came responsibility for the budget. Sometime after midnight she decided that, whatever happened, she was going to have to get an accountant to help her. Ingela Oskarsson, who did the bookkeeping two days a week, had no responsibility for the budget and was not at all helpful when it came to making decisions about how much a freelancer should be paid or whether they could afford to buy a new laser printer that was not already included in the sum earmarked for capital investments or IT upgrades. It was a ridiculous situation—*Millennium* was making a profit, but that was because Berger had always managed to balance an extremely tight budget. Instead of investing in something as fundamental as a new colour laser printer for 45,000 kronor, they would have to settle for a black-and-white printer for 8,000.

For a moment she envied Berger. At *SMP* she had a budget in which such a cost would be considered pin money.

Millennium's financial situation had been healthy at the last annual general meeting, but the surplus in the budget was primarily made up of the profits from Blomkvist's book about the Wennerström affair. The revenue that had been set aside for investment was shrinking alarmingly fast. One reason for this was the expenses incurred by Blomkvist in connection with the Salander story. *Millennium* did not have the resources to keep any employee on an open-ended budget with all sorts of expenses in the form of rental cars, hotel rooms, taxis, the purchase of research material and new mobiles and the like.

Eriksson signed an invoice from Daniel Olsson in Göteborg. She sighed. Blomkvist had approved a sum of 14,000 kronor for a week's research on a story that was not going to be published. Payment to an Idris Ghidi went into the budget under fees to sources who could not be named, which meant that the accountant would remonstrate about the lack of an invoice or receipt and insist that the matter have the board's approval. *Millennium* had paid a fee to Advokat Giannini which was supposed to come out of the general fund, but she had also invoiced *Millennium* for train tickets and other costs.

Eriksson put down her pen and looked at the totals. Blomkvist had blown 150,000 kronor on the Salander story, way beyond their budget. Things could not go on this way.

She was going to have to have a talk with him.

Berger spent the evening not on her sofa watching TV, but in the ER at Nacka hospital. The shard of glass had penetrated so deeply that the bleeding would not stop. It turned out that one piece had broken off and was still in her heel, and would have to be removed. She was given a local anaesthetic and the wound was sewn up with three stitches.

Berger cursed the whole time she was at the hospital, and she kept trying to call her husband or Blomkvist. Neither chose to answer the phone. By 10:00 she had her foot wrapped in a thick bandage. She was given crutches and took a taxi home.

She spent a while limping around the living room, sweeping up the floor. She called Emergency Glass to order a new window. She was in luck. It had been a quiet evening and they arrived within twenty minutes. But the living-room window was so big that they did not have the glass in stock. The glazier offered to board up the window with plywood for the time being, and she accepted gratefully.

As the plywood was being put up, she called the duty officer at Nacka Integrated Protection and asked why the hell their expensive burglar alarm had not gone off when someone threw a brick through her biggest window.

Someone from NIP came out to look at the damage. It turned out that whoever had installed the alarm several years before had neglected to connect the leads from the windows in the living room.

Berger was furious.

The man from NIP said they would fix it first thing in the morning. Berger told him not to bother. Instead she called the duty officer at Milton Security and explained her situation. She said that she wanted to have a complete alarm package installed the next morning. "I know I have to sign a contract, but tell Armansky that Erika Berger called and make damn sure someone comes around in the morning."

Then, finally, she called the police. She was told that there was no car available to come and take her statement. She was advised to contact her local station in the morning. *Thank you. Fuck off.*

Then she sat and fumed for a long time until her adrenaline level dropped, and it began to sink in that she was going to have to sleep alone in a house without an alarm while somebody was running around the neighbourhood calling her a whore and smashing her windows.

She wondered whether she ought to go into the city to spend the night at a hotel, but Berger was not the kind of person who liked to be threatened. And she liked giving in to threats even less.

But she did take some elementary safety precautions.

Blomkvist had told her once how Salander had put paid to the serial killer Martin Vanger with a golf club. So she went to the garage and spent several minutes looking for her golf bag, which she had hardly even thought about for fifteen years. She chose an iron that she thought had a certain heft to it and laid it within easy reach of her bed. She left a putter in the hall and an 8-iron in the kitchen. She took a hammer from the tool box in the basement and put that in the master bathroom.

She put the canister of Mace from her shoulder bag on her bedside table. Finally she found a rubber doorstop and wedged it under the bedroom door. And then she almost hoped that the moron who had called her a whore and destroyed her window would be stupid enough to come back that night.

By the time she felt sufficiently entrenched it was 1:00. She had to be at *SMP* at 8:00. She checked her calendar and saw that she had four meetings, the first at 10:00. Her foot was aching badly. She undressed and crept into bed.

Then, inevitably, she lay awake and worried.

Whore.

She had received nine emails, all of which had contained

the word *whore,* and they all seemed to come from sources in the media. The first had come from her own newsroom, but the source was a fake.

She got out of bed and took out the new Dell laptop that she had been given when she had started at *SMP.*

The first email—which was also the most crude and intimidating, with its suggestion that she would be fucked with a screwdriver—had come on May 16, a couple of weeks ago.

Email number two had arrived two days later, on May 18.

Then a week went by before the emails started coming again, now at intervals of about twenty-four hours. Then the attack on her home. Again, *whore.*

During that time Carlsson on the culture pages had received an ugly email purportedly sent by Berger. And if Carlsson had received an email like that, it was entirely possible that the emailer had been busy elsewhere too—that other people had gotten mail apparently from her that she did not know about.

It was an unpleasant thought.

The most disturbing was the attack on her house.

Someone had taken the trouble to find out where she lived, drive out here, and throw a brick through the window. It was obviously premeditated—the attacker had brought his can of spray paint. The next moment she froze when she realized that she could add another attack to the list. All four of her tyres had been slashed when she spent the night with Blomkvist at the Slussen Hilton.

The conclusion was just as unpleasant as it was obvious. She was being stalked.

Someone, for some unknown reason, had decided to harass her.

The fact that her home had been subject to an attack was understandable—it was where it was and impossible to disguise. But if her car had been damaged on some random street in Södermalm, her stalker must have been somewhere nearby when she parked it. He must have been following her.

CHAPTER 18

Thursday, June 2

Berger's mobile was ringing. It was 9:05.

"Good morning, Fru Berger. Dragan Armansky. I understand you called last night."

Berger explained what had happened and asked whether Milton Security could take over the contract from Nacka Integrated Protection.

"We can certainly install an alarm that will work," Armansky said. "The problem is that the closest car we have at night is in Nacka centre. Response time would be about thirty minutes. If we took the job I'd have to subcontract out your house. We have an agreement with a local security company, Adam Security in Fisksätra, which has a response time of ten minutes if all goes as it should."

"That would be an improvement over NIP, which doesn't bother to turn up at all."

"Adam Security is a family-owned business, a father, two sons, and a couple of cousins. Greeks, good people. I've known the father for many years. They handle coverage about three hundred twenty days a year. They tell us in advance the days they aren't available because of holidays or something else, and then our car in Nacka takes over."

"That works for me."

"I'll be sending a man out this morning. His name is David Rosin, and in fact he's already on his way. He's going to do a security assessment. He needs your keys if you're not going to be home, and he needs your authorization to do a thorough examination of your house, from top to bottom. He's going to take pictures of the entire property and the immediate surroundings."

"All right."

"Rosin has a lot of experience, and we'll make you a proposal. We'll have a complete security plan ready in a few days, which will include a personal attack alarm, fire security, evacuation plan, and break-in protection."

"OK."

"If anything should happen, we also want you to know what to do in the ten minutes before the car arrives from Fisksätra."

"Sounds good."

"We'll install the alarm this afternoon. Then we'll have to sign a contract."

Only after she had finished her conversation with Armansky did Berger realize that she had overslept. She called Fredriksson and explained that she had hurt herself. He would have to cancel the 10:00.

"What's happened?" he said.

"I cut my foot," Berger said. "I'll hobble in as soon as I've pulled myself together."

She used the toilet in the master bathroom and then pulled on some black pants and borrowed one of Greger's slippers for her injured foot. She chose a black blouse and put on a jacket. Before she removed the doorstop from the bedroom door, she armed herself with the canister of Mace.

She made her way cautiously through the house and switched on the coffeemaker. She had her breakfast at the kitchen table, listening for sounds in the vicinity. She had just poured a second cup of coffee when there was a firm knock on the front door. It was David Rosin from Milton Security.

Figuerola walked to Bergsgatan and summoned her four colleagues for an early morning conference.

"We have a deadline now," she said. "Our work has to be done by July 13, the day the Salander trial begins. We have just under six weeks. Let's agree on what's most important right now. Who wants to go first?"

Berglund cleared his throat. "The blond man with Mårtensson. Who is he?"

"We have photographs, but no idea how to find him. We can't put out an APB."

"What about Gullberg, then? There must be a story to track down there. We have him in the Security Police from the early fifties to 1964, when SIS was founded. Then he vanishes."

Figuerola nodded.

"Should we conclude that the Zalachenko club was an association formed in 1964? That would be some time before Zalachenko even came to Sweden."

"There must have been some other purpose . . . a secret organization within the organization."

"That was after Stig Wennerström. Everyone was paranoid."

"A sort of secret spy police?"

"There are in fact parallels overseas. In the States a special group of internal spy chasers was created within the CIA in the fifties. It was led by a James Jesus Angleton, and it very nearly sabotaged the entire CIA. Angleton's gang were as fanatical as they were paranoid—they suspected everyone in the CIA of being a Russian agent. As a result, the agency's effectiveness in large areas was paralysed."

"But that's all speculation . . ."

"Where are the old personnel files kept?"

"Gullberg isn't in them. I've checked."

"But what about a budget? An operation like this has to be financed."

The discussion went on until lunchtime, when Figuerola excused herself and went to the gym for some peace, to think things over.

Berger did not arrive in the newsroom until lunchtime. Her foot was hurting so badly that she could not put any weight on it. She hobbled over to her glass cage and sank into her chair with relief. Fredriksson looked up from his desk, and she waved him in.

"What happened?" he said.

"I stepped on a piece of glass and a shard lodged in my heel."

"That . . . wasn't so good."

"No. It wasn't good. Peter, has anyone received any more weird emails?"

"Not that I've heard."

"Keep your ears open. I want to know if anything odd happens around *SMP*."

"What sort of odd?"

"I'm afraid some idiot is sending really vile emails and he seems to have targeted me. So I want to know if you hear of anything going on."

"The type of email Eva Carlsson got?"

"Right, but anything strange at all. I've had a whole string of crazy emails accusing me of being all kinds of things—and suggesting various perverse things that ought to be done to me."

Fredriksson's expression darkened. "How long has this been going on?"

"A couple of weeks. Keep your eyes peeled. . . . So tell me, what's going to be in the paper tomorrow?"

"Well . . ."

"Well, *what*?"

"Holm and the head of the legal section are on the warpath."

"Why is that?"

"Because of Frisk. You extended his contract and gave him a feature assignment. And he won't tell anybody what it's about."

"He is forbidden to talk about it. My orders."

"That's what he says. Which means that Holm and the legal editor are up in arms."

"I can see that they might be. Set up a meeting with Legal at 3:00. I'll explain the situation."

"Holm is not pleased—"

"I'm not pleased with Holm, either, so we're even."

"He's so upset that he's complained to the board."

Berger looked up. *Damn it. I'm going to have to face up to the Borgsjö problem.*

"Borgsjö is coming in this afternoon and wants a meeting with you. I suspect it's Holm's doing."

"What time?"

"Two o'clock," said Fredriksson, and he went back to his desk to write the midday memo.

Jonasson visited Salander during her lunch. She pushed away a plate of the hospital's vegetable stew. As always, he did a brief examination of her, but she noticed that he was no longer putting much effort into it.

"You've recovered nicely," he said.

"Hmm. You'll have to do something about the food at this place."

"What about it?"

"Couldn't you get me a pizza?"

"Sorry. Way beyond the budget."

"I was afraid of that."

"Lisbeth, we're going to have a discussion about the state of your health tomorrow—"

"Understood. And I've recovered nicely."

"You're now well enough to be moved to Kronoberg prison. I might be able to postpone the move for another week, but my colleagues are going to start wondering."

"You don't need to do that."

"Are you sure?"

She nodded. "I'm ready. And it had to happen sooner or later."

"I'll give the go-ahead tomorrow, then," Jonasson said. "You'll probably be transferred pretty soon."

She nodded.

"It might be as early as this weekend. The hospital administration doesn't want you here."

"Who could blame them."

"Er . . . that device of yours—"

"I'll leave it in the recess behind the table here." She pointed.

"Good idea."

They sat in silence for a moment before Jonasson stood up.

"I have to check on my other patients."

"Thanks for everything. I owe you one."

"Just doing my job."

"No. You've done a great deal more. I won't forget it."

Blomkvist entered police headquarters on Kungsholmen through the entrance on Polhemsgatan. Figuerola accompanied him up to the offices of the Constitutional Protection Unit. They exchanged only silent glances in the elevator.

"Do you think it's such a good idea for me to be hanging around at police HQ?" Blomkvist said. "Someone might see us together and start to wonder."

"This will be our only meeting here. From now on we'll meet in an office we've rented at Fridhemsplan. We get access tomorrow. But this will be OK. Constitutional Protection is a small and more or less self-sufficient unit, and nobody else at SIS cares about it. And we're on a different floor from the rest of Säpo."

He greeted Edklinth without shaking hands and said hello to two colleagues who were apparently part of his team. They introduced themselves only as Stefan and Anders. He smiled to himself.

"Where do we start?" he said.

"We could start by having some coffee. . . . Monica?" Edklinth said.

"Thanks, that would be nice," Figuerola said.

Edklinth had probably meant for her to serve the coffee. Blomkvist noticed that the chief of the Constitutional Protection Unit hesitated for only a second before he got up and brought the coffee over to the conference table, where place settings were already laid out. Blomkvist saw that Edklinth was also smiling to himself, which he took to be a good sign. Then Edklinth turned serious.

"I honestly don't know how I should be managing this. It must be the first time a journalist has sat in on a meeting of the Security Police. The issues we'll be discussing now are in many respects confidential and highly classified."

"I'm not interested in military secrets. I'm only interested in the Zalachenko club."

"But we have to strike a balance. First of all, the names of today's participants must not be mentioned in your articles."

"Agreed."

Edklinth gave Blomkvist a look of surprise.

"Second, you may not speak with anyone but me and Monica Figuerola. We're the ones who will decide what we can tell you."

"If you have a long list of requirements, you should have mentioned them yesterday."

"Yesterday I hadn't yet thought through the matter."

"Then I have something to tell you too. This is probably the first and only time in my professional career that I will reveal the contents of an unpublished story to a police officer. So, to quote you, I honestly don't know how I should be managing this."

A brief silence settled over the table.

"Maybe we—"

"What if we—"

Edklinth and Figuerola had started talking at the same time before falling silent.

"My target is the Zalachenko club," Blomkvist said. "You want to bring charges against the Zalachenko club. Let's stick to that."

Edklinth nodded.

"So, what do you have?" Blomkvist said.

Edklinth explained what Figuerola and her team had unearthed. He showed Blomkvist the photograph of Evert Gullberg with Colonel Wennerström.

"Good. I'll take a copy of that."

"It's in Åhlén and Åkerlund's archive," Figuerola said.

"It's on the table in front of me. With a note on the back," Blomkvist said.

"Give him a copy," Edklinth said.

"That means that Zalachenko was murdered by the Section."

"Murder, coupled with the suicide of a man who was dying of cancer. Gullberg's still alive, but the doctors don't give him more than a few weeks. After his suicide attempt he sustained such severe brain damage that he is for all intents and purposes a vegetable."

"And he was the person with primary responsibility for Zalachenko when he defected."

"How do you know that?"

"Gullberg met Prime Minister Fälldin six weeks after Zalachenko's defection."

"Can you prove that?"

"I can. With the visitors' log of the government secretariat. Gullberg arrived together with the then chief of SIS."

"And the chief has since died."

"But Fälldin is alive and willing to talk about the matter."

"Have you—"

"No, I haven't. But someone else has. I can't give you the name. Source protection."

Blomkvist explained how Fälldin had reacted to the information about Zalachenko and how he had travelled to The Hague to interview Janeryd.

"So the Zalachenko club is somewhere in this building," Blomkvist said, pointing at the photograph.

"Partly. We think it's an organization inside the organization. What you call the Zalachenko club cannot exist without the support of key people in this building. But we think that the so-called Section for Special Analysis set up shop somewhere outside."

"So that's how it works? A person can be employed by Säpo, have his salary paid by Säpo, and then in fact report to another employer?"

"Something like that."

"So who in the building is working for the Zalachenko club?"

"We don't know yet. But we have several suspects."

"Mårtensson," Blomkvist suggested.

Edklinth nodded.

"Mårtensson works for Säpo, and when he's needed by the Zalachenko club he's released from his regular job," Figuerola said.

"How does that work in practice?"

"That's a very good question," Edklinth said with a faint smile. "Wouldn't you like to come and work for us?"

"Not on your life," Blomkvist said.

"I jest, of course. But it's a good question. We have a suspect, but we're unable to verify our suspicions just yet."

"Let's see . . . it must be someone with administrative authority."

"We suspect Chief of Secretariat Albert Shenke," Figuerola said.

"And here we are at our first stumbling block," Edklinth said. "We've given you a name, but we have no proof. So how do you intend to proceed?"

"I can't publish a name without proof. If Shenke is innocent he would sue *Millennium* for libel."

"Good. Then we are agreed. This cooperative effort has to be based on mutual trust. Your turn. What do you have?"

"Three names," Blomkvist said. "The first two were members of the Zalachenko club in the eighties."

Edklinth and Figuerola were instantly alert.

"Hans von Rottinger and Fredrik Clinton. Von Rottinger is dead. Clinton is retired. But both of them were part of the circle closest to Zalachenko."

"And the third name?" Edklinth said.

"Teleborian has a link to a person I know only as Jonas. We don't know his last name, but we do know that he was with the Zalachenko club. . . . We've actually speculated a bit that he might be the man with Mårtensson in the pictures from Café Copacabana."

"And in what context did the name Jonas crop up?"

Salander hacked Teleborian's computer, and we can follow the correspondence that shows how Teleborian is conspiring with Jonas in the same way he conspired with Björck in 1991.

"He gives Teleborian instructions. And now we come to

another stumbling block," Blomkvist said to Edklinth with a smile. "I can prove my assertions, but I can't give you the documentation without revealing a source. You'll have to accept what I'm saying."

Edklinth looked thoughtful.

"Maybe one of Teleborian's colleagues in Uppsala. OK. Let's start with Clinton and von Rottinger. Tell us what you know."

Borgsjö received Berger in his office next to the boardroom. He looked concerned.

"I heard that you hurt yourself," he said, pointing to her foot.

"It'll pass," Berger said, leaning her crutches against his desk as she sat down in the guest chair.

"Well . . . that's good. Erika, you've been here a month and I want us to have a chance to catch up. How do you feel it's going?"

I have to discuss Vitavara with him. But how? When?

"I've begun to get a handle on the situation. There are two sides to it. On the one hand, *SMP* has financial problems and the budget is strangling the newspaper. On the other, *SMP* has a huge amount of dead meat in the newsroom."

"Aren't there any positive aspects?"

"Of course there are. A whole bunch of experienced professionals who know how to do their jobs. The problem is the ones who won't let them do their jobs."

"Holm has spoken to me. . . ."

"I know."

Borgsjö looked puzzled. "He has a number of opinions about you. Almost all of them are negative."

"That's OK. I have a number of opinions about him too."

"Also negative? It's no good if the two of you can't work together—"

"I have no problem working with him. But he does have a problem with me." Berger sighed. "He's driving me nuts. He's very experienced and doubtless one of the most competent news chiefs I've come across. At the same time, he's a bastard of exceptional proportions. He enjoys indulging in intrigue and playing people against one another. I've worked in the media for twenty-five years, and I have never met a person like him in a management position."

"He has to be tough to handle the job. He's under pressure from every direction."

"Tough, by all means. But that doesn't mean he has to behave like an idiot. Unfortunately, Holm is a walking disaster, and he's one of the chief reasons why it's almost impossible to get the staff to work as a team. He takes divide-and-rule as his job description."

"Harsh words."

"I'll give him one month to sort out his attitude. If he hasn't managed it by then, I'm going to remove him as news editor."

"You can't do that. It's not your job to take apart the operational organization."

Berger studied the CEO.

"Forgive me for pointing this out, but that was exactly why you hired me. We also have a contract which explicitly gives me free rein to make the editorial changes I deem necessary. My task here is to rejuvenate the newspaper, and I can do that only by changing the organization and the work routines."

"Holm has devoted his life to *SMP*."

"Right. And he's fifty-eight, with seven years to go before retirement. I can't afford to keep him on as a dead weight all that time. Don't misunderstand me, Magnus. From the moment I sat down in that glass cage, my life's goal has been to raise *SMP*'s quality as well as its circulation figures. Holm has a choice: either he can do things my way, or he can do something else. I'm going to bulldoze anyone who is obstructive or who tries to damage *SMP* in some other way."

Damn . . . I have to bring up the Vitavara thing. Borgsjö is going to be fired.

Suddenly Borgsjö smiled. "By God, I think you're pretty tough too."

"Yes, I am, and in this case it's regrettable since it shouldn't be necessary. My job is to produce a good newspaper, and I can do that only if I have a management that functions and colleagues who enjoy their work."

After the meeting with Borgsjö, Berger limped back to the glass cage. She felt depressed. She had been with Borgsjö for forty-five minutes without mentioning one syllable about Vitavara. She had not, in other words, been particularly straight or honest with him.

When she sat at her computer she found a message from <MikBlom@millennium.nu>. She knew perfectly well that no such address existed at *Millennium*. She opened the email:

YOU THINK THAT BORGSJÖ CAN SAVE YOU, YOU
LITTLE WHORE: HOW DOES YOUR FOOT FEEL?

She raised her eyes involuntarily and looked out across the newsroom. Her gaze fell on Holm. He looked back at her. Then he smiled.

It can only be someone at SMP.

The meeting at the Constitutional Protection Unit lasted until after 5:00, and they agreed to have another meeting the following week. Blomkvist could contact Figuerola if he needed to be in touch with SIS before then. He packed away his laptop and stood up.

"How do I get out of here?" he asked.

"You certainly can't go running around on your own," Edklinth said.

"I'll show him out," Figuerola said. "Give me a couple of minutes; I just have to pick up a few things from my office." They walked together through Kronoberg park towards Fridhemsplan.

"So what happens now?" Blomkvist said.

"We stay in touch," Figuerola said.

"I'm beginning to like my contact with Säpo."

"Do you feel like having dinner later?"

"Bosnian again?"

"No, I can't afford to eat out every night. I was thinking of something simple at my place."

She stopped and smiled at him.

"Do you know what I'd like to do now?" she said.

"No."

"I'd like to take you home and undress you."

"This could get a bit awkward."

"I know. But I wasn't planning on telling my boss."

"We don't know how this story's going to turn out. We could end up on opposite sides of the barricades."

"I'll take my chances. Now, are you going to come quietly or do I have to handcuff you?"

The consultant from Milton Security was waiting for Berger when she got home at around 7:00. Her foot was throbbing painfully, and she limped into the kitchen and sank onto the nearest chair. He had made coffee, and he poured her some.

"Thanks. Is making coffee part of Milton's service agreement?"

He gave her a polite smile. David Rosin was a short, plump man in his fifties with a reddish goatee. "Thanks for letting me borrow your kitchen today."

"It's the least I could do. What's the situation?"

"Our technicians were here and installed a proper alarm. I'll show you how it works in a minute. I've also gone over every inch of your house from the basement to the attic and studied the area around it. I'll review your situation with my colleagues at Milton, and in a few days we'll present an assessment that we'll go over with you. But before that there are one or two things we ought to discuss."

"Go ahead."

"First of all, we have to take care of a few formalities. We'll work out the final contract later—it depends what services we agree on—but this is an agreement saying that you've commissioned Milton Security to install the alarm we put in today. It's a standard document saying that we at Milton require certain things of you and that we commit to certain things—client confidentiality and so forth."

"You require things of me?"

"Yes. An alarm is an alarm and is completely pointless if some nutcase is standing in your living room with an automatic weapon. For the security to work, we want you and your husband to be aware of certain things and to take certain routine measures. I'll go over the details with you."

"OK."

"I'm jumping ahead and anticipating the final assessment, but this is how I view the general situation. You and your husband live in a detached house. You have a beach at the back of the house and a few large houses in the immediate vicinity. Your neighbours do not have an unobstructed view of your house. It's relatively isolated."

"That's correct."

"Therefore an intruder would have a good chance of approaching your house without being observed."

"The neighbours on the right are away for long periods, and on the left is an elderly couple who go to bed quite early."

"In addition, the houses are positioned with their gables facing each other. There are few windows, and so on. Once an intruder comes onto your property—and it takes only five seconds to turn off the road and arrive at the rear of the house—the view is completely blocked. The rear is screened by your hedge, the garage, and that large freestanding building."

"That's my husband's studio."

"He's an artist, I take it?"

"That's right. Then what?"

"Whoever smashed your window and sprayed your outside wall was able to do so undisturbed. There might have been some risk that the sound of the breaking window would be heard and someone might have reacted . . . but your house sits at an angle and the sound was deflected by the façade."

"I see."

"The second thing is that you have a large property here with a living area of approximately 2,700 square feet, not counting the attic and basement. That's eleven rooms on two floors."

"The house is a monster. It's my husband's old family home."

"There are also a number of different ways to get into the house. Via the front door, the balcony at the back, the porch on the upper floor, and the garage. There are also windows on the ground floor and six basement windows that were left without alarms by our predecessors. Finally, I could break in by using the fire escape at the back of the house and entering through the roof hatch leading to the attic. The trapdoor is secured by nothing more than a latch."

"It sounds as if there are revolving doors into the place. What do we have to do?"

"The alarm we installed today is temporary. We'll come back next week and do the proper installation with alarms on every window on the ground floor and in the basement. That's your protection against intruders in the event that you and your husband are away."

"That's good."

"But the present situation has arisen because you have been subject to a direct threat from a specific individual. That's much more serious. We don't know who this person is, what his motives are, or how far he's willing to go, but we can make a few assumptions. If it were just a matter of anonymous hate mail we would make a decreased threat assessment, but in this case a person has actually taken the trouble to drive to your house—and it's pretty far to Saltsjöbaden—to carry out an attack. That is worrisome."

"I agree with you there."

"I talked with Dragan today, and we're of the same mind: until we know more about the person making the threat, we have to play it safe."

"Which means?"

"First of all, the alarm we installed today contains two components. On the one hand, it's an ordinary burglar alarm which is on when you're not at home, but it's also a sensor for the ground floor that you'll have to turn on when you're upstairs at night."

"Hmm."

"It's an inconvenience because you have to turn off the alarm every time you come downstairs."

"Understood."

"Second, we changed your bedroom door today."

"You changed the whole door?"

"Yes. We installed a steel safety door. Don't worry . . . it's painted white and looks just like a normal bedroom door. The difference is that it locks automatically when you close it. To open the door from the inside you just have to press down the handle as with any normal door. But to open the door from the outside, you have to enter a three-digit code on a plate on the door handle."

"And you did all this today?"

"If you're threatened in your home, then you have a safe room in which you can barricade yourself. The walls are sturdy, and it would take quite a while to break down that door, even if your assailant had tools at hand."

"That's a comfort."

"Third, we're going to install surveillance cameras, so that you'll be able to see what's going on in the garden and on the ground floor when you're in the bedroom. That will be done later this week, at the same time as we install the motion detectors outside the house."

"It sounds like the bedroom won't be such a romantic place in the future."

"It's a small monitor. We can put it inside a wardrobe or a cabinet so that it isn't in full view."

"Thank you."

"Later in the week I'll change the doors in your study and in a downstairs room too. If anything happens you should quickly seek shelter and lock the door while you wait for assistance."

"All right."

"If you trip the burglar alarm by mistake, then you'll have to call Milton's alarm centre immediately to cancel the emergency vehicle. To cancel it you'll have to give a password that will be registered with us. If you forget the password, the emergency vehicle will come out anyway and you'll be charged a fee."

"Understood."

"Fourth, there are now attack alarms in four places inside the house. Here in the kitchen, in the hall, in your study upstairs, and in your bedroom. The attack alarm consists of two buttons that you press simultaneously and hold down for three seconds. You can do it with one hand, but you can't do it by mistake. If the attack alarm is sounded, three things will happen. First, Milton will send cars out here. The closest car will come from Adam Security in Fisksätra. Two men will be here in ten to twelve minutes. Second, a car from Milton will come down from Nacka. For that the response time is at best twenty minutes, but more likely twenty-five. Third, the police will be alerted automatically. In other words, several cars will arrive at the scene within a short time, a matter of minutes."

"OK."

"An attack alarm can't be cancelled the same way you would cancel the burglar alarm. You can't call and say that it was a mistake. Even if you meet us in the driveway and say it was a mistake, the police will enter the house. We want to be sure that nobody's holding a gun to your husband's head or anything like that. So you use the attack alarm, obviously, only when there is real danger."

"I understand."

"It doesn't have to be a physical attack. It could be if someone is trying to break in or turns up in the garden or something like that. If you feel threatened in any way, you should set off the alarm, but use your good judgement."

"I will."

"I notice that you have golf clubs planted here and there around the house."

"Yes. I slept here alone last night."

"I myself would have checked into a hotel. I have no problem with you taking safety precautions on your own. But you ought to know that you could easily kill an intruder with a golf club."

"Hmm."

"And if you did that, you would most probably be charged

with manslaughter. If you admitted that you put golf clubs around the place with the intent of arming yourself, it could also be classified as murder."

"If someone attacks me, chances are I do intend to bash in that person's skull."

"I understand. But the point of hiring Milton Security is so that you have an alternative to doing that. You should be able to call for help, and above all, you shouldn't end up in a situation where you have to bash in someone's skull."

"I'm only too happy to hear it."

"And, by the way, what would you do with the golf clubs if an intruder had a gun? The key to good security is all about staying one step ahead of anyone who means you harm."

"Tell me how I'm supposed to do that if I have a stalker after me?"

"You see to it that he never has a chance to get close to you. Now, we won't be finished with the installations here for a couple of days, and then we'll also have to have a talk with your husband. He'll have to be as safety-conscious as you are."

"He will be."

"Until then I'd rather you didn't stay here."

"I can't move anywhere else. My husband will be home in a couple of days. But both he and I travel fairly often, and one or the other of us has to be here alone from time to time."

"I understand. But I'm only talking about a couple of days, until we have all the installations ready. Isn't there a friend you could stay with?"

Berger thought for a moment about Blomkvist's apartment but remembered that just now it was not such a good idea.

"Thanks, but I'd rather stay here."

"I was afraid you'd say that. In that case, I'd like you to have company here for the rest of the week."

"Well . . ."

"Do you have a friend who could come and stay with you?"

"Sure. But not at 7:30 in the evening if there's a nutcase on the prowl outside."

Rosin thought for a moment. "Do you have anything against a Milton employee staying here? I could call and find out if my colleague Susanne Linder is free tonight. She certainly wouldn't mind earning a few hundred kronor on the side."

"What would it cost exactly?"

"You'd have to negotiate that with her. It would be outside all our formal agreements. But I really don't want you to stay here alone."

"I'm not afraid of the dark."

"I didn't think you were or you wouldn't have slept here last night. Susanne Linder is also a former policewoman. And it's only temporary. If we had to arrange for bodyguard protection that would be a different matter—and it would be rather expensive."

Rosin's seriousness was having an effect. It dawned on her that here he was calmly talking of the possibility of there being a threat to her life. Was he exaggerating? Should she dismiss his professional caution? In that case, why had she called Milton Security in the first place and asked them to install an alarm?

"OK. Call her. I'll get the guest room ready."

· · ·

It was not until after 10:00 p.m. that Figuerola and Blomkvist wrapped sheets around themselves and went to her kitchen to make a cold pasta salad with tuna and bacon from the leftovers in her fridge. They drank water with their dinner.

Figuerola giggled.

"What's so funny?"

"I'm thinking that Edklinth would be a little bit disturbed if he saw us right now. I don't believe he intended for me to go to bed with you when he told me to keep a close eye on you."

"You started it. I had the choice of being handcuffed or coming quietly," Blomkvist said.

"True, but you weren't very hard to convince."

"Maybe you aren't aware of this—though I doubt that—but you give off the most incredible sexual vibrations. Who on earth do you think can resist that?"

"You're very kind, but I'm not that sexy. And I don't have sex that often either."

"You amaze me."

"Really, I don't end up in bed with that many men. I was going out with a guy this spring. But it ended."

"Why was that?"

"He was sweet, but it turned into a wearisome sort of arm-wrestling contest. I was stronger than he was and he couldn't bear it. Are you the kind of man who'll want to arm-wrestle me?"

"You mean, am I someone who has a problem with the fact that you're fitter and physically stronger than I am? No, I'm not."

"Thanks for being honest. I've noticed that quite a few

men get interested, but then they start challenging me and looking for ways to dominate me. Especially if they discover I'm a policewoman."

"I'm not going to compete with you. I'm better than you are at what I do. And you're better than I am at what you do."

"I can live with that attitude."

"Why did you pick me up?"

"I give in to impulses. And you were one of them!"

"But you're an officer in Säpo, of all places, and we're in the middle of an investigation in which I'm involved. . . ."

"You mean it was unprofessional of me. You're right. I shouldn't have done it. And I'd have a serious problem if it became known. Edklinth would go through the roof."

"I won't tell him."

"Very chivalrous."

They were silent for a moment.

"I don't know what this is going to turn into. You're a man who gets more than his fair share of action, as I gather. Is that accurate?"

"Yes, unfortunately. And I may not be looking for a steady girlfriend."

"Fair warning. I'm probably not looking for a steady boyfriend either. Can we keep it on a friendly level?"

"I think that would be best. Monica, I'm not going to tell anybody that we got together. But if we aren't careful I could end up in one hell of a conflict with your colleagues."

"I don't think so. Edklinth is as straight as an arrow. And we share the same objective, you and my people."

"We'll see how it goes."

"You had a thing with Lisbeth Salander too."

Blomkvist looked at her. "Listen . . . I'm not an open book for everyone to read. My relationship with Lisbeth is none of anyone's business."

"She's Zalachenko's daughter."

"Yes, and she has to live with that. But she isn't Zalachenko. There's the world of difference."

"I didn't mean it that way. I was wondering about your involvement in this story."

"Lisbeth is my friend. That should be enough of an explanation."

Susanne Linder from Milton Security was dressed in jeans, a black leather jacket, and running shoes. She arrived in Saltsjöbaden at 9:00 in the evening and Rosin showed her around the house. She had brought a green duffel bag containing her laptop, a spring baton, a Mace canister, handcuffs, and a toothbrush, which she unpacked in Berger's guest room.

Berger made coffee.

"Thanks for the coffee. You're probably thinking of me as a guest you have to entertain. The fact is, I'm not a guest at all. I'm a necessary evil that's suddenly appeared in your life, albeit just for a couple of days. I was in the police for six years and I've worked at Milton for four. I'm a trained bodyguard."

"I see."

"There's a threat against you and I'm here to be a gatekeeper so that you can sleep in peace or work or read a book or do whatever you feel like doing. If you need to talk, I'm happy to listen. Otherwise, I brought my own book."

"Understood."

"What I mean is that you should go on with your life and

not feel as though you need to entertain me. Then I'd just be in the way. The best thing would be for you to think of me as a temporary work colleague."

"Well, I'm certainly not used to this kind of situation. I've had threats before, when I was editor in chief at *Millennium,* but then it had to do with my work. Right now it's some seriously unpleasant individual—"

"Who has a hang-up about you in particular."

"Something along those lines."

"If we have to arrange full bodyguard protection, it'll cost a lot of money. And for it to be worth the cost, there has to be a very clear and specific threat. This is just an extra job for me. I'll ask you for 500 kronor a night to sleep here the rest of the week. It's cheap and far below what I would charge if I took the job for Milton. Is that OK with you?"

"It's completely OK."

"If anything happens, I want you to lock yourself in your bedroom and let me handle the situation. Your job is to press the attack alarm. That's all. I don't want you underfoot if there's any trouble."

Berger went to bed at 11:00. She heard the click of the lock as she closed her bedroom door. Deep in thought, she undressed and climbed into bed.

She had been told not to feel obliged to entertain her "guest," but she had spent two hours with Linder at the kitchen table. She discovered that they got along famously. They had discussed the psychology that causes certain men to stalk women. Linder told her that she did not hold with psychological mumbo-jumbo. She thought the most important thing was simply to stop the bastards, and she enjoyed

her job at Milton Security a great deal, since her assignments
were largely to act as a counter-force to raging lunatics.

"So why did you resign from the police force?" Berger said.

"A better question would be why did I become a police
officer in the first place."

"Why *did* you become a police officer?"

"Because when I was seventeen a close friend of mine was
mugged and raped in a car by three utter bastards. I became
a police officer because I thought, rather idealistically, that
the police existed to prevent crimes like that."

"Well?"

"I couldn't prevent shit. As a policewoman I invariably
arrived on the scene *after* a crime had been committed. I
couldn't cope with the arrogant lingo on the squad. And I
soon found out that some crimes are never even investigated.
You're a typical example. Did you try to call the police about
what happened?"

"Yes."

"And did they bother to come out here?"

"Not really. I was told to file a report at the local station."

"So now you know. I work for Armansky, and I come into
the picture *before* a crime is committed."

"Mostly concerning women who are threatened?"

"I work with all kinds of things. Security assessments,
bodyguard protection, surveillance, and so on. But the work
often concerns people who have been threatened. I get on
considerably better at Milton than on the force, although
there's a drawback."

"What's that?"

"We are only there for clients who can pay."

As she lay in bed Berger thought about what Linder had

said. Not everyone can afford security. She herself had accepted Rosin's proposal for several new doors, engineers, backup alarm systems, and everything else without blinking. The cost of all that work would be almost 50,000 kronor. But she could afford it.

She pondered for a moment her suspicion that the person threatening her had something to do with *SMP*. Whoever it was had known that she had hurt her foot. She thought of Holm. She did not like him, which added to her mistrust of him, but the news that she had been injured had spread fast from the second she appeared in the newsroom on crutches.

And she had the Borgsjö problem.

She suddenly sat up in bed and frowned, looking around the bedroom. She wondered where she had put Cortez's file on Borgsjö and Vitavara Inc.

She got up, put on her bathrobe, and leaned on a crutch. She went to her study and turned on the light. No, she had not been in her study since . . . since she had read through the file in the bath the night before. She had put it on the windowsill.

She looked in the bathroom. It was not on the windowsill.

She stood there for a while, worrying.

She had no memory of seeing the folder that morning. She had not moved it anywhere else.

She turned ice-cold and spent the next five minutes searching the bathroom and going through the stacks of papers and newspapers in the kitchen and bedroom. In the end she had to admit that the folder was gone.

Between the time when she had stepped on the shard of glass and Rosin's arrival that morning, somebody had gone into her bathroom and taken *Millennium*'s material about Vitavara Inc.

Then it occurred to her that she had other secrets in the house. She limped back to the bedroom and opened the bottom drawer of the chest by her bed. Her heart sank like a stone. Everyone has secrets. She kept hers in the chest of drawers in her bedroom. Berger did not regularly write a diary, but there were periods when she had. There were also old love letters which she had kept from her teenage years.

There was an envelope with photographs that had been cool at the time, but ... When Berger was twenty-five she had been involved in Club Xtreme, which arranged private dating parties for people who were into leather. There were photographs from various parties, and if she had been sober then, she would have recognized that she looked completely demented.

And—most disastrous of all—there was a video taken on vacation in the early nineties when she and Greger had been guests of the glass artist Torkel Bollinger at his villa on the Costa del Sol. During the vacation Berger had discovered that her husband had a definite bisexual tendency, and they had both ended up in bed with Torkel. It had been a pretty wonderful vacation. Video cameras were still a relatively new phenomenon. The movie they had playfully made was definitely not for general release.

The drawer was empty.

How could I have been so fucking stupid?

On the bottom of the drawer someone had spray-painted the familiar five-letter word.

CHAPTER 19

Friday, June 3– Saturday, June 4

Salander finished her autobiography at 4:00 on Friday morning and sent a copy to Blomkvist via the Yahoo group [Idiotic_Table]. Then she lay still in bed and stared at the ceiling.

She knew that on Walpurgis Night she had had her twenty-seventh birthday, but she had not even reflected on the fact at the time. She was imprisoned. She had experienced the same thing at St. Stefan's. If things did not go right for her, there was a risk that she would spend many more birthdays in some form of confinement.

She was not going to accept a situation like that.

The last time she had been locked up she was barely into her teens. She was grown up now, and had more knowledge and skills. She wondered how long it would take for her to escape and settle down safely in some other country to create a new identity and a new life for herself.

She got up from the bed and went to the bathroom, where she looked in the mirror. She was no longer limping. She ran her fingers over her hip where the wound had healed to a scar. She twisted her arms and stretched her left shoulder back and forth. It was tight, but she was more or less healed. She tapped herself on the head. She supposed that her brain had not been too greatly damaged after being perforated by a bullet with a full-metal jacket.

She had been extraordinarily lucky.

Until she had access to a computer, she had spent her time trying to work out how to escape from this locked room at Sahlgrenska.

Then Dr. Jonasson and Blomkvist had upset her plans by smuggling in her Palm. She had read Blomkvist's articles and brooded over what he had to say. She had done a risk assessment and pondered his plan, weighing her chances. She had decided that for once she was going to do as he advised. She would test the system. Blomkvist had convinced her that she had nothing to lose, and he was offering her a chance to escape in a very different way. If the plan failed, she would simply have to plot her escape from St. Stefan's or whichever other nuthouse they put her in.

What actually convinced her to decide to play the game Blomkvist's way was her desire for revenge.

She forgave nothing.

Zalachenko, Björck, and Bjurman were dead.

Teleborian, on the other hand, was alive.

So too was her brother, the so-called Ronald Niedermann, even though in reality he was not her problem. Certainly, he had helped in the attempt to murder and bury her, but he seemed peripheral. *If I run into him sometime, we'll see, but until such time, he's the police's problem.*

Yet Blomkvist was right: behind the conspiracy there had

to be others not known to her who had contributed to the shaping of her life. She had to put names and social security numbers to these people.

So she had decided to go along with Blomkvist's plan. That was why she had written the plain, unvarnished truth about her life in a cracklingly terse autobiography of forty pages. She had been quite precise. Everything she had written was true. She had accepted Blomkvist's reasoning that she had already been so savaged in the Swedish media by such grotesque libels that a little sheer nonsense could not possibly further damage her reputation.

The autobiography was a fiction in the sense that she had not, of course, told the *whole* truth. She had no intention of doing that.

She went back to bed and pulled the covers over her.

She felt a niggling irritation that she could not identify. She reached for a notebook, given to her by Giannini and hardly used. She turned to the first page, where she had written:

$$(x^3 + y^3 = z^3)$$

She had spent several weeks in the Caribbean last winter working herself into a frenzy over Fermat's Last Theorem. When she came back to Sweden, before she got mixed up in the hunt for Zalachenko, she had kept on playing with the equations. What was maddening was that she had the feeling she had seen a solution . . . *that she had discovered a solution.*

But she could not remember what it was.

Not being able to remember something was a phenomenon unknown to Salander. She had tested herself by going on the Net and picking out random HTML codes that she glanced at, memorized, and reproduced exactly.

She had not lost her photographic memory, which she had always considered a curse.

Everything was running as usual in her head.

Save for the fact that she thought she recalled seeing a solution to Fermat's theorem, but she could not remember how, when, or where.

The worst thing was that she did not have the least interest in it. Fermat's theorem no longer fascinated her. That was ominous. That was just the way she usually functioned. She would be fascinated by a problem, but as soon as she had solved it, she lost interest.

That was how she felt about Fermat. He was no longer a demon riding on her shoulder, demanding her attention and vexing her intellect. It was an ordinary formula, some squiggles on a piece of paper, and she felt no desire at all to engage with it.

This bothered her. She put down the notebook.

She should get some sleep.

Instead she took out her Palm again and went on the Net. She thought for a moment and then went into Armansky's hard drive, which she had not done since she got the handheld. Armansky was working with Blomkvist, but she had not had any particular need to read what he was up to.

Absentmindedly she read his email.

She found the assessment Rosin had carried out of Berger's house. She could scarcely believe what she was reading.

Erika Berger has a stalker.

She found a message from Susanne Linder, who had evidently stayed at Berger's house the night before and who had emailed a report late that night. She looked at the time of the message. It had been sent just before 3:00 in the morning and reported Berger's discovery that diaries, letters, and photographs, along with a video of a personal nature, had been stolen from a chest of drawers in Berger's bedroom.

```
After discussing the matter, Fru Berger and I
determined that the theft must have occurred
during the time she was at Nacka hospital. That
left a period of c. 2.5 hours when the house was
empty, and the defective alarm from NIP was not
switched on. At all other times either Berger or
David was in the house until the theft was
discovered.

Conclusion: Berger's stalker remained in her area
and was able to observe that she was picked up by
a taxi, also possibly that she was injured. The
stalker then took the opportunity to get into the
house.
```

Salander updated her download of Armansky's hard drive and then switched off the Palm, lost in thought. She had mixed feelings.

She had no reason to love Berger. She remembered still the humiliation she had felt when she saw her walk off down Hornsgatan with Blomkvist the day before New Year's Eve a year and a half ago.

It had been the stupidest moment of her life and she would never again allow herself those sorts of feelings.

She remembered the terrible hatred she had felt, and her desire to run after them and hurt Berger.

Embarrassing.

She was cured.

But she had no reason to sympathize with Berger.

She wondered what the video "of a personal nature" contained. She had her own film of a personal nature, which showed how Advokat Bastard Bjurman had raped her. And it was now in Blomkvist's keeping. She wondered how she would have reacted if someone had broken into her place and stolen the DVD. Which Blomkvist by definition had actually done, even though his motives were not to harm her.

Hmm. An awkward situation.

Berger had not been able to sleep on Thursday night. She hobbled restlessly back and forth while Linder kept a watchful eye on her. Her anxiety lay like a heavy fog over the house.

At 2:30 Linder managed to talk Berger into getting into bed to rest, even if she did not sleep. She heaved a sigh of relief when Berger closed her bedroom door. She opened her laptop and summarized the situation in an email to Armansky. She had scarcely sent the message before she heard that Berger was up and moving about again.

At 7:30 she made Berger call *SMP* and take a sick day. Berger had reluctantly agreed and then fallen asleep on the living-room sofa in front of the boarded-up picture window. Linder spread a blanket over her. Then she made some coffee and called Armansky, explaining her presence at the house and that she had been called in by Rosin.

"Stay there with Berger," Armansky told her, "and get a couple of hours' sleep yourself."

"I don't know how we're going to bill this—"

"We'll work that out later."

Berger slept until 2:30. She woke up to find Linder sleeping in a recliner on the other side of the living room.

Figuerola slept late on Friday morning; she did not have time for her morning run. She blamed Blomkvist for this state of affairs as she showered and then rousted him out of bed.

Blomkvist drove to *Millennium,* where everyone was surprised to see him up so early. He mumbled something, made some coffee, and called Eriksson and Cortez into his office. They spent three hours going over the articles for the themed issue and keeping track of the book's progress.

"Dag's book went to the printer yesterday," Eriksson said. "We're going down the perfect-bound trade paperback route."

"The special issue is going to be called 'The Lisbeth Salander Story,'" Cortez said. "They're bound to move the date of the trial, but at the moment it's set for Wednesday, July 13. The magazine will be printed by then, but we haven't fixed on a distribution date yet. You can decide nearer the time."

"Good. That leaves the Zalachenko book, which right now is a nightmare. I'm calling it *The Section.* The first half is basically what's in the magazine. It begins with the murders of Dag and Mia, and then follows the hunt for Salander first, then Zalachenko, and then Niedermann. The second half will be everything we know about the Section."

"Mikael, even if the printer breaks every record for us, we're going to have to send them the files by the end of this month—at the latest," Eriksson said. "Christer will need a couple of days for the layout, the typesetter, say, a week. So we have about two weeks left for the text. I don't know how we're going to make it."

"We won't have time to dig up the whole story," Blomkvist conceded. "But I don't think we could manage that even if we had a whole year. What we're going to do in this book is to state what happened. If we don't have a source for something, then I'll say so. If we're flying kites, we'll make that clear. So, we're going to write about what happened, what we can document, and what we believe to have happened."

"That's pretty vague," Cortez said.

Blomkvist shook his head. "If I say that a Säpo agent broke into my apartment and I can document it—and him—with a video, then it's documented. If I say that he did it on behalf of the Section, then that's speculation, but in the light of all the facts we're setting out, it's a reasonable speculation. Does that make sense?"

"It does."

"I won't have time to write all the missing pieces myself. I have a list of articles here that you, Henry, will have to cobble together. It corresponds to about fifty pages of book text. Malin, you're backup for Henry, just as when we were editing Dag's book. All three of our names will be on the cover and on the title page. Is that all right with you two?"

"That's fine," Eriksson said. "But we have other urgent problems."

"Such as?"

"While you were concentrating on the Zalachenko story, we had a hell of a lot of work to do here—"

"You're saying I wasn't available?"

Eriksson nodded.

"You're right. I'm sorry."

"No need to apologize. We all know that when you're in the throes of a story, nothing else matters. But that won't work for the rest of us, and it definitely doesn't work for me. Erika had me to lean on. I have Henry, and he's an ace, but he's putting in an equal amount of time on your story. Even if we count you in, we're still two people short in editorial."

"Two?"

"And I'm not Erika. She had a routine that I can't compete with. I'm still learning this job. Monika is working her back-side off. And so is Lotta. Nobody has a moment to stop and think."

"This is all temporary. As soon as the trial begins—"

"No, Mikael. It won't be over then. When the trial begins, it'll be sheer hell. Remember what it was like during the Wennerström affair? We won't see you for three months while you hop from one TV interview sofa to another."

Blomkvist sighed. "What do you suggest?"

"If we're going to run *Millennium* effectively during the fall, we're going to need new blood. Two people at least, maybe three. We just don't have the editorial capacity for what we're trying to do, and . . ."

"And?"

"And I'm not sure that I'm ready to do it."

"I hear you, Malin."

"I mean it. I'm a damn good managing editor—it's a piece of cake with Erika as your boss. We said that we were going to try this over the summer . . . well, we've tried it. I'm not a good editor in chief."

"Nonsense," Cortez said.

Eriksson shook her head.

"I hear what you're saying," Blomkvist said, "but remember that it's been an extreme situation."

Eriksson smiled at him sadly. "You could take this as a complaint from the staff," she said.

The operations unit of Constitutional Protection spent Friday trying to get a handle on the information they had received from Blomkvist. Two of their team had moved into a temporary office at Fridhemsplan, where all the documentation was being assembled. It was inconvenient because the police intranet was at headquarters, which meant that they had to walk back and forth between the two buildings several times a day. Even if it was only a ten-minute walk, it was tiresome. By lunchtime they already had extensive documentation of the fact that both Fredrik Clinton and Hans von Rottinger had been associated with the Security Police in the sixties and early seventies.

Von Rottinger came originally from the military intelligence service and worked for several years in the office that coordinated military defence with the Security Police. Clinton's background was in the air force, and he began working for the Personal Protection Unit of the Security Police in 1967.

They had both left SIS: Clinton in 1971 and von Rottinger in 1973. Clinton had gone into business as a management consultant, and von Rottinger had entered the civil service to do investigations for the Swedish Atomic Energy Agency. He was based in London.

It was late afternoon by the time Figuerola was able to convey to Edklinth with some certainty the discovery that Clinton's and von Rottinger's careers after they left SIS were falsifications. Clinton's career was hard to follow. Being a consultant for industry can mean almost anything at all, and a person in that role is under no obligation to report his activities to the government. From his tax returns it was clear that he made good money, but his clients were for the most part corporations with home offices in Switzerland or Liechtenstein, so it was not easy to prove that his work was a fabrication.

Von Rottinger, on the other hand, had never set foot in the office in London where he supposedly worked. In 1973 the office building where he had claimed to be working was in fact torn down and replaced by an extension to King's Cross station. No doubt someone made a blunder when the cover story was devised. In the course of the day Figuerola's team had interviewed a number of people now retired from the Swedish Atomic Energy Agency. Not one of them had heard of Hans von Rottinger.

"Now we know," Edklinth said. "We just have to discover what it was they really were doing."

Figuerola said: "What do we do about Blomkvist?"

"In what sense?"

"We promised to give him feedback if we uncovered anything about Clinton and von Rottinger."

Edklinth thought about it. "He's going to be digging up that stuff himself if he keeps at it for a while. It's better that we stay on good terms with him. You can give him what you've found. But use your judgement."

Figuerola promised that she would. They spent a few minutes making arrangements for the weekend. Two of Figuerola's team were going to keep working. She would be taking the weekend off.

Then she clocked out and went to the gym at St. Eriks-plan, where she spent two hours driving herself hard to catch up on lost training time. She was home by 7:00. She showered, made a simple dinner, and turned on the TV to listen to the news. But then she got restless and put on her running clothes. She paused at the front door to think. *Fucking Blomkvist.* She flipped open her mobile and called his Ericsson.

"We found out a certain amount about von Rottinger and Clinton."

"Tell me."

"I will if you come over."

"Sounds like blackmail," Blomkvist said.

"I've just changed into jogging things to work off a little of my surplus energy," Figuerola said. "Should I go now or should I wait for you?"

"Would it be OK if I came after 9:00?"

"That'll be fine."

At 8:00 on Friday evening Salander had a visit from Dr. Jonasson. He sat in the guest chair and leaned back.

"Are you going to examine me?" Salander said.

"No. Not tonight."

"OK."

"We studied all your notes today and we've informed the prosecutor that we're prepared to discharge you."

"I understand."

"They want to take you over to the prison in Göteborg tonight."

"So soon?"

He nodded. "Stockholm is making noises. I said I had a

number of final tests to run on you tomorrow and that I couldn't discharge you until Sunday."

"Why's that?"

"Don't know. I was just annoyed they were being so pushy."

Salander actually smiled. Given a few years she would probably be able to make a good anarchist out of Dr. Anders Jonasson. In any case he had a penchant for civil disobedience on a private level.

"Fredrik Clinton," Blomkvist said, staring at the ceiling above Figuerola's bed.

"If you light that cigarette I'll stub it out in your navel," Figuerola said.

Blomkvist looked in surprise at the cigarette he had extracted from his jacket.

"Sorry," he said. "Could I borrow your balcony?"

"As long as you brush your teeth afterwards."

He tied a sheet around his waist. She followed him to the kitchen and filled a large glass with cold water. Then she leaned against the door frame by the balcony.

"Clinton first?"

"If he's still alive, he's the link to the past."

"He's dying; he needs a new kidney and spends a lot of his time in dialysis or some other treatment."

"But he's alive. We should contact him and put the question to him directly. Maybe he'll talk."

"No," Figuerola said. "First of all, this is a preliminary investigation, and the police are handling it. In that sense, there is no 'we' about it. Second, you're receiving this information in accordance with your agreement with Edklinth, but you've given your word not to take any initiatives that could interfere with the investigation."

Blomkvist smiled at her. "Ouch," he said. "The Security Police are pulling on my leash." He stubbed out his cigarette.

"Mikael, this is not a joke."

Berger drove to the office on Saturday morning still feeling queasy. She had thought she was beginning to come to grips with the actual process of producing a newspaper and had planned to reward herself with a weekend off—the first since she started at *SMP*—but the discovery that her most personal and intimate possessions had been stolen, and the Borgsjö report too, made it impossible for her to relax.

During a sleepless night spent mostly in the kitchen with Linder, Berger had expected the "Poison Pen" to strike, disseminating pictures of her that would be deplorably damaging. What an excellent tool the Internet was for freaks. *Good grief . . . a video of me fucking my husband and another man—I'm going to end up on half the websites in the world.*

Panic and terror had dogged her through the night.

It took all of Linder's powers of persuasion to send her to bed.

At 8:00 she got up and drove to *SMP*. She could not stay away. If a storm was brewing, then she wanted to face it first, before anyone else got wind of it.

But in the half-staffed Saturday newsroom everything was normal. People greeted her as she limped past the central desk. Holm was off today. Fredriksson was the acting news editor.

"Morning. I thought you were taking today off," he said.

"Me too. But I wasn't feeling well yesterday and there are things I have to do. Anything happening?"

"No, it's pretty slow today. The hottest thing we've got is that the timber industry in Dalarna is reporting a boom, and there was a robbery in Norrköping in which one person was injured."

"Right. I'll be in the cage for a while."

She sat down, leaned her crutches against the book-shelves, and logged on. First she checked her email. She had several messages, but nothing from Poison Pen. She frowned. It had been two days now since the break-in, and he had not yet acted on what had to be a treasure trove of opportunities. *Why not? Maybe he's going to change tactics. Blackmail? Maybe he just wants to keep me guessing.*

She had nothing specific to work on, so she clicked on the strategy document she was writing for *SMP*. She stared at the screen for fifteen minutes without seeing the words.

She tried to call Greger, but with no success. She did not even know if his mobile worked in other countries. Of course she could have tracked him down with a bit of effort, but she felt lazy to the core. Wrong—she felt helpless and paralysed.

She tried to call Blomkvist to tell him that the Borgsjö folder had been stolen, but he did not answer.

By 10:00 she had accomplished nothing and decided to go home. She was just reaching out to shut down her computer when her ICQ account pinged. She looked in astonishment at the icon bar. She knew what ICQ was but she seldom chatted, and she had not used the programme since starting at *SMP*.

She clicked hesitantly on Answer.

\<Hi, Erika.\>

\<Hi. Who's this?\>

\<Private. Are you alone?\>

A trick? Poison Pen?

\<Who are you?\>

\<We met at Kalle Blomkvist's place when he came home from Sandhamn.\>

Berger stared at the screen. It took her a few seconds to make the connection. *Lisbeth Salander. Impossible.*

\<Are you there?\>

\<Yes.\>

\<No names. You know who I am?\>

\<How do I know this isn't a bluff?\>

\<I know how Mikael got that scar on his neck.\>

Berger swallowed. Only four people in the world knew how he had come by that scar. Salander was one of them.

\<But how can you be chatting with me?\>

\<I'm pretty good with computers.\>

Salander is a devil with computers. But how the hell is she managing to communicate from Sahlgrenska, where she's been isolated since April?

\<I believe it.\>

\<Can I trust you?\>

\<How do you mean?\>

\<This conversation must not be leaked.\>

She doesn't want the police to know she has access to the Net. Of course not. Which is why she's chatting with the editor in chief of one of the biggest newspapers in Sweden.

\<No problem. What do you want?\>

\<To pay my debt.\>

\<What do you mean?\>

\<Millennium backed me up.\>

\<We were just doing our job.\>

\<No other publication did.\>

\<You're not guilty of what you were
accused of.\>

\<You have a stalker.\>

Berger's heart beat furiously.

\<What do you know?\>

\<Stolen video. Break-in.\>

\<Correct. Can you help?\>

Berger could not believe she was asking this question. It was absurd. Salander was in rehabilitation at Sahlgrenska and was up to her neck in her own problems. She was the most unlikely person Berger could turn to with any hope of getting help.

\<Dunno. Let me try.\>

\<How?\>

\<Question. You think the creep is at SMP?\>

\<I can't prove it.\>

\<Why do you think so?\>

Berger thought for a while before she replied.

\<Just a hunch. It started when I began working
at SMP. Other people here have received crude
messages from Poison Pen that looked as though
they came from me.\>

\<Poison Pen?\>

\<My name for the creep.\>

<OK. Why did you become the object of Poison
Pen's attention?>

<No idea.>

<Is there anything to suggest that it's per-
sonal?>

<How do you mean?>

<How many employees at SMP?>

<230 give or take, including the publishing
company.>

<How many do you know personally?>

<Can't say. I've met several journalists and
other colleagues over the years.>

<Anyone you argued with before you went to
SMP?>

<Nobody that I can think of.>

<Anyone who might want to get revenge?>

<Revenge? What for?>

<Revenge is a powerful motive.>

Berger stared at the screen as she tried to work out what
Salander was getting at.

<Still there?>

<Yes. Why do you ask about revenge?>

<I read Rosin's list of all the incidents
you connect to Poison Pen.>

Why am I not surprised?

<And???>

<Doesn't feel like a stalker.>

<Why not?>

<Stalkers are driven by sexual obsession. This
looks like somebody imitating a stalker.

Screwdriver in your cunt . . . hello? Pure
parody.>

<You think?>

<I've seen real stalkers. They're considerably
more perverted, coarse, and grotesque. They
express love and hate at the same time. This
just doesn't feel right.>

<You don't think it's perverted enough?>

<No. Mail to Eva Carlsson all wrong. Somebody
who wants to get even.>

<Wasn't thinking along those lines.>

<Not a stalker. Personal against you.>

<OK. What do you suggest?>

<Can you trust me?>

<Maybe.>

<I need access to SMP's intranet.>

<Whoa, hold everything.>

<Now. I'm going to be moved soon and lose
the Net.>

Berger hesitated for ten seconds. Open up *SMP* to . . .
what? A complete loony? Salander might be innocent of
murder, but she was definitely not normal.

But what did she have to lose?

<How?>

<I have to load a programme into your com-
puter.>

<We have firewalls.>

<You have to help. Start the Internet.>

<Already logged on.>

<Explorer?>

<Yes.>

<I'll type an address. Copy and paste it into Explorer.>

<Done.>

<Now you see a list of programmes. Click on Asphyxia Server and download it.>

Berger followed the instruction.

<Done.>

<Start Asphyxia. Click on Install and choose Explorer.>

It took three minutes.

<Done. OK. Now you have to reboot your computer. We'll lose contact for a minute.>

<Got you.>

<When we reboot I'm going to copy your hard disk to a server on the Net.>

<OK.>

<Restart. Talk to you soon.>

Berger stared in fascination at the screen as her computer slowly rebooted. She wondered whether she was crazy. Then her ICQ pinged.

<Hi again.>

<Hi.>

<It'll be faster if you do it. Start up the Internet and copy in the address I email you.>

<Done.>

<Now you see a question. Click on Start.>

<Done.>

<Now you're asked to name the hard disk. Call it SMP-2.>

<Done.>

```
<Go and get a coffee. This is going to take a
while.>
```

Figuerola woke at 8:00 on Saturday morning, about two hours later than usual. She sat up in bed and looked at the man beside her. He was snoring. *Well, nobody's perfect.*

She wondered where this affair with Blomkvist was going to lead. He was obviously not the faithful type, so no point in looking forward to a long-term relationship. She knew that much from his biography. Anyway, she was not so sure she wanted a stable relationship herself—with a partner and a mortgage and kids. After a dozen failed relationships since her teens, she was tending towards the theory that stability was overrated. Her longest had been with a colleague in Uppsala—they had shared an apartment for two years.

But she was not someone who went in for one-night stands, although she did think that sex was an underrated therapy for just about all ailments. And sex with Blomkvist, out of shape as he was, was just fine. More than just fine, actually. Plus, he was a good person. He made her want more.

A summer romance? A love affair? Was she in love?

She went to the bathroom and washed her face and brushed her teeth. Then she put on her shorts and a thin jacket and quietly left the apartment. She stretched and went on a forty-five-minute run out past Rålambshov hospital and around Fredhäll and back via Smedsudden. She was home by 9:00 and discovered Blomkvist still asleep. She bent down and bit him on the ear. He opened his eyes in bewilderment.

"Good morning, darling. I need somebody to scrub my back."

He looked at her and mumbled something.

"What did you say?"

"You don't need to take a shower. You're soaked to the skin already."

"I've been running. You should come along."

"If I tried to go at your pace, I'd have a heart attack on Norr Mälarstrand."

"Nonsense. Come on, time to get up."

He scrubbed her back and soaped her shoulders. And her hips. And her stomach. And her breasts. And after a while she had completely lost interest in her shower and pulled him back to bed.

They had their coffee at the outdoor café beside Norr Mälarstrand.

"You could turn out to be a bad habit," she said. "And we've only known each other a few days."

"I find you incredibly attractive. But you know that already."

"Why do you think that is?"

"Sorry, can't answer that question. I've never understood why I'm attracted to one woman and totally uninterested in another."

She smiled thoughtfully. "I have today off," she said.

"But I don't. I have a mountain of work before the trial begins, and I've spent the last three evenings with you instead of getting on with it."

"What a shame."

He stood up and gave her a kiss on the cheek. She took hold of his shirtsleeve.

"Blomkvist, I'd like to spend some more time with you."

"Same here. But it's going to be a little up and down until we put this story to bed."

He walked away down Hantverkargatan.

Berger got some coffee and watched the screen. For fifty-three minutes absolutely nothing happened except that her screen saver started up from time to time. Then her ICQ pinged again.

```
<Ready. You have a whole bunch of shit on your
hard drive, including a couple of viruses.>
<Sorry. What's the next step?>
<Who's the admin for SMP's intranet?>
<Don't know. Probably Peter Fleming, our IT
manager.>
<Right.>
<What should I do?>
<Nothing. Go home.>
<Just like that?>
<I'll be in touch.>
<Should I leave the computer on?>
```

But Salander was gone from her ICQ. Berger stared at the screen in frustration. Finally she turned off the computer and went out to find a café where she could sit and think.

CHAPTER 20

Saturday, June 4

Blomkvist spent twenty-five minutes on the tunnelbana changing lines and going in different directions. He finally got off a bus at Slussen, jumped on the Katarina lift up to Mosebacke, and took a circuitous route to Fiskargatan 9. He had bought bread, milk, and cheese at the mini-mart next to the County Council building, and he put the groceries straight into the fridge. Then he turned on Salander's computer.

After a moment's thought he also turned on his Ericsson T10. He ignored his normal mobile because he did not want to talk to anyone who was not involved in the Zalachenko story. He saw that he had missed a number of calls in the past twenty-four hours: three from Cortez, two from Eriksson, and several from Berger.

First he called Cortez, who was in a café in Vasastad and had a few details to discuss, nothing urgent.

Eriksson had only called, she told him, to keep in touch.

Then he called Berger, whose line was busy.

He opened the Yahoo group [Idiotic_Table] and found the

final version of Salander's autobiographical statement. He smiled, printed out the document, and began to read it at once.

Salander switched on her Palm Tungsten T3. She had spent an hour infiltrating and charting the intranet at *SMP* with the help of Berger's account. She had not tackled the Peter Fleming account because she did not need to have full administrator rights. What she was interested in was access to *SMP*'s personnel files. And Berger's account had complete access to those.

She fervently wished that Blomkvist had been kind enough to smuggle in her PowerBook with a real keyboard and a seventeen-inch screen instead of only the hand-held. She downloaded a list of everyone who worked at *SMP* and began to check them off. There were 223 employees, 82 of whom were women.

She began by crossing off all the women. She did not exclude women on the grounds of their being incapable of such folly, but statistics showed that the absolute majority of people who harassed women were men. That left 141 individuals.

Statistics also argued that the majority of poison pen artists were either teenagers or middle-aged. Since *SMP* did not have any teenagers on its staff, she drew an age curve and deleted everyone over fifty-five and under twenty-five. That left 103.

She thought for a moment. She did not have much time. Maybe not even twenty-four hours. She made a snap decision. She eliminated all employees in distribution, advertising, the photo department, maintenance, and IT. She focused on a group of journalists and editorial staff, forty-eight men between the ages of twenty-six and fifty-four.

Then she heard the rattle of a set of keys. She turned off the Palm and put it under the covers, between her thighs. This would be her last Saturday lunch at Sahlgrenska. She took stock of the cabbage stew with resignation. After lunch she would not, she knew, be able to work undisturbed for a while. She put the Palm in the recess behind the bedside table and waited while two Eritrean women vacuumed the room and changed her bed linen.

One of the women had regularly smuggled in a few Marlboro Lights for Salander during the past month. She had also given her a lighter, now hidden behind the bedside table. Salander gratefully accepted two cigarettes, which she planned to smoke by the vent window during the night.

Not until 2:00 p.m. was everything quiet again in her room. She took out the Palm and connected to the Net. She had intended to go straight back to *SMP*'s administration, but she also had to deal with her own problems. She made her daily sweep, starting with the Yahoo group [Idiotic_Table]. She saw that Blomkvist had not uploaded anything new for three days and wondered what he was working on. *The son of a bitch is probably out screwing around with some bimbo with big boobs.*

She then proceeded to the Yahoo group [The_Knights] and checked whether Plague had added anything. He had not.

Then she checked the hard drives of Ekström (some routine correspondence about the trial) and Teleborian.

Every time she accessed Teleborian's hard drive she felt as if her body temperature dropped a few degrees.

She found that he had already written her forensic psychiatric report, even though he was obviously not supposed to write it until after he had been given the opportunity to examine her. He had brushed up his prose, but there was nothing much new. She downloaded the report and sent it off to [Idiotic_Table]. She checked Teleborian's emails from the past twenty-four hours, clicking through one after another. She almost missed the terse message:

Saturday, 3:00 at the Ring in Central Station.
Jonas

Shit. Jonas. He was mentioned in a lot of correspondence with Teleborian. Used a Hotmail account. Not identified.

Salander glanced at the digital clock on her bedside table—2:28. She immediately pinged Blomkvist's ICQ. No response.

Blomkvist printed out the 220 pages of the manuscript that were finished. Then he shut off the computer and sat down at Salander's kitchen table with a red pencil.

He was pleased with the text. But there was still a gigantic, gaping hole. How could he find the remainder of the Section? Eriksson might be right: it might be impossible. He was running out of time.

Salander swore in frustration and pinged Plague. He did not answer either. She looked again at the clock—2:30.

She sat on the edge of the bed and tried Cortez next and then Eriksson. *Saturday. Everybody's off work.* 2:32.

Then she tried to reach Berger. *No luck. I told her to go home. Shit.* 2:33.

She should be able to send a text message to Blomkvist's mobile . . . but it was tapped. She bit her lip.

Finally, in desperation, she rang for the nurse.

It was 2:35 when she heard the key in the lock and Nurse Agneta looked in on her.

"Hello. Are you OK?"

"Is Dr. Jonasson on duty?"

"Aren't you feeling well?"

"I feel fine. But I need to have a few words with him. If possible."

"I saw him a little while ago. What's it about?"

"I just have to talk to him."

Nurse Agneta frowned. Lisbeth Salander had seldom rung for a nurse if she did not have a severe headache or some other equally serious problem. She never pestered them for anything and had never before asked to speak to a specific doctor. But Nurse Agneta had noticed that Dr. Jonasson had spent time with the patient who was under arrest and otherwise seemed withdrawn from the world. It was possible that he had established some sort of rapport.

"I'll find out if he has time," Nurse Agneta said gently, and closed the door. And then locked it. It was 2:36, and then the clock clicked over to 2:37.

Salander got up from the edge of the bed and went to the window. She kept an eye on the clock. 2:39. 2:40.

At 2:44 she heard steps in the corridor and the rattle of the Securitas guard's key ring. Jonasson gave her an inquisitive glance and stopped in his tracks when he saw her desperate look.

"Has something happened?"

"Something is happening *right now*. Do you have a mobile on you?"

"A what?"

"A mobile. I have to make a call."

Jonasson looked over his shoulder at the door.

"Anders, I need a mobile. *Now!*"

When he heard the desperation in her voice he dug into his pants pocket and handed her his Motorola. Salander grabbed it from him. She could not call Blomkvist because he had not given her the number of his Ericsson T10. It had never come up, and he had never supposed that she would be able to call him from her isolation. She hesitated a tenth of a second and punched in Berger's number. It rang three times before Berger answered.

Berger was in her BMW half a mile from home in Saltsjöbaden when her mobile rang.

"Berger."

"Salander. No time to explain. Do you have the number of Mikael's second mobile? The one that's not tapped."

"Yes."

Salander had already surprised her once today.

"Call him. Now! Teleborian is meeting Jonas at the Ring in Central Station at 3:00."

"What's—"

"Just hurry. Teleborian. Jonas. The Ring in Central Station. 3:00. He has fifteen minutes."

Salander flipped the phone shut so that Berger would not be tempted to waste precious seconds with unnecessary questions.

Berger pulled over to the curb. She reached for the address

book in her bag and found the number Blomkvist had given her the night they met at Samir's Cauldron.

Blomkvist heard his mobile beeping. He got up from the kitchen table, went to Salander's office, and picked up the phone from the desk.

"Yes?"

"Erika."

"Hi."

"Teleborian is meeting Jonas at the Ring in Central Station at 3:00. You only have a few minutes."

"What? What? What?"

"Teleborian—"

"I heard you. How do you know about that?"

"Stop arguing and make it snappy."

Mikael glanced at the clock—2:47. "Thanks. Bye."

He grabbed his laptop case and took the stairs instead of waiting for the elevator. As he ran he called Cortez on his T10.

"Cortez."

"Where are you now?"

"At the Academy bookshop."

"Teleborian is meeting Jonas at the Ring in Central Station at 3:00. I'm on my way, but you're closer."

"Oh, boy. I'm on my way."

Blomkvist jogged down to Götgatan and sped up towards Slussen. When he reached Slussplan he was badly out of breath. Maybe Figuerola had a point. He was not going to make it. He looked around for a taxi.

Salander handed the mobile back to Dr. Jonasson.

"Thanks," she said.

"Teleborian?" Jonasson could not help overhearing the name.

She met his gaze. "Teleborian is a real, real bastard. You have no idea."

"No, but I could see that something happened just now that got you more agitated than I've seen you in all the time you've been in my care. I hope you know what you're doing."

Salander gave Jonasson a lopsided smile.

"You should have the answer to that question very soon," she said.

Cortez left the Academy bookshop running like a madman. He crossed Sveavägen on the viaduct at Mäster Samuelsgatan and went straight down to Klara Norra, where he turned up the Klaraberg viaduct and across Vasagatan. He flew across Klarabergsgatan between a bus and two cars, one of whose drivers punched his windshield in fury, and through the doors of Central Station as the station clock ticked over to 3:00 sharp.

He took the escalator three steps at a time down to the main ticket hall and jogged past the Pocket bookshop before slowing down so as not to attract attention. He scanned every face of every person standing or walking near the Ring.

He did not see Teleborian or the man Malm had photographed outside Café Copacabana, whom they believed to be Jonas. He looked back at the clock—3:01. He was gasping as if he had just run a marathon.

He took a chance and hurried across the hall and out through the doors onto Vasagatan. He stopped and looked around, checking one face after another, as far as his eyes could see. No Teleborian. No Jonas.

He turned back into the station—3:03. The Ring area was almost deserted.

Then he looked up and got a split second's glimpse of Teleborian's dishevelled profile and goatee as he came out of Pressbyrån on the other side of the ticket hall. A second later the man from Malm's photograph materialized at Teleborian's side. *Jonas.* They crossed the concourse and went out onto Vasagatan by the north door.

Cortez exhaled in relief. He wiped the sweat from his brow with the back of his hand and set off in pursuit of the two men.

Blomkvist's taxi got to Central Station at 3:07. He walked rapidly into the ticket hall, but he could see neither Teleborian nor anyone looking like he might be Jonas. Nor Cortez for that matter.

He was about to call Cortez when the T10 rang in his hand.

"I've got them. They're sitting in the Tre Remmare pub on Vasagatan by the stairs down to the Akalla line."

"Thanks, Henry. Where are you?"

"I'm at the bar. Having my afternoon beer. I earned it."

"Very good. They know what I look like, so I'll stay out of it. I don't suppose you have any chance of hearing what they're saying."

"Not a hope. I can only see Jonas's back, and that fucking psychiatrist mumbles when he speaks, so I can't even see his lips move."

"I get it."

"But we may have a problem."

"What's that?"

"Jonas has put his wallet and mobile on the table. And he put his car keys on top of the wallet."

"OK. I'll handle it."

Figucrola's mobile played the theme from *Once Upon a Time in the West.* She put down her book about God in antiquity. It did not seem as though she would ever be able to finish it.

"Hi. It's Mikael. What are you up to?"

"I'm sitting at home sorting through my collection of photographs of old lovers. I was ignominiously ditched earlier today."

"Do you have your car nearby?"

"The last time I checked it was in the parking space outside."

"Good. Do you feel like an afternoon on the town?"

"Not particularly. What's going on?"

"A psychiatrist named Teleborian is having a beer with an undercover agent—code name Jonas—down on Vasagatan. And since I'm cooperating with your Stasi-style bureaucracy, I thought you might be amused to tag along."

Figuerola was on her feet and reaching for her car keys.

"This is not your little joke, is it?"

"Hardly. And Jonas has his car keys on the table in front of him."

"I'm on my way."

Eriksson did not answer the phone, but Blomkvist got lucky and caught Karim, who had been at Åhléns department store buying a birthday present for her husband. He asked her to please—on overtime—hurry over to the pub as backup for Cortez. Then he called Cortez.

"Here's the plan. I'll have a car in place in five minutes. It'll be on Järnvägsgatan, down the street from the pub. Lotta is going to join you in a few minutes as backup."

"Good."

"When they leave the pub, you tail Jonas. Keep me posted by mobile. As soon as you see him approach a car, we have to know. Lotta will follow Teleborian. If we don't get there in time, make a note of his registration number."

"OK."

Figuerola parked beside the Nordic Light Hotel next to the Arlanda Express platforms. Blomkvist opened the driver's door a minute later.

"Which pub are they in?"

Blomkvist told her.

"I have to call for backup."

"I'd rather you didn't. We've got them covered. Too many cooks might wreck the whole dish."

Figuerola gave him a sceptical look. "And how did you know that this meeting was going to take place?"

"I have to protect my source. Sorry."

"Do you have your own fucking intelligence service at *Millennium*?" she burst out.

Blomkvist looked pleased. It was cool to outdo Säpo in their own field of expertise.

In fact he did not have the slightest idea how Berger came to call him out of the blue to tell him of the meeting. She had not had access to ongoing editorial work at *Millennium* since early April. She knew about Teleborian, to be sure, but Jonas had not come into the picture until May. As far as he knew, Berger had not even known of his existence, let alone that he was the focus of intense speculation both at Säpo and at *Millennium*.

He needed to talk to Berger.

Salander pressed her lips together and looked at the screen of her hand-held. After using Jonasson's mobile, she had pushed all thoughts of the Section to one side and concentrated on Berger's problem. She had next, after careful consideration, eliminated all the men in the twenty-six to fifty-four age group who were married. She was working with a broad brush, of that she was perfectly aware. The selection was scarcely based on any statistical, sociological, or scientific rationale. Poison Pen might easily be a married man with five children and a dog. He might also be a man who worked in maintenance. "He" could even be a woman.

She simply needed to prune the number of names on the list, and her group was down from forty-eight to eighteen since her latest cut. The list was made up largely of the better-known reporters, managers, or middle managers aged thirty-five or older. If she did not find anything of interest in that group, she could always widen the net again.

At 4:00 she logged on to Hacker Republic and uploaded the list to Plague. He pinged her a few minutes later.

<18 names. What is this?>

<A little project on the side. Consider it a training exercise.>

<OK, I guess.>

<One of the guys on the list is a stalker.
Find him.>

<What are the parameters?>

<Have to work fast. Tomorrow they're pulling
the plug on me. Need to find him before then.>
She outlined the Poison Pen situation.

<Is there any profit in this?>

<Yes. I won't come out to the Swamp and set
your place on fire.>

<Would you really?>

<I pay you every time I ask you to do something for me. This isn't for me. View it as a
tax write-off.>

<You're beginning to exhibit signs of a social
conscience.>

<Oh yeah?>

She sent him the access codes for *SMP*'s newsroom and then logged off from ICQ.

It was 4:20 before Cortez called.

"They're showing signs of leaving."

"We're ready."

Silence.

"They're going their separate ways outside the pub. Jonas heading north. Teleborian south. Lotta's going after him."

Blomkvist raised a finger and pointed as Jonas flashed past them on Vasagatan. Figuerola nodded and started the engine. Seconds later Blomkvist could also see Cortez.

"He's crossing Vasagatan, heading towards Kungsgatan," Cortez said into his mobile.

"Keep your distance so he doesn't spot you."

"Quite a few people out."

Silence.

"He's turning north on Kungsgatan."

"North on Kungsgatan," Blomkvist said.

Figuerola changed gears and turned up Vasagatan. They were stopped by a red light.

"Where is he now?" Blomkvist said as they turned onto Kungsgatan.

"Opposite PUB department store. He's walking fast. Whoops, he's turned up Drottninggatan heading north."

"Drottninggatan heading north," Blomkvist said.

"Right," Figuerola said, making an illegal turn onto Klara Norra and heading towards Olof Palmes Gata. She turned and braked outside the SIF building. Jonas crossed Olof Palmes Gata and turned up towards Sveavägen. Cortez stayed on the other side of the street.

"He turned east—"

"We can see you both."

"He's turning down Holländargatan. *Hello* . . . Car. Red Audi."

"Car," Blomkvist said, writing down the registration number Cortez read off to him.

"Which way is he facing?" Figuerola said.

"Facing south," Cortez reported. "He's pulling out in front of you on Olof Palmes Gata . . . *now*."

Monica was already on her way and passing Drottninggatan. She signalled and headed off a couple of pedestrians who tried to sneak across even though their light was red.

"Thanks, Henry. We'll take him from here."

The red Audi turned south on Sveavägen. As Figuerola followed she flipped open her mobile with her left hand and punched in a number.

"Could I get an owner of a red Audi?" she said, rattling off the number.

"Jonas Sandberg, born 1971. What did you say? Helsing-örsgatan, Kista. Thanks."

Blomkvist wrote down the information.

They followed the red Audi via Hamngatan to Strand-vägen and then straight up to Artillerigatan. Jonas parked a block away from the Armémuseum. He walked across the street and through the front door of an 1890s building.

"Interesting," Figuerola said, turning to Blomkvist.

Jonas Sandberg had entered a building that was only a block away from the apartment the prime minister had bor-rowed for their private meeting.

"Nicely done," Figuerola said.

Just then Karim called and told them that Teleborian had gone up onto Klarabergsgatan via the escalators in Central Station and from there to police headquarters on Kungshol-men.

"Police headquarters at 5:00 on a Saturday afternoon?"

Figuerola and Blomkvist exchanged a sceptical look. Monica pondered this turn of events for a few seconds. Then she picked up her mobile and called Criminal Inspector Jan Bublanski.

"Hello, it's Monica from SIS. We met on Norr Mälar-strand a while back."

"What do you want?" Bublanski said.

"Do you have anybody on duty this weekend?"

"Modig," Bublanski said.

"I need a favour. Do you know if she's at headquarters?"

"I doubt it. It's beautiful weather and Saturday afternoon."

"Could you possibly reach her or anyone else on the investigative team who might be able to take a look in Prosecutor Ekström's hallway . . . to see if there's a meeting going on in his office at the moment."

"What sort of meeting?"

"I can't explain just yet. I just need to know if he's in a meeting with anybody right now. And if so, who."

"You want me to spy on a prosecutor who happens to be my superior?"

Figuerola paused. "Yes, I do."

"I'll do what I can," he said and hung up.

Sonja Modig was closer to police headquarters than Bublanski had thought. She was having coffee with her husband on the balcony of a friend's place in Vasastaden. Their children were away with her parents, who had taken them on a week's vacation, and they planned to do something as old-fashioned as have a bite to eat and go to the movies.

Bublanski explained why he was calling.

"And what sort of excuse would I have to barge in on Ekström?" Modig asked.

"I promised to give him an update on Niedermann yesterday, but in fact I forgot to deliver it to his office before I left. It's on my desk."

"OK," said Modig. She looked at her husband and her friend. "I have to go in to HQ. I'll take the car and with a little luck I'll be back in an hour."

Her husband sighed. Her friend sighed.

"I'm on call this weekend," Modig said in apology.

She parked on Bergsgatan, took the elevator up to Bublanski's office, and picked up the three pages that comprised the meagre results of their search for Niedermann. Not much to hang on the Christmas tree, she thought.

She took the stairs up to the next floor and stopped at the door to the hallway. Headquarters was almost deserted on this summer afternoon. She was not exactly sneaking around. She was just walking very quietly. She stopped outside Ekström's closed door. She heard voices and all of a sudden her courage deserted her. She felt like a fool. In any normal situation she would have knocked on the door, pushed it open, and exclaimed, "Hello! So you're still here?" and then sailed right in. Now it seemed all wrong.

She looked around.

Why had Bublanski called her? What was this meeting about?

She glanced across the hall. Opposite Ekström's office was a conference room big enough for ten people. She had sat through a number of presentations there herself. She went into the room and closed the door. The blinds were down, and the glass partition to the hallway was covered by curtains. It was dark. She pulled up a chair and sat down, then opened the curtains a crack so that she would have a view of the hallway.

She felt uneasy. If anyone opened the door she would have quite a problem explaining what she was doing there. She took out her mobile and looked at the time display. Just before 6:00. She set the phone to vibrate and leaned back in her chair, watching the door of Ekström's office.

* * *

At 7:00 Plague pinged Salander.

```
<OK. I'm the admin for SMP.>
<Where?>
```

He sent over a URL.

```
<We won't be able to make it in 24 hours. Even
if we have email addresses for all 18, it's
going to take days to hack their home PCs.
Most probably aren't even online on a Saturday
night.>
<Concentrate on their home PCs and I'll take
care of the ones at SMP.>
<I thought of that. Your Palm is a bit lim-
ited. Anything you want me to focus on?>
<No. Just try them.>
<OK.>
<Plague?>
<Yeah.>
<If we don't find anything by tomorrow I want
you to keep at it.>
<OK.>
<In which case I'll pay you.>
<Forget about it. This is just fun.>
```

She logged out and went to the URL where Plague had uploaded all the administrator rights for *SMP*. She started by checking whether Fleming was online and at work. He was not. So she borrowed his identity and went into *SMP*'s mail server. That way she could look at all the activity in the email system, even messages that had long since been deleted from individual accounts.

She started with Ernst Teodor Billinger, one of the night

editors at *SMP*, forty-three years old. She opened his mail
and began to click back in time. She spent about two seconds
on each message, just long enough to get an idea of who had
sent it and what it was about. After a few minutes she had
worked out what was routine mail in the form of daily
memos, schedules, and other uninteresting stuff. She started
to scroll past these.

She went through three months' worth of messages one
by one. Then she skipped month to month and read the subject lines, opening the message only if it was something that
caught her attention. She learned that Billinger was going out
with a woman named Sofia and that he used an unpleasant
tone with her. She saw that this was nothing unusual, since
Billinger took an unpleasant tone with most of the people to
whom he wrote messages—reporters, layout artists, and others. Even so, she thought it odd that a man would consistently address his girlfriend with the words *fucking fatty,
fucking airhead,* or *fucking cunt.*

After an hour of searching, she shut down Billinger and
crossed him off the list. She moved on to Lars Örjan Wollberg,
a veteran reporter of fifty-one who was on the legal desk.

Edklinth walked into police headquarters at 7:30 on Saturday
evening. Figuerola and Blomkvist were waiting for him. They
were sitting at the same conference table at which Blomkvist
had sat the day before.

Edklinth reminded himself that he was on very thin ice
and that a host of regulations had been violated when he
gave Blomkvist access to the hallway. Figuerola most
definitely had no right to invite him here on her own authority. Even the spouses of his colleagues were not permitted in

the halls of SIS, but were asked instead to wait on the landings if they were meeting their partner. And to cap it all, Blomkvist was a journalist. From now on Blomkvist would be allowed only into the temporary office at Fridhemsplan.

But outsiders *were* allowed into the hallways by special invitation. Foreign guests, researchers, academics, freelance consultants . . . he put Blomkvist into the category of freelance consultant. All this nonsense about security classification was little more than words anyway. Someone decides that a certain person should be given a particular level of clearance. And Edklinth had decided that if criticism were raised, he would say that he personally had given Blomkvist clearance.

If something went wrong, that is. He sat down and looked at Figuerola.

"How did you find out about the meeting?"

"Blomkvist called me at around 3:00," she said with a satisfied smile.

Edklinth turned to Blomkvist. "And how did you find out about the meeting?"

"Tipped off by a source."

"Am I to conclude that you're running some sort of surveillance on Teleborian?"

Figuerola shook her head. "That was my first thought too," she said in a cheerful voice, as if Blomkvist were not in the room. "But it doesn't add up. Even if somebody were following Teleborian for Blomkvist, that person could not have known in advance that he was on his way to meet Jonas Sandberg."

"So, what else? Illegal tapping or something?" Edklinth said.

"I can assure you," Blomkvist said to remind them that he was there in the room, "that I'm not conducting illegal eavesdropping on anyone. Be realistic. Illegal tapping is the domain of government authorities."

Edklinth frowned. "So you aren't going to tell us how you heard about the meeting?"

"I've already told you that I won't. I was tipped off by a source. The source is protected. Why don't we concentrate on what we've discovered?"

"I don't like loose ends," Edklinth said. "But OK. What have you found out?"

"His name is Jonas Sandberg," Figuerola said. "Trained as a navy frogman and then attended the police academy in the early nineties. Worked first in Uppsala and then in Södertälje."

"You're from Uppsala."

"Yes, but we missed each other by about a year. He was recruited by SIS Counter-Espionage in 1998. Reassigned to a secret post abroad in 2000. According to our documents, he's at the embassy in Madrid. I checked with the embassy. They have no record of a Jonas Sandberg on their staff."

"Just like Mårtensson. Officially moved to a place where he doesn't exist."

"The chief of Secretariat is the only person who could make this sort of arrangement."

"And in normal circumstances everything would be dismissed as muddled red tape. We've noticed it only because we're specifically looking for it. And if anyone starts asking awkward questions, they'll say it's confidential or that it has something to do with terrorism."

"There's quite a bit of budget work to check up on."

"The chief of Budget?"

"Maybe."

"Anything else?"

"Sandberg lives in Sollentuna. He's not married, but he has a child with a teacher in Södertälje. No black marks on his record. Licence for two handguns. Conscientious and a teetotaller. The only thing that doesn't quite fit is that he seems to be an evangelical and was a member of the Word of Life in the nineties."

"Where did you find that out?"

"I had a word with my old chief in Uppsala. He remembers Sandberg quite well."

"A Christian frogman with two weapons and offspring in Södertälje. More?"

"We only ID'd him about three hours ago. This is pretty fast work, you have to admit."

"Fair enough. What do we know about the building on Artillerigatan?"

"Not a lot yet. Stefan went to chase someone up from the city building office. We have blueprints of the building. Six floors with a total of twenty-two apartments, plus eight apartments in a small building in the courtyard. I looked up the tenants but didn't find anything that stood out. Two of the people living in the building have police records."

"Who are they?"

"Lindström on the second floor, sixty-three. Convicted of insurance fraud in the seventies. Wittfelt on the fourth floor, forty-seven. Twice convicted for beating his ex-wife. Otherwise what sounds like a cross-section of middle-class Sweden. There's one apartment that raises a question mark though."

"What?"

"It's on the top floor. Eleven rooms and apparently a bit of a snazzy joint. It's owned by a company called Bellona Inc."

"And what's their stated business?"

"God only knows. They do marketing analyses and have annual sales of around thirty million kronor. All the owners live abroad."

"Aha."

"Aha what?"

"Nothing. Just 'aha.' Do some more checks on Bellona."

At that moment the officer Blomkvist knew only as Stefan entered the room.

"Hi, Chief," he greeted Edklinth. "This is really cool. I checked out the story behind the Bellona apartment."

"And?" Figuerola said.

"Bellona Inc. was founded in the seventies. They bought the apartment from the estate of the former owner, a woman by the name of Kristina Cederholm, born in 1917, married to Hans Wilhelm Francke, the loose cannon who quarrelled with P. G. Vinge at the time SIS was founded."

"Good," Edklinth said. "Very good. Monica, we want surveillance on that apartment around the clock. Find out what phones they have. I want to know who goes in and who comes out, and what vehicles drop anyone off at that address. The usual."

Edklinth turned to Blomkvist. He looked as if he wanted to say something, but he restrained himself. Blomkvist looked at him expectantly.

"Are you satisfied with the information flow?" Edklinth said at last.

"Very satisfied. Are you satisfied with *Millennium*'s contribution?"

Edklinth nodded reluctantly. "You do know that I could get into very deep water for this."

"Not because of me. I regard the information that I receive here as source-protected. I'll report the facts, but I won't mention how or where I got them. Before I go to press I'm going to do a formal interview with you. If you don't want to give me an answer to something, you just say 'No comment.' Or else you could expound on what you think about the Section for Special Analysis. It's up to you."

"Indeed." Edklinth nodded.

Blomkvist was happy. Within a few hours the Section had taken on tangible form. A real breakthrough.

To Modig's great frustration, the meeting in Ekström's office was lasting a long time. Mercifully someone had left a full bottle of mineral water on the conference table. She had twice texted her husband to tell him that she was still held up, promising to make it up to him as soon as she could get home. She was starting to get restless and felt like an intruder.

The meeting did not end until 7:30. She was taken completely by surprise when the door opened and Faste came out. And then Dr. Teleborian. Behind them came an older, grey-haired man Modig had never seen before. Finally Prosecutor Ekström, putting on a jacket as he switched off the lights and locked the door to his office.

Modig held up her mobile to the gap in the curtains and took two low-res photographs of the group outside Ekström's door. Seconds later they had set off down the hall.

She held her breath until they were some distance from the conference room in which she was trapped. She was in a cold sweat by the time she heard the door to the stairwell close. She stood up, weak at the knees.

Bublanski called Figuerola just after 8:00.

"You wanted to know if Ekström had a meeting."

"Correct," Figuerola said.

"It just ended. Ekström met with Dr. Peter Teleborian, my former colleague Criminal Inspector Faste, and an older gentleman we didn't recognize."

"Just a moment," Figuerola said. She put her hand over the mouthpiece and turned to the others. "Teleborian went straight to Ekström."

"Hello, are you still there?"

"Sorry. Do we have a description of the third man?"

"Even better. I'm sending you a picture."

"A picture? I'm in your debt."

"It would help if you'd tell me what's going on."

"I'll get back to you."

They sat in silence around the conference table for a moment.

"So," Edklinth said at last. "Teleborian meets with the Section and then goes directly to see Prosecutor Ekström. I'd give a lot of money to find out what they talked about."

"Or you could just ask me," Blomkvist said.

Edklinth and Figuerola looked at him.

"They met to finalize their strategy for nailing Salander at her trial."

Figuerola gave him a look. Then she nodded slowly.

"That's a guess," Edklinth said. "Unless you happen to have paranormal abilities."

"It's no guess," said Mikael. "They met to discuss the forensic psychiatric report on Salander. Teleborian has just finished writing it."

"Nonsense. Salander hasn't even been examined."

Blomkvist shrugged and opened his laptop case. "That hasn't stopped Teleborian in the past. Here's the latest version. It's dated, as you can see, the week the trial is scheduled to begin."

Edklinth and Figuerola read through the report before them. At last they exchanged glances and then looked at Blomkvist.

"And where the devil did you get ahold of this?" Edklinth said.

"From a source I have to protect," said Blomkvist.

"Blomkvist, we have to be able to trust each other. You're withholding information. Do you have any more surprises up your sleeve?"

"Yes. I do have secrets, of course. Just as I'm persuaded that you haven't given me carte blanche to look at everything you have here at Säpo."

"It's not the same thing."

"It's precisely the same thing. This arrangement involves cooperation. You said it yourself: we have to trust each other. I'm not holding back anything that could be useful to your investigation of the Section or could throw light on the various crimes that have been committed. I've already handed over evidence that Teleborian committed crimes with Björck in 1991, and I told you that he would be hired to do the same thing again now. And this is the document that proves me right."

"But you're still withholding key material."

"Naturally, and you can either suspend our cooperation or you can live with that."

Figuerola held up a diplomatic finger. "Excuse me, but does this mean that Ekström is working for the Section?"

Blomkvist frowned. "That I don't know. My sense is that he's more a useful fool being used by the Section. He's ambitious, but I think he's honest, if a little stupid. One source did tell me that he swallowed most of what Teleborian fed him about Salander at a presentation of reports when the hunt for her was still on."

"So you don't think it takes much to manipulate him?"

"Exactly. And Criminal Inspector Faste is an unadulterated idiot who believes that Salander is a lesbian Satanist."

Berger was at home. She felt paralysed and unable to concentrate on any real work. All the time she expected someone to call and tell her that pictures of her were posted on some website.

She caught herself thinking over and over about Salander, although she realized that her hopes of getting help from her were most likely in vain. Salander was locked up at Sahlgrenska. She was not allowed visitors and could not even read the newspapers. But she was an oddly resourceful young woman. Despite her isolation she had managed to contact Berger on ICQ and then by phone. And two years ago she had single-handedly destroyed Wennerström's financial empire and saved *Millennium*.

At 8:00 Linder arrived and knocked on the door. Berger jumped as though someone had fired a shot in her living room.

"Hello, Erika. You're sitting here in the dark looking glum."

Berger nodded and turned on a light. "Hi. I'll put on some coffee—"

"No. Let me do it. Anything new?"

You can say that again. Lisbeth Salander got in touch with me and took control of my computer. And then she called to say that Teleborian and somebody named Jonas were meeting at Central Station this afternoon.

"No. Nothing new," she said. "But I have something I'd like to bounce off you."

"Go ahead."

"What do you think the chances are that this isn't a stalker but somebody I know who wants to fuck with me?"

"What's the difference?"

"To me a stalker is someone I don't know who's become fixated on me. The alternative is a person who wants to take some sort of revenge and sabotage my life for personal reasons."

"Interesting thought. Why did this come up?"

"I was . . . discussing the situation with someone today. I can't give you her name, but she suggested that threats from a real stalker would be different. She said a stalker would never have written the email to the girl on the culture desk. It seems completely beside the point."

Linder said: "There is something to that. You know, I never read the emails. Could I see them?"

Berger set up her laptop on the kitchen table.

· · ·

Figuerola escorted Blomkvist out of police headquarters at
10:00 p.m. They stopped at the same place in Kronoberg park
as the day before.

"Here we are again. Are you going to disappear to work or
do you want to come to my place and come to bed with me?"

"Well . . ."

"You don't have to feel pressured, Mikael. If you have to
work, then do it."

"Listen, Figuerola, you're worryingly habit-forming."

"And you don't want to be dependent on anything. Is that
what you're saying?"

"No. That's not what I'm saying. But there's someone I
have to talk to tonight and it'll take a while. You'll be asleep
before I'm done."

She shrugged.

"See you."

He kissed her cheek and headed for the bus stop on Fridhemsplan.

"Blomkvist," she called.

"What?"

"I'm free tomorrow morning as well. Come and have
breakfast if you can."

CHAPTER 21

Saturday, June 4–
Monday, June 6

Salander picked up a number of ominous vibrations as she browsed the emails of the news editor, Holm. He was fifty-eight and thus fell outside the group, but Salander had included him anyway because he and Berger had been at each other's throats. He was a schemer who wrote messages to various people telling them how someone had done a rotten job.

It was obvious to Salander that Holm did not like Berger, and he certainly wasted a lot of space talking about how "the bitch" had said this or done that. He used the Net exclusively for work-related sites. If he had other interests, he must Google them in his own time on some other machine.

She kept him as a candidate for the title of Poison Pen, but he was not a favourite. Salander spent some time thinking about why she did not believe he was the one, and arrived at the conclusion that he was so damned arrogant he did not have to go to the trouble of using anonymous email. If he wanted to call Berger a whore, he would do it openly. And he did not seem the type to go sneaking into Berger's home in the middle of the night.

At 10:00 in the evening she took a break and went into [Idiotic_Table]. She saw that Blomkvist had not come back yet. She felt slightly peeved and wondered what he was up to, and whether he had made it in time to Teleborian's meeting.

Then she went back into *SMP*'s server.

She moved to the next name on the list, assistant sports editor Claes Lundin, twenty-nine. She had just opened his email when she stopped and bit her lip. She closed it again and went instead to Berger's.

She scrolled back in time. There was relatively little in Berger's in-box, since her email account had only been opened on May 2. The very first message was a midday memo from Peter Fredriksson. In the course of Berger's first day several people had emailed her to welcome her to *SMP*.

Salander carefully read each message in Berger's in-box. She could see how even from day one there had been a hostile undertone in her correspondence with Holm. They seemed unable to agree on anything, and Salander saw that Holm was already trying to exasperate Berger by sending several emails about complete trivialities.

She skipped over ads, spam, and news memos. She focused on any kind of personal correspondence. She read budget calculations, advertising and marketing projections, an exchange with CFO Sellberg that went on for a week and was virtually a brawl over staff layoffs. Berger had received irritated messages from the head of the legal department about some temp by the name of Johannes Frisk. She had apparently assigned him to work on some story and this had not been appreciated. It seemed as if no-one at management level could see anything positive in any of Berger's arguments or proposals.

After a while Salander scrolled back to the beginning and did a statistical calculation in her head. Of all the upper-level managers at *SMP*, only four did not engage in sniping. They were CEO Magnus Borgsjö, assistant editor Fredriksson, assistant front-page editor Magnusson, and culture editor Sebastian Strandlund.

Had they never heard of women at *SMP*? All the heads of department were men.

Of these, the one that Berger had least to do with was Strandlund. She had exchanged only two emails with the culture editor. The friendliest and most engaging messages came from assistant front-page editor Gunnar Magnusson. Borgsjö's were terse and to the point.

Why the hell had this group of boys hired Berger at all, if all they did was tear her limb from limb?

The colleague Berger seemed to have the most to do with was Fredriksson. His role was to act as a kind of shadow, to sit in on her meetings as an observer. He prepared memos, briefed Berger on various articles and issues, and got the jobs moving.

He emailed Berger a dozen times a day.

Salander sorted all of Fredriksson's emails to Berger and read them through. In a number of instances he had objected to some decision Berger had made and presented counter-proposals. Berger seemed to have confidence in him since she would then often change her decision or accept his argument. He was never hostile. But there was not a hint of any personal relationship to her.

Salander closed Berger's email and thought for a moment. She opened Fredriksson's account.

Plague had been fooling around with the home computers of various employees of *SMP* all evening without much success. He had managed to get into Holm's machine because it had an open line to his desk at work; any time of the day or night he could go in and access whatever he was working on. Holm's PC was one of the most boring Plague had ever hacked. He had no luck with the other seventeen names on Salander's list. One reason was that none of the people he tried to hack was online on a Saturday night. He was beginning to tire of this impossible task when Salander pinged him at 10:30.

<What's up?>

<Peter Fredriksson.>

<OK.>

<Forget the others. Focus on him.>

<Why?>

<Just a hunch.>

<This is going to take a while.>

<There's a shortcut. Fredriksson is assistant editor and uses a programme called Integrator to keep track of what's happening on his work computer from home.>

<I don't know anything about Integrator.>

<A little programme that was released a couple of years ago. It's obsolete now. Integrator has a bug. It's in the archive at Hacker Rep. In theory you could reverse the

programme and get into his home computer
from SMP.>

Plague sighed. This girl who had once been his student
now had a better handle on things than he did.

<OK. I'll try.>

<If you find anything and I'm not online, give
it to Kalle Blomkvist.>

Blomkvist was back at Salander's apartment on Mosebacke
just before midnight. He was tired. He took a shower and put
on some coffee, and then he booted up Salander's computer
and pinged her ICQ.

<It's about time.>

<Sorry.>

<Where've you been the past few days?>

<Having sex with a secret agent. And chasing
Jonas.>

<Did you make it to the meeting?>

<Yep. You tipped off Erika?>

<Only way to reach you.>

<Smart.>

<I'm being moved to prison tomorrow.>

<I know.>

<Plague's going to help out on the Net.>

<Good.>

<So all that's left is the finale.>

<Sally, we're going to do what we have to.>

<I know. You're predictable.>

<As always, my little charmer.>

<Is there anything else that I need to know?>

```
<No.>
<In that case, I have a lot of work to finish
up online.>
<Good luck.>
```

Linder woke with a start when her earpiece beeped. Someone had just tripped the motion detector she had placed in the hall on the ground floor. She propped herself up on her elbow. It was 5:23 on Sunday morning. She slipped silently out of bed and pulled on her jeans, a T-shirt, and sneakers. She stuffed the Mace in her back pocket and picked up her spring-loaded baton.

She passed the door to Berger's bedroom without a sound, noticing that it was closed and therefore locked.

She stopped at the top of the stairs and listened. She heard a faint clinking sound and movement from the ground floor. Slowly she went down the stairs and paused in the hall to listen again.

A chair scraped in the kitchen. She held the baton in a firm grip and crept to the kitchen door. She saw a bald, unshaven man sitting at the kitchen table with a glass of orange juice, reading *SMP*. He sensed her presence and looked up.

"And who the hell are you?"

Linder relaxed and leaned against the door jamb. "Greger Beckman, I presume. Hello. I'm Susanne Linder."

"I see. Are you going to hit me over the head or would you like a glass of juice?"

"Yes, please," Linder said, putting down her baton. "Juice, that is."

Beckman reached for a glass from the draining board and poured some for her.

"I work for Milton Security," Linder said. "I think it's probably best if your wife explains what I'm doing here."

Beckman stood up. "Has something happened to Erika?"

"Your wife is fine. But there's been some trouble. We tried to get ahold of you in Paris."

"Paris? Why Paris? I've been in Helsinki, for God's sake."

"All right. I'm sorry, but your wife thought you were in Paris."

"That's next month," said Beckman on his way out the door.

"The bedroom is locked. You need a code to open the door," Linder said.

"I beg your pardon? What code?"

She told him the three numbers he had to punch in to open the bedroom door. He ran up the stairs.

At 10:00 on Sunday morning Jonasson came into Salander's room.

"Hello, Lisbeth."

"Hello."

"Just thought I'd warn you: the police are coming at lunchtime."

"Fine."

"You don't seem worried."

"I'm not."

"I have a present for you."

"A present? What for?"

"You've been one of my most interesting patients in a long time."

"You don't say," Salander said sceptically.

"I heard that you're fascinated by DNA and genetics."

"Who's been gossiping? That psychologist lady, I bet."

Jonasson nodded. "If you get bored in prison . . . this is the latest thing on DNA research."

He handed her a brick of a book titled *Spirals—Mysteries of DNA,* by Professor Yoshito Takamura of Tokyo University. Salander opened it and studied the table of contents.

"Beautiful," she said.

"Someday I'd be interested to hear how it is that you can read academic texts that even I can't understand."

As soon as Jonasson had left the room, she took out her Palm. Last chance. From *SMP*'s personnel department Salander had learned that Fredriksson had worked at the paper for six years. During that time he had been out sick for two extended periods: two months in 2003 and three months in 2004. From the personnel files she concluded that the reason in both instances was burnout. Berger's predecessor Morander had on one occasion questioned whether Fredriksson should indeed stay on as assistant editor.

Yak, yak, yak. Nothing concrete to go on.

At 11:45 Plague pinged her.

\<What?\>

\<Are you still at Sahlgrenska?\>

\<What do you think?\>

\<It's him.\>

\<Are you sure?\>

\<He accessed his work computer from home half an hour ago. I took the opportunity to go in. He has pictures of Berger scanned onto his hard drive at home.\>

```
<Thanks.>
<She looks pretty tasty.>
<Plague, please.>
<I know. What do you want me to do?>
<Did he post the pictures on the Net?>
<Not that I can see.>
<Can you mine his computer?>
<Already done. If he tries to email or upload
anything bigger than 20 KBs, his hard drive
will crash.>
<Cool.>
<I'm going to bed. Take care of yourself.>
<As always.>
```

Salander logged off from ICQ. She glanced at the clock and realized that it would soon be lunchtime. She rapidly composed a message that she addressed to the Yahoo group [Idiotic_Table]:

```
Mikael. Important. Call Berger right away and
tell her Fredriksson is Poison Pen.
```

The instant she sent the message she heard movement in the corridor. She polished the screen of her Palm Tungsten T3, then switched it off and placed it in the recess behind the bedside table.

"Hello, Lisbeth." It was Giannini in the doorway.

"Hello."

"The police are coming for you in a while. I've brought you some clothes. I hope they're the right size."

Salander looked distrustfully at the selection of neat, dark-coloured linen pants and pastel blouses.

· · ·

Two uniformed Göteborg policewomen came to get her. Giannini was to go with them to the prison.

As they walked from her room down the hall, Salander noticed that several members of the staff were watching her with curiosity. She gave them a friendly nod, and some of them waved back. As if by chance, Jonasson was standing by the reception desk. They looked at each other and nodded. Even before they had turned the corner, Salander noticed that he was heading for her room.

During the entire procedure of transporting her to the prison, Salander did not say a word to the police.

Blomkvist had closed his iBook at 7:00 on Sunday morning. He sat for a moment at Salander's desk, listless, staring into space.

Then he went to her bedroom and looked at her gigantic king-size bed. After a while he went back to her office and flipped open his mobile to call Figuerola.

"Hi. It's Mikael."

"Hello there. Are you already up?"

"I've just finished working and I'm on my way to bed. I just wanted to call and say hello."

"Men who just call to say hello generally have ulterior motives."

He laughed.

"Blomkvist . . . you could come here and sleep if you like."

"I'd be terrible company."

"I'll get used to it."

He took a taxi to Pontonjärgatan.

· · ·

Berger spent Sunday in bed with her husband. They lay there talking and dozing. In the afternoon they got dressed and went for a walk down to the steamship wharf.

"*SMP* was a mistake," Berger said when they got home.

"Don't say that. Right now it's tough, but you knew it would be. Things will calm down after you've been there awhile."

"It's not the job. I can handle that. It's the atmosphere."

"I see."

"I don't like it there, but on the other hand, I can't walk out after a few weeks."

She sat at the kitchen table and stared morosely into space. Beckman had never seen his wife so stymied.

Inspector Faste met Salander for the first time at 12:30 on Sunday afternoon when a female police officer brought her into Erlander's office at Göteborg police headquarters.

"You were difficult enough to catch," Faste said.

Salander gave him a long look, satisfied herself that he was an idiot, and decided that she would not waste too many seconds concerning herself with his existence.

"Inspector Gunilla Wäring will accompany you to Stockholm," Erlander said.

"All right," Faste said. "Then we'll leave at once. There are quite a few people who want to have a serious talk with you, Salander."

Erlander said goodbye to her. She ignored him.

They had decided for simplicity's sake to do the prisoner transfer to Stockholm by car. Wäring drove. At the start of the journey Hans Faste sat in the front passenger seat with his head turned towards the back as he tried to have some exchange with Salander. By the time they reached Alingsås his neck was aching and he gave up.

Salander looked at the countryside. In her mind Faste did not exist.

Teleborian was right. She's fucking retarded, Faste thought. *We'll see about changing that attitude when we get to Stockholm.*

Every so often he glanced at Salander and tried to form an opinion of the woman he had been desperate to track down for such a long time. Even he had some doubts when he saw the skinny girl. He wondered how much she could weigh. He reminded himself that she was a lesbian and consequently not a real woman.

But it was possible that the bit about Satanism was an exaggeration. She did not look the type.

The irony was that he would have preferred to arrest her for the three murders she was originally suspected of, but reality had caught up with his investigation. Even a skinny girl can handle a weapon. Instead she had been taken in for assaulting the top leadership of Svavelsjö MC, and she was guilty of that crime, no question. There was forensic evidence related to the incident, which she no doubt intended to refute.

Figuerola woke Blomkvist at 1:00 in the afternoon. She had been sitting on her balcony and had finished reading her book about the idea of God in antiquity, listening all the while to Blomkvist's snores from the bedroom. It had been peaceful. When she went in to look at him it came to her, acutely, that she was more attracted to him than she had been to any other man in years.

It was a pleasant yet unsettling feeling. There he was, but he was not a stable element in her life.

They went down to Norr Mälarstrand for a coffee. Then she took him home and to bed for the rest of the afternoon. He left her at 7:00. She felt a vague sense of loss a moment after he kissed her cheek and was gone.

At 8:00 on Sunday evening Linder knocked on Berger's door. She would not be sleeping there now that Beckman was home, and this visit was not connected with her job. But during the time she had spent at Berger's house they had both grown to enjoy the long conversations they had in the kitchen. She had a great liking for Berger. She recognized in her a desperate woman who succeeded in concealing her true nature. She went to work apparently calm, but in reality she was a bundle of nerves.

Linder suspected that her anxiety was not solely due to Poison Pen. But Berger's life and problems were none of her business. It was a friendly visit. She had come out here just to see Berger and to be sure that everything was all right. The couple were in the kitchen in a solemn mood. It seemed as though they had spent their Sunday working their way through one or two serious issues.

Beckman put on some coffee. Linder had been there only a few minutes when Berger's mobile rang.

Berger had answered every call that day with a feeling of impending doom.

"Berger," she said.

"Hello, Ricky."

Blomkvist. Shit. I haven't told him the Borgsjö file has disappeared.

"Hi, Micke."

"Salander was moved to the prison in Göteborg this evening, to wait for transport to Stockholm tomorrow."

"OK."

"She sent you a . . . well, a message."

"Oh?"

"It's pretty cryptic."

"What did she say?"

"She said: 'Fredriksson is Poison Pen.'"

Erika sat for ten seconds in silence while thoughts rushed through her head. *Impossible. Peter isn't like that. Salander has to be wrong.*

"Was that all?"

"That's the whole message. Do you know what it's about?"

"Yes."

"Ricky, what are you and that girl up to? She rang you to tip me off about Teleborian, and—"

"Thanks, Micke. We'll talk later."

She turned off her mobile and looked at Linder with an expression of absolute astonishment.

"Tell me," Linder said.

Linder was of two minds. Berger had been told that her assistant editor was the one sending the vicious emails. She talked non-stop. Then Linder had asked her *how* she knew Fredriksson was her stalker. Berger was silent. Linder noticed her eyes and saw that something had changed in her attitude. She was all of a sudden totally confused.

"I can't tell you."

"What do you mean you can't tell me?"

"Susanne, I just know that Fredriksson is responsible. But I can't tell you how I got that information. What can I do?"

"If I'm going to help you, you have to tell me."

"I . . . I can't. You don't understand."

Berger got up and stood at the kitchen window with her back to Linder. Finally she turned.

"I'm going to his house."

"You'll do nothing of the sort. You're not going anywhere, least of all to the home of somebody who obviously hates you."

Berger looked torn.

"Sit down. Tell me what happened. It was Blomkvist calling you, right?"

Berger nodded.

"I . . . today I asked a hacker to go through the home computers of the staff."

"Aha. So you've probably by extension committed a serious computer crime. And you don't want to tell me who your hacker is?"

"I promised I would never tell anyone. Other people are involved. Something that Mikael is working on."

"Does Blomkvist know about the emails and the break-in here?"

"No; he was just passing on a message."

Linder cocked her head to one side, and all of a sudden a chain of associations formed in her mind.

Erika Berger. Mikael Blomkvist. Millennium. *Rogue policemen who broke in and bugged Blomkvist's apartment. Linder*

watching the watchers. Blomkvist working like a madman on a
story about Lisbeth Salander.

The fact that Salander was a wizard at computers was
widely known at Milton Security. No-one knew how she had
come by her skills, and Linder had never heard any rumours
that Salander might be a hacker. But Armansky had once said
something about Salander's delivering quite incredible reports
when she was doing personal investigations. A hacker . . .

But Salander is under guard on a ward in Göteborg.

It was absurd.

"Is it Salander we're talking about?" Linder said.

Berger looked as though she had touched a live wire.

"I can't discuss where the information came from. Not
one word."

Linder laughed aloud.

*It was Salander. Berger's confirmation of it could not have
been clearer. She's completely off balance.*

Yet it's impossible.

*Under guard as she was, Salander nevertheless took on the
job of finding out who Poison Pen was. Sheer madness.*

Linder thought hard.

She could not understand the whole Salander story. She
had met her maybe five times during the years she had
worked at Milton Security and had never had so much as
a single conversation with her. She regarded Salander as a
sullen and asocial individual with a skin like a rhino. She
had heard that Armansky himself had taken on Salander,
and since she respected Armansky she assumed that he
had good reason for his endless patience towards the sullen
girl.

Fredriksson is Poison Pen.

Could she be right? What was the proof?

Linder then spent a long time questioning Erika on everything she knew about Fredriksson, what his role was at *SMP*, and how their relationship had been. The answers did not help her at all.

Berger had displayed a frustrating indecision. She had wavered between a determination to drive out to Fredriksson's place and confront him and an unwillingness to believe that it could really be true. Finally Linder convinced her that she could not storm into Fredriksson's apartment and launch into an accusation—if he was innocent, she would make an utter fool of herself.

So Linder had promised to look into the matter. It was a promise she regretted as soon as she made it, because she did not have the faintest idea how she was going to proceed.

She parked her Fiat Strada as close to Fredriksson's apartment building in Fisksätra as she could. She locked the car and looked around. She was not sure what she was going to do, but she supposed she would have to knock on his door and somehow get him to answer a number of questions. She was acutely aware that this was a job that lay well outside her purview at Milton, and she knew Armansky would be furious if he found out what she was doing.

It was not a good plan, and in any case it fell apart before she had managed to put it into practice. She had reached the courtyard and was approaching Fredriksson's apartment when the door opened. Linder recognized him at once from the photograph in his personnel file, which she had studied on Berger's computer. She kept walking and they passed each other. He disappeared in the direction of the garage. It was just before 11:00 and Fredriksson was on his way somewhere. Linder turned and ran back to her car.

Blomkvist sat for a long time looking at his mobile after Berger hung up. He wondered what was going on. In frustration he looked at Salander's computer. By now she had been moved to the prison in Göteborg, and he had no chance of asking her anything.

He opened his Ericsson T10 and called Idris Ghidi in Angered.

"Hello. Mikael Blomkvist."

"Hello," Ghidi said.

"Just to tell you that you can stop that job you were doing for me."

Ghidi had already worked out that Blomkvist would call since Salander had been taken from the hospital.

"I understand," he said.

"You can keep the mobile, as we agreed. I'll send you the final payment this week."

"Thanks."

"I'm the one who should thank you for your help."

Blomkvist opened his iBook. The events of the past twenty-four hours meant that a significant part of the manuscript had to be revised, and that in all probability a whole new section would have to be added.

He sighed and got to work.

At 11:15 Fredriksson parked three blocks away from Berger's house. Linder had already guessed where he was going and had stopped trying to keep him in sight. She drove past his car fully two minutes after he parked. The car was empty. She went on a short distance past Berger's house and stopped well out of sight. Her palms were sweating.

She opened her tin of Catch Dry snuff and tucked some inside her upper lip.

Then she opened her car door and looked around. As soon as she could tell that Fredriksson was on his way to Salt-sjöbaden, she knew that Salander's information must be correct. And obviously he had not come all this way for fun. Trouble was brewing. Which was fine by her, so long as she could catch him red-handed.

She took her telescopic baton from the side pocket of her car door and weighed it in her hand for a moment. She pressed the lock in the handle and out shot a heavy, spring-loaded steel cable. She clenched her teeth.

That was why she had left the Södermalm force.

She had had one mad outbreak of rage when for the third time in as many days the squad car had driven to an address in Hägersten after the same woman had called the police and screamed for help because her husband had abused her. And just as on the first two occasions, the situation had resolved itself before they arrived.

They had detained the husband on the staircase while the woman was questioned. No, she did not want to file a police report. No, it was all a mistake. No, he was fine; it was actually all her fault. She had provoked him. . . .

And the whole time the bastard had stood there grinning, looking Linder straight in the eye.

She could not explain why she did it. But suddenly something snapped in her, and she took out her baton and slammed it across his face. The first blow had lacked power. She had only given him a fat lip and forced him to his knees. In the next ten seconds—until her colleagues grabbed her and half dragged, half carried her out of the hallway—she had let the blows rain down on his back, kidneys, hips, and shoulders.

Charges were never filed. She had resigned the same evening and gone home and cried for a week. Then she pulled herself together and went to see Dragan Armansky. She explained what she had done and why she had left the force. She was looking for a job. Armansky had been sceptical and said he would need some time to think it over. She had given up hope by the time he called six weeks later and told her he was ready to take her on trial.

Linder frowned and stuck the baton into her belt at the small of her back. She checked that she had the Mace canister in her right-hand pocket and that the laces of her sneakers were securely tied. She walked back to Berger's house and slipped into the garden.

She knew that the outside motion detector had not yet been installed, and she moved soundlessly across the lawn, along the hedge at the border of the property. She could not see Fredriksson. She went around the house and stood still. Then she spotted him as a shadow in the darkness near Beckman's studio.

He can't know how stupid it is for him to come back here.

He was squatting down, trying to see through a gap in a curtain in the room next to the living room. Then he moved up onto the veranda and looked through the cracks in the drawn blinds at the big picture window.

Linder suddenly smiled.

She crossed the lawn to the corner of the house while he still had his back to her. She crouched behind some currant bushes by the gable end and waited. She could see him through the branches. From his position, Fredriksson would be able to look down the hall and into part of the kitchen. Apparently he had found something interesting to look at, and it was ten minutes before he moved again. This time he came closer to Linder.

As he rounded the corner and passed her, she stood up and spoke in a low voice.

"Hello there, Herr Fredriksson."

He stopped short and spun towards her.

She saw his eyes glistening in the dark. She could not see his expression, but she could hear that he was holding his breath and she could sense his shock.

"We can do this the easy way or we can do it the hard way," she said. "We're going to walk to your car and—"

He turned and made to run away.

Linder raised her baton and directed a devastatingly painful blow to his left kneecap.

He fell with a moan.

She raised the baton a second time, but then caught herself. She thought she could feel Armansky's eyes on the back of her neck.

She bent down, flipped Fredriksson over onto his stomach, and put her knee in the small of his back. She took hold of his right hand and twisted it around onto his back and handcuffed him. He was frail, and he put up no resistance.

Berger turned off the lamp in the living room and limped upstairs. She no longer needed the crutches, but the sole of her foot still hurt when she put any weight on it. Beckman turned off the light in the kitchen and followed his wife upstairs. He had never before seen her so unhappy. Nothing he said could soothe her or alleviate the anxiety she was feeling.

She got undressed, crept into bed, and turned her back to him.

"It's not your fault, Greger," she said when she heard him get in beside her.

"You're not well," he said. "I want you to stay at home for a few days."

He put an arm around her shoulders. She did not push him away, but she was completely passive. He bent over, kissed her cautiously on the neck, and held her.

"There's nothing you can say or do to make the situation any better. I know I need to take a break. I feel as though I've climbed onto an express train and discovered that I'm on the wrong track."

"We could go sailing for a few days. Get away from it all."

"No. I can't get away from it all."

She turned to him. "The worst thing I could do now would be to run away. I have to sort things out first. Then we can go."

"OK," Beckman said. "I'm not being much help."

She smiled wanly. "No, you're not. But thanks for being here. I love you insanely—you know that."

He mumbled something inaudible.

"I simply can't believe it's Fredriksson," Berger said. "I've never felt the least bit of hostility from him."

Linder was just wondering whether she should ring Berger's doorbell when she saw the lights go off on the ground floor. She looked down at Fredriksson. He had not said a word. He was quite still. She thought for a long time before she made up her mind.

She bent down and grabbed the handcuffs, pulled him to his feet, and leaned him against the wall.

"Can you stand by yourself?" she said.

He did not answer.

"Right, we'll make this easy. You struggle in any way and you'll get the same treatment on your right leg. You struggle even more and I'll break your arms. Do you understand?"

She could hear him breathing heavily. Fear?

She pushed him along in front of her out onto the street and all the way to his car. He was limping badly, so she held him up. Just as they reached the car, they met a man out walking his dog. The man stopped and looked at Fredriksson in his handcuffs.

"This is a police matter," Linder said in a firm voice. "You go home." The man turned and walked away in the direction he had come from.

She put Fredriksson in the back seat and drove him home to Fisksätra. It was 12:30 and they saw no-one as they walked into his building. Linder fished out his keys and followed him up the stairs to his apartment on the fourth floor.

"You can't go into my apartment," said Fredriksson.

It was the first thing he had said since she cuffed him. She opened the apartment door and shoved him inside.

"You have no right. You have to have a search warrant—"

"I'm not a police officer," she said in a low voice.

He stared at her suspiciously.

She took hold of his shirt and dragged him into the living room, pushing him down onto a sofa. He had a neatly kept two-bedroom apartment. Bedroom to the left of the living room, kitchen across the hall, a small office off the living room.

She looked in the office and heaved a sigh of relief. *The smoking gun.* Right away she saw photographs from Berger's album spread out on a desk next to a computer. He had pinned up thirty or so pictures on the wall behind the computer. She regarded the exhibition with raised eyebrows. Berger was a fine-looking woman. And her sex life was more active than Linder's own.

She heard Fredriksson moving and went back to the living room, rapped him once across his lower back, and then dragged him into the office and sat him down on the floor.

"You stay there," she said.

She went into the kitchen and found a paper shopping bag from Konsum. She took down one picture after another and then found the stripped album and Berger's diaries.

"Where's the video?" she said.

Fredriksson did not answer. Linder went into the living room and turned on the TV. There was a tape in the VCR, but it took a while before she found the video channel on the remote so she could check it. She popped out the video and looked around to ensure that he had not made any copies.

She found Berger's teenage love letters and the Borgsjö folder. Then she turned her attention to Fredriksson's computer. She saw that he had a Microtek scanner hooked up to his PC, and when she lifted the lid she found a photograph of Berger at a Club Xtreme party—New Year's Eve 1986, according to a banner on the wall.

She booted up the computer and discovered that it was password-protected.

"What's your password?" she asked.

Fredriksson sat obstinately silent and refused to answer.

Linder suddenly felt utterly calm. She knew that technically she had committed one crime after another this evening, including unlawful restraint and even aggravated kidnapping. She did not care. On the contrary, she felt almost exhilarated.

After a while she shrugged and dug in her pocket for her Swiss Army knife. She unplugged all the cables from the computer, turned it around, and used the screwdriver to open the back. It took her fifteen minutes to take it apart and remove the hard drive.

She had taken everything, but for safety's sake she did a thorough search of the desk drawers, the stacks of paper, and the shelves. Suddenly her gaze fell on an old school yearbook lying on the windowsill. She saw that it was from Djursholm Gymnasium, 1978. Did Berger not come from Djursholm's upper class? She opened the yearbook and began to look through the pictures of that year's graduating class.

She found Erika Berger, eighteen years old, with a mortarboard and a sunny smile with dimples. She wore a thin white cotton dress and held a bouquet of flowers in her hand. She looked the epitome of an innocent teenager with top grades.

Linder almost missed the connection, but there it was on the next page. She would never have recognized him but for the caption. Peter Fredriksson. He was in a different class from Berger. Linder studied the photograph of a thin boy who looked into the camera with a serious expression.

Her eyes met Fredriksson's.

"Even then she was a whore."

"Fascinating," Linder said.

"She fucked every guy in the school."

"I doubt that."

"She was a fucking—"

"Don't say it. So what happened? Couldn't you get into her pants?"

"She treated me as though I didn't exist. She laughed at me. And when she started at *SMP* she didn't even recognize me."

"Right," said Linder wearily. "I'm sure you had a terrible childhood. How about we have a serious talk?"

"What do you want?"

"I'm not a police officer," Linder said. "I'm someone who takes care of people like you."

She paused and let his imagination do the work.

"I want to know if you put photographs of her anywhere on the Internet."

He shook his head.

"Are you quite sure about that?"

He nodded.

"Berger will have to decide for herself whether she wants to make a formal complaint against you for harassment, threats, and breaking and entering, or whether she wants to settle things amicably."

He said nothing.

"If she decides to ignore you—and I think that's about what you're worth—then I'll be keeping an eye on you."

She held up her baton.

"If you ever go near her house again, or send her email or otherwise molest her, I'll be back. I'll beat you so hard that even your own mother won't recognize you. Do I make myself clear?"

Still he said nothing.

"So you have the opportunity to influence how this story ends. Are you interested?"

He nodded slowly.

"In that case, I'm going to recommend to Fru Berger that she let you off, but don't think about coming in to work again. As of right now you're fired."

He nodded.

"You will disappear from her life and move out of Stockholm. I don't give a shit what you do with your life or where you end up. Find a job in Göteborg or Malmö. Go on sick leave again. Do whatever you like. But leave Berger in peace. Are we agreed?"

Fredriksson began to sob.

"I didn't mean any harm," he said. "I just wanted—"

"You just wanted to make her life a living hell, and you certainly succeeded. Do I or do I not have your word?"

He nodded.

She bent over, turned him onto his stomach, and unlocked the handcuffs. She took the Konsum bag containing Berger's life and left him there on the floor.

It was 2:30 a.m. on Monday when Linder left Fredriksson's building. She considered letting the matter rest until the next day, but then it occurred to her that if she had been the one involved, she would have wanted to know right away. Besides, her car was still parked out in Saltsjöbaden. She called a taxi.

Beckman opened the door even before she managed to ring the bell. He was wearing jeans and did not look as if he had just got out of bed.

"Is Erika awake?" Linder asked.

He nodded.

"Has something else happened?" he said.

She smiled at him.

"Come in. We're just talking in the kitchen."

They went in.

"Hello, Erika," Linder said. "You need to learn to get some sleep once in a while."

"What's happened?"

Linder held out the Konsum bag.

"Fredriksson promises to leave you alone from now on. God knows if we can trust him, but if he keeps his word it'll be less painful than hassling with a police report and a trial. It's up to you."

"So it *was* him?"

Linder nodded. Beckman poured her a coffee, but she did not want one. She had drunk much too much coffee over the past few days. She sat down and told them what had happened outside their house that night.

Berger sat in silence for a moment. Then she went upstairs and came back with her copy of the school yearbook. She looked at Fredriksson's face for a long time.

"I do remember him," she said at last. "But I had no idea it was the same Peter Fredriksson. I wouldn't even have remembered his name if it weren't written here."

"What happened?" Linder asked.

"Nothing. Absolutely nothing.. He was a quiet and

totally uninteresting boy in another class. I think we might have had some subjects together. French, if I remember correctly."

"He said you treated him as though he didn't exist."

"I probably did. He wasn't somebody I knew, and he wasn't in our group."

"I know how cliques work. Did you bully him or anything like that?"

"No . . . no, for God's sake. I hated bullying. We had campaigns against bullying in the school, and I was president of the student council. I don't remember that he ever spoke to me."

"OK," Linder said. "But he obviously had a grudge against you. He was out sick for two long periods, suffering from stress and overwork. Maybe there were other reasons for his being out that we don't know about."

She got up and put on her leather jacket.

"I've got his hard drive. Technically it's stolen goods, so I shouldn't leave it with you. You don't have to worry—I'll destroy it as soon as I get home."

"Wait, Susanne. How can I ever thank you?"

"Well, you can back me up when Armansky's wrath hits me like a bolt of lightning."

Berger gave her a concerned look.

"Will you get into trouble for this?"

"I don't know. I really don't know."

"Can we pay you for—"

"No. But Armansky may bill you for tonight. I hope he does, because that would mean he approves of what I did and probably won't decide to fire me."

"I'll make sure he sends us a bill."

Berger stood up and gave Linder a long hug.

"Thanks, Susanne. If you ever need a friend, you've got one in me. If there's anything I can do for you . . ."

"Thanks. Don't leave those pictures lying around. And while we're on the subject, Milton could install a much better safe for you."

Berger smiled as Beckman walked Linder back to her car.

CHAPTER 22

Monday, June 6

Berger woke up at 6:00 on Monday morning. She had not slept for more than an hour, but she felt strangely rested. She supposed it was a physical reaction of some sort. For the first time in several months she put on her jogging clothes and went for a furious and excruciatingly painful sprint down to the steamboat wharf. But after a hundred yards or so her heel hurt so much that she had to slow down and go on at a more leisurely pace, relishing the pain in her foot with each step she took.

She felt reborn. It was as though the Grim Reaper had passed by her door and at the last moment changed his mind and moved on to the next house. She could still not take in how fortunate she was that Fredriksson had had her pictures in his possession for four days and done nothing with them. The scanning he had done indicated that he had something planned, but he had simply not gotten around to whatever it was.

She decided to give Susanne Linder a very expensive Christmas present this year. She would think of something really special.

She left her husband asleep and at 7:30 drove to *SMP*'s office at Norrtull. She parked in the garage, took the elevator to the newsroom, and settled down in the glass cage. Before she did anything else, she called someone from maintenance.

"Peter Fredriksson has left the paper. He won't be back," she said. "Please bring as many boxes as you need to empty his desk of personal items and have them delivered to his apartment this morning."

She looked over towards the news desk. Holm had just arrived. He met her gaze and nodded to her.

She nodded back.

Holm was a bastard, but after their altercation a few weeks earlier he had stopped trying to cause trouble. If he continued to show the same positive attitude, he could possibly survive as news editor. Possibly.

She should, she felt, be able to turn things around.

At 8:45 she saw Borgsjö come out of the elevator and disappear up the internal staircase to his office on the floor above. *I have to talk to him today.*

She got some coffee and spent a while on the morning memo. It looked like it was going to be a slow news day. The only item of interest was an agency report, to the effect that Lisbeth Salander had been moved to the prison in Stockholm the day before. She OK'd the story and forwarded it to Holm.

At 8:59 Borgsjö called.

"Berger, come up to my office right away." He hung up.

He was white in the face when Berger found him at his desk. He stood up and slammed a thick wad of papers on his desk.

"What the hell is this?" he roared.

Berger's heart sank like a stone. She only had to glance at the cover to see what Borgsjö had found in the morning mail.

Fredriksson hadn't managed to do anything with her photographs. But he had sent a copy of Cortez's article and research to Borgsjö.

Calmly she sat down across from him.

"That's an article written by a reporter named Henry Cortez. *Millennium* had planned to run it in last week's issue."

Borgsjö looked desperate.

"How dare you? I brought you into *SMP* and the first thing you do is to start digging up dirt. What kind of a media whore are you?"

Berger's eyes narrowed. She turned ice-cold. She had had enough of the word *whore*.

"Do you really think anyone is going to care about this? Do you think you can trap me with this crap? And why the hell did you send it to me anonymously?"

"That's not what happened, Magnus."

"Then tell me what did happen."

"The person who sent that article to you anonymously was Fredriksson. He was fired from *SMP* yesterday."

"What the hell are you talking about?"

"It's a long story. But I've had a copy of the article for more than two weeks, trying to figure out a way to raise the subject with you."

"You're behind this article?"

"No, I am not. Cortez researched and wrote the article entirely on his own. I didn't know anything about it."

"You expect me to believe that?"

"As soon as my old colleagues at *Millennium* saw how you were implicated in the story, Blomkvist stopped its publication. He called me and gave me a copy, out of concern for my position. It was then stolen from me, and now it's ended up with you. *Millennium* wanted me to have a chance to talk with you before they printed it. Which they mean to do in the August issue."

"I've never met a more unscrupulous media whore in my whole life. It defies belief."

"Now that you've read the story, perhaps you have also considered the research behind it. Cortez has an iron-clad story. You know that."

"What the hell is that supposed to mean?"

"If you're still here when *Millennium* goes to press, that will hurt *SMP*. I've worried myself sick and tried to find a way out . . . but there isn't one."

"What do you mean?"

"You'll have to go."

"Don't be absurd. I haven't done anything illegal."

"Magnus, don't you understand the impact of this exposé? I don't want to have to call a board meeting. It would be too embarrassing."

"You're not going to call anything at all. You're finished at *SMP*."

"Wrong. Only the board can sack me. Presumably you're allowed to call them in for an extraordinary meeting. I would suggest you do that for this afternoon."

Borgsjö came around the desk and stood so close to Berger that she could feel his breath.

"Berger, you have one chance to survive this. You have to go to your damned colleagues at *Millennium* and get them to kill this story. If you do a good job I might even forget what you've done."

Berger sighed.

"Magnus, you aren't understanding how serious this is. I have no influence whatsoever on what *Millennium* publishes. This story is going to come out no matter what I say. The only thing I care about is how it affects *SMP*. That's why you have to resign."

Borgsjö put his hands on the back of her chair.

"Berger, your cronies at *Millennium* might change their minds if they knew that you would be fired the instant they leak this bullshit."

He straightened up.

"I'll be at a meeting in Norrköping today." He looked at her, furious and arrogant. "At Svea Construction."

"I see."

"When I'm back tomorrow you will report to me that this matter has been taken care of. Understood?"

He put on his jacket. Berger watched him with her eyes half closed.

"Maybe then you'll survive at *SMP*. Now get out of my office."

She went back to the glass cage and sat quite still in her chair for twenty minutes. Then she picked up the phone and asked Holm to come to her office. This time he was there within a minute.

"Sit down."

Holm raised an eyebrow and sat down.

"What did I do wrong this time?" he said sarcastically.

"Anders, this is my last day at *SMP*. I'm resigning here and now. I'm calling in the deputy chairman and as many members of the board as I can find for a meeting over lunch."

He stared at her with undisguised shock.

"I'm going to recommend that you be made acting editor in chief."

"What?"

"Are you OK with that?"

Holm leaned back in his chair and looked at her.

"I've never wanted to be editor in chief," he said.

"I know that. But you're tough enough to do the job. And you'll walk over corpses to be able to publish a good story. I just wish you had more common sense."

"So what happened?"

"I have a different style than you. You and I have always argued about what angle to take, and we'll never agree."

"No," he said. "We never will. But it's possible that my style is old-fashioned."

"I don't know if *old-fashioned* is the right word. You're a very good newspaperman, but you behave like a bastard. That's totally unnecessary. But what we were most at odds about was that you claimed that as news editor you couldn't allow personal considerations to affect how the news was assessed."

Berger suddenly gave Holm a sly smile. She opened her bag and took out a copy of the Borgsjö story.

"Let's test your sense of news assessment. I have a story here that came to us from a reporter at *Millennium*. This morning I'm thinking that we should run this article as today's top story." She tossed the folder into Holm's lap. "You're the news editor. I'd be interested to hear whether you share my assessment."

Holm opened the folder and began to read. Even the introduction made his eyes widen. He sat up straight in his chair and stared at Berger. Then he lowered his eyes and read through the article to the end. He studied the source material for ten more minutes before he slowly put the folder aside.

"This is going to cause one hell of an uproar."

"I know. That's why I'm leaving. *Millennium* was planning to run the story in their June issue, but Mikael Blomkvist stopped publication. He gave me the article so that I could talk with Borgsjö before they run it."

"And?"

"Borgsjö ordered me to suppress it."

"I see. So you're planning to run it in *SMP* out of spite?"

"Not out of spite, no. There's no other way. If *SMP* runs the story, we have a chance of getting out of this mess with our honour intact. Borgsjö has no choice but to go. But it also means that I can't stay here any longer."

Holm sat in silence for two minutes.

"Damn it, Berger. . . . I didn't think you were that tough. I never thought I'd ever say this, but if you're that thick-skinned, I'm actually sorry you're leaving."

"You could stop publication, but if both you and I OK it . . . Do you think you'll run the story?"

"Damn right we'll run it. It would leak anyway."

"Exactly."

Holm got up and stood uncertainly by her desk.

"Get to work," said Berger.

After Holm left her office she waited five minutes before she picked up the phone and rang Eriksson.

"Hello, Malin. Is Henry there?"

"Yes, he's at his desk."

"Could you call him into your office and put on the speakerphone? We have to have a conference."

Cortez was there within fifteen seconds.

"What's up?"

"Henry, I did something immoral today."

"Oh, you did?"

"I gave your story about Vitavara to the news editor here at *SMP*."

"You *what*?"

"I told him to run the story in *SMP* tomorrow. Your byline. And you'll be paid, of course. In fact, you can name your price."

"Erika, what the hell is going on?"

She gave him a brisk summary of what had happened during the last weeks, and how Fredriksson had almost destroyed her.

"Jesus Christ," Cortez said.

"I know that this is your story, Henry. But I have no choice. Can you agree to this?"

Cortez was silent for a long while.

"Thanks for asking," he said. "It's OK to run the story with my byline. If it's OK with Malin, I should say."

"It's OK with me," Eriksson said.

"Thank you both," Berger said. "Can you tell Mikael? I don't suppose he's in yet."

"I'll talk to Mikael," Eriksson said. "But, Erika, does this mean that you're out of work from today?"

Berger laughed. "I've decided to take the rest of the year off. Believe me, a few weeks at *SMP* was enough."

"I don't think you ought to start thinking in terms of a vacation yet," Eriksson said.

"Why not?"

"Could you come here this afternoon?"

"What for?"

"I need help. If you want to come back to being editor in chief here, you could start tomorrow morning."

"Malin, you're the editor in chief. Anything else is out of the question."

"Then you could start as managing editor." Eriksson laughed.

"Are you serious?"

"Oh, Erika, I miss you so much that I'm ready to die. One reason I took the job here was so that I'd have a chance to work with you. And now you're somewhere else."

Berger said nothing for a minute. She had not even thought about the possibility of making a comeback at *Millennium.*

"Do you think I'd really be welcome?" she said hesitantly.

"What do you think? I bet we'd begin with a huge celebration, which I would arrange myself. And you'd be back just in time for us to publish you-know-what."

Berger checked the clock on her desk—10:55. In a couple of hours her whole world had been turned upside down. She realized what a longing she had to walk up the stairs at *Millennium* again.

"I have a few things to take care of here over the next few hours. Is it OK if I pop in at around 4:00?"

Linder looked Armansky directly in the eye as she told him exactly what had happened during the night. The only thing she left out was her sudden intuition that the hacking of Fredriksson's computer had something to do with Salander.

She kept that to herself for two reasons. First, she thought it sounded too implausible. Second, she knew that Armansky was somehow up to his neck in the Salander affair along with Blomkvist.

Armansky listened intently. When Linder finished her account, he said: "Beckman called about an hour ago."

"Oh?"

"He and Berger are coming in later this week to sign a contract. He wants to thank us for what Milton has done, and above all for what you have done."

"I see. It's nice to have a satisfied client."

"He also wants to order a safe for the house. We'll install it and finish up the alarm package before this weekend."

"That's good."

"He says he wants us to invoice him for your work over the weekend. That'll make it quite a sizable bill we'll be sending them." Armansky sighed. "Susanne, you do know that Fredriksson could go to the police and get you into very deep water on a number of counts."

She nodded.

"Mind you, he'd end up in prison so fast it would make his head spin, but he might think it was worth it."

"I doubt he has the balls to go to the police."

"You may be right, but what you did far exceeded instructions."

"I know."

"So how do you think I should react?"

"Only you can decide that."

"How did you think I *would* react?"

"What I think has nothing to do with it. You could always fire me."

"Hardly. I can't afford to lose a professional of your calibre."

"Thanks."

"But if you do anything like this again, I'm going to get very angry."

Linder nodded.

"What did you do with the hard drive?"

"It's destroyed. I put it in a vise this morning and crushed it."

"Then we can forget about all this."

Berger spent the rest of the morning calling the board members of *SMP*. She reached the deputy chairman at his summer house near Vaxholm and persuaded him to drive to the city as quickly as he could. A rather makeshift board assembled over lunch. Berger began by explaining how the Cortez folder had come to her, and what consequences it had already had.

When she finished, it was proposed, as she had anticipated, that they try to find another solution. Berger told them that *SMP* was going to run the story the next day. She also told them that this would be her last day of work and that her decision was final.

She got the board to approve two decisions and enter them in the minutes. Magnus Borgsjö would be asked to vacate his position as CEO, effective immediately, and Anders Holm would be appointed acting editor in chief. Then she excused herself and left the board members to discuss the situation among themselves.

At 2:00 she went down to the personnel department and had a contract drawn up. Then she went to speak to Sebastian Strandlund, the culture editor, and the reporter Eva Carlsson.

"As far as I can tell, you consider Eva to be a talented reporter."

"That's true," said Strandlund.

"And in your budget requests over the past two years you've asked that your staff be increased by at least two."

"Correct."

"Eva, in view of the email to which you were subjected, there might be ugly rumours if I were to hire you full-time. But are you still interested?"

"Of course."

"In that case my last act here at *SMP* will be to sign this employment contract."

"Your last act?"

"It's a long story. I'm leaving today. Could you two be so kind as to keep quiet about it for an hour or so?"

"What . . . ?"

"There'll be a memo coming around soon."

Berger signed the contract and pushed it across the desk towards Carlsson.

"Good luck," she said, smiling.

"The older man who participated in the meeting with Ekström on Saturday is Georg Nyström, a police superintendent," Figuerola said as she put the surveillance photographs from Modig's mobile on Edklinth's desk.

"Superintendent," Edklinth muttered.

"Stefan identified him last night. He went to the apartment on Artillerigatan."

"What do we know about him?"

"He comes from the regular police and has worked for SIS since 1983. Since 1996 he's been serving as an investigator with his own area of responsibility. He does internal checks and examines cases that SIS has completed."

"OK."

"Since Saturday morning six persons of interest have been to the building. Besides Sandberg and Nyström, Clinton is definitely operating from there. This morning he was taken by ambulance to have dialysis."

"Who are the other three?"

"A man named Otto Hallberg. He was in SIS in the eighties but he's actually connected to the Defence General Staff. He works for the navy and the military intelligence service."

"I see. Why am I not surprised?"

Figuerola laid down one more photograph. "This man we haven't identified yet. He went to lunch with Hallberg. We'll have to see if we can get a better picture when he goes home tonight. But the most interesting one is this man." She laid another photograph on the desk.

"I recognize him," Edklinth said.

"His name is Wadensjöö."

"Precisely. He worked on the terrorist detail around fifteen years ago. A desk man. He was one of the candidates for the post of top boss here at the Firm. I don't know what became of him."

"He resigned in 1991. Guess who he had lunch with an hour or so ago?"

She put her last photograph on the desk.

"Chief of Secretariat Shenke and Chief of Budget Gustav Atterbom. I want to have surveillance on these gentlemen around the clock. I want to know exactly who they meet."

"That's not practical," Edklinth said. "I have only four men available."

Edklinth pinched his lower lip as he thought. Then he looked up at Figuerola.

"We need more people," he said. "Do you think you could reach Inspector Bublanski discreetly and ask him if he might like to have dinner with me today? Around 7:00, say?"

Edklinth then reached for his phone and dialled a number from memory.

"Hello, Armansky. It's Edklinth. Might I reciprocate for that wonderful dinner? No, I insist. Shall we say 7:00?"

Salander had spent the night in Kronoberg prison in a seven-by-thirteen-foot cell. The furnishings were pretty basic, but she had fallen asleep within minutes of the key being turned in the lock. Early on Monday morning she was up and obediently doing the stretching exercises prescribed for her by the physical therapist at Sahlgrenska. Breakfast was then brought to her, and she sat on her cot and stared into space.

At 9:30 she was led to an interrogation cell at the end of the hall. The guard was a short, bald, old man with a round face and horn-rimmed glasses. He was polite and cheerful.

Giannini greeted her affectionately. Salander ignored Faste. She was meeting Prosecutor Ekström for the first time, and she spent the next half hour sitting on a chair staring stonily at a spot on the wall just above Ekström's head. She said nothing, and she did not move a muscle.

At 10:00 Ekström broke off the fruitless interrogation. He was annoyed not to be able to get the slightest response out of her. He began to feel uncertain as he observed the thin, doll-like young woman. How was it possible that she could have beaten up those two thugs Lundin and Nieminen in

Stallarholmen? Would the court really believe that story, even if he did have convincing evidence?

Salander was brought a simple lunch at noon and spent the next hour solving equations in her head. She focused on an area of spherical astronomy from a book she had read two years earlier.

At 2:30 she was led back to the interrogation cell. This time her guard was a young woman. Salander sat on a chair in the empty cell and pondered a particularly intricate equation.

After ten minutes the door opened.

"Hello, Lisbeth." A friendly tone. It was Teleborian.

He smiled at her, and she froze. The components of the equation she had constructed in the air before her came tumbling to the ground. She could hear the numbers and mathematical symbols bouncing and clattering as if they had physical form.

Teleborian stood still for a minute and looked at her before he sat down on the other side of the table. She continued to stare at the same spot on the wall.

After a while she met his eyes.

"I'm sorry that you've ended up in this situation," Teleborian said. "I'm going to try to help you in every way I can. I hope we can establish some level of mutual trust."

Salander examined every inch of him. The dishevelled hair. The goatee. The little gap between his front teeth. The thin lips. The brand-new brown jacket. The shirt open at the neck. She listened to his smooth and treacherously friendly voice.

"I also hope that I can be of more help to you than the last time we met."

He placed a small notebook and pen on the table. Salander lowered her eyes and looked at the pen. It was a pointed, silver-coloured tube.

Risk assessment.

She suppressed an impulse to reach out and grab the pen.

Her eyes sought the little finger of his left hand. She saw a faint white mark where fifteen years earlier she had sunk in her teeth and locked her jaws so hard that she almost bit his finger off. It had taken three guards to hold her down and prise open her jaw.

I was a scared little girl barely into my teens then. Now I'm a grown woman. I can kill you whenever I want.

Again she fixed her eyes on the spot on the wall, and gathered up the scattered numbers and symbols and began to reassemble the equation.

Teleborian studied Salander with a neutral expression. He had not become an internationally respected psychiatrist for nothing. He had a gift for reading emotions and moods. He could sense a cold shadow passing through the room, and interpreted this as a sign that the patient felt fear and shame beneath her imperturbable exterior. He assumed that she was reacting to his presence, and was pleased that her attitude towards him had not changed over the years. *She's going to hang herself in court.*

Berger's final act at *SMP* was to write a memo to the staff. She was angry, and she filled two pages explaining why she was resigning, including her opinion of various colleagues. Then she deleted the whole text and started again in a calmer tone.

She did not refer to Fredriksson. If she had, all interest

would have focused on him, and her real reasons would be drowned out by the sensation a case of sexual harassment would inevitably cause.

She gave two reasons. The principal one was that she had met implacable resistance from management to her proposal that managers and owners should reduce their salaries and bonuses. Which meant that she would have had to start her tenure at *SMP* with damaging cutbacks in staff. This was not only a breach of the promise she had been given when she accepted the job, but it would undercut her every attempt to bring about long-term change in order to strengthen the newspaper.

The second reason she gave was the revelation about Borgsjö. She wrote that she had been instructed to cover up the story, and this flew in the face of all she believed to be her job. It meant that she had no choice but to resign her position as editor. She concluded by saying that *SMP*'s dire situation was not a personnel problem, but a management problem.

She read through the memo, corrected the typos, and emailed it to all the paper's employees. She sent a copy to *Pressens Tidning*, a media journal, and also to the trade magazine *Journalisten*. Then she packed away her laptop and went to see Holm at his desk.

"Goodbye," she said.

"Goodbye, Berger. It was hellish working with you."

They smiled at each other.

"One last thing," she said.

"Tell me."

"Frisk has been working on a story I commissioned."

"Right, and nobody has any idea what it's about."

"Give him some support. He's come a long way, and I'll be staying in touch with him. Let him finish the job. I guarantee you'll be pleased with the result."

He looked wary. Then he nodded.

They did not shake hands. She left her card key on his desk and took the elevator down to the garage. She parked her BMW near the *Millennium* offices at a little after 4:00.

PART 4

Rebooting System

JULY 1–OCTOBER 7

Despite the rich variety of Amazon legends from ancient Greece, South America, Africa, and elsewhere, there is only one historically documented example of female warriors. This is the women's army that existed among the Fon of Dahomey in West Africa, now Benin.

These female warriors have never been mentioned in the published military histories; no romanticized films have been made about them, and today they exist as no more than footnotes to history. Only one scholarly work has been written about these women, *Amazons of Black Sparta* by Stanley B. Alpern (C. Hurst & Co., London, 1998), and yet they made up a force that was the equal of every contemporary body of male elite soldiers from among the colonial powers.

It is not clear exactly when Fon's female army was founded, but some sources date it to the 1600s. It was originally a royal guard, but it developed into a military collective of 6,000 soldiers with a semi-divine status. They were not merely window dressing. For almost 200 years they constituted the vanguard of the Fon against European colonizers. They were feared by the French forces, who lost several battles against them. This army of women was not defeated until 1892, when France sent troops with artillery, the Foreign Legion, a marine infantry regiment, and cavalry.

It is not known how many of these female warriors fell in battle. For many years survivors continued to wage guerrilla warfare, and veterans of the army were interviewed and photographed as late as the 1940s.

CHAPTER 23

Friday, July 1–
Sunday, July 10

Two weeks before the trial of Lisbeth Salander began, Malm finished the layout of the 352-page book tersely titled *The Section*. The cover was blue with yellow type. Malm had positioned seven postage-stamp-sized black-and-white images of Swedish prime ministers along the bottom. Superimposed over them hovered a photograph of Zalachenko. He had used Zalachenko's passport photograph as an illustration, increasing the contrast so that only the darkest areas stood out, like a shadow across the whole cover. It was not a particularly sophisticated design, but it was effective. Blomkvist, Cortez, and Eriksson were named as the authors.

It was 5:00 in the morning and he had been working all night. He felt slightly sick and badly wanted to go home and sleep. Eriksson had sat up with him doing final corrections page by page as Malm OK'd them and printed them out. By now she was asleep on the sofa.

Malm put the entire text plus illustrations into a folder. He started up the Toast programme and burned two CDs.

One he put in the safe. The other was collected by a sleepy Blomkvist just before 7:00.

"Go and get some rest," Blomkvist said.

"I'm on my way."

They left Eriksson asleep and turned on the door alarm. Cortez would be in at 8:00 to take over.

Blomkvist walked to Lundagatan, where he again borrowed Salander's abandoned Honda without permission. He drove to Hallvigs Reklam, the printers near the railway tracks in Morgongåva, west of Uppsala. This was a job he would not entrust to the mail.

He drove slowly, refusing to acknowledge the stress he felt, and then waited until the printers had checked that they could read the CD. He made sure that the book would indeed be ready to distribute on the first day of the trial. The problem was not the printing but the binding, which could take time. But Jan Köbin, Hallvigs's manager, promised to deliver at least 500 copies of the first printing of 10,000 by that day.

Finally, Blomkvist made sure that everyone understood the need for the greatest secrecy, although this reminder was probably unnecessary. Two years earlier Hallvigs had printed Blomkvist's book about Hans-Erik Wennerström under very similar circumstances.

Blomkvist drove back to Stockholm in no particular hurry. He parked outside Bellmansgatan 1 and went to his apartment to pack a change of clothes and toiletries. He drove to Stavsnäs wharf in Värmdö, where he parked the Honda and took the ferry out to Sandhamn.

It was the first time since Christmas that he had been to

the cabin. He unfastened the window shutters to let in the air and drank a Ramlösa. As always when a job was finished and at the printer, and nothing could be changed, he felt empty.

He spent an hour sweeping and dusting, scouring the shower tray, switching on the fridge, checking the water pipes, and changing the bedding up in the sleeping loft. He went to the grocery and bought everything he would need for the weekend. Then he started up the coffeemaker and sat outside on the veranda, smoking a cigarette and not thinking about anything in particular.

Just before 5:00 he went down to the steamboat wharf and met Figuerola.

"I thought you said you couldn't take time off," he said, kissing her on the cheek.

"That's what I thought too. But I told Edklinth I've been working every waking minute for the past few weeks and I'm starting to burn out. I said I needed two days off to recharge my batteries."

"In Sandhamn?"

"I didn't tell him where I was going," she said with a smile.

Figuerola ferreted around in Blomkvist's 270-square-foot cabin. She subjected the kitchen area, the bathroom, and the loft to a critical inspection before she nodded in approval. She washed and changed into a thin summer dress while Blomkvist cooked lamb chops in red wine sauce and set the table on the veranda. They ate in silence as they watched the parade of sail boats on their way to or from the marina. They shared the rest of the bottle of wine.

"It's a wonderful cabin. Is this where you bring all your girlfriends?" Figuerola said.

"Just the important ones."

"Has Erika Berger been here?"

"Many times."

"And Salander?"

"She stayed here for a few weeks when I was writing the book about Wennerström. And we spent Christmas here two years ago."

"So both Berger and Salander are important in your life?"

"Erika is my best friend. We've been friends for twenty-five years. Lisbeth is a whole different story. She's certainly unique, and she's the most antisocial person I've ever known. You could say that she made a big impression on me when we first met. I like her. She's a friend."

"You don't feel sorry for her?"

"No. She has herself to blame for a lot of the crap that's happened to her. But I do feel enormous sympathy for and solidarity with her."

"But you aren't in love either with her or with Berger?"

He shrugged. Figuerola watched an Amigo 23 coming in late with its navigation lights glowing as it chugged past a motorboat on the way to the marina.

"If love is liking someone an awful lot, then I suppose I'm in love with several people," Blomkvist said.

"And now with me?"

Blomkvist nodded. Figuerola frowned and looked at him.

"Does it bother you?"

"That you've brought other women here? No. But it does bother me that I don't really know what's happening between us. And I don't think I can have a relationship with a man who screws around whenever he feels like it."

"I'm not going to apologize for the way I've led my life."

"And I guess that in some way I'm falling for you because you are who you are. It's easy to sleep with you because there's no bullshit and you make me feel safe. But this all started because I gave in to a crazy impulse. It doesn't happen very often, and I hadn't planned it. And now we've gotten to the stage where I've become just another one of the girls you invite out here."

They sat in silence for a moment.

"You didn't have to come."

"Yes, I did. Oh, Mikael . . ."

"I know."

"I'm unhappy. I don't want to fall in love with you. It'll hurt far too much when it's over."

"Listen, I've had this cabin for twenty-five years, since my father died and my mother moved back to Norrland. My sister got our apartment and I got the cabin. Apart from some casual acquaintances in the early years, there are five women who have been here before you: Erika; Lisbeth; my ex-wife, who I was with in the eighties; a woman I was in a serious relationship with in the late nineties; and someone I met two years ago, whom I still see occasionally. It's sort of special circumstances. . . ."

"I bet it is."

"I keep this cabin so that I can get away from the city and have some quiet time. I'm mostly here on my own. I read books, I write, and I relax and sit on the wharf and look at the boats. It's not a secret love nest."

He stood up to get the bottle of wine he had put in the shade.

"I won't make any promises. My marriage broke up because Erika and I couldn't keep away from each other," he said, and then he added in English, "Been there, done that, got the T-shirt."

He filled their glasses.

"But you're the most interesting person I've met in a long time. It's as if our relationship took off at full speed from a standing start. I think I fell for you the moment you picked me up outside my apartment. The few times I've slept at my place since then, I've woken up in the middle of the night needing you. I don't know if I want a steady relationship, but I'm terrified of losing you." He looked at her. "So what do you think we should do?"

"Let's think about things," Figuerola said. "I'm really attracted to you too."

"This is starting to get serious," Blomkvist said.

She suddenly felt a great sadness. They did not say much for a long time. When it got dark they cleared the table, went inside, and closed the door.

On the Friday before the week of the trial, Blomkvist stopped at the Pressbyrån news-stand at Slussen and read the headlines for the morning papers. *Svenska Morgon-Posten*'s CEO and chairman of the board, Magnus Borgsjö, had capitulated and tendered his resignation. Blomkvist bought the papers and walked to Java on Hornsgatan to have a late breakfast. Borgsjö cited family reasons as the explanation for his unexpected resignation. He would not comment on claims that Berger had also resigned after he ordered her to cover up a story about his involvement in the wholesale enterprise

Vitavara Inc. But in a sidebar it was reported that the chair of Svenskt Näringsliv, the confederation of Swedish enterprise, had decided to set up an ethics committee to investigate the dealings of Swedish companies with businesses in Southeast Asia known to explcit child labour.

Blomkvist burst out laughing, and then he folded the morning papers and flipped open his Ericsson to call the woman who hosted *She* on TV4, who was in the middle of a lunchtime sandwich.

"Hello, darling," Blomkvist said. "I'm assuming you'd still like dinner sometime."

"Hi, Mikael," she said, laughing. "Sorry, but you couldn't be further from my type."

"Still, how about coming out with me this evening to discuss a job?"

"What do you have going?"

"Erika Berger made a deal with you two years ago about the Wennerström affair. I want to make a similar deal that will work just as well."

"I'm all ears."

"I can't tell you about it until we've agreed on the terms. I have a story in the works. We're going to publish a book and a themed issue of the magazine, and it's going to be huge. I'm offering you an exclusive look at all the material, provided you don't leak anything before we publish. This time the publication is extra complicated because it has to happen on a specific day."

"How big is the story?"

"Bigger than Wennerström," Blomkvist said. "Are you interested?"

"Are you serious? Where shall we meet?"

"How about Samir's Cauldron? Erika's going to sit in on the meeting."

"What's going on with her? Is she back at *Millennium* now that she's been thrown out of *SMP*?"

"She didn't get thrown out. She resigned because of differences of opinion with Magnus Borgsjö."

"He seems to be a real creep."

"You're not wrong there," Blomkvist said.

Clinton was listening to Verdi through his earphones. Music was pretty much the only thing left in life that could take him away from dialysis machines and the growing pain in the small of his back. He did not hum to the music. He closed his eyes and followed the notes with his right hand, which hovered and seemed to have a life of its own alongside his disintegrating body.

That is how it goes. We are born. We live. We grow old. We die. He had played his part. All that remained was the disintegration.

He felt strangely satisfied with life.

He was playing for his friend Evert Gullberg.

It was Saturday, July 9. Only four days until the trial, and the Section could set about putting this whole wretched story behind them. He had gotten the message that morning. Gullberg had been tougher than almost anyone he had known. When you fire a 9mm full-metal-jacketed bullet into your own temple, you expect to die. Yet it was three months before Gullberg's body gave up at last. That was probably due as much to chance as to the stubbornness with which the doctors had waged the battle for Gullberg's life. And it was the cancer, not the bullet, that had finally determined his end.

Gullberg's death had been painful, and that saddened Clinton. Although incapable of communicating with the outside world, he had at times been in a semi-conscious state, smiling when the hospital staff stroked his cheek or grunting when he seemed to be in pain. Sometimes he had tried to form words and even sentences, but nobody was able to understand anything he said.

He had no family, and none of his friends came to his sickbed. His last contact with life was an Eritrean night nurse by the name of Sara Kitama, who kept watch at his bedside and held his hand as he died.

Clinton realized that he would soon be following his former comrade-in-arms. No doubt about that. The likelihood of his surviving a transplant operation decreased each day. His liver and intestinal functions appeared to have declined at each examination.

He hoped to live past Christmas.

Yet he was content. He felt an almost spiritual, giddy satisfaction that his final days had involved such a sudden and surprising return to service.

It was a boon he could not have anticipated.

The last notes of Verdi faded away just as somebody opened the door to the small room in which he was resting at the Section's headquarters on Artillerigatan.

Clinton opened his eyes. It was Wadensjöö.

He had come to the conclusion that Wadensjöö was a deadweight. He was entirely unsuitable as director of the most important vanguard of Swedish national defence. He could not conceive how he and von Rottinger could ever have made such a fundamental miscalculation as to imagine that Wadensjöö was the appropriate successor.

Wadensjöö was a warrior who needed a fair wind. In a crisis he was feeble and incapable of making a decision. A timid encumbrance lacking steel in his backbone who would most likely have remained in paralysis, incapable of action, and let the Section go under.

It was this simple. Some had it. Others would always falter when it came to the crunch.

"You wanted a word?"

"Sit down," Clinton said.

Wadensjöö sat.

"I'm at a stage in my life when I can no longer waste time. I'll get straight to the point. When all this is over, I want you to resign from the management of the Section."

"You do?"

Clinton tempered his tone.

"You're a good man, Wadensjöö. But unfortunately you were completely unsuited to succeed Gullberg. You should not have been given that responsibility. Von Rottinger and I were at fault when we failed to deal properly with the succession after I got sick."

"You've never liked me."

"You're wrong about that. You were an excellent administrator when von Rottinger and I were in charge of the Section. We would have been helpless without you, and I have great admiration for your patriotism. It's your inability to make decisions that lets you down."

Wadensjöö smiled bitterly. "After this, I don't know if I even want to stay in the Section."

"Now that Gullberg and von Rottinger are gone, I've had

to make the crucial decisions myself," Clinton said. "And you've obstructed every decision I've made during the past few months."

"And I maintain that the decisions you've made are absurd. It's going to end in disaster."

"That's possible. But your indecision would have guaranteed our collapse. Now at least we have a chance, and our plan seems to be working. *Millennium* doesn't know which way to turn. They may suspect that we're somewhere out here, but they lack documentation, and they have no way of finding it—or us. And we know at least as much as they do."

Wadensjöö looked out the window and across the rooftops.

"The only thing we still have to do is to get rid of Zalachenko's daughter," Clinton said. "If anyone starts digging around in her past and listening to what she has to say, there's no knowing what might happen. But the trial starts in a few days, and then it'll be over. This time we have to bury her so deep that she'll never come back to haunt us."

Wadensjöö shook his head.

"I don't understand your attitude," Clinton said.

"I can see that. You're sixty-eight years old. You're dying. Your decisions are not rational, and yet you seem to have bewitched Nyström and Sandberg. They obey you as if you were God the Father."

"I am God the Father in everything that has to do with the Section. We're working according to a plan. Our decision to act has given the Section a chance. And it is with the utmost conviction that I say that the Section will never find itself in such an exposed position again. When all this is over, we're going to implement a complete overhaul of our activities."

"I see."

"Nyström will be the new director. He's really too old, but he's the only choice we have, and he's promised to stay on for six years at least. Sandberg is too young and—as a direct result of your management policies—too inexperienced. He should have been fully trained by now."

"Clinton, don't you see what you've done? You've murdered a man. Björck worked for the Section for thirty-five years, and you ordered his death. Do you not understand—"

"You know quite well that it was necessary. He betrayed us, and he would never have withstood the pressure when the police closed in."

Wadensjöö stood up.

"I'm not finished."

"Then we'll have to continue later. I have a job to do while you lie here fantasizing that you're the Almighty."

"If you're so morally indignant, why don't you go to Bublanski and confess your crimes?"

"Believe me, I've considered it. But whatever you may think, I'm doing everything in my power to protect the Section."

He opened the door and met Nyström and Sandberg on their way in.

"Hello, Fredrik," Nyström said. "We have to talk."

"Wadensjöö was just leaving."

Nyström waited until the door had closed. "Fredrik, I'm seriously worried."

"What's going on?"

"Sandberg and I have been thinking. Things are happening that we don't understand. This morning Salander's lawyer lodged her autobiographical statement with the prosecutor."

"*What?*"

. . . .

Inspector Faste scrutinized Advokat Giannini as Ekström poured coffee from a thermos carafe. The document Ekström had been handed when he arrived at work that morning had taken both of them by surprise. He and Faste had read the forty pages of Salander's story and discussed the extraordinary document at length. Finally he felt compelled to ask Giannini to come in for an informal chat.

They were sitting at the small conference table in Ekström's office.

"Thank you for agreeing to come in," Ekström said. "I have read this . . . hmm . . . account that arrived this morning, and there are a few matters I'd like to clarify."

"I'll do what I can to help," Giannini said.

"I don't know exactly where to start. Let me say from the outset that both Inspector Faste and I are profoundly astonished."

"Indeed?"

"I'm trying to understand what your objective is."

"How do you mean?"

"This autobiography, or whatever you want to call it . . . What's the point of it?"

"The point is perfectly clear. My client wants to set down her version of what has happened to her."

Ekström gave a good-natured laugh. He stroked his goatee, an oft-repeated gesture that was beginning to irritate Giannini.

"Yes, but your client has had several months to explain herself. She hasn't said a word in all her interviews with Faste."

"As far as I know there is no law that forces my client to talk only when it suits Inspector Faste."

"No, but I mean . . . Salander's trial will begin in four days' time, and at the eleventh hour she comes up with this. To tell the truth, I feel a responsibility here which is beyond my duties as prosecutor."

"You do?"

"I do not wish to sound at all offensive. That is not my intention. But we have a procedure for trials in this country. You, Fru Giannini, are a lawyer specialising in women's rights, and you have never before represented a client in a criminal case. I did not charge Lisbeth Salander because she is a woman, but on a charge of aggravated assault and attempted murder. Even you, I believe, must have realized that she suffers from a serious mental illness and needs the protection and assistance of the state."

"You're afraid that I won't be able to provide Lisbeth Salander with an adequate defence," Giannini said in a friendly tone.

"I do not wish to be judgemental," Ekström said, "and I don't question your competence. I'm simply making the point that you lack experience."

"I do understand, and I completely agree with you. I am woefully inexperienced when it comes to criminal cases."

"And yet you have all along refused the help that has been offered by lawyers with considerably more experience—"

"At the express wish of my client. Lisbeth Salander wants me to be her lawyer, and accordingly, I will be representing her in court." She gave him a polite smile.

"Very well, but I do wonder whether in all seriousness you intend to offer this statement to the court."

"Of course. It's her story."

Ekström and Faste glanced at each other. Faste raised his

eyebrows. He could not see what Ekström was fussing about. If Giannini did not understand that she was on her way to sinking her client, then that certainly was not the prosecutor's fault. All they needed to do was to say thank you, accept the document, and put the issue aside.

As far as he was concerned, Salander was off her rocker. He had employed all his skills to persuade her to tell them, at the very least, where she lived. But in interview after interview that damn girl had just sat there, silent as a stone, staring at the wall behind him. She had refused the cigarettes he offered, and had never so much as accepted a coffee or a cold drink. Nor had she registered the least reaction when he pleaded with her, or when he raised his voice in moments of extreme annoyance. Faste had never conducted a more frustrating set of interviews.

"Fru Giannini," Ekström said at last, "I believe that your client ought to be spared this trial. She is not well. I have a psychiatric report from a highly qualified doctor to fall back on. She should be given the psychiatric care that for so many years she has badly needed."

"I take it that you will be presenting this recommendation to the district court."

"That's exactly what I'll be doing. It's not my business to tell you how to conduct her defence. But if this is the line you seriously intend to take, then the situation is, quite frankly, absurd. This statement contains wild and unsubstantiated accusations against a number of people, in particular against her guardian, Advokat Bjurman, and Dr. Peter Teleborian. I hope you do not in all seriousness believe that the court will accept an account that casts suspicion on Dr. Teleborian without offering a single shred of evidence. This document is going to be the final nail in your client's coffin, if you'll pardon the metaphor."

"I hear what you're saying."

"In the course of the trial you may claim that she is not ill and request a supplementary psychiatric assessment, and then the matter can be submitted to the medical board. But to be honest, her statement leaves me in very little doubt that every other forensic psychiatrist will come to the same conclusion as Dr. Teleborian. Its very existence confirms all documentary evidence that she is a paranoid schizophrenic."

Giannini smiled politely. "There is an alternative view," she said.

"What's that?"

"That her account is in every detail true and that the court will elect to believe it."

Ekström looked bewildered by the notion. Then he smiled and stroked his goatee.

Clinton was sitting at the little side table by the window in his office. He listened attentively to Nyström and Sandberg. His face was furrowed, but his peppercorn eyes were focused and alert.

"We've been monitoring the telephone and email traffic of *Millennium*'s key employees since April," Clinton said. "We've confirmed that Blomkvist and Eriksson and this Cortez fellow are pretty downcast on the whole. We've read the outline version of the next issue. It seems that even Blomkvist has reversed his position and is now of the view that Salander is mentally unstable after all. There is a socially linked defence for her—he's claiming that society let her down, and that as a result it's somehow not her fault that she tried to murder her father. But that's hardly an argument. There isn't one word about the break-in at his apartment or the fact that his sister was attacked in Göteborg, and there's no mention of the missing reports. He knows he can't prove anything."

"That is precisely the problem," Sandberg said. "Blomkvist must know that someone has their eye on him. But he seems to be completely ignoring his suspicions. Forgive me, but that isn't *Millennium*'s style. Besides, Erika Berger is back in editorial and yet this whole issue is so bland and devoid of substance that it seems like a joke."

"What are you saying? That it's a decoy?"

Sandberg nodded. "The summer issue should have come out in the last week of June. According to one of Malin Eriksson's emails, it's being printed by a company in Södertälje, but when I rang them this morning, they told me they hadn't even gotten the CRC. All they'd had was a request for a quote about a month ago."

"Where have they printed before?" Clinton said.

"At a place called Hallvigs in Morgongåva. I called to ask how far they had gotten with the printing—I said I was calling from *Millennium*. The manager wouldn't tell me a thing. I thought I'd drive up there this evening and take a look."

"Makes sense. Georg?"

"I've reviewed all the telephone traffic from the past week," Nyström said. "It's bizarre, but the *Millennium* staff never discusses anything to do with the trial or Zalachenko."

"Nothing at all?"

"No. They mention it only when they're talking with someone outside *Millennium*. Listen to this, for instance. Blomkvist gets a call from a reporter at *Aftonbladet* asking whether he has any comment to make on the upcoming trial."

He put a tape recorder on the table.

"Sorry, but I have no comment."

"You've been involved with the story from the start. You were the one who found Salander down in Gosseberga. And you haven't published a single word since. When do you intend to publish?"

"When the time is right. Provided I have anything to say."

"Do you?"

"Well, you can buy a copy of *Millennium* and see for yourself."

He turned off the recorder.

"We didn't think about this before, but I went back and listened to bits at random. It's been like this the entire time. He hardly discusses the Zalachenko business except in the most general terms. He doesn't even discuss it with his sister, and she's Salander's lawyer."

"Maybe he really doesn't have anything to say."

"He consistently refuses to speculate about anything. He seems to live at the offices around the clock; he's hardly ever at his apartment. If he's working night and day, then he ought to have come up with something more substantial than whatever's going to be in the next issue of *Millennium*."

"And we still haven't been able to tap the phones at their offices?"

"No," Sandberg said. "There's been somebody there twenty-four hours a day—and that's significant—ever since we went into Blomkvist's apartment the first time. The office lights are always on, and if it's not Blomkvist it's Cortez or Eriksson, or that faggot . . . er, Christer Malm."

Clinton stroked his chin and thought for a moment.

"Conclusions?"

Nyström said: "If I didn't know better, I'd think they were putting on an act for us."

Clinton felt a cold shiver run down the back of his neck. "Why hasn't this occurred to us before?"

"We've been listening to what they've been saying, not to what they haven't been saying. We've been gratified when we've heard their confusion or noticed it in an email. Blomkvist knows damn well that someone stole copies of the 1991 Salander report from him and his sister. But what the hell is he doing about it?"

"And they didn't report her mugging to the police?"

Nyström shook his head. "Giannini was present at the interviews with Salander. She's polite, but she never says anything of any weight. And Salander herself never says anything at all."

"But that will work in our favour. The more she keeps her mouth shut, the better. What does Ekström say?"

"I saw him a couple of hours ago. He'd just been given Salander's statement." He pointed to the pages in Clinton's lap.

"Ekström is confused. It's fortunate that Salander is no good at expressing herself in writing. To an outsider this would look like a totally insane conspiracy theory with added pornographic elements. But she still shoots very close to the mark. She describes exactly how she came to be locked up at St. Stefan's, and she claims that Zalachenko worked for Säpo and so on. She says she thinks everything is connected with a little club inside Säpo, pointing to the existence of something corresponding to the Section. All in all it's fairly accurate. But as I said, it's not plausible. Ekström is in a dither because this also seems to be the line of defence Giannini is going to use at the trial."

"Shit," Clinton said. He bowed his head and thought intently for several minutes. Finally he looked up.

"Jonas, drive up to Morgongåva this evening and find out if anything is going on. If they're printing *Millennium*, I want a copy."

"I'll take Falun with me."

"Good. Georg, I want you to see Ekström this afternoon and take his pulse. Everything has gone smoothly until now, but I can't ignore what you two are telling me."

Clinton sat in silence for a moment more.

"The best thing would be if there wasn't any trial," he said at last.

He raised his eyes and looked at Nyström. Nyström nodded. Sandberg nodded.

"Nyström, can you investigate our options?"

Sandberg and the locksmith known as Falun parked a short distance from the railway tracks and walked through Morgongåva. It was 8:30 in the evening. It was too light and too early to do anything, but they wanted to reconnoitre and get a look at the place.

"If the building is alarmed, I'm not doing it," Falun said. "It would be better to have a look through the window. If there's anything lying around, you can just chuck a rock through, jump in, grab what you need, and run like hell."

"That'll work," Sandberg said.

"If you only need one copy of the magazine, we can check the trash cans around the back. There must be overruns and test printings and things like that."

Hallvigs Reklam printing factory was in a low, brick building. They approached from the south on the other side of the street. Sandberg was about to cross when Falun took hold of his elbow.

"Keep going straight," he said.

"What?"

"Keep going straight, as if we're out for an evening stroll."

They passed Hallvigs and made a tour of the neighbourhood.

"What was all that about?" Sandberg said.

"You have to keep your eyes peeled. The place isn't just alarmed. There was a car parked alongside the building."

"You mean somebody's there?"

"It was a car from Milton Security. The factory is under surveillance, for Christ's sake."

"Milton Security?" Clinton felt the shock hit him in the gut.

"If it hadn't been for Falun, I would have walked right into their arms," Sandberg said.

"There's something fishy going on," Nyström said. "There is no rationale for a small out-of-town printer to hire Milton Security for twenty-four-hour surveillance."

Clinton's lips were pressed tight. It was after 11:00 and he needed to rest.

"And that means *Millennium* really is up to something," Sandberg said.

"I can see that," Clinton said. "OK. Let's analyse the situation. What's the worst-case scenario? What could they know?" He gave Nyström an urgent look.

"It has to be the Salander report," he said. "They beefed up their security after we stole the copies. They must have guessed that they're under surveillance. The worst case is that they still have a copy of the report."

"But Blomkvist was at his wits' end when it went missing."

"I know. But we may have been duped. We can't shut our eyes to that possibility."

"We'll work on that assumption," Clinton said. "Sandberg?"

"We do know what Salander's defence will be. She's going to tell the truth as she sees it. I've read this autobiography of hers. In fact it plays right into our hands. It's full of such outrageous accusations of rape and violation of her civil rights that it will come across as the ravings of a paranoid personality."

Nyström said: "Besides, she can't prove a single one of her claims. Ekström will use the account against her. He'll annihilate her credibility."

"And Teleborian's new report is excellent. There is, of course, the possibility that Giannini will call in her own expert, who'll say that Salander isn't crazy, and the whole thing will end up before the medical board. But again, unless Salander changes tactics, she's going to refuse to talk to them too, and then they'll conclude that Teleborian is right. She's her own worst enemy."

"The best thing would still be if there was no trial," Clinton said.

Nyström shook his head. "That's virtually impossible. She's in Kronoberg prison and she has no contact with other prisoners. She gets an hour's exercise each day in the little area on the roof, but we can't get to her up there. And we have no contacts among the prison staff."

"There may still be time."

"If we'd wanted to dispose of her, we should have done it when she was at Sahlgrenska. The likelihood that a hit man would do time is almost 100 percent. And where would we find a gun who'd agree to that? And on such short notice it would be impossible to arrange a suicide or an accident."

"I was afraid of that. And unexpected deaths have a tendency to invite questions. OK; we'll have to see how the trial goes. In reality, nothing has changed. We've always anticipated that they would make some sort of counter-move, and it seems to be this so-called autobiography."

"The problem is *Millennium*," Sandberg said.

"*Millennium* and Milton Security," Clinton said pensively. "Salander has worked for Armansky, and Blomkvist once had a thing with her. Should we assume that they've joined forces?"

"It doesn't seem unreasonable that Milton Security is watching the factory where *Millennium* is being printed. And it can't be a coincidence."

"When are they going to publish? Sandberg, you said that they're almost two weeks behind schedule. If we assume that Milton is keeping an eye on the printers to make sure that nobody gets hold of a copy, that means either that they're publishing something that they don't want to leak, or that the magazine has already been printed."

"To coincide with the opening of the trial," Sandberg said. "That's the only reasonable explanation."

Clinton nodded. "What's going to be in the magazine?"

They thought for a while, until Nyström broke the silence.

"In the worst case they have a copy of the 1991 report, as we said."

Clinton and Sandberg had reached the same conclusion.

"But what can they do with it?" Sandberg said. "The report implicates Björck and Teleborian. Björck is dead. They can press hard with Teleborian, but he'll claim that he was doing a routine forensic psychiatric examination. It'll be their word against his."

"And what can we do if they publish the report?" Nyström said.

"I think we're holding the trump card," Clinton said. "If there's a ruckus over the report, the focus will be on Säpo, not the Section. And when reporters start asking questions, Säpo will just pull it out of the archive."

"And it won't be the same report," Sandberg said.

"Shenke has put the modified version in the archive—that is, the version Ekström was given to read. It was assigned a case number. So we could swiftly present a lot of disinformation to the media. . . . We have the original, which Bjurman got ahold of, and *Millennium* only has a copy. We could even spread information to suggest that it was Blomkvist himself who falsified the original."

"Good. What else could *Millennium* know?"

"They can't know anything about the Section. That wouldn't be possible. They'll have to focus on Säpo, and that would mean Blomkvist being cast as a conspiracy theorist."

"By now he's rather well known," Clinton said slowly. "Since the resolution of the Wennerström affair, he's been taken pretty seriously."

"Could we somehow reduce his credibility?" Sandberg said.

Nyström and Clinton exchanged glances. Clinton looked at Nyström.

"Do you think you could put your hands on . . . let's say, fifty grams of cocaine?"

"Maybe from the Yugos."

"Give it a try. And get a move on. The trial starts in three days."

"I don't get it," Sandberg said.

"It's a trick as old as the profession. But still extremely effective."

"Morgongåva?" Edklinth said with a frown. He was sitting in his bathrobe on his sofa at home, reading through Salander's autobiography for the third time, when Figuerola called. Since it was after midnight, he assumed that something was up.

"Morgongåva," Figuerola repeated. "Sandberg and Lars Faulsson were there at 8:30 this evening. They were tailed by Inspector Andersson from Bublanski's gang, and we had a radio transmitter planted in Sandberg's car. They parked near the old railway station, walked around for a while, and then returned to the car and drove back to Stockholm."

"I see. Did they meet anyone, or—"

"No. That was the strange thing. They just got out of the car and walked around a little, then drove straight back to Stockholm, Andersson told me."

"I see. And why are you calling me at 12:30 in the morning to tell me this?"

"It took a little while to work it out. They walked past Hallvigs printers. I talked to Blomkvist about it. That's where *Millennium*'s being printed."

"Oh, shit," Edklinth said. He saw the implications immediately.

"Since Faulsson was along, I have to suppose that they were intending to pay the printers a late-night visit, but they abandoned the expedition," Figuerola said.

"Why?"

"Because Blomkvist asked Armansky to keep an eye on the factory until the magazine was distributed. They probably saw the car from Milton Security. I thought you'd want to know right away."

"You're right. It means that they've begun to smell a rat."

"Alarm bells must have gone off in their heads when they saw the car. Sandberg dropped Faulsson off in town and then went back to Artillerigatan. We know that Clinton is there. Nyström arrived at about the same time. The question is, what are they going to do?"

"The trial starts on Wednesday. . . . Can you reach Blomkvist and urge him to double up on security at *Millennium*? Just in case."

"They already have good security. And they blew smoke rings around their tapped phones—like old pros. Blomkvist is so paranoid already that he's using diversionary tactics we could learn from."

"I'm happy to hear it, but call him anyway."

Figuerola closed her mobile and put it on the bedside table. She looked up and studied Blomkvist as he lay naked with his head against the foot of the bed.

"I'm supposed to call you and tell you to beef up security at *Millennium*," she said.

"Thanks for the suggestion," he said wryly.

"I'm serious. If they start to smell a rat, there's a danger that they'll go and do something without thinking. They might break in."

"Henry's sleeping there tonight. And we have a burglar alarm that goes straight to Milton Security, three minutes away."

He lay in silence with his eyes shut.

"Paranoid," he muttered.

CHAPTER 24

Monday, July 11

It was 6:00 on Monday morning when Linder from Milton Security called Blomkvist on his T10.

"Don't you people ever rest?" Blomkvist said, drunk with sleep.

He glanced at Figuerola. She was up already and had changed into jogging shorts, but had not yet put on her T-shirt.

"Sure. But the night duty officer woke me. The silent alarm we installed at your apartment went off at 3:00."

"Did it?"

"I drove down to see what was going on. This is a bit tricky. Could you come to Milton this morning? As soon as possible, that is."

"This is serious," Armansky said.

It was just after 8:00 when Armansky, Blomkvist, and Linder were gathered in front of a TV monitor in a conference room at Milton Security. Armansky had also called in Johan Fräklund, a retired criminal inspector in the Solna police, now chief of Milton's operations unit, and the former inspector Sonny Bohman, who had been involved in the Salander affair from the start. They were pondering the surveillance video that Linder had just shown them.

"What we see here is Säpo officer Jonas Sandberg opening the door to Mikael's apartment at 3:17. He has his own keys. You will recall that Faulsson, the locksmith, made copies of the spare set when he and Göran Mårtensson broke in several weeks ago."

Armansky nodded sternly.

"Sandberg is in the apartment for approximately eight minutes. During that time he does the following things. First, he takes a small plastic bag from the kitchen, which he fills. Then he unscrews the back plate of a speaker which you have in the living room, Mikael. That's where he places the bag. The fact that he takes a bag from your kitchen is significant."

"It's a Konsum bag," Blomkvist said. "I save them to put cheese and stuff in."

"I do the same. What matters, of course, is that the bag has your fingerprints on it. Then he takes a copy of *SMP* from the recycling bin in the hall. He tears off a page to wrap up an object, which he puts on the top shelf of your wardrobe. Same thing there: the paper has your fingerprints on it."

"I get you," Blomkvist said.

"I drive to your apartment at around 5:00," Linder said. "I find the following items: in your speaker there are now approximately a hundred and eighty grams of cocaine. I've taken a sample, which I have here."

She put a small evidence bag on the conference table.

"What's in the wardrobe?" Blomkvist said.

"About 120,000 kronor in cash."

Armansky motioned to Linder to turn off the TV. He turned to Fräklund.

"So Mikael Blomkvist is involved in cocaine dealing," Fräklund said good-naturedly. "Apparently they've started to get a little worried about what Blomkvist is working on."

"This is a counter-move," Blomkvist said.

"A counter-move to what?"

"They ran into Milton's security patrol in Morgongåva last night."

He told them what he had heard from Figuerola about Sandberg's expedition to the printing factory.

"That busy little rascal," Bohman said.

"But why now?"

"They must be nervous about what *Millennium* might publish when the trial starts," Fräklund said. "If Blomkvist is arrested for dealing cocaine, his credibility will drop dramatically."

Linder nodded. Blomkvist looked sceptical.

"How are we going to handle this?" Armansky said.

"We should do nothing," Fräklund said. "We hold all the cards. We have crystal-clear evidence of Sandberg planting the stuff in your apartment. Let them spring the trap. We can prove your innocence in a second, and besides, this will be further proof of the Section's criminal activities. I would so love to be prosecutor when those guys are brought to trial."

"I don't know," Blomkvist said slowly. "The trial starts the day after tomorrow. The magazine is on the stands on Friday, day three of the trial. If they plan to frame me for dealing cocaine, I'll never have the time to explain how it happened before the magazine comes out. I risk sitting in prison and missing the beginning of the trial."

"So, all the more reason for you to stay out of sight this week," Armansky said.

"Well . . . I have to work with TV4, and I have a number of other things to do. It would be enormously inconvenient—"

"Why right now?" Linder said suddenly.

"How do you mean?" Armansky said.

"They've had three months to smear Blomkvist. Why do it right now? Whatever happens, they're not going to be able to prevent publication."

They all sat in silence for a moment.

"It might be because they don't have a clue what you're going to publish, Mikael," Armansky said. "They have to suppose that you have something in the offing, but they might think all you have is Björck's report. They have no reason to know that you're planning on rolling up the whole Section. If it's only about Björck's report, then it's certainly enough to blacken your reputation. Any revelations you might come up with would be drowned out when you're arrested and charged. Big scandal. The famous Mikael Blomkvist arrested on a drug charge. Six to eight years in prison."

"Could I have two copies of the video?" Blomkvist said.

"What are you going to do with them?"

"Lodge one copy with Edklinth. And in three hours I'm going to be at TV4. I think it would be prudent to have this ready to run on TV if or when all hell breaks loose."

Figuerola turned off the DVD player and put the remote on the table. They were meeting in the temporary office on Fridhemsplan.

"Cocaine," Edklinth said. "They're playing a very dirty game here."

Figuerola looked thoughtful. She glanced at Blomkvist.

"I thought it best to keep all of you up to date," he said with a shrug.

"I don't like this," Figuerola said. "It implies a recklessness. Someone hasn't really thought this through. They must realize that you wouldn't go quietly and let yourself be thrown into Kumla bunker under arrest on a drugs charge."

"I agree," Blomkvist said.

"Even if you were convicted, there's still a strong likelihood that people would believe what you have to say. And your colleagues at *Millennium* wouldn't keep quiet either."

"Furthermore, this is costing them a great deal," Edklinth said. "They have a budget that allows them to distribute 120,000 kronor here and there without blinking, plus whatever the cocaine costs them."

"I know, but the plan is actually not bad," Blomkvist said. "They're counting on Salander landing back in the asylum while I disappear in a cloud of suspicion. They're also assuming that any attention would be focused on Säpo—not on the Section."

"But how are they going to convince the narcotics unit to search your apartment? I mean, an anonymous tip will hardly be enough for someone to kick in the door of a star journalist. And if this is going to work, suspicion would have to be cast on you within forty-eight hours."

"Well, we don't really know anything about their schedule," Blomkvist said.

He felt exhausted and longed for all this to be over. He got up.

"Where are you off to?" Figuerola said. "I'd like to know where you're going to be for the next few days."

"I have a meeting with TV4 at lunchtime. And at 6:00 I'm going to catch up with Erika Berger over a lamb stew at Samir's. We're going to fine-tune the press release. The rest of the afternoon and evening I'll be at *Millennium,* I imagine."

Figuerola's eyes narrowed slightly at the mention of Berger.

"I need you to stay in touch during the day. I'd prefer it if you laid low until the trial starts."

"Maybe I could move in with you for a few days," Blomkvist said with a playful smile.

Figuerola's face darkened. She cast a hasty glance at Edklinth.

"Monica's right," Edklinth said. "I think it would be best if you stay more or less out of sight for the time being."

"You take care of your end," Blomkvist said, "and I'll take care of mine."

The host of *She* on TV4 could hardly conceal her excitement over the video material that Blomkvist had delivered. Blomkvist was amused at her undisguised glee. For a week they had worked like dogs to put together coherent material about the Section that they could use on TV. Her producer and the news editor at TV4 were in no doubt as to what a scoop the story would be. It was being produced in the utmost secrecy, with only a few people involved. They had agreed to Blomkvist's insistence that the story be the lead the evening of the third day of the trial. They had decided to do an hour-long news special.

Blomkvist had given her a quantity of still photographs to work with, but on television nothing compares to the moving image. She was simply delighted when he showed her the video—in razor-sharp definition—of an identifiable police officer planting cocaine in his apartment.

"This is great TV," she said. "Camera shot: 'Here is Säpo planting cocaine in the reporter's apartment.'"

"Not Säpo . . . the Section," Blomkvist corrected her. "Don't make the mistake of confusing the two."

"Sandberg works for Säpo, for God's sake," she said.

"Sure, but in practice he should be regarded as an infiltrator. Keep the boundary line very clear."

"Understood. It's the Section that's the story here. Not Säpo. Mikael, can you explain to me how it is that you keep getting mixed up in these sensational stories? And you're right. This is going to be bigger than the Wennerström affair."

"Sheer talent, I guess. Ironically enough, this story also begins with a Wennerström. The spy scandal of the sixties, that is."

Berger called at 4:00. She was in a meeting with the newspaper publishers' association, sharing her views on the planned cutbacks at *SMP*, which had given rise to a major conflict in the industry after she had resigned. She would not be able to make it to their dinner before 6:30.

Sandberg helped Clinton move from the wheelchair to the daybed in the room that was his command centre in the Section's headquarters on Artillerigatan. Clinton had just returned from a whole morning spent in dialysis. He felt ancient, infinitely weary. He had hardly slept the past few days and wished that all this would soon come to an end. He had managed to make himself comfortable, sitting up in the bed, when Nyström appeared.

Clinton concentrated his energy. "Is it ready?"

"I've just come from a meeting with the Nikolich brothers," Nyström said. "It's going to cost 50,000."

"We can afford it," Clinton said.

Christ, if only I were young again.

He turned his head and studied Nyström and Sandberg in turn.

"No qualms of conscience?" he said.

They shook their heads.

"When?" Clinton said.

"Within twenty-four hours," Nyström said. "It's difficult to pin down where Blomkvist is staying, but if worst comes to worst they'll do it outside *Millennium*'s offices."

"We have a possible opportunity tonight, two hours from now," said Sandberg.

"Oh, really?"

"Erika Berger called him a while ago. They're going to have dinner at Samir's Cauldron. It's a restaurant near Bellmansgatan."

"Berger . . . ," Clinton said hesitantly.

"I hope for God's sake that she doesn't—" Nyström began.

"That wouldn't be the end of the world," Sandberg interrupted.

Clinton and Nyström both stared at him.

"We're agreed that Blomkvist is our greatest threat, and that he's going to publish something damaging in the next issue of *Millennium*. We can't prevent publication, so we have to destroy his credibility. If he's killed in what appears to be a typical underworld hit and the police then find drugs and cash in his apartment, the investigators will draw certain conclusions. They won't initially be looking for conspiracies involving the Security Police."

"Go on," Clinton said.

"Erika Berger is actually Blomkvist's lover," Sandberg said

with some force. "She's unfaithful to her husband. If she too were to be a victim, that would lead to further speculation."

Clinton and Nyström exchanged glances. Sandberg had a natural talent when it came to creating smokescreens. He learned fast. But Clinton and Nyström felt a surge of anxiety. Sandberg was too cavalier about life-and-death decisions. That was not good. Extreme measures were not to be employed just because an opportunity had presented itself. Murder was no easy solution; it should be resorted to only when there was no alternative.

Clinton shook his head.

Collateral damage, he thought. He suddenly felt disgust for the whole operation.

After a lifetime in service to the nation, here we sit like primitive mercenaries. Zalachenko was necessary. Björck was . . . regrettable, but Gullberg was right: Björck would have caved in. Blomkvist is . . . possibly necessary. But Erika Berger could only be an innocent bystander.

He looked steadily at Sandberg. He hoped that the young man would not develop into a psychopath.

"How much do the Nikolich brothers know?"

"Nothing. About us, that is. I'm the only one they've met. I used another identity and they can't trace me. They think the killing has to do with trafficking."

"What happens to them after the hit?"

"They leave Sweden at once," Nyström said. "Just like after Björck. If the murder investigation yields no results, they can very cautiously return after a few weeks."

"And the method?"

"Sicilian style. They walk up to Blomkvist, empty a magazine into him, and walk away."

"Weapon?"

"They have an automatic. I don't know what type."

"I do hope they won't spray the whole restaurant—"

"No danger of that. They're cold-blooded; they know what they have to do. But if Berger is sitting at the same table . . ."

Collateral damage.

"Look here," Clinton said. "It's important that Wadensjöö doesn't get wind of this. Especially not if Berger becomes a victim. He's stressed to the breaking point as it is. I'm afraid we're going to have to put him out to pasture when this is over."

Nyström nodded.

"Which means that when we get word that Blomkvist has been shot, we're going to have to put on a good show. We'll call a crisis meeting and act thunderstruck by the development. We can speculate who might be behind the murder, but we'll say nothing about the drugs until the police find the evidence."

Blomkvist took leave of the host of *She* just before 5:00. They had spent the afternoon filling in the gaps in the material. Then Blomkvist had gone to make-up and subjected himself to a long interview on film.

One question had been put to him which he struggled to answer in a coherent way, and they had to film that section several times.

"How is it possible that civil servants in the Swedish government will go so far as to commit murder?"

Blomkvist had brooded over the question long before *She*'s host had asked it. The Section must have considered

Zalachenko an unacceptable threat, but it was still not a satisfactory answer. The reply he eventually gave was not satisfactory either:

> "The only reasonable explanation I can give is that over the years the Section developed into a cult in the true sense of the word. They became like Knutby, or the pastor Jim Jones, or something like that. They write their own laws, within which concepts like right and wrong have ceased to be relevant. And through these laws they imagine themselves isolated from normal society."
>
> "It sounds like some sort of mental illness, don't you think?"
>
> "That wouldn't be an inaccurate description."

Blomkvist took the tunnelbana to Slussen. It was too early to go to Samir's Cauldron. He stood on Södermalmstorg for a while. He was worried still, yet all of a sudden life felt right again. It was not until Berger came back to *Millennium* that he realized how terribly he had missed her. Besides, her retaking of the helm had not led to any internal strife; Eriksson had reverted happily to the position of managing editor, indeed was almost ecstatic—as she put it—that life would now return to normal.

Berger's coming back had also meant that everyone discovered how incredibly understaffed they had been during the past three months. Berger had had to resume her duties at *Millennium* at a run, and she and Eriksson managed to tackle together some of the organizational issues that had been piling up.

Blomkvist decided to buy the evening papers and have coffee at Java on Hornsgatan to kill time before he met Berger.

Prosecutor Ragnhild Gustavsson of the National Prosecutors' Office set her reading glasses on the conference table and studied the group. She had a lined but apple-cheeked face and short, greying hair. She had been a prosecutor for twenty-five years and had worked at the NPO since the early nineties. She was fifty-eight.

Only three weeks had passed since she had been summoned to the NPO to meet Superintendent Edklinth, director of Constitutional Protection. That day she had been busily finishing up one or two routine matters so she could begin her six-week leave at her cabin on the island of Husarö with a clear conscience. Instead she had been assigned to lead the investigation of a group of civil servants who went by the name of "the Section." Her vacation plans had to be shelved. She had been advised that this would be her priority for the foreseeable future, and she had been given more or less free rein to shape her operational team and make the necessary decisions.

"This may prove to be one of the most sensational criminal investigations this country has witnessed," the prosecutor general had told her.

She was beginning to think he was right.

She had listened with increasing amazement to Edklinth's summary of the situation and the investigation he had undertaken at the instruction of the prime minister. The investigation was not yet complete, but he believed that his team had come far enough to be able to present the case to a prosecutor.

First Gustavsson had reviewed all the material that Edklinth had delivered. When the sheer scope of the criminal activity began to emerge, she realized that every decision she made would someday be pored over by historians and their readers. Since then she had spent every waking minute trying to come to grips with the numerous crimes. The case was unique in Swedish law, and since it involved charting criminal activity that had gone on for at least thirty years, she recognized the need for a very particular kind of operational team. She was reminded of the Italian government's anti-Mafia investigators who had been forced in the seventies and eighties to work almost underground in order to survive. She knew why Edklinth himself had been bound to work in secret. He did not know whom he could trust.

Her first action was to call in three colleagues from the NPO. She selected people she had known for many years. Then she hired a renowned historian who had worked on the Crime Prevention Council to help with an analysis of the growth of Security Police responsibilities and powers over the decades. She formally appointed Inspector Figuerola head of the investigation.

At this point the investigation of the Section had taken on a constitutionally valid form. It could now be viewed like any other police investigation, even though its operation would be conducted in absolute secrecy.

Over the past two weeks Prosecutor Gustavsson had summoned a large number of individuals to official but extremely discreet interviews. As well as with Edklinth and Figuerola, interviews had been conducted with Criminal Inspectors Bublanski, Modig, Andersson, and Holmberg. She had called in Mikael Blomkvist, Malin Eriksson, Henry Cortez, Christer

Malm, Advokat Giannini, Dragan Armansky, and Susanne Linder, and she had herself gone to visit Lisbeth Salander's former guardian Holger Palmgren. Apart from the members of *Millennium*'s staff who on principle did not answer questions that might reveal the identity of their sources, all had readily provided detailed answers, and in some cases supporting documentation as well.

Prosecutor Gustavsson had not been at all pleased to have been presented with a timetable that had been determined by *Millennium*. It meant that she would have to order the arrest of a number of individuals on a specific date. She knew that ideally she would have had several months of preparation before the investigation reached its present stage, but she had no choice. Blomkvist had been adamant. *Millennium* was not subject to any governmental ordinances or regulations, and he intended to publish the story on day three of Salander's trial. Gustavsson was thus compelled to adjust her own schedule to strike at the same time, so that those individuals who were under suspicion would not be given a chance to disappear along with the evidence. Blomkvist received a surprising degree of support from Edklinth and Figuerola, and the prosecutor came to see that Blomkvist's plan had certain clear advantages. As prosecutor she would get just the kind of fully focused media backup she needed to push forward the prosecution. In addition, the whole process would move ahead so quickly that this complex investigation would not have time to leak into the halls of the bureaucracy and thus risk being unearthed by the Section.

"Blomkvist's first priority is to achieve justice for Salander. Nailing the Section is merely a by-product," Figuerola said.

The trial of Lisbeth Salander was to commence on Wednesday, in two days' time. The meeting on Monday involved doing a review of the latest material available to them and dividing up the work assignments.

Thirteen people participated in the meeting. From NPO, Ragnhild Gustavsson had brought her two closest colleagues. From Constitutional Protection, Inspector Monica Figuerola had come with Bladh and Berglund. Edklinth, as director of Constitutional Protection, was sitting in as an observer.

But Gustavsson had decided that a matter of this importance could not credibly be restricted to SIS. She had therefore called in Inspector Bublanski and his team, consisting of Modig, Holmberg, and Andersson from the regular police force. They had, after all, been working on the Salander case since Easter and were familiar with all the details. Gustavsson had also called in Prosecutor Jervas and Inspector Erlander from the Göteborg police. The investigation of the Section had a direct connection to the investigation of the murder of Alexander Zalachenko.

When Figuerola mentioned that former prime minister Thorbjörn Fälldin might have to take the stand as a witness, Holmberg and Modig were scarcely able to conceal their discomfort.

For five hours they examined one individual after another who had been identified as an activist in the Section. After that they established the various crimes that could be linked to the apartment on Artillerigatan. A further nine people had been identified as being connected to the Section, although they never visited Artillerigatan. They worked primarily at SIS on Kungsholmen, but had met with some of the Section's activists.

"It is still impossible to say how widespread the conspiracy is. We do not know under what circumstances these people meet with Wadensjöö or with anyone else. They could be informers, or they may have been given the impression that they're working for internal affairs or something similar. So there is some uncertainty about the degree of their involvement, and that can be resolved only after we've had a chance to interview them. Furthermore, these are merely those individuals we have observed during the weeks the surveillance has been in effect; there could be more that we do not yet know about."

"But the chief of Secretariat and the chief of Budget—"

"We have to assume that they're working for the Section."

It was 6:00 on Monday when Gustavsson gave everyone an hour's break for dinner, after which they would reconvene.

It was just as everyone had stood up and begun to move about that Jesper Thoms, Figuerola's colleague from CP's operations unit, drew her aside to report on what had developed during the last few hours of surveillance.

"Clinton has been in dialysis for most of the day and got back to Artillerigatan at 3:00. The only one who did anything of interest was Nyström, although we aren't quite sure what it was he did."

"Tell me," said Figuerola.

"At 1:30 he drove to Central Station and met up with two men. They walked across to the Sheraton and had coffee in the bar. The meeting lasted for about twenty minutes, after which Nyström returned to Artillerigatan."

"So who were they?"

"They're new faces. Two men in their mid-thirties who

seem to be of eastern European origin. Unfortunately, our observer lost them when they went into the tunnelbana."

"I see," Figuerola said wearily.

"Here are the pictures," Thoms said. He handed her a series of surveillance photographs.

She glanced at the enlargements of two faces she had never set eyes on before.

"Thanks," she said, laying out the photographs on the conference table. She picked up her handbag to go and find something to eat.

Andersson, who was standing nearby, bent to look more closely at the pictures.

"Oh, shit," he said. "Are the Nikolich brothers involved in this?"

Figuerola stopped in her tracks. "Who did you say?"

"These two are seriously rotten apples," Andersson said. "Tomi and Miro Nikolich."

"Have you had dealings with them?"

"Sure. Two brothers from Huddinge. Serbs. We had them under observation several times when they were in their twenties and I was in the gangs unit. Miro is the dangerous one. He's been wanted for about a year for aggravated assault. I thought they'd both gone back to Serbia to become politicians or something."

"Politicians?"

"Right. They went to Yugoslavia in the early nineties and helped carry out ethnic cleansing. They worked for a Mafia leader, Arkan, who was running some sort of private fascist militia. They got a reputation for being shooters."

"Shooters?"

"Hit men. They've been flitting back and forth between

Belgrade and Stockholm. Their uncle has a restaurant in Norrmalm, and they've apparently worked there once in a while. We've had reports that they were mixed up in at least two of the killings in what was known as the 'cigarette war,' but we never got close to charging them with anything."

Figuerola gazed mutely at the photographs. Then suddenly she turned pale as a ghost. She stared at Edklinth.

"Blomkvist," she cried with panic in her voice. "They're not just planning to involve him in a scandal, they're planning to murder him. Then the police will find the cocaine during the investigation and draw their own conclusions."

Edklinth stared back at her.

"He's supposed to be meeting Erika Berger at Samir's Cauldron," Figuerola said. She grabbed Andersson by the shoulder. "Are you armed?"

"Yes."

"Come with me."

Figuerola rushed out of the conference room. Her office was three doors down. She ran in and took her service weapon from the desk drawer. Against all regulations she left the door to her office unlocked and wide open as she raced off towards the elevators. Andersson hesitated for a second.

"Go," Bublanski told him. "Sonja, you go with them too."

Blomkvist got to Samir's Cauldron at 6:20. Berger had just arrived and found a table near the bar, not far from the entrance. He kissed her on the cheek. They both ordered lamb stew and strong beers from the waiter.

"How was the *She* woman?" Berger said.

"Cool, as usual."

Berger laughed. "If you don't watch out you're going to

become obsessed by her. Imagine, a woman who can resist the famous Blomkvist charm."

"There are in fact several women who haven't fallen for me over the years," Blomkvist said. "How has your day been?"

"Wasted. But I accepted an invitation to be on a panel to debate the whole *SMP* business at the Publicists' Club. That will be my final contribution."

"Great."

"It's just such a relief to be back at *Millennium*."

"You have no idea how good it is that you're back. I'm still elated."

"It's fun to be at work again."

"Mmm."

"I'm happy."

"And I have to go to the gents," Blomkvist said, getting up.

He almost collided with a man who had just walked in. Blomkvist noticed that he looked vaguely eastern European and was staring at him. Then he saw the sub-machine gun.

As they passed Riddarholmen, Edklinth called to tell them that neither Blomkvist nor Berger was answering their mobiles. They had presumably turned them off for dinner.

Figuerola swore and passed Södermalmstorg at a speed of close to fifty miles an hour. She kept her horn pressed down and made a sharp turn onto Hornsgatan. Andersson had to brace himself against the door. He had taken out his gun and checked the magazine. Modig did the same in the back seat.

"We have to call for backup," Andersson said. "You don't play games with the Nikolich boys."

Figuerola ground her teeth.

"This is what we'll do," she said. "Sonja and I will go

straight into the restaurant and hope they're sitting inside. Curt, you know what these guys look like, so you stay outside and keep watch."

"Right."

"If all goes well, we'll take Blomkvist and Berger straight out to the car and drive them down to Kungsholmen. If we suspect anything's wrong, we'll stay inside the restaurant and call for backup."

"OK," Modig said.

Figuerola was nearly at the restaurant when the police radio crackled beneath the dashboard.

All units. Shots fired on Tavastgatan on Södermalm. Samir's Cauldron restaurant.

Figuerola felt a sudden lurch in her chest.

Berger saw Blomkvist bump into a man as he was heading past the entrance towards the gents'. She frowned without really knowing why. She saw the other man stare at Blomkvist with a surprised expression. She wondered if it was somebody he knew.

Then she saw the man take a step back and drop a bag to the floor. At first she did not know what she was seeing. She sat paralysed as he raised some kind of gun and aimed it at Blomkvist.

Blomkvist reacted without stopping to think. He flung out his left hand, grabbed the barrel of the gun, and twisted it up towards the ceiling. For a microsecond the muzzle passed in front of his face.

The burst of fire from the sub-machine gun was deafening in the small room. Mortar and glass from the overhead lights rained down on Blomkvist as Miro Nikolich squeezed off eleven shots. For a moment Blomkvist looked directly into the eyes of his attacker.

Then Nikolich took a step back and yanked the gun towards him. Blomkvist was unprepared and lost his grip on the barrel. He knew at once that he was in mortal danger. Instinctively he threw himself at the attacker instead of crouching down or trying to take cover. Later he realized that if he had ducked or backed away, he would have been shot on the spot. He got a new grip on the barrel of the sub-machine gun and used his entire weight to drive the man against the wall. He heard another six or seven shots go off and tore desperately at the gun to direct the muzzle at the floor.

Berger instinctively took cover when the second series of shots was fired. She stumbled and fell, hitting her head on a chair. As she lay on the floor, she looked up and saw that three holes had appeared in the wall just behind where she had been sitting.

In shock she turned her head and saw Blomkvist struggling with the man by the door. He had fallen to his knees and was gripping the gun with both hands, trying to wrench it loose. She saw the attacker struggling to get free. He kept smashing his fist over and over into Blomkvist's face and temple.

Figuerola braked hard opposite Samir's Cauldron, flung open the car door, and ran across the road towards the restaurant. She had her Sig Sauer in her hand with the safety off when she noticed the car parked right outside the restaurant.

She saw one of the Nikolich brothers behind the wheel and pointed her weapon at his face behind the driver's door.

"Police. Hands up," she screamed.

Tomi Nikolich held up his hands.

"Get out of the car and lie facedown on the pavement," she roared, fury in her voice. She turned and glanced at Andersson and Modig beside her. "The restaurant," she said.

Modig was thinking of her children. It was against all police protocol to charge into a building with her weapon drawn without first having backup in place and without knowing the exact situation.

Then she heard the sound of more shots from inside.

Blomkvist had his middle finger between the trigger and the trigger guard as Miro Nikolich tried to keep shooting. He heard glass shattering behind him. He felt a searing pain as the attacker squeezed the trigger again and again, crushing his finger. As long as his finger was in place the gun could not be fired. But as Nikolich's fist pummelled the side of his head, it suddenly occurred to him that he was too old for this sort of thing.

Have to end it, he thought.

That was his first rational thought since he had become aware of the man with the sub-machine gun.

He clenched his teeth and shoved his finger farther into the space behind the trigger.

Then he braced himself, rammed his shoulder into the attacker's body, and forced himself back onto his feet. He let go of the gun with his right hand and raised his elbow up to protect his face from the pummelling. Nikolich switched to hitting him in the armpit and ribs. For a second they stood eye to eye again.

The next moment Blomkvist felt the attacker being pulled away from him. He felt one last devastating pain in his finger and became aware of Andersson's huge form. The police officer literally picked up Nikolich with a firm grip on his neck and slammed his head into the wall by the door. Nikolich collapsed to the ground.

"Police! Get down! Stay still!" he heard Modig yell.

He turned his head and saw her standing with her legs apart and her gun held in both hands as she surveyed the chaos. At last she raised her gun to point it at the ceiling and looked at Blomkvist.

"Are you hurt?" she said.

In a daze Blomkvist looked back at her. He was bleeding from his forehead and his nose.

"I think I broke a finger," he said, sitting down on the floor.

Figuerola received backup from the Södermalm armed response team less than a minute after she forced Tomi Nikolich to the pavement at gunpoint. She showed her ID and left the officers to take charge of the prisoner. Then she ran inside. She stopped in the entrance to take stock of the situation.

Blomkvist and Berger were sitting side by side. His face was bloodied and he seemed to be in shock. She sighed in relief. He was alive. Then she frowned as Berger put her arm around his shoulder. At least her face was bruised.

Modig was squatting down next to them, examining Blomkvist's hand. Andersson was handcuffing Nikolich, who looked as though he had been hit by a truck. She saw a Swedish army model M/45 sub-machine gun on the floor.

Figuerola looked up and saw shocked restaurant staff and terror-stricken patrons, along with shattered china, overturned chairs and tables, and debris from the rounds that had been fired. She smelled cordite. But she was not aware of anyone dead or wounded in the restaurant. Officers from the armed response team began to squeeze into the room with their weapons drawn. She reached out and touched Andersson's shoulder. He stood up.

"You said that Miro Nikolich was on our wanted list?"

"Correct. Aggravated assault. About a year ago. A street fight down in Hallunda."

"OK. Here's what we'll do," Figuerola said. "I'll take off as fast as I can with Blomkvist and Berger. You stay here. The story is that you and Modig came here to have dinner and you recognized Nikolich from your time in the gangs unit. When you tried to arrest him he pulled a weapon and started shooting. So you sorted him out."

Andersson looked completely astonished. "That's not going to hold up. There are witnesses."

"The witnesses will say that somebody was fighting and shots were fired. It only has to hold up until tomorrow's evening papers. The story is that the Nikolich brothers were apprehended by sheer chance because you recognized them."

Andersson surveyed the shambles all around him.

Figuerola pushed her way through the knot of police officers out on the street and put Blomkvist and Berger in the back seat of her car. She turned to the armed response team leader and spoke in a low voice with him for half a minute. She gestured towards the car in which Blomkvist and Berger were now sitting. The leader looked puzzled but at last he nodded. She drove to Zinkensdamm, parked, and turned around to her passengers.

"How badly are you hurt?"

"I took a few punches. I still have all my teeth, but my middle finger's hurt."

"I'll take you to the ER at St. Göran's."

"What happened?" Berger said. "And who are you?"

"I'm sorry," Blomkvist said. "Erika, this is Inspector Monica Figuerola. She works for Säpo. Monica, this is Erika Berger."

"I worked that out all by myself," Figuerola said in a neutral tone. She did not spare Berger a glance.

"Monica and I met during the investigation. She's my contact at SIS."

"I understand," Berger said, and she began to shake as suddenly the shock set in.

Figuerola stared hard at Berger.

"What went wrong?" Blomkvist said.

"We misinterpreted the reason for the cocaine," Figuerola said. "We thought they were setting a trap for you, to create a scandal. Now we know they wanted to kill you. They were going to let the police find the cocaine when they went through your apartment."

"What cocaine?" Berger said.

Blomkvist closed his eyes for a moment.

"Take me to St. Göran's," he said.

"Arrested?" Clinton barked. He felt a butterfly-light pressure around his heart.

"We think it's all right," Nyström said. "It seems to have been sheer bad luck."

"Bad luck?"

"Miro Nikolich was wanted on some old assault story. A policeman from the gangs unit happened to recognize him when he went into Samir's Cauldron and wanted to arrest him. Nikolich panicked and tried to shoot his way out."

"And Blomkvist?"

"He wasn't involved. We don't even know if he was in the restaurant at the time."

"This cannot be fucking true," Clinton said. "What do the Nikolich brothers know?"

"About us? Nothing. They think Björck and Blomkvist were both hits that had to do with trafficking."

"But they know that Blomkvist was the target?"

"Sure, but they're hardly going to start blabbing about being hired to do a hit. They'll keep their mouths shut all the way to district court. They'll do time for possession of illegal weapons and, as like as not, for resisting arrest."

"Those damned fuck-ups," Clinton said.

"Well, they seriously screwed up. We've had to let Blomkvist give us the slip for the moment, but no harm was actually done."

It was 11:00 by the time Linder and two hefty bodyguards from Milton Security's personal protection unit collected Blomkvist and Berger from Kungsholmen.

"You really do get around," Linder said.

"Sorry," Berger said gloomily.

Berger had been in a state of shock as they drove to St. Göran's. It had dawned on her all of a sudden that both she and Blomkvist had very nearly been killed.

Blomkvist had spent an hour in the ER having his head X-rayed and his face bandaged. His left middle finger was put in a splint. The end joint was badly bruised and he would lose the fingernail. Ironically, the main injury was caused when Andersson came to his rescue and pulled Nikolich off him. Blomkvist's middle finger had been caught in the trigger guard of the M/45 and had snapped straight across. It hurt a lot, but the injury was hardly life-threatening.

For Blomkvist the shock did not set in until two hours later, when he had arrived at Constitutional Protection at SIS and reported to Inspector Bublanski and Prosecutor Gustavsson. He began to shiver and felt so tired that he almost fell asleep between questions. At that point a certain amount of palavering ensued.

"We don't know what they're planning, and we have no idea whether Mikael was the only intended victim," Figuerola said. "Or whether Erika here was supposed to die too. We don't know if they will try again or if anyone else at *Millennium* is being targeted. And why not kill Salander? After all, she's the truly serious threat to the Section."

"I called my colleagues at *Millennium* while Mikael was being patched up," Berger said. "Everyone's going to lie extremely low until the magazine comes out. The office will be left unstaffed."

Edklinth's immediate reaction had been to order bodyguard protection for Blomkvist and Berger. But on reflection he and Figuerola decided that it would not be the smartest move to contact SIS's Personal Protection unit. Berger solved the problem by declining police protection. She called Armansky to explain what had happened, which was why, later that night, Linder was called in for duty.

Blomkvist and Berger were lodged on the top floor of a safe house just beyond Drottningholm on the road to Ekerö. It was a large 1930s villa overlooking Lake Mälaren. It had an impressive garden, outbuildings, and extensive grounds. The estate was owned by Milton Security, but Martina Sjögren lived there. She was the widow of Hans Sjögren, their colleague of many years, who had died in an accident on assignment fifteen years earlier. After the funeral, Armansky had talked with Fru Sjögren and then hired her as housekeeper and general caretaker of the property. She lived rent-free in a wing of the ground floor and kept the top floor ready for those occasions, a few times each year, when Milton Security needed to hide away individuals who for real or imagined reasons feared for their safety.

Figuerola went with them. She sank onto a chair in the kitchen and allowed Fru Sjögren to serve her coffee, while Berger and Blomkvist settled in upstairs and Linder checked the alarm and electronic surveillance equipment around the property.

"There are toothbrushes and so on in the chest of drawers outside the bathroom," Sjögren called up the stairs.

Linder and Milton's bodyguards installed themselves in rooms on the ground floor.

"I've been on the go ever since I was woken at 4:00," Linder said. "You can put together a watch schedule, but let me sleep till at least 5:00."

"You can sleep all night. We'll take care of this," one of the bodyguards said.

"Thanks," Linder said, and she went straight to bed.

Figuerola listened absent-mindedly as the bodyguards switched on the motion detector in the courtyard and drew straws to see who would take the first watch. The one who lost made himself a sandwich and went into the TV room next to the kitchen. Figuerola studied the flowery coffee cups. She too had been on the go since early morning and was feeling fairly exhausted. She was just thinking about driving home when Berger came downstairs and poured herself a cup of coffee. She sat down across from Figuerola.

"Mikael went out like a light as soon as his head hit the pillow."

"Reaction to the adrenaline," Figuerola said.

"What happens now?"

"You'll have to lie low for a few days. Within a week this will all be over, whichever way it ends. How are you feeling?"

"So-so. A bit shaky still. It's not every day something like this happens. I just called my husband to explain why I wouldn't be coming home."

"Hmm."

"I'm married to—"

"I know who you're married to."

Silence. Figuerola rubbed her eyes and yawned.

"I have to go home and get some sleep," she said.

"Oh, for God's sake, stop talking nonsense and go and lie down with Mikael," Berger said.

Figuerola looked at her.

"Is it that obvious?" she said.

Berger nodded.

"Did Mikael say anything?"

"Not a word. He's generally rather discreet when it comes to his lady friends. But sometimes he's an open book. And you're clearly hostile every time you even look at me. The two of you obviously have something to hide."

"It's my boss," Figuerola said.

"Where does he come into it?"

"He'd fly off the handle if he knew that Mikael and I were—"

"I can see that."

Silence.

"I don't know what's going on between you two, but I'm not your rival," Berger said.

"You're not?"

"Mikael and I sleep together now and then. But I'm not married to him."

"I heard that you two had a special relationship. He told me about you when we were out at Sandhamn."

"So you've been to Sandhamn? Then it *is* serious."

"Don't make fun of me."

"Monica, I hope that you and Mikael . . . I'll try to stay out of your way."

"And if you can't?"

Berger shrugged. "His ex-wife flipped out big time when Mikael was unfaithful with me. She threw him out. It was my fault. As long as Mikael is single and available, I would have no compunction. But I promised myself that if he was ever serious about someone, then I'd keep my distance."

"I don't know if I dare count on him."

"Mikael is special. Are you in love with him?"

"I think so."

"All right, then. Just don't tell him too soon. Now go to bed."

Figuerola thought about it for a moment. Then she went upstairs, undressed, and crawled into bed next to Blomkvist. He mumbled something and put his arm around her waist.

Berger sat alone in the kitchen for a long time. She felt deeply unhappy.

CHAPTER 25

Wednesday, July 13–
Thursday, July 14

Blomkvist had always wondered why the loudspeakers in the district court were so faint, discreet almost. He could hardly make out the words of the announcement that the trial of Lisbeth Salander would begin in courtroom 5 at 10:00. But he had arrived in plenty of time and positioned himself to wait right by the entrance to the courtroom. He was one of the first to be let in. He chose a seat in the public gallery on the left-hand side of the room, where he would have the best view of the defence table. The seats filled up fast. Media interest had steadily increased in the weeks leading up to the trial, and over the past week Prosecutor Ekström had been interviewed daily.

Lisbeth Salander was charged with aggravated assault in the case of Carl-Magnus Lundin; with unlawful threats, attempted murder, and aggravated assault in the case of Karl Axel Bodin, alias Alexander Zalachenko, now deceased; with two counts of breaking and entering—the first at the summer cabin of the deceased lawyer Nils Erik Bjurman in Stallarholmen, the second at Bjurman's home on Odenplan; with the theft of a vehicle—a Harley-Davidson owned by one Sonny Nieminen of Svavelsjö MC; with three counts of possession of illegal weapons—a canister of Mace, a Taser, and a Polish P-83 Wanad, all found in Gosseberga; with the theft of or withholding of evidence—the formulation was imprecise but it referred to the documentation she had found in Bjurman's summer cabin; and with a number of further misdemeanours. In all, sixteen charges had been filed against Lisbeth Salander.

Ekström had been busy.

He had also leaked information indicating that Salander's mental state was cause for alarm. He cited first the forensic psychiatric report by Dr. Jesper H. Löderman that had been compiled at the time of her eighteenth birthday, and second, a report which, in accordance with a decision by the district court at a preliminary hearing, had been written by Dr. Peter Teleborian. Since the mentally ill girl had, true to form, refused categorically to speak to psychiatrists, the analysis was made on the basis of "observations" carried out while she was detained at Kronoberg prison in Stockholm during the month before her trial. Teleborian, who had many years of experience with the patient, had determined that Salander was suffering from a serious mental disturbance and employed terms such as *psychopathy, pathological narcissism,* and *paranoid schizophrenia.*

The press had also reported that seven police interviews had been conducted with Salander. At each of these interviews the defendant had declined even to say good morning to those who were leading the interrogation. The first few interviews had been conducted by the Göteborg police; the remainder had taken place at police headquarters in Stockholm. The tape recordings of the interview protocol revealed that the police had used every means of persuasion and repeated questioning, but had not received the favour of a single reply.

She had not even bothered to clear her throat.

Occasionally Advokat Giannini's voice could be heard on the tapes, at such points as she realized that her client evidently was not going to answer any questions. The charges against Salander were accordingly based exclusively on forensic evidence and on whatever facts the police investigation had been able to determine.

Salander's silence had at times placed her defence lawyer in an awkward position, since she was compelled to be almost as silent as her client. What Giannini and Salander discussed in private was confidential.

Ekström made no secret of the fact that his primary objective was secure psychiatric care for the defendant; of secondary interest to him was a substantial prison sentence. The normal process was the reverse, but he believed that in her case there were such transparent mental disturbances and such an unequivocal forensic psychiatric assessment that he was left with no alternative. It was highly unusual for a court to decide against a forensic psychiatric assessment.

He also believed that Salander's declaration of incompetence should not be rescinded. In an interview he had explained with a concerned expression that in Sweden there were a number of sociopaths with such grave mental disturbances that they presented a danger to themselves as well as to others, and modern medicine could offer no alternative to keeping these individuals safely locked up. He cited the case from the seventies of a violent girl who had been a frequent focus of attention in the media, and who thirty years later was still in a secure psychiatric institution. Every endeavour to ease the restrictions had resulted in her launching reckless and violent attacks on relatives and caretakers, or in attempts to injure herself. Ekström was of the view that Salander suffered from a similar form of psychopathic disturbance.

Media interest had also increased for the simple reason that Salander's defence lawyer, Annika Giannini, had made not a single statement to the press. She had refused all requests to be interviewed, so that members of the media were, as they many times put it, "unable to have an opportunity to present the views of the other side of the case." Journalists were therefore in a difficult situation: the prosecution kept on shovelling out information while the defence, uncharacteristically, gave not the slightest hint of Salander's reaction to the charges against her, nor of what strategy the defence might employ.

This state of affairs was commented on by the legal expert engaged to follow the trial in one of the evening newspapers. The expert had stated in his column that Advokat Giannini was a respected women's rights lawyer, but that she had absolutely no experience in criminal law outside this case. He concluded that she was unsuitable for the purpose of defending Salander. From his sister Blomkvist had also learned that several distinguished lawyers had offered their services. Giannini had, on behalf of her client, courteously turned down every such proposal.

As he waited for the trial to begin, Blomkvist glanced around at the other spectators. He caught sight of Armansky sitting near the exit and their eyes met for a moment.

Ekström had a large stack of papers on his table. He greeted several journalists.

Giannini sat at her table across from Ekström. She had her head down and was sorting through her papers. Blomkvist thought his sister looked a bit tense. Stage fright, he supposed.

Then the judge, assessor, and lay assessors entered the courtroom. Judge Jörgen Iversen was a white-haired, fifty-seven-year-old man with a gaunt face and a spring in his step. Blomkvist had researched Iversen's background and found that he was an exacting judge of long experience who had presided over many high-profile cases.

Finally Salander was brought into the courtroom.

Even though Blomkvist was used to Salander's penchant for shocking clothing, he was amazed that his sister had allowed her to show up to the courtroom in a black leather miniskirt with frayed seams and a black top—with the legend I AM ANNOYED—which barely covered her many tattoos. She had ten piercings in her ears, and a ring through her left eyebrow. Her head was covered in three months' worth of uneven stubble after her surgery. She wore grey lipstick and more black mascara than Blomkvist had ever seen her wear. Her eyebrows were heavily darkened. In the days when he and Salander had spent time together, she had shown almost no interest in make-up.

She looked a bit vulgar, to put it mildly. It was almost a Goth look. She reminded him of a vampire in some pop-art movie from the sixties. Blomkvist was aware of some of the reporters in the press gallery catching their breath in astonishment or smiling broadly. They were at last getting a look at the scandal-ridden young woman they had written so much about, and she was certainly living up to all their expectations.

Then he realized that Salander was in costume. Usually her style was sloppy and rather tasteless. Blomkvist had assumed that she was not really interested in fashion, but that she tried instead to accentuate her own individuality. Salander always seemed to mark her private space as hostile territory, and he had thought of the rivets in her leather jacket as a defence mechanism, like the quills of a hedgehog. To everyone around her it was as good a signal as any: *Don't try to touch me—it will hurt.*

But here in the district court she had exaggerated her style to the point of parody.

It was no accident; it was part of Giannini's strategy.

If Salander had come in with her hair smoothed down and wearing a twin-set and pearls and sensible shoes, she would have came across as a con artist trying to sell a story to the court. It was a question of credibility. She had come as herself and no-one else. Way over the top—for clarity. She was not pretending to be someone she was not. Her message to the court was that she had no reason to be ashamed or to put on a show. If the court had a problem with her appearance, it was no concern of hers. The state had accused her of a multitude of things, and the prosecutor had dragged her into court. With her very appearance she had already indicated that she intended to brush aside the prosecutor's accusations as nonsense.

She moved with confidence and sat down next to her lawyer. She surveyed the spectators. There was no curiosity in her gaze. She seemed instead to be defiantly observing and registering those who had already convicted her in the press.

It was the first time Blomkvist had seen her since she lay like a bloody rag doll on the bench in that kitchen in Gosseberga, and a year and a half or more since he had last seen her under normal circumstances. If the term "normal circumstances" could ever be used in connection with Salander. For a matter of seconds their eyes met. Hers lingered on him, but she betrayed no sign of recognition. Yet she did seem to study the bruises that covered Blomkvist's cheek and temple and the surgical tape over his right eyebrow. Blomkvist thought he discerned the merest hint of a smile in her eyes but could not be sure he had not imagined it. Then Judge Iversen pounded his gavel and called the court to order.

The spectators were allowed to be present in the courtroom for all of thirty minutes. They listened to Ekström's introductory presentation of the case.

Every reporter except Blomkvist was busily taking notes, even though by now all of them knew the charges Ekström intended to bring. Blomkvist had already written his story.

Ekström's introductory remarks went on for twenty-two minutes. Then it was Giannini's turn. Her presentation took thirty seconds. Her voice was firm.

"The defence rejects all the charges brought against my client except one. She admits to possession of an illegal weapon, that is, one spray canister of Mace. To all other counts, my client pleads not guilty of criminal intent. We will show that the prosecutor's assertions are flawed and that my client has been subjected to grievous violations of her civil rights. I will demand that my client be acquitted of all charges, that her declaration of incompetence be revoked, and that she be released."

There was a murmuring from the press gallery. Advokat Giannini's strategy had at last been revealed. It was obviously not what the reporters had been expecting. Most had speculated that Giannini would in some way exploit her client's mental illness to her advantage. Blomkvist smiled.

"I see," Judge Iversen said, making a swift note. He looked at Giannini. "Are you finished?"

"That is my presentation."

"Does the prosecutor have anything to add?" Judge Iversen said.

It was at this point that Ekström requested a private meeting in the judge's chambers. There he argued that the case hinged upon one vulnerable individual's mental state and welfare, and that it also involved matters which, if explored before the public in court, could be detrimental to national security.

"I assume that you are referring to what may be termed the Zalachenko affair," Judge Iversen said.

"That is correct. Alexander Zalachenko came to Sweden as a political refugee and sought asylum from a terrible dictatorship. There are elements in the handling of his situation, personal connections and the like, that are still classified, even though Herr Zalachenko is now deceased. I therefore request that the deliberations be held behind closed doors and that a rule of confidentiality be applied to those sections of the deliberations that are particularly sensitive."

"I believe I understand your point," Judge Iversen said, knitting his brows.

"In addition, a large part of the deliberations will deal with the defendant's guardianship. This touches on matters which in all normal cases become classified almost automatically, and it is out of respect for the defendant that I am requesting a closed court."

"How does Advokat Giannini respond to the prosecutor's request?"

"For our part it makes no difference."

Judge Iversen consulted his assessor and then returned to the courtroom and announced, to the annoyance of the reporters present, that he had accepted the prosecutor's request. So Blomkvist left the courtroom.

Armansky waited for Blomkvist at the bottom of the stairs in the courthouse. It was sweltering in the July heat and Blomkvist could feel sweat in his armpits. His two bodyguards joined him as he emerged from the courthouse. Both nodded to Armansky and then busied themselves studying the surroundings.

"It feels strange to be walking around with bodyguards," Blomkvist said. "What's all this going to cost?"

"It's on the firm. I have a personal interest in keeping you alive. But, since you ask, we've spent roughly 250,000 kronor on pro bono work in the past few months."

"Coffee?" Blomkvist said, pointing to the Italian café on Bergsgatan.

Blomkvist ordered a latte and Armansky a double espresso with a teaspoon of milk. They sat in the shade on the sidewalk outside. The bodyguards sat at the next table drinking Cokes.

"Closed court," Armansky said.

"That was expected. And it's OK, since it means that we can control the news flow better."

"You're right, it doesn't matter to us, but my opinion of Prosecutor Ekström is sinking fast," Armansky said.

They drank their coffee and contemplated the courthouse in which Salander's future would be decided.

"Custer's last stand," Blomkvist said.

"She's well prepared," Armansky said. "And I must say I'm impressed with your sister. When she began planning her strategy I thought it made no sense, but the more I think about it, the more effective it seems."

"This trial won't be decided in there," Blomkvist said. He had been repeating these words like a mantra for several months.

"You're going to be called as a witness," Armansky said.

"I know. I'm ready. But it won't happen before the day after tomorrow. At least that's what we're counting on."

Ekström had left his reading glasses at home and had to push his glasses up onto his forehead and squint to be able to read the last-minute handwritten additions to his text. He stroked his blond goatee before he readjusted his glasses once more and surveyed the room.

Salander sat with her back ramrod straight and gave the prosecutor an unfathomable look. Her face and eyes were impassive, and she did not appear to be wholly present. It was time for the prosecutor to begin questioning her.

"I would like to remind Fröken Salander that she is speaking under oath," Ekström said at last.

Salander did not move a muscle. Prosecutor Ekström seemed to be anticipating some sort of response and waited for a few seconds. He looked at her expectantly.

"You are speaking under oath," he said.

Salander tilted her head very slightly. Giannini was busy reading something in the preliminary investigation protocol and seemed unconcerned by whatever Prosecutor Ekström was saying. Ekström shuffled his papers. After an uncomfortable silence he cleared his throat.

"Very well then," Ekström said. "Let us proceed directly to the events at the late Advokat Bjurman's summer cabin outside Stallarholmen on April 6 of this year, which was the starting point of my presentation of the case this morning. We shall attempt to bring clarity to how it happened that you drove down to Stallarholmen and shot Carl-Magnus Lundin."

Ekström gave Salander a challenging look. Still she did not move a muscle. The prosecutor suddenly seemed resigned. He threw up his hands and looked pleadingly at the judge. Judge Iversen seemed wary. He glanced at Giannini, who was still engrossed in some papers, apparently unaware of her surroundings.

Judge Iversen cleared his throat. He looked at Salander. "Are we to interpret your silence to mean that you don't want to answer any questions?" he asked.

Salander turned her head and met Judge Iversen's eyes.

"I will gladly answer questions," she said.

Judge Iversen nodded.

"Then perhaps you can answer the question," Ekström put in.

Salander looked at Ekström and said nothing.

"Could you please answer the question?" Judge Iversen urged her.

Salander looked back at the judge and raised her eyebrows. Her voice was clear and distinct.

"Which question? Until now that man there"—she nodded towards Ekström—"has made a number of unverified statements. I haven't yet heard a question."

Giannini looked up. She propped her elbow on the table and leaned her chin on her hand with an interested expression.

Ekström lost his train of thought for a few seconds.

"Could you please repeat the question?" Judge Iversen said.

"I asked whether . . . you drove down to Advokat Bjurman's summer cabin in Stallarholmen with the intention of shooting Carl-Magnus Lundin."

"No. You said that you were going to try to bring clarity to how it happened that I drove down to Stallarholmen and shot Carl-Magnus Lundin. That was not a question. It was a general assertion in which you anticipated my answer. I'm not responsible for the assertions you are making."

"Don't quibble. Answer the question."

"No."

Silence.

"No what?"

"No is my answer to the question."

Prosecutor Ekström sighed. This was going to be a long day. Salander watched him expectantly.

"It might be best to take this from the beginning," he said. "Were you at the late Advokat Bjurman's summer cabin in Stallarholmen on the afternoon of April 6 this year?"

"Yes."

"How did you get there?"

"I went by shuttle train to Södertälje and took the Strängnäs bus."

"What was your reason for going to Stallarholmen? Had you arranged a meeting there with Carl-Magnus Lundin and his friend Sonny Nieminen?"

"No."

"How was it that they showed up there?"

"You'll have to ask them that."

"I'm asking you."

Salander did not reply.

Judge Iversen cleared his throat. "I presume that Fröken Salander is not answering because—purely semantically—you have once again made an assertion," the judge said helpfully.

Giannini suddenly snickered just loud enough to be heard. She pulled herself together at once and studied her papers again. Ekström gave her an irritated glance.

"Why do you think Lundin and Nieminen went to Bjurman's summer cabin?"

"I don't know. I suspect that they went there to commit arson. Lundin had half a gallon of gasoline in a plastic bottle in the saddlebag of his Harley-Davidson."

Ekström pursed his lips. "Why did you go to Advokat Bjurman's summer cabin?"

"I was looking for information."

"What sort of information?"

"The information that I suspect Lundin and Nieminen were there to destroy, and which could contribute to clarifying who murdered the bastard."

"Is it your opinion that Advokat Bjurman was a bastard? Is that correctly construed?"

"Yes."

"And why do you think that?"

"He was a sadistic pig, a pervert, and a rapist—and therefore a bastard."

She was quoting the text that had been tattooed on the late Advokat Bjurman's stomach and thus indirectly admitting that she was responsible for it. This incident, however, was not included in the charges against Salander. Bjurman had never filed a report of assault, and it would be impossible now to prove whether he had allowed himself to be tattooed or whether it had been done against his will.

"In other words, you are alleging that your guardian forced himself on you. Can you tell the court when these assaults are supposed to have taken place?"

"They took place on Tuesday, February 18, 2003, and again on Friday, March 7, of the same year."

"You have refused to answer every question asked by the police in their attempts to interview you. Why?"

"I had nothing to say to them."

"I have read the so-called autobiography that your lawyer delivered without warning a few days ago. I must say it is a strange document, and we'll come back to it in more detail later. But in it you claim that Advokat Bjurman allegedly forced you to perform oral sex on the first occasion, and on the second subjected you to an entire night of repeated rape and severe torture."

Lisbeth did not reply.

"Is that correct?"

"Yes."

"Did you report the rapes to the police?"

"No."

"Why not?"

"The police never listened before when I tried to tell them something. So there seemed no point in reporting anything to them then."

"Did you discuss these assaults with any of your acquaintances? A girlfriend?"

"No."

"Why not?"

"Because it's none of their business."

"Did you try to contact a lawyer?"

"No."

"Did you go to a doctor to be treated for the injuries you claim to have sustained?"

"No."

"And you didn't go to any women's crisis centre either."

"Now you're making an assertion again."

"Excuse me. Did you go to any women's crisis centre?"

"No."

Ekström turned to the judge. "I want to make the court aware that the defendant has stated that she was subjected to sexual assaults on two occasions, the second of which should be considered exceptionally severe. The person she claims committed these rapes was her guardian, the late Nils Bjurman. The following facts should be taken into account at this juncture." Ekström consulted the papers in front of him. "In the investigation carried out by the violent crimes division, there was nothing in Advokat Bjurman's past to support the credibility of Lisbeth Salander's account. Bjurman was never convicted of any crime. He has never been reported to the police or been the subject of an investigation. He had previously been a guardian or trustee to several other young people, none of whom have claimed that they were subjected to any sort of attack. On the contrary, they assert that Bjurman invariably behaved correctly and kindly towards them."

Ekström turned a page.

"It is also my duty to remind the court that Lisbeth Salander has been diagnosed as a paranoid schizophrenic. This is a young woman with a documented violent tendency, who since her early teens has had serious problems in her interactions with society. She spent several years in a children's psychiatric institution and has been under guardianship since the age of eighteen. However regrettable this may be, there are reasons for it. Lisbeth Salander is a danger to herself and to those around her. It is my conviction that she does not need a prison sentence. She needs psychiatric care."

He paused for effect.

"Discussing a young person's mental state is an innately disagreeable task. So much is an invasion of privacy, and her mental state becomes the subject of interpretation. In this case, however, we have Lisbeth Salander's own confused worldview on which to base our decision. It becomes manifestly clear in what she has termed her 'autobiography.' Nowhere is her want of a foothold in reality as evident as it is here. In this instance we need no witnesses or interpretations to invariably contradict one another. We have her own words. We can judge for ourselves the credibility of her assertions."

His gaze fell on Salander. Their eyes met. She smiled. She looked malicious. Ekström frowned.

"Does Advokat Giannini have anything to say?" Judge Iversen said.

"No," Giannini said. "Other than that Prosecutor Ekström's conclusions are nonsensical."

The afternoon session began with the cross-examining of witnesses. The first was Ulrika von Liebenstaahl from the guardianship agency. Ekström had called her to the stand to establish whether complaints had ever been lodged against Advokat Bjurman. This was strongly denied by von Liebenstaahl. Such assertions were defamatory.

"There exists a rigorous supervision of guardianship cases. Advokat Bjurman had been active on behalf of the guardianship agency for almost twenty years before he was so shockingly murdered."

She gave Salander a withering look, despite the fact that Salander was not accused of murder; it had already been established that Bjurman was murdered by Ronald Niedermann.

"In all these years there has not been a single complaint against Advokat Bjurman. He was a conscientious person who evidenced a deep commitment to his wards."

"So you don't think it's plausible that he would have subjected Lisbeth Salander to aggravated sexual assault?"

"I think that statement is ridiculous. We have monthly reports from Advokat Bjurman, and I personally met him on several occasions to go over the assignment."

"Advokat Giannini has presented a request that Lisbeth Salander's guardianship be rescinded, effective immediately."

"No-one is happier than we who work at the agency when a guardianship can be rescinded. Unfortunately, we have a responsibility, which means that we have to follow the appropriate regulations. For the agency's part, we are required in accordance with normal protocol to see to it that Lisbeth Salander is declared fit by a psychiatric expert before there can be any talk of changes to her legal status."

"I understand."

"This means that she has to submit to a psychiatric examination. Which, as everyone knows, she has refused to do."

The questioning of Ulrika von Liebenstaahl lasted for about forty minutes, during which time Bjurman's monthly reports were examined.

Giannini asked only one question before Ulrika von Liebenstaahl was dismissed.

"Were you in Advokat Bjurman's bedroom on the night of March 7, 2003?"

"Of course not."

"In other words, you haven't the faintest idea whether my client's statement is true or not?"

"The accusation against Advokat Bjurman is preposterous."

"That is your opinion. Can you give him an alibi or in any other way document that he did not assault my client?"

"That's impossible, naturally. But the probability—"

"Thank you. That will be all," Giannini said.

Blomkvist met his sister at Milton's offices near Slussen at around 7:00 to go through the day's proceedings.

"It was pretty much as expected," Giannini said. "Ekström has bought Salander's autobiography."

"Good. How's she holding up?"

Giannini laughed.

"She's holding up very well, coming across as a complete psychopath. She's merely being herself."

"Wonderful."

"Today has mostly been about what happened at the cabin in Stallarholmen. Tomorrow it'll be about Gosseberga, interrogations of people from forensics and so forth. Ekström is going to try to prove that Salander went down there intending to murder her father."

"Well . . ."

"But we may have a technical problem. This afternoon Ekström called Ulrika von Liebenstaahl from the guardianship agency. She started going on about how I had no right to represent Lisbeth."

"Why?"

"She says that Lisbeth is under guardianship and therefore isn't entitled to choose her own lawyer. So, technically, I may not be her lawyer if the guardianship agency hasn't rubber-stamped it."

"And?"

"Judge Iversen is going to decide tomorrow morning. I had a brief word with him after today's proceedings. I *think* he'll decide that I can continue to represent her. My point was that the agency has had three whole months to raise the objection—to show up with that kind of objection after proceedings have started is an unwarranted provocation."

"Teleborian will testify on Friday, I gather. You *have* to be the one who cross-examines him."

On Thursday Prosecutor Ekström explained to the court that after studying maps and photographs and listening to extensive technical conclusions about what had taken place in Gosseberga, he had determined that the evidence indicated that Salander had gone to her father's farmhouse in Gosseberga with the intention of killing him. The strongest link in the chain of evidence was that she had taken a weapon with her, a Polish P-83 Wanad.

The fact that Alexander Zalachenko (according to Salander's account) or possibly the cop killer Ronald Niedermann (according to testimony that Zalachenko had given before he was murdered at Sahlgrenska) had in turn attempted to kill Salander and bury her in a trench in woods nearby could in no way be held in mitigation of the fact that she had tracked down her father to Gosseberga with the express intention of killing him. Moreover, she had all but succeeded in that objective when she struck him in the face with an axe. Ekström demanded that Salander be convicted of attempted murder or premeditation with the intent to kill and, in that case, aggravated assault.

Salander's own account stated that she had gone to Gosseberga to confront her father, to persuade him to confess to the murders of Dag Svensson and Mia Johansson. This statement was of dramatic significance in the matter of establishing intent.

When Ekström had finished questioning the witness Melker Hansson from the technical unit of the Göteborg police, Advokat Giannini had asked some succinct questions.

"Herr Hansson, is there anything at all in your investigation or in all the technical documentation that you have compiled which could in any way establish that Lisbeth Salander is lying about her intent regarding the visit to Gosseberga? Can you prove that she went there with the intention of murdering her father?"

Hansson thought for a moment.

"No," he said at last.

"Do you have anything to say about her intent?"

"No."

"Prosecutor Ekström's conclusion, eloquent and extensive as it is, is therefore speculation?"

"I believe so."

"Is there anything in the forensic evidence that contradicts Lisbeth Salander's statement that she took with her the Polish weapon, a P-83 Wanad, by chance simply because it was in her bag, and she didn't know what she should do with the weapon, having taken it the day before from Sonny Nieminen in Stallarholmen?"

"No."

"Thank you," Giannini said and sat down. Those were her only words throughout Hansson's testimony, which had lasted one hour.

Wadensjöö left the Section's apartment on Artillerigatan at 6:00 on Thursday evening with a feeling that he was under ominous clouds of turmoil, of imminent ruin. For several weeks he had known that his title as director—that is, chief of the Section for Special Analysis—was but a meaningless label. His opinions, protests, and entreaties carried no weight. Clinton had taken over all decision-making. If the Section had been an open and public institution, this would not have been a problem—he would simply have gone to his superior and lodged his protests.

As things stood now, there was no-one he could protest to. He was alone and subject to the mercy or disfavour of a man whom he regarded as insane. And the worst of it was that Clinton's authority was absolute. Snot-nosed kids like Sandberg and faithful retainers like Nyström . . . they all seemed to jump to obey the fatally ill lunatic's every whim.

No question that Clinton was a soft-spoken authority who was not working for his own gain. He would even acknowledge that Clinton was working in the best interests of the Section, or at least in what he regarded as its best interests. The whole organization seemed to be in free fall, indulging in a collective fantasy in which experienced colleagues refused to admit that their every movement, every decision that was made and implemented, only led them one step closer to the abyss.

Wadensjöö felt a pressure in his chest as he turned onto Linnégatan, where he had found a parking spot earlier that day. He disabled the alarm and was about to open the car door when he heard a movement behind him. He turned around, squinting against the sun. It was a few seconds before he recognized the stately man on the sidewalk before him.

"Good evening, Herr Wadensjöö," Edklinth said. "I haven't been out in the field in ten years, but today I felt that my presence might be appropriate."

Wadensjöö looked in confusion at the two plain-clothes policemen flanking Edklinth. Bublanski he knew, but not the other man.

Suddenly he guessed what was going to happen.

"It is my unenviable duty to inform you that the prosecutor general has decided that you are to be arrested for such a long string of crimes that it will surely take weeks to compile a comprehensive catalogue of them."

"What's going on here?" Wadensjöö said indignantly.

"What is going on at this moment is that you are being arrested, suspected of being an accessory to murder. You are also suspected of extortion, bribery, illegal telephone tapping, several counts of criminal forgery, criminal embezzlement of funds, participation in breaking and entering, misuse of authority, espionage, and a long list of other lesser, but that's not to say insignificant, offences. The two of us are going to Kungsholmen to have a very serious talk in peace and quiet."

"I haven't committed murder," Wadensjöö said breathlessly.

"That will have to be established by the investigation."

"It was Clinton. It was always Clinton," Wadensjöö said.

Edklinth nodded in satisfaction.

Every police officer knows that there are two classic ways to conduct the interrogation of a suspect. The bad cop and the good cop. The bad cop threatens, swears, slams his fist on the table, and generally behaves aggressively with the intent of scaring the suspect into submission and confession. The good cop, often a small, grey-haired, elderly man, offers cigarettes and coffee, nods sympathetically, and speaks in a reasonable tone.

Many policemen—though not all—also know that the good cop's interrogation technique is by far a superior way to get results. The tough-as-nails veteran thief will be least impressed by the bad cop. And the uncertain amateur, who might be frightened into a confession by a bad cop, would in all likelihood have confessed everything anyway, regardless of the technique used.

Blomkvist listened to the questioning of Birger Wadensjöö from an adjoining room. His presence had been the topic of a good deal of internal argument before Edklinth decided that he would probably have use for Blomkvist's observation.

Blomkvist noticed that Edklinth was using a third variant on the police interrogator, the uninterested cop, which in this particular case seemed to be working even better. Edklinth strolled into the interrogation room, served coffee in china cups, turned on the tape recorder, and leaned back in his chair.

"This is how it is: we already have every conceivable forensic evidence against you. We have, accordingly, no interest whatsoever in hearing your story save as confirmation of what we already know. But the question we might want an answer to is: why? How could you be so idiotic as to decide to begin liquidating individuals in Sweden just as we saw happen in Chile under the Pinochet dictatorship? The tape is rolling. If you have anything to say, now is the time. If you don't want to talk, I'll turn off the tape recorder and then we'll remove your tie and shoelaces and accommodate you in a cell upstairs while we wait for a lawyer, a trial, and in due course, sentencing."

Edklinth then took a sip of coffee and sat in silence. When nothing was said for two minutes, he reached out and turned off the tape recorder. He stood up.

"I'll see that you're taken upstairs in a few minutes. Good evening."

"I didn't murder anyone," Wadensjöö said when Edklinth had already opened the door. Edklinth paused on the threshold.

"I'm not interested in having a general discussion with you. If you want to explain yourself, then I'll sit down and turn the tape recorder back on. All of Swedish officialdom— and the prime minister in particular—is eagerly waiting to hear what you have to say. If you tell me, then I can go and see the prime minister tonight to give him your version of events. If you don't tell me, you will be charged and convicted anyway."

"Please sit down," Wadensjöö said.

It was evident to everyone that he was resigned to his fate. Blomkvist exhaled. He was there with Figuerola, Prosecutor

Gustavsson, the otherwise anonymous Säpo officer Stefan, and two other altogether nameless individuals. Blomkvist suspected that one of them at least was there to represent the minister of justice.

"I had nothing to do with the murders," Wadensjöö said when Edklinth started the tape recorder again.

"*Murders?*" Blomkvist whispered to Figuerola.

"Ssshh," she said.

"It was Clinton and Gullberg. I had no idea what they intended. I swear. I was utterly shocked when I heard that Gullberg had shot Zalachenko. I couldn't believe it. . . . I simply couldn't believe it. And when I heard about Björck I thought I was going to have a heart attack."

"Tell me about Björck's murder," Edklinth said without altering his tone. "How was it carried out?"

"Clinton hired some people. I don't even know how it happened, but it was two Yugoslavs. Serbs, if I'm not mistaken. Georg Nyström gave them the contract and paid them afterwards. When I found out, I knew it would end in disaster."

"Should we take this from the beginning?" Edklinth said. "When did you first start working for the Section?"

Once Wadensjöö had begun to talk he could not be stopped. The interview lasted for almost five hours.

CHAPTER 26

Friday, July 15

Teleborian's appearance inspired confidence as he sat in the witness box in the courtroom on Friday morning. He was questioned by Prosecutor Ekström for some ninety minutes, and he replied with calm authority to every question. The expression on his face was sometimes concerned and sometimes amused.

"To sum up," Ekström said, leafing through his sheaf of papers, "it is your judgement as a psychiatrist of long standing that Lisbeth Salander suffers from paranoid schizophrenia?"

"I have said that it is unusually difficult to make a precise evaluation of her condition. The patient is, as you know, almost autistic in her relation to doctors and other figures of authority. My assessment is that she suffers from a serious mental disorder, but that at the present time I cannot give an exact diagnosis. Nor can I determine what stage of the psychosis she is in without more extensive study."

"At any rate, you don't consider her to be sane."

"Indeed her entire history presents most compelling proof that she is not."

"You have been allowed to read what Lisbeth Salander has termed her 'autobiography,' which she has presented to the district court. What are your comments on this?"

Teleborian threw up his hands and shrugged.

"How would you judge the credibility of her account?"

"There is no credibility. It is a series of assertions about various individuals, one story more fantastical than the other. Taken as a whole, her written explanation confirms our suspicions that she suffers from paranoid schizophrenia."

"Could you give an example?"

"The most obvious is of course the description of the alleged rape by her guardian Advokat Bjurman."

"Could you expand on that?"

"The description is extremely detailed. It is a classic example of the sort of grotesque fantasy that children are capable of. There are plenty of parallel examples from familial incest cases in which the child gives an account which falls through due to its utter improbability, and for which there is no forensic evidence. These are erotic fantasies which even children of a very young age can have . . . almost as if they were watching a horror film on television."

"But Lisbeth Salander is not a child; she is a grown woman," Ekström said.

"That is correct. Although it remains to be seen exactly what her mental level may be. But basically you are correct. She is a grown woman, and presumably she believes in the account she has presented."

"So you're saying it is all lies."

"No. If she believes what she says, then it is not a lie. It's a story which shows that she cannot distinguish fantasy from reality."

"So she was not raped by Advokat Bjurman?"

"No. There is no likelihood of that at all. She needs expert care."

"You yourself appear in Lisbeth Salander's account—"

"Yes, and that is rather intriguing. But once again, it's a figment of her imagination. If we are to believe the poor girl, then I'm something approximate to a paedophile." He smiled and continued. "But this is all just another expression of what I was speaking of before. In Salander's autobiography we are told that she was abused by being placed in restraints for long spells at St. Stefan's. And that I came to her room at night . . . This is a classic manifestation of her inability to interpret reality; or rather, she is giving reality her own interpretation."

"Thank you. I leave it to the defence, if Fru Giannini has any questions."

Since Giannini had not had many questions or objections during the first two days of the trial, those in the courtroom expected that she would once again ask some obligatory questions and then bring the questioning to an end. *This really is an embarrassingly deficient effort by the defence,* Ekström thought.

"Yes, I do," Giannini said. "I do in fact have a number of questions, and they may take some time. It's 11:30 now. May I propose that we break for lunch, and that I be allowed to carry out my cross-examination of the witness after lunch without interruption?"

Judge Iversen agreed that the court should adjourn for lunch.

· · ·

Andersson was accompanied by two uniformed officers when he placed his huge hand on Superintendent Nyström's shoulder outside the Mäster Anders restaurant on Hantverkargatan at noon precisely. Nyström looked up in amazement at the man who was shoving his police ID right under his nose.

"Hello. You're under arrest, suspected of being an accessory to murder and attempted murder. The charges will be explained to you by the prosecutor general at a hearing this afternoon. I suggest that you come along peacefully," he said.

Nyström did not seem to process what Andersson was saying, but he could see that he was a man you went along with without protest.

Inspector Bublanski was accompanied by Modig and seven uniformed officers when Stefan Bladh of the Constitutional Protection Unit admitted them at exactly noon into the locked section that comprised the domain of the Security Police at Kungsholmen. They walked through the halls behind Bladh until he stopped and pointed at an office door. The chief of Secretariat's assistant looked up and was utterly perplexed when Bublanski held up his ID.

"Kindly remain where you are. This is a police action."

He strode to the inner door. Chief of Secretariat Albert Shenke was on the phone.

"What is this interruption?" Shenke said.

"I am Criminal Inspector Jan Bublanski. You are under arrest for violation of the Swedish constitution. There is a long list of specific points in the charge, all of which will be explained to you this afternoon."

"This is outrageous," Shenke said.

"It most certainly is," Bublanski said.

He had Shenke's office sealed and then placed two officers on guard outside the door, with instructions to let no-one cross the threshold. They had permission to use their batons and even draw their service weapons if anyone tried to enter the sealed office by force.

They continued their procession down the hall until Bladh pointed to another door, and the procedure was repeated with Chief of Budget Gustav Atterbom.

Inspector Holmberg had the Södermalm armed response team as backup when at exactly noon he knocked on the door of an office rented temporarily on the fourth floor just across the street from *Millennium*'s offices on Götgatan.

Since no-one opened the door, Holmberg ordered the Södermalm police to force the lock, but the door was opened a crack before the crowbar was used.

"Police," Holmberg said. "Come out with your hands up."

"I'm a policeman myself," Inspector Mårtensson said.

"I know. And you have licences for a great many guns."

"Yes, well . . . I'm on assignment."

"I think not," Holmberg said.

He accepted the assistance of his colleagues in placing Mårtensson against the wall so he could confiscate his service weapon.

"You are under arrest for illegal telephone tapping, gross dereliction of duty, repeated break-ins at Mikael Blomkvist's apartment on Bellmansgatan, and additional counts. Handcuff him."

Holmberg took a swift look around the room and saw that

there was enough electronic equipment to furnish a recording studio. He detailed an officer to guard the premises, but told him to sit still on a chair so he would not leave any fingerprints.

As Mårtensson was being led through the front door of the building, Cortez took a series of twenty-two photographs with his Nikon. He was, of course, no professional photographer, and the quality left something to be desired. But the best images were sold the next day to an evening newspaper for an obscene sum of money.

Figuerola was the only police officer participating in the day's raids who encountered an unexpected incident. She had backup from the Norrmalm team and three colleagues from SIS when at noon she walked through the front door of the building on Artillerigatan and went up the stairs to the top-floor apartment, registered in the name of Bellona Inc.

The operation had been planned on short notice. As soon as the group was assembled outside the door of the apartment, she gave the go-ahead. Two burly officers from the Norrmalm team raised an eighty-five-pound steel battering ram and opened the door with two well-aimed blows. The team, equipped with bulletproof vests and assault rifles, took control of the apartment within ten seconds of the door's being forced.

According to surveillance carried out at dawn, five individuals identified as members of the Section had arrived at the apartment that morning. All five were apprehended and put in handcuffs.

Figuerola was wearing a bulletproof vest. She went through the apartment, which had been the headquarters of the Section since the sixties, and flung open one door after another. She was going to need an archaeologist to sort through the reams and reams of paper that filled the rooms.

A few seconds after she entered the apartment, she opened the door to a small room towards the back and discovered that it was used for overnight stays. She found herself eye to eye with Jonas Sandberg. He had been a question mark during that morning's assignment of tasks, as the surveillance officer detailed to watch him had lost track of him the evening before. His car had been parked on Kungsholmen and he had not been home to his apartment during the night. This morning they had not expected to locate and apprehend him.

They man the place at night for security reasons. Of course. And Sandberg sleeps over after the night shift.

Sandberg had on only his underpants and seemed to be dazed with sleep. He reached for his service weapon on the bedside table, but Figuerola bent over and swept the weapon away from him onto the floor.

"Jonas Sandberg, you are under arrest as a suspect and accessory to the murders of Gunnar Björck and Alexander Zalachenko, and as an accomplice in the attempted murders of Mikael Blomkvist and Erika Berger. Now get your trousers on."

Sandberg threw a punch at Figuerola. She blocked it instinctively.

"You must be joking," she said. She took hold of his arm and twisted his wrist so hard that he was forced backwards to the floor. She flipped him over onto his stomach and put her knee in the small of his back. She handcuffed him herself. It was the first time she had used handcuffs on an assignment since she began at SIS.

She handed Sandberg over to one of the backup team and continued her passage through the apartment until she opened the last door, at the very back. According to the blueprints, this was a small cubbyhole looking out onto the courtyard. She stopped in the doorway and looked at the most emaciated figure she had ever seen. She did not for one second doubt that here was a person who was mortally ill.

"Fredrik Clinton, you are under arrest as an accomplice to murder, for attempted murder, and for a long list of further crimes," she said. "Stay where you are in bed. We've called an ambulance to take you to Kungsholmen."

Malm was stationed immediately outside the building on Artillerigatan. Unlike Cortez, he knew how to handle his digital Nikon. He used a short telephoto lens, and the pictures he took were of excellent quality.

They showed the members of the Section, one by one, being led out through the front door and down to the police cars. And finally the ambulance that arrived to pick up Clinton. His eyes were fixed on the lens as the shutter clicked. Clinton looked nervous and confused.

The photograph later won the Picture of the Year award.

CHAPTER 27

Friday, July 15

Judge Iversen banged his gavel at 12:30 and decreed that district court proceedings were thereby resumed. He noticed that a third person had appeared at Advokat Giannini's table. It was Holger Palmgren, in a wheelchair.

"Hello, Holger," Judge Iversen said. "I haven't seen you in a courtroom in quite a while."

"Good day to you, Judge Iversen. Some cases are so complicated that these younger lawyers need a little assistance."

"I thought you had retired."

"I've been ill. But Advokat Giannini engaged me as assistant counsel in this case."

"I see."

Giannini cleared her throat.

"It is germane to the case that Advokat Palmgren was until his illness Lisbeth Salander's guardian."

"I have no intention of commenting on that matter," Judge Iversen said.

He nodded to Giannini to begin, and she stood up. She had always disliked the Swedish tradition of carrying on court proceedings informally while sitting around a table, almost as though the occasion were a dinner party. She felt better when she could speak standing up.

"I think we should begin with the concluding comments from this morning. Dr. Teleborian, what leads you so consistently to dismiss as untrue everything that Lisbeth Salander says?"

"Because her statements so obviously *are* untrue," replied Teleborian.

He was relaxed. Giannini turned to the judge.

"Judge Iversen, Dr. Teleborian claims that Lisbeth Salander tells lies and that she fantasizes. The defence will now demonstrate that every word in her autobiography is true. We will present copious documentation, both visual and written, as well as the testimony of witnesses. We have now reached the point in this trial when the prosecutor has presented the principal elements of his case. We have listened, and we now know the exact nature of the accusations against Lisbeth Salander."

Giannini's mouth was suddenly dry, and she felt her hands shake. She took a deep breath and sipped her mineral water. Then she placed her hands in a firm grip on the back of the chair so that they would not betray her nervousness.

"From the prosecutor's presentation we may conclude that he has a great many opinions but a woeful shortage of evidence. He *believes* that Lisbeth Salander shot Carl-Magnus Lundin in Stallarholmen. He *claims* that she went to Gosseberga to kill her father. He *assumes* that my client is a paranoid schizophrenic and mentally ill in every sense. And he *bases* this assumption on information from a single source: to wit, Dr. Peter Teleborian."

She paused to catch her breath and forced herself to speak slowly.

"As it now stands, the case presented by the prosecutor rests on the testimony of Dr. Teleborian. If he is right, then my client would be best served by receiving the expert psychiatric care that both he and the prosecutor are seeking."

Pause.

"But if Dr. Teleborian is wrong, this prosecution case must be seen in a different light. Furthermore, if he is lying, then my client is now, here in this courtroom, being subjected to a violation of her civil rights, a violation that has gone on for many years."

She turned to face Ekström.

"What we shall do this afternoon is to show that your witness is a false witness, and that you as prosecutor have been deceived into accepting these false testimonies."

Teleborian flashed a smile. He held out his hands and nodded to Giannini, as if applauding her presentation. Giannini now turned to the judge.

"Your honour. I will show that Dr. Teleborian's so-called forensic psychiatric investigation is nothing but a deception from start to finish. I will show that he is lying about Lisbeth Salander. I will show that my client has in the past been subjected to a gross violation of her rights. And I will show that she is just as sane and intelligent as anyone in this room."

"Excuse me, but—" Ekström began.

"Just a moment." She raised a finger. "I have for two days allowed you to talk uninterrupted. Now it's my turn."

She turned back to Judge Iversen.

"I would not make so serious an accusation before the court if I did not have ample evidence to support it."

"By all means, continue," the judge said. "But I don't want to hear any long-winded conspiracy theories. Bear in mind that you can be charged with slander for false statements that are made before a court."

"Thank you. I will bear that in mind."

She turned to Teleborian. He still seemed entertained by the situation.

"The defence has repeatedly asked to be allowed to examine Lisbeth Salander's medical records from the time when she, in her early teens, was committed to your care at St. Stefan's. Why have we not been shown those records?"

"Because a district court decreed that they were classified. That decision was made out of solicitude for Lisbeth Salander, but if a higher court were to rescind that decision, I would naturally hand them over."

"Thank you. For how many nights during the two years that Lisbeth Salander spent at St. Stefan's was she kept in restraints?"

"I couldn't recall that offhand."

"She herself claims that it was 380 out of the total of 786 days and nights she spent at St. Stefan's."

"I can't possibly answer as to the exact number of days, but that is a fantastic exaggeration. Where do those figures come from?"

"From her autobiography."

"And you believe that today she is able to remember accurately each night she was kept in restraints? That's preposterous."

"Is it? How many nights do you recall?"

"Lisbeth Salander was an extremely aggressive and

violence-prone patient, and undoubtedly she was placed in a stimulus-free room on a number of occasions. Perhaps I should explain the purpose of a stimulus-free room—"

"Thank you, that won't be necessary. According to theory, it is a room in which a patient is denied any sensory input that might provoke agitation. For how many days and nights did thirteen-year-old Lisbeth Salander lie strapped down in such a room?"

"It would be . . . I would estimate perhaps on 30 occasions during the time she was at the hospital."

"Thirty. Now that's only a fraction of the 380 that she claims."

"Undeniably."

"Not even 10 percent of her figure."

"Yes . . ."

"Would her medical records perhaps give us more accurate information?"

"It's possible."

"Excellent," Giannini said, taking out a large sheaf of paper from her briefcase. "Then I ask to be allowed to hand over to the court a copy of Lisbeth Salander's medical records from St. Stefan's. I have counted the number of notes about the restraining straps and find that the figure is 381, one more than my client claims."

Teleborian's eyes widened.

"Stop . . . this is classified information. Where did you get that from?"

"I got it from a reporter at *Millennium* magazine. It can hardly be classified if it's lying around a newspaper's offices. Perhaps I should add that extracts from these medical records were published today in *Millennium*. I believe, therefore, that even this district court should have the opportunity to look at the records themselves."

"This is illegal—"

"No, it isn't. Lisbeth Salander has given her permission for the extracts to be published. My client has nothing to hide."

"Your client has been declared incompetent and has no right to make any such decision for herself."

"We'll come back to the declaration of incompetence. But first we need to examine what happened to her at St. Stefan's."

Judge Iversen frowned as he accepted the papers that Giannini handed to him.

"I haven't made a copy for the prosecutor; he received a copy of this privacy-invading document more than a month ago."

"How did that happen?" the judge said.

"Prosecutor Ekström got a copy of these classified records from Teleborian at a meeting which took place in his office at 5:00 p.m. on Saturday, June 4, this year."

"Is that correct?" Judge Iversen said.

Ekström's first impulse was to deny it. Then he realized that Giannini might somehow have evidence.

"I requested permission to read parts of the records if I signed a confidentiality agreement," Ekström said. "I had to make sure that Salander had the history she was alleged to have."

"Thank you," Giannini said. "This means that we now have confirmation that Dr. Teleborian not only tells lies but also broke the law by disseminating records that he himself claims are classified."

"Duly noted," said the judge.

. . .

Judge Iversen was suddenly very alert. In a most unorthodox way, Giannini had launched a serious attack on a witness, and she had already made mincemeat of an important part of his testimony. *And she claims that she can document everything she says.* Judge Iversen adjusted his glasses.

"Dr. Teleborian, based on these records which you yourself wrote, could you now tell me how many days Lisbeth Salander was kept in restraints?"

"I have no recollection that it could have been so extensive, but if that's what the records say, then I have to believe it."

"A total of 381 days and nights. Does that not strike you as excessive?"

"It is unusual, yes."

"How would you perceive it if you were thirteen years old and someone strapped you to a steel-framed bed for more than a year? Would it feel like torture?"

"You have to understand that the patient was dangerous to herself as well as to others—"

"OK. Let's look at whether she was dangerous to herself. Has Lisbeth Salander ever injured herself?"

"There were such misgivings—"

"I'll repeat the question: has Lisbeth Salander ever injured herself? Yes or no?"

"As psychiatrists we must teach ourselves to interpret the overall picture. With regard to Lisbeth Salander, you can see on her body, for example, a multitude of tattoos and piercings, which are a form of self-destructive behaviour and a way of damaging one's own body. We can interpret that as a manifestation of self-hate."

Giannini turned to Salander.

"Are your tattoos a manifestation of self-hate?" she said.

"No," Salander said.

Giannini turned back to Teleborian. "So you believe that I am also dangerous to myself because I wear earrings and actually have a tattoo in a private place?"

Palmgren snickered, but he managed to transform the snicker into a clearing of his throat.

"No, not at all . . . tattoos can also be part of a social ritual."

"Are you saying that Lisbeth Salander is not part of this social ritual?"

"You can see for yourself that her tattoos are grotesque and extend over large parts of her body. That is no normal measure of fetishism or body decoration."

"What percentage?"

"Excuse me?"

"At what percentage of tattooed body surface does it stop being fetishism and become a mental illness?"

"You're distorting my words."

"Am I? How is it that, in your opinion, it is part of a wholly acceptable social ritual when it applies to me or to other young people, but it becomes dangerous when it's a matter of evaluating my client's mental state?"

"As a psychiatrist I have to look at the whole picture. The tattoos are merely an indicator. As I have already said, it is one of many indicators which need to be taken into account when I evaluate her condition."

Giannini was silent for a few seconds as she fixed Teleborian with her gaze. She now spoke very slowly.

"But Dr. Teleborian, you began strapping down my client

when she was twelve years old, going on thirteen. At that time she did not have a single tattoo, did she?"

Teleborian hesitated, and Giannini went on.

"I presume that you did not strap her down because you predicted that she would begin tattooing herself sometime in the future."

"Of course not. Her tattoos had nothing to do with her condition in 1991."

"With that we are back to my original question. Did Lisbeth Salander ever injure herself in a way that would justify keeping her bound to a bed for a whole year? For example, did she cut herself with a knife or a razor blade or anything like that?"

Teleborian looked unsure for a second.

"No ... I used the tattoos as an *example* of self-destructive behaviour."

"And we have just agreed that tattoos are a legitimate part of a social ritual. I asked why you restrained her for a year, and you replied that it was because she was a danger to herself."

"We had reason to believe that she was a danger to herself."

"'Reason to believe.' So you're saying that you restrained her because you guessed something?"

"We carried out assessments."

"I have now been asking the same question for about five minutes. You claim that my client's self-destructive behaviour was one reason why she was strapped down for a total of more than a year out of the two years she was in your care. Can you please finally give me some examples of the self-destructive behaviour she evidenced at the age of twelve?"

"The girl was extremely undernourished, for example. This was partially due to the fact that she refused food. We suspected anorexia."

"I see. Was she anorexic? As you can see, my client is even today uncommonly thin and fine-boned."

"Well, it's difficult to answer that question. I would have to observe her eating habits for quite a long time."

"You did observe her eating habits—for two years. And now you're suggesting that you confused anorexia with the fact that my client is small and thin. You say that she refused food."

"We were compelled to force-feed her on several occasions."

"And why was that?"

"Because she refused to eat, of course."

Giannini turned to her client.

"Lisbeth, is it true that you refused to eat at St. Stefan's?"

"Yes."

"And why was that?"

"Because that bastard was mixing psychotropic drugs into my food."

"I see. So Dr. Teleborian wanted to give you medicine. Why didn't you want to take it?"

"I didn't like the medicine I was being given. It made me sluggish. I couldn't think, and I was sedated for most of the time I was awake. And the bastard refused to tell me what the drugs contained."

"So you refused to take the medicine?"

"Yes. Then he began putting the crap in my food instead.

So I stopped eating. Every time something had been put in my food, I stopped eating for five days."

"So you had to go hungry."

"Not always. Several of the attendants smuggled sandwiches in to me on various occasions. One in particular gave me food late at night. That happened quite often."

"So you think that the nursing staff at St. Stefan's saw that you were hungry and gave you food so that you would not have to starve?"

"That was during the period when I was battling with this bastard over psychotropic drugs."

"Tell us what happened."

"He tried to drug me. I refused to take his medicine. He started putting it in my food. I refused to eat. He started force-feeding me. I began vomiting up the food."

"So there was a completely rational reason why you refused the food."

"Yes."

"It was not because you didn't want food?"

"No. I was often hungry."

"And since you left St. Stefan's, do you eat regularly?"

"I eat when I'm hungry."

"Would it be correct to say that a conflict arose between you and Dr. Teleborian?"

"You could say that."

"You were sent to St. Stefan's because you had thrown gasoline at your father and set him on fire."

"Yes."

"Why did you do that?"

"Because he abused my mother."

"Did you ever explain that to anyone?"

"Yes."

"And who was that?"

"I told the police who interviewed me, the social workers, the doctors, a pastor, and that bastard."

"By 'that bastard' you are referring to . . . ?"

"That man." She pointed at Dr. Teleborian.

"Why do you call him a bastard?"

"When I first arrived at St. Stefan's I tried to explain to him what had happened."

"And what did Dr. Teleborian say?"

"He didn't want to listen to me. He claimed that I was fantasizing. And as punishment I was to be strapped down until I stopped fantasizing. And then he tried to force-feed me psychotropic drugs."

"This is nonsense," Teleborian said.

"Is that why you won't speak to him?"

"I haven't said a word to the bastard since the night I turned thirteen. I was strapped to the bed. It was my birthday present to myself."

Giannini turned to Teleborian. "This sounds as if the reason my client refused to eat was that she did not want the psychotropic drugs you were forcing upon her."

"It's possible that she views it that way."

"And how do you view it?"

"I had a patient who was abnormally difficult. I maintain that her behaviour showed that she was a danger to herself, but this might be a question of interpretation. However, she was violent and exhibited psychotic behaviour. There is no doubt that she was dangerous to others. She came to St. Stefan's after she tried to murder her father."

"We'll get to that later. For 381 of those days you kept her in restraints. Could it have been that you used strapping as a way to punish my client when she didn't do as you said?"

"That is utter nonsense."

"Is it? I notice that according to the records the majority of the strapping occurred during the first year . . . 320 of 381 instances. Why was the strapping discontinued?"

"I suppose the patient changed her behaviour and became less agitated."

"Is it not true that your measures were considered unnecessarily brutal by other members of the staff?"

"How do you mean?"

"Is it not true that the staff lodged complaints against the force-feeding of Lisbeth Salander, among other things?"

"Inevitably people will arrive at differing evaluations. This is nothing unusual. But it became a burden to force-feed her because she resisted so violently—"

"Because she refused to take psychotropic drugs which made her listless and passive. She had no problem eating when she was not being drugged. Wouldn't that have been a more reasonable method of treatment than resorting to forcible measures?"

"If you don't mind my saying so, Fru Giannini, I am actually a physician. I suspect that my medical expertise is rather more extensive than yours. It is my job to determine what medical treatments should be employed."

"It's true, I'm not a physician, *Doctor* Teleborian. However, I am not entirely lacking in expertise. Besides my qualifications as a lawyer I was also trained as a psychologist at Stockholm University. This is necessary background training in my profession."

You could have heard a pin drop in the courtroom. Both

Ekström and Teleborian stared in astonishment at Giannini. She continued inexorably.

"Is it not correct that your methods of treating my client eventually resulted in serious disagreements between you and your superior, Dr. Johannes Caldin, head physician at the time?"

"No, that is not correct."

"Dr. Caldin passed away several years ago and cannot give testimony. But here in court we have someone who met Dr. Caldin on several occasions. Namely, my assistant counsel, Holger Palmgren."

She turned to him.

"Can you tell us how that came about?"

Palmgren cleared his throat. He still suffered from the after-effects of his stroke and had to concentrate to pronounce the words.

"I was appointed as trustee for Lisbeth Salander after her mother was so severely beaten by Lisbeth's father that she was disabled and could no longer take care of her daughters. She suffered permanent brain damage and repeated brain haemorrhages."

"You're speaking of Alexander Zalachenko, I presume." Ekström was leaning forward attentively.

"That's correct," Palmgren said.

Ekström said: "I would ask you to remember that we are now on a subject which is highly classified."

"It's hardly a secret that Alexander Zalachenko persistently abused Lisbeth's mother," Giannini said.

Teleborian raised his hand.

"The matter is probably not quite as self-evident as Fru Giannini is presenting it."

"What do you mean by that?" Giannini said.

"There is no doubt that Lisbeth Salander witnessed a family tragedy . . . that something triggered a serious beating in 1991. But there is no documentation to suggest that this was a situation that went on for many years, as Fru Giannini claims. It could have been an isolated incident or a quarrel that got out of hand. If truth be told, there is not even any documentation to point towards Herr Zalachenko as Lisbeth's mother's aggressor. We have been informed that she was a prostitute, so there could have been a number of other possible perpetrators."

Giannini looked in astonishment at Teleborian. She seemed to be speechless for a moment. Then her eyes bored into him.

"Could you expand on that?" she said.

"What I mean is that in practice we have only Lisbeth Salander's assertions to go on."

"And?"

"First of all, there were two sisters. Twins, in fact. Camilla Salander has never made any such claims; indeed, she has denied that such a thing occurred. And if there was abuse to the extent your client maintains, then it would naturally have been noted in social welfare reports and so forth."

"Is there an interview with Camilla Salander that we might examine?"

"Interview?"

"Do you have any documentation to show that Camilla Salander was even asked about what occurred at their home?"

Salander squirmed in her seat at the mention of her sister. She glanced at Giannini.

"I presume that the social welfare agency filed a report—"

"You have just stated that Camilla Salander never made any assertions that Alexander Zalachenko abused their mother, that on the contrary she denied it. That was a categorical statement. Where did you get that information?"

Teleborian sat in silence for several seconds. Giannini could see his eyes change when he realized he had made a mistake. He could anticipate what it was that she wanted to introduce, but there was no way to avoid the question.

"I seem to remember that it appeared in the police report," he said at last.

"You 'seem to remember.' I myself have searched high and low for police reports about the incident on Lundagatan during which Alexander Zalachenko was severely burned. The only ones available are the brief reports written by the officers at the scene."

"That's possible—"

"So I would very much like to know how it is that you were able to read a police report that is not available to the defence."

"I can't answer that," Teleborian said. "I was shown the report in 1991 when I wrote a forensic psychiatric report on your client after the attempted murder of her father."

"Was Prosecutor Ekström shown this report?"

Ekström squirmed. He stroked his goatee. By now he knew that he had underestimated Advokat Giannini. However, he had no reason to lie.

"Yes, I've seen it."

"Why wasn't the defence given access to this material?"

"I didn't consider it of interest to the trial."

"Could you please tell me how you were allowed to see

this report? When I asked the police, I was told only that no such report exists."

"The report was written by the Security Police. It's classified."

"So Säpo wrote a report on a case involving aggravated assault on a woman and decided to make the report classified."

"It was because of the perpetrator, Alexander Zalachenko. He was a political refugee."

"Who wrote the report?"

Silence.

"I don't hear anything. What name was on the title page?"

"It was written by Gunnar Björck from the immigration division of SIS."

"Thank you. Is that the same Gunnar Björck who my client claims worked with *Doctor* Teleborian to fabricate the forensic psychiatric report about her in 1991?"

"I assume it is."

Giannini turned her attention back to Teleborian.

"In 1991 you committed Lisbeth Salander to the secure ward of St. Stefan's children's psychiatric clinic—"

"That's not correct."

"Is it not?"

"No. Lisbeth Salander was *sentenced* to the secure psychiatric ward. This was the outcome of an entirely routine legal action in a district court. We're talking about a seriously disturbed minor. That was not my own decision—"

"In 1991 a district court decided to lock up Lisbeth Salander in a children's psychiatric clinic. Why did the district court make that decision?"

"The district court made a careful assessment of your

client's actions and mental condition—she had tried to murder her father with a gasoline bomb, after all. This is not an activity that a normal teenager would engage in, whether they are tattooed or not." Teleborian gave her a polite smile.

"And what did the district court base their judgement on? If I've understood correctly, they had only one forensic medical assessment to go on. It was written by yourself and a policeman by the name of Gunnar Björck."

"This is about Fröken Salander's conspiracy theories, Fru Giannini. Here I would have to—"

"Excuse me, but I haven't asked a question yet," Giannini said and turned once again to Palmgren. "Holger, we were talking about your meeting Dr. Teleborian's superior, Dr. Caldin."

"Yes. In my capacity as trustee for Lisbeth Salander. At that stage I had met her only very briefly. Like everyone else, I got the impression that she had a serious mental illness. But since it was my job, I undertook to research her general state of health."

"And what did Dr. Caldin say?"

"She was Dr. Teleborian's patient, and Dr. Caldin had not paid her any particular attention except in routine assessments and the like. It wasn't until she had been there for more than a year that I began to discuss how she could be rehabilitated back into society. I suggested a foster family. I don't know exactly what went on internally at St. Stefan's, but after about a year Dr. Caldin began to take an interest in her."

"How did that manifest itself?"

"I discovered that he had arrived at an opinion that differed from Dr. Teleborian's," Palmgren said. "He told me once that he had decided to change the type of care she was receiving. I did not understand until later that he was referring to the strap restraints. Dr. Caldin had decided that she should not be restrained. He didn't think there was any reason for it."

"So he went against Dr. Teleborian's directives?"

Ekström interrupted. "Objection. That's hearsay."

"No," Palmgren said. "Not entirely. I asked for a report on how Lisbeth Salander was supposed to re-enter society. Dr. Caldin wrote that report. I still have it today."

He handed a document to Giannini.

"Can you tell us what it says?"

"It's a letter from Dr. Caldin to me dated October 1992, which is when Lisbeth had been at St. Stefan's for nineteen months. Here Dr. Caldin expressly writes, I quote, 'My decision for the patient not to be restrained or force-fed has also produced the noticeable effect that she is now calm. There is no need for psychotropic drugs. However, the patient is extremely withdrawn and uncommunicative and needs continued supportive therapies.' End quote."

"So he *expressly writes* that it *was* his decision," Giannini said.

"That is correct. It was also Dr. Caldin himself who decided that Lisbeth should be able to re-enter society by being placed with a foster family."

Salander nodded. She remembered Dr. Caldin the same way she remembered every detail of her stay at St. Stefan's. She had refused to talk to Dr. Caldin. He was a "crazy-doctor," another man in a white coat who wanted to root around in her emotions. But he had been friendly and good-natured. She had sat in his office and listened to him when he explained things to her.

He had seemed hurt when she did not want to speak to him. Finally she had looked him in the eye and explained her decision: *I will never ever talk to you or any other crazy-doctor. None of you listen to what I have to say. You can keep me locked up here until I die. That won't change a thing. I won't talk to any of you.* He had looked at her with surprise and hurt in his eyes. Then he had nodded as if he understood.

"Dr. Teleborian," Giannini said, "we have established that you had Lisbeth Salander committed to a children's psychiatric clinic. You were the one who furnished the district court with the report, and this report constituted the only basis for the decisions that were made. Is this correct?"

"That is essentially correct. But I think—"

"You'll have plenty of time to explain what you think. When Lisbeth Salander was about to turn eighteen, you once again interfered in her life and tried to have her locked up in a clinic."

"This time I wasn't the one who wrote the forensic medical report—"

"No, it was written by Dr. Jesper H. Löderman, a doctoral candidate at that time. And you just happened to be his supervisor. So it was your assessments that caused the report to be approved."

"There's nothing unethical or incorrect in these reports. They were done according to the proper regulations of my profession."

"Now Lisbeth Salander is twenty-seven years old, and for the third time we are in a situation in which you are trying to convince a district court that she is mentally ill and must be committed to a secure psychiatric ward."

· · ·

Teleborian took a deep breath. Giannini was well prepared. She had surprised him with a number of tricky questions, and she had succeeded in distorting his replies. She had not fallen for his charms, and she completely ignored his authority. He was used to having people nod in agreement when he spoke.

How much does she know?

He glanced at Prosecutor Ekström but realized that he could expect no help from that quarter. He had to ride out the storm alone.

He reminded himself that, in spite of everything, he *was* an authority.

It doesn't matter what she says. It's my assessment that counts.

Giannini picked up his forensic psychiatric report.

"Let's take a closer look at your latest report. You expend a great deal of energy analysing Lisbeth Salander's emotional life. A large part deals with your interpretation of her personality, her behaviour, and her sexual habits."

"In this report I have attempted to give a complete picture."

"Good. And based on this complete picture you came to the conclusion that Lisbeth suffers from paranoid schizophrenia."

"I prefer not to restrict myself to a precise diagnosis."

"But you have not reached this conclusion through conversations with my client, have you?"

"You know very well that your client resolutely refuses to answer questions that I or any other person in authority might put to her. This behaviour is in itself particularly telling. One can conclude that the patient's paranoid traits have progressed to such an extent that she is literally incapable of having a simple conversation with anyone in authority. She believes that everyone is out to harm her and feels so threatened that she shuts herself inside an impenetrable shell and goes mute."

"I notice that you're expressing yourself very carefully. You say, for example, that one *can* conclude—"

"Yes, that's right. I *am* expressing myself carefully. Psychiatry is not an exact science, and I must be careful with my conclusions. At the same time, it is not true that we psychiatrists sit around making assumptions that have no basis in fact."

"What you are being very precise about is protecting yourself. The literal fact is that you have not exchanged one single word with my client since the night of her thirteenth birthday because she has refused to talk to you."

"Not only to me. She appears unable to have a conversation with any psychiatrist."

"This means that, as you write here, your conclusions are based on 'experience' and on 'observations' of my client."

"That's right."

"What can you learn by studying a girl who sits on a chair with her arms crossed and refuses to talk to you?"

Teleborian sighed as though he thought it was irksome to have to explain the obvious. He smiled.

"From a patient who sits and says nothing, you can learn only that this is a patient who is good at sitting and saying nothing. Even this is disturbed behaviour, but that's not what I'm basing my conclusions on."

"Later this afternoon I will call upon another psychiatrist. His name is Svante Brandén, and he's senior physician at the

Institute of Forensic Medicine and a specialist in forensic psychiatry. Do you know him?"

Teleborian felt confident again. He had expected Giannini to call upon another psychiatrist to question his own conclusions. It was a situation for which he was ready, and in which he would be able to dismiss every objection without difficulty. Indeed, it would be easier to handle an academic colleague in a friendly debate than someone like Advokat Giannini, who had no inhibitions and was bent on distorting his words. He smiled.

"He is a highly respected and skilled forensic psychiatrist. But you must understand, Fru Giannini, that producing a report of this type is an academic and scientific process. You may disagree with my conclusions, and another psychiatrist may interpret an action or an event in a different way. You may have dissimilar points of view, or perhaps it would be a question purely of how well one doctor or another knows the patient. He might arrive at a very different conclusion about Lisbeth Salander. That is not at all unusual in psychiatry."

"That's not why I'm calling him. He has not met or examined Lisbeth Salander, and he will not be making any evaluations about her mental condition."

"Oh, is that so?"

"I have asked him to read your report and all the documentation you have produced on Lisbeth Salander and to look at her medical records from St. Stefan's. I have asked him to make an assessment, not about the state of my client's health, but about whether, from a purely scientific point of view, there is adequate foundation for your conclusions in the material you recorded."

Teleborian shrugged.

"With all due respect, I think I have a better understanding of Lisbeth Salander than any other psychiatrist in the country. I have followed her development since she was twelve, and regrettably my conclusions were always confirmed by her actions."

"Very well," Giannini said. "Then we'll take a look at your conclusions. In your statement you write that her treatment was interrupted when she was placed with a foster family at the age of fifteen."

"That's correct. It was a serious mistake. If we had been allowed to complete the treatment we might not be here in this courtroom today."

"You mean that if you had had the opportunity to keep her in restraints for another year she might have become more tractable?"

"That is unfair."

"I do beg your pardon. You cite extensively the report that your doctoral candidate Jesper Löderman put together when Lisbeth Salander was about to turn eighteen. You write that, quote, 'Her self-destructive and antisocial behaviour is confirmed by drug abuse and the promiscuity which she has exhibited since she was discharged from St. Stefan's,' unquote. What did you mean by this statement?"

Teleborian sat in silence for several seconds.

"Well . . . now I'll have to go back a bit. After Lisbeth Salander was discharged from St. Stefan's she developed, as I had predicted, problems with alcohol and drug abuse. She was repeatedly arrested by the police. A social welfare report also determined that she had had profligate sexual relations with older men and that she was very probably involved in prostitution."

"Let's analyse this. You say that she abused alcohol. How often was she intoxicated?"

"I'm sorry?"

"Was she drunk every day from when she was released until she turned eighteen? Was she drunk once a week?"

"Naturally, I can't answer that."

"But you have just stated that she had problems with alcohol abuse."

"She was a minor and arrested repeatedly by the police for drunkenness."

"That's the second time you have said that she was arrested repeatedly. How often did this occur? Was it once a week or once every other week?"

"It's not a matter of so many individual occasions. . . ."

"Lisbeth Salander was arrested on two occasions for drunkenness when she was seventeen. She was so blind drunk that she was taken to the hospital. These are the 'repeated arrests' you refer to. Was she intoxicated on more than these occasions?"

"I don't know, but one might fear that her behaviour was—"

"Excuse me, did I hear you correctly? You *do not know* whether she was intoxicated on more than two occasions during her teenage years, but you *fear* that this was the case. And yet you write reports maintaining that Lisbeth Salander was engaged in repeated alcohol and drug abuse?"

"That is the social service's information, not mine. It has to do with Lisbeth Salander's whole lifestyle. Not surprisingly, her prognosis was dismal after her treatment was interrupted, and her life became a round of alcohol abuse, police intervention, and uncontrolled promiscuity."

"You say 'uncontrolled promiscuity.'"

"Yes. That's a term which indicates that she had no control over her own life. She had sexual relations with older men."

"That's not against the law."

"No, but it's abnormal behaviour for a seventeen-year-old girl. The question might be asked as to whether she participated in such encounters of her own free will or whether she was in a situation of uncontrollable compulsion."

"But you said that she was very probably a prostitute."

"That may have been a natural consequence of the fact that she lacked education, was incapable of completing school or continuing on to higher education, and therefore could not get a job. It's possible that she viewed older men as father figures and that financial remuneration for sexual favours was simply a convenient bonus. In which case I perceive it as neurotic behaviour."

"So you think that a seventeen-year-old girl who has sex is neurotic?"

"You're twisting my words."

"But you do not know whether she ever took money for sexual favours."

"She was never arrested for prostitution."

"And she hardly could be, since prostitution is not a crime in our country."

"Well, yes, that's right. In her case this has to do with compulsive neurotic behaviour."

"And you did not hesitate to conclude that Lisbeth Salander is mentally ill based on these unverifiable assumptions? When I was sixteen years old, I drank myself silly on half a bottle of vodka which I stole from my father. Do you think that makes me mentally ill?"

"No, of course not."

"If I may be so bold, is it not a fact that when you were seventeen you went to a party and got so drunk that you and your friends went out on the town and smashed the windows around the square in Uppsala? You were arrested by the police, detained until you were sober, and then let off with a fine."

Teleborian looked shocked.

"Is that not a fact, Dr. Teleborian?"

"Well, yes. People do so many stupid things when they're seventeen. But—"

"But that doesn't lead you—or anyone else—to believe that you have a serious mental illness?"

Teleborian was angry. That infernal lawyer kept twisting his words and homing in on details. She refused to see the larger picture. And his own childish escapade . . . How the hell had she gotten ahold of that information?

He cleared his throat and spoke in a raised voice.

"The reports from social services were unequivocal. They confirmed that Lisbeth Salander had a lifestyle that revolved around alcohol, drugs, and promiscuity. Social services also said that she was a prostitute."

"No, social services never said that she was a prostitute."

"She was arrested at—"

"No. She was not arrested," Giannini said. "She was searched in Tantolunden at the age of seventeen when she was in the company of a much older man. That same year she was arrested for drunkenness, also in the company of a much older man. Social services *feared* that she *might* be engaged in prostitution. But no *evidence* was ever presented."

"She had very loose sexual relations with a large number of individuals, both male and female."

"In your own report, you dwell on my client's sexual habits. You claim that her relationship with her friend Miriam Wu 'confirms the misgivings about a sexual psychopathy.' Why does it *confirm* any such thing?"

Teleborian gave no answer.

"I sincerely hope that you are not thinking of claiming that homosexuality is a mental illness," Giannini said. "That might even be an illegal statement."

"No, of course not. I'm alluding to the elements of sexual sadism in the relationship."

"You think that she's a sadist?"

"I—"

"We have Miriam Wu's statement here. There was, it says, no violence in their relationship."

"They engaged in S and M sex and—"

"Now I'm beginning to think you've been reading too many evening newspapers. Lisbeth Salander and her friend Miriam Wu engaged in sexual games on some occasions which involved Miriam Wu tying up my client and giving her sexual satisfaction. That is neither especially unusual nor against the law. Is that why you want to lock up my client?"

Teleborian waved a hand in a dismissive gesture.

"When I was sixteen and still at school I was intoxicated on a good many occasions. I have tried drugs. I have smoked marijuana, and I even tried cocaine on one occasion about twenty years ago. I had my first sexual experience with a school friend when I was fifteen, and I had a relationship with a boy who tied my hands to the bedposts when I was twenty. When I was twenty-two I had a relationship with a man who was forty-seven that lasted several months. Am I, in your view, mentally ill?"

"Fru Giannini, you joke about this, but your sexual experiences are irrelevant in this case."

"Why is that? When I read your so-called psychiatric assessment of Lisbeth Salander, I find point after point which, taken out of context, would apply to myself. Why am I healthy and sound while Lisbeth Salander is considered a dangerous sadist?"

"These are not the details that are relevant. You didn't twice try to murder your father—"

"Dr. Teleborian, the reality is that it's none of your business whom Lisbeth Salander wants to have sex with. It's none of your business which gender her partner is or how they conduct their sexual relations. And yet in her case you pluck out details from her life and use them as the basis for saying that she is sick."

"Lisbeth Salander's whole life—from the time she was in junior school—is a document of unprovoked and violent outbursts of anger against teachers and other pupils."

"Just a moment." Giannini's voice was suddenly like an ice scraper on a car window. "Look at my client."

Everyone looked at Salander.

"My client grew up in abominable family circumstances. Over a period of years her father persistently abused her mother."

"That's—"

"Let me finish. Lisbeth Salander's mother was mortally afraid of Alexander Zalachenko. She did not dare to protest. She did not dare to go to a doctor. She did not dare to go to a women's crisis centre. She was ground down and eventually beaten so badly that she suffered irreversible brain damage. The person who had to take responsibility, the only person who tried to take responsibility for the family long before she reached her teens even, was Lisbeth Salander. She had to shoulder that burden all by herself, since Zalachenko the spy was more important to the state and its social services than Lisbeth's mother."

"I cannot—"

"The result, excuse me, was a situation in which society abandoned Lisbeth's mother and her two children. Are you surprised that Lisbeth had problems at school? Look at her. She's small and skinny. She has always been the smallest girl in her class. She was introverted and eccentric, and she had no friends. Do you know how children tend to treat fellow students who are *different*?"

Teleborian sighed.

Giannini continued. "I can go back to her school records and examine one situation after another in which Lisbeth turned violent. The incidents were always preceded by some kind of provocation. I can easily recognize the signs of bullying. Let me tell you something."

"What?"

"I admire Lisbeth Salander. She's tougher than I am. If I had been strapped down for a year when I was thirteen, I would probably have broken down altogether. She fought back with the only weapon she had available—her contempt for you."

Her nervousness was long gone. She felt that she was in control.

"In your testimony this morning you spoke a great deal about fantasies. You stated, for instance, that Lisbeth Salander's account of her rape by Advokat Bjurman is a fantasy."

"That's correct."

"On what do you base your conclusion?"

"On my experience of the way she usually fantasizes."

"On your experience of the way she usually fantasizes? How do you decide when she is fantasizing? When she says that she was strapped to a bed for 380 days and nights, in your opinion it's a fantasy, despite the fact that your very own records tell us that this was indeed the case."

"This is something entirely different. There is not a shred of evidence that Bjurman committed rape against Lisbeth Salander. I mean, needles through her nipples and such gross violence that she unquestionably should have been taken by ambulance to the hospital? It's obvious that this could not have taken place."

Giannini turned to Judge Iversen. "I asked to have a projector available today . . ."

"It's in place," the judge said.

"Could we close the curtains, please?"

Giannini opened her PowerBook and plugged in the cables to the projector. She turned to her client.

"Lisbeth. We're going to look at the film. Are you ready for this?"

"I lived through it," Salander said dryly.

"And I have your approval to show it here?"

Salander nodded. She fixed her eyes on Teleborian.

"Can you tell us when the film was made?"

"On March 7, 2003."

"Who shot the film?"

"I did. I used a hidden camera, standard equipment at Milton Security."

"Just one moment," Prosecutor Ekström shouted. "This is beginning to resemble a circus act."

"What is it we are about to see?" Judge Iversen said with a sharp edge to his voice.

"Dr. Teleborian claims that Lisbeth Salander's account of her rape by Advokat Bjurman is a fantasy. I am going to show you evidence to the contrary. The film is ninety minutes long, but I will show only a few short excerpts. I warn you that it contains some very unpleasant scenes."

"Is this some sort of trick?" Ekström said.

"There's a good way to find out," said Giannini and started the DVD in her laptop.

"Haven't you even learned to tell the time?" Advokat Bjurman greets Salander gruffly. The camera enters his apartment.

After nine minutes Judge Iversen banged his gavel. Advokat Bjurman was being shown violently shoving a dildo into Lisbeth Salander's anus. Giannini had turned up the volume. Salander's half-stifled screams through the duct tape that covered her mouth were heard throughout the courtroom.

"Turn off the film," Judge Iversen said in a very loud and commanding voice.

Giannini pressed Stop, and the ceiling lights were turned back on. Judge Iversen was red in the face. Prosecutor Ekström sat as if turned to stone. Teleborian was as pale as a corpse.

"Advokat Giannini, how long is this film, did you say?"

"Ninety minutes. The rape itself went on in stages for about five or six hours, but my client has only a vague sense of the violence inflicted upon her in the last few hours."

Giannini turned to Teleborian. "There is a scene, however, in which Bjurman pushes a needle through my client's nipple, something that *Doctor* Teleborian maintains is an expression of Lisbeth Salander's wild imagination. It takes place in minute seventy-two, and I'm offering to show the episode here and now."

"Thank you, that won't be necessary," the judge said. "Fröken Salander . . ."

For a second he lost his train of thought and did not know how to proceed.

"Fröken Salander, why did you record this film?"

"Bjurman had already subjected me to one rape and was demanding more. The first time, he made me blow him, the old creep. I thought it was going to be a repeat. I thought I'd be able to get such good evidence of what he did that I could then blackmail him into staying away from me. I misjudged him."

"But why did you not go to the police when you have such . . . irrefutable evidence?"

"I don't talk to policemen," Salander said flatly.

Palmgren stood up from his wheelchair. He supported himself by leaning on the edge of the table. His voice was very clear.

"Our client on principle does not speak to the police or to other persons of authority, and least of all to psychiatrists. The reason is simple. From the time she was a child she tried time and again to talk to police and social workers to explain that her mother was being abused by Alexander Zalachenko. The result in every instance was that she was punished because government civil servants had decided that Zalachenko was more important than she was."

He cleared his throat and continued.

"And when she eventually concluded that nobody was listening to her, her only means of protecting her mother was to fight Zalachenko with violence. And then this bastard who calls himself a doctor"—he pointed at Teleborian—"wrote a fabricated psychiatric diagnosis which described her as mentally ill, and it gave him the opportunity to keep her in restraints at St. Stefan's for 380 days. What a bastard."

Palmgren sat down. Judge Iversen was surprised by this outburst. He turned to Salander.

"Would you perhaps like to take a break . . . ?"

"Why?" Salander said.

"All right, then we'll continue. Advokat Giannini, the recording will be examined, and I will require a technical opinion to verify its authenticity. But I cannot tolerate seeing any more of these appalling scenes at present. Let's proceed."

"Gladly. I too find them appalling," said Giannini. "My client has been subjected to multiple instances of physical and mental abuse and legal misconduct. And the person most to blame for this is Dr. Peter Teleborian. He betrayed his oath as a physician, and he betrayed his patient. Together with a member of an illegal group within the Security Police, Gunnar Björck, he patched together a forensic psychiatric assessment for the purpose of locking up an inconvenient witness. I believe that this case must be unique in Swedish jurisprudence."

"These are outrageous accusations," Teleborian said. "I have done my best to help Lisbeth Salander. She tried to murder her father. It's perfectly obvious that there's something wrong with her—"

Giannini interrupted him.

"I would now like to bring to the attention of the court Dr. Teleborian's second forensic psychiatric assessment of my client, presented at this trial today. I maintain that it is a lie, just as the report from 1991 was a lie."

"Well, this is simply—" Teleborian spluttered.

"Judge Iversen, could you please ask the witness to stop interrupting me?"

"Herr Teleborian . . ."

"I will be quiet. But these are outrageous accusations. It's not surprising that I'm upset—"

"Herr Teleborian, please be quiet until a question is directed to you. Go on, Advokat Giannini."

"This is the forensic psychiatric assessment that Dr. Teleborian has presented to the court. It is based on what he has termed 'observations' of my client which were supposed to have taken place after she was moved to Kronoberg prison on June 5. The examination was supposed to have been concluded on July 5."

"Yes, so I have understood," Judge Iversen said.

"Dr. Teleborian, is it the case that you did not have the opportunity to examine or observe my client before June 6? Before that she was at Sahlgrenska hospital in Göteborg, where she was being kept in isolation, as we know."

"Yes."

"You made attempts on two separate occasions to gain access to my client at Sahlgrenska. Both times you were denied admittance."

Giannini opened her briefcase and took out a document. She walked around her table and handed it to Judge Iversen.

"I see," the judge said. "This appears to be a copy of Dr. Teleborian's report. What is your point?"

"I would like to call two witnesses. They are waiting outside the courtroom now."

"Who are these witnesses?"

"They are Mikael Blomkvist from *Millennium* magazine and Superintendent Torsten Edklinth, director of the Constitutional Protection Unit of the Security Police."

"And they are outside?"

"Yes."

"Show them in," Judge Iversen said.

"This is highly irregular," Prosecutor Ekström said.

Ekström had watched in extreme discomfort as Giannini shredded his key witness. The film was devastating evidence. The judge ignored Ekström and gestured to the bailiff to open the door to admit Blomkvist and Edklinth.

"I would first like to call Mikael Blomkvist."

"Then I would ask that Herr Teleborian stand down for a while," Judge Iversen said.

"Are you finished with me?" Teleborian said.

"No, not by any means," Giannini said.

Blomkvist replaced Teleborian in the witness box. Judge Iversen swiftly dealt with the formalities, and Blomkvist took the oath.

"Mikael," Giannini said, and then she smiled. "I would find it difficult, if your honour will forgive me, to call my brother Herr Blomkvist, so I will settle for his first name."

She went to Judge Iversen's bench and asked for the forensic psychiatric report which she had just handed to him. She then gave it to Blomkvist.

"Have you seen this document before?"

"Yes, I have. I have three versions in my possession. The first I acquired on May 12, the second on May 19, and the third—this one—on June 3."

"Can you tell us how you acquired the copies?"

"I received them in my capacity as a journalist from a source I do not intend to name."

Salander stared at Teleborian. He was once more deathly pale.

"What did you do with the report?"

"I gave it to Torsten Edklinth at Constitutional Protection."

"Thank you, Mikael. Now I'd like to call Torsten Edklinth," Giannini said, taking back the report. She handed it to Judge Iversen, and the procedure with the oath was repeated.

"Superintendent Edklinth, is it correct that you received a forensic psychiatric report on Lisbeth Salander from Mikael Blomkvist?"

"Yes, it is."

"When did you receive it?"

"It was logged in at SIS on June 4."

"And this is the same report I have just handed to Judge Iversen?"

"If my signature is on the back, then it's the same one."

The judge turned over the document and saw Edklinth's signature there.

"Superintendent Edklinth, could you explain how you happened to have a forensic psychiatric report in your possession which claims to have analysed a patient who was still in isolation at Sahlgrenska?"

"Yes, I can. Dr. Teleborian's report is a sham. It was put

together with the help of a person by the name of Jonas Sandberg, just as he produced a similar document in 1991 with Gunnar Björck."

"That's a lie," Teleborian said in a weak voice.

"Is it a lie?" Giannini said.

"No, not at all," Edklinth said. "I should perhaps mention that Jonas Sandberg is one of a dozen or so individuals who were arrested today by order of the prosecutor general. Sandberg is being held as an accomplice to the murder of Gunnar Björck. He is part of a criminal unit operating within the Security Police which has been protecting Alexander Zalachenko since the seventies. This same group of officers was responsible for the decision to lock up Lisbeth Salander in 1991. We have incontrovertible evidence, as well as a confession from the unit's director."

The courtroom was hushed, transfixed.

"Would Dr. Teleborian like to comment on what has just been said?" Judge Iversen asked.

Teleborian shook his head.

"In that case it is my duty to tell you that you risk being charged with perjury and possibly other counts in addition," Judge Iversen said.

"If you'll excuse me, your honour," Blomkvist said.

"Yes?"

"Dr. Teleborian has bigger problems than this. Outside the courtroom are two police officers who would like to bring him in for questioning."

"I see," the judge said. "Is it a matter which concerns this court?"

"I believe it is, your honour."

Judge Iversen gestured to the bailiff, who admitted Inspector Modig and a woman Prosecutor Ekström did not immediately recognize. Her name was Lisa Collsjö, and she was a criminal inspector for the special investigations division, the unit within the National Police Board responsible for investigating cases of child pornography and sexual assault on children.

"And what is your business here?" Judge Iversen said.

"We are here to arrest Peter Teleborian with your permission, and without wishing to disturb the court's proceedings."

Judge Iversen looked at Advokat Giannini.

"I'm not quite finished with him . . . but the court may have heard enough of Dr. Teleborian."

"You have my permission," Judge Iversen said to the police officers.

Collsjö walked across to Teleborian. "Peter Teleborian, you are under arrest for violation of the law on child pornography."

Teleborian sat still, hardly breathing. Giannini saw that all the light in his eyes seemed to have been extinguished.

"Specifically, for possession of approximately nine thousand pornographic photographs of children found on your computer."

She bent down to pick up his laptop, which he had brought with him.

"This is confiscated as evidence," she said.

As he was being led from the courtroom, Salander's blazing eyes bored into Teleborian's back.

CHAPTER 28

Friday, July 15–
Saturday, July 16

Judge Iversen tapped his pen on the edge of his table to quell the murmuring that had arisen in the wake of Teleborian's departure. He seemed unsure how to proceed. Then he turned to Prosecutor Ekström.

"Do you have any comment to make to the court on what has been seen and heard in the past hour?"

Ekström stood up and looked at Judge Iversen and then at Edklinth before he turned his head and met Salander's unwavering gaze. He understood that the battle was lost. He glanced over at Blomkvist and realized with sudden terror that he too risked being exposed to *Millennium*'s investigators . . . which could ruin his career.

He was at a loss to comprehend how this had happened. He had come to the trial convinced that he knew everything about the case.

He had understood the delicate balance sought by national security after his many candid talks with Superintendent Nyström. It had been explained to him that the

Salander report from 1991 had been fabricated. He had received the inside information he needed. He had asked questions—hundreds of questions—and received answers to all of them. A deception in the national interest. And now Nyström had been arrested, according to Edklinth. He had believed in Teleborian, who had, after all, seemed so . . . so competent. So convincing.

Good Lord. What sort of a mess have I landed in?

And then, *How the hell am I going to get out of it?*

He stroked his goatee. He cleared his throat. Slowly he removed his glasses.

"I regret to say that it seems I have been misinformed on a number of essential points in this investigation."

He wondered if he could shift the blame onto the police investigators. Then he had a vision of Inspector Bublanski. Bublanski would never back him up. If Ekström made one wrong move, Bublanski would call a press conference and sink him.

Ekström met Salander's gaze. She was sitting there patiently, and in her eyes he read both curiosity and vengeance.

No compromises.

He could still get her convicted of aggravated assault in Stallarholmen. And he could probably get her convicted for the aggravated assault and attempted murder of her father in Gosseberga. That would mean changing his strategy immediately; he would drop everything that had anything to do with Teleborian. All claims that she was a psychopath had to go, but that meant that her story would be strengthened all the way back to 1991. The whole declaration of incompetence was bogus, and with that . . .

Plus she has that blasted film . . .

Then it struck him.

Good God. She's a victim, pure and simple.

"Judge Iversen, I believe I can no longer rely on the documents I have here in my hand."

"I suppose not," Judge Iversen said.

"I'm going to have to ask for a recess, or that the trial be suspended until I am able to make certain adjustments to my case."

"Advokat Giannini?" the judge said.

"I request that my client be at once acquitted on all counts and be released immediately. I also request that the district court take a definite position on the question of Fröken Salander's declaration of incompetence. Moreover, I believe that she should be adequately compensated for the violations of her rights that have occurred."

Lisbeth Salander turned towards Judge Iversen.

No compromises.

Judge Iversen looked at Salander's autobiography. He then looked over at Prosecutor Ekström.

"I too believe we would be wise to investigate exactly what has happened that brings us to this sorry pass. I fear that you are probably not the right person to conduct that investigation. In all my years as a jurist and judge, I have never been party to anything even approaching the legal dilemma in this case. I confess that I am at a loss for words. I have never even heard of a case in which the prosecutor's chief witness is arrested during a court in session, or of a convincing argument turning out to be an utter fabrication. I honestly do not see what is left of the prosecutor's case."

Palmgren cleared his throat.

"Yes?" Iversen said.

"As a representative for the defence, I can only share your feelings. Sometimes one must step back and allow common sense to guide the formal procedures. I'd like to state that you, in your capacity as judge, have seen only the first stage of a scandal that is going to rock the whole establishment. Today twelve police officers from within Säpo have been arrested. They will be charged with murder and a list of crimes so long that it will take quite some time to draw up the report."

"I presume that I must decide on a suspension of this trial."

"If you'll excuse me for saying so, I think that would be an unfortunate decision."

"I'm listening."

"Lisbeth Salander is innocent. Her 'fantastical' autobiography, as Dr. Teleborian so contemptuously dismissed it, is in fact true. And it can all be proven. She has suffered an outrageous violation of her rights. As a court we could now stick with formal procedure and continue with the trial until finally we arrive at an acquittal, but there is an obvious alternative: to let a new investigation take over everything concerning Lisbeth Salander. An investigation is already under way to sort out an integral part of this mess."

"I see what you mean."

"As the judge of this case you have a choice. The wise thing to do would be to reject the prosecutor's entire preliminary investigation and request that he do his homework."

Judge Iversen looked long and hard at Ekström.

"The *just* thing to do would be to acquit my client at once. She also deserves an apology, but the redress will take time and will depend upon the rest of the investigation."

"I understand the points you're making, Advokat Palmgren. But before I can declare your client innocent I will have to have the whole story clear in my mind. That will probably take a while. . . ."

He hesitated and looked at Giannini.

"If I decide that the court will adjourn until Monday and accommodate your wishes insofar as I see no reason to keep your client in custody any longer—which would mean that you could expect that, no matter what else happens, she will not be given a prison sentence—can you guarantee that she will appear for continued proceedings when summoned?"

"Of course," Palmgren said quickly.

"No," Salander said in a sharp voice.

Everyone's eyes turned to the person who was at the heart of the entire drama.

"What do you mean by that?" Judge Iversen said.

"The moment you release me I'm going to leave the country. I do not intend to spend one more minute of my time on this trial."

"You would refuse to appear?"

"That is correct. If you want me to answer more questions, then you'll have to keep me in prison. The moment you release me, this story is settled as far as I'm concerned. And that does not include being available for an indefinite time to you, to Ekström, or to any police officers."

Judge Iversen sighed. Palmgren looked bewildered.

"I agree with my client," Giannini said. "It is the government and the authorities who have committed crimes against Lisbeth Salander, not the other way around. At the very least she deserves to be able to walk out that door with an acquittal and the chance to put this whole story behind her."

No compromises.

Judge Iversen glanced at his watch.

"It is 3:00. That means that you're going to force me to keep your client in custody."

"If that's your decision, then we accept it. As Fröken Salander's representative I request that she be acquitted of the charges brought by Prosecutor Ekström. I request that you release my client without restrictions, and without delay. And I request that the previous declaration of incompetence be rescinded and that her civil rights be immediately restored."

"The matter of the declaration of incompetence is a significantly longer process. I would have to get statements from psychiatric experts after she has been examined. I cannot simply make a snap decision about that."

"We do not accept that," Giannini said.

"Why not?"

"Lisbeth Salander must have the same civil rights as any other citizen of Sweden. *She* has been the victim of a crime. She was *falsely* declared incompetent. We have heard evidence of that falsification. The decision to place her under guardianship therefore lacks a legal basis and must be unconditionally rescinded. There is no reason whatsoever for my client to submit to a psychiatric examination. No-one else has to prove that they are not mentally ill if they are the victim of a crime."

Judge Iversen considered the matter for a moment. "Advokat Giannini, I realize that this is an exceptional situation. I'm calling a recess of fifteen minutes so that we can stretch our legs and gather our thoughts. I have no wish that your client be kept in custody tonight if she is innocent, but that means that this trial will have to continue today until we are done."

"That sounds good to me," said Giannini.

· · ·

Blomkvist hugged his sister. "How did it go?"

"Mikael, I was brilliant against Teleborian. I annihilated him."

"I told you you'd be unbeatable. When it comes down to it, this story is not primarily about spies and secret government agencies; it's about violence against women, and the men who enable it. From what little I heard and saw, you were phenomenal. She's going to be acquitted."

"You're right. There's no longer any doubt."

Judge Iversen banged his gavel.

"Could you please sum up the facts from beginning to end, so that I can get a clear picture of what actually happened?"

"Let's begin," Giannini said, "with the astounding story of a group within the Security Police who call themselves 'the Section,' and who got ahold of a Soviet defector in the mid-seventies. The story was published today in *Millennium* magazine. I imagine it will be the lead story on all the news broadcasts this evening. . . ."

At 6:00 that evening Judge Iversen decided to release Salander and to revoke her declaration of incompetence.

But the decision was made on one condition: Judge Iversen demanded that Salander submit to an interview in which she would formally testify to her knowledge of the Zalachenko affair. At first she refused. This refusal brought about a moment's wrangling until Judge Iversen raised his voice. He leaned forward and fixed his gaze on Salander.

"Fröken Salander, if I rescind your declaration of incompetence, that will mean that you have exactly the same rights as all other citizens. It also means that you have the same obligations. It is therefore your duty to manage your finances, pay taxes, obey the law, and assist the police in investigations of serious crimes. So I am summoning you to be questioned like any other citizen who has information that might be vital to an investigation."

The force of this logic seemed to sink in. She pouted and looked angry, but she stopped arguing.

"When the police have interviewed you, the leader of the preliminary investigation—in this case the prosecutor general—will decide whether you will be summoned as a witness in any future legal proceedings. Like any other Swedish citizen, you can refuse to obey such a summons. How you act is none of my concern, but you do not have carte blanche. If you refuse to appear, then like any other adult you may be charged with obstruction of justice or perjury. There are no exceptions."

Salander's expression darkened even more.

"So, what is your decision?" Judge Iversen said.

After thinking it over for a minute, Salander gave a curt nod.

OK. A little compromise.

During her summary of the Zalachenko affair that evening, Giannini launched a savage attack on Prosecutor Ekström. Eventually Ekström admitted that the course of events had proceeded more or less as Giannini had described. He had been helped during the preliminary investigation by Superintendent Nyström, and he had received his information from Dr. Teleborian. In Ekström's case there was no conspiracy. He had gone along with the Section in good faith in his capacity as leader of the preliminary investigation. When the whole extent of the conspiracy finally dawned on him, he decided to withdraw all charges against Salander, and that decision meant that a raft of bureaucratic formalities could be set aside. Judge Iversen looked relieved.

Palmgren was exhausted after his day in court, the first in many years. He needed to go back to the Ersta rehabilitation home and go to bed. He was driven there by a uniformed guard from Milton Security. As he was leaving, he put a hand on Salander's shoulder. They looked at each other, saying nothing. After a moment she nodded.

Giannini called Blomkvist at 7:00 to tell him that Salander had been acquitted of all charges, but that she was going to have to stay at police headquarters for what might be another couple of hours for her interview.

The news came as the entire staff of *Millennium* was gathered at the office. The phones had been ringing incessantly since the first copies of the magazine had been distributed by messenger at lunchtime to other newsrooms across the city. In the early evening, TV4 had broadcast its first special programme on Zalachenko and the Section. The media was having a field day.

Blomkvist walked into the main office, stuck his fingers in his mouth, and gave a loud whistle.

"Great news. Salander has been acquitted on all counts."

Spontaneous applause broke out. Then everyone went back to talking on their phones as if nothing had happened.

Blomkvist looked up at the television that had been turned on in the editorial office. The news on TV4 was just starting. The trailer was a brief clip of the film showing Sandberg planting cocaine in his apartment on Bellmansgatan.

"Here we can clearly see a Säpo officer planting what we later learn is cocaine at the apartment of Mikael Blomkvist, journalist at *Millennium* magazine."

Then the anchorman came on the screen.

"Twelve officers of the Security Police were today arrested on a range of criminal charges, including murder. Welcome to this extended news broadcast."

Blomkvist turned off the sound when *She* came on and he saw himself sitting in a studio armchair. He already knew what he had said. He looked over at the desk where Svensson had sat. All his research documents on the sex-trafficking industry were gone, and the desk was once more home to stacks of newspapers and piles of unsorted paper that nobody had time to deal with.

For Blomkvist, it was at that desk that the Zalachenko affair had begun. He wished that Svensson had been able to see the conclusion of it. A pile of copies of his just-published book was on the table next to Blomkvist's own about the Section.

You would have loved this moment, Dag.

He heard the phone in his office ringing, but he could not face picking it up. He pulled the door shut and went into Berger's office and sank into a comfortable chair by the window. Berger was on the phone. He looked around. She had been back a month but had not yet had a chance to put up the paintings and photographs she had taken away when she left in April. The bookshelves were still bare.

"How does it feel?" she said when she hung up.

"I think I'm happy," he said.

She laughed. "*The Section* is going to be a sensation. Every newsroom is going crazy for it. Do you feel like appearing on *Aktuellt* at 9:00 for an interview?"

"I think not."

"I suspected as much."

"We're going to be talking about this for several months. There's no rush."

She nodded.

"What are you doing later this evening?" Berger said.

"I don't know." He bit his lip. "Erika, I . . ."

"Figuerola," Berger said with a smile.

He nodded.

"So it's serious?"

"I don't know."

"She's in love with you."

"I think I'm in love with her too," he said.

"I promise I'll keep my distance until, you know . . . well, maybe," she said.

At 8:00 Armansky and Linder appeared at *Millennium*'s offices. They thought the occasion called for champagne, so they had brought over a crate from the liquor store. Berger hugged Linder and introduced her to everyone. Armansky took a seat in Blomkvist's office.

They drank their champagne. Neither of them said anything for quite a while. It was Armansky who broke the silence.

"You know what, Blomkvist? The first time we met, on that job in Hedestad, I didn't much care for you."

"You don't say."

"You came over to sign a contract when you hired Lisbeth as a researcher."

"I remember."

"I think I was jealous of you. You'd known her only a couple of hours, yet she was laughing with you. For some years I'd tried to be Lisbeth's friend, but I have never once made her smile."

"Well, I haven't really been that successful either."

They sat in silence once again.

"Great that all this is over," Armansky said.

"Amen to that," Blomkvist said, and they raised their glasses in salute.

Inspectors Bublanski and Modig conducted the formal interview with Salander. They had both been at home with their families after a particularly taxing day but were immediately summoned to return to police headquarters.

Salander was accompanied by Giannini. She gave precise responses to all the questions that Bublanski and Modig asked, and Giannini had little occasion to comment or intervene.

Salander lied consistently on two points. In her description of what had happened in Stallarholmen, she stubbornly maintained that it was Nieminen who had accidentally shot "Magge" Lundin in the foot at the instant that she nailed him with the Taser. Where had she gotten the Taser? She had confiscated it from Lundin, she explained.

Bublanski and Modig were both sceptical, but there was

no evidence and no witnesses to contradict her story. Nieminen was no doubt in a position to protest, but he refused to say anything about the incident; in fact he had no notion of what had happened in the seconds after he was stunned with the Taser.

As far as Salander's journey to Gosseberga was concerned, she claimed that her only objective had been to convince her father to turn himself in to the police.

Salander looked completely guileless; it was impossible to say whether she was telling the truth or not. Giannini had no reason to arrive at an opinion on the matter.

The only person who knew for certain that Salander had gone to Gosseberga with the intention of terminating any relationship she had with her father once and for all was Blomkvist. But he had been sent out of the courtroom shortly after the proceedings were resumed. No-one knew that he and Salander had carried on long conversations online by night while she was confined to Sahlgrenska.

The media missed her release from custody altogether. If the time of it had been known, a huge contingent would have descended on police headquarters. But many of the reporters were exhausted after the chaos and excitement that had ensued when *Millennium* reached the news-stands and certain members of the Security Police were arrested by other Security Police officers.

The host of *She* on TV4 was the only journalist who knew what the story was all about. Her hour-long broadcast became a classic, and some months later she won the award for Best TV News Story of the Year.

Modig got Salander away from police headquarters by

simply taking her and Giannini down to the garage and driving them to Giannini's office on Kungholm's Kyrkoplan. There they switched to Giannini's car. When Modig had driven away, Giannini headed for Södermalm. As they passed the Parliament building she broke the silence.

"Where to?" she said.

Salander thought for a few seconds.

"You can drop me somewhere on Lundagatan."

"Miriam isn't there."

Salander looked at her.

"She went to France soon after she got out of the hospital. She's staying with her parents if you want to get ahold of her."

"Why didn't you tell me?"

"You never asked. She said she needed some space. This morning Mikael gave me these and said you'd probably like to have them back."

She handed her a set of keys. Salander took it and said: "Thanks. Could you drop me somewhere on Folkungagatan instead?"

"You don't even want to tell me where you live?"

"Later. Right now I want to be left in peace."

"OK."

Giannini had switched on her mobile when they left police headquarters. It started beeping as they were passing Slussen. She looked at the display.

"It's Mikael. He's called every ten minutes for the past couple of hours."

"I don't want to talk to him."

"Tell me . . . Can I ask you a personal question?"

"Yes."

"What did Mikael do to you that you hate him so much? I mean, if it weren't for him, you'd probably be back on a secure ward tonight."

"I don't hate Mikael. He hasn't done anything to me. I just don't want to see him right now."

Giannini glanced across at her client. "I don't mean to pry, but you fell for him, didn't you?"

Salander looked out the window and did not answer.

"My brother is completely irresponsible when it comes to relationships. He screws his way through life and doesn't seem to grasp how much it can hurt those women who think of him as more than a casual affair."

Salander met her gaze. "I don't want to discuss Mikael with you."

"Right," Giannini said. She pulled over just before the junction with Erstagatan. "Is this OK?"

"Yes."

They sat in silence for a moment. Salander made no move to open the door. Then Giannini turned off the engine.

"What happens now?" Salander said at last.

"What happens now is that as of today you are no longer under guardianship. You can live your life however you want. Even though we won in the district court, there's still a ton of red tape to get through. There will be reports on accountability within the guardianship agency and the question of compensation and things like that. And the criminal investigation will continue."

"I don't want any compensation. I want to be left in peace."

"I understand. But what you want won't play much of a role here. This process is beyond your control. I suggest you get yourself a lawyer to represent you."

"Don't you want to go on being my lawyer?"

Giannini rubbed her eyes. After all the stress of the day she felt utterly drained. She wanted to go home and have a shower. She wanted her husband to massage her back.

"I don't know. You don't trust me. And I don't trust you. I have no desire to be drawn into a long process during which I encounter nothing but frustrating silence when I make a suggestion or want to discuss something."

Salander said nothing for a long moment. "I . . . I'm not good at relationships. But I do trust you."

It sounded almost like an apology.

"That may be. And it needn't be my problem if you're bad at relationships. But it does become my problem if I have to represent you."

Silence.

"Would you want me to go on being your lawyer?"

Salander nodded. Giannini sighed.

"I live at Fiskargatan 9. Above Mosebacke Torg. Could you drive me there?"

Giannini looked at her client and then started the engine. She let Salander direct her to the address. They stopped short of the building.

"OK," Giannini said. "We'll give it a try. Here are my conditions. I agree to represent you. When I call you I want you to answer. When I need to know what you want me to do, I want clear answers. If I call you and tell you that you have to talk to a policeman or a prosecutor or do anything else that has to do with the criminal investigation, then I have already decided that it's necessary. You will have to turn up at the appointed place, on time, and not make a fuss about it. Can you live with that?"

"I can."

"And if you start acting up, I stop being your lawyer. Understood?"

Salander nodded.

"One more thing. I don't want to get involved in a big drama between you and my brother. If you have a problem with him, you'll have to work it out. But, for the record, he's not your enemy."

"I know. I'll deal with it. But I need some time."

"What do you plan to do now?"

"I don't know. You can reach me via email. I promise to reply as soon as I can, but I might not be checking it every day."

"You won't become a slave just because you have a lawyer. OK, that's enough for the time being. Out you get. I'm dead tired and I want to go home and sleep."

Salander opened the door and got out. She paused as she was about to close the car door. She looked as though she wanted to say something but could not find the words. For a moment she appeared almost vulnerable.

"That's all right, Lisbeth," Giannini said. "Go and get some sleep. And stay out of trouble for a while."

Salander stood at the curb and watched Giannini drive away until her tail lights disappeared around the corner.

"Thanks," she said at last.

CHAPTER 29

Saturday, July 16–
Friday, October 7

Salander found her Palm Tungsten T3 on the hall table. Next to it were her car keys and the shoulder bag she had lost when Lundin attacked her outside the door to her apartment building on Lundagatan. She also found both opened and unopened mail that had been collected from her P.O. box on Hornsgatan. *Mikael Blomkvist.*

She took a slow tour through the furnished part of her apartment. She found traces of him everywhere. He had slept in her bed and worked at her desk. He had used her printer, and in the wastepaper basket she found drafts of the manuscript of *The Section,* along with discarded notes.

He had bought a quart of milk, bread, cheese, caviar, and a jumbo pack of Billy's Pan Pizza and put them in the fridge.

On the kitchen table she found a small white envelope with her name on it. It was a note from him. The message was brief. His mobile number. That was all.

She knew that the ball was in her court. He was not going to get in touch with her. He had finished the story, given back the keys to her apartment, and he would not call her. If she wanted something, then she could call him. *Pig-headed bastard.*

She put on a pot of coffee, made four open sandwiches, and went to sit in her window seat to look out towards Djurgården. She lit a cigarette and brooded.

It was all over, and yet now her life felt more claustrophobic than ever.

Miriam Wu had gone to France. *It was my fault that you almost died.* She had shuddered at the thought of having to see Mimmi, but had decided that that would be her first stop when she was released. But she had gone to France.

All of a sudden she was in debt to people.

Palmgren. Armansky. She ought to contact them to say thank you. Paolo Roberto. And Plague and Trinity. Even those damned police officers, Bublanski and Modig, who had so obviously been in her corner. She did not like feeling beholden to anyone. She felt like a chess piece in a game she could not control.

Kalle Fucking Blomkvist. And maybe even Erika Fucking Berger with the dimples and the expensive clothes and all that self-assurance.

But it was over. Giannini had said so as they left police headquarters. Right. The trial was over. It was over for Giannini. And it was over for Blomkvist. He had published his book and would end up on TV and probably win some fucking prize too.

But it was not over for Lisbeth Salander. This was only the first day of the rest of her life.

At 4:00 in the morning she stopped thinking. She discarded her punk outfit on the floor of her bedroom and went to the bathroom and took a shower. She cleaned off all the make-up she had worn in court, put on loose, dark linen pants, a white top, and a thin jacket. She packed an overnight bag with a change of underwear and a couple of tops and put on some simple walking shoes.

She picked up her Palm and called a taxi to collect her from Mosebacke Torg. She rode out to Arlanda Airport and arrived just before 6:00. She studied the departure board and booked a ticket for the morning flight to Málaga. She used her own passport in her own name. She was surprised that nobody at the ticket desk or at the check-in counter seemed to recognize her or react to her name.

She landed in Málaga in the blazing midday heat. She stood inside the terminal building for a moment, feeling uncertain. Then she bought a pair of sunglasses at an airport shop, went out to the taxi stand, and climbed into the back seat of the first taxi.

"Gibraltar. I'm paying with a credit card."

The trip took three hours via the new motorway along the coast. The taxi dropped her off at British passport control and she walked across the border and over to the Rock Hotel on Europa Road, partway up the slope of the 1,398-foot monolith. She asked if they had a room and was told there was a double room available. She booked it for two weeks and handed over her credit card.

She showered and sat on the balcony wrapped up in a bath towel, looking out over the Straits of Gibraltar. She could see freighters and a few yachts. She could just make out Morocco in the haze on the other side of the straits. It was peaceful.

After a while she went in and lay down and slept.

· · ·

The next morning Salander woke at 5:00. She got up, showered, and had a coffee in the hotel bar on the ground floor. At 7:00 she left the hotel and set out to buy mangoes and apples. She took a taxi to the Peak and walked over to the apes. She was so early that few tourists had yet appeared, and she was practically alone with the animals.

She liked Gibraltar. It was her third visit to the strange rock that housed an absurdly densely populated English town on the Mediterranean. Gibraltar was a place that was not like anywhere else. The town had been isolated for decades, a colony that obstinately refused to be incorporated into Spain. The Spaniards protested the occupation, of course. (But Salander thought that the Spaniards should keep their mouths shut on that score so long as they occupied the enclave of Ceuta on Moroccan territory across the straits.) It was a place that was comically shielded from the rest of the world, consisting of a bizarre rock, about three quarters of a square mile of town, and an airport that began and ended in the sea. The colony was so small that every square inch of it was used, and any expansion had to be over the sea. Even to get into the town, visitors had to walk across the landing strip at the airport.

Gibraltar gave the concept of "compact living" a whole new meaning.

Salander watched a big male ape climb up onto a wall next to the path. He glowered at her. He was a Barbary ape. She knew better than to try to stroke any of the animals.

"Hello, friend," she said. "I'm back."

The first time she visited Gibraltar she had not even heard about these apes. She had gone up to the top just to look at the view, and she was surprised when she followed some tourists and found herself in the midst of a group of apes climbing and scrambling on both sides of the pathway.

It was a peculiar feeling to be walking along a path and suddenly have two dozen apes around you. She looked at them with great wariness. They were not dangerous or aggressive, but they were certainly capable of giving you a bad bite if they got agitated or felt threatened.

She found one of the guards and showed him her bag of fruit and asked if she could give it to the apes. He said it was OK.

She took out a mango and put it on the wall a little way away from the male ape.

"Breakfast," she said, leaning against the wall and taking a bite of an apple.

The male ape stared at her, bared his teeth, and contentedly picked up the mango.

In the middle of the afternoon five days later, Salander fell off her stool in Harry's Bar on a side street off Main Street, two blocks from her hotel. She had been drunk almost continuously since she left the apes on the rock, and most of her drinking had been done with Harry O'Connell, who owned the bar and spoke with a phoney Irish accent, having never in his life set foot in Ireland. He had been watching her anxiously.

When she had ordered her first drink several days earlier, he had asked to see her ID. Her name was Lisbeth, he knew, and he called her Liz. She would come in after lunch and sit on a high stool at the far end of the bar with her back against the wall. Then she would drink an impressive number of beers or shots of whisky.

When she drank beer she did not care what brand or type

it was; she accepted whatever he served her. When she ordered whisky she always chose Tullamore Dew, except on one occasion when she studied the bottles behind the bar and asked for Lagavulin. When the glass was brought to her, she sniffed at it, stared at it for a moment, and then took a tiny sip. She set down her glass and stared at it for a minute with an expression that seemed to indicate that she considered its contents to be a mortal enemy.

Finally she pushed the glass aside and asked Harry to give her something that could not be used to tar a boat. He poured her another Tullamore Dew and she went back to her drinking. Over the past four days she had consumed almost a whole bottle. He had not kept track of the beers. Harry was surprised that a young woman with her slender build could hold so much, but he took the view that if she wanted alcohol she was going to get it, whether in his bar or somewhere else.

She drank slowly, did not talk to any of the other customers, and did not make any trouble. Her only activity apart from the consumption of alcohol seemed to be to play with a hand-held computer which she connected to a mobile now and then. He had several times tried to start a conversation but was met with a sullen silence. She seemed to avoid company. Sometimes, when there were too many people in the bar, she moved outside to a table on the sidewalk, and at other times she went two doors down to an Italian restaurant and had dinner. Then she would come back to Harry's and order another Tullamore Dew. She usually left the bar at around 10:00 and made her way unsteadily off, always to the north.

Today she had drunk more and at a faster rate than on the other days, and Harry had kept a watchful eye on her. When she had put away seven glasses of Tullamore Dew in a little over two hours, he decided not to give her anymore. It was then that he heard the crash as she fell off the bar stool.

He put down the glass he was drying and went around the counter to pick her up. She seemed offended.

"I think you've had enough, Liz," he said.

She looked at him, bleary-eyed.

"I believe you're right," she said in a surprisingly lucid voice.

She held on to the bar with one hand as she dug some notes out of her top pocket and then wobbled off towards the door. He took her gently by the shoulder.

"Hold on a minute. Why don't you go to the toilet and throw up the last of that whisky and then sit at the bar for a while? I don't want to let you go in this condition."

She did not object when he led her to the toilet. She stuck her fingers down her throat. When she came back out to the bar he had poured her a large glass of club soda. She drank the whole glass and burped. He poured her another.

"You're going to feel like death in the morning," Harry said.

She nodded.

"It's none of my business, but if I were you I'd sober up for a couple of days."

She nodded. Then she went back to the toilet and threw up again.

She stayed at Harry's Bar for another hour, until she looked sober enough to be turned loose. She left the bar on unsteady legs, walked down to the airport, and followed the shoreline around the marina. She walked until after 8:00, when the ground at last stopped swaying under her feet.

Then she went back to the hotel. She took the elevator to her room, brushed her teeth and washed her face, changed her clothes, and went back down to the hotel bar to order a cup of black coffee and a bottle of mineral water.

She sat there, silent and unnoticed next to a pillar, studying the people in the bar. She saw a couple in their thirties engaged in quiet conversation. The woman was wearing a light-coloured summer dress, and the man was holding her hand under the table. Two tables away sat a black family, the man with the beginnings of grey at his temples, the woman wearing a lovely, colourful dress in yellow, black, and red. They had two young children with them. She studied a group of businessmen in white shirts and ties, their jackets hung over the backs of their chairs. They were drinking beer. She saw a group of elderly people, without a doubt American tourists. The men wore baseball caps, polo shirts, and loose-fitting trousers. She watched a man in a light-coloured linen jacket, grey shirt, and dark tie come in from the street and pick up his room key at the front desk before he headed over to the bar and ordered a beer. He sat down nine feet away from her. She gave him an expectant look as he took out his mobile and began to speak in German.

"Hello, is that you? . . . Is everything all right? . . . It's going fine; we're having our next meeting tomorrow afternoon. . . . No, I think it'll work out. . . . I'll be staying here five or six days at least, and then I go to Madrid. . . . No, I won't be home before the end of next week. . . . Me too. I love you. . . . Sure. . . . I'll call you later in the week. . . . Kiss kiss."

He was a little over six feet tall, about fifty years old (maybe fifty-five), with blond hair that was turning grey and was a bit on the long side, a weak chin, and too much weight around the middle. But still reasonably well preserved. He was reading the *Financial Times*. When he finished his beer and headed for the elevator, Salander got up and followed him.

He pushed the button for the sixth floor. Salander stood next to him and leaned her head against the side of the elevator.

"I'm drunk," she said.

He smiled down at her. "Oh, really?"

"It's been one of those weeks. Let me guess. You're a businessman of some sort, from Hanover or somewhere in northern Germany. You're married. You love your wife. And you have to stay here in Gibraltar for another few days. I gathered that much from your phone call in the bar."

The man looked at her, astonished.

"I'm from Sweden myself. I'm feeling an irresistible urge to have sex with somebody. I don't care if you're married and I don't want your phone number."

He looked startled.

"I'm in room 711, on the floor above yours. I'm going to go up to my room, take a bath, and get into bed. If you want to keep me company, knock on the door within half an hour. Otherwise I'll be asleep."

"Is this some kind of joke?" he said as the elevator stopped.

"No. It's just that I can't be bothered to go out to some pick-up bar. Either you knock on my door or you don't."

Twenty-five minutes later there was a knock on the door of Salander's room. She had a bath towel around her when she opened the door.

"Come in," she said.

He stepped inside and looked around the room suspiciously.

"I'm alone here," she said.

"How old are you, actually?"

She reached for her passport on top of a chest of drawers and handed it to him.

"You look younger."

"I know," she said, taking off the bath towel and throwing it onto a chair. She went over to the bed and pulled off the bedspread.

She glanced over her shoulder and saw that he was staring at her tattoos.

"This isn't a trap. I'm a woman, I'm single, and I'll be here for a few days. I haven't had sex for months."

"Why did you choose me?"

"Because you were the only man in the bar who looked as if you were here alone."

"I'm married—"

"And I don't want to know who she is, or even who you are. And I don't want to discuss sociology. I want to fuck. Take off your clothes or go back down to your room."

"Just like that?"

"Yes. Why not? You're a grown man—you know what you're supposed to do."

He thought about it for all of thirty seconds. He looked as if he was going to leave. She sat on the edge of the bed and waited. He bit his lip. Then he took off his trousers and shirt and stood hesitantly in his boxer shorts.

"Take it all off," Salander said. "I don't intend to fuck somebody in his underwear. And you have to use a condom. I know where I've been, but I don't know where you've been."

He took off his shorts and went over to her and put his hand on her shoulder. Salander closed her eyes when he bent down to kiss her. He tasted good. She let him tip her back onto the bed. He was heavy on top of her.

Jeremy Stuart MacMillan, Esq., felt the hairs rise on the back of his neck as soon as he tried to unlock the door to his office at Buchanan House on Queensway Quay above the marina. It was already unlocked. He opened it and smelled tobacco smoke and heard a chair creak. It was just before 7:00, and his first thought was that he had surprised a burglar.

Then he smelled the coffee from the machine in the kitchenette. After a couple of seconds he stepped hesitantly over the threshold and walked down the hall to look into his spacious and elegantly furnished office. Salander was sitting in his desk chair with her back to him and her feet on the windowsill. His PC was turned on. Obviously she had not had any problem cracking his password. Nor had she had any problem opening his safe. She had a folder with his most private correspondence and bookkeeping on her lap.

"Good morning, Miss Salander," he said at last.

"Ah, there you are," she said. "There's freshly brewed coffee and croissants in the kitchen."

"Thanks," he said, sighing in resignation.

He had, after all, bought the office with her money and at her request, but he had not expected her to turn up without warning. What's more, she had found and apparently read a gay porn magazine that he kept hidden in a desk drawer.

So embarrassing.

Or maybe not.

When it came to Salander, he felt that she was the most judgemental person he had ever met. But she never once raised an eyebrow at people's weaknesses. She knew that he was officially heterosexual, but his dark secret was that he was attracted to men; since his divorce fifteen years ago he had been making his most private fantasies a reality.

It's funny, but I feel safe with her.

Since she was in Gibraltar anyway, Salander had decided to visit MacMillan, the man who handled her finances. She had not been in touch with him since just after the New Year, and she wanted to know if he had been busy ruining her ever since.

But there had not been any great hurry, and it was not for him that she had gone straight to Gibraltar after her release. She did it because she felt a burning desire to get away from everything, and in that respect Gibraltar was an excellent choice. She had spent almost a week getting drunk, and then a few days having sex with the German businessman, who eventually introduced himself as Dieter. She doubted it was his real name but had not bothered to check. He spent the days sitting in meetings and the evenings having dinner with her before they went back to his or her room.

He was not at all bad in bed, Salander thought, although he was a bit out of practice and sometimes needlessly rough.

Dieter seemed genuinely astonished that on sheer impulse she had picked up an overweight German businessman who was not even looking for it. He was indeed married, and he was not in the habit of being unfaithful or seeking female company on his business trips. But when the opportunity was presented on a platter in the form of a thin, tattooed young woman, he could not resist the temptation. Or so he said.

Salander did not much care what he said. She had not been looking for anything more than recreational sex, but she was gratified that he actually made an effort to satisfy her. It was not until the fourth night, their last together, that he had a panic attack and started going on about what his wife would say. Salander thought he should keep his mouth shut and not tell his wife a thing.

But she did not tell him what she thought.

He was a grown man and could have said no to her invitation. It was not her problem if he was now attacked by feelings of guilt, or if he confessed anything to his wife. She had lain with her back to him and listened for fifteen minutes, until finally she rolled her eyes in exasperation, turned over, and straddled him.

"Do you think you could take a break from the worrywart stuff and get me off again?" she said.

Jeremy MacMillan was a very different story. He held zero erotic attraction for her. He was a crook. Amusingly enough, he looked a lot like Dieter. He was forty-eight, a bit overweight, with greying, dark-blond curly hair that he combed straight back from a high forehead. He wore thin gold-rimmed glasses.

Cambridge-educated, he had once been a business lawyer and a stockbroker in London. He had had a promising future and was a partner in a law firm that was engaged by big corporations and wealthy yuppies interested in real estate and tax planning. He had spent the go-go eighties hanging out with nouveau riche celebrities. He had drunk hard and snorted coke with people that he really did not want to wake up with the next morning. He had never been charged with anything, but he did lose his wife and two kids along with his job when he mismanaged several transactions and tottered drunk into a mediation hearing.

Without thinking too much about it, he sobered up and

fled London with his tail between his legs. Why he picked Gibraltar he did not know, but in 1991 he went into partnership with a local attorney and opened a modest back-street law office which officially dealt with much less glamorous matters: estate planning, wills, and the like. Unofficially, MacMillan & Marks also helped to set up P.O. box companies and acted as gatekeepers for a number of shady figures in Europe. The firm was barely making ends meet when Salander selected Jeremy MacMillan to administer the 2.5 billion Swedish kronor she had stolen from the collapsing empire of the Swedish financier Hans-Erik Wennerström.

MacMillan was a crook, no doubt about it, but she regarded him as *her* crook, and he had surprised himself by being impeccably honest in his dealings with her. She had first hired him for a simple task. For a modest fee he had set up a string of P.O. box companies for her to use; she put a million dollars into each of them. She had contacted him by telephone and had been nothing more than a voice from afar. He never tried to discover where the money came from. He had done what she asked and took a 5 percent commission. A little while later she had transferred a large sum of money that he was to use to set up a corporation, Wasp Enterprises, which then acquired a substantial apartment in Stockholm. His dealings with Salander were becoming quite lucrative, even if still on a modest scale.

Two months later she had paid a visit to Gibraltar. She had called him and suggested dinner in her room at the Rock Hotel, which was if not the biggest hotel in Gibraltar, then certainly the most famous. He was not sure what he had expected, but he could not believe that his client was this doll-like girl who looked as if she were in her early teens. He thought he was the butt of some outlandish practical joke.

He soon changed his mind. The strange young woman talked with him impersonally, without ever smiling or showing any warmth. Or coolness, for that matter. He had sat paralysed as, over the course of a few minutes, she obliterated the professional façade of sophisticated respectability that he was always so careful to maintain.

"What is it that you want?" he had asked.

"I've stolen a sum of money," she replied with great seriousness. "I need a crook who can administer it."

He had stared at her, wondering whether she was deranged, but politely he played along. She might be a possible mark for a con game that could bring in a small income. Then he had sat as if struck by lightning when she explained whom she had stolen the money from, how she'd done it, and what the amount was. The Wennerström affair was the hottest topic of conversation in the world of international finance.

"I see."

The possibilities flew through his head.

"You're a skilled business lawyer and stockbroker. If you were an idiot you would never have gotten the jobs you did in the eighties. However, you behaved like an idiot and managed to get yourself fired."

He winced.

"In the future I will be your only client."

She had looked at him with the most ingenuous expression he had ever seen.

"I have two conditions. The first is that you never ever

commit a crime or get mixed up in anything that could create problems for us and focus the authorities' attention on my companies and accounts. The second is that you never lie to me. Never ever. Not a single time. And not for any reason. If you lie to me, our business relationship will terminate instantly, and if you make me angry enough I will ruin you."

She poured him a glass of wine.

"There's no reason to lie to me. I already know everything worth knowing about your life. I know how much you make in a good month and how much in a bad month. I know how much you spend. I know that you never really have enough money. I know that you owe £120,000 in both long-term and short-term debts, and that you always have to take risks and skim some money to make the loan payments. You wear expensive clothes and try to keep up appearances, but in reality you've gone to the dogs and haven't bought a new sports jacket in several months. But you did take an old jacket in to have the lining mended two weeks ago. You used to collect rare books but have been gradually selling them off. Last month you sold an early edition of *Oliver Twist* for £760."

She stopped talking and fixed him with her gaze. He swallowed hard.

"Last week you actually made a killing. A quite clever fraud perpetrated against that widow you represent. You robbed her of £6,000, which she'll probably never miss."

"How the hell do you know that?"

"I know that you were married, that you have two children in England who don't want to see you, and that you've taken the big leap since your divorce and now have primarily homosexual relationships. You're probably ashamed of that and avoid the gay clubs, and you avoid being seen in town with any of your male friends. You regularly cross the border into Spain to meet men."

MacMillan was shaken to the core. And he was suddenly terrified. He had no idea how she had come by all this information, but she knew enough to destroy him.

"And I'm only going to say this one time. I don't give a shit who you have sex with. It's none of my business. I want to know who you are, but I will never use what I know. I won't threaten you or blackmail you."

MacMillan was no fool. He was perfectly aware, of course, that her knowledge of all that information about him constituted a threat. She was in control. For a moment he considered picking her up and throwing her over the edge of the terrace, but he restrained himself. He had never in his life been so scared.

"What do you want?" he managed to say.

"I want to have a partnership with you. You will bring to a close all the other business you're handling and will work exclusively for me. You will make more money from my company than you could ever dream of making any other way."

She explained what she required him to do, and how she wanted the arrangements to be made.

"I want to be invisible," she said. "And I want you to take care of my affairs. Everything has to be legitimate. Whatever money I make on my own will not have any connection to our business together."

"I understand."

"You have one week to phase out your other clients and put a stop to all your little schemes."

He also realized that he had been given an offer that would never come around again. He thought about it for sixty seconds and then accepted. He had only one question.

"How do you know that I won't swindle you?"

"Don't even think about it. You'd regret it for the rest of your miserable life."

He had no reason to cook the books. Salander had made him an offer that had the potential of such a silver lining that it would have been idiotic to risk it for bits of change on the side. As long as he was relatively discreet and did not get involved in any financial chicanery, his future would be assured.

Accordingly, he had no thought of swindling Ms. Salander.

So he went straight, or as straight as a burned-out lawyer who was administering an astronomical sum of stolen money could go.

Salander was simply not interested in the management of her finances. MacMillan's job was to invest her money and see to it that there were funds to cover the credit cards she used. She told him how she wanted her finances to be handled. His job was to make sure it was done.

A large part of the money had been invested in gilt-edged funds that would provide her with economic independence for the rest of her life, even if she chose to live it recklessly and dissolutely. It was from these funds that her credit card bills were paid.

The rest of the money he could play with and invest as he saw fit, provided that he did not invest in anything that might cause problems with the police in any way. She forbade him to engage in stupid petty crimes and cheap con games which—if he was unlucky—might prompt investigations which in turn could put her under scrutiny.

All that remained was to agree on how much he would make on the transactions.

"I'll pay you £500,000 as a retainer. With that you can pay off all your debts and have a good deal left over. After that you'll earn money for yourself. You will start a company with the two of us as partners. You get 20 percent of all the profits generated. I want you to be rich enough that you won't be tempted to cheat, but not so rich that you won't make an effort."

He had started his new job on February 1 the year before. By the end of March he had paid off all his debts and stabilized his personal finances. Salander had insisted that he make cleaning up his own affairs a priority so that he would be solvent. In May he dissolved the partnership with his alcoholic colleague George Marks. He felt a twinge of conscience towards his former partner, but getting Marks mixed up in Salander's business was out of the question.

He discussed the matter with Salander when she returned to Gibraltar on another unheralded visit in early July and discovered that MacMillan was working out of his apartment instead of from the office he had previously occupied.

"My partner's an alcoholic and wouldn't be able to handle this. And he would be an enormous risk factor. At the same time, fifteen years ago he saved my life when he took me into his business."

She pondered this for a while as she studied MacMillan's face.

"I see. You're a crook who's loyal. That could be a commendable quality. I suggest you set up a small account that he can play around with. See to it that he makes a couple of thousand a month so he gets by."

"Is that OK with you?"

She nodded and looked around his bachelor pad. He lived in a studio apartment with a kitchen nook on one of the alleys near the hospital. The only pleasant thing about the place was the view. On the other hand, it was a view that was hard to avoid in Gibraltar.

"You need an office and a nicer place to live," she said.

"I haven't had time," he said.

Then she went out and found an office for him, choosing a 1,400-square-foot place with a little balcony facing the sea in Buchanan House on Queensway Quay, which was definitely upmarket in Gibraltar. She hired an interior decorator to renovate and furnish it.

MacMillan recalled that while he had been busy shuffling papers, Salander had personally supervised the installation of an alarm system, computer equipment, and the safe that she had already rummaged through by the time he entered the office that morning.

"Am I in trouble?" he said.

She put down the folder with the correspondence she had been perusing.

"No, Jeremy. You're not in trouble."

"That's good," he said as he poured himself some coffee. "You have a way of popping up when I least expect it."

"I've been busy lately. I just wanted to get an update on what's been happening."

"I believe you were suspected of killing three people, you

got shot in the head, and you were charged with a whole assortment of crimes. I was pretty worried for a while. I thought you were still in prison. Did you break out?"

"No. I was acquitted of all the charges and released. How much have you heard?"

He hesitated a moment. "Well, when I heard that you were in trouble, I hired a translation agency to comb the Swedish press and give me regular updates. I'm familiar with the details."

"If you're basing your knowledge on what you read in the papers, then you're not familiar at all. But I dare say you discovered a number of secrets about me."

He nodded.

"What's going to happen now?" he said.

She gave him a surprised look. "Nothing. We keep on exactly as before. Our relationship has nothing to do with my problems in Sweden. Tell me what's been happening since I've been away. Have you been doing all right?"

"I'm not drinking, if that's what you mean."

"No. Your private life doesn't concern me so long as it doesn't encroach on our business. I mean, am I richer or poorer than I was a year ago?"

He pulled out the guest chair and sat down. Somehow it did not matter to him that she was sitting in his chair.

"You turned over 2.5 billion Swedish kronor to me. We put 200 million into personal funds for you. You gave me the rest to play with."

"And?"

"Your personal funds haven't grown by much more than the amount of interest. I could increase the profit if—"

"I'm not interested in increasing the profit."

"OK. You've spent a negligible amount. The principal expenses have been the apartment I bought for you and the fund you started for that lawyer Palmgren. Otherwise you've just had normal expenses. The interest rate has been favourable. You're running about even."

"Good."

"The rest I invested. Last year we didn't make very much. I was a little rusty and spent the time learning the market again. We've had expenses. We didn't really start generating income until this year. Since the start of the year we've taken about seven million. Dollars, that is."

"Of which 20 percent goes to you."

"Of which 20 percent goes to me."

"Are you satisfied with that?"

"I've made more than a million dollars in six months. Yes, I'm satisfied."

"You know . . . you shouldn't get too greedy. You can cut back on your hours when you're satisfied. Just make sure you spend a few hours on my affairs every so often."

"Ten million dollars," he said.

"Excuse me?"

"When I get ten million together I'll pack it in. It was good that you turned up in my life. We have a lot to discuss."

"Fire away."

He threw up his hands.

"This is so much money that it scares the shit out of me. I don't know how to handle it. I don't know the purpose of the company besides making more money. What's all the money going to be used for?"

"I don't know."

"Me neither. But money can become an end in itself. It's crazy. That's why I've decided to call it quits when I've earned ten million for myself. I don't want the responsibility any longer."

"Fair enough."

"But before I call it a day I want you to decide how this fortune is to be administered in the future. There has to be a purpose and guidelines and some kind of organization that can take over."

"Mmm."

"It's impossible to conduct business this way. I've divided up the sum into long-term fixed investments—real estate, securities, and so forth. There's a complete list on the computer."

"I've read it."

"The other half I've put into speculation, but it's so much money to keep track of that I can't keep up. So I set up an investment company on Jersey. At present you have six employees in London. Two talented young brokers and some clerical staff."

"Yellow Ballroom Ltd.? I was wondering what that could be."

"Our company. Here in Gibraltar I've hired a secretary and a promising young lawyer. They'll be here in half an hour, by the way."

"I know. Molly Flint, forty-one, and Brian Delaney, twenty-six."

"Do you want to meet them?"

"No. Is Brian your lover?"

"What? No." He looked shocked. "I don't mix—"

"Good."

"By the way, I'm not interested in young guys . . . inexperienced ones, I mean."

"No, you're more attracted to men with a tough attitude than to some snot-nosed kid. It's none of my business. But, Jeremy . . ."

"Yes?"

"Be careful."

Salander had not planned to stay in Gibraltar for more than two weeks; just long enough, she thought, to get her bearings. But she suddenly discovered that she had no idea what she was going to do or where she should go. She stayed for three months. She checked her email once a day and replied promptly to messages from Giannini on the few occasions her lawyer got in touch. She did not tell her where she was. She did not answer any other email.

She still went to Harry's Bar, but now she came in only for a beer or two in the evenings. She spent large parts of her days at the Rock Hotel, either on her balcony or in bed. She got together with a thirty-year-old Royal Navy officer, but it was a one-night stand and all in all an uninteresting experience.

She was bored.

Early in October she had dinner with MacMillan. They had met up only a few times during her stay. It was dark and they drank a fruity white wine and discussed what they should use her billions for. And then he surprised her by asking what was upsetting her.

She studied his face for a long time and pondered the matter. Then she, just as surprisingly, told him about her relationship with Miriam Wu, and how Mimmi had been beaten and almost killed. And she, Lisbeth, was to blame. Apart from one greeting sent by way of Giannini, Salander had not heard a word from Mimmi. And now she was in France.

MacMillan listened in silence.

"Are you in love with her?" he said at last.

Salander shook her head.

"No. I don't think I'm the type who falls in love. She was a friend. And we had good sex."

"Nobody can avoid falling in love," he said. "They might want to deny it, but friendship is probably the most common form of love."

She looked at him in astonishment.

"Will you get angry if I say something personal?"

"No."

"Go to Paris, for God's sake," he said.

She landed at Charles de Gaulle Airport at 2:30 in the afternoon, took the airport bus to the Arc de Triomphe, and spent two hours wandering around the nearby neighbourhoods trying to find a hotel room. She walked south towards the Seine and finally found a room at a small hotel, the Victor Hugo on rue Copernic.

She took a shower and called Miriam Wu. They met that evening at a bar near Notre-Dame. Mimmi was dressed in a white shirt and jacket. She looked fabulous. Salander instantly felt shy. They kissed each other on the cheek.

"I'm sorry I haven't called, and that I didn't come to the trial," Mimmi said.

"That's OK. The trial was behind closed doors anyway."

"I was in the hospital for three weeks, and then it was

chaos when I got home to Lundagatan. I couldn't sleep. I had nightmares about that bastard Niedermann. I called my mother and told her I wanted to come here, to Paris."

Salander said she understood.

"Forgive me," Mimmi said.

"Don't be such an idiot. I'm the one who's come here to ask you to forgive me."

"For what?"

"I wasn't thinking. It never occurred to me that I was putting you in such danger by turning over my old apartment to you. It was my fault that you were almost murdered. You'd have every right to hate me."

Mimmi looked shocked. "Lisbeth, I never even gave it a thought. It was Ronald Niedermann who tried to murder me, not you."

They sat in silence for a while.

"All right," Salander said finally.

"Right," Mimmi said.

"I didn't follow you here because I'm in love with you," Salander said.

Mimmi nodded.

"We had great sex, but I'm not in love with you."

"Lisbeth, I think—"

"What I wanted to say was that I hope you . . . *damn.*"

"What?"

"I don't have many friends. . . ."

Mimmi nodded. "I'm going to be in Paris for a while. My studies at home were a mess so I signed up at the university here instead. I'll probably stay at least one academic year. After that I don't know. But I'm going to go back to Stockholm. I'm still paying the service charges on Lundagatan and I mean to keep the apartment. If that's OK with you."

"It's your apartment. Do what you want with it."

"Lisbeth, you're a very special person," Mimmi said. "I'd still like to be your friend."

They talked for two hours. Salander did not have any reason to hide her past from Miriam Wu. The Zalachenko business was familiar to everyone who had access to a Swedish newspaper, and Mimmi had followed the story with great interest. She gave Salander a detailed account of what had happened in Nykvarn the night Paolo Roberto saved her life.

Then they went back to Mimmi's student lodgings near the university.

Friday, December 2– Sunday, December 18

Giannini met Salander in the bar of the Södra theatre at 9:00. Salander was drinking beer and was already coming to the end of her second glass.

"Sorry I'm late," Giannini said, glancing at her watch. "I had to deal with another client."

"That's OK," said Lisbeth.

"What are you celebrating?"

"Nothing. I just feel like getting drunk."

Giannini looked at her sceptically and took a seat.

"Do you often feel that way?"

"I drank myself stupid after I was released, but I have no tendency to alcoholism. It just occurred to me that for the first time in my life I have a legal right to get drunk here in Sweden."

Giannini ordered a Campari.

"Do you want to drink alone," she said, "or would you like some company?"

"Preferably alone. But if you don't talk too much you can

sit with me. I take it you don't feel like coming home with me and having sex."

"I beg your pardon?" Giannini said.

"No, I didn't think so. You're one of those insanely heterosexual people."

Giannini suddenly looked amused.

"That's the first time in my life that one of my clients has propositioned me."

"Are you interested?"

"No, not in the least, sorry. But thanks for the offer."

"So what was it you wanted, counsellor?"

"Two things. Either I quit as your lawyer here and now or you start answering your phone when I call. We've already had this discussion, when you were released."

Salander looked at Giannini.

"I've been trying to reach you for a week. I've called, I've sent letters, I've emailed."

"I've been away."

"In fact you've been impossible to get ahold of for most of the fall. This just isn't working. I said I would represent you in all negotiations with the government. There are formalities that have to be taken care of. Papers to be signed. Questions to be answered. I have to be able to reach you, and I have no wish to be made to feel like an idiot because I don't know where the hell you are."

"I was away again for two weeks. I came home yesterday and called you as soon as I knew you were looking for me."

"That's not good enough. You have to keep me informed of where you are and get in touch at least once a week until all the issues about compensation and such are resolved."

"I don't give a shit about compensation. I just want the government to leave me alone."

"But the government isn't going to leave you alone, no matter how much you may want it to. Your acquittal has set in motion a long chain of consequences. It's not just about you. Teleborian is going to be charged for what he did to you. You're going to have to testify. Ekström is the subject of an investigation for dereliction of duty, and he may even be charged too if it turns out that he deliberately disregarded his duty at the behest of the Section."

Salander raised her eyebrows. For a moment she looked interested.

"I don't think it's going to come to an indictment. He was led up the garden path by the Section and in fact he had nothing to do with them. But as recently as last week a prosecutor initiated a preliminary investigation against the guardianship agency. It involves several reports being sent to the parliamentary ombudsman, as well as a report to the ministry of justice."

"I didn't report anyone."

"No. But it's obvious that there has been gross dereliction of duty. You're not the only person affected."

Salander shrugged. "This has nothing to do with me. But I promise to be in closer contact with you. These last two weeks have been an exception. I've been working."

Giannini did not look as though she believed her. "What are you working on?"

"Consulting."

"I see," she said. "The other thing is that the inventory of the estate is now ready."

"Inventory of what estate?"

"Your father's. The state's legal representative contacted me since nobody seemed to know how to get in touch with you. You and your sister are the sole heirs."

Salander looked at Giannini blankly. Then she caught the waitress's eye and pointed at her glass.

"I don't want any inheritance from my father. Do whatever the hell you want with it."

"Wrong. *You* can do what you want with the inheritance. My job is to see to it that you have the opportunity to do so."

"I don't want a single öre from that pig."

"Then give the money to Greenpeace or something."

"I don't give a shit about whales."

Giannini's voice suddenly softened. "Lisbeth, if you're going to be a legally responsible citizen, then you're going to have to start behaving like one. I don't give a damn what you do with your money. Just sign here that you received it, and then you can get drunk in peace."

Salander glanced at her and then looked down at the table. Annika assumed this was some kind of conciliatory gesture that perhaps corresponded to an apology in Salander's limited repertoire of expressions.

"What kind of figures are we talking about?"

"They're not insignificant. Your father had about 300,000 kronor in shares. The property in Gosseberga would sell for around 1.5 million—there's a little woodland included. And there are three other properties."

"What sort of properties?"

"It seems that he invested a significant amount of money. There's nothing of enormous value, but he owns a small building in Uddevalla with six apartments, and they bring in some income. But the property is not in good shape. He didn't bother with upkeep. You won't get rich, but you'd get a good price if you sold it. He also owns a summer cabin in Småland that's worth around 250,000 kronor. Plus he owns a dilapidated industrial site outside Norrtälje."

"Why in the world did he buy all this shit?"

"I have no idea. However, the estate could bring in over four million kronor after taxes. But . . ."

"But what?"

"The inheritance has to be divided equally between you and your sister. The problem is that nobody knows where your sister is."

Salander looked at Giannini in silence.

"Well?"

"Well what?"

"Where is your sister?"

"I have no idea. I haven't seen her for ten years."

"Her file is classified, but I found out that she is listed as out of the country."

"I see," Salander said, showing little interest.

Giannini sighed in exasperation.

"I would suggest that we liquidate all the assets and deposit half the proceeds in the bank until your sister can be found. I can initiate the negotiations if you give me the go-ahead."

Salander shrugged. "I don't want anything to do with his money."

"I understand that. But the balance sheet still has to be sorted out. It's part of your responsibility as a citizen."

"Sell the crap, then. Put half in the bank and send the rest to whoever you like."

Giannini stared at her. She had understood that Salander

had money stashed away, but she had not realized that her client was so well off that she could ignore an inheritance that might amount to a million kronor or more. What's more, she had no idea where Salander had gotten her money, or how much was involved. On the other hand, she was keen to finalize the bureaucratic procedure.

"Lisbeth, please . . . could you read through the estate inventory and give me the green light so that we can get this matter resolved?"

Salander grumbled for a moment, but finally she acquiesced and stuffed the folder into her shoulder bag. She promised to read through it and send instructions as to what she wanted Giannini to do. Then she went back to her beer. Giannini kept her company for an hour, drinking mostly mineral water.

It was not until several days later, when Giannini called to remind her about the estate inventory, that Salander took out the crumpled papers. She sat at the kitchen table, smoothed out the documents, and read through them.

The inventory covered several pages. There was a detailed list of all kinds of junk—the china in the kitchen cupboards in Gosseberga, clothing, cameras, and other personal effects. Zalachenko had not left behind much of real value, and none of the objects had the slightest sentimental value for Salander. She decided that her attitude had not changed since she met with Giannini at the theatre bar. Sell the crap and give the money away. Or something. She was positive that she did not want a single öre of her father's wealth, but she also was pretty sure that Zalachenko's real assets were hidden where no tax inspector would look for them.

Then she opened the title deeds for the property in Norrtälje.

It was an industrial site of three buildings totalling 215,000
square feet in the vicinity of Skederid, between Norrtälje and
Rimbo.

The estate appraiser had apparently paid a cursory visit
and noted that it was an old brickworks that had been more
or less empty and abandoned since it was shut down in the
sixties, apart from a period in the seventies when it had been
used to store lumber. He noted that the buildings were in
"extremely poor condition" and could not in all likelihood be
renovated for any other activity. The term "poor condition"
was also used to describe the "north building," which had in
fact been destroyed by fire and collapsed. Some repairs, he
wrote, had been made to the "main building."

What gave Salander a jolt was the site's history. Zalachenko had acquired the property for a song on March 12,
1984, but the signatory on the purchase documents was
Agneta Sofia Salander.

So Salander's mother had in fact been the owner of the
property. Yet in 1987 her ownership had ceased. Zalachenko
had bought her out for 2,000 kronor. After that the property
had stood unused for fifteen years. The inventory showed
that on September 17, 2003, KAB Import AB had hired the
builders NorrBygg Inc. to do renovations which included
repairs to the floor and roof, as well as improvements to the
water and electrical systems. Repair work had gone on for
two months, until the end of November, when it was discontinued. NorrBygg had sent an invoice, which had been paid.

Of all the assets in her father's estate, this was the only surprising entry. Salander was puzzled. Ownership of the indus-

trial site made sense if her father had wanted to give the impression that KAB Import was carrying on legitimate activities or owned certain assets. It also made sense that he had used her mother as a front in the purchase and had then for a pittance bought back the property.

But why in heaven's name would he spend almost 440,000 kronor to renovate a ramshackle building, which according to the appraiser was still not being used for anything in 2005?

She could not understand it, but she was not going to waste time wondering. She closed the folder and called Giannini.

"I've read the inventory. What I said still holds. Sell the shit and do whatever you like with the money. I want nothing from him."

"Very well. I'll see to it that half the revenue is deposited in an account for your sister, and I'll suggest some suitable recipients for the rest."

"Right," Salander said and hung up without further discussion.

She sat in her window seat, lit a cigarette, and looked out towards Saltsjön.

Salander spent the next week helping Armansky with an urgent matter. She had to help track down and identify a person suspected of being hired to kidnap a child in a custody battle resulting from a Swedish woman divorcing her Lebanese husband. Salander's job amounted to checking the email of the person who was presumed to have hired the kidnapper. Milton Security's role was discontinued when the parties reached a legal solution.

On December 18, the Sunday before Christmas, Salander

woke at 6:00 and remembered that she had to buy a Christmas present for Palmgren. For a moment she wondered whether there was anyone else she should buy presents for—Giannini, perhaps. She got up and took a shower in no particular hurry, and ate a breakfast of toast with cheese and marmalade and a coffee.

She had nothing special planned for the day and spent a while clearing papers and magazines from her desk. Then her gaze fell on the folder with the estate inventory. She opened it and reread the page about the title registration for the site in Norrtälje. She sighed. *OK. I have to find out what the hell he had going on there.*

She put on warm clothes and boots. It was 8:30 when she drove her burgundy Honda out of the garage beneath Fiskargatan 9. It was icy cold but beautiful, sunshine and a pastel blue sky. She took the road via Slussen and Klarabergsleden and wound her way onto the E18 going north, heading for Norrtälje. She was in no hurry. At 10:00 she turned into a gas station a few miles outside Skederid to ask the way to the old brickworks. No sooner had she parked than she realized that she did not even need to ask.

She was on a hillside with a good view across the valley on the other side of the road. To the left towards Norrtälje she could see a warehouse, some sort of builder's yard, and another yard with bulldozers. To the right, at the edge of the industrial area, about 400 yards from the road, was a dismal brick building with a crumbling chimney stack. The factory stood like a last outpost of the industrial area, somewhat isolated beyond a road and a narrow stream. She surveyed the building thoughtfully and asked herself what on earth had possessed her to drive all the way up to Norrtälje.

She turned and glanced at the gas station, where a long-distance truck and trailer with the emblem of the International Road Transport Union had just pulled in. She remembered that she was on the main road from the ferry terminal at Kapellskär, through which a good deal of the freight traffic between Sweden and the Baltic countries passed.

She started the car and drove out onto the road towards the old brickworks. She parked in the middle of the yard and got out. It was below freezing outside, and she put on a black knitted cap and leather gloves.

The main building was on two floors. On the ground floor all the windows had been boarded up with plywood, and she could see that on the floor above many of them had been broken. The factory was a much bigger building than she had imagined, and it was incredibly dilapidated. She could see no evidence of repairs. There was no trace of a living soul, but she saw that someone had discarded a used condom in the yard, and that graffiti artists had attacked part of the façade.

Why had Zalachenko owned this building?

She walked around the factory and found the ramshackle north building to the rear. She saw that the doors to the main building were locked. In frustration she studied a door at one end of the building. All the other doors had padlocks attached with iron bolts and galvanized security strips, but the lock on the gable end seemed weaker and was in fact attached only with rough spikes. *Damn it, it's my building.* She looked around and found a narrow iron pipe in a pile of rubbish. She used it to lever open the fastening of the padlock.

She entered a stairwell with a doorway to the ground floor area. The boarded-up windows meant that it was pitch-black inside, except for a few shafts of light seeping in at the edges of the boards. She stood still for several minutes, until her eyes adjusted to the darkness. She saw a sea of junk—wooden pallets, old machine parts, and lumber—in a workshop that was 150 feet long and about 65 feet wide, supported by massive pillars. The old brick ovens seemed to have been disassembled, and in their place were big pools of water and patches of mould on the floor. There was a stale, foul smell from all the debris. She wrinkled her nose in disgust.

She turned back and went up the stairs. The top floor was dry and consisted of two similar rooms, each about sixty-five feet square, and at least twenty-five feet high. There were tall, inaccessible windows close to the ceiling which provided no view but let in plenty of light. The upper floor, like the workshop downstairs, was full of junk. There were dozens of three-foot-high packing cases stacked on top of one another. She gripped one of them but could not move it. The label on the crate read: MACHINE PARTS 0-A77, with an apparently corresponding label in Russian underneath. She noticed an open freight elevator halfway down one wall of the first room.

It was a machine warehouse of some sort, but that would hardly generate income so long as the machinery stood there rusting.

She went into the inner room and discovered that this was where the repair work must have been carried out. The room was again full of rubbish, boxes, and old office furniture arranged in some sort of labyrinthine order. A section of the floor was exposed where new floor planks had been laid. Salander guessed that the renovation work had been stopped abruptly. A crosscut saw and a circular saw, a nail gun, a crowbar, an iron rod, and tool boxes were still there. She frowned. Even if the work had been discontinued, the joiners should have picked up their tools. But this question too was answered when she held a screwdriver up to the light and saw that the writing on the handle was Russian. Zalachenko had imported the tools, and probably the workers as well.

She switched on the circular saw and a green light went on. There was power. She turned it off.

At the far end of the room were three doors to smaller rooms, perhaps the old offices. She tried the handle of the door on the north side of the building. Locked. She went back to the tools and got a crowbar. It took her a while to break open the door.

It was pitch-black inside the room and smelled musty. She ran her hand along the wall and found a switch that lit a bare bulb in the ceiling. Salander looked around in astonishment.

The furniture in the room consisted of three beds with soiled mattresses and another three mattresses on the floor. Filthy bed linen was strewn around. To the right was a two-ring electric stove and some pots next to a rusty water tap. In a corner stood a tin bucket and a roll of toilet paper.

Somebody had lived here. Several people.

Then she saw that there was no handle on the inside of the door. She felt an ice-cold shiver run down her back.

There was a large linen cupboard at the far end of the room. She opened it and found two suitcases. Inside the one on top were some clothes. She rummaged through them and held up a dress with a Russian label. She found a handbag and emptied the contents on the floor. From among the cosmetics and other bits and pieces she retrieved a passport belonging to a young, dark-haired woman. It was a Russian passport, and she sounded out the name as Valentina.

Salander walked slowly from the room. She had a feeling of déjà vu. She had done the same kind of crime scene examination in a basement in Hedeby two and a half years earlier. Women's clothes. A prison. She stood there for a long time, thinking. It bothered her that the passport and clothes had been left behind. It did not feel right.

Then she went back to the assortment of tools and rummaged about until she found a powerful flashlight. She checked that there was life in the batteries and went downstairs into the larger workshop. The water from the puddles on the floor seeped into her boots.

The nauseating stench of rotting matter grew stronger the farther into the workshop she went; it seemed to be worst when she was in the middle of the room. She stopped next to the foundation of one of the old brick furnaces, which was filled with water almost to the brim. She shone her flashlight onto the coal-black surface of the water but could not make anything out. The surface was partly covered by algae that had formed a green slime. Nearby she found a long steel rod, which she stuck into the pool and stirred around. The water was only about twenty inches deep. Almost immediately the rod bumped into something. She manipulated it this way and that for several seconds before a body rose to the surface, face first, a grinning mask of death and decomposition. Breathing through her mouth, Salander looked at the face in the beam of the flashlight and saw that it was a woman, possibly the woman from the passport photograph. She knew nothing about the speed of decay in cold, stagnant water, but the body seemed to have been in the pool for a long time.

There was something moving on the surface of the water. Larvae of some sort.

She let the body sink back beneath the surface and poked around more with the rod. At the edge of the pool she came across something that might have been another body. She left it there and pulled out the rod, letting it fall to the floor as she stood thinking next to the pool.

Salander went back up the stairs. She used the crowbar to break open the middle door. The room was empty.

She went to the last door and slotted the crowbar in place, but before she began to force it, the door swung open a crack. It was not locked. She nudged it open with the crowbar and looked around.

The room was about a hundred feet square. It had windows at a normal height with a view of the yard in front of the brickworks. She could see the gas station on the hill. There was a bed, a table, and a sink with dishes. Then she saw a bag lying open on the floor. There were banknotes in it. Surprised, she took two steps forward before she noticed that the room was warm and saw an electric heater in the middle of the room. Then she saw that the red light was on on the coffee machine.

Someone was living here. She was not alone in the building.

She spun around and ran through the inner room, out the doors, and towards the exit in the outer workshop. She stopped five steps short of the stairwell when she saw that the exit had been closed and padlocked. She was locked in. Slowly she turned and looked around, but there was no-one.

"Hello, little sister," came a cheerful voice from somewhere to her right.

She turned to see Niedermann's vast form materialize from behind some packing crates.

In his hand was a large knife.

"I was hoping I'd have a chance to see you again," Niedermann said. "Everything happened so fast the last time."

Salander looked around.

"Don't bother," Niedermann said. "It's just you and me, and there's no way out except through the locked door behind you."

Salander turned her eyes to her half-brother.

"How's the hand?" she said.

Niedermann was smiling at her. He raised his right hand and showed her. His little finger was missing.

"It got infected. I had to chop it off."

Niedermann could not feel pain. Salander had sliced his hand open with a spade at Gosseberga only seconds before Zalachenko had shot her in the head.

"I should have aimed for your skull," Salander said in a neutral tone. "What the hell are you doing here? I thought you'd left the country months ago."

He smiled at her again.

If Niedermann had tried to answer Salander's question as to what he was doing in the dilapidated brickworks, he probably would not have been able to explain. He could not explain it to himself.

He had left Gosseberga with a feeling of liberation. He was counting on the fact that Zalachenko was dead and that he would take over the business. He knew he was an excellent organizer.

He had changed cars in Alingsås, put the terror-stricken dental hygienist, Anita Kaspersson, in the trunk, and driven towards Borås. He had no plan. He improvised as he went.

He had not reflected on Kaspersson's fate. It made no difference to him whether she lived or died, and he assumed that he would be forced to do away with a bothersome witness. Somewhere on the outskirts of Borås it came to him that he could use her in a different way. He turned south and found a desolate forest outside Seglora. He tied her up in a barn and left her there. He reckoned that she would be able to work her way loose within a few hours and then lead the police south in their hunt for him. And if she did not manage to free herself, and starved or froze to death in the barn, it did not matter; it was no concern of his.

Then he drove back to Borås and from there east towards Stockholm. He had driven straight to Svavelsjö, but he avoided the clubhouse itself. It was a drag that Lundin was in prison. He went instead to the home of the club's sergeant-at-arms, Hans-Åke Waltari. He said he was looking for a place to hide, which Waltari sorted out by sending him to Göransson, the club's treasurer. But he had stayed there only a few hours.

Niedermann had, theoretically, no money worries. He had left behind almost 200,000 kronor in Gosseberga, but he had access to considerably larger sums that had been deposited abroad. His problem was that he was short of actual cash. Göransson was responsible for Svavelsjö MC's finances, and it had not been difficult for Niedermann to persuade him to take him to the cabinet in the barn where the cash was kept. Niedermann was in luck. He had been able to help himself to 800,000 kronor.

He seemed to remember that there had been a woman in the house too, but he had forgotten what he had done with her.

Göransson had also provided a car that the police were not yet looking for. Niedermann went north. He had a vague plan to make it onto one of the ferries at Kapellskär that would take him to Tallinn.

When he got to Kapellskär he sat in the parking lot for half an hour, studying the area. It was crawling with policemen.

He drove on aimlessly. He needed a place where he could lie low for a while. When he passed Norrtälje he remembered the old brickworks. He had not even thought about the place in more than a year, since the time when repairs had been under way. The brothers Harry and Atho Ranta were using the brickworks as a depot for goods moving to and from the Baltic ports, but they had both been out of the country for several weeks, ever since that journalist Svensson had started snooping around the whore trade. The brickworks would be empty.

He had driven Göransson's Saab into a shed behind the factory and gone inside. He had had to break open a door on the ground floor, and one of the first things he did was to create an emergency exit through a loose plywood board at one end of the ground floor. He later replaced the broken padlock. Then he had made himself at home in a cosy room on the upper floor.

A whole afternoon had passed before he heard the sounds coming through the walls. At first he thought these were his familiar phantoms. He sat alert and listened for almost an hour before he got up and went out to the workshop to listen more closely. At first he heard nothing, but he stood there patiently until he heard more scraping noises.

He found the key next to the sink.

Niedermann had seldom been as amazed as when he opened the door and found the two Russian whores. They were skin and bones. They seemed to have had no food for several weeks and had been living on tea and water since the last packet of rice had run out.

One of the girls was so exhausted that she could not get up from the bed. The other was in better shape. She spoke only Russian, but he knew enough of the language to understand that she was thanking God and him for saving them. She fell on her knees and threw her arms around his legs. He pushed her away, then left the room and locked the door behind him.

He had not known what to do with the whores. He heated up some soup from the cans he found in the kitchen and gave it to them while he thought. The weaker woman on the bed seemed to be getting some of her strength back. He spent the evening questioning them. It was a while before he understood that the two women were not whores at all, but students who had paid the Ranta brothers to get them into Sweden. They had been promised visas and work permits. They had come from Kapellskär in February and were taken straight to the warehouse, and there they were locked up.

Niedermann's face had darkened with anger. Those bastard Ranta brothers were collecting an income that they had not told Zalachenko about. Then they had completely forgotten about the women, or maybe had knowingly left them to their fate when they fled Sweden in such a hurry.

The question was: what was he supposed to do with them? He had no reason to harm them, and yet he could not really let them go, considering that they would probably lead the police to the brickworks. It was that simple. He could not send them back to Russia, because that would mean he would have to drive them down to Kapellskär. That seemed too difficult. The dark-haired woman, whose name was Valentina, had offered him sex if he helped them. He was not the least bit interested in having sex with the girls, but the offer had turned her into a whore too. All women were whores. It was that simple.

After three days he had tired of their incessant pleading, nagging, and knocking on the wall. He could see no other way out. So he unlocked the door one last time and swiftly solved the problem. He asked Valentina to forgive him before he reached out and in one movement broke her neck between the second and third cervical vertebrae. Then he went over to the blond girl on the bed whose name he did not know. She lay there passively, did not put up any resistance. He carried the bodies downstairs and put them in one of the flooded pits. At last he could feel some sort of peace.

Niedermann had not intended to stay long at the brickworks. He thought he would have to lie low only until the initial police manhunt had died down. He shaved his head and let his beard grow to half an inch, and that altered his appearance. He found a pair of overalls belonging to one of the workers from NorrBygg which were almost big enough to fit him. He put on a Beckers Paints baseball cap and stuffed a folding ruler into a leg pocket. At dusk he drove to the gas station shop on the hill and bought supplies. He had all the cash he needed from Svavelsjö MC's piggy bank. He looked like any workman stopping on his way home, and nobody seemed to pay him any attention. He shopped once or twice a week at the same time of day. At the shop they were always perfectly friendly to him.

From the very first day he had spent a considerable amount of time fending off the creatures that inhabited the building. They lived in the walls and came out at night. He could hear them wandering around the workshop.

He barricaded himself in his room. After several days he had had enough. He armed himself with a large knife which he had found in a kitchen drawer and went out to confront the monsters. It had to end.

All of a sudden he discovered that they were retreating. For the first time in his life he had been able to dominate his phantoms. They shrank back when he approached. He could see their deformed bodies and their tails slinking off behind the packing crates and cabinets. He howled at them. They fled.

Relieved, he went back to his room and sat up all night, waiting for them to return. They mounted a renewed attack at dawn and he faced them down once more. They fled.

He was teetering between panic and euphoria.

All his life he had been haunted by these creatures in the dark, and for the very first time he felt that he was in control of the situation. He did nothing. He slept. He ate. He thought. It was peaceful.

The days turned into weeks and spring turned to summer. From his transistor radio and the evening papers he could tell that the hunt for the killer Ronald Niedermann was winding down. He read with interest the reports of the murder of Zalachenko. *What a laugh. A psycho put an end to Zalachenko.* In July his interest was again aroused when he followed the reports of Salander's trial. He was appalled when she was acquitted and released. It did not feel right. She was free while he was forced to hide.

He bought the *Millennium* special issue at the gas station shop and read all about Salander and Zalachenko and Niedermann. A journalist named Blomkvist had described Niedermann as a pathological murderer and a psychopath. He frowned.

Fall came suddenly, and still he had not made a move. When it got colder he bought an electric heater at the shop. He did not know what kept him from leaving the brickworks.

Occasionally some young people drove into the yard and parked there, but no-one had disturbed him or tried to break into the building. In September a car drove up and a man in a blue Windbreaker tried the doors and snooped around the property. Niedermann had watched him from the window on the upper floor. The man kept writing in his notebook. He had stayed for twenty minutes before he looked around one last time and got in his car and drove away. Niedermann breathed a sigh of relief. He had no idea who the man was or what business had brought him there, but he appeared to be doing a survey of the property. It did not occur to Niedermann that Zalachenko's death had prompted an inventory of his estate.

He thought a lot about Salander. He had never expected to see her again, but she fascinated and frightened him. He was not afraid of any living person. But his sister—his half-sister—had made a particular impression on him. No-one else had ever defeated him the way she had. She had come back to life, even though he had buried her. She had come back and hunted him down. He dreamed about her every night. He would wake up in a cold sweat, and he recognized that she had replaced his usual phantoms.

In October he made a decision. He was not going to leave Sweden before he had found his sister and destroyed her. He did not have a plan, but at least his life now had a purpose. He did not know where she was or how he would trace her. He just sat in his room on the upper floor of the brickworks, staring out the window, day after day, week after week.

Until one day a burgundy Honda parked outside the building and, to his complete astonishment, he saw Salander get out of the car. *God is merciful,* he thought. Salander would join the two women in the pool downstairs. His wait was over, and he could at last get on with his life.

Salander assessed the situation and saw that it was anything but under control. Her brain was working at high speed. *Click, click, click.* She still held the crowbar in her hand but she knew that it was a feeble weapon against a man who could not feel pain. She was locked inside an area of about 10,000 square feet with a murderous robot from hell.

When Niedermann suddenly moved towards her she threw the crowbar at him. He dodged it easily. Salander moved fast. She stepped onto a pallet, swung herself up onto a packing crate and kept climbing, like a monkey, up two more crates. She stopped and looked down at Niedermann, now thirteen feet below her. He was looking up at her and waiting.

"Come down," he said patiently. "You can't escape. The end is inevitable."

She wondered if he had a gun of some sort. Now, that *would* be a problem.

He bent down and picked up a chair and threw it at her. She ducked.

Niedermann was getting annoyed. He put his foot on the pallet and started climbing up after her. She waited until he was almost at the top before she took a running start of two quick steps and jumped across an aisle to land on top of another crate. She swung down to the floor and grabbed the crowbar.

Niedermann was not actually clumsy, but he knew that he could not risk jumping from the stack of crates and perhaps breaking a bone in his foot. He had to climb down carefully and set his feet on the floor. He always had to move slowly and methodically, and he had spent a lifetime mastering his body. He had almost reached the floor when he heard footsteps behind him and turned just in time to block a blow from the crowbar with his shoulder. He lost his grip on the knife.

Salander dropped the crowbar just as she delivered the blow. She did not have time to pick up the knife, but she kicked it away from him along the pallets, dodging a backhand blow from his huge fist and retreating back up onto the packing crates on the other side of the aisle. Out of the corner of her eye she saw Niedermann reach for her. Quick as lightning she pulled up her feet. The crates stood in two rows, stacked up three high next to the centre aisle and two high along the outside. She swung down onto the two crates and braced herself, using all the strength in her legs and pushing her back against the crate next to her. It must have weighed more than 400 pounds. She felt it begin to move and then tumble down towards the centre aisle.

Niedermann saw the crate coming and threw himself to one side. A corner of the crate struck him on the chest, but he seemed not to have been injured. He picked himself up. She was resisting. He started climbing up after her. His head was just appearing over the third crate when she kicked at him. Her boot struck him with full force in the forehead. He grunted and heaved himself up on top of the packing crates. Salander fled, leaping back to the crates on the other side of the aisle. She dropped over the edge and vanished immediately from his sight. He could hear her footsteps and caught a glimpse of her as she passed through the doorway to the inner workshop.

Salander took an appraising look around. *Click.* She knew that she did not have a chance. She could survive for as long as she could avoid Niedermann's enormous fists and keep her distance. But when she made a mistake—which would happen sooner or later—she was dead. She had to evade him. He would only have to grab hold of her once, and the fight would be over.

She needed a weapon.

A pistol. A sub-machine gun. A rocket-propelled grenade. A personnel mine.

Any fucking thing at all.

But there was nothing like that at hand.

She looked everywhere.

No weapons.

Only tools. *Click.* Her eyes fell on the circular saw, but he was hardly going to lie down on the saw bench. *Click. Click.* She saw an iron rod that could be used as a spear, but it was probably too heavy for her to handle effectively. *Click.* She glanced through the door and saw that Niedermann was down from the crates and no more than fifty feet away. He was coming towards her again. She started to move away from the door. She had maybe five seconds left before Niedermann was upon her. She glanced one last time at the tools.

A weapon . . . or a hiding place.

Niedermann was in no hurry. He knew that there was no way out and that sooner or later he would catch his sister. But she was dangerous, no doubt about it. She was, after all, Zalachenko's daughter. And he did not want to be injured. It was better to let her run around and wear herself out.

He stopped in the doorway to the inner room and looked around at the jumble of tools, furniture, and half-finished floorboards. She was nowhere to be seen.

"I know you're in here. And I'm going to find you."

Niedermann stood still and listened. All he could hear was his own breathing. She was hiding. He smiled. She was challenging him. Her visit had suddenly turned into a game between brother and sister.

Then he heard a clumsy rustling noise from somewhere in the centre of the room. He turned his head but at first could not tell where the sound was coming from. Then he smiled again. In the middle of the floor, set slightly apart from the other debris, stood a sixteen-foot-long wooden workbench with a row of drawers and sliding cabinet doors beneath it.

He approached the workbench from the side and glanced behind it to make sure that she was not trying to fool him. Nothing there.

She was hiding inside the cabinet. So stupid.

He slid open the first door on the far left.

He instantly heard movement inside the cabinet, from the middle section. He took two quick steps and opened the middle door with a triumphant expression on his face.

Empty.

Then he heard a series of sharp cracks that sounded like pistol shots. The sound was so close that at first he could not tell where it was coming from. He turned to look. Then he felt a strange pressure against his left foot. He felt no pain, but he looked down at the floor just in time to see Salander's hand moving the nail gun over to his right foot.

She was underneath the cabinet.

He stood as if paralysed for the seconds it took her to put the mouth of the nail gun against his boot and fire another five seven-inch nails straight through his foot.

He tried to move.

It took him precious seconds to realize that his feet were nailed solidly to the newly laid plank floor. Salander's hand moved the nail gun back to his left foot. It sounded like an automatic weapon getting shots off in bursts. She managed to shoot in another four nails as reinforcement before he was able to react.

He reached down to grab her hand, but immediately lost his balance and regained it only by bracing himself against the workbench as he heard the nail gun being fired again and again, *ka-blam, ka-blam, ka-blam*. She was back to his right foot. He saw that she was firing the nails diagonally through his heel and into the floor.

Niedermann howled in sudden rage. He lunged again for Salander's hand.

From her position under the cabinet Salander saw his pant leg slide up, a sign that he was trying to bend down. She let go of the nail gun. Niedermann saw her hand disappear quick as a lizard beneath the cabinet just before he reached her.

He reached for the nail gun, but the instant he touched it with the tips of his fingers she drew it under the cabinet.

The gap between the floor and the cabinet was about eight inches. With all the strength he could muster he toppled the cabinet onto its back. Salander looked up at him with big eyes and an offended expression. She aimed the nail gun and fired it from a distance of twenty inches. The nail hit him in the middle of his shin.

The next instant she dropped the nail gun, rolled fast as lightning away from him, and got to her feet beyond his reach. She backed up several feet and stopped.

Niedermann tried to move and again lost his balance, swaying backwards and forwards with his arms flailing. He steadied himself and bent down in rage.

This time he managed to grab hold of the nail gun. He pointed it at Salander and pulled the trigger.

Nothing happened. He looked in dismay at the nail gun and then at Salander again. She looked back at him blankly and held up the plug. In fury he threw the nail gun at her. She dodged to the side.

Then she plugged in the cord again and hauled in the nail gun.

He met Salander's expressionless eyes and was amazed. She had defeated him. *She's supernatural.* Instinctively he tried to pull one foot from the floor. *She's a monster.* He could lift his foot only a fraction of an inch before his boot hit the heads of the nails. They had been driven into his feet at different angles, and to free himself he would have to rip his feet to shreds. Even with his almost superhuman strength he was unable to pull himself loose. For several seconds he swayed back and forth as if he were swimming. He saw a pool of blood slowly forming between his shoes.

Salander sat down on a stool and watched for signs that he might be able to tear his feet loose. Since he could not feel pain, it was a matter of whether he was strong enough to pull the heads of the nails straight through his feet. She sat stock-still and observed his struggle for ten minutes. The whole time her eyes were frozen blank.

After a while she stood up and walked behind him and held the nail gun to his spine, just below the nape of his neck.

Salander was thinking hard. This man had transported, drugged, abused, and sold women both retail and wholesale. He had murdered at least eight people, including a police-man in Gosseberga and a member of Svavelsjö MC and his wife. She had no idea how many other lives her half-brother might have on his account, if not his conscience, but thanks to him she had been hunted all over Sweden like a mad dog, suspected of three of the murders he had committed.

Her finger rested heavily on the trigger.

He had murdered the journalist Dag Svensson and his partner, Mia Johansson.

With Zalachenko he had also murdered *her* and buried her in Gosseberga. And now he had resurfaced to murder her again.

You could get pretty angry with less provocation.

She saw no reason to let him live any longer. He hated her with a passion that she could not even fathom. What would happen if she turned him over to the police? A trial? A life sentence? When would he be granted parole? How soon

would he escape? And now that her father was finally gone . . .
How many years would she have to look over her shoulder,
waiting for the day when her brother would suddenly turn up
again? She felt the heft of the nail gun. She could end this thing
once and for all.

Risk assessment.

She bit her lip.

Salander was afraid of no-one and nothing. She realized
that she lacked the necessary imagination—and that was evidence enough that there was something wrong with her brain.

Niedermann hated her, and she responded with an
equally implacable hatred towards him. He joined the ranks
of men like Magge Lundin and Martin Vanger and Zalachenko and dozens of other creeps who in her estimation
had absolutely no claim to be among the living. If she could
put them all on a desert island and set off an atomic bomb,
then she would be satisfied.

But murder? Was it worth it? What would happen to her if
she killed him? What were the odds that she would avoid discovery? What would she be ready to sacrifice for the satisfaction of firing the nail gun one last time?

I could claim self-defence . . . no, not with his feet nailed to
the floorboards.

She suddenly thought of Harriet Fucking Vanger, who had
also been tormented by her father and her brother. She
recalled the exchange she had had with Mikael Fucking Blomkvist in which she cursed Harriet Vanger in the harshest possible terms. It was Harriet Vanger's fault that her brother
Martin had been allowed to go on murdering women year
after year.

"What would you do?" Blomkvist had said.

"I'd kill the fucker," she had said with a conviction that came from the depths of her cold soul.

And now she was standing in exactly the same position in which Harriet Vanger had found herself. How many more women would Niedermann kill if she let him go? She had the legal right of a citizen and was socially responsible for her actions. How many years of her life did she want to sacrifice? How many years had Harriet Vanger been willing to sacrifice?

Suddenly the nail gun felt too heavy for her to hold against his spine, even with both hands.

She lowered the weapon and felt as though she had come back to reality. She was aware of Niedermann muttering something incoherent. He was speaking German. He was talking about a devil that had come to get him.

She knew that he was not talking to her. He seemed to see somebody at the other end of the room. She turned her head and followed his gaze. There was nothing there. She felt the hairs rise on the back of her neck.

She turned on her heel, grabbed the iron rod, and went to the outer room to find her shoulder bag. As she bent to retrieve it she caught sight of the knife. She still had her gloves on, and she picked up the weapon.

She hesitated a moment and then placed it in full view in the centre aisle between the stacks of packing crates. With the iron rod she spent three minutes prising loose the padlock so that she could get outside.

She sat in her car and thought for a long time. Finally she flipped open her mobile. It took her two minutes to locate the number for Svavelsjö MC's clubhouse.

"Yeah?"

"Nieminen," she said.

"Wait."

She waited for three minutes before Sonny Nieminen came to the phone.

"Who's this?"

"None of your fucking business," Salander said in such a low voice that he could hardly make out the words. He could not even tell whether it was a man or a woman.

"All right, so what do you want?"

"You want a tip about Niedermann?"

"Do I?"

"Don't give me shit. Want to know where he is or not?"

"I'm listening."

Salander gave him directions to the brickworks outside Norrtälje. She said that he would be there long enough for Nieminen to find him if he hurried.

She closed her mobile, started the car, and drove up to the gas station across the road. She parked so that she had a clear view of the brickworks.

She had to wait for more than two hours. It was just before 1:30 in the afternoon when she saw a van drive slowly past on the road below her. It stopped at the turning off the main road, stood there for five minutes, and then drove down to the brickworks. On this December day, twilight was setting in.

She opened the glove box and took out a pair of Minolta 16 × 50 binoculars and watched as the van parked. She identified Nieminen and Waltari with three men she did not recognize. *New blood. They had to rebuild their operation.*

When Nieminen and his pals had found the open door at

the end of the building, she opened her mobile again. She composed a message and sent it to the police station in Norr-tälje.

COP KILLER R. NIEDERMANN IN OLD
BRICKWORKS BY THE GAS STATION OUTSIDE
SKEDERID. ABOUT TO BE MURDERED BY S. NIEMI-
NEN AND MEMBERS OF SVAVELSJÖ MC. WOMEN
DEAD IN PIT ON GROUND FLOOR.

She could not see any movement from the factory.

She bided her time.

As she waited she removed the SIM card from her phone and cut it up with some nail scissors. She rolled down the window and tossed out the pieces. Then she took a new SIM card from her wallet and inserted it in her phone. She was using a Comviq cash card, which was virtually impossible to track. She called Comviq and credited 500 kronor to the new card.

Eleven minutes after her message was sent, two police vans with their sirens off but with blue lights flashing drove at high speed up to the factory from the direction of Norr-tälje. They parked in the yard next to Nieminen's van. A minute later two squad cars arrived. The officers conferred and then moved together towards the brickworks. Salander raised her binoculars. She saw one of the policemen radio through the registration number of Nieminen's van. The officers stood around waiting. Salander watched as another team approached at high speed two minutes later.

Finally it was all over.

The story that had begun on the day she was born had ended at the brickworks.

She was free.

When the officers took out assault rifles from their vehicles, put on Kevlar vests, and started to fan out around the factory site, Salander went inside the shop and bought a coffee and a sandwich wrapped in cellophane. She ate standing at a counter in the café.

It was dark by the time she got back to her car. Just as she opened the door, she heard two distant reports from what she assumed were handguns on the other side of the road. She saw several black figures, presumably policemen, pressed against the wall near the entrance at one end of the building. She heard sirens as another squad car approached from the direction of Uppsala. A few cars had stopped at the side of the road below her to watch the drama.

She started the Honda, turned onto the E18, and drove home.

It was 7:00 that evening when Salander, to her great annoyance, heard the doorbell ring. She was in the bath and the water was still steaming. There was really only one person who could be at her front door.

At first she thought she would ignore it, but at the third ring she sighed, got out of the bath, and wrapped a towel around her. Pouting, she trailed water down the hall floor. She opened the door a crack.

"Hello," Blomkvist said.

She did not answer.

"Did you hear the evening news?"

She shook her head.

"I thought you might like to know that Ronald Niedermann is dead. He was murdered today in Norrtälje by a gang from Svavelsjö MC."

"Really?" Salander said.

"I talked to the duty officer in Norrtälje. It seems to have been some sort of internal dispute. Apparently Niedermann had been tortured and slit open with a knife. They found a bag at the factory with several hundred thousand kronor."

"Jesus."

"The Svavelsjö mob was arrested, but they put up quite a fight. There was a shoot-out and the police had to send for a backup team from Stockholm. The bikers surrendered at around 6:00."

"Is that so?"

"Your old friend Sonny Nieminen bit the dust. He went completely nuts and tried to shoot his way out."

"That's nice."

Blomkvist stood there in silence. They looked at each other through the crack in the door.

"Am I interrupting something?" he said.

She shrugged. "I was in the bath."

"I can see that. Do you want some company?"

She gave him an acid look.

"I didn't mean in the bath. I've brought some bagels," he said, holding up a bag. "And some espresso. Since you own a Jura Impressa X7, you should at least learn how to use it."

She raised her eyebrows. She did not know whether to be disappointed or relieved.

"Just company?"

"Just company," he confirmed. "I'm visiting a good friend. If I'm welcome, that is."

She hesitated. For two years she had kept as far away from Mikael Blomkvist as she could. And yet he kept sticking to her life like gum on the sole of her shoe, either on the Net or in real life. On the Net it was OK. There he was no more than electrons and words. In real life, standing on her doorstep, he was still fucking attractive. And he knew her secrets just as she knew all of his.

She looked at him for a moment and realized that she now had no feelings for him. At least not those kinds of feelings.

He had in fact been a good friend to her over the past year.

She trusted him. Maybe. It was troubling that one of the few people she trusted was a man she spent so much time avoiding.

Then she made up her mind. It was absurd to pretend that he did not exist. It no longer hurt her to see him.

She opened the door wide and let him into her life again.

NOTES

Olof Palme was the leader of the Social Democratic Party and prime minister of Sweden at the time of his assassination on February 28, 1986. He was an outspoken politician, popular with the left and detested by the right. Two years after his death a petty criminal and drug addict was convicted of his murder but was later acquitted on appeal. Although a number of alternative theories as to who carried out the murder have since been proposed, to this day the crime remains unsolved.

Prompted by Olof Palme's assassination, Prime Minister **Ingvar Carlsson** called an investigation into the procedures of the Swedish Security Police (Säpo) in the fall of 1987. Carl Lidbom, then Swedish ambassador to France, was given the task of leading the investigation. One of his old acquaintances, the publisher **Ebbe Carlsson,** firmly believed that the Kurdish organization PKK was involved in the murder and was given resources to start a private investigation. The Ebbe Carlsson affair exploded as a major political scandal in 1988, when it was revealed that the publisher had been secretly supported by the then minister of justice, Anna-Greta Leijon. She was subsequently forced to resign.

Informationsbyrån (IB) was a secret intelligence agency without official status within the Swedish armed forces. Its main purpose was to gather information about communists and other individuals who were perceived to be a threat to the nation. It was thought that these findings were passed on to key politicians at cabinet level, most likely the defence minister at the time, Sven Andersson, and Prime Minister Olof Palme. The exposure of the agency's operations by journalists Jan Guillou and Peter Bratt in the magazine *Folket i Bild/Kulturfront* in 1973 became known as **the IB affair.**

Carl Bildt was prime minister of Sweden between 1991 and 1994 and leader of the liberal conservative Moderate Party from 1986 to 1999.

Anna Lindh was a Swedish Social Democratic politician who served as foreign minister from 1998 until her assassination in 2003. She was considered by many as one of the leading candidates to succeed Göran Persson as leader of the Social Democrats and prime minister of Sweden. In the final weeks of her life she was intensely involved in the pro-euro campaign preceding the Swedish referendum on the euro.

Colonel Stig Wennerström of the Swedish air force was convicted of treason in 1964. During the fifties he was suspected of leaking air defence plans to the Soviets, and in 1963 he was informed upon by his maid, who had been recruited by Säpo. He was initially sentenced to life imprisonment, but his sentence was commuted to twenty years in 1973, of which he served only ten. He died in 2006. He is not to be confused with Hans-Erik Wennerström, the crooked financier who appears in *The Girl with the Dragon Tattoo* and *The Girl Who Played with Fire.*

In the late eighties and early nineties there was an immigration crisis in Sweden. The number of asylum seekers increased, and the resulting unemployment and backlash from local government prompted the city of Sjöbo to hold a referendum in 1998, where the population voted against accepting immigrants. The subsequent political debate, called **the Sjöbo debate,** led to a combined immigration and integration system in the Aliens Act of 1989.

ALSO BY STIEG LARSSON

THE GIRL WITH THE DRAGON TATTOO

An international publishing sensation, *The Girl with the Dragon Tattoo* combines murder mystery, family saga, love story, and financial intrigue into one satisfyingly complex and entertainingly atmospheric novel. Harriet Vanger, a scion of one of Sweden's wealthiest families disappeared over forty years ago. All these years later, her aged uncle continues to seek the truth. He hires Mikael Blomkvist, a crusading journalist recently trapped by a libel conviction, to investigate. He is aided by the pierced and tattooed punk prodigy Lisbeth Salander. Together they tap into a vein of unfathomable iniquity and astonishing corruption.

Crime Fiction

THE GIRL WHO PLAYED WITH FIRE

Part blistering espionage thriller, part riveting police procedural, and part piercing exposé on social injustice, *The Girl Who Played with Fire* is a masterful, endlessly satisfying novel. Mikael Blomkvist, crusading publisher of the magazine *Millennium*, has decided to run a story that will expose an extensive sex-trafficking operation. On the eve of its publication, the two reporters responsible for the article are murdered, and the fingerprints found on the murder weapon belong to his friend, the troubled genius hacker Lisbeth Salander. Blomkvist, convinced of Salander's innocence, plunges into an investigation. Meanwhile, Salander herself is drawn into a murderous game of cat and mouse, which forces her to face her dark past.

Crime Fiction

VINTAGE CRIME/BLACK LIZARD
Available wherever books are sold.
www.randomhouse.com
www.weeklylizard.com